2010

PUSHCART PRIZE XXXIV BEST OF THE SMALL PRESSES

EDITED BY BILL HENDERSON
WITH THE PUSHCART PRIZE EDITORS

Note: nominations for this series are invited from any small, independent, literary book press or magazine in the world, print or online. Up to six nominations—tear sheets or copies, selected from work published, or about to be published, in the calendar year—are accepted by our December 1 deadline each year. Write to Pushcart Press, P.O. Box 380, Wainscott, N.Y. 11975 for more information or consult our websites www.pushcartprize.com. or pushcartpress.org.

Acknowledgments

Selections for The Pushcart Prize are reprinted with the permission of authors and presses cited. Copyright reverts to authors and presses immediately after publication.

Distributed by W. W. Norton & Co.
500 Fifth Ave., New York, N.Y. 10110

Library of Congress Card Number: 76–58675
ISBN (hardcover): 978-1-888889-55-0
ISBN (paperback): 978-1-888889-54-3
ISSN: 0149–7863

For Ruth Wittman

INTRODUCTION

Despite the election of a president who can actually read, write, feel, think and govern, it can be tough to find hope these days, especially in the publishing world. Giant commercial firms like Houghton Mifflin Harcourt, dozens of respected newspapers and magazines, seem bound for oblivion. Writers are now called "content providers" at McGraw Hill's textbook division and books and journals long ago were denigrated to mere "units" identified by their scan numbers not by title. And of course the book or journal may yet succumb to the rise of Kindle—you can replace your bookshelves with blank walls. It's all good for efficient business, the experts say.

As the conglomerates have taken over (and destroyed) much of publishing, it falls to small presses to carry on. Donna Seaman noted in her *Booklist* review of last year's Pushcart Prize, "open the latest Pushcart gathering of the best of the small presses and enter a cosmos of candor, humor, conviction and lyricism . . . generous, glimmering and hopeful."

Hopeful, I think, because small presses remain close to the human heart and not lodged in hedge funds. Our universe of presses does not depend on money (the love of which is "the root of all evil," you may recall from your Bible) but on inspiration, dedication, perseverance, empathy, talent and, may I say it, love.

Bloated business giants were said to be too big to fail. So we tax payers bailed them out. Well, small presses are too small to fail. We are at rock bottom now and we are grounded there.

The behemoths of banking, insurance and automobiles and their publishing clones worshiped growth. Their aim was not to the heavens but to elephantiasis. With their eyes firmly fixed on more, more, more (money, power), they didn't notice they had lost their souls as their sham financial scaffolding collapsed under them and their clay footings too.

As I said years ago in this annual sermon, the Pushcart Prize is to me "a small good thing"—the title of my favorite Ray Carver story. We will stay small because we and now all the country can see the horrors of money lust. A computerless shack in the backyard is our World Headquarters and we intend to make no expansions or office upgrades to the 8x8 edifice set on concrete blocks, our ears close to the spiritual ground with the help of our 232 staff contributors and hundreds of small press editors across the country.

Another lust that consumes our culture today is speed, not the drug but the electronic version. This is especially deadly to writers. On-demand vanity publishers will zip out your efforts, no questions asked (and usually no readers found). It's a mistake for writers to be in a huge hurry to be noticed. YouTube, My Space, a zillion blogs—everybody wants to be a celebrity, and fast. The electronic juggernaut drives their frenzy for renown and is very destructive, particularly to young authors. It takes years, maybe a lifetime, to figure out what you want to say and how to say it. Because you can burp out a poem or short story online, you will not immediately join the ranks of the immortals. Indeed you will be embraced in the Pantheon of Twitter. Or maybe The Kingdom of Kindle will admit you. Fast books, no binding needed. Toss when done. Another electronic absurdity. Remember: speed kills.

Speaking of long, thoughtful and slow—Pushcart is pleased to commence an association with the Jentel Artist Residency Program in Banner, Wyoming. Jentel, founded in 2001, has generously offered a month of room and board, peace and quiet for a selected group of Pushcart winners in "a spectacularly beautiful place to peacefully work and achieve personal artistic goals . . . with views to the majestic Big Horn Mountains." The Jentel complex (a former ranch) affords writers an opportunity to "roam in an uncultivated and natural expanse". We thank Pushcart Endowment board member Jim Charlton and Jentel for the welcome gift of slow time.

Pushcart may be determinedly small but our effort is large. Over 7000 nominations are considered each year by our staff of prose editors (Peter Orner, Joe Hurka, Jack Driscoll and Carolyn Waite) and this year by guest poetry co-editors, Rosanna Warren and Wesley McNair.

Wesley McNair's volumes of poetry include seven collections and two limited editions. He has also published books of essays and several anthologies. A recipient of Fulbright and Guggenheim fellowships, he has won two NEA grants and has twice received Rockefeller fellowships for creative work at the Bellagio Center in Italy. His honors in poetry include the Theodore Roethke Prize, the Eunice Tietjens Prize, the Jane Kenyon Award, the Sarah Josepha Hale Medal and a Pushcart Prize. In 2006 he was awarded a United States Artist Fellowship for poetry. His two forthcoming books are *Lovers of the Lost: New and Selected Poems* and *The Words I Chose: a memoir of family and poetry*.

On his Pushcart selection experience, Wesley comments: "What surprised me was that there were so many good poems, and that they came from everywhere—internet sites, independent magazines, university periodicals. To read poems for the Pushcart anthology is to discover how strong and vital the poetry scene in this country really is."

Rosanna Warren is Professor of Humanities at Boston University. She has received fellowships from the Guggenheim, Lila Wallace, and Ingram Merrill foundations. Her prizes include: the Award of Merit for Poetry from the American Academy of Arts and Letters, the Lamont Prize from the Academy of American Poets and two Pushcart Prizes. Her most recent book is *Fables of the Self: Studies In Lyric Poetry* (2008, WW Norton) and a poetry collection, *Departure*, (2003, WW Norton).

Emerging from under the stack of Pushcart Prize nominations she comments: "On the evidence of the hundreds (perhaps over a thousand?) poems I read for Pushcart this year, poetry in the United States seems in a vigorous state. It exhibits a blessed profusion not easily categorized—thank heavens—into schools . . . the real is stranger than we think. And it is poetry's task to show us that year after year."

And so our funky little commune advances into its 35th year—thanks to our editors and the generosity of donors to our Endowment. We intend to stick around. In fact as we go to press our stock (if we had any) is now higher than Bank of America's.

Our readers are the heart of the enterprise. Without you, nothing. May you find greatness in the 62 selections from 41 presses that follow. Blessings on you.

THE PEOPLE WHO HELPED

FOUNDING EDITORS—Anaïs Nin (1903–1977), Buckminster Fuller (1895–1983), Charles Newman (1938–2006), Daniel Halpern, Gordon Lish, Harry Smith, Hugh Fox, Ishmael Reed, Joyce Carol Oates, Len Fulton, Leonard Randolph, Leslie Fiedler (1917–2003), Nona Balakian (1918–1991), Paul Bowles (1910–1999), Paul Engle (1908–1991), Ralph Ellison (1914–1994), Reynolds Price, Rhoda Schwartz, Richard Morris, Ted Wilentz (1915–2001), Tom Montag, William Phillips (1907–2002). Poetry editor: H. L. Van Brunt

CONTRIBUTING EDITORS FOR THIS EDITION—*Kim Addonizio, Dan Albergotti, Carolyn Alessio, Dick Allen, John Allman, Keith Althaus, Daniel Anderson, Philip Appleman, Antler, Tony Ardizzone, Renee Ashley, David Baker, Jim Barnes, Kim Barnes, Catherine Barnett, Tony Barnstone, Ellen Bass, Rick Bass, Claire Bateman, Charles Baxter, Bruce Beasley, Marvin Bell, Pinckney Benedict, Molly Bendall, Karen Bender, Ciaran Berry, Marie-Helene Bertino, Linda Bierds, Diann Blakley, Robert Bly, Marianne Boruch, Laure-Anne Bosselaar, Michael Bowden, Betsy Boyd, John Bradley, Kurt Brown, Rosellen Brown, Michael Dennis Browne, Christopher Buckley, Andrea Hollander Budy, E. S. Bumas, Richard Burgin, Shannon Cain, Kathy Callaway, Bonnie Jo Campbell, Dan Chaon, Katie Chase, Kim Chinquee, Suzanne Cleary, Michael Collier, Billy Collins, Martha Collins, Joan Connor, Robert Cording, Stephen Corey, Michael Czyzniejewski, Philip Dacey, Claire Davis, Chard deNiord, Ted Deppe, Sharon Dilworth, Stuart Dischell, Matt Donovan, Rita Dove, Jack Driscoll, John Drury, Karl Elder, Angie Estes, Kathy Fagan, Tom Filer, Gary Fincke, Chris Forhan, Ben Fountain, H.E. Francis, John*

Fulton, Kenneth Gangemi, Richard Garcia, Scott Geiger, Reginald Gibbons, Gary Gildner, Herbert Gold, Sarah Green, Susan Hahn, Mark Halliday, Jeffrey Hammond, James Harms, Jeffrey Harrison, Michael Heffernan, Robin Hemley, Daniel Henry, DeWitt Henry, Bob Hicok, Kathleen Hill, Jane Hirshfield, Daniel Hoffman, Helen H. Houghton, Christopher Howell, Joe Hurka, Colette Inez, Mark Irwin, Richard Jackson, David Jauss, Jeff P. Jones, Beena Kamlani, Laura Kasischke, Deborah Keenan, George Keithley, Brigit Kelly, Thomas E. Kennedy, Kristen King, David Kirby, John Kistner, Judith Kitchen, Richard Kostelanetz, Maxine Kumin, Wally Lamb, Dorianne Laux, Nam Le, Sydney Lea, Don Lee, Dana Levin, Philip Levine, Jack Livings, E. J. Levy, Daniel S. Libman, Gerald Locklin, Rachel Loden, Clancy Martin, Sage Marsters, Michael Martone, Nicola Mason, Dan Masterson, Alice Mattison, Tracy Mayor, Robert McBrearty, Nancy McCabe, Rebecca McClanahan, Erin McGraw, Elizabeth McKenzie, Wesley McNair, Nadine Meyer, Joseph Millar, Brenda Miller, Susan Mitchell, Jim Moore, Joan Murray, Kirk Nesset, Aimee Nezhukumatathil, Joyce Carol Oates, Ed Ochester, Lance Olson, Dzvinia Orlowsky, Pamela Painter, Alan Michael Parker, Edith Pearlman, Lydia Peelle, Benjamin Percy, Lucia Perillo, Donald Platt, Andrew Porter, Joe Ashby Porter, C. E. Poverman, Kevin Prufer, Lia Purpura, James Reiss, Donald Revell, Nancy Richard, Atsuro Riley, Katrina Roberts, Jessica Roeder, Gibbons Ruark, Vern Rutsala, Kay Ryan, David St. John, Maureen Seaton, Alice Schell, Brandon Schrand, Grace Schulman, Philip Schultz, David Schuman, Lloyd Schwartz, Salvatore Scibona, Gerald Shapiro, Gary Short, Floyd Skloot, Tom Sleigh, Arthur Smith, R.T. Smith, Anna Solomon, Debra Spark, Elizabeth Spires, Maura Stanton, Maureen P. Stanton, Patricia Staton, Gerald Stern, Pamela Stewart, Pat Strachan, Terese Svoboda, Joan Swift, Janet Sylvester, Elizabeth Tallent, Ron Tanner, Katherine Taylor, Lysley Tenorio, Susan Terris, Robert Thomas, Jean Thompson, Melanie Rae Thon, Pauls Toutonghi, Natasha Trethewey, Lee Upton, Dennis Vannatta, G.C. Waldrep, B. J. Ward, Rosanna Warren, Sylvia Watanabe, Don Waters, Michael Waters, Charles H. Webb, Roger Weingarten, William Wenthe, Philip White, Dara Wier, Naomi J. Williams, Eleanor Wilner, S.L. Wisenberg, Mark Wisniewski, David Wojahn, Robert Wrigley, Matt Yurdana, Christina Zawadisky, Paul Zimmer

PAST POETRY EDITORS—H.L. Van Brunt, Naomi Lazard, Lynne Spaulding, Herb Leibowitz, Jon Galassi, Grace Schulman, Carolyn

CONTENTS

MODULATION

fiction by RICHARD POWERS

from CONJUNCTIONS

DO

From everything that Toshi Yukawa could later determine, the original file was uploaded to one of those illegal Brigadoon sites that appeared, drew several thousand ecstatic hits from six continents, then disappeared traceless, twelve hours later, compressing the whole arc of human history into a single day: rough birth, fledgling colonies, prospering community, land grabs and hoarding, shooting wars, imperial decay, and finally, much gnashing of teeth after the inevitable collapse, which seemed to happen faster each time through the cycle. The kind of site that spelled *music* t-u-n-z.

Yukawa—or the artist formerly known as free4yu—was paid to spend his days trawling such sites. When he was twenty-six, the Recording Industry Association of America surrounded his apartment, coming after him to the tune of $50,000 and four years in prison. He was now twenty-eight, out on parole, and working for his old enemies. His job was to study the latest escalations in the arms race that kept a motley army of hackers, crackers, and slackers running roughshod over a multibillion-dollar industry, and then to develop the next counteroffensive to try to reclaim file-sharing no-man's-land.

By Yukawa's count, the average illegal file server could satisfy half a million happy customers across the planet before being shut down. Most looters rushed to grab this week's tops of the pops. But even files with no identifying description could rack up hundreds of downloads before the well went dry. Much later, Yukawa guessed that the infected track might have installed itself onto as few as fifty initial machines. But as his friends in digital epidemiology were quick to point out, all it took to start a full-fledged epidemic was a single Typhoid Mary surprise package slipping through quarantine.

DI

A week before the music changed, Brazilian journalist Marta Mota was grilling a strike brigade attached to the Second Infantry Division near Baqubah in the explosive Iraqi province of Diyala. She was looking for a story for the *Folha de S. Paulo,* some new angle in the endless war that hadn't already been done to death. The stress the combatants had lived with for years had broken her in three days. All she wanted was to get back to her apartment in Tatuapé and write some harmless feature about local rampant corruption.

On the day before she left Baqubah, she interviewed a young American specialist who called himself Jukebox. He described, in more detail than anyone needed, how part of his informal job description involved rigging up one of the M1127 Stryker Reconnaissance vehicles with powerful mounted speakers, in order to pound out morale-boosting music for the unit during operations. "What does this music do?" Marta asked the soldier, in her lightly accented English. The question bewildered him, so she asked again. Jukebox cut her off, somewhere between impatience and amusement. "What does it *do*? That depends on who's listening." When she pressed for details, Jukebox just said, "You *know* what the hell it does."

At his words, Marta Mota snapped back in time to Panama, listening as American Marines tried to flush Manuel Noriega out of his bunker with massive waves of surround-sound Van Halen. That was two decades ago, when she was still a fledgling journalist in her twenties, absolutely convinced that the right story could change the conscience of the species. Since then, in combat zones on three continents, she had written up far more soul-crushing sounds.

She asked what music the Stryker vehicle pumped out, and Jukebox gave a rapid-fire list: the soundtrack of the globe's inescapable future. She asked for a listen. He pulled out something that looked like those slender, luxury matchboxes set out on the tables in her favorite Vila Madalena jazz club. She inserted the ear buds and he fired up the player. She yanked the buds out of her ear, howling in pain. Jukebox

16

just laughed and adjusted her volume. Even at almost mute, the music was ear-stabbing, brain-bleeding, spine-crushing stuff.

"Can you copy some of these tracks onto my player?" she asked, and fished her device out of her bag. She would write up the musical recon operations later, in Frankfurt, while on her way back home.

The sight of her three-year-old player reduced Jukebox to tears of mirth. He pretended to be unable to lift it. "What does this beast weigh, like half a *pound*?"

RE

On the campus of a midwestern college dead center in one of the I-states, in the middle of a cornfield that stretched three hundred miles in every direction, a recently retired professor of ethnomusicology walks through a dusting of snow across the quad to his office in the music building to begin his permanent evacuation. Jan Steiner was supposed to have vacated back in August, to surrender his coveted space to a newly hired junior faculty member; it's now mid-December, the semester over, and he's still not started culling.

Born in the late twenties to a German-speaking family in Prague, Steiner came to the States just before half his extended family was rounded up and sent east. He moved from a Czech enclave in Queens to Berkeley and Princeton, and from there, he went on to change the way that academics thought about concert music. He has taught at his privileged college for as long as anyone alive, and he has occupied his office one semester longer than the college allows.

He follows the stone path through a break in a hedge and comes alongside the Doric temple to Harmony. For the first time in years, he notices the names chiseled into the building's limestone frieze: Palestrina, Bach, Mozart, Beethoven, Schumann, Brahms, and—after decades, he still can't help smiling—Carl Maria von Weber. It could've been worse; there's a University of California music building that celebrates the immortality of Rameau and Dittersdorf. His parents revered these names above any humanitarian's; beyond these names, they said, the rest was noise. Steiner's father went to his grave holding his son partly responsible for the twilight of these gods.

Once, at the peak of the iconoclastic sixties, Jan Steiner suggested that all these names be unceremoniously chiseled out of their limestone and replaced by thousands of names from all places and times, names so numerous and small they would be legible only to those willing to come up close and look. Like all his writing from those heady days, his jest had been deadly serious. The whole sleepy campus was outraged; he'd almost been driven to finding work elsewhere. Now, a third of a century on, when the college would probably leap at such a venture, Jan Steiner no longer has the heart to propose it again.

Before Steiner and his like-minded colleagues set to work, scholars wrote about music mostly as an aesthetic experience, masterpieces to be celebrated in religious terms. After his generation's flood of publications, music took its place among all other ambiguous cultural work—a matter of power relations, nationalism, market forces, class contestation, and identity politics.

Jan Steiner gazes up at the Doric temple's entablature, circa 1912, and squints in pain. Could he still tell Palestrina from Allegri, in an aural police lineup? When did he last listen to anything for pleasure? If this building were to collapse tomorrow, what would he advocate, for the replacement frieze? Just spelling out the solfège syllables of the chromatic scale smacked of Eurocentrism.

He lets himself into the building's side door and makes his way up to the second story. Even on a snowy December Sunday, the practice rooms are going full tilt. He walks past the eight cubicles of baby grands—Pianosaurus Rex in full, eighty-eight-key sprint. The repertoire has certainly expanded in his half a century on campus. The only fragment of sound in the whole polychordal gauntlet he can name is the John Cage emanating from the empty cubicle on the end.

Other voices, other rooms: he's given his life to promote that, and the battle is all but won. Scholarship has discovered the ninety-eight percent of world music it hitherto suppressed. Elitism is dead; all ears are forever opened wide. So why this pall he's been unable to shake for these last several months? Perhaps it's the oppressiveness that Paul Hindemith once attributed to Bach in his last years in Leipzig: the melancholy of accomplishment.

He unlocks his oaken office door and flicks on the light. The tomb is overflowing. Every flat surface including the dark linoleum floor is piled with precarious paper towers. Monographs bulge off the shelves. Folders and collection boxes stack almost to the fluorescent lights. But he can still put his finger on any desired item, in no more than a few minutes. The problem is desire.

Now he must judge every scrap. There's too much to save, but it would stop his valve-repaired heart to throw any of it out. Five decades of iconoclasm. The college library might sift through it and keep anything of value. But who in the last five years has set foot in the college library?

He drops into his desk chair and stares again at the awful severance gift from his retirement party. The department presented the mobile device to him in a teary ceremony: a clock, calendar, appointment book, phone, Web browser, and matter transporter, but mostly a bribe to get him to quit quietly. The thing also, incidentally, plays music. Even the name sounds like *Invasion of the Body Snatchers*. He should have known, half a century ago, that music, like the most robust of weeds, would eventually come in *pods*.

And this one came preloaded with every piece of music he has ever written about, recorded, or championed. Turkish hymns and Chinese work-camp songs, gamelan orchestras and Albanian wedding choirs, political prisoners' anthems and 1930s radio jingles: his entire life's work arranged for an instrument that everyone could learn to play without any effort. What were his colleagues thinking, giving him his own back? What he needs is music he hasn't yet discovered, any sound at all that hasn't disappeared into the oversold, derivative, or market branded. He grabs the device, flips it on, and blunders through the menu screens, looking for a song he might somehow, by accident, have blessedly forgotten.

RI

On the night before the exploit launched, Mitchell Payne was on his way from Los Angeles to the Sydney 8-Bit Chiptune Blowout. The first humans to grow up from infancy on video games had stumbled inadvertently into young adulthood, a condition that left them stricken with nostalgia for the blips and bleeps of their Atari child-hood. And where there was nostalgia, there were always live concerts. The Sydney event was Mitchell's third such extravaganza. The chip-tune phenomenon had hit North America ten months ago, which meant it would soon erupt into mass consciousness and be dead by this time next year. But until such demise, Mitchell Payne, leading Futurepop composer and perhaps the greatest real-time Roland MC-909 Groovebox performer of his generation, had found another way to help pay off his Sarah Lawrence student loans.

The one-hundred-and-fifty-grand debt didn't worry him so much. What bothered him, as he hunkered down over Palmyra Atoll for the next hour's installment of in-flight entertainment from the Homeland

Security Channel, was the growing conviction that at twenty-three, he no longer had his finger on the pulse. He had lost his lifelong ability to keep one measure ahead of the next modulation. He'd recently scored only seventy-two percent on an online musical genre test, making stupid mistakes such as confusing acid groove, acid croft, acid techno, and acid lounge. He blamed how busy he had been, trying to master the classic eight-bit repertoire. He told himself that he had just overthought the test questions, but in reality, there was no excuse. Truth was, he was slipping. Things were happening, whole new genres crossbreeding, and he was going to be one of those people who didn't even hear it until the next big thing was already in its grave and all over the cover of *Rolling Stone*.

But he had more pressing worries. In Sydney, he'd be up against some classic composers, the true giants of the international chiptune movement. Without some serious art on his part, they'd laugh him off the stage. Fortunately, his material was beyond awesome. He pulled his laptop out of his carry-on and fired up the emulator. He flipped through his sequences again, checking tempi, fiddling with the voicing of chords. Then he peeked again at the climax of his set, an inspiration he still couldn't quite believe he'd pulled off. He'd managed to contrapuntally combine the theme from Nintendo's *Donkey Kong* with Commodore 64's *Skate or Die*, in retrograde inversion. The sheer ecumenical beauty of the gesture once more brought tears to his eyes.

When he looked up again, the in-flight entertainment had graduated to that new reality show, *Go for the Green*, where ten illegal alien families compete against each other to keep from getting deported. He watched for a few minutes, then returned to his hard drive's 160 GB of tracks. But before he could determine where he'd gone wrong in discriminating between epic house, progressive house, filtered house, and French house, the stewardess was on the sound system asking everyone to turn off and stow all portable devices in preparation for landing in Sydney.

MI

Toshi Yukawa took too long to realize the danger of the virus. He'd seen the chatter on the pirate music discussion boards, the reports of files that downloaded just fine then disappeared from the receiving directory. Some guy named Jarod would complain that his file count was broken after syncing with his Nano. Some guy named Jason would report that the same thing was true on his Shuffle. Another guy named Justin would confirm for his Zen. Then another guy named Dustin would chime in, "Get a Touch, you freaking noobs, it's been out for weeks."

Any file that hid itself was trouble. He ran some tests on the twelve machines behind his router firewall: five subdirectories were compromised. He could discover nothing else until he synchronized these machines with portable devices. After syncing, three different handhelds—a music player, a pocket PC, and even a cell phone—showed flaky file counts. Yukawa realized that he was looking at something technologically impossible: the very first backdoor infection of multiple music players.

The ingenuity of the code humbled Yukawa. The main file seemed to figure out what kind of mobile device was attached to the host computer, then loaded in the appropriate code. But the ingenuity got better, and worse. On next check, Yukawa's five suspicious desktop directories had multiplied to twelve. The malicious payload was attaching itself to other files.

What kind of person would want to punish music traffickers? There were the geek hacker athletes, virtuosi like Toshi had been, simply giving their own kind of concert on their own astonishing instruments, regardless of the effect on the audience. There were always the terrorists, of course. Once you hated freedom, it was just a matter of time before you hated two-part harmony. But when he saw how this new virus could spread, Toshi Yukawa wondered if he wasn't being set up. Maybe some of his colleagues at the Recording Industry Association had developed the ultimate counterstrike for a world where two hundred million songs a day were sold, and even more were borrowed. And maybe his colleagues had simply neglected to tell him about the new weapon.

Some days he wasn't even sure why the RIAA had hired him. So much music could be had by so many for so little that Toshi should have long ago been driven into honest work, say eclectic format discjockeying for Starbucks. There was pay what you want and genetic taste matching and music by statistical referral. Customers who liked Radiohead also listened to Slipknot. If you like Slipknot, you may also like the Bulgarian Women's Chorus. The vendors had your demographic, and would feed it to you in unlimited ninety-nine-cent doses or even free squirts that vanished after three listens. He owed his job to saltwater syndrome. Drinking made you thirsty. Buffets bred hunger.

And some kind of strange musical hunger had bred this virus. Whoever had made the payload had made something beautiful. Yukawa had no other word for it, and the way the thing worked scared the hell out of him. Three days into his hunt, he discovered that four other computers behind his firewall were now infected. These boxes had gone nowhere near an illegal download site. The virus had somehow uploaded itself back up to shared music service software, and was spreading itself through automatic synchronization onto innocent bystanders.

A sick and brilliant mind: that's what Toshi Yukawa was fighting. He felt a wave of disgust for anyone who couldn't put such gifts to better use. Then he remembered himself, just four years ago: a collector so obsessed with liberating music that he'd all but stopped listening to it.

FA

Marta Mota woke up in her economy hotel on the Schönstraße near the Frankfurt Hauptbahnhof with a tune in her head. Not a tune, exactly: more like a motif. She couldn't altogether sing it, but she couldn't shake it, either.

It lasted through her hot shower—a marvelous indulgence, after Iraq. It persisted through the heavy black breads and sausages of German breakfast. It was still there as she handled her e-mail and filed another story with *Folha* on the Diyala campaign. She had contracted what the German called an *Uhrwurm*, what Brazilian Portuguese called *chiclete de ouvido*: a gum tune stuck in her relentlessly chewing brain.

As earworms went, this one wasn't bad. She'd spent an hour yesterday listening to the testosterone storms that the American soldier had copied for her. She'd needed two hours of Django Reinhardt and Eliane Elias to drive that throbbing from her mind. What she hummed now, she felt sure, was nothing she'd heard in the last five days.

She Skyped her mate Andre at the appointed hour. He was consulting, in Bahrain. The world was insane, and far too mobile for its own well-being. She only thanked God for dispensing Voice Over Internet just in time.

Andre asked about Iraq. There was nothing to say. Everyone knew already, and no one could help. She told him about the earworm. Andre laughed. "Oh yes. I had that for three months once. Kylie Minogue. I thought I was going to have to check into a hospital. You see? The Americans will get us all, one way or the other."

She told him she thought Kylie Minogue was Australian.

"Alabama, Arizona, Australia: it's all a World Bank thing, right?"

He asked how the tune went. She tried to describe it. Words were as effective at holding music as smoke was at holding water.

"Sing it," he commanded.

She swore colorfully. "Sing it! Here? In public?"

The man seemed to do nothing but laugh. Wasn't there grimness enough, out in Bahrain?

"The Internet is not public," he told her. "Don't you know that? Everything you do on the Internet instantly disappears."

She tried to sing a few notes, but it was hopeless. The earworm wasn't even a motif. It was more a harmony, a sequence of magical chords that receded when she focused on them.

"Where do you think you heard it?"

She had no clue.

"I read an article about why this happens, but I can't remember it. Would you like the garbled version?"

She said yes. That was the beauty of free communication. They could be as silly as if they were lying next to each other in bed. Andre recounted his jumbled article, something about a cognitive itch, some combination of simplicity and surprise, the auditory cortex singing to itself. He thought he remembered something about the most common stuck tunes coming from the first fifteen years of a person's life.

"You need an eraser tune," he told her. "A good eraser tune is as sticky as the original, and they cancel each other out. Here's the one that worked for me." And into his tinny laptop computer microphone in Bahrain, in a frail but pretty baritone she hadn't heard for way too long, he sang a few notes that rematerialized in her Frankfurt hotel as the theme song from *Mission Impossible*.

It didn't help, and she went to bed that night with the phantom chords taunting her, just out of reach.

FI

Jan Steiner sits in his windowless office, listening to his life's work. It isn't bad, as life's work goes. But all these sounds have become so

23

achingly predictable. He can't listen to anything for more than thirty seconds without hearing political agendas. Somebody preserving their social privileges. Somebody else subverting them. Groups of people bonding together with branded tunes that assert their superiority over everyone with different melodies.

He has recorded hundreds of hours of what people now call "world music," and written about thousands more. He always paid the performers out of his modest grant money and gave them any rare recording profits. But he has never taken out a single copyright. Music belonged to everyone alive, or to no one. Every year, in his Introduction to Music lecture, he told his freshmen the story about how the Vatican tried to keep Allegri's *Miserere* a trade secret, refusing even to show the score, but insisting that, for the full mystic aura of the piece, one had to come to Rome and pay top dollar. And the protectionism worked until the fourteen-year-old Mozart, in Rome for a concert, transcribed it perfectly from memory, freeing it for performance everywhere. And every year, Jan Steiner got his freshmen cheering the original bootlegger.

The idea was simple: put your song out in the world, free of all motives, and see what other people do with it. When his scandalized colleagues asked how musicians were supposed to make a living, he pointed out that musicians in hundreds of countries had eked out a living for millennia without benefit of copyright. He said that most music should be amateur, or served up like weekly cantatas knocked out for the Glory of God alone.

He sits on his green padded office chair, tipped back on the cracked linoleum, under the humming fluorescent lights, listening. He listens to a traditional Azerbaijani mourning song, as personal a lament as has ever been put into tones. He found it gut-wrenching when he first recorded it, two decades back. Now all he can hear is the globally released feature film from a year ago that used the song as its novel theme music. The movie seemed to be mostly about potential residuals and the volatile off-screen escapades of its two stars. The soundtrack made more money in six months than any Azerbaijani musician had made in a lifetime, and the performers on his track—the one that had brought the haunted melody to North America—had seen not a penny.

Just to further torture himself, he switches to his other great recent hit: an ecstatic Ghanaian instrumental performed entirely on hubcaps and taxi horns that only six months before had been turned into an exultant commercial for global financial services. This one also made a mint as a cell phone ring tone.

He has no one to blame for these abuses but himself. All music was theft, he has maintained over a lifetime of scholarly writing, since long before sampling even had a name. Europe used to call it cantus firmus. Renaissance magpies used to dress up millennium-old Gregorian Psalmodic chants in bright polyphony. Whole musical systems— Persian dastgáhs and Indian ragas—knew nothing about ownership and consisted entirely of brilliant improvisations on pre-existing themes. The best songs, the ones that God wanted, were the ones that someone else transposed and sang back to you, from another country, in a distant key. But God hadn't anticipated global financial services jingles.

Back in the 1970s Steiner had predicted that the rise of computing would save music from death by commodity. Armed with amazing new ways to write, arrange, record, and perform, everyone alive would become a composer and add to the world's ongoing song. Well, his prediction had come true. More music of more variety was being produced by more people than any ethnomusicologist would ever be able to name again. His own illiterate grandson was a professional digital musician, and Jan Steiner finds the boy's every measure unbearably predictable.

He works his way through the towering stacks of offprints, pitching mercilessly. While he works, he leaves the player on shuffle, letting it select his life's tracks at random. By the time he leaves, hours later, he has thrown out two large garbage bins, and it's made no visible dent on the office. He stashes the player in his coat pocket as he leaves the building and heads back toward the snowy quad. Outside, it's night, and silent, the only track he can bear.

But as he rounds the corner of the Georgian psychology building, a tune comes back to him. *Comes back* isn't quite right, since this one is nothing he's listened to this evening. He can't quite say whether he's ever heard it before, or even what scale or mode or key it wants to be in. As far as he can tell, this track—if it is a *track*—has gotten away safely, innocent, never repackaged, let alone heard by anyone.

SOL

In Sydney, Mitchell Payne felt a song coming on. It had banged around his head since deplaning. This was dangerous: when melodies came to him out of the blue, it usually meant he was ripping someone off. He wasn't alone. There were only so many notes—twelve, to be precise—and they could be combined in only so many sensible ways. Someday soon, a garage band out in Cos Cob was going to string together the last viable melody, and music would be pure plagiarism and mash-ups, from then on.

The industry was already pretty much there anyway. Covers and remakes, quotations and allusions, homage, sampling, and down and dirty five-fingered discounts. A Korean kid covering a Taiwanese kid whose arrangement imitated the video game *Pump It Up* whose soundtrack mimicked an old Brian Eno performance uploads an electrifying guitar video of Pachelbel's Canon in D, already the most hacked-at piece of the last three hundred years, and immediately, people from Panama to Turkmenistan post hundreds of shot-perfect recreations, faithful down to every detail of tempo and ornament. . . .

The melody nibbling at Mitchell's brain as he set up his loopers, shifters, sequencers, and MPCs on the stage of the small Haymarket theater might have come from anywhere. It was at once oddly familiar and deeply strange. He cursed the snippet, even as it haunted him. He couldn't afford Stuck Tune Syndrome just before performing. He had to settle into the chiptune groove, that quantized trance that the children of Mario demanded.

But by the time he finished testing the gear, Mitchell was flipping. He stood inside the circle of banked electronics, his Mission Control of waveform generators, wanting to pull the plug on everything and crawl off to a Buddhist monastery until the monster tune scratching at his brain either came forward and said what it wanted from him or left him for dead.

While the house filled, Mitchell sat backstage in the green room answering questions from an editor of New South Wales's most prestigious online chiptune zine. What was the most influential mix he'd ever listened to? What would be the most important developments in the eight-bit scene over the next few weeks? If he could put only one video game soundtrack into an interplanetary spacecraft, which would it be? He could barely hear the questions over the stunning harmonic tension in his head. The stage manager had to call him twice before he heard.

Nerves almost doubled him over as he jogged out of the wings in front of a restive crowd already clapping in frenzied, synchronized downbeats. He had that sick flash of doubt: *Why do I put myself through this! I could retire to something safe, write a music blog or something.* But as soon as he got the backing tracks looping, the MSX emulator bumping, and his Amiga kicking out the MIDI jambs to the principal theme from the old blockbuster game *Alternate Reality*, he remembered just what Face-to-Face was all about, and why nothing would ever replace live performance.

SI

By the time Toshi Yukawa realized he needed help from coders beyond himself, it was too late. He'd taken too long to isolate the virus and even longer to break-point and trace the logic, trying to determine exactly what the multiple payloads meant to do to the hundreds of thousands, perhaps even millions of music players already infected. The code was so idiosyncratic and original that Toshi couldn't understand it, even as it stared him in the face. The weapon was cryptic, evanescent, awful, awesome, protean, full of fearsome intelligence and unfathomable routines: a true work of art. He isolated a subroutine devoted to hijacking the player and beaming out music in subaudible frequencies. Yukawa didn't get it: why spend such incredible intellectual effort to take over millions of devices, just to play a tune no one could hear? That had to be just a private amusement, a warm-up act for the headline show. Yukawa dug deeper, bracing for the real mayhem. A person who could write such code could sow destruction on an operatic scale.

Then Toshi stumbled onto a portion of the initializer that made his blood run cold. It checked the host's time zone and adjusted another routine that made continuous calls to the music player's clock. A timed detonator: the code was going to launch a synchronized event to go off at a single moment across all the world's time zones. But what event? The code was inscrutable assembly language. Deleting songs at random? Scrambling the firmware or flash memory?

Yukawa logged in to the best professional discussion board for tracking the thousands of viruses, worms, Trojans, and assorted malicious code in the wild. There it was: growing chatter about something already code-named *counterpoint*. Yukawa posted his discoveries, and four hours later, one of the big boys at Norton found the trigger date for Yukawa's detonator routine. A day obvious after the fact: *counterpoint* was set to premiere on December 21, the winter solstice. The day after tomorrow.

27

Time had run out. In two days, many, many people were going to be walking around earbudless, their billions of dollars' worth of portable media centers bricked. Personalized music would never be safe again. People would be thrown back on singing to each other.

A South American journalist reporting on the eternal hackers' arms race had once asked Yukawa what would happen if the white hats lost. He'd laughed her off, but here it was. Toshi sat back in his Aeron chair, gazed out his window down the glens that hid the unsuspecting venture capitalists along Sand Hill Road, and gave up. Then he did what any artist would, faced with imminent destruction: he turned back to study the beauties of the inscrutable score. He worked on without point, and all the while, unconsciously, under his breath, in the key of hopeless and exhilarating work, he hummed.

LA

São Paulo did not help Marta Mota. In fact, the relative safety of home only worsened her earworm. It got so bad she had to take a few days' leave from *Folha*. Andre actually suggested she get help. Only the fact that several friends were also suffering from a barely audible *chiclete de ouvido* running through their minds kept her from losing hers.

More confirmation awaited her online. She turned up hundreds of posts, each one plagued by unsingable music. A reporter to the end, she traced the blind leads. She found herself in ancient backwaters, Krishna's healing flute, Ling Lun's discovery of the foundation tone, Orpheus raising the dead and animating stones, the Pythagoreans with their vibrations the length of a planetary orbit, the secret music that powered the building of the Pyramids, the horns that felled Jericho, the drumming dance of Ame no Uzume, the rain goddess, luring the sun goddess, Amaterasu Omikami, from out of hiding in the rock cave of heaven. She read about African maloya, outlawed because of its power to stir revolution. She found a fantastic article by an old Czech-American musicologist tracing the myth of sublime sound, from Ulysses, tied to the mast to hear the Sirens, through Sufi mystics, Cædmon's angel-dictated hymn, and on into songs on all continents that yearned for the lost chord. God's own court composer seemed to be baiting her for a libretto.

On the solstice, Andre was consulting in Kamchatka. Marta worked late, too wired to sleep. She drew a hot bath, trying to calm down. Her player was docked in the living room, whispering soft, late Vinicius de Moraes, one of the few human-made things capable of temporarily curing her of the human-made world. Right at a key change, the music stopped, plunging her into the night's silence. Then another tune began, one that, in four measures, lifted her bodily out of the water. She sprang from the tub and dashed into the living room, nude and dripping. By the time she reached the player, the harmonies were done.

She fiddled with the interface in a naked daze, but the tune had erased its tracks. Whatever had visited was gone faster than it came. She shut her eyes and tried to take down that sublime dictation before it faded, but could make out only vague hope, vaguer reassurance. What was left of the tune said, *Keep deep down; you'll hear me again someday.* She stood on the soaking carpet, midway between bitter and elated. The song had ended. But the melody lingered on.

LI

Mitchell Payne was deep into a smoking rendition of *The Last Ninja* that was burning down the house when the music died. The backing track piped out by his 160 GB classic simply quit. The iPod brought down the master sequencer, which in turn crashed the Roland, a chain reaction that pretty much left Mitchell noodling away clueless on a couple of MIDI controllers in the empty air. The silence lasted no longer that it takes to change a track, an onstage eternity.

His first thought was that his old partner in crime, free4yu, had come back to wreak electronic revenge on Mitchell for walking away scot-free when their trading concession got rounded up by the federales. But before Mitchell had the presence of mind to power anything down, the iPod started up again.

The thumping audience fell silent and listened. The harmonies passed through a series of changes, each a strangely familiar surprise. Afterward, no two people described the sequence the same way. It was the weaving antiphony of a dream, the tune your immigrant nanny made you laugh with, the unsuspecting needle dropping onto a virgin *Sgt. Pepper*, a call to desert prayer, an archaic fauxbourdon, that tape you tried to make with your high school garage band, the last four measures of something amazing on the radio that you could never subsequently identify, highland temple bells, an evening sing-along, the keys you pressed chasing after your grandmother's player piano, a garbled shortwave "Happy Birthday" from the other side of the planet, a first slow dance, a hymn from back when you were just setting out on the game of consciousness, all resonance, sphinxlike, aching with possibility, a little incandescent phrase transporting all listeners back into timeless time.

That's how the world described it the next day, those who were lucky enough not to rip their buds out of their ears or fiddle with their rebellious players. The nations' blogs resounded with endless variations on one simple theme: *OMG—did you hear that?*

The world on that day had half a billion music-capable mobile devices. If a tenth of those were infected and turned on when the tune got loose, then more people heard the ghost tune at the same time than were alive when music was first recorded into the Samaveda. And here it was again, after an eternity away: a tune that sold nothing, that had no agenda, that required no identity or allegiance, that was not disposable background product, that came and went for no reason, brief as thunder on a summer night.

For his part, Mitchell heard the song he'd been hallucinating for the last two days. And in that instant before the crowd broke out into stunned applause, Mitchell Payne thought, *This is it—a totally new genre.* The first person to transcribe the thing was going to make a fortune. *Bow, you sucker, bow!*

TI

The quad is dark and empty, the snow gathering. Flakes pour out of the woolen air. The sky above him is a lambent orange, scattering the lights of the town. Jan Steiner takes the long diagonal path toward the neoclassical English building. The phantom tune still nags at him. The harmonies take an amazing turn, he calls out in surprise, his foot slips on the icy walk, and he slams to the pavement. Hot current shoots through his brain. Pain such as he has never felt tears up the fuse of his spine and he blacks out.

When he comes to, he feels nothing. Some part of him understands: shock. He tries to stand but can't. His right thigh comes through his hip in a way that it shouldn't. The front part of his pelvis is as powdered as the snow.

He lies on his back, paralyzed, looking up into the rust of night. He calls out, but his voice doesn't carry much beyond the globe of his body's warmth. He always was a feeble little tenor, even in the prime of life. Those who can't sing, teach.

He rolls his head to the left, the empty Colonial anthropology building. He rolls to the right, the abandoned Brutalist auditorium. He can't see past his body to the music building, with the seven names on its confident pediment. Winter's first night. The college is closed, evacuated for the holidays. He'll lie here until morning, undiscovered. The temperature is falling and the pain starts a vast, slow crescendo. He can't imagine how the piece will end.

He's amazed that this fate has been lying in wait his entire life. He looks up into snowy emptiness, recalling the words of the stunned Mozart, when the natives in provincial Leipzig forced him to listen to their old Capellmeister's archaic motet they'd kept alive like some forgotten relic: *What is this? Here at last is something one can learn from.*

Then he remembers: invasion of the pod phone players. By a mighty effort of will, he manages to crane his shattered right hand around into his coat pocket. He shovels the device out onto the pavement in little Lego pieces. No saving call. Not even a diverting tune while waiting to go numb.

He inserts the buds anyway, to keep the warmth from leaking out his ears. World's smallest earmuffs. Snow falling on the wool of his coat and his cotton cap. Snow falling on concrete, on frozen earth, freezing skin, snow on snow. In the hush, his ears sharpen. Through the dead buds, he hears the crushed device whisper a vast and silent fantasia: the wired world recovering a theme it long ago misplaced.

He lies still in the ravishing dark, listening to a need as big as lust or hunger, an urge with no reason on earth ever to have evolved. The only fundamental human pleasure with no survival value whatsoever: Music. . . .

> Ah, music for a while,
> will all your cares beguile.

A few measures more, and the cold returns him to Do.

Nominated by Conjunctions

MIDSUMMER

by LOUISE GLÜCK

from POETRY

On nights like this we used to swim in the quarry,
the boys making up games requiring them to tear off the girls' clothes
and the girls cooperating, because they had new bodies since last
    summer
and they wanted to exhibit them, the brave ones
leaping off the high rocks—bodies crowding the water.

The nights were humid, still. The stone was cool and wet,
marble for graveyards, for buildings that we never saw,
buildings in cities far away.

On cloudy nights, you were blind. Those nights the rocks were
    dangerous,
but in another way it was all dangerous, that was what we were after.
The summer started. Then the boys and girls began to pair off
but always there were a few left at the end—sometimes they'd keep
    watch,
sometimes they'd pretend to go off with each other like the rest,
but what could they do there, in the woods? No one wanted to be
    them.
But they'd show up anyway, as though some night their luck would
    change,
fate would be a different fate.

At the beginning and at the end, though, we were all together.
After the evening chores, after the smaller children were in bed,

then we were free. Nobody said anything, but we knew the nights
    we'd meet
and the nights we wouldn't. Once or twice, at the end of summer,
we could see a baby was going to come out of all that kissing.

And for those two, it was terrible, as terrible as being alone.
The game was over. We'd sit on the rocks smoking cigarettes,
worrying about the ones who weren't there.

And then finally walk home through the fields,
because there was always work the next day.
And the next day, we were kids again, sitting on the front steps in the
    morning,
eating a peach. Just that, but it seemed an honor to have a mouth.
And then going to work, which meant helping out in the fields.
One boy worked for an old lady, building shelves.
The house was very old, maybe built when the mountain was built.

And then the day faded. We were dreaming, waiting for night.
Standing at the front door at twilight, watching the shadows lengthen.
And a voice in the kitchen was always complaining about the heat,
wanting the heat to break.

Then the heat broke, the night was clear.
And you thought of the boy or girl you'd be meeting later.
And you thought of walking into the woods and lying down,
practicing all those things you were learning in the water.
And though sometimes you couldn't see the person you were with,
there was no substitute for that person.

The summer night glowed; in the field, fireflies were glinting.
And for those who understood such things, the stars were sending
    messages:
You will leave the village where you were born
and in another country you'll become very rich, very powerful,
but always you will mourn something you left behind, even though
    you can't say what it was,
and eventually you will return to seek it.

Nominated by David St. John, Philip Levine, Joan Murray, Lucia Perillo,

TWO HOSPICE ESSAYS

by SPENCER REECE

from THE AMERICAN POETRY REVIEW

It is strange how people seem to belong to places, especially to places where they were not born.

—Christopher Isherwood, *The Berlin Stories*

I. A Call

"You don't see this often," the chaplain said to me. On my first rounds at Hospice I entered a room: a baby, born without her brain's frontal lobes, gurgled on her mother's chest. The baby lived with the mother for months, much longer than the doctor expected. The baby's face grew gravely unencumbered. We prayed over that baby every day. When the baby died, words never explained it. The mother walked out of the room, her arms slackening at her sides like old latches to a door of an abandoned house.

I have decided to become a priest. No light decision. Each piece of my sentence is weighted. The wild, oval-flourish of the "I," the firm, charged, unequivocal "decided," the blossoming, fleshy "to become," and finally that stern, indelible object, "a priest"—all yoked together, coming out of my hand, onto a keyboard, displayed on a screen, projected outwards, by wires, into space. Who invests in such architecture? I hammer my antique sentence on air.

Unfortunately, sentences are no longer immortal. E-mail has wrecked the intimate tenacity of handwritten sentences. A letter, breathed on, spilled on with coffee, ink-smudged, the paper torn, words crossed out, nails time. Today e-mails disappear fast as Japanese bullet trains. When Paul wrote in his letter to the Philippians, "Let the same mind be in you that was in Christ Jesus," his ink was concrete. I am glad that sentence was saved. Nowadays, cavalier deletions crowd us. Instant messages quicken me.

I often wonder these days if this departure from the slowly personal is affecting that fragile thing we call the spiritual world. As our glaciers melt and the lakes dry up, and Beijing's sky is a complete ceiling of pollution so that the citizens no longer can see the moon or the stars, so too has some of the patient, ponderous care we took in communicating with each other begun to completely evaporate. Archeologists will have a harder time finding e-mails than they did the ancient Roman letter from Vindolanda.

No doubt, this rushed, charged atmosphere I breathe and walk through every day, is also pushing me towards the priesthood. I want to be quiet. I want to be still with others. I want to let others know Jesus loved them. If Jesus sets off alarms, I want to let people know, simply, they were loved.

I have been called. That sounds arrogant, unstable even, I know. But that is not how I mean it. I mean to express obedience and transformation. No cell-phone, answering machine or labyrinthine voice-mail system reached me. I got quiet. Through silent retreats, spiritual direction from nuns, Hospice courses, volunteering, and simply aging, I began to listen. Exiting the Tower of Babel, my message came, clear and direct. There was a tentative quality in what I heard. I think sometimes Jesus is tentative: his spirit always managing to live in both the divine and the human world, without taking sides. He commanded me in a gentle, invisible, determined way. Yes, that is better. There are those that have been put on locked units for hearing voices; conversely, the voice I heard gave me the keys. The voice I heard was coming through the patients I have been meeting. Perhaps you know of what I speak? For this is a long legacy of one whisper that came down from a horrible day on a hill.

Two years ago, I began volunteering at the Gerstenberg Center in Palm Beach County as a pastoral care volunteer. Although I had attended the Harvard Divinity School and graduated with a masters of theology in 1990, I had not used that education for twenty years. Often, as the years went by, I thought my choice a mistake. Perhaps, as Marjorie Thompson suggests in her book, *Soul Feast*, I was "anxious over what God might demand of [me] if [I] got too close. Maybe God would ask [me] to give up certain relationships, life dreams, or things

[I] enjoy." I was 27 when I graduated. Dependent on my parents, who had generously paid for my education, at the time, I felt beholden to produce something more than prayers. A religious career seemed impractical—401Ks repellent to speaking of blessings.

These days, the word "spiritual" is palatable and welcomed, spreading like wild fire through twelve-step groups that fill church basements like gatherings of early Christians, but who uses the word "pious"? The image of a "pious Christian" is nearly always bad, someone prim, prudish. As Thompson writes: "Our caricature of a pious Christian has eyes rolled heavenward and hands permanently joined at the fingertips. Indeed, many would rather be taken for secular humanists than pious Christians." I see this, on an etymological level, as a deepening schism in our modern world, the spirit being blocked by ring tones. I don't feel Christ is a dirty word. I wish my little Episcopal church in Tequesta, Florida, to be as irresistible as a treatment center. But, perhaps zealous piety is too idealistic.

As I look back at my impossibly young self, I see there was another reason I did not become a priest in my twenties. I was immature. I could not draw on depths to help others in a priestly manner, or more frankly, I could not help in any manner. I was, embarrassingly, shallow. My faith had not been tested. I had not come through doubt. Nor did I know grief.

Psalm 34: "O, taste and see that the Lord is good!" I sipped, but I did not commit. I needed to dance in the wrangles of the world. I did. Although definitely fascinated with religion, I left academe and wound up in the Mall of America, working for Brooks Brothers, eventually in various locations, as a salesman and manager, for twelve years. In 2008, I turn 45 and qualify for that nearly extinct commodity, a small pension, to be collected in my dotage. I have applied to the Yale Divinity School. Southeast Florida's Bishop has blessed my call. My discernment committee has formed. A board of priests awaits with a list of piercing questions.

At 40, one January evening, returning home late from the mall in Florida, after submitting my first manuscript of poems to over three hundred competitions for over fifteen years, my answering machine blinked its little bright red light. There was a message from Louise Glück, soon to be Poet Laureate of the United States, that she wished to select my manuscript, *The Clerk's Tale*, for the Bakeless Prize. Did I really work in haberdashery? Yes. Would I be willing to work on edits with her over the next six months?

I had been sitting in a small room for years with green shag carpet from the 70s, working on a desk that consisted of two saw horses and a door from Home Depot, and a typewriter and an antiquated heavy crashing laptop, waiting for someone to knock on the door. Here was the knock. I welcomed my guest with eager hospitality. For days I lived in a beautiful, calm shock. In public, I was quieter than I had ever been, stunned by a long held prayer manifesting itself into the world, something from the mind and soul was being incarnated into the visible. In private, over the telephone with my new poetry friend, words came in a torrent.

This turn of events led to three major grants, and for the first time in years, I was able to step down from the frenzy of retail scheduling. I worked three days a week to keep my benefits, but was able to, as the French say, *"reculer pour mieux sauter,"* translated, it means, to back up and assess the view before leaping. In a rare moment in my life, everything seemed quite clear, I recalled my old intentions, the years spent at the Divinity School, a door opened in my mind: I picked up the telephone and called Hospice.

For the last two years I have been whispering into the ears of the dying, and they have been whispering back to me. I have been bringing my own broken spirit to the altar of these divine appointments in the little rooms at the Gerstenberg Center on my day off from Brooks Brothers. I meet with Chaplain Frank Cebollero, and he gives me a list of patients who need to be visited.

No matter how carefully I read the face sheets, each room surprises: a black woman my age, with, what she herself calls, "full-blown AIDS," speaking frankly about sex and broken relationships, a mother who doesn't speak to her, her need for human touch; an elderly woman who did not speak to me for months, her wisps of gray hair top-knotted, her mouth caved in without teeth, until one day, she looked at me directly, and told me how her husband beat her; a customer of mine from Brooks Brothers, who came with his navy blue slippers and pajamas neatly folded—an observed formality that took my breath away; a young man named Ed, with two small children, frightened, but believing, not understanding why God was calling him home quickly—what would happen to his children?

Christians, Muslims, Jews, Buddhists, agnostics enter Hospice. We, the nondenominational volunteers, sometimes proselytize, but more often than not hold a hand, read a chapter from the Bible or the Koran, or even, sometimes, a poem. Priests hired by Hospice cater to all faith traditions. Hospice is a welcoming, churchy circus of trapdoors.

On July 26th, 2007, Dr. Gail Gazelle wrote in *The New England Journal of Medicine:*

> Introduced in the United States as a grassroots movement more than 30 years ago and added as a Medicare entitlement in 1983, hospice care is now considered part of mainstream medicine, as evidenced by growing patient enrollment and Medicare expenditure. In 2005, more than 1.2 million Americans received hospice care, and between 2000 and 2004, the percentage of Medicare decedents that had been enrolled in hospice programs increased by almost 50%.

The amount of priests has not kept up with these numbers. When I began to volunteer, I saw this almost immediately. I began to think, of course, about my own singular, circuitous life. Perhaps thirteen years in an Episcopal prep school, a seemingly dead-end graduate degree, twelve years in retail, a first book published in middle age, a priest could make. Why not?

There were many well-meaning, personality-driven fundamentalist volunteers willing to file your nails and speak to you about being saved, but not enough trained clergy. Not everyone wants a revival tent next to their oxygen machine. There are no Catholic priests on staff and only one Buddhist.

Fundamentalism makes me uncomfortable. Forcing Jesus on people feels arrogant to me. I am a person imprinted by a Connecticut mother and a Connecticut college. Still one must respect the land where one lands and certainly Florida is not New England. Florida is home to mega-churches the size of shopping malls led by former football coaches and Pentecostal churches in soaped store fronts next to hair salons. As I move among my fog-horning brethren in Hospice, I see I have led a somewhat unconventional life, somewhat gypsylike, bookish, frequently observing rather than holding forth, always at home in the foreign. Yet, I have always cleaved to conventions that worked, perhaps as a source of stability. Even though I am a minority where I volunteer, I have begun to feel my decorous Episcopal understatement has a place at Hospice. Rowan Williams writes, "There is no *one* way to be a priest." By extrapolation, then, there is no one way to assist the dying, some will beg for speaking in tongues, but some might prefer a middle-aged, tall, bespectacled man, with thinning hair, a tattered bible in one hand, who has found wisdom, on occasion, in holding his tongue.

Personal anxiety and hesitation have visited me. What am I afraid of? There is much I don't understand. Intimate relationships have not always been my strong suit. But each door I open at Hospice, I move closer to something brightly intimate.

There, in the broken places, good-byes filling the sanitized air, I knock, I listen, I leap.

2. In Praise of George Herbert

"Speak, Lord, your servant is listening," says I Samuel (3:10). If I am to do anything in the realm of the spirit, I *have* to listen. A doctor has a scalpel, an engineer a slide rule, a priest ears: we must use them with precision.

If I monologue, what can I hear but the sound of my own voice? If I enter the rooms of the dying at Hospice to deliver soliloquies, I'd be better off on Broadway. There is a quiet meditation that comes with the dying in the rooms at the Gerstenberg. The rooms are small with linoleum floors, those enormous mechanical beds like speedboats, a comfortable couch, some metal folding chairs, and windows that look out on lush, moist Floridian flora—banana trees, pin oak, Malaysian, Kiwi and Sabal palms. There, everyone waits. Some talk. Some listen to the silence in the room. Some speak of the nurses. Some want to know about me. Some speak of what is out the window. No one has much of a schedule. The words of Madame de Stael come to mind: "The human mind always makes progress, but it is progress in spirals." Hospice is a world of circles and progress that is rarely linear. Indeed, the floor plan consists of a central two-story atrium with a fountain surrounded by the various wards. Doctors, nurses and chaplains, literally, go in circles all day.

It strikes me that the way I read a poem is similar to the way I visit patients. Poems are artifacts left behind, messages left from fellow travelers that say, in a sense, "I was here," "I saw this," or "I did this." Poems want to matter: they are not embarrassed about their sacred disclosures. Patients, too, universally, I can say, want to matter, they want to know their lives, brief or very long, meant something to somebody, if only to themselves. In my mind, I go back over the poems I've read for years, ruminating peacefully. Similarly, when my hands come together in prayer and I think of the patients I see, so many faces flash before me, like a photo booth constantly running—yes, it is mainly the faces—and I think of what they said, what they did, their fears, their perceptions, the spirals the years took them in.

Of all the poets that come back to me as time charges ahead, as the patients die weekly (each week I return it is usually an entirely new set), no voice speaks to me more strongly now than the 17th Century English country parson, George Herbert. His voice is clear, direct, ever-yearning for a deeper connection to God. Rather than a poet of vistas or histories, Herbert's poems are nearly entirely vertical, wholly concerned with the relationship between the speaker and God. I think, sometimes, it is the most intimate voice. And that is the voice you need at Hospice.

Herbert wrote one book of poems, *The Temple*, published after his death. There are one hundred and fifty poems on the progress of his soul. Some are fretful, often spoken between Jesus and the speaker, but however truculent Herbert becomes in a poem, ultimately, we see Herbert and Jesus as friends. The emotion is so tender, made all the more poignant by the fact that the relationship memorialized is between a human being with a pen and paper and the other participant is in the ether. "Pitch thy behavior low, thy projects high," Herbert writes in "The Church Porch," "So shalt thou humble and magnanimous be." (l. 331–32). Herbert always feels teachable and there is something about that humble perspective which has always welcomed me in. He's not the *prima donna* John Donne was, as W. H. Auden wryly pointed out. Donne with all his floods and trumpets, his infinities of souls and "Death be not proud," is the ultimate contrast to Herbert's soft, metrically uneventful "Love bade me welcome yet my soul drew back." If both were on stage, Donne would be front and center and Herbert might very well be offstage, quietly stitching costumes for understudies. At this stage in my life, I want to be back stage.

On August 15th, 2007, I received a shock. Liam Rector, head of the Bennington Writers Program, who had championed my poems, had invited me up into the lovely, chilly Vermont hills to meet students, had talked to me in his deep baritone over the phone for hours (using, I believe, the word "groovy"), had gushed at my reading in a very masculine way (if such a thing is possible), had pushed me ardently to deliver my lecture on James Merrill, cajoled me behind his horn-rimmed spectacles for my scatter-brained moments, had smiled when I entered a room, had loved the idea of my work at Brooks Brothers in contrast with my poetry life (he made a point of mentioning the weft and weave of fabrics knowing he and I were engaged in a secret conversation—we could have been speaking Dutch in front of the fellow poets), had treated my syllables as if they were events, took his grandfather's gun out in his Greenwich Village apartment after putting on a tuxedo and blew his brains out. He was 57 years old.

I had never known someone this closely who had played the trump card of suicide. As I asked fellow colleagues who knew more, I learned his health had been bad for some time, a reoccurrence of colon cancer and a strained heart. In my youth, reading Sylvia Plath, I'd romanticized the idea of dying young, the sheer sweep and violent, unreasoning refusal of her leaving her brilliant poems on a desk and stuffing the tea towels under her kitchen door before she turned on the gas oven in that coldest of winters in London in 1963. But now, past 40, having celebrated so much life with dozens of Hospice patients and the call to become a priest, I had simply wished Liam hadn't have done it. I wished I had known more. I wished I could have said something to alter his choice. He wrote in his own poem, "The Remarkable Objectivity of Your Old Friends," "it was the thing/ You wanted and we'd just have to live with that." No going in circles there. If the spiritual journey can be compared to walking a labyrinth then this was a sealed-off dead-end. There was no room to reason.

Novelist Patricia Volk e-mailed, "Liam blew his brains out. Everyone shocked. Nothing else to say." *The New York Times* wrote: "Mr. Rector, who had been treated for cancer and heart trouble in the past, left a note in which he expressed distress over his health." I picked up Herbert's "Prayer." At my small black desk, I read the following:

> Prayer, the Churches banquet, Angel's age,
>   God's breath in man returning to his birth,
>   The soul in paraphrase, heart in pilgrimage,
> The Christian plummet sounding in heav'n and earth;
> Engine against th'Almightie, sinners towre,
>   Reversed thunder, Christ-side-piercing spear,
>   The six-daies world transposing in an hour,
> A kind of tune, which all things heare and fear;
> Softnesse, and peace, and joy, and love, and blisse,
>   Exalted Manna, gladnesse of the best,
>   Heaven in ordinarie, man well drest,

41

The milkie way, the bird of Paradise,
  Church-bels beyond the starres heard, the soul's bloud,
  The land of spices; something understood.

In the Benedictine tradition of *Lectio Divina*, I looked at this poem spiritually, listening to the words as if I could play them like a spiritual piano. How could the words form me rather than inform me? I began the four basic phases of the practice, *lectio, meditatio, oratio*, and *contemplatio* (add an "n" to translate into English). I begin them now, working over the page: I read the poem, the poem reads me. I've always liked "engine against th' Almightie" as praying seems like the least mechanical thing of all, the choice of words feels so improbably triumphant, "Prayer" like a Mini-Cooper driving alongside the tractor trailer of John Milton's *Paradise Lost*.

The 17th Century Carmelite Brother Lawrence wrote:

When He finds a soul penetrated with living faith, He pours out grace on it in abundance. God's grace is like a torrent. When it is stopped from taking its ordinary course, it looks for another outlet, and when it finds one, it spreads out with impetuosity and abundance.

Impetuous and abundant, this poem sits closely to me in my pew. Herbert feels open to the torrent, whereas Plath writes her poems on ice. This poem is a bubbling recipe, a quiet meditative exercise built on a series of analogies, Christ entering briefly. The poem is the first hint, I think, of surrealism before there was surrealism, with its wild, almost Plathian logical leaps. As Titian's *The Rape of Europa* has at the bottom that surrealistic fish at Europa's feet, so I have often felt Herbert's poem indicates some of the places where poetry will go. Rimbaud here we come.

The first quatrain focuses on the relationship between man and God from the perspective of heaven. The image of the Eucharist comes first and remains throughout. Prayer gets close to the angels who worship unceasingly. Prayer resuscitates us. We do not only come to life, we expand, as the Reverend F. E. Hutchinson has pointed out that "paraphrase" implies expansion in *The Works of George Herbert*.

In the second quatrain, the focus is on man and his use of prayer as a power of love. Meditating upon Christ's crucifixion is an example of

God's love. The poem is opening, the speaker, whom I like to think of as Herbert, turning his head upwards. The whole poem is built on trust and assurance. Mother Maria, in an essay, "George Herbert: Aspects of His Theology," described Herbert's type of piety this way:

> Trust is the key word for Anglican spirituality. It is the truth which within the most intimate striving after unity, overcomes the terror of the transcendence, which opens therein, and bends it back into the union. The trust is the faith lived, which comprehends itself as love, and bears within itself the sovereignty of humility, the integrating power of reconciliation.

Herbert's simplicity feels earned, to me "Prayer" is a document of faith lived, ending with a riveting glissando, "Something understood." Prayer clarifies.

He wrote without public embrace, which perhaps makes his abiding faith in God's grace more intense. His poems were written out of a completely private world, he passionately disclosed to God, his only audience. I imagine his prayers like the ones Frederick Buechner imagines the angel Raphael knowing; "There are prayers of such power that you might almost say they carry me rather than the other way around—the way a bird with outstretched wings is carried higher and higher on the back of the wind."

If poems are elemental, then Herbert's are made of air, barely anchored by dirt and water. Neither do they blaze with the fires of rancor and frustration as John Donne's battering of the heart does. This begins with "The Sacrifice," where the plangent refrain, "Was ever grief like mine?" repeats like the dripping of Christ's blood on the cross. Each of his poems is influenced by the reality of Christ on the cross. I can think of few poets with such singularity of purpose.

I have been listening to Herbert whisper to me for decades now. Auden wrote that he thought Herbert would be "exceptionally nice" if he were to meet up with him. Nice, yes, perhaps, but also made humble and direct by difficulty. Comforting his mother in a time of sickness, before she died, he wrote: "I beseech you to be cheerful, and comfort yourself in the God of all Comfort . . . why should our afflictions here, have so much power or boldness as to oppose the hope of our Joyes hereafter." Nice, then, but strong. Herbert is always trying to bridge to God, but always there is the tension of distance, as seen in "Love" (III), "Love bade me welcome, yet my soul drew back." It is not an uncommon tension at Hospice, where the volunteer is joining with strangers in search of solace in the invisible.

No doubt, Herbert, born to wealth, educated at Trinity College, Cambridge, skilled in oratory and rhetoric, fluent in five languages, was being groomed for an elite government job. In one black year, his two greatest aristocratic patrons and King James the 1st, who also took a shine to Herbert, died. It is never easy to descend the ladders of money and fame. It couldn't have been easy to close the door on English opulence. Instead, he accepted an unsophisticated parish of unschooled farmers in the tiny village of Bemerton, near Salisbury.

He must have stood out dramatically. He would have been quite alone. Perhaps this explains, partly, the singular clarity of his verse; he was speaking every day to people with simple faiths. When placed in a world of unfamiliars, I imagine he must have been listening more intensely than ever before. I know I do at Hospice. Perhaps such a tension in his life imbues the poems with their power. Over and over again, there is a sense of yearning and distance in his poems. Helen Vendler writes in her essay, "George Herbert and God": "The inconstancy of God's felt presence is the source of much of Herbert's pain in *The Temple*: at the same time, paradoxically, it is the occasion for some of Herbert's most intimate tones of reproach." Not always tapping into God's presence when at Hospice can also be a source of pain and reproach—maybe I talked too much about myself, maybe something distracted us, maybe my mind was elsewhere—and perhaps this is why I return to Herbert again and again. E. M. Forster's motto was, "Only connect." Herbert's would be, "Only connect to God."

More than twenty years ago, with a sky weighted down with tarps of deep blue and some of lighter grayish blue, stacked, jolting London clustered behind me, I was trying to direct a taxi driver to Herbert's Bemerton: Yes, yes, he knew Salisbury Cathedral with its famous spires (where Herbert would go and play the lute). The taxi driver had taken visitors to the cathedral many times. But where I wanted to go, he had only a vague idea. We kept on. I didn't have a map, only the name of the church, St. Andrew's, and the knowledge that I was close. I came upon wheat fields, stretching wide—a pleasure for the eye in a place of so much memorable architecture. Wasn't it the Zwinglians that worshiped open spaces?

When, finally, I found the little church, no bigger than the Grolier Bookshop in Cambridge, Massachusetts, I was stunned by the smallness, the place humbled me as the poems had. I asked the taxi driver to wait.

Ralph Waldo Emerson in his essay, "Nature," presents a convincing case for the power of architecture, particularly church architecture, as evoking a signature of the time, the place, and in this case, the man who self-effacingly left behind a packet of poems and if his friend, Nicholas Ferrar, didn't like them, he asked for him to destroy them. Emerson writes: "The American who has been confined, in his own country, to the sight of buildings designed after foreign models, is surprised on entering the York Minster or St. Peter's in Rome, by the feeling that the structures are imitations also,—faint copies of an invisible archetype." Before me was an archetype of humility.

The little church I went to was first built in the 13th Century. A front section was probably added during Herbert's time. His first biographer, Sir Isaac Walton, tells us Herbert had "to rebuild almost three parts" of his rectory. This would have been like building three tool-sheds. The church was sparse, the beams plain, the walls white, the chairs small, even uncomfortable, the stone floor bumpy.

I went forward. The Anglican element of having the altar close to the congregants was still evident and had not changed much since Herbert's time. At the front of the church, behind the altar, there are three small stained glass windows depicting Christ on the cross with Mary Magdalene on the one side and Mary on the other.

Protestants have never been overly zealous interior decorators. England has always felt more driven by the pen than by the paint brush, so it is no surprise the church is sparse. However, the Reformation in England seemed to be slightly less stark than in Germany and Switzerland. One need only refer to Sir Thomas Moore's forlorn reaction to the Lutheran Reformation: "Now the parish churches in many places are not only defaced, all ornaments withdrawn, the holy images pulled down and either broken or burned, but also holy sacraments cast out."

As I paused—the taxi driver waiting, tapping his dirty fingernails on his dashboard—I saw clearly Herbert's poem, "The Altar," perhaps one of the few successful concrete poems. It takes guts for a poet to sublimate words and try to paint a picture with words instead. The enterprise sounds childish. So easily could the thing fail. But here we have some architecture that stands up:

A broken A L T A R, Lord, thy servant reares,
Made of a heart, and cemented with teares:
Whose parts are as thy hand did frame;
No workmans tool hath touch'd the same.
A H E A R T alone
Is such a stone,
As nothing but
Thy pow'r doth cut.
Wherefore each part
Of my hard heart
Meets in this frame,
To praise thy Name:
That, if chance to hold my peace,
These stones to praise thee may not cease
O let thy blessed S A C R I F I C E be mine,
And sanctifie the A L T A R to be thine.

Again, Emerson writes in "Nature":

> Not only resemblances exist in things whose analogy is obvi-
> ous, as when we detect the type of the human hand in the
> flipper of the *fossil saurus*, but also in objects wherein there
> is great superficial unlikeness. Thus architecture is called
> "frozen music," by De Stael and Goethe. Vitruvius thought
> an architect should be a musician. "A Gothic church," said
> Coleridge, "is petrified religion."

The church and the poem merge in an unlikely analogy—"The
Altar" 's fasting from adjectives and adverbs, its minimalism mimics
the building. Indeed, the poem combines all the arts—with its meter
it is like song, in its design it is like painting, in its structure it is like
architecture. How like Herbert to yoke all the arts in praise of his
God. Few poets can claim the splendor of his simplicity. I've often
thought poems begin as prayers and it might well be this poem that
first gave me that thought. All a Hospice priest can offer the dying are
words. Flimsy words. The words themselves are quite useless. At Hos-
pice, as chaplains, faith is the concrete we use to make the words
something strong.

"The Altar" is about pausing and gazing: image first, words second.
The poem is rich with Biblical allusions, but let me unearth one. The

poem works from an allusion in Psalm 51, line 17: "The sacrifice acceptable to God is/ a broken spirit;/a broken and contrite heart." In line three and four, I become aware that the rearing of this altar is internal. God is responsible for rearing the stone. Herbert's reliance on God appears effortless, whether or not it actually was we'll never know. I imagine there was struggle before such graceful writing, for grace comes often after much strife.

The poem casts a much smaller shadow than the looming effigy of Donne at St. Paul's. How different the two men were at the same time. One so afraid of death, tortured by love, while Herbert married briefly, died young and wrote every poem straight to God. The vexed, quixotic winds of romance appear not to have blown over Herbert. Donne wrote, "Death is the last, and in that respect, the worst enemy." I think Herbert might question that. Herbert advocates peace, acceptance and rarely does the reader feel there are adversaries in his midst. Herbert surrenders as he writes at the base of his altar: "let thy blessed sacrifice be mine." The sacrifice balances the architecture of his life. I wish the same for my Hospice work.

For me there have been moments of doubt, taking my own will back, and being humbled by that. My altar could use some work. Herbert's "The Altar," nudges me gently: I need God to build. Architect Louise Sullivan wrote that "form follows function." Herbert made a temple: there I dwell. When Liam pulled his trigger, I entered *The Temple*. It was quiet, peaceful, warm. Safely inside, I could look out the windows on the dark, cruel world and go on. I imagine Anne Frank felt the same about her diary.

The taxi driver was impatient. He honked. Despite his large bill, he had things to do, schedules to keep. At the altar was a chubby, jolly English lady tending flowers. I asked her if she knew where Herbert was buried. Outside, she thought, maybe around the corner, she thought again. O yes, she'd heard that name before. A poet, was he? I looked and looked and looked. The taxi waited behind the stone wall. I left without finding the tombstone, only to learn he was buried with a small plaque before the altar.

Nominated by American Poetry Review, Joan Murray

WHY SOME GIRLS LOVE HORSES

by **PAISLEY REKDAL**

from THE MISSOURI REVIEW

And then I thought, Can I have more
of this, would it be possible
for every day to be a greater awakening: more light,
more light, your face on the pillow
with the sleep creases rudely
fragmenting it, hair so stiff
from paint and Sheetrock it feels
like the dirty short hank
of mane I used to grab on Dandy's neck
before he hauled me up and forward,
white flanks flecked green
with shit and the satin of his dander,
the livingness, the warmth
of all that blood just under the skin
and in the long, thick muscle of the neck—
he was smarter than most of the children
I went to school with. He knew
how to stand with just the crescent

of his hoof along a boot toe and press,
incrementally, his whole weight down. The pain
so surprising when it came,
its iron intention sheathed in stealth, the decisive
sudden twisting of his leg until the hoof
pinned one's foot completely to the ground,
we'd have to beat and beat him with a brush
to push him off, that hot
insistence with its large horse eye trained
deliberately on us, to watch—

Like us, he knew how to announce through violence
how he didn't hunger, didn't want
despite our practiced ministrations; too young
not to try to empathize
with this cunning: this thing
that was and was not human we must respect
for itself and not our imagination of it: I loved him because
I could not love him anymore
in the ways I'd taught myself,
watching the slim bodies of teenagers
guide their geldings in figure eights around the ring
as if they were one body, one fluid motion
of electric understanding I would never feel
working its way through fingers to the bit: this thing
had a name, a need, a personality; it possessed
an indifference that gave me
logic and a measure: I too might stop wanting
the hand placed on back or shoulder
and never feel the longed-for response.
I loved the horse for the pain it could imagine

and inflict on me, the sudden jerking
of head away from halter, the tentative nose
inspecting first before it might decide
to relent and eat. I loved
what was not slave or instinct, that when you turn to me
it is a choice, it is always a choice to imagine pleasure
might be blended, one warmth
bleeding into another as the future

49

bleeds into the past, more light, more light,
your hand against my shoulder, the image
of the one who taught me disobedience
is the first right of being alive.

Nominated by Donald Platt, The Missouri Review

OUR POINTY BOOTS

fiction by BROCK CLARKE

from ECOTONE

THE REPORTERS STAND BETWEEN ALL FOURTEEN OF US and our transport; they put their microphones and cameras in our faces and say, "You're going home for Christmas. What's the first thing you're going to do when you get home?"

We ask, "What are our choices?"

"The usual two," the reporters say. "Are you going to hold your babies and sweet babies real tight? Or, are you going to lay your fallen comrade to rest while the chaplain conveys the gratitude of the president and the entire nation and then prays to God for the state of your comrade's immortal soul?" Then they consult their notes and ask, "You do have a fallen comrade, don't you?"

"Yes," we say. "Saunders."

"Well," they say. "What's the first thing you're going to do when you get home? Are you going to bury him? Or, are your going to hold your babies and sweet babies real tight?"

"Neither," we tell then. "The first thing we're going to do when we get home is put on our pointy boots and parade around the Public Square."

Before we graduated from high school, before we met and married our sweet babies, before we had babies with our sweet babies, before we got the jobs that we didn't want to work at for the rest of our lives, before we realized that we probably *would* work at them for the rest of our lives if we didn't do something about it, before we did something about it and joined up, before we went to Iraq, before what happened to Saunders, before any of this happened, we were sitting around on a Friday just before graduation, skipping school, which, as graduating seniors, we were of course expected to do, feeling bored, feeling like we were missing something in our lives. And so we decided to go to the Public Square, to the Bon Ton, which had a little of everything, to see if they had what we were missing.

They were terrified of us at the Bon Ton because we were young and noisy, and we seemed even noisier than we were because we were the only customers in the store, because the store was the only store left on the Public Square that hadn't pulled out and moved to the mall, and they were terrified of us because we couldn't, at first, find what we were missing, and this disappointed us and so we let them know about it. They tried to sell us fedoras in the Men's department, and we put our fists through their tops and then wore them around our wrists like bracelets. They tried to sell us stirrup pants in the Ladies' department and those of us who are Ladies said stirrup pants were an abomination and so we all liberated the stirrups with our hands and feet and teeth and then reshelved what remained with the other, normal pants, thus diminishing their retail value. We wondered what the people at Bon Ton had to say about *that*. The people at Bon Ton didn't have anything to say; they scattered, hiding in dressing rooms and locking the slatted doors behind them; or crouching behind checkout counters, armed only with their bar code guns. And so there was no one to help us when we entered Footwear and saw the rows and rows of boots, their pointy toes pointing at us, as if to say they wanted us as much as we, we realized, wanted them.

Once we've finished talking to the reporters, we get on the transport that takes us to Germany and then another one that takes us home. We get off the transport and there, standing on the base's tarmac, are our sweet babies, waving at us. We can see that our sweet babies don't have our babies with them, for which we are grateful. Because that means there's one fewer person between us and our pointy boots. The tarmac has been cleared, but the snowbanks surrounding it are ten, fifteen feet high, high enough that you can't see the electric fences somewhere on the other side of them. It's sunny out, the sky is crystal blue, but it's so, so cold that our eyes start to water, immediately, the way they did when we first got to the desert and sand got into our eyes and they started to water, immediately. This is one of the things we've learned: not that people are the same wherever you go, but that we don't change, no matter where we are. We shoulder our duffel bags and walk toward our sweet babies. As we get closer, our sweet babies stop waving, run toward us, arms out in front of them, preparing to hold us. Their faces look hopeful, but nervous. Because they know that Saunders is dead, and they also know about the usual choices, know that we could choose him instead of them. When they get close enough, they put their arms around us and hold us real tight. But we don't hold them back. We keep one arm to our sides; the other keeps shouldering our duffels. When our sweet babies realize this they push themselves away, like they're the ships and we're the shore.

"You bastard," our sweet babies say to those of us who are men. "You bitch," our sweet babies say to those of us who are women. "You chose Saunders, didn't you? You chose burying Saunders over holding us real tight."

"We didn't choose Saunders," we say.

"Well, you obviously didn't choose us," they say.

"That's true," we say.

They look at us, confusion displacing anger on their faces for a second, before they figure out what's going on, before they figure out what we've chosen. "Oh no," they say.

"Oh yes," we say. And then we ask them to please take us home, where our pointy boots are in our closets, waiting for us to put them on and parade around the Public Square.

We have seen and done some things: When we first killed an enemy, we were glad, because for the first time ever we found that we could actually do what we were trained to do; when we first killed someone who we weren't sure was an enemy, we were happy that the word *enemy* existed so that we could call him one anyway; when we first saw one of our own comrades killed, we were ecstatic that it wasn't us; and when we were done being ecstatic, then we were so so ashamed. We've seen and done all of that. Plus, there's Saunders. But we're truly ashamed of only one thing: that once we first saw the pointy boots in the Bon Ton, we had a fight over what kind we should get.

Those of us who grew up on a farm refused to buy Luccheses for fear of being mistaken for wops. Those of us who were Italians refused to buy Fryes for fear of being mistaken for rednecks. Some of us didn't want to get Acmes because they sounded like joke boots. Some of us didn't want to get Bearpaws because the name was too close to the name of the pastry. Some of us had no trouble getting Durangos

53

except for those of us who had trucks that went by the same name. We all, finally, agreed on Saunders, except for Saunders, who said it was a stupid name for a boot. It was like giving a dog a human name, he said. "I would never name *my* dog 'Saunders,'" one of us said, and then Saunders wanted to know what the hell *that* was supposed to mean. And how does life turn out this way? How does the thing that promises to be different, the thing that promises to make you feel good, end up making you feel as bad as everything else? And when that happens, do you take it out on the thing that has promised so much, or do you take it out on yourself for believing the promise?

We did both: We took it out on ourselves and on the boots. We hurled them at each other, at close range; we gouged each other's eyes with the pointy toes; we clubbed each other with the hard heels; we put the boots over our hands, like gloves, and then boxed each other with them; we fell on the floor and wept at how pathetic and ridiculous we had become, how pathetic and ridiculous we always had been and always would be. And then, after we had wept but before we could figure out what else to do that we might later weep over, we were quiet, just for a moment, just long enough to hear one of the salesladies say meekly from inside her locked, slatted dressing room door: "What I'm hearing is that it doesn't really matter what *kind* of boots you're wearing, just as long as they're pointy."

It was like hearing the voice of God: not a vengeful God, but a practical, reasonable God, a God who didn't keep tabs on all the bad things you did, but who listened, really listened to you while you did those bad things, so as to help you get what you wanted so you'd stop doing them. When you hear that voice, you don't stop and ask how it got so wise, or question its wisdom. You just do what it tells you to do. We did what the saleslady told us to do. We gathered up the boots, found their partners. We located our size and our preferred brand and put them on, no matter how damaged they were, how damaged we had made them. Then we lined up and proceeded past the locked dressing room door; as we went past the door, we put our mouths to the slats and thanked the saleslady for her help. "I guess you're welcome," was her blessing. And then we left the Bon Ton and went out onto the Public Square.

Once our sweet babies figure out what we've chosen, they say, to themselves, "Poor Saunders. Poor us." And then, to us: "You fuckers can just go ahead and walk home," and then they run to their cars and lay rubber out of the parking lot. So, we re-shoulder our duffels and start walking.

Just outside the base, on the other side of the street from the entrance gate, are two protestors, both dressed head to toe in insulated camo, layers and layers of it, with only their faces uncovered. One, a woman, her cheeks round and fiery red, her gray hair peeking out from under a camo ski hat, is holding a cardboard sign with the words NO MORE WAR written on it in red marker, with a green peace symbol drawn underneath. The other protestor is a man. Ice hangs from his gray beard, and snot from his red nose, like Christmas tree ornaments. He chants "NO MORE WAR" into a bullhorn, drowning out whatever it is the woman is chanting, which is also probably "NO MORE WAR." They are exactly like us: There should be more of them, and they should have better ideas, and they should have better ways to tell people about their ideas. When they see us walk out of the gate, they stop chanting and come over to talk with us.

"Welcome home," the guy with the bullhorn says, although not through the bullhorn, which he holsters in what looks like an enormous, weird-looking widemouthed wine sack.

"We're proud of you," says the woman, who is probably his wife. "We feel it's important you know that."

"Okay," we say.

"This"—and here she taps her sign with the hand that's not holding it—"this doesn't mean we're not proud of you."

"Thank you," we say.

"We know you don't want to be there any more than we do," she says.

"But we volunteered," we say.

"You didn't think you were volunteering for this," she says. She looks at her sign and points to the word WAR, so we know exactly what's she's talking about.

"What *did* we think we were volunteering for, then?" we ask. We know the answer, and she doesn't, but even if she did, she'd look at us the way she looks at us now—in huge disappointment, as though we're not the people she thought we were, not the people she needs us to be. Still, she's not quite ready to give up on us. We know this, because we know her. She really is the kind of person who wants to give peace a chance, and since she's giving peace a chance, she figures she might as well give us one, too. "We," she says. "You keep talking about yourselves as 'We,' and not 'I.' You poor people. I bet the army taught you to talk like that, to think like that."

"Actually," we tell her, "we've talked and thought this way ever since the day we first put on our pointy boots and paraded around the Public Square."

"What?" she says, but she doesn't wait for any answer. She slowly backs away from us, and across the street, where she stands holding her sign over her chest with both hands, as though out of modesty. "Are you coming, Harold?" she shouts. But Harold is not coming, not quite yet.

"Tell us something about what it's like over there," he says, eagerly. We know him, too. He's the kind of guy—with his camo, his questions, his bullhorn, his homemade holster, his gear—who spends every minute he's not protesting the war fantasizing about what it's like to be in one. "Tell us something we might not have heard from someone else."

"Well," we say, "one of the things you might not have heard is that when we're interrogating someone we say that if they don't tell us what we want to know, we'll cut off their heads and then fuck their skulls."

"Always?" Harold asks.

"Every time," we say.

"You say it in English?"

"No, we don't say it in English," we say, even though we do say it in English. Because we trust that if we say it the right way, whomever we're saying it to will get the point, more or less.

"Has anyone ever told you what you wanted to know?"

"No," we say.

"I wouldn't think so," he says, then glances at those of us who are women, then looks away from them before they see him looking. It's too late; they see.

"What?" those of us who are women say. "You got some kind of problem?"

"No, no problem," the guy says, his hand moving instinctively to the bullhorn in his holster. "I just have a hard time imagining it, that's all. Can, you know, a gal actually do that, physically? I mean, it's not much of a threat, is it?"

"That's *it*," those of us who are women say. They drop their duffel bags and charge Harold. Those of us who are men have to restrain

56

them while he retreats across the street. He stands next to his wife and shouts through his bullhorn, "It's kind of funny, if you think about it," and then his wife snatches the bullhorn out of his hands and tucks it into her parka.

"Saunders wouldn't have thought it was funny," we say.

"Who is Saunders?" Harold's wife wants to know.

"Saunders is dead," we say. "We're going to lay him to rest tomorrow."

"I bet Saunders didn't think he was volunteering for *that*," the woman says.

"No, he didn't," we say as we start walking home. Because we know what Saunders thought he was volunteering for. He thought he was volunteering for the same thing we did: for the chance to feel the way we felt when we first put on our pointy boots and paraded around the Public Square.

It was lunchtime when we got out of the Bon Ton that day and onto the Public Square. It was sunny, hot, almost summer. The county courthouse workers were sitting in the shadow of the statue of our locally significant revolutionary war general with their bagged lunches, struggling to unwrap their cellophane-wrapped meat and cheese sandwiches. The guys from the halfway house were lying back-down and shirtless on the grass, wolfing their cigarettes, then lighting their new butts with the remainders of the old without once opening their eyes. The bail bondsmen stood near their storefronts, across the square from the courthouse, sipping burnt coffee out of Styrofoam cups, eyeing the cuffed as they were led into the courthouse, making bets on how much their bail would be, on who would end up jumping and who would not.

And then there was us, fifteen teenagers, boys and girls, standing in front of the Bon Ton. For a while, we did nothing but look down and admire our new pointy boots. There is no love so true as one's love for one's new pair of shoes, and we loved our pointy boots even more truly than that. We turned our feet this way and that, watched as the boots glinted in the sun; we squatted down and traced our fingers over the stitched patterns, or if we'd chosen boots with no patterns, we ran our fingers over the smooth, stitchless surfaces; we stuck our toes into the smallest sidewalk cracks and marveled at how pointy the toes really were. We looked around the square, and saw that no one else was wearing anything remotely like them. We pitied these people. Be-

57

cause this is what it means to be in love: You feel sorry for people who aren't. And then you feel happy that no one feels sorry for you. You feel so happy that it's not enough just to sit there and admire the beloved. You have to do something that shows the beloved how much you love it. And if you love your pointy boots the way we loved ours, you show them so by parading in them around the Public Square.

We did that. We proceeded loosely, not in formation, as we later learned to do at the base; not single file, or on our hands and knees, as we learned to do in the desert; but some of us in twos and threes, some of us by ourselves, some of us stopping, momentarily, to admire our boots in the windows of the empty storefronts, or to wipe some dust or dirt off our pointy boots, and then moving on again. Around and around we went. We did it for the joy of the thing, and not necessarily to be noticed by the poor people who were not us. But they noticed us anyway. The county courthouse workers looked up from their sandwiches, the bail bondsmen from those who might soon be bail bonded; the guys from the halfway house actually sat up and opened their eyes and let their butts die out without lighting another. One of the most fully gone of the halfway house guys even got up and started parading with us. He wore sweatpants—with one sweatpant leg down to the ankle, the other pushed up to the knee—and beat-up white leather high-top basketball sneakers with no socks. He brought his knees up high as he marched and waved his unlit cigarette like a baton. He was mocking us, probably, and we let him, rather than kicking his ass, which we could have done, easily. We practiced restraint. We figured ass kicking was unnecessary, figured he'd get tired and sooner or later return to the grass with his halfway house brothers. Which is exactly what happened. After a lap or two around the square, he went back to the grass and sat down and watched us. Everyone did. We knew what they were seeing: They were seeing fifteen teenagers, some boys, some girls, parading together but not together, all wearing pointy boots but not the same pointy boots. Fifteen individuals, but also a group, a group people could identify and admire: those kids who paraded around the Public Square in their pointy boots. They could see what we, and they, and everyone, were told in school was all around us: a nation of individuals, united. They could see the promise of America, in other words, made flesh by us and our pointy boots.

It's dark by the time we get home. We knock on our front doors, and our sweet babies unlock them and let us in. But before we're able to get our boots out of our closets and on our feet and start parading around the Public Square, our sweet babies try to stop us. We keep aiming for the bedroom, for the closet where our pointy boots are waiting for us, and they keep edging in front of us, blocking the room, asking us questions. They ask us if we want something to eat. They ask if we want to take a rest, or watch some TV, or maybe play a board game. They ask us to admire the Christmas tree (there is a Christmas tree, in the corner, next to the TV, a pretty, droopy Scotch pine with colored lights and presents piled underneath it and a wooden nativity scene with baby Jesus and His mom and dad facing outward and the donkeys and wise men facing the presents). They tell us that they were waiting for us to get home to put the star on the top of the tree. They ask us if we'd like to put the star on the top of the tree now or a little bit later. Why don't we do it a little bit later? our sweet babies say. But for right now, would we like some hot chocolate? We know what they're doing. We know they've taken a seminar, at the base, about what to do when your soldier comes home. We know they've been warned to expect us to be a little different. To be a little *off*. We know they've been told to be patient with us, not to force us to talk about things we might not want to talk about. We know this because we were made to take a seminar at the base in Iraq, telling us to ex- pect the same thing about ourselves, to treat ourselves with the same caution, the same care.

When we don't answer any of their questions, our sweet babies put their hands on our shoulders and look into our eyes and say, "We missed you."

"Yes," we say.

"I bet you miss Saunders," they say.

"Yes," we say.

"Poor Saunders," they say.

"Yes," we say. And then: "About those pointy boots . . ."

"*Fine*," they say. They take their hands off our shoulders, step to the side, and make a sweeping motion with their arms in the direction of the bedroom, the closet, the boots, as if to say, *It's all yours*. We can see the hurt on their faces. We can see what we've done to them, what we've always done to them. We are not heartless, and to show we're not heartless, we say, "Sorry."

"You've always cared more about your pointy boots than you've cared about us, haven't you?" they ask.

"Yes," we say, and run past them, into the bedroom.

At the end of lunch hour, the county workers finished their sandwiches and went back into the courthouse. The bail bondsmen finished their coffee and went back into their storefronts. The halfway house guys finished their cigarettes and went back into their halfway houses. And we, we finished our parading and sat down at the foot of the statue of our local revolutionary war general. We'd paraded for almost an hour, but we didn't feel at all tired, not even our feet, which we would have expected to feel tired, considering we'd been parading in brandnew pointy boots. But we didn't have one blister, one strained arch, one bruised heel, one rubbed-raw toe. We felt *good*. And if we felt so good, some of us wondered, if we weren't tired, if we weren't footsore, then what did we think we were doing, sitting down? Let's get up and *parade*, for crying out loud, some of us said. But others of us said no. Because hadn't we felt good before? Hadn't we felt good on the basketball court, or while smoking cigarettes behind the art room, or while sitting on the hoods of our parents' second cars on the dirt roads outside town and drinking beer, or while doing things to each other—in the cornfields next to the dirt roads—that we'd always wanted to do but couldn't get up the nerve to without the help of the beer? And hadn't we then ruined those good things? Hadn't we then taken and missed a terrible shot we had no business taking, at exactly the worst possible moment, and lost the game, or smoked an extra cigarette and got caught doing it by the art teacher, or drunk ten beers too many and then later wrecked our parents' cars, or before we wrecked those cars done things we shouldn't have with each other in the cornfields and then regretted it afterward? Hadn't we ruined good things before? some of us asked. And it should be said that Saunders was one of us who asked it. Looking back, you would think, after everything Saunders had done in Iraq, that he was one of us who wanted to get up and parade and ruin our good feeling, but no: He was one of us who spoke eloquently about not ruining it. He was one of us who said that we should always keep the memory, the vision, of our parading around the square in our pointy boots close by, and we shouldn't ruin it by going out and parading around the Public Square in our pointy boots whenever we felt a little sad, a little lonely, a little useless. He said that we should try to find that feeling somewhere else—through our work, through our marriages, through *whatever*—that we should go looking for that feeling everywhere. And even if we never found it, even if our lives ended up as lousy as they'd been before we put on our pointy boots, then at least we'd have the memory of that time when it wasn't lousy, when we felt *good*; at least we'd have the memory of the one good thing we *didn't* ruin. And no matter what, we should agree to do this together, to do everything together, as one. Then, those of us who hadn't wanted to parade again asked, Agreed? And those of us who had wanted to parade again said, Agreed. Then we went home and took off our pointy boots and put them in our closets. We polished them regularly, religiously, treated them more tenderly, more lovingly than we ever did our sweet babies, which our sweet babies never failed to notice and comment upon. Whenever we moved, we took the boots with us, moved them from bedroom closet to bedroom closet, but we never put them on, not once, until now. Because we promised Saunders we would wear them when we laid him to rest.

We're sitting on our beds, trying to put on our pointy boots, which is difficult, more difficult than we remember, more difficult than it used to be, because our feet have been in round-toed boots for so long they've stopped being the kind of feet that will slip easily into pointy boots. A few seconds later we hear soft, muffled, thumping sounds coming toward us. We look up and see our sweet babies standing in the doorway. They have crazed, I'm-determined-to-try-one-more-time smiles on their faces, and in front of them, in front of us, stand our babies, wearing overlarge T-shirts that read DADDY'S LITTLE GIRL, or MOMMY'S LITTLE BOY, or DADDY'S LITTLE GIRL, or MOMMY'S LITTLE GIRL, depending. Our babies are so much bigger than the last time we saw them; they hardly even look like our babies anymore. Our babies turn to look at our sweet babies, who nod; then our babies turn back to us, and smile in their shy, distracted, happy way. On the transport, we warned each other about this moment, the moment when our babies would be produced, when our babies and sweet babies would conspire to melt our hearts. We reminded each other that our hearts had melted when our babies had first been born, too. We reminded each other of how we had each said to our newborn babies, "You are mine. You are mine and you melted my heart and I will never let you down." And then, of course, we did let them down, in thousands of small and large ways, every day of their lives, including by leaving them to go to Iraq. We resented them because of it—there is no resentment so pure as that for the people whom you love and have let down, and our resentment was even purer than that, because we were comparing our babies to our pointy boots, which we had never let down after we'd first put them on and which we had never resented. We look away from our babies now and pull even harder on our boots, trying to jam our feet into them.

"Don't you want to hold your baby?" our sweet babies ask as we pull and grunt, pull and grunt. Our babies are closer now. They are on the verge of calling to us by name, or, at least, by little. Their lips open and close, open and close, as though practicing to say the word. It is almost impossible to resist a baby who is on the verge of saying your name for the first time. Still we resist. This infuriates our sweet babies; this *pisses them off*. They pick up our babies, and pull them away from us and to their chests, as though we're not worthy of them. This is another thing the seminars have taught them: that they will become infuriated by us; but no matter how infuriated they get, they should never, the seminars tell them, never ever act as though we're not worthy. But what if we *aren't* worthy? What do they do then? On this, the seminars are silent. Figure that out for yourself, the seminars seem to say.

Our babies start to cry; they start to struggle in our sweet babies' arms. They want to get down; they want to come to us. But our sweet babies won't let them.

"Jesus, what kind of person *are* you?" our sweet babies want to know.

We stop trying to put on our boots, and look at our sweet babies, wondering if they *really* want to know. Do they really want to know what the two protestors know: that we are the kind of people who, when interrogating someone, shove our rifles in his face and say, "If you don't tell us what we want to know, we are going to chop off your head and fuck your skull"? Do they want to know what the two protestors don't know? Do they want to know that we are also the kind of people who then, when it comes down to it, will not do what we've threatened, except for Saunders, once, kind of? We say "kind of" because the woman was already dead. She was already dead. We had killed her while storming the house, or someone in the house had shot her beforehand, or during, or she had shot herself. In any case, she was dead, slumped against the wall. There was a small hole in her chest and there was a lot of blood still coming out of it and staining her robes. She was wearing so many robes, so many layers of clothing, even though it was so hot; her headscarf had slipped down and was covering her face. We removed it. Her face looked like ash, but we put our hands inches from her mouth to feel if she was breathing; we put our fingers on her neck to see if she had a pulse. She wasn't and didn't; she was dead. Her son (we assumed he was her son; he was the right age, around ten or so) was still alive, face down on the floor, hands behind his head. There was no one else in the house; we'd checked. We assumed we would do what we normally did: We would tell the boy who was still alive that if he didn't tell us what we wanted to know that we would cut off his head and fuck his skull. And then, when he didn't tell us, we'd bring him to the people who did the real interrogating, the people we knew nothing about except that they used better threats than we did. Or, they used the same threat, just more effectively. But before we could say what we usually said, Saunders blurted out, "If you don't tell me what I want to know, I'm going to fuck your dead mother's skull." And then, before we could give him hell for deviating from the script, Saunders dropped his pants and tried to do what he'd threatened. Do our sweet babies want to know that? Do they want to know that, when Saunders started to do it, we laughed? That all of us laughed? Maybe because we were so startled that he deviated from the script, or that he tried to do what he'd threatened. Or maybe because he kept saying, "It's not working, it's not working," and we said, "Well, *of course* it's not working, Saunders, she's dead." "That's not what I mean," Saunders said. "I'm talking about *it*. *It* isn't working." "Well, Jesus, Saunders," we said, "of course *it* isn't working." And then we laughed, we couldn't help ourselves. Because it *was* kind of funny, if you thought about it. Do our sweet babies want to know that? Do they want to know that we are the kind of people who laugh at Saunders trying and failing to skull-fuck that dead mother? That we are the kind of people who laugh harder when Saunders, his pants still around his ankles, the *it* that wasn't working hanging out for anyone with eyes to see, waddles over to the son, his rifle in his right hand? The son is lying facedown on the dirt floor of his house—if it is his house, or if you can call it a house, just a stack of cinder blocks with planks of wood resting on top, really. The son is crying, the dirt around his head getting wet from his tears, his hands still clamped behind his head, keeping his head still while the rest of his body shakes and writhes and convulses, like a snake with its head nailed to the ground. "Look at me," Saunders says to the son. The boy turns his head in Saunders's direction. "You're next," he says, cupping his crotch with his left hand, and we laugh harder. *That's* the kind of people we are. Or maybe that's *not* the kind of people we are. But it is the kind of people we've become.

But our sweet babies don't want to know this, any of this. So, instead, we say, "We are the kind of people, who when we get home, before we do anything else, put on our pointy boots and parade around the Public Square." And then, finally, we cram our round-toed boot feet into our pointy boots, and go do that.

It is hard sledding, getting to the Public Square. For one, it's snowing, again, again, and there is nowhere left to put the snow—the snowbanks are too high already—and so the walks are unshoveled, the roads unplowed. For another, our pointy boots have shit for traction and we slip and fall, a lot, as we walk. By the time we all get to the Public Square, we are soaked and sore from all the falling. Cold, too. Because all we have on are our travel camo pants and jackets, our berets, and, of course, our pointy boots—which are at least waterproof, and a good thing, too, because they're completely buried in the snow. It is dark, after six o'clock. The county office building's windows are dark; everyone has gone home. On the corner of State and Lewis, the bail bonds office has an illuminated Western Union sign in the window, but otherwise the place is dark as well. The guys in the halfway house are nowhere to be seen. It's possible that the halfway house has closed. It's possible that they've joined up, too, that the army is where the halfway house guys are sent when the halfway house closes. The Bon Ton is no longer the Bon Ton, is no longer anything, but the city has decorated its front windows with white blinking Christmas lights. The streetlight poles are wrapped with green garland and red bows. The statue of the revolutionary war general is buried up to the waist in snow, the falling snow piling up on his plumed hat. Other than him, we are the only ones on the square. It is not how we pictured it, not how we remembered it. For that matter, we're not sure how we pictured ourselves, how we remembered ourselves. We do a quick head count and find that we're not all here, not even close.

"Where the hell is everyone?" we ask. But we know. We can see them putting the silver stars on top of their Christmas trees; we can see them holding their sweet babies real tight; we can hear their babies calling them by name, each and every one of them.

"Those bastards," one of us says.

"Those bitches," another one of us says.

"This is ridiculous," the third of us says.

"Maybe we should just go home," the fourth of us says.

"Our poor babies," the fifth of us says.

"Our poor sweet babies," the sixth of us says.

"Poor Saunders," the last of us says, and then we remember why we can't go home. His funeral is at nine in the morning. We can picture it: His sweet baby and baby will be there, trying to be brave, trying not to cry while the chaplain conveys the thanks of the president and prays to God for the state of Saunders's immortal soul. We'll be there, too, wearing our pointy boots. Because we promised Saunders, right before he died. He said, "When you lay me to rest, will you please wear your pointy boots?" We promised we would. But first, we need to do what we've come here to do. We have fifteen hours to parade around the public square in our pointy boots; fifteen hours to forget what happened to Saunders, so we can help bury him.

"Are we ready?" we ask each other. And then we start parading around the Public Square. We walk slowly at first, take tiny steps, because of the footing. But then we start going faster. We don't mean to. It's the blinking Christmas lights: They blink too fast and when we look at them, they make us walk too fast, too. Right in front of the Bon Ton, after only one lap around the Public Square, we slip, and fall on our backs, and because it's impossible not to laugh when someone slips and falls in the snow, we laugh. Then we remember laughing at Saunders and we stop laughing. Then we remember when we stopped laughing at Saunders and looked around. There was the mother, lying on the dirt floor faceup, the way Saunders had left her. There was the son, lying there, his face down and to the side, still weeping, still looking at Saunders, who was still grabbing his crotch with one hand and holding his rifle with the other. But Saunders wasn't looking at the son, or at the mother, or at us. His eyes were closed, his face pinched in concentration. We knew what he was doing: He was trying to picture the day we'd paraded around the Public Square in our pointy boots; he was trying to replace the picture of what he'd just done with the picture of us, our boots, the square, us parading around it, people watching us, us feeling so good. We knew that's what he was doing, because we did the same thing: We closed our eyes and tried to picture it, tried to remember it. We tried so hard. But the harder we tried to picture the boots, the Public Square, the office workers and bail bondsmen and halfway house guys, the farther away all of that was. All we could see was the mother, Saunders kneeling over her, us laughing; Saunders getting up and waddling over to the son, us laughing even harder. Go away, we told the memory we didn't want. Please come back, we told the one we did. Please come back, we begged our pointy boots. But they didn't.

We opened our eyes. Saunders was lying on his back next to the son. They were both crying now—the son because he didn't know what was going to happen, Saunders because he did.

"I'm sorry," Saunders said.

"I am, too," each of us said.

"Will you promise me something?" Saunders said. "When you lay me to rest, will you please wear your pointy boots?"

"We will," we said, and then without saying another word, we aimed our guns at him and one by one—Carson, Marocco, Smoot, Mayfair, Penfield, Rovazzo, Zyzk, Palmer, Reese, Appleton, Exley, Scarano, Loomis, Olearzyck—we shot him, and then we shot the son, too. Then we closed our eyes again. But we saw the same thing as before, except that there was another Saunders in it and another son, and they were both dead and we'd killed them.

"Are you still seeing it?" we ask ourselves. But of course we know the answer. We lie there, in the snow, waiting to see whether one of us, any of us, will get up, brush off our pointy boots, and try again.

Nominated by Ecotone, Nicola Mason

SUNFLOWER

by HENRI COLE

from ALASKA QUARTERLY REVIEW

When Mother and I first had the do-not-
resuscitate conversation, she lifted her head,
like a drooped sunflower, and said,
"Those dying always want to stay."
Months later, on the kitchen table,
Mars red gladiolus sang *Ode to Joy*,
and we listened. House flies swooped and veered
around us, like the Holy Spirit. "Nature
is always expressing something human,"
Mother commented, her mouth twisting,
as I plucked whiskers from around it.
"Yes, no, please." Tenderness was not yet dust.
Mother sat up, rubbed her eyes drowsily, her breaths
like breakers, the living man the beach.

Nominated by Alaska Quarterly Review, Elizabeth Spires, Jane Hirshfield, Philip White

I CAN'T WRITE A MEMOIR OF CZESLAW MILOSZ

by ADAM ZAGAJEWSKI

from THE THREEPENNY REVIEW

I CAN'T WRITE A MEMOIR of Czeslaw Milosz. For some reason it seems impossible to me though I had almost no trouble when I wrote about the late Zbigniew Herbert, for example (but, on the other hand, I wouldn't envisage writing this kind of essay about Joseph Brodsky either, someone I knew well). Why is it so? Was Herbert more of a "unified person"? Not really. All three of them, Milosz, Herbert, Brodsky—so different as poets and human beings—enjoyed, or suffered, the complexity of a life divided between the utmost seriousness of their work and the relative jocularity of what the other people perceived as their socially visible personalities. All three enjoyed joking, being with other people, dominating the conversation, laughing (Milosz's laugh was the loudest, the most majestic), as if needing a respite from the gravity of their vocation.

And yet, again, some time ago I was able to write a few pages about Herbert's life. Was it because I met him briefly when I was almost a child, when he visited my high school in Silesia? Because his personal predicament, his illness, stamped him with a drama which was so gripping in its ferocity and made him differ even more from the music of his noble poetry than was the case with other poets and artists (who, none of them, are ever identical with their work)? Because I had the feeling that, as we were born in the same city of Lvov, some twenty years apart and only two hundred yards away from each other, I had a special claim on his fate, the way veterans from two different wars but from the same regiment may feel close, almost like members of the same tribe, the same family?

I had read Milosz for many years before I met him in person. In the late Sixties and in the Seventies I didn't believe I'd ever meet him. He was then for me a legend, a unicorn, somebody living on a different planet; California was but a beautiful name to me. He belonged to a chapter of the history of Polish literature that seemed to be, seen from the landscape of my youth, as remote as the Middle Ages. He was a part of the last generation that had been born into the world of the impoverished gentry (impoverished but still very much defining themselves as gentry): he grew up in a small manor house in the Lithuanian countryside where woods, streams, and water snakes were as evident as streetcars and apartment houses in the modest, industrial city of my childhood. His Poland was so totally different from mine—it had its wings spread to the East. When he was born in 1911 he was a subject of the Russian Tsar; everything Russian, including the language which he knew so well, was familiar to him (though, as his readers well know, he was also very critical of many things Russian). I was born into a Poland that had changed its shape; like a sleeper who turns from one side to another, my country spread its arms toward the West—of course only physically, because politically it was incorporated into the Eastern bloc.

I grew up in a post-German city; almost everything in the world of my childhood looked and smelled German. Cabbage seemed to be German, trees and walls recalled Bismarck, blackbirds sang with a Teutonic accent. My primary school could have belonged in any of Berlin's middle-class suburbs—its Prussian bricks were dark red like the lips of Wagnerian singers. The first radio in our apartment (a radio I worshipped—it received signals from an invisible realm, it had music, it brought strange sounds from different continents) was German and probably still nostalgic about Adolph Hitler's endless speeches. The first foreign language I had begun to learn (unwillingly), because of my grandfather, himself a Germanist, was German, too. For Milosz, who was a polyglot, learning German never existed as a possibility, especially after World War II, and German poetry never played a major role in the vast universe of his reading.

69

There were no manor houses and water snakes in my childhood. Coal mines and chimneys played the part of woods and meadows. Aristocratic families were squatting in the smallest apartments, surviving on minimal wages. (My family, I hasten to make it clear, was not aristocratic at all.) I was supposed to be a lucky inhabitant of a classless society in which falcons and sparrows were condemned to mandatory friendship. Classless society: practically, it meant that everybody was very poor, with the exception of Party dignitaries and a few cunning merchants who were able to outwit the Party but whose sleep was rather nervous; the wealth they accumulated could have been taken away from them in one day, no solid law protected them. The language we spoke was a plebeian Polish, hard, ugly, filled with typical Communist acronyms, abbreviations, and clichés, punctuated with giggles, swear-words, and ironies—a language of slaves, good only for basic communication in a kind of a Boolean algebra of resentment. In the mid-Seventies I venerated a performance of Adam Mickiewicz's *Dziady* (*Forefathers*) staged at the Teatr Stary in Krakow; it was directed by Konrad Swinarski, who before long died tragically in an airplane accident in Syria. Soon afterwards I was told that Milosz, who had been offered the recording of the piece, commented sourly: "I can't stand the way these actors speak the Polish language." He found their pronunciation barbaric. These barbarians were my peers, my contemporaries: I knew many of them from rather benign military training sessions at the university. When they played the rebels from the Mickiewicz generation they sounded to me like my friends; I was transported back to turn-of-the-century Vilna, I was one of them. They spoke my language, a language that didn't have the sweet music of Russian nor the elegance of French.

Also in the Seventies, one of my friends, a painter, Leszek Sobocki, traveled regularly to the United States (his mother was living in Los Angeles then). He was a part of a vague constellation of young artists and poets who were critical of the Communist system, though they hadn't known any other from personal experience, and who tried, being faithful to a more or less realistic aesthetic, to create art that would matter socially and politically. I belonged to the same archipelago. Sobocki, on one of his trips to L.A., mailed to Berkeley a package which contained excerpts from poetry and fiction produced by us, as well as reproductions of the paintings and prints made by him and his friends. After a while, a long letter written in response by Milosz arrived; it couldn't have been more devastating. Milosz basically dismissed the whole business of socially critical art, reducing our efforts to the well-meaning but aesthetically uninteresting and totally predictable reactions of inexperienced youngsters. He extolled "metaphysical distance," quoting Aleksander Wat's sentence on the necessity of fighting against Communism on metaphysical grounds. Which meant going to the very foundations of somebody's convictions. The letter was a cold shower for us, for me. Was Milosz right? I was of two minds even then . . . He gave me pause. Now I think he was mostly right, though there must have been also a bit of jealousy in his judgment, jealousy of the directness of our action; an intellectual in exile is often "metaphysical" by necessity—for him it's not a matter of free choice since he has lost access to the unmediated spectacle of life in his own country. A much younger Milosz, the Milosz of the great poems written under the Nazi occupation or right after it, was after all somebody who didn't disdain directness at all.

And yet against all odds I fell in love with Milosz's poetry; its melodies seemed at times ancient, but its intellectual content couldn't have been more modern, more attractive, more complex, more intoxicating. I say I fell in love with it, which is true—still, first I had to find Milosz's poems, which was very difficult indeed. My parents had a significant library (where, it's true, fiction dwarfed poetry) but there was nothing by Milosz on the shelves. His name was erased from all the text-books. My high school literature teacher never mentioned the name of Czeslaw Milosz. In an encyclopedia there was an entry under Milosz, but it was devoted to "Milosz Obrenovic," a brave Serbian prince, not to the author of *Native Realm*. Since 1951, the year of his defection, Milosz had been an outcast, a non-person. If his name did appear somewhere in print, it was frequently accompanied by the official Byzantine formula "an enemy of the People's Republic of Poland." Poor republic, having such a potent enemy!

In order to be able to read his poems and his prose, I needed a special permit from the dean of my college, and even once I got it—which wasn't easy—I was not allowed to check these books out; I could only study them in one of the reading rooms in the Jagellonian Library, my Krakow alma mater's crown jewel. Each day I had to say good-night to a pile of books: they had to stay on the shelf while I walked home. I was assigned to the Professor's Reading Room, which in my eyes, the eyes of a young graduate student, added to the importance of the occasion. And there I sat for hours, discovering the writings of the enemy of our republic. Sweet hours! And they were made even sweeter by the conspiratorial conditions under which I approached Milosz's poetry.

The richness of this work was overwhelming; I wasn't able right away to grasp the whole extent of the poet's achievement. I was swallowing lines of his poems like somebody given only a short moment in a magical orchard, a trespasser avidly reaching out for cherries, pears, peaches. I didn't have enough time and leisure—nor maturity, I'm afraid—to discern the different layers within his work, to understand the meandering of his thought, to define the stages of Milosz's complicated poetic evolution. I read for enchantment, not for any critical insights. I remember walking home after these sessions in the library and repeating lines from his poems—I was inebriated with them. Had I been a driver then, the police could have arrested me for driving in a state of drunkenness. But as I was only a chaotic walker, nobody could stop me; even a totalitarian state was not able to control my daydreams, my poetic fascinations, the pattern of my walking.

What was it that attracted me to Milosz's poetry? Precisely everything that was different from my own experience, my own situation, from my "people's republic" language. I fell in love with the freedom with which Milosz both respected and defied the rules of poetic modernism. He was saying more than the poets I had known before—I mean he didn't keep a strict diet of purist metaphors: he was willing to tell the reader more than was accepted among contemporary poets. The reader knew that Milosz believed in something and hated something else, knew what Milosz's *Weltanschauung* was, and yet many of his poems were violent quarrels of the poet with himself, not at all easy to decipher—he was never doctrinaire, he never quite agreed with himself. I was also struck by a constant, energetic quest for the invisible in his poetry, a quest that arose amidst the most concrete, sensual images, not in an ascetic monastery chapel. In his oeuvre, ecstatic tones mixed with sober reflection; there was no easy way to classify this poetry—it burst taxonomies. It was not "nature poetry," it was not a "poetic meditation on History," neither was it "autobiographical lyric"—it was all of those. The ambition of this poet knew no limits; he tried to drink in the cosmos.

After so much intimacy gained from the contact with his work, the shock of meeting him in person was still considerable. And the contrast between the immense, complicated territory of his powerful work and the gentleman I finally met (a seventy-year-old "smiling public man") was sizeable, too. How can a single person embody all the nuances and contradictions of a vast opus? I don't want to say that I was disappointed with Milosz's human incarnation. Not at all; I admired him, I loved him, every moment spent with him was fascinating. He was a kind friend; he wrote a most generous preface to *Tremor*, my first collection of poems in the United States; he showed interest in my life and work; and much later, in Krakow, we became almost neighbors, and I saw him often. And yet I know that for him I always remained a younger friend, not somebody he would confide in the way, I imagine, some from his generation might have enjoyed—or endured.

I met him for the first time in June 1983, in Paris, in the spacious apartment of Leonor Fini and Konstanty Jelenski near Place des Victoires. I was then somebody who had recently left Poland and who had no idea how long his Parisian emigration would last. Konstanty Jelenski was an exile like Milosz, a brilliant critic and a great admirer of Milosz's poetry. The Milosz I met then was an elder statesman—old and yet strangely young and handsome, serene, witty, radiating an energy which made him the center of every social event; wild and tame at the same time, rescued by the renown of the Stockholm accolade from the trials of his Berkeley solitude.

In January 1986 I read with him and some other famous poets during the PEN conference in New York, in the Cooper Union Hall, where a huge and enthusiastic audience that consisted mostly, it seemed, of very young poets greeted the readers—what a wonderful audience it was! After that I saw him now and then in Paris, in California, in New York, in Indianapolis . . . In Houston, where I taught creative writing, I introduced his reading.

Later, in Krakow, I'd visit him many times in his apartment in Boguslawski Street, where he eventually settled down with Carol. I saw him walking—more and more slowly—in the Krakow Old Town, where almost everybody recognized him and looked at him with awe. Given the slow pace of his walks, the awe had enough time to be richly deployed. He was like Goethe in Weimar, though his apartment was so much more modest than the house in Frauenplan—but the centrality of his position in the small world of Krakow and Poland was never questioned. This in itself was an enormous achievement for an exile who had returned to his country after so many decades of absence. His intellectual authority was overwhelming. In the restaurants he spoke very loudly because he was hard of hearing, so loudly that it was a bit embarrassing for his friends—not much privacy in these conversations. And yet he was never diminished by his great old age. His memory was invincible, his laughter irresistible, his mind alert.

In 2002 and 2003 he was enthusiastically received by American poets, very young ones and also the well-known ones, during summer conferences I organized with Edward Hirsch in Krakow; Milosz refused to participate in panels because he couldn't hear what the others said, but agreed to meet students from Houston. He gave several Q & A's, answering endless questions, embarking on long, unforgettable soliloquies (someone would always help him by repeating the question near his better ear). And he read with the other poets: I'll always remember him at a reading in the beautifully restored Krakow reform synagogue, a yarmulka on his regal head—old David speaking to his nation, feeble and yet so strong, solemn but also visibly savoring with a courteous, contented smile the din of the ovation that went on and on.

There was something absolutely splendid in the way he stood up to the challenges of his last years. He never withdrew into the comfort of a well-deserved retirement. With those he loved or liked, he was tender, magnanimous, charming; he received many friends and many strangers, young or old admirers of his work, poets and critics, but when he spoke in public he retained the tone of an angry prophet. He had always attacked the pettiness of his compatriots; he defended the visionary homeland of his dreams, pluralistic and tolerant, but at the same time he castigated the vices of the existing society: he hated anti-Semitism, narrow-mindedness, nationalism, stupidity. He had a religious mind but he also believed in liberal, democratic principles and tried to teach his contemporaries the implications of this complex creed.

I witnessed his deep sadness after Carol died; by then he knew he would face the end of his life in an empty apartment whose every corner bore traces of Carol's tender hand and imagination. Even then, after he returned from his last trip to California, where he bade her goodbye, he was able to write the beautiful elegy for Carol, "Orpheus and Eurydice." His gift for transforming life's sorrows into poetry was intact, but he was tired and, it seems to me, maybe even a bit ashamed of always succeeding in being a magician against all odds, all catastrophes, all deaths. "What is poetry which does not save / Nations or people?" he asked in the mid-Forties. What's the use of magic that doesn't assuage despair? There was always his religious hope, his faith, sometimes dreams brought him signals of divine presence, but—we know it from the poems—despair was also one of his frequent visitors. His laughter still triumphed over the baseness of biology, but the last years made him frail.

This great life had its secrets: how many times had Milosz told us in his poems that he was an "evil person"? His friends never believed it, though I think he wanted us maybe not to accept it as true but at least to considered it more seriously. Friends are usually too well-meaning, too polite, too well-bred. They always tell you "you'll be fine," "you exaggerate"; they want to cheer you up—that's their business. Which is probably the last thing someone coping with the grave images at life's end wants to hear. The poet who decided early on that poetry was about communicating with other people, not about lofty hermeticism and language games, was dying in the silence of his solitary days and nights. One of the last humans who spoke to him in his hours of agony was an uneducated woman who took care of his small household, a wonderful person with a great heart. I like to think of it: in the vast polyphony of the almost hundred years of his dramatic existence, the ultimate sound he heard was an unschooled voice of goodness. Perhaps in this soothing voice he found something like an arch between his early idyllic childhood in the Lithuanian countryside and his closing moments; and in between there remained, bracketed out for once, the rage of modern history, the loneliness of his long exile, the violence of his struggles, of his thought, his imagination, his rebellions.

I can't write a memoir of Milosz: so much was hidden in his life. Besides, he was an ecstatic poet and an ecstatic person. We'll never really know people like that. They hide their great moments of elation; they never share with others the short joys of their sudden discoveries, and the sadness when the vision fades. They thrive in solitude. With their friends they are usually correct, measured, just like everybody else. They are like a ship we sometimes see in a peaceful port: a huge immobile mass of metal covered by spots of rust, a few sailors lazily sunbathing on the deck, a blue shirt drying on a rope. One wouldn't guess that this ship was once struggling with the hurricane, barely surviving the onslaught of big waves, singing an iron song . . . No, I didn't know him enough. I have to return to his poems, to his essays.

Nominated by Threepenny Review, Philip Levine

FRIEDA PUSHNIK

by B. H. FAIRCHILD

from IMAGE

> *"Little Frieda Pushnik, the Armless, Legless Girl Wonder,"* who spent years as a
> touring attraction for Ripley's Believe It or Not and Ringling Brothers and Barnum
> and Bailey. . . .
>
> —from the *Los Angeles Times* Obituaries

I love their stunned, naked faces. Adrift with wonder,
big-eyed as infants and famished for that *strangeness*
in the world they haven't known since early childhood,
they are monsters of innocence who gladly shoulder
the burden of the blessed, the unbroken, the beautiful,
the lost. They should be walking on their lovely knees
like pilgrims to that shrine in Guadalupe, where
I failed to draw a crowd. I might even be their weird
little saint, though God knows *I've wanted everything
they've wanted*, and more, of course. When we toured Texas, west
from San Antonio, those tiny cow towns flung
like pearls from the broken necklace of the Rio Grande,
I looked out on a near infinity of rangeland
and far blue mountains, avatars of emptiness,
minor gods of that vast and impossibly pure nothing
to whom I spoke my little still-born, ritual prayer.

I'm not on those posters they paste all over town,
those silent orgies of secondary colors—jade,
burnt orange, purple—each one a shrieking anthem
to the exotic: Bengal tigers, ubiquitous

as alley cats, raw with not inhuman but
superhuman beauty, demonic spider monkeys,
absurdly buxom dancers clad in gossamer,
and spiritual gray elephants, trunks raised like arms
to Allah. Franciscan murals of plenitude,
brute vitality ripe with the fruit of eros,
the faint blush of sin, and I am not there. Rather,
my role is the unadvertised, secret, wholly
unexpected thrill you find within. A discovery.
Irresistible, like sex.

           So here I am. The crowd
leaks in—halting, unsure, a bit like mourners
at a funeral but without the grief. And there is
always something damp, interior, and, well,
sticky about them, cotton-candy souls that smear
the bad air, funky, bleak. All quite forgettable,
except for three. A woman, middle-aged, plain
and unwrinkled as her Salvation Army uniform,
bland as oatmeal but with this heavy, leaden sorrow
pulling at her eyelids and the corners of her mouth.
Front row four times, weeping, weeping constantly,
then looking up, lips moving in a silent prayer,
I think, and blotting tears with a kind of practiced,
automatic movement somehow suggesting that
the sorrow is her own and I'm her mirror now,
the little well of suffering from which she drinks.
A minister once told me to embrace my sorrow.
To hell with that, I said, *embrace your own*. And then
there was that nice young woman, Arbus, who came and talked,
talked brilliantly, took hours setting up the shot,
then said, *I'm very sorry*, and just walked away.
The way the sunlight plunges through the opening
at the top around the center tent pole like a spotlight
cutting through the smutty air, and it fell on him,
the third, a boy of maybe sixteen, hardly grown,
sitting in the fourth row, not too far but not too close,
red hair flaring numinous, ears big as hands,
gray eyes that nailed themselves to mine. My mother,
I remember, looked at me that way. And a smile
not quite a smile. He came twice. And that second time,

just before I thanked the crowd, *I'm so glad you could
drop by, please tell your friends*, his hand rose—floated,
really—to his chest. It was a wave. The slightest,
shyest wave good-bye, hello (and what's the difference,
anyway) as if he knew me, *truly* knew me, as if,
someday, he might return. His eyes. His hair, as vivid
as the howdahs on those elephants. In the posters
where I'm not. That day the crowd seemed to slither out,
to ooze, I thought, like reptiles—sluggish, sleek, gut-hungry
for the pleasures of the world, the prize, the magic number,
the winning shot, the doll from the rifle booth, the girl
he gives it to, the snow cone dripping, the popcorn dyed
with all the colors of the rainbow, the *rainbow*, the sky
it crowns, and whatever lies beyond, the One, perhaps,
we're told, enthroned there who in love or rage or spasm
of inscrutable desire made that teeming, oozing,
devouring throng borne now into the midway's sunlight,
that vanished God of the unborn to whom I say
again my little prayer: *let me be one of them.*

Nominated by Image, Ted Deppe, Joyce Carol Oates, Charles Harper Webb

BONOBO MOMMA

fiction by JOYCE CAROL OATES

from MICHIGAN QUARTERLY REVIEW

THAT DAY, I met my "estranged" mother in the lobby of the Carlisle Hotel on Fifth Avenue, New York City. It was a few weeks following the last in a series of surgeries to correct a congenital malformation in my spine, and one of the first days when I could walk unassisted for any distance and didn't tire too quickly. This would be the first time I'd seen my mother since Fall Fashion Week nearly two years ago. Since she'd divorced my father when I was eight years old my mother—whose professional name was Adelina—spent most of her time in Paris. At thirty she'd retired from modeling and was now a consultant for one of the couture houses—a much more civilized and rewarding occupation than modeling, she said. For the world is "pitiless" to aging women, even former *Vogue* models.

As soon as I entered the Carlisle Hotel lobby, I recognized Adelina waiting for me on a velvet settee. Quickly she rose to greet me and I was struck another time by the fact that my mother was so *tall*. To say that Adelina was a striking woman is an understatement. The curvature of my spine had stunted my growth and even now, after my first surgery, I more resembled a girl of eleven than thirteen. On the way to the hotel I'd become anxious that my beautiful mother might wince at the sight of me, as sometimes she'd done in the past, but she was smiling happily at me—joyously—her arms opened for an embrace. I felt a jolt of love for her like a kick in the belly that took my breath away and left me faint-headed. *Is that my mother? My—mother?*

Typical of Adelina, for this casual luncheon engagement with her thirteen-year-old daughter she was dressed in such a way—

cream-colored coarse-knit coat, very short very tight sheath in a material like silver vinyl, on her long sword-like legs patterned stockings, and on her feet elegantly impractical high-heeled shoes—to cause strangers to glance at her, if not to stare. Her ash-blond hair fell in sculptured layers about her angular face. Hiding her eyes were stylish dark glasses in oversized frames. Bracelets clattered on both her wrists and her long thin fingers glittered with rings. In a hotel like the Carlisle it was not unreasonable for patrons to assume that this glamorous woman was *someone*, though no one outside the fashion world would have recalled her name.

My father too was "famous" in a similar way—he was a painter/sculptor whose work sold in the "high six figures"—famous in contemporary Manhattan art circles but little-known elsewhere.

"Darling! Look at *you*—such a tall girl—"

My mother's arms were thin but unexpectedly strong. This I recalled from previous embraces, when Adelina's strength caught me by surprise. Surprising too was the flatness of Adelina's chest, her breasts small and resilient as knobs of hard rubber. I loved her special fragrance—a mixture of flowery perfume, luxury soap, something drier and more acrid like hair bleach and cigarette smoke. When she leaned back to look at me her mouth worked as if she were trying not to cry. Adelina had not been able to visit me in the hospital at the time of my most recent operation though she'd sent cards and gifts to my room at the Hospital for Special Surgery overlooking the East River: flowers, candies, luxurious stuffed animals and books more appropriate for a younger girl. It had been her plan to fly to New York to see me except an unexpected project had sent her to Milan instead.

"Your back, darling!—you are all mended, are you?—yet so *thin*."

Before I could draw away Adelina unzipped my jacket, slipped her hands inside and ran her fingers down my spine in a way that made me giggle for it was ticklish, and I was embarrassed, and people were watching us. Over the rims of her designer sunglasses she peered at me with pearl-colored eyes that seemed dilated, the lashes sticky-black with mascara. "But—you are very *pretty*. Or would be if—"

Playfully seizing my lank limp no-color brown hair in both her beringed hands, pulling my hair out beside my face and releasing it. Her fleshy lips pouted in a way I knew to be distinctly French.

"A haircut, *chérie!* This very day."

Later I would remember that a man had moved away from Adelina when I'd first entered the lobby. As I'd pushed through the revolving door and stepped inside I'd had a vague impression of a man in a dark suit seated beside the striking blond woman on the settee and as this woman quickly rose to greet me he'd eased away, and was gone.

Afterward I would think *There might be no connection. Much is accident.*

"You're hungry for lunch, I hope? I am famished—*très petit déjeuner* this morning—'jet lag'—come!"

We were going to eat in the sumptuous hotel restaurant. Adelina had made a "special reservation."

So many rings on Adelina's fingers, including a large glittery emerald on the third finger of her left hand, there was no room for a wedding band and so there was no clear sign if Adelina had remarried. My father did not speak of my "estranged" mother, and I would not have risked upsetting him with childish inquiries. On the phone with me, in her infrequent calls, my mother was exclamatory and vague about her personal life and lapsed into breathless French phrases if I dared to ask prying questions.

Not that I was an aggressive child. Even in my desperation I was wary, hesitant. With my S-shaped spine that had caused me to walk oddly, and to hold my head at an awkward angle, and would have coiled back upon itself in ever-tighter contortions except for the corrective surgery, I had always been shy and uncertain. Other girls my age hoped to be perceived as beautiful, sexy, "hot"—I was grateful not to be stared at.

As the maitre d' was seating us in the restaurant, it appeared that something was amiss. In a sharp voice Adelina said, "No. I don't like this table. This is not a good table."

It was one of the small tables, for two, a banquette seat against a mirrored wall, close by other diners; one of us would be seated on the banquette seat and the other on the outside, facing in. Adelina didn't want to sit with her back to the room nor did Adelina want to sit facing the room. Nor did Adelina like a table so close to other tables.

The maitre d' showed us to another table, also small, but set a little apart from the main dining room; now Adelina objected that the table was too close to the restrooms: "I hate this table!"

By this time other diners were observing us. Embarrassed and unhappy, I stood a few feet away. In her throaty aggrieved voice Adelina was telling the maitre d' that she'd made a reservation for a "quiet" table—her daughter had had "major surgery" just recently—what was required was a table for four, that we would not be "cramped." With an expression of strained courtesy the maitre d' showed my mother to a table for four, also at the rear of the restaurant, but this table too had something fatally wrong with it, or by now the attention of the other diners had become offensive to Adelina, who seized my hand and huffily pulled me away. In a voice heavy with sarcasm she said, "We will go elsewhere, *monsieur! Merci beaucoup!*"

Outside on Fifth Avenue, traffic was thunderous. My indignant mother pulled me to the curb, to wait for a break in the stream of vehicles before crossing over into the park. She was too impatient to walk to the intersection, to cross at the light. When a taxi passed too slowly, blocking our way, Adelina struck its yellow hood with her fist. "Go on! *Allez!*"

In the park, Adelina lit a cigarette and exhaled bluish smoke in luxurious sighs as if only now could she breathe deeply. Her mood was incensed, invigorated. Her wide dark nostrils widened further, with feeling. Snugly she linked her arm through mine. I was having trouble keeping pace with her but I managed not to wince in pain for I knew how it would annoy her. On the catwalk—"catwalk" had been a word in my vocabulary for as long as I could remember—Adelina had learned to walk in a brisk assured stride no matter how exquisitely impractical her shoes.

"Lift your head, *chérie*. Your chin. You are a pretty girl. Ignore if they stare. Who are *they*!"

With singular contempt Adelina murmured *they*. I had no idea what she was talking about but was eager to agree.

It was a sunny April day. We were headed for the Boat House Restaurant to which Adelina had taken me in the past. On the paved walk beside a lagoon excited geese and mallards rushed to peck at pieces of bread tossed in their direction, squawking at one another and flapping their wings with murderous intent. Adelina crinkled her nose. "Such a *clatter*! I hate noisy birds."

It was upsetting to Adelina, too, that the waterfowl droppings were everywhere underfoot. How careful one had to be, walking beside the lagoon in such beautiful shoes.

"Not good to feed wild creatures! And not good for the environment. You would think, any idiot would know."

Adelina spoke loudly, to be overheard by individuals tossing bread at the waterfowl.

I was hoping that she wouldn't confront anyone. There was a fiery sort of anger in my mother, that was fearful to me, yet fascinating.

"Excuse me, *chérie*: turn here."

With no warning Adelina gripped my arm tighter, pivoting me to ascend a hilly incline. When I asked Adelina what was wrong she hissed in my ear, "Eyes straight ahead. Ignore if they stare."

I dared not glance back over my shoulder to see who or what was there.

Because of her enormously busy professional life that involved frequent travel to Europe, Adelina had relinquished custody of me to my father at the time of their divorce. It had been a "tortured" decision, she'd said. But "for the best, for all." She had never heard of the private girl's school in Manhattan to which my father was sending me and alluded to it with an air of reproach and suspicion for everyone knew, as Adelina said, that my father was "stingy—*perfide*." Now when she questioned me about the school—teachers, courses, classmates—I sensed that she wasn't really listening as she responded with murmurs of *Eh? Yes? Go on!* Several times she turned to glare at someone who'd passed us saying sharply, "Yes? Is there some problem? Do I know you?"

To me she said, frowning, "Just look straight ahead, darling! Ignore them."

Truly I did not know if people were watching us—either my mother or me—but it would not have surprised me. Adelina dressed like one who expects attention, yet seemed sincere in rebuffing it. Especially repugnant to her were the openly aggressive, sexual stares of men, who made a show of stopping dead on the path to watch Adelina walk by. As a child with a body that had been deformed until recently, I'd become accustomed to people glancing at me in pity, or children staring at me in curiosity, or revulsion; but now with my repaired spine that allowed me to walk more or less normally, I did not see that I merited much attention. Yet on the pathway to the Boat House my mother paused to confront an older woman who was walking a miniature schnauzer, and who had in fact been staring at both Adelina and me, saying in a voice heavy with sarcasm, "Excuse me, *madame*? My daughter would appreciate not to be stared at. *Merci!*"

Inside the Boat House, on this sunny April day, many diners were awaiting tables. The restaurant took no phone reservations. There was a crowd, spilling over from the bar. Adelina raised her voice to give her name to the hostess and was told that we would have a forty-minute wait for a table overlooking the lagoon. Other tables were more readily available but Adelina wanted a table on the water: "This is a special occasion. My daughter's first day out, after major surgery."

The hostess cast me a glance of sympathy. But a table on the lagoon was still a forty-minute wait.

My disappointed mother was provided with a plastic device like a remote control that was promised to light up and "vibrate" when our table was ready. Adelina pushed her way to the bar and ordered a drink—"Bloody Mary for me, Virgin Mary for my daughter."

The word *virgin* was embarrassing to me. I had never heard it in association with a drink and had to wonder if my capricious mother had invented it on the spot.

In the crowded Boat House, we waited. Adelina managed to capture a stool at the bar, and pulled me close beside her as in a windstorm. We were jostled by strangers in a continuous stream into and out of the dining area. Sipping her blood-red drink, so similar in appearance to mine which turned out to be mere tomato juice, my mother inquired about my surgery, and about the surgeon; she seemed genuinely interested in my physical therapy sessions, which involved strenuous swimming; another time she explained why she hadn't been able to fly to New York to visit me in the hospital, and hoped that I understood. (I did! Of course.) "My life is not so fixed, *chérie*. Not like your father so settled out there on the island."

My father owned two residences: a brownstone on West Eighty-ninth Street and, at Montauk Point at the easternmost end of Long Island, a rambling old shingleboard house. It was at Montauk Point that my father had his studio, overlooking the ocean. The brownstone, which was where I lived most of the time, was maintained by a housekeeper. My father preferred Montauk Point though he tried to get into the city at least once a week. Frequently on weekends I was brought out to Montauk Point—by hired car—but it was a long, exhausting journey that left me writhing with back pain, and when I was there, my father spent most of the time in his studio or visiting with artist friends. It was not true, as Adelina implied, that my father neglected me, but it was true that we didn't see much of each other during the school year. As an artist/bachelor of some fame my father was eagerly sought as a dinner guest and many of his evenings both at Montauk Point and in the city were spent with dealers and collectors. Yet he'd visited me each day while I'd been in the hospital. We'd had serious talks about subjects that faded from my memory afterward—art, religion?—whether God "existed" or was a "universal symbol"—whether there was "death" from the perspective of "the infinite universe." In my hospital bed when I'd been dazed and delirious from painkillers it was wonderful how my father's figure melted and eased into my dreams with me, so that I was never lonely. Afterward my father revealed that when I'd been sleeping he had sketched me—in charcoal—in the mode of Edvard Munch's "The Sick Child"—but the drawings were disappointing, he'd destroyed them.

My father was much older than my mother. One day I would learn that my father was eighteen years older than my mother, which seemed to me such a vast span of time, there was something obscene about it. My father loved me very much, he said. Still, I saw that he'd begun to lose interest in me once my corkscrew spine had been repaired, and I was released from the hospital: my medical condition had been a problem to be solved, like one of my father's enormous canvases or sculptures, and once such a problem was solved, his imagination detached from it.

I could understand this, of course. I understood that, apart from my physical ailments, I could not be a very interesting subject to any adult. It was a secret plan of mine to capture the attention of both my father and my mother in my life to come. I would be something unexpected, and I would excel: as an archeologist, an Olympic swimmer, a poet. A neurosurgeon.

At the Boat House bar, my mother fell into conversation with a man with sleek oiled hair and a handsome fox face; this man ignored me, as if I did not exist. When I returned from using the restroom, I saw the fox-faced man was leaving, and my mother was slipping a folded piece of paper into her oversized handbag. The color was up in Adelina's cheeks. She had a way of brushing her ash-blond hair from her face that reminded me of the most popular girls at my school who exuded at all times an air of urgency, expectation. "*Chérie*, you are all right? You are looking pale, I think." This was a gentle admonition. Quickly I told Adelina that I was fine. For some minutes a middle-aged couple a few feet away had been watching my mother, and whispering together, and when the woman at last approached my mother to ask if she was an actress—"Someone on TV, your face is so familiar"—I steeled myself for Adelina's rage, but unexpectedly she laughed and said no, she'd never been an actress, but she had been a model and maybe that was where they'd seen her face, on a *Vogue* cover. "Not for a while, though! I'm afraid." Nonetheless the woman was impressed and asked Adelina to sign a paper napkin for her, which Adelina did, with a gracious flourish.

85

More than a half-hour had passed, and we were still waiting to be seated for lunch. Adelina went to speak with the harried young hostess who told her there might be a table opening in another ten-fifteen minutes. "The wand will light up, ma'am, when your table is ready. You don't have to check with me." Adelina said, "No? When I see other people being seated, who came after us?" The hostess denied that this was so. Adelina indignantly returned to the bar. She ordered a second Bloody Mary and drank it thirstily. "She thinks that I'm not aware of what she's doing," my mother said. "But I'm very aware. I'm expected to slip her a twenty, I suppose. I hate that!" Abruptly then my mother decided that we were leaving. She paid the bar bill and pulled me outside with her; in a trash can she disposed of the plastic wand. Again she snugly linked her arm through mine. The Bloody Marys had warmed her, a pleasant yeasty-perfumy odor lifted from her body. The silver-vinyl sheath, which was a kind of tunic covering her legs to her mid-thighs, made a shivery sound as she moved. "Never let anyone insult you, darling. Verbal abuse is as vicious as physical abuse." She paused, her mouth working as if she had more to say but dared not. In the Boat House she'd removed her dark glasses and shoved them into her handbag and now her pearly-gray eyes were exposed to daylight, beautiful glistening eyes just faintly bloodshot, tinged with yellow like old ivory.

"*Chérie*, your shoulder! Your left, you carry it lower than the other. Are you aware?"

Quickly I shook my head *no*.

"You don't want to appear hunchbacked. What was he—*Quasimodo*—A terrible thing for a girl. Here—"

Briskly like a physical therapist Adelina gripped my wrists and pulled them over my head, to stretch me. I was made to stand on my toes, like a ballerina.

Adelina scolded: "I don't like how people look at you. With pity, that is a kind of scorn. I hate that!"

Her mouth was wide, fleshy. Her forehead was low. Her features seemed somehow in the wrong proportions and yet the effect of my mother was a singular kind of beauty, it was not possible to look away from her. At about the time of their divorce my father had painted a sequence of portraits titled *Bonobo Momma* which was his best-known work as it was his most controversial: enormous unfinished canvases with raw, primitive figures of monkey-like humanoid females. It was possible to see my beautiful mother in these simian fig-

86

ures with their wide fleshy mouths, low brows, breasts like dugs, swollen and flushed female genitalia. When I was older I would stare at the notorious *Bonobo Momma* in the Museum of Modern Art and I would realize that the female figure most closely resembling Adelina was unnervingly sexual, with large hands, feet, genitalia. This was a rapacious creature to inspire awe in the merely human viewer.

I would see that there was erotic power greater than beauty. My father had paid homage to that, in my mother. Perhaps it was his loathing of her, that had allowed him to see her clearly.

Approaching us on the path was a striking young woman—walking with two elegant borzoi dogs—dark glasses masking half her face—in tight designer jeans crisscrossed with zippers like stitches—a tight sweater of some bright material like crinkled plastic. The girl's hair was a shimmering chestnut-red ponytail that fell to her hips. Adelina stared with grudging admiration as the girl passed us without a glance.

"That's a distinctive look."

We walked on. I was becoming dazed, light-headed. Adelina mused: "On the catwalk, it isn't beauty that matters. Anyone can be beautiful. Mere beauty is boring, an emptiness. Your father knew that, at least. With so much else he did not know, at least he knew that. It's the walk—the authority. A great model announces 'Here I am—there is only me'."

Shyly I said, " 'There is only I.' "

"What?"

" 'There is only I.' You said 'me.' "

"What on earth are you talking about? Am I supposed to know?"

My mother laughed, perplexed. She seemed to be having difficulty keeping me in focus.

I'd meant to speak in a playful manner with Adelina, as I often did with adults who intimidated me and towered over me. It was a way of seeming younger than I was. But Adelina interpreted most remarks literally. Jokes fell flat with her, unless she made them herself, punctuated with her sharp barking laughter.

Adelina hailed a taxi, to take us to Tavern on the Green.

The driver, swarthy-skinned, with a short-trimmed goatee, was speaking on a cell phone in a lowered voice, in a language unknown to us. At the same time, the taxi's radio was on, a barrage of noisy advertising. Adelina said, "Driver? Please turn off that deafening radio, will you?"

With measured slowness as if he hadn't quite heard her, the driver turned off his radio. Into the cell phone he muttered an expletive in an indecipherable language.

Sharply Adelina said, "Driver? I'd prefer that you didn't speak on the phone while you're driving. If you don't mind."

In the rear view mirror the driver's eyes fixed us with scarcely concealed contempt.

"Your cell phone, please. Will you turn it off. There's a law against taxi drivers using their cell phones while they have fares, you must know that. It's dangerous. I hate it. I wouldn't want to report you to the taxi authority."

The driver mumbled something indistinct. Adelina said, "It's rude to mumble, *monsieur*. You can let us off here."

"Ma'am?"

"Don't pretend to be stupider than you are, *monsieur!* You understand English perfectly well. I see your name here, and I'm taking down your license number. Open this damned door. Immediately."

The taxi braked to a stop. I was thrown forward against the scummy plastic partition that separated us from the furious driver. Pain like an electric shock, fleeting and bright, throbbed in my spine. Adelina and the swarthy-skinned driver exchanged curses as Adelina yanked me out of the taxi and slammed the door, and the taxi sped away.

"Yes, I will report him! Illegal immigrant—I wouldn't be surprised."

We were stranded inside the park, on one of the drives traversing the park from Fifth Avenue to Central Park West. We had some distance to walk to Tavern on the Green and I was feeling light-headed, concerned that I wasn't going to make it. But when Adelina asked me if I was all right, quickly I told her that I was fine.

"Frankly, darling, you don't look 'fine.' You look sick. What on earth is your father thinking, entrusting you with a *housekeeper*?"

I wanted to protest, I loved Serena. A sudden panic came over me that Adelina might have the authority to fire her, and I would have no one.

"Darling, if you could walk straighter. This shoulder!—*try*. I hate to see people looking at my daughter in *pity*."

Adelina shook her head in disgust. Her ash-blond hair stirred in the wind, stiffly. At the base of her throat was a delicate hollow I had not seen before. The bizarre thought came to me, I could insert my fingers into this hollow. I could push down, using all of my weight. My mother's brittle skeleton would shatter.

"—what? What are you saying, darling?"

I was trying to protest something. Trying to explain. As in a dream in which the right words won't come. Not ten feet from us stood a disheveled man with a livid boiled-beet face. He too was muttering to himself—or maybe to us—grinning and showing an expanse of obscenely pink gum. Adelina was oblivious of him. He'd begun to follow us, lurching and flapping his arms as if in mockery of my gorgeous mother.

Adelina chided: "You shouldn't have come out today, darling. If you're not really mended. I could have come to see you, we could have planned that. We could have met at a restaurant on the West Side."

Briskly Adelina was signaling for another taxi, standing in the street. She was wearing her dark-tinted glasses now. Her manner was urgent, dramatic. A taxi braked to a stop, the driver was an older man, darker-skinned than the other driver, more deferential. Adelina opened the rear door, pushed me inside, leaned into the window to instruct the driver: "Please take my daughter home. She'll tell you the address. She's just thirteen, she has had major surgery and needs to get home, right away. Make sure she gets to the actual door, will you? You can wait in the street and watch her. Here"—thrusting a bill at the driver, which must have been a large bill for the man took it from Adelina's fingers with a terse smile of thanks.

Awkwardly Adelina stooped to kiss my cheek. She was juggling her designer handbag and a freshly lit cigarette, breathing her flamy-sweet breath into my face. "Darling, goodbye! Take a nap when you get home. You look ghastly. I'll call you. I'm here until Thursday. Auvoir!"

The taxi sprang forward. On the curb my mother stood blowing kisses after us. In the rear view mirror the driver's narrowed eyes shifted to my face.

A jarring ride through the park! Now I was alone, unobserved. I wiped at my eyes. Through the smudged window beside me flowed a stream of strangers on the sidewalk—all that I knew in my life that would be permanent, and my own.

Nominated by Michigan Quarterly Review, Bonnie Jo Campbell,
Joan Murray, Christina Zawadiwsky

O, ELEGANT GIANT

by LAURA KASISCHKE

from NEW AMERICAN WRITING

AND JEHOVAH. And Alzheimer. And a diamond of extraordinary size on the hand of a starving child. The quiet mob in a vacant lot. My father asleep in a chair in a warm corridor. While his boat, the Unsinkable, sits at the bottom of the ocean. While his boat, the Unsinkable, waits marooned on the shore. While his boat, the Unsinkable, sails on, and sails on.

nominated by New American Writing, Pinckney Benedict, Diann Blakely,

James Harms, Mark Irwin, Debra Spark

RAIN

by PETER EVERWINE

from PLOUGHSHARES

Toward evening, as the light failed
and the pear tree at my window darkened,
I put down my book and stood at the open door,
the first raindrops gusting in the eaves,
a smell of wet clay in the wind.
Sixty years ago, lying beside my father,
half asleep, on a bed of pine boughs as rain
drummed against our tent, I heard
for the first time a loon's sudden wail
drifting across that remote lake—
a loneliness like no other,
though what I heard as inconsolable
may have been only the sound of something
untamed and nameless
singing itself to the wilderness around it
and to us until we slept. And thinking of my father
and of good companions gone
into oblivion, I heard the steady sound of rain
and the soft lapping of water, and did not know
whether it was grief or joy or something other
that surged against my heart
and held me listening there so long and late.

Nominated by Ploughshares, Christopher Buckley, Katherine Taylor, David St. John

RETURN TO
HAYNEVILLE

by GREGORY ORR

from THE VIRGINIA QUARTERLY REVIEW

I WAS BORN AND RAISED in rural, upstate New York, but who I am began with a younger brother's death in a hunting accident when I was twelve and he was eight. I held the gun that killed him. But if my life began at twelve with my brother's sudden, violent death, then my end, determined by the trajectory of that harsh beginning, could easily have taken place a scant six years later, when, in June 1965, I was kidnapped at gunpoint by vigilantes near the small town of Hayneville, Alabama.

When I was sixteen, in my senior year of high school, I became involved in the civil rights movement partly because I hoped I could lose myself in that worthwhile work. I became a member of CORE (Congress of Racial Equality) and canvassed door-to-door in poorer neighborhoods in the nearby city of Kingston. I traveled down to Atlantic City with a carload of CORE members to picket the Democratic National Convention in August 1964. Earlier that summer, the Mississippi Freedom Democratic Party—another civil rights group— had chosen a slate of racially-integrated delegates to challenge Mississippi's all-white official Democratic Party delegates for seats at the convention. The goal was to put Lyndon Johnson and the whole liberal wing of the party on the spot—testing their commitment to change. I was one of about twenty or so people parading in a small circle on the dilapidated boardwalk outside the convention hall. We carried signs urging on the drama inside: SUPPORT THE FREEDOM DELEGATION and ONE MAN, ONE VOTE. I felt confused and thrilled and purposeful all at the same time.

Three marchers carried poles, each bearing a huge charcoal portrait of a different young man. Their larger-than-life faces gazed down at us as we walked our repetitious circle. They were renditions of Andrew Goodman, James Chaney, and Michael Schwerner, SNCC (Student Nonviolent Coordinating Committee) volunteers who had been missing for months, whose bodies had only recently been discovered. They had last been seen alive on June 21, driving away from the Neshoba County sheriff's office in Philadelphia, Mississippi. When an informer led investigators to the spot where their tortured bodies had been bulldozed into a clay dam, the mystery of their whereabouts ended abruptly and they began a second life—the life of martyrs to a cause. Those three faces mesmerized us as we circled the boardwalk, singing and trying to ignore the heckling from bystanders. The artist who had drawn them had resolved their faces into a few bold lines that gave them a subtle dignity. They seemed at peace, all their uncertainties and inner complexities over. I longed to be like them, to transcend my confusions and the agonies of my past and be taken up into some noble simplicity beyond change. I longed to sacrifice myself and escape myself—to become a martyr for the movement. If it took death to gain access to the grandeur of meaning, so be it. And thus are young soldiers born.

I was too young, only seventeen, to go to Mississippi that summer, but a year later I was on my way. I drove south, alone, in a '56 Ford my father had bought me for the trip. And so it commenced—my instruction in the grim distance between the myth of the martyr and the intimate reality of violence.

Cut to November 2006—over forty years have passed since my late-adolescent misadventures in the Deep South. I'm a poet and a professor—that's how I've spent my life. One of the happier perquisites of my profession is that I'm sometimes asked to read my poems at various colleges and universities. One such invitation has come my way— a former student of mine, a poet named Chris, is teaching at Auburn University and has invited me down. I'm reading that same week in Atlanta, and as I look over my Rand McNally, I see that I can not only drive from Atlanta to Auburn, I can proceed an hour or so farther and drive straight through time and into my own past. I decide to go back to Hayneville—the tiny town that has been so long lodged like a sliver in my memory.

Chris says he'll take the trip with me, and he brings Brian, a former student of his own. I'm glad of the company. Three poets from three generations: I'll turn sixty within the year, Chris is in his early forties, Brian in his midtwenties. As we leave town in my rented, economy-size Hyundai, pulling onto the interstate in the late-afternoon drizzle, Brian asks where we're headed. For several days, I've felt a quiet tension about this trip, and suddenly it seems I can release some of the tension by telling Brian and Chris the story of that long-ago summer. At first, I try to talk about what happened to me in Hayneville itself, but I quickly see that I'll have to start further back in order to make a coherent story of it.

As we drive down the highway toward Montgomery, I feel like one of those pilgrims in Chaucer, challenged by my travel companions to entertain them on the journey. Brian's in the back seat, and as I begin my story, I occasionally turn my head slightly as if acknowledging I'm aware of him as an audience, but soon I'll become so caught up in the narrative that I'll lose all sense of my companions and of time and distance passing. I'll drive steadily toward Hayneville, as though the story and the highway were a single, fused flowing.

It was late May 1965. After brief training, another volunteer, a man from Pittsburgh named Steve, and I were assigned to work in Bolivar County, Mississippi—the Delta region, where COFO (Council of Federated Organizations) was trying to gain momentum for a strike of field workers. The going wage was $4 a day—dawn to dusk hoeing the cotton by hand, everyone from seven-year-old kids to octogenarians. We'd been in Bolivar only a week or so, helping out at the office. Suddenly, there was a summons from headquarters: everyone who could be mustered and spared from their local work—any new volunteers and all the local residents who could be persuaded—should report to the state capital in Jackson. The governor of Mississippi had called a secret session of the legislature, and the movement was organizing a mass demonstration to draw national attention to what it suspected was serious political skulduggery.

At ten in the morning on June 14, about five hundred of us—men, women, teenagers, old folks—assembled in Jackson. We walked two abreast down the sidewalk toward the capitol building. Our leaders told us we'd be stopped by the police and warned we could not parade without a permit. At that point, we would have to choose to be arrested or to disperse. We were urged to let ourselves be arrested—the plan was to fill the jail to overflowing and apply the steady pressure of media and economics (they'll have to feed and house us at city expense). The powers-that-be had learned to present a sanitized image to the media, so our arrest was very polite—journalists and photographers there watched each of us ushered onto a truck by two city policemen who held us by both arms, firmly but calmly. The trucks themselves were large, enclosed vehicles—the kind you'd use to transport chairs for a rally or municipal lawnmowers. They packed about thirty of us inside, then closed the doors. And we were off—each truck with its own motorcycle escort gliding through red lights, heading, we presumed, toward the city jail. But the actual destination was our first big surprise. We activists may have had a plan to demonstrate, but the State of Mississippi and the City of Jackson had their own plan. We were taken to the county fairgrounds—twenty or so fenced acres of clear-cut land set with half a dozen long, low, tin-roofed barns. Another thing we didn't know: when each truck entered the fairgrounds, the gate swung shut behind it, and police turned back anyone else who tried to enter.

The truck I was on stopped, backed up, then came to a final halt. When the doors opened and our eyes adjusted to the flood of light, we saw we weren't at the jail at all—but in a narrow alley between two barns. A score of uniformed officers were gathered there, wearing the uniforms of motorcycle cops—tall leather boots, mirrored sunglasses, and blue helmets with the black earflaps pulled down. Each tanned face was almost indistinguishable under its partial disguise—only the nose and mouth showing—some already grinning at the joke of our surprise and what was in store for us. Each of them had his nightstick out—some tapping their clubs rhythmically in the palms of their hands, others just standing there expectantly with the stick held at each end. I didn't notice until I was up close and even then, in my confusion, didn't comprehend that the lower half of each officer's silver badge, where the identifying number should have been displayed, was neatly covered with black tape. An officer ordered us to climb down, and when some of us didn't, two officers climbed up and pushed us to the edge where others pulled us down. And it began. They swung their clubs right and left, randomly but thoroughly, for about ten minutes. It made no difference what you did, whether you screamed or were silent—you were struck again and again and, if you fell to the ground, kicked. It hurts—to be beaten over the head or back or shoulders with a wooden club. It's also terrifying. Then an order came and the clubbing stopped—we were told to get up (one kid couldn't and was dragged away somewhere, his leg too damaged to stand on).

We filed through a door into one of the barns. Inside, there was a calm that felt surreal after the violence outside. In the middle of the empty concrete floor, five card tables had been set up in a row, each with a typewriter and a city policeman seated in a folding chair. The far end of the barn, half hidden in shadow, was a milling cluster of frightened women and girls who, their initial beating and processing over, had been told to assemble there. Our dazed group lined up, and each of us in turn was formally processed and charged. The women from our truck were sent to join the other women at the far end of the barn. I was told to go out one of the side doors to the next barn where the men were being confined. Just as I was about to go through the door, an officer told me to take my straw hat off and carry it in my hands. I emerged into the outdoors and the bright sunlight and saw them—two lines of about fifteen highway patrolmen on either side. I was ordered to walk, not run, between them. Again, I was beaten with nightsticks, but this time more thoroughly as I was the only target. When I covered my head with raised arms to ward off the first blow from the officer on my right, I was jabbed in the ribs with a club from the other side. Instinctively, I pivoted in that direction, only to be left vulnerable in the other. I heard blows and felt sharp pokes or slaps fall flat and hard across my ribs and back from both directions—whether they were simultaneous or alternating, it made no difference; my defense was hopeless. By the time I neared the end of this gantlet, I was cringing from feinted blows—the humiliation of my fear and their laughter far worse than the physical pain.

Inside the other barn, men and boys were assembled in a dense clump surrounded by a loose ring of officers. Later that afternoon we would go through another ritually structured set of beatings. When anyone tried to sit down or move out to the edge of the impacted group to get some air, two or three officers dashed across the small, intervening space and beat him with clubs. This technique was designed to make us prisoners panic and fight one another to get to the safer center of the mass. But it didn't work. We tried to protect ourselves as best we could and keep the most vulnerable, especially the children, safe in the middle. A bearded young man in our group was noticeably defiant, and at a certain point an officer ran in and deftly struck him with a slicing motion of the blunt end of his nightstick in such a way that the taut skin of his forehead split and blood streamed down over the whole of his face. To see an individual human face suddenly turned into a mask of blood is to witness the eradication of the personal, and, if you're standing nearby as I was, to be sickened and unnerved.

The hours went by as more prisoners were processed and our group continued to grow—there were over a hundred and fifty men and boys in the barn. Evening fell. We were ordered to sit in rows on the concrete floor—three feet apart, three feet between the rows. We didn't know it, but we were waiting for mattresses to be delivered. We were told to sit bolt upright and not move; officers walked up and down the rows. If you leaned a hand down to rest or shifted your weight, a shouting patrolman rushed up with his club raised.

A black kid of maybe ten or twelve sat next to me. We'd been there for an hour and things were pretty quiet when a state patrolman stopped in front of the boy. He looked him over for a minute, then ordered him to take off the pin he was wearing—one of those movement buttons that said FREEDOM NOW or ONE MAN, ONE VOTE. No safety clasp, just an open pin. The guard told the kid to pull the pin off his shirt. He did. "Put it in your mouth," the guard said. I turned my head to the right and saw the boy place it in his mouth. "Swallow it," the guard said, his voice menacing, but not loud. If the kid tried to swallow it, the pin would choke him or pierce his throat and lodge there until he bled to death in agony.

Watching the scene, I felt murderous rage fill my whole being, geysering up in the single second it took to see what seemed about to happen. I became nothing but the impulse to scramble to my feet, grab the guard's pistol before he knew what was happening, and shoot him as many times as possible. Nothing but that intense impulse and a very small voice inside me that said: "You don't stand a chance. It would take longer than you imagine—long enough for him to turn on you, for his buddies to rush up and grab you. And then what? You would be their sudden and absolute target."

How long did that moment last? How long did the guard loom over the boy with his threats? How long did the boy sit there with the pin in his mouth, tasting its metallic bitterness but refusing to swallow, or unable to swallow? It could have been five minutes; it could have been less. The guard repeated his command several times, along with profanities. And then, other officers were there, urging him to give it up, persuading him to move on, to move away.

The mattresses finally arrived, and each of us dragged one off to his place in a row. We were officially segregated according to the laws of the sovereign state of Mississippi—a vigilantly patrolled lane separated two imaginary cell-blocks, one for blacks and one for whites. We lay down to sleep. The pounding of nightsticks on the concrete floor woke us at dawn, and we realized the highway patrolmen who had abused us with such relish and impunity the previous day were nowhere in sight. They'd been replaced by Fish and Game wardens who looked altogether more rustic and thoughtful (some even had moustaches) and made no effort to conceal their badge numbers and even wore name tags. Later that morning, a plainclothes officer entered our barn and announced that the FBI had arrived and that if anyone had complaints about their treatment, they should step forward to be interviewed. I did so and was ushered out into the same alley where we'd first been greeted and beaten. The narrow lane had been rigged at one end with an awning for shade. Under the awning, four FBI agents sat at small desks. When my turn came, I told my narrative about the beatings, but how could I identify the perpetrators? The agent asked if I could specify hair or eye color, or badge number? I couldn't. Could I point out now, in person, any of the officers who had beaten me? They weren't there, of course—they'd left in the middle of the night. The agent recorded my story of the previous day's beatings and violence and thanked me for my time. If they had actually wanted to protect us, the FBI could easily have arrived any time the preceding day. Many in the movement already knew what was inconceivable to me at the time—that events like this were stage-managed and that the FBI wasn't a friend or even a neutral ally of the civil rights movement.

For the next ten days, we lay each morning on our mattresses until breakfast—grits and a molasses syrup and powdered milk so watered-down I could see all the way to the bottom of the fifty-gallon pot that held it. After breakfast, we rolled up our mattresses and either sat all day on the concrete floor or paced the imaginary confines of our collective cell. Twice a day, we were lined up for the bathroom—it was then or never as we stood pressed up against one another, waiting for our brief turn in one of the five stinking stalls. No showers, no chance to wash at all, the same, reeking clothes day after day. Hot as hell once

98

the sun heated the tin roof, but chill at night when we huddled, blanketless, in the dark on our bare mattresses. The mosquito fogger sprayed around the outside of the barn each evening, sending its toxic cloud in under the closed doors to set us all coughing. Boredom, stench, heat. Word came from outside—we could, at any time, be released by posting a $50 bond that the movement would provide, but the plan called for as many as possible to stay inside for as long as we could. There was hope we would seriously inconvenience the state by staying, that another demonstration in support of us might take place—there was even talk of Martin Luther King Jr. himself showing up for it. Rumors and hope; and a request to persevere. Most of us stayed, though some of the youngest and oldest chose to leave. The violence mostly gone; if it occurred, it was sporadic and spontaneous and ended quickly without major consequence. Exhausted by lack of substantial food, worn down by boredom and discomfort, I gradually lost heart. I had dreamed of meaningful work and even heroic martyrdom, but here I was merely cannon fodder. I held a place; I counted— but only as an integer in the calculus of a complex political game playing out in rooms far above me. And close up, as close as the arc of a swung billy club, I had discovered that for every martyr whose life was resolved into a meaningful death, there were hundreds of others who were merely beaten, terrorized, humiliated. Even as I sank into depression and brooded in the stifling heat of that jail-barn, I was learning that I wanted to live.

On the tenth day there, my name was called and I was led outside and taken to a pay phone attached to a post near our barn. Picking up the receiver, I heard the voice of my father's lawyer, who was calling from upstate New York. We'd only met once; I hardly knew him. He began by saying he couldn't stand me or any of the causes I believed in, but my father was his dear friend and was frantic with worry. My fine had been paid. I was to leave now and drive back north immediately if I cared a damn about my family. End of story. His tongue-lashing eliminated the last of my resolve. The officer standing beside me took me in a patrol car to where I'd left the Ford ten days ago, as if the whole thing had been prearranged.

I should have called the COFO office and told them I was leaving, was heading north that very day—but I was ashamed. I was deserting—a frightened and confused teenager. The map told me my quickest route north was by state roads from Jackson to Selma, Alabama, and then on to Montgomery, where the interstate began. When I passed through Selma it was early evening and I was starved (we'd been fed nothing but vegetables and grits for ten days), but I was too afraid to stop for dinner.

It was dusk on US 80, past Selma and within fifteen miles of Montgomery, when I heard a siren. A white car pulled up close behind me, flashing its lights. I thought it was a police car and pulled over, but the two men who jumped out, one tall and rather thin, the other shorter and stout, wore no uniforms. They did each wear holsters, and as they approached, one on each side of my car, they drew their pistols. I rolled up my windows and locked my doors. Rap of a pistol barrel on the window two inches from my head: "Get out, you son of a bitch, or I'll blow your head off."

I got out and stood on the road's shoulder, beside my car. They prodded me with their guns and told me they were going to kill me. They searched my car and found SNCC pamphlets in the trunk. They were sure I was an agitator rumored to be coming to their town—my New York license plates had been a strong clue that the pamphlets confirmed. The men made two promises about my immediate future, the first was that they would kill me and dump my body in the swamps. The second, made a few moments later, was that they were going to take me to a jail where I would rot. With those two contradictory threats left floating in the air, they took my wallet and went back to their vehicle, ordering me to follow them in my own car. They pulled onto the highway and zoomed off. I started my car and followed them. We hadn't driven more than a mile when they signaled and turned off to the right, onto a smaller road. I hesitated, uncertain what to do, then made the turn and followed.

I pause in this story I'm telling Chris and Brian when I realize we've reached the green sign marking the turnoff for Hayneville. I'd been so caught up in telling it that I hardly noticed we'd passed through Montgomery and were speeding down Route 80 toward Selma. Suddenly, I realize the old story and my present journey are eerily coinciding at this forlorn intersection. It's as if my ghost Ford from forty years ago is approaching the turnoff from the west, coming from Selma, at the same moment that my shiny, white rental reaches that same turn from the direction of Montgomery. The terrified boy in the ghost Ford drives right into us, and for a moment, we and the story are one and the same. Now, I'm driving slowly down that backroad toward Hayneville, telling Chris and Brian what it felt like the first time

100

I took this road, alone, following the car driven by my would-be killers.

Their car was newer than mine and faster. It sped up. A voice in my head started screaming: "What are you doing? You are obligingly speeding to your own death—driving to your own grave! Turn around and make a run for it!" But how could I? They had my wallet with my license and all my money. It was pitch-dark now. The road was so narrow there was no place to turn around; there were swamps on either side. If I tried to make a getaway, their car could easily overtake mine, and they would surely shoot me. This hysterical dialogue raged in my head for the ten long minutes of that ride, and then we emerged out of the dark into Hayneville. We passed the courthouse, pulled into a narrow street, and stopped in back of a small jail.

Even as I describe that terrifying drive, I see that the wooded swamps are gone. (Or were they imagined in the dark so long ago?) It's mostly fields and pasture with a pond here and there gleaming like oil in the deepening gloom. And now we're arriving in the town itself. Again, as with the first time I was here, it's almost completely dark under the overarching trees, only a glimpse of a gray sky from which all trace of light is gone. I recognize things: there is the courthouse—no wonder it stood out—white and two stories high on its tree-filled lawn in a town of twenty or so tiny houses and bungalows. And there is something completely new in town (the only new thing as far as I can see)—a BP convenience store where I stop for gas. The station is shiny and all lit up, its blue-green signs glowing intensely in the dark like those roadside stores in Edward Hopper paintings, gleaming forlornly against the primeval dark of rural Anywhere, America. I'm trembling with a kind of giddy excitement as I pump the gas. Even here I can see changes—the man behind the counter in the station, whom I take to be the owner, is black, so are most of his customers. Back then, whites owned everything. As I pull my car out of the station across from the courthouse, I see that the sheriff's car, just now parking beside the small police bungalow behind the courthouse, is driven by a black officer.

When we got to the jail forty years ago, I felt relieved. At least the terrifying drive was over. But my torment was only entering another phase. I'd be held there in solitary confinement without charges for eight days. I was kept on the second floor the entire time, separate from all other prisoners and personnel, seeing and talking to no one

101

except the silent trustee who brought me food twice a day and took away my empty tray. Why was I so isolated from the rest of the prisoners? It was possible they didn't want people to know where I was as they waited to find out if anyone was aware that I was "missing." Ever since the murders of Goodman, Schwerner, and Chaney, volunteers were under strict orders to check in with headquarters before traveling any distance, to record their destination and expected arrival time, so that if anything went wrong an alert could be sent out for an immediate search. I hadn't called, so no one knew I was in Hayneville's jail.

Four days into my incarceration, my father's lawyer called the DA in Jackson, Mississippi, to ask if he knew why I hadn't arrived home. The DA didn't know; they'd let me go. Then he tried the state attorney general's office in Montgomery, which was run at the time by Richmond Flowers, a racial moderate. His office made inquiries and learned I was being held in Hayneville, but they couldn't offer any help. They told Dad's lawyer that Lowndes County resisted all outside interference, even from Alabama state authorities. On my fifth day there, my father's lawyer managed to call the jail and was told (by the sheriff himself, slyly posing as a deputy) that indeed a young man named Greg Orr was there and was at that moment playing checkers with the sheriff.

Of course this was a lie. I had no knowledge of the call, no sense that anyone in the world knew where I was. Each day I spent in that cell was an eternity. I was unmoored from structures except food and the alternation of day and night. I didn't know when my spell in solitary would end. If someone had said to me: "You'll be kept alone in a small cell with no one to speak to for eight days," I could have tried to organize the ordeal in my mind—I could have, for starters, kept track of the days and known that each one passing brought me closer to the end. But there was no known end point and so no measurement—it was wholly arbitrary and made me even more aware of my own powerlessness. Already depressed and disoriented by the ten days in "jail" in Jackson, I was even more frightened in Hayneville: I had a better sense of how dangerous my situation was, and my imagination took over from there.

In the middle of my eighth day the sheriff came to my cell, unlocked it, and told me I was free to go. That was it: no apology, no formal charges, no anything. I was taken to my car, told to get out of town. I was set free as abruptly and mysteriously as I had been captured and incarcerated. I got in my car and drove. I drove and drove.

I have one memory of stopping in some rest area in South Carolina in the middle of the night and trying to wash and shave, but my hands were shaking too much to control the razor. I slept whenever I couldn't drive any longer, pulling into parking lots and climbing into the back seat. By the time I reached New Jersey, I was hallucinating huge rats running across the highway in front of my headlights. And then I was home, back in the Hudson River Valley town I'd left only a month or so earlier.

I spent July in my hometown, but in early August I took a job in New York with a small film company, synchronizing sound and picture. On my way home from work one August day, I bought a *New York Times* to read on the subway. When I looked at the front page, I saw a story about a murder that had just taken place in Hayneville. I turned to the inner page to finish the article and was stunned to see a photograph of one of the men who had kidnapped me on the highway. The news article related that he had shotgunned Jonathan Daniels, an Episcopalian seminary student and civil rights volunteer, in broad daylight on the courthouse lawn, in front of half a dozen witnesses. From what I could tell, the victim and the others with him might have been the "outside agitators" whom I had been mistaken for. According to the newspaper, they, like me, had been arbitrarily arrested and held without charges for days in the jail and then suddenly released. But unlike me, they had no car. They spent several hours desperately trying to find someone to drive them to Montgomery, while the murderer, a friend of the sheriff's and a "special unpaid deputy," became more and more agitated. He found the released organizers near the courthouse and aimed his shotgun at a young black woman, Ruby Sales. The seminary student pushed her aside and stood in front just as the gun went off.

Though he was charged with murder, the verdict, given by a local, all-white jury in that very courthouse, was "not guilty" on the basis of self-defense. The same courthouse later saw the trial of the killers of Viola Liuzzo, the Detroit housewife who, three months before my arrival in town, had participated in the Selma to Montgomery march. On the evening of March 25, she was killed by gunfire while ferrying marchers in her car on Route 80. Her slayers, quickly apprehended, were also found not-guilty by another all-white Hayneville jury, even though eye-witness prosecution testimony was given by one of the four Klansmen (a paid FBI informer) present that night in the murder car.

My situation in Hayneville resembled the seminary student's: arbitrary arrest, jail time without arraignment or trial, and then sudden release. But I had a car, and timing mattered: the *New York Times* article stressed that the killer had been upset about the passage of the Voting Rights Act—as if part of his motivation was a kind of crazed act of political protest. When I was apprehended and jailed, the status quo in Hayneville seemed secure—if my presence there was a sign of change, it was the sort of change they felt they could easily contain and control.

Two others died there; a murder in March; another in August—and in between, in late June, my own narrow escape as I slipped through the same violent landscape. "Slipped through" makes me sound like a fish that found a hole in the net, but surely I was trapped in it, surely it was luck that pulled me from its entanglements and casually tossed me back into the sea.

And here I am again, forty-one years later, approaching the jail, that brick edifice in which all my emotions and memories of Hayneville are concentrated. Not the memory or idea of jail, but this dingy incarnation of incarceration—a building full of little cages where people are captive. I've been monologuing until now, spewing out non-stop the whole story that brought me here, but as we travel the last few blocks, I go silent with anticipation. Chris and Brian are also quiet but excited—now that we're in the town itself, certain key nouns connect to real things—there is the courthouse pretty much as I described it. And here, down this little lane a half block past the courthouse, is the jail itself, that brick, L-shaped building I've been talking about. But how different it is from what I remembered and described! It's an empty husk. Boarded up—from the looks of it, abandoned a number of years ago. Deserted, dilapidated, the mortar rotted out between the grimy bricks. The only thing not in utter disrepair is a small exercise yard attached to the back, behind a chain-link fence topped with razor wire.

When I stop in the cinder parking lot and hop out of the car I feel like a kid who has arrived at a playground. I'm surprised by my responses. Here, at a place that was a locus of some of the most intense misery I've ever known, I'm feeling curiously happy. Chris and Brian have also climbed out. I can see they're glad, too—pleased to have found some real, palpable thing at the end of a tunnel of words burrowing from the distant past. Chris has a camera and begins to take pictures, though it's night now and there's no way of knowing if anything will register. The doors to the building are locked, but Brian, exploring the fence's gate, finds it's open, and we're able to enter the yard. We climb some rusty steps to a second-floor landing; from there I can point to the window that was across the corridor from my cell and that I peered out of after shinnying up my cell door's bars and craning my neck. That giddiness I felt when I first set my feet on the parking lot has been growing more intense—I'm laughing now, and when I'm not laughing, I'm unable to stop grinning. Earlier, in the car, telling the stories of my long-ago misadventures, the words had zipped directly from my brain's private memory to my tongue in a kind of nonstop narrative that mostly bypassed my emotions. Now my brain has stopped functioning almost entirely, and I'm taken over by this odd laughter that's bubbling up from some wordless source far down in my body—some deep, cellular place.

Brian and Chris poke around the weed-grown yard, looking for anything interesting, some rusty artifact to point to or pick up and ponder. I'm ordinarily a person who likes souvenirs—a shell from a beach, a rock from a memorable walk in the woods—but I have no wish to take anything physical from this place. Even a pebble would weigh me down, and the truth is I feel weightless right now, as if I'm a happy spirit moving through a scene of desolation.

My beginning was a rifle shot and someone innocent suddenly dead. My end might well have been something eerily similar: perhaps a pistol shot, my own death in this tiny town so far from my home—a beginning and end so close to each other as to render the life cryptic and tragic by way of its brevity. Only, Hayneville *wasn't* my end. It was a place where my life could have ended but didn't, and now, almost half a century later, I stand beside that closed-down, dilapidated jail, laughing. But laughing at what, at whom? Not at the confused and earnest kid I was all those years ago, the one who blundered through and escaped thanks to blind luck. What is this laughter that's fountaining up through me?

As we're leaving and I pause in the cindery parking lot with one hand on my car-door handle, taking a last look at the old jail, a single word comes to me: *joy*. It's joy I'm feeling—joy is at the heart of this peculiar laughter. Joy is my body's primal response to the enormity of the gift it has been given—a whole life! A whole life was there waiting for me the day I left this town. A life full of joys I couldn't imagine

105

back then: a long, deeply satisfying marriage to a woman I love, two wonderful daughters, forty years of writing poems and teaching the craft of poetry. Laughing to think that the kid I was had come south seeking the dark blessing of death in a noble cause, but had instead been given the far more complex blessing of life, given his whole existence and all the future struggle to sort it out and make it significant— to himself and, if he was lucky as a writer, to others also. Laughing at how my life went on past this town and blossomed into its possibilities, one of which (shining in the dark) was love.

Nominated by John Kistner, Floyd Skloot, Virginia Quarterly Review

TOM & JERRY

fiction by CHRISTIE HODGEN

from PLOUGHSHARES

October

Another night in the hospital and nothing makes sense to you but that yellow-eyed cat, seething, slobbering, Ahab-mad, nightly one a.m., TV38. You are stuck in bed on an intravenous paralytic, so many sites blown, bruised to hell, the nurses have had to work their way up one arm and down another, all of this—the mindless, layabout life of a cat—to keep a baby from coming too soon.

Something to pass the time. Flipping channels and how happy you'd been to see them, cat and mouse, still running in circles around the same old house, Mammy Two Shoes giving chase in her slippers, slapping her broom, just as they'd always done all those years when you'd sat watching cross-legged on the basement floor of your grand-mother's house. You'd been delighted to see them in the way people tend to be delighted when they find things unchanged by time. That slavering hunger, that slapdash pursuit, everything just as it was in childhood, the violence as spectacular, as thrilling, as brilliant as fire-works. At first, the fun was in watching the cat take his lumps; now the fun comes in the moments just beforehand, when you sense what is coming but the cat does not, in such moments you feel clairvoyant, su-perior, you feel the satisfaction of a God watching his subjects make flagrant disasters of their tiny lives. *If only the cat would learn*, you think. *If only he would take instruction.* There are certain laws of mo-tion particular to his universe—there's a certain Murphy's law of grav-ity operating about his person—that he'd do well to study. Each night, after the show ends, you entertain yourself with the enumeration of these phenomena in a formal letter to the cat.

Dear Tom: you think.

Kindly allow me to fill you in on a few of life's inevitabilities. Believe me, it is for your own good that I warn you: while attempting to smite Jerry with an umbrella you will trip, fall, and swallow said umbrella, it will spring open and distort your face to its shape; all raised piano lids will collapse on your fingers and likewise with kitchen windows; when you launch explosives towards your enemies they will fail to detonate, for unknown reasons you will follow up with them—those red sticks of dynamite, those black balls with hissing wicks—and demand to know their ailments, you will shake them, hold them to your ear, your face will be blasted off; at various times, without your noticing, your own tail will be substituted for other objects, such as hot dogs and cigars, and you will bite down into or set fire to yourself, you will scream the scream of the dying; when lauching a bowling ball down a lane, your fingers will, without question stick in its holes, your entire body will soar through the air and strike down every last pin, you will come tumbling out of the return chute to the delight of your opponents; now and then you will be flattened by anvils falling from great heights and cars traveling at high speeds; as a general rule, every blow to your head will result in the rising of an equal and opposite red welt.

What I am writing to tell you, Dear Tom, is that with a minimal increase in cognizance I believe you'll find these dangers to be entirely avoidable. Really, it is all quite simple.

This is what one does when confined to bed. Like Proust, one lies about making grand philosophies out of other people's suffering. You do this because there is literally nothing else to do. You are four months' pregnant and have gone into preterm labor, you are completely effaced, you have been drugged senseless in an effort to stop contractions, but the efforts are thought to be futile. You are waiting to deliver what you have been told will be a stillborn, or at the very best a baby that will gasp for an hour in your arms before dying, the baby being, in the strictest medical terms, the size of a potato and too small to save: any day now, you're told. The medication you're on is a poison, a chemical compound that has the effect of shutting down your body's functioning and thereby labor. What it feels like is mercury in the veins, an unbearable heaviness, a dozen x-ray aprons piled atop you. You can move, but only slowly and with great effort against a formidable invisible force; you move, that is, like a mime. Side effects include but are not limited to: nausea and vomiting, migraine, profuse sweating, hypotension, arrhythmia, double vision. Possible complications include cardiac arrest, lung failure, profound muscular paralysis, fetal death, maternal death, all of the above. When you were first admitted, it was thought you'd deliver before nightfall. But it has been three weeks. Your life, it seems, has been turned into some loathsome French novel in which, in order to illustrate certain theories of plotlessness, the main character does nothing, absolutely nothing, the main character is so motionless one is left to wonder if she is alive or dead.

Only a month ago, you were a fully functioning human being, a French teacher at a Catholic girls' high school. You had a schedule, a checking account, a small basement apartment you'd appointed to the best of your ability given the limitations of your budget and taste; you had a green bicycle with a wicker basket in which you carried around clothbound library books that hadn't, in most cases, been checked out by a living soul since nineteen fifty-seven; you had a cactus, a goldfish; five days a week and five classes a day you had a profusion of verbs to conjugate aloud, in multiple tenses, in front of dozens of indifferent students; you had a longstanding predilection for the subjunctive; you had an expensive block of Irish cheese in your refrigerator, a pile of unwanted mail, including a jury duty summons, sitting on the kitchen table which doubled as your desk; you had blue eyes and pale, freckled skin; you had a pleasant face, not a beautiful one, more like a beautiful face reflected in a spoon, but still it was something you didn't mind looking at, it was something with which you could get by; you had, in other words, a life, not a great one but yours, it was something.

Now here you are in perpetual pajamas like Hugh Hefner, the absurd protagonist of a dreadful story, cruelly paused just short of the crisis, with nothing to do but wait. Something bad is about to happen and you are waiting, the contractions mounting and quelling, you are waiting, day running into night into day. All the while, people come in and out of your room performing their assigned functions: they roll you to the side and yank down your underpants and administer steroid shots into the flesh of your hip, your hindquarters as it were; they hook new bags of fluid to your IV pole—those glistening bags of poison—and set them running; they draw blood; they consult monitors and charts and frown; they take your blood pressure and ask you if you are alive because, they say, according to their calculations you are dead; every three days, they warm a special bonnet in the microwave and then place it over your head, massage the bonnet with their fingers to activate its inner chemical lining, they tell you this has the same hygienic results as a shower and shampoo, but you're not convinced, like dry cleaning, it seems to you the main talents of the bonnet have to do with fragrance; they settle bedpans underneath you and command you to fill them, they squeeze cold jelly onto your stomach and run sensors across it, they pronounce the estimated weight of the baby at thirteen ounces.

You have to do something to pass the time and so while you wait you watch television, you watch like you used to as a child, which is to say you watch without discrimination, watch with equal interest comedies and dramas and game shows and talk shows and the commercials between them. You watch even the unwatchable—weather conditions reported by the voice of a robot who seems to be speaking from the very back of its robot throat, channels plagued with static, telethons. One of the public broadcasting stations is immersed in its annual fund drive and the stakes, to you, seem as monumental as the Cuban missile crisis. Behind the telecaster (fat, bald, plaid-suited, appealingly pathetic) is a handmade chart in the shape of a thermometer with the raised funds shown in red rising toward the projected goal. The raised funds are pathetically low, the mercury stays sunken in its well, in the background a single telephone rings and is answered, and now the broadcaster has something on his mind, a serious question: whether or not the station you are currently watching will live to see another day or whether it will fold, shut down its signal, send its sad employees home laid-off to their small children, the question to you is, considering how much public television contributes to your life and mind, will you rise to the occasion, will you please help?

On another channel, the question is whether or not you will rise to the aid of Central American orphans. Asking the question are their big, wet eyes and their distended stomachs, asking the question is a slow-motion montage of images, children running barefoot through puddles of sewage and drinking from the same pails as their goats.

On still another channel, the question is whether or not you will contribute your heart, mind, and ten percent gross earnings to the ministry of Dr. Creflo A. Dollar. *Can this really be the name of a televangelist?* you think to yourself. You smirk, you scoff, you take note of his brilliant, shimmering, double-breasted suits, his diamond rings, and you wonder how it is that he manages to convince people, poor people, to send *him* money, he of the polished shoe and silk tie, he of the glistening cufflinks. You laugh—*Ha!*—but only in your head.

You watch all of this as if a stranger to this world looking through its window in the hopes of understanding its inhabitants. You watch and you wait.

The idea is to immerse yourself in something, anything other than the wait itself, which is projected by all experts to end in tragedy, you are waiting for the story to end, waiting to lose your firstborn, as is the fate of all stupid girls in fairytales who, in exchange for good looks and a handsome prince, promise their babies to witches. You are waiting and turning every moment into a narrative. Like Rapunzel, like a spider, like a planet, like a drunk, you are spinning and spinning and endlessly spinning, spinning a tale, constantly a voice runs in your head, translating all that happens to you into the second person. This voice is female, with a slight British accent, like yours but more mellifluous and intelligent; this voice will not shut up, it will not *shut the fuck up* though you keep telling it to and you start to wonder if—no, you're quite sure of this—maniacs live this way, if after only three weeks you have already gone batshit, bonkers, berserk, Howard Hughes crazy, Joan of Fucking Arc crazy, crazy from which there is no return. The voice, it doesn't stop, it simply won't stop.

On the rare occasions when the voice *does* stop it is only because it has been preempted by the voice of Peter Jennings, who breaks in with his own newscast. Once or twice a day, you imagine Peter Jennings reporting your condition from behind his desk, you can see his head cocked slightly, the slender gleam of his tiepin. He says things like: *For those of you tuning in tonight, I am pleased to report that in the case of our favorite patient there has been, as of yet, no delivery. Another day has come and gone and the doctors, working tirelessly around the clock, have managed to quell the contractions once again. As for our patient, she is still drugged into paralysis, but is said to be bearing up admirably. Do we have a live feed?* he asks. *May we see into the room for a moment?* From an aerial view you see the room, a small box with a bed in the middle, with hulking, blinking equipment on either side, you see yourself lying pathetically in bed, you see the wires snaking out from the neck and sleeves of your hospital gown, you see the computer screens crawling with the information fed to them by the wires attached to you, the waves of contractions rolling across, the spikes of the fetal and maternal heartbeats, you see your hair, squid-like in dark tendrils, slick with grease, spread across the pillow, you are lying on one side and holding something in your hand. What could it be? The camera pans in and all comes into focus. What you are doing is staring at the ultrasound picture, the picture of your firstborn in utero. White on black, you see the outline of its skull and belly, you see its nose and lips, its spine, its arms. You see that it has raised its fist to its mouth. The camera pans back again and Peter says: *And so it continues.* He says that he will break into regular programming with any updates. He says good night.

One particular nurse—Edith, your favorite—comes in and out of the room constantly, rustling the cellophane wrappers of popsicles. Always she tells you to eat, though it is true you will only throw it up afterwards (the drug you're hooked up to causes you to vomit on the hour, with the precision of certain geysers), she tells you to eat anyway. "You got," says Edith, fat and black as Hattie McDaniel, with the same gruff voice and the same flair for stealing a scene, "to eat something. Put some meat," she tells you, "on that baby! That baby no bigger than a stick of butter and what your job is to eat this popsicle whether you like it or not, and the whole mess of others I'm gonna bring you after." Edith is the only nurse kind enough to suggest that this story of yours will end as a fairytale, in the happily ever after. She has a story of her own and tells it loud, tells it from on high, walks in the room mid-sentence already telling it: the story involves a girl, *just like you*, who came in the October prior, *twenty weeks along just like you, whitest of white girls just like you*, a girl who stayed paralyzed in bed for four solid months, stayed unspooked through Halloween and All Saint's Day, stayed gratefully through Thanksgiving, stayed proud through Pearl Harbor Day, stayed rejoicing through Christmas and New Years all the way through the birthday of Dr. Martin Luther King, Jr., stayed all that time and gave birth, finally, to healthy twins, the fattest pinkest twins she's ever seen in all her years on the maternity ward. "That mother," she says one day, "had a positive attitude, and that's what made all the difference. She didn't lay around moping with her back turned to the world, she didn't lay around staring out the window like *some* people. It was a positive attitude that made all the difference, a positive attitude that saved those twins, you ask me I'll tell you."

The twins, the twins, the twins, always and everywhere she talks of those twins. One day she walks in and asks you to guess, go on ahead and guess who you just missed passing by the hallway: the twins come for a visit dressed up in pumpkin suits, the twins gurgling and drool-

112

ing, the twins by the name of Jaime and David and their mother, who after four months paralyzed was so weak she couldn't turn a door knob but who recovered in no time and recently ran a charitable half-marathon. Every time Edith brings you a Popsicle, she tells you something of those twins and their glorious mother. At the end of Edith's shift your mouth is so rimmed in red you have the smile of a circus clown, of a vampire, you have enough stained wooden sticks to build a scale model of your entire hospital room and the equipment inside it. Also at the end of Edith's shift, you have puked so many times into that clever kidney-shaped plastic bowl, that tiny vomitorium, that you think of consulting the Guinness to see if you have broken a world record.

A social worker comes by, then a psychiatrist. They come separately, but say almost the exact same thing.

"We've noticed," says one.

"It has been brought to our attention," says the other. They both speak this way, in the first person plural, like royalty.

"We've noticed you put yourself on NO VISITOR status."

"It has been brought to our attention that you are alone here."

"And that you aren't speaking."

"We're told you run the television and stare out the window all day, like you're doing now."

"Just staring out at the parking lot. Is that the doctor's parking lot? They sure get special treatment, right next to the front entrance, don't they? Boy."

"The nurses are concerned about you."

"The nurses have mentioned you."

"It's not that they're angry or insulted or anything like that, with your not speaking to them or anyone, not even a single word."

"They're professionals and they can work around any kind of circumstance, even complete silence."

"It's just that they, and we, believe the outcome of your situation can be affected by your state of mind."

"They think—we all think—that you have a better chance of pulling through this, the baby has a better chance, if you reach out for help and companionship."

"We can get you some help, some drugs. You'd be amazed."

"We can arrange for visitors if you like. Volunteers. Most of them teenagers. But sometimes the humane society comes by with puppies. They're clinically proven to lift patient spirits, puppies."

"You just think about it."

"Take your time and think about it."

"Let us know."

Visitors! You decide to allow visitors. Mindy and Cindy, your upstairs neighbors, come to visit. Like you, they are teachers at Sacred Heart Academy for Girls, English and History, like you they are doughy, flaccid people who almost never see the light of day. You have lived below them for several years. Your friendship has been forged on the same complaints: students and their papers, perpetual lack of money, the cruel and impenetrable Sacred Heart administration. When Mindy and Cindy come into the room, they smell of the outdoors, of a delicious arctic breeze. They have snowflakes, bits of the outside world, on the shoulders of their jackets, and what you want to do is lick them, actually lick the snowflakes right off their skin, hair and clothing.

"We called and called!" says Mindy.

"We've been calling your hospital room all day and night for weeks, but you've had your phone turned off."

"And we keep coming by but they haven't let us in!"

"It's been terrible."

"Awful, really."

"The thing is," says Cindy.

"What we don't understand," Mindy says.

"Is that we didn't even know you were pregnant!"

"Here we are your best friends and everything."

"Your only friends."

"And you didn't even tell us."

"Obviously it would have been awkward, an unmarried pregnant woman at a Catholic school."

"But really if anyone should understand that kind of thing—"

"When you stop to think about it, if anyone's going to be sympathetic to an unmarried pregnant woman—"

"It would be the Catholics."

"It should be Catholics."

"Obviously the other teachers aren't very nice."

"They're not exactly *warm* or anything."

"In three years, they've hardly spoken to you."

"You'd think after doing a good job for three years they might, but they don't."

"They've been disapproving of your wardrobe."

114

"And your hair."

"Too much black, they say."

"They've dropped hints."

"And certainly your not going to mass hasn't helped."

"No, that's been a disappointment to everyone."

"They're old-fashioned, they don't understand how it is today, to be young in a time like this."

"But you'd like to think in a crisis."

"In a crisis, you'd like to think they'd rise to the occasion."

"They haven't replaced you or anything."

"They've just got a substitute. A series of substitutes."

"There's still hope for you, we think."

"Anyway we missed you at work, and then at home, we called and called."

"The police and everything."

"And they called the hospital and told us you were here."

"But you didn't call."

"It made us feel weird."

"Sad, in a way."

"We were so worried."

"And then when we found out you were pregnant we were like . . ."

"We were like, *Oh my God!*"

"How exciting!"

"But how terrible! Because it's too early."

"And then we figured you didn't want us to know."

"Which we couldn't figure out."

"Because we totally would have been okay with it."

"Totally!"

"Regardless of how we feel about the father."

"That would have been put aside."

"Entirely put to the side."

There is an awkward silence. You can't think of anything to say.

"Otherwise there's no news," says Cindy. "You haven't missed much."

"Except the fish," says Mindy. "Mr. Muckle died."

"Not that we weren't taking good care of him," says Cindy. "My feeling is that it was bound to happen anyway and not really our fault."

"Because you never clean the bowl."

"And you forget to feed it sometimes."

115

"But we didn't come here to tell you that."

"That's true, we didn't."

"What we more or less came here to say—"

"What we've both been thinking is—"

"Maybe all this trouble you're having—"

"Maybe this whole awful business—"

"Maybe," they say in unison, "it's all for the best."

They kiss you on the forehead. These kinds of gestures don't usually pass between you and you are moved. When they go to leave, you have the urge to claw at the hems of their garments and pull them down with you into your private hell, but of course you don't.

By far the most important part of the day is *Tom & Jerry*, which, like all of your life's past pleasures, you have managed to ruin with obsessive analysis. Lately, you have begun to sympathize with the cat, to suspect that the cat's continued failures are speaking to you personally, you feel now as if the cat's tribulations are mocking reenactments of your own life. Watching him, you feel anxious, wounded, mortified. Most painful are the moments when the cat is walking around satisfied with himself. He has done something clever, he has shut away the mouse deep within a series of nesting suitcases, he has licked clean a saucer full of cream, he has exacted revenge, he has spotted a girl and commanded her attention, he has done any or all of these things and so walks on his hind legs with his chest thrust out. But the problem with the cat's walking like this—as it is for you and likewise all the world—is that in such a position his heart and genitals are exposed, they are right out there tempting some violence, and sure enough it comes calling. At the height of his glory the cat is knocked down in the most humiliating fashion and what hurts to watch is not the fall itself, but the perfect confidence with which the cat carries himself directly into the clutches of certain doom. Watching these scenes over and over, you are moved, you feel in those moments something like the pity and compassion you were always instructed to feel in church but could never muster.

One episode in particular you almost can't make it through. Here Tom is shown in pursuit of his intended. He lugs a string bass to her back yard and plays beneath her bedroom window, plays right there next to the dog house, without regard for peril. He cries up to the lighted window: *Is you is or is you ain't my baby? The way you acting lately makes me doubt.* And the intended comes to the window. She pouts, she blinks, she sighs, she props her chin on her paw, she watches with boredom as Tom is dismembered, utterly torn to pieces by a spike-collared bulldog. *Yes*, you think. *That's just how it went.*

After *Tom & Jerry*, you always turn off the TV and wait for sleep, which doesn't come. You stare out the window conjugating verbs. *Je dormirai*, you say. *Je dormirais. Si je dorme.*

NOVEMBER

Something about the weather, the nurses say, the cycle of the moon combined with a drastic barometric shift, there's a snow-storm, and right in the middle of it the hospital is overflowing with women gone into labor. You hear their cries, you hear the cries of the newly born. Past your door you see them wheeled in beds and chairs and isolettes. One day, a bed is wheeled into your room—what you have come to think of as your own personal room—with a hugely pregnant woman lying on it. She has brown hair, brown eyes, and a freckled face, her hair is done up in braided pigtails, she reminds you of a grown-up Laura from *Little House on the Prairie*.

"It's crazy in here," says Edith, "and we outta room so you two have to be roommates for a bit." As if to prove Edith's point, someone cries out in pain from the next room, and she leaves, leaves you with this new roommate, this pigtailed settler.

"You pregnant?" says the roommate. "You don't look none pregnant."

You nod.

"Watcha in labor or something?"

You shrug.

"I'm three weeks early but it looks like I gone into labor."

You nod.

"Boy you sure did keep your figure," she says. "You're lucky you didn't blow up like a whale like me."

Her name is Amanda and she is determined to tell you her life story in as much painful detail as she can manage to recall, starting, like David Copperfield, at birth. "I was born right here in this here hospital—maybe even in this very room, who knows, that'd be funny, wouldn't it? My momma had me right here, right in this same place if you can believe that." She tells you of her childhood in a trailer park on the edge of town, her brothers and sisters and the trouble they got into vandalizing other trailers, how they slept outside in sleeping bags all summer and how she once rolled her brother, asleep, into a creek, her parents who worked in the dog food factory, her father the day shift and her mother the night. She tells you about her first sex, age thirteen, her first pregnancy at the age of sixteen, how she dropped out of high school and always planned to go back, or at least get her GED, but didn't, the birth of her son—*right here, maybe even right here in this room, I can't remember, but wouldn't that be funny?*—her first son who's eighteen now and just started college, but she can't remember where because when he turned ten he went to live with his Daddy in St. Louis and she hasn't seen him since. "That was right about the time," she says, "when Michael left for his Daddy's, that was right about the time I had my second baby, Dean, who's half-black. Michael always said it didn't make no difference to him, Dean being half-black, but I always thought that's why he left for his Daddy's, he said it was the noise and him not being able to do his school work with a baby in the house, but secretly I always thought it was Dean being half-black, nobody liked it, nobody never said anything but you know how people are, nobody likes a white woman and a black man together, it gives people the willies, who knows why but it does."

After forty solid minutes, she asks you about yourself. But by this time you've rolled away from her. You don't say anything, pretend you're asleep.

"Well," she says. "I didn't know I was in the presence of *greatness* or nothing like that. Sorry to bother you. I didn't know you were thinking all kinds of deep personal thoughts over there. Excuse *me*." She turns on the television, a talk show in which an estranged mother and daughter relay messages of hatred and resentment to one another through the host. "Tell her," says the mother, "she's an ungrateful little monster."

"Well you tell *her*," says the daughter, "she's a pathetic fat cow and to mind her own business."

"I won't bother you anymore," Amanda says. "I'll be quiet over here. Nice and quiet."

On another channel, two drag queens are fighting over a third, relaying messages of hatred and resentment to one another through the host. "Would you please tell her?" says the first drag queen, "that she's a pathetic fat cow?"

"Well you tell *her*," says the second, "she's an ungrateful little monster."

"I think," Amanda says, "those are men." She shuts off the TV and sighs, then sighs again. "Well we gotta pass the time *somehow*," she says. "I'm alone like you. Ain't nobody come here to visit me. My boyfriend? Jimmy? He works construction and he don't get off 'til seven. By the time he gets home, he's so tired he just passes right out. He ain't good for nothing when he gets home. He just comes on home and clean passes out on the couch, ain't nothing can wake him. You could hit him with a hammer and he wouldn't even flinch, I swear it. One time me and my friends, we did him all up in lipstick and eye-shadow and he didn't even notice, he just got up in the morning and went on into work like that, I swear."

She picks up the phone—she isn't on bed rest and can do whatever she wants—and calls Jimmy at his apartment but he doesn't answer. "I bet he done passed out already," she says, "once he falls asleep ain't nothing can wake him. I bet you anything I go into labor and he sleeps through the whole thing, you wait and see."

She tries to call her twelve-year-old son, Dean, home alone with no one there to watch him, probably drunk and truant from school. "I'd have Jimmy watch him, but he and Dean don't get along none," she says. "Jimmy won't have nothing to do with Dean, that's why me and Jimmy don't live together. He says it's cause Dean's a brat, but I think it's because Dean's half-black and Jimmy don't like blacks for nothing. I do. I don't see no difference black or white or half-black or Chinese or whatever, but some people do, most people do, which is why it's hard for me and Dean to make friends, him being half-black and peo-ple being able to tell by looking at him I slept with a black person." Never, never, never does she speak his name without including the phrase "half-black," as in: *My son? Dean? The half-black one?* That phrase, *half-black, half-black, half-black* going around him all his life, attached to him in the prefix and suffix, *half-black Dean, Dean-who's half-black, my half-black son Dean who's half-black, bless his heart.*

"Well he's probably over at the neighbor's," she says. "The neighbor got a boy who's retarded and him and Dean stick together, they get along real good because they ain't got no other friends; they're both outsiders on account of Sam being a retard and Dean being half-black and all."

You can't think of anything to say to this, but it doesn't matter. "Af-ter the baby comes me and Jimmy gonna get married. We got rings picked out on layaway, real pretty rings on layaway."

Peter Jennings breaks in. *A new development tonight,* he says, *is putting a strain on our young heroine. Tonight it seems as if the Gods have seen fit to pair her with a roommate scientifically calculated to vi-*

olate every last one of her sensibilities. As some of you may know she is a person of few words who believes in carrying around her thoughts and experiences deep in the privacy of her own mind. Now she is literally trapped in a room with a person of the exact opposite temperament. Do we have a feed? he says. You see the room from above, you lying with your back turned to Amanda, looking out the window as always. Into the phone, Amanda is saying, "Thank God you answered. They got me stuck in a room with this roommate who doesn't talk? I mean here I am with nothing to pass the time and I get Quiet Mc-Churchmouse over here, won't say two words for nothing, I swear." She laughs. "Quiet McChurchmouse!" she says.

Amanda stays, talking constantly, for eight days. She rings the call button like a contestant on *Jeopardy!*, keeps it in her hand, calls and calls and calls the nurses, calls them not ten seconds apart, calls and asks them through the intercom: "Can you bring me a Coke? Can you bring me a ham sandwich with a little mustard? Can you bring me just a little more mustard? Can you bring me some chips, some pretzels, some of them twisty cheesy pouffy things? What about a milkshake? Can somebody wheel me outside so I can have a smoke? Would you get me one of them wet wipes? You got any Mylanta, any Tums, any orange-flavor Metamucil? What about Oxycontin, you got any of that? Got any cough syrup with codeine? Extended-release ibuprofen? Gum, at least, you got any gum?" She simply won't kick over into active labor. The nurses keep trying to send her home, but as soon as they get together the paperwork she claims to be afflicted with some grievous ailment. "I can't feel nothing in my left leg," she tells them, "nothing at all, and my right foot is tingling like crazy. I think I might be having a stroke or something. Can someone get me a Coke?"

The worst part is that unlike you, Amanda sleeps at night and so you can't watch *Tom & Jerry*. You watch the clock, 12:30, 12:45, 12:57, and finally one a.m. You wonder which episode is playing. You hear the theme song in your head, all those horns and strings. You feel better just thinking about them.

Every night, well after Amanda is asleep, an old Volvo wagon pulls into a space in the doctor's lot just outside your window. Since the blizzard there has been, perched on the roof of the Volvo, a snowman, complete with stick arms and a carrot nose, complete with a striped scarf. The doctor who owns the car always looks to be in a tremendous hurry. He slams the door and runs for the entrance, his white coat flapping behind him like the cape of a superhero. You like this doctor very much. You like to think of his life, of the kid who looked at him and said, "Hey Dad, can we make a snowman on the roof of your car?" and him saying no at first, thinking of the technical difficulties, and the embarrassment of riding around like that, but then thinking to himself, "Why the hell not?" You like to think you'd be the same, the same kind of parent.

"You awake?" Amanda says one night, "cause I feel like talking."
You roll toward her.
"I just wish my momma and daddy were here is all," she says. "I wish they was here to see Kyle when he gets born. I picked the name Kyle myself. It's classy. What you gonna name your kid?"
You speak to her for the first time. You tell her the names you're thinking of—this is the first time you've spoken them out loud—and she bursts into sobs. At first you don't know what has happened but what has happened, apparently, is this: you have just spoken the names of her dead parents. "It's a sign!" she says. "It's a miracle. Those names right there are the names of my dead parents, my momma's dead of breast cancer and my father, he killed himself, but those were their exact names, and what this is is a sign, it's them speaking to me through you and telling me they're here. And right now from this moment." She stops to blow her nose, here, on her bed sheet. "You and me are sisters and you and me are gonna be friends forever, I knew it the minute I saw you!"
Your parents are dead, too, you remember them vaguely, they died drunk in a car crash when you were six, they died and left you to your grandparents, your grandmother who wore handmade smock dresses that buttoned down the center, who went around the house and neighborhood in her slippers and curlers, your grandmother who, when people stopped her on the street to speak of her misfortune—of her having to raise a child again just when she should have been rest-ing, after a lifetime of working and raising kids of her own here she was with another one—always said to them, in a fierce whisper: *I try not to let her know it, but I can't keep up with her much longer, I'm too old and she's too much for me, no I can't keep up. Luckily she has a fine imagination, she plays by herself, she has two little girlfriends, imaginary girlfriends with rhyming names I forget what they are, she certainly entertains herself which is nice, she sits quiet down in the basement in front of the television and has tea parties with those two little girls in her head, I forget their names, but they rhyme, and most*

121

days she's quiet as a mouse and you can't even tell she's there. When you think of those years, you think only of the television, that animated universe, its songs, its glare, the people on it enjoying their lives and how you watched them as if trying to decode something, as if trying to pick some kind of lock, yes, your parents are dead too, all your life you have been alone, this business in the hospital, this not talking to anyone, this isn't out of the ordinary at all, this isn't a muteness brought on by trauma, this is pretty much who you are all the time, with a single extraordinary exception, you have been alone your whole life, but you don't tell her this. You keep this, as everything, to yourself.

Edith comes in and out delivering Amanda's food. "Guess who just came by in little Pilgrim outfits?' she asks you one day. "Guess who showed up dressed like Pilgrims, looking fat as turkeys, so juicy and plump I'd like to stick some paper socks on their feet and roast them in a pan, pull them out the oven from time to time and baste them? Guess who just came by in little black coats and hats, little patent leather belts and boots and suchlike?"

"Who?" says Amanda. "Who?"

The day before Thanksgiving Amanda goes into active labor—that morning she gets up to use the bathroom and says, "Well, shit! My water broke!," and she is taken away, wheeled off. By now you have lost all sense of time and it seems to you that as soon as she leaves she turns right around and comes back carrying a baby, although she tells you later that two days have passed and she is on her way home. This child, too, is half-black, the lovely color of an almond, with a full head of curly hair. "This here is Kyle," she says. "Turns out he weren't Jimmy's after all. I knew it was either one or the other," she says. "Jimmy didn't take the news too good." She tells you how Jimmy, miraculously roused from his nightly coma, had made it to the hospital just in time for the birth, just in time to see for himself the face of the baby he thought was his but plainly wasn't. She tells you how she called him and called him, tried to work things out, but *he wasn't about to have none of it,* no, Jimmy has already packed his things and struck out to make his living in the Alaskan canneries. She hands you the baby—there is some difficulty with the wires but you manage— and you hold him tight. You regard his hands, so small, so impossibly small, tucked under his chin. His eyes are pressed shut. He squirms, he moves his tiny mouth. "Kyle's Daddy," Amanda says, "I don't even remember his name, I was drunk and don't remember nothing about him practically except he was real good looking and of course he was black." She sighs. "I guess those wedding rings just gonna sit there on layaway until they figure out we're not coming." You hold Kyle a long time, longer than necessary or reasonable, you stare into his fat face, you think: *Maybe I'll just keep him. Maybe I'll hold him a while on a layaway plan. Maybe she'll just leave him to me.* For several whole minutes you actually think this. Finally Amanda takes him away—she is suddenly in a great hurry to leave. "Good luck and all," she says. She props the baby on her shoulder and as she walks out the door you watch his face, bunched in pain, you watch him and think: *Kyle, you're fucked.*

That night Tom and Jerry continue to clobber each other's brains out, Tom occasionally getting the best of Jerry but never, never in the end. *Most of all I relate to the cat*, you think, *because of its desperate yearning for what it cannot have.* Time and again you watch him, crazed with hunger, pass up a perfectly good meal in pursuit of the one meal he is forbidden. Time and again he goes mad with rage, the thing he most wants just, just out of reach. He thrusts his arm into Jerry's mouse hole, he slaps his fat white paws around, he crushes flat Jerry's dining set, knocks from Jerry's mouse walls the oval silhouette portraits of his mouse parents, he demolishes Jerry's clever bed, made of four matches and their box, but he never gets what he truly wants. Often in the course of his chase he is cast from his home, Mammy Two Shoes calling from the kitchen: "One more breaking and you is out, O-U-T, Out!" It is sad to watch. *Dear Tom*, you think. *Aretez-vous. Please, please stop.*

DECEMBER

By now people around the hospital have begun to take notice of your situation. Something extraordinary is happening and it is happening to you. Nurses who initially wanted nothing to do with you—you were clearly just another sad case, another mother to be sent home empty-handed—start to linger. They tell you about their own pregnancies, their own children. They produce photographs from their pocket-books, children of various ages, each a stereoisomer of its mother. Your baby is now twenty-nine weeks gestation, has a decent chance of survival. The neonatologist comes by for a chat. He tells you that one does not worry about death at this point so much as blindness, paralysis, retardation, heart and lung problems, bleeding in the brain, weeks upon weeks in intensive care, years of medication and physical therapy. He speaks of these things in a bright, high voice. These things are manageable! These things are better than nothing! A child of this sort amounts to a consolation prize, but still it is better than nothing!

Edith comes by one afternoon, laughing, to tell you about a rumor she heard. "They're saying," she tells you, and stops to laugh—*Ha! Woooh!*—"they're saying around here you're some kind of religious figure. You know with the baby staying in there all this time even with no medical reason it should be, what they're saying is," she stops to laugh again—*Ha!*—"what they're saying is you're some kind of martyr or saint-like figure." You smirk. A corner of your mouth turns up. This is the closest you've come to smiling in months. "I *knew*," Edith says, "you'd get a kick out of that one."

A nun stops by from Sacred Heart, the retired headmistress. Her name is Sister Isabelle and you have been together in the same room on several prior occasions, but have never actually met. She has a large mole on her chin, a brown mole in the shape of Florida, and you have often wondered—you are the kind of petty person who wonders about these things—if in fact she joined the convent because of the mole, because of the dark shadow it cast on her any hope of love or marriage. She tells you that word has gotten out, she has been told by several people of your situation and now of the miracle surrounding it, and she believes, she says, that God is going about his strange work in this room at the end of the hall. She presses her palm against your forehead. *All is forgiven you*, she says. She is in full habit—wimple and all!—robed head to toe in black. She is old, trembling old, her face wrinkled as seersucker. For a long moment, she stands with her hand pressed to your forehead as if by doing so she might read your mind. *No*, she says. *You are not alone.* Now one of her hands is on your head and one on your stomach, and you feel something coursing through you, some kind of electricity. A light, a yellow light, absolutely fills the room, so bright you have to close your eyes. You are warm, warm, warmer than you have ever been. *A miracle is happening here*, says the nun. The baby, which almost never moves because it is drugged into the same kind of paralysis you are, rolls over. *And lo*, she says, *they were sore afraid.* She says, *Be still.*

You have never in your adult life cried in front of another person and won't do it now—no, you won't, you won't, you won't do it, you look away, look out the window.

After that moment—so bizarre you can't think of the words to describe it, Peter Goddamned Jennings can't even think of the words—everything changes. You, even you, start to believe that something extraordinary might happen. You start to think that you have been transformed, converted, rescued from the lonely person you have always been and brought into the fold of humanity. One day you happen again upon the ministry of Dr. Creflo Dollar, and instead of flipping past him, you stay. Then he points his finger directly at you and speaks the word *longsuffering*. His message is this: that life is difficult, that life requires of you a never-ending series of sacrifices and offers in return but meager restitution and sometimes not even that, that we are as a human population essentially rode hard and put away wet—here the crowd before him claps and howls, springs to its feet, they raise their hands in the air as a means of testifying, of bearing witness, they shout *Amen*, someone cries out *Tell it!* and Dr. Creflo A. Dollar tells you that your longsuffering will one day be rewarded, that this life and its agonies are nothing compared with the life of the world to come, nothing, nothing, not a single thing can happen to you in this life that won't be made good later, and already you find yourself nodding, already you find swelling in your chest a fiery emotion you can't name, if you could sit up you would, if you could shout you would, if you could dial a phone and state the numbers of your credit card, you would.

One night, Amanda calls from home. In the background you hear Kyle screaming, screaming his half-black lungs out. "He's got colic," she says. "He won't stop screaming for nothing." She asks you to come over. You tell her you can't right now and she says, "Oh yeah, I forgot, it's just that I didn't want to be alone tonight. I'm so glad we're sisters," she says, "because you can call up your sister any time of the day or night and it's okay, it's just what family does, and family shouldn't never be alone on a night like tonight." Through the window, you see the Volvo drive up. The snowman is still on its roof, but its arms have fallen off and someone has done something obscene with the carrot. Amanda is saying something, but you only catch the end of it. "Tonight of all nights," she says. Only later, when channel 38 runs a *Tom & Jerry* Christmas episode, does it occur to you that it is Christmas Eve.

In this episode, Tom and Jerry have their usual fight. Tom casts

Jerry out into the snow but then, in the spirit of Christmas, lets him back into the house. They shake hands. *Maybe*, you think, *it just might be possible.*

Days pass, a week. On New Year's Eve, your IV pops out. You've blown another vein and you need to place a new line before the magnesium wears off and you kick into labor. It is seven o'clock, the end of Edith's shift, and she stops by to find a vein. Unlike the other nurses, she always warms up your arm with a hot cloth before sticking you, and this makes all the difference. "I wish you could have seen those twins in they Santa suits," she says. "Little fur-trimmed coats, little hats, little patent-leather boots, shaking those bellies like little bowls full of jelly. It was something else."

You look at her, look her in the eye. She sticks you, gets the IV running again, tapes it down, flicks the bag with her finger. "I'll see you tomorrow," she says. "Don't go nowhere." A little joke between you.

Whenever you blow a vein, they reload you on a double dose, a bolus. Someone is supposed to come by in an hour and dial you down to a regular dose, but that night no one does. You lie there you know not how long. By this stage of the game, you have been on the paralytic so long you hardly take notice its effects. Sometimes you can move and sometimes you can't, from day to day you feel more, or less, trapped under a pile of stones like Giles Corey, your breathing is more difficult or less from hour to hour, you have gotten so used to these things that you don't notice, that night, for a while, you simply don't notice that you have crossed over into another territory altogether, that you can't move and that your heart is doing something it has never done before, it seems to be flapping in your chest like a bird attempting flight. When it *does* hit you, the fact that something has gone very wrong, you try to move your arm toward the call button, which you can see but can't reach—true paralysis has set in, your arm won't work, you lie there staring at it—you try to call out but can't so much as open your mouth. You struggle with these things—these most basic of tasks—for quite some time. You realize that your fate, the baby's fate, depends on the off chance that someone comes to check on you. But from all your nights awake—how many of them, now?—you know that one never does, no one will.

You stare out the window at the falling snow. You think of Robert Frost and his promises left to keep, the poem you were made to memorize in third grade. You remember Mrs. Smith trying to explain the repetition of the last line: *and miles to go before I sleep*. This repetition, she claimed, was no matter of the poet running out of things to say and so therefore saying the same thing twice, no, you were all quite wrong about that. Rather it was meant to suggest that our tired traveler was giving in, that he was about to fall prey to the woods, lovely dark and deep, that he would freeze to death in their midst. You can just make out the monitors to the side of the bed, your heart rate making only the faintest spikes and the same with the baby's, in fact it seems to you that the baby's line is flat—you keep watching it and sometimes it seems okay and others it doesn't, your vision is blurred and it's hard to tell, you just can't tell, but what you know for a fact, what you know absolutely, is that if the baby is gone there is nothing left to live for. These months here have, you realize, meant something, in fact the act of lying still, of doing nothing, for the sake of another person, your child, all these months of nothing have amounted to the greatest trial and triumph of your life, these months you have been closer to someone than you have ever been before, and if, at the end of this, the baby is gone, then there is nothing left to live for indeed. This is what you're thinking when everything goes quiet. A quiet comes over you such as you've never known before, you can't see or hear or feel anything, for a long moment you are just floating, and then you are dead.

You die! For a few minutes you are actually dead! There is a break in the narrative. An alarm sounds. People come in the dark to do their desperate, frantic work, like stagehands changing scenery, they come with the crash cart, they work your chest, all of this happens unbeknownst to you because as mentioned previously you have ceased to live. You are quite offstage.

Peter Jennings interrupts the regularly scheduled programming to report your death. *Sad news tonight*, he says, his voice slow and heavy. His shirt is rumpled, his tie loose, even his impeccable hair is mussed. He has been sitting behind the news desk, constantly sitting there, for weeks now and your story has taken its toll on him, too. He is heartbroken, anyone can see this, anyone can see that he wants to go home and take a hot shower and sleep for a month and a half.

The next day, having been brought back to life, you wake to find Edith standing over you. Her hand rests on your heart. You open your eyes and close them, open them again.

"You just rest," says Edith. You do. You start to drift off but you can

127

still feel her hand on your chest. As yet you have no memory of the night before and you fall into a peaceful half-sleep. But then Edith says something that wakes you up, wakes you terribly and completely. "I never seen," she says, "a girl suffer long as you."

And you're back in it.

A question forms in your mind, a series of questions. What you want to know is plain and simple. What you want to know is elaborate and difficult. You want to know if the baby made it through. You want to know if, after all this time, you have lost it in the end. Your plans—the things you have dared to dream about these last weeks, how you'd have the baby and hold it, how you'd bring it home and love it—you want to know if these things are still possible. You want to know something of your hopes concerning the man you've loved for years—the man you followed west to graduate school and waited around for, six years now, the man who was always going back and forth, loving you and then not, calling you over and then sending you home, the only man you've ever loved. Because he was difficult, because he was troubled, because he was alone, too, and always had been, you had loved him for this and loved him still even when he sent you away, pregnant this last time, you'd *still* believed he would come around in the end. What you want to know is: your hopes involving the baby, and its father, are they still possible? You want to know if you are alone now, alone again, this time more alone than you have ever been. You want to know what Edith meant—what did she mean when she said she'd never seen this before, never seen anyone suffer so long? You want to know all of this, but it tangles in your mind and the only think you can think to say is this: "What about that other girl," you say, "just like me, what about her, the one with the twins, just like me?"

You look into Edith's eyes, lovely dark and deep, you look into them and have your answer even before she speaks, in that moment you realize your mistake, all is revealed to you then, what a fool you are, what a fool you have always been and ever will be, you know all of this even before she says: *Oh, honey. Weren't no girl. Weren't never no girl like that.*

Nominated by Ploughshares, Tony Ardizzone, Rosellen Brown, Clancy Martin, Gerald Shapiro

COLLECTOR

by FRANK BIDART

from THE AMERICAN SCHOLAR

As if these vessels by which the voices of
the dead are alive again

were something on which to dream, without

which you cannot dream—
without which you cannot, hoarder, breathe.

Tell yourself what you hoard

commerce or rectitude cannot withdraw.
Your new poem must, you suspect, steal from

The Duchess of Malfi. Tonight, alone, reread it.

❁

By what steps can the Slave become
the Master, and is

becoming the master its only release?

It is not release. When your stepfather
went broke, you watched as your mother's

money allowed survival—

It is not release. You watched her pay him
back by multitudinous

daily humiliations. In the back seat of

the car you were terrified as Medea
invented new ways to tell

Jason what he had done to her.

✿

You cannot tell that it is there
but it is there, falling.

Once you leave any surface

uncovered for a few hours
you see you are blind.

Your arm is too heavy to wipe

away what falls on a lifetime's
accumulations. The rituals

you love imply that, repeating them,

you store seeds that promise
the end of ritual. Not this. Wipe this

away, tomorrow it is back.

✿

*The curator, who thinks he made his soul
choosing each object that he found he chose,*

wants to burn down the museum.

✿

Stacked waist-high along each
increasingly unpassable

130

corridor, whole lifeworks

wait, abandoned or mysteriously
never even tested by your

promiscuous, ruthless attention.

✿

The stratagems by which briefly you
ameliorated, even seemingly

untwisted what still twists within you—

you loved their taste and lay there
on your side

nursing like a puppy.

✿

Lee Wiley, singing in your bathroom
about "ghosts in a lonely parade,"

is herself now one—

erased era you loved, whose maturity
was your youth, whose blindness

you became you by loathing.

✿

Cities at the edge of the largest
holes in the ground

are coastal: the rest, inland.

The old age you fear is Lady
Macbeth wiping away

what your eyes alone can see.

Each of us knows that there is a black
hole within us. No place you hole up is

adequately inland.

✿

The song that the dead sing is at one
moment as vivid, various, multi-voiced

as the dead were living—

then violated the next moment, flattened
by the need now to speak in

such a small space, you.

✿

He no longer arrives even
in dreams.

You learned love is addiction

when he to whom you spoke on
the phone every day

dying withdrew his voice—

more than friends, but
less than lovers.

There, arranged in a pile, are his letters.

✿

The law is that you
must live

in the house you have built.

The law is absurd: it is
written down nowhere.

132

You are uncertain what crime

is, though each life writhing to
elude what it has made

feels like punishment.

                    ✿

Tell yourself, again, *The rituals*
you love imply that, repeating them,

you store seeds that promise

the end of ritual. You store
seeds. Tell yourself, again,

what you store are seeds.

Nominated by The American Scholar, Atsuro Riley

HOW TO SUCCEED
IN PO BIZ

by KIM ADDONIZIO

from NEW LETTERS

MANY WRITERS HARBOR THE DESIRE to become successful poets and rise to the top of their profession. To see one's name on the cover of a slender paperback, to have tens and perhaps even hundreds of readers, to ascend to a lecture podium in a modest-sized auditorium after being introduced by the less successful poet who has been introduced in turn by an earnest graduate student unsure of the pronunciation of your name—these are heady rewards. Beyond these lie the true grail: generous grants, an endowed chair at a university, the big money that will allow you to write and remodel your kitchen, while freeing you from reading the incoherent ramblings of inferior wannabes. How can you realize your dreams? Follow this step-by-step advice.

First, receive some measure of recognition as a writer. Publish in a few literary journals of small circulation, then publish a book or two with a struggling non-profit press and receive a pittance of an advance on royalties. This is step one. Step one is not as simple as it sounds. Think of a little baby, of how long it takes to raise its head without a hand cradling it, then how long to flail its arms about, until the happy day it manages to roll over of its own accord. Think of the months of crawling; multiply them times one-hundred-to-the-tenth power, and you will have some idea of the difficulty of step one.

Yet babies do stand, and eventually walk, and soon no one thinks anything of it. Of course, some babies will never learn to walk, and if you are one of these unfortunates, it is true that you may never reach step one. If so, be grateful that you don't face the challenges of those who must make their way on two legs. Cats and dogs, opossums and peccaries, rabbits and armadillos and scarab beetles—these are all more content than humans, and all are equally valuable—are, in fact, beneficial to the earth rather than a blight upon it. Humans who are writers are a devastation. Writers plunder, excavate, and strip mine without regard for the consequences to others. They suck their loved ones dry of vital fluids, revealing their beloveds' deepest fears and yearnings. They expose the most precious secrets of their friends and families, and then take the credit and get the applause.

But if you can manage to stand, and are willing to be such a vampire, a succubus from the realms of depredation and darkness, read on. Step two is to win some small, local awards, and then, after half a lifetime of literary labor, finally to be nominated for a major award. For the ceremony at which the winners will be announced, fly to New York City with the miles it has taken you seven years to accrue. Bring your boyfriend with you, even though the two of you are breaking up, because you are afraid to go alone. Spend an afternoon having your makeup professionally done for the taping of a Barnes & Noble interview in which you say things like, "If you want to be a writer, you must simply persist." Say this while looking directly at the camera, like an actor in a movie who has dropped all pretense of being a believable character, like a politician feigning sincerity while laying the groundwork to rip away every freedom you hold dear. This interview will never air. Try to get through the next twenty-four hours without washing or even touching your face, so your makeup will be intact for the ceremony.

At the ceremony, stand beneath a four-by-six-foot black-and-white photo of your face that makes your actual self look ugly, overweight, and slovenly. Smile. Later, you will weep in the empty ballroom—everyone else will be at the cocktail party—while your almost ex-boyfriend (all wrong for you, not to mention fourteen years younger, but what an amazing body, you will never feel those muscled arms holding you again, sob, weep, weep) goes around to each table loading up on the leftover stacks of free books. Later still, you will watch a revered male writer, honored earlier with a Lifetime Achievement Award, relieve his compromised old bladder in a potted plant in a corner of the lobby. When asked by a concerned publisher if he needs help, he will respond, *What, do you want to hold it for me?* and you will weep again. Not because of the frailty of human beings, no matter what the scope of their accomplishments, but because, when the winner of the major award was announced, it was not your name that was spoken by the celebrity MC, not your folded-up speech thanking your mother that was heard by the hundreds of people pushing the berries-and-chocolate dessert around their plates.

It is crucial not to win the major award, because then you might feel too great a sense of achievement. Be a finalist, but not a winner. This will keep you forever unsure of the scope of your talent, and you will be able to continue the habits of excruciating self-doubt and misery that stood you in such good stead during the many years you received no recognition at all. Notice that all around you, people of little imagination and even less heart are being honored with prizes, with obscene sums of money, with publications of their execrable twaddle in prestigious magazines like *The New Yorker*. Hold fast to the simultaneous sense of moral superiority and abject failure this observation inspires.

At this juncture, pay attention to your e-mail. Your account name should be chosen from among these: poetrybabe, writelikecrazy, hatemyjob, writergrrl, rimbaudsister54. Check your inbox compulsively to see if anyone wants to offer you money to give a reading or workshop. These offers will be few, so you will find yourself reading spam to justify running to the computer every three minutes. You will begin to seriously consider adjusting the size of your nonexistent penis, or giving your bank account number to the stranger in Nigeria offering to split his inheritance with you. You will become fascinated by strange strings of words such as bullyboy bangorcumberland jehovahmonetarist antares driftdeadline embeddable ephesusmyrtle, and wonder if you can use them somehow in a piece of writing. Ordering a large, unaffordable prescription of anxiety-relieving drugs will be a constant temptation. Resist that temptation, and steal your new boyfriend's Xanax instead.

Once or twice a week, drink a little vodka mixed with lemonade in the middle of the day, while your new boyfriend is at his real job, making four times as much money as you. You are a poet, after all; a little something to take the edge off is allowed. You work part-time in order to write, and lately you aren't writing much of anything. What you do write, you realize, is crap, garbage, shit. That major award nomination, which once seemed to promise such a heady future, was in fact the apex of your career. Since the nomination, you have received numerous form rejections, no grants or fellowships, and several fan e-mails from people who clearly meet the legal definition for insanity. These are the people who want to date you. They have pored over your poems and concluded that you will not only share your naked body with them, but also read their demented poetry and thrust it into the hands of editors they are sure you must see socially, or how else would you have become a recognized writer in the first place?

Occasionally, the subject heading of the e-mails will say "Offer of Reading" or "We Would Be Honored. . . ." Open these e-mails and respond immediately. Don't wait the few days you give the insane fans so that they will assume you are a busy, wildly successful writer with no time to correspond. Accept with alacrity all offers that contain the magic word "honorarium." Reject the others, no matter how nice and gushing the offer, because you are likely to end up sitting through a three-hour open mike during which someone will sing, someone else will break into cathartic sobs, a third person will drum, and the technician recording the evening will step out from behind the camera to read his first-ever poem that he just now wrote, he was so moved and inspired. When formulating your rejection, it is acceptable to lie. If the reading is nearby, respond, "I'm so sorry but I have a previous commitment." If the reading is farther away, say, "I'm so sorry, but I was recently injured and my doctor has not cleared me for travel."

Once a bona fide, i.e., paying, invitation has been extended, try to obtain as high a fee as possible. Tell yourself you are worth every penny, but secretly feel the way you did when you were on food stamps—other people need and deserve this more than you. Feel anxious about the upcoming trip because you hate to travel. Feel anxious because you are basically a private person and can't live up to the *persona* that is floating out there in the world acting tougher and braver than you. You are a writer, after all, and prefer to be alone in your own house with your cat. You don't really like your fellow humans, except for your lover, whose stories and mannerisms can be usefully stolen and put into your writing. When he traveled with a carnival as a young man, he learned to eat fire and to put a nail up his nose. Sensibly, he left the carnival to work in sales, while you suspect that you have become a sideshow act, a fake mermaid shriveling in her tank, uselessly flipping her plastic scales.

As the event approaches, ramp up your level of anxiety and focus on these specific possibilities: the presenters will not have obtained a single copy of your books to offer for sale. There will be an audience of three in a six-hundred seat auditorium. You will miss your ride from the airport and end up lost in a strange city late at night, in the rain, trying to climb in the window of a private citizen's apartment you have mistaken for the university guest residence. Two teenage girls will come to the window and ask you for cigarettes, and then their redneck father, who thinks you are a prostitute, will show up and tell you to get the fuck away from his daughters and drive you back out into the freezing elements. These things have all happened to you, so your anxiety will be well-founded. Go ahead and have a little more vodka with lemonade, and get slightly drunk by dusk. Try to write a few good lines and then give up in despair. Tell yourself you are foolish, feeling terrible when you have actually been asked to share your work with other people. It is the work that you love, and sometimes you even get paid for it. Tell yourself you are lucky, that people envy you. Tell yourself this is what you toiled and sweated your whole life to be able to do, and now you are doing it, and above all, don't be such a goddamned little baby.

Nominated by New Letters

DADDY: 1933

by GEOFFREY BROCK

from POETRY

If one takes
a walk on a clear sunny
day in middle April,

when the first
willows are in bloom,
one may often see

young bumblebee queens
eagerly sipping
nectar from the catkins—

thus begins
the one book written
by Otto Emil Plath.

It is a delightful thing
to pause and watch
these queens, clad

in their costumes of rich
velvet, their wings
not yet torn—

he wrote it the year after
Sylvia was born—
by the long foraging

flights which
they will be obliged
to take later.

Nominated by Poetry, Philip Levine, Michael Heffernan, Philip White

WORK AND INDUSTRY IN
THE NORTHERN MIDWEST

fiction by LUTHER MAGNUSSEN

from THE YALE REVIEW

The Whitefish Bay Merchant and Traders Bank

In 1947 I traveled from my family's summer residence in Interlaken to Whitefish Bay, Michigan, to inspect the books of a bank that my father had acquired in a set of complicated financial trades that also involved shares in a petroleum company in Libya and a spice estate in Indonesia. Normally my father would have sold off the bank in a separate package without thinking much about it, but he had always adored novels about rural America and thought that it might be interesting to own a financial institution in the Great Lakes region. Additionally, the bank (called the Whitefish Bay Merchant and Traders Bank) had become extremely profitable in the previous several years, mostly because of holdings in a company called Kindersley Provisioners, and my father wanted an assessment of what exactly Kindersley Provisioners did and why they were making so much money. I made the trip from Switzerland, following a two-week stopover in New York and then another week in Cleveland, where a friend of mine owned a now-defunct munitions factory, and finally arrived in Whitefish Bay at the beginning of August.

I was fairly young at this point although the man they sent to meet me in Detroit was extremely deferential, as I suppose he would be given that I was the new owner's son. But he was also very kind, and asked numerous questions about my mother and my sisters, and every time we passed a roadside restaurant or bar he asked if I'd like to stop for something to eat or drink. I was, in fact, very much looking forward to a cocktail and was pleased when he finally reached into his breast pocket and pulled out a flask. He apologized for the quality of the liquor—it was made locally at a still built on the back lot of an old sawmill—but it was surprisingly good, and by the time we were approaching Whitefish Bay we were both drunk.

Toward the end of the drive, and afterward at a formal dinner where we were served calves' livers cooked in milk, turnips, salted cod, and endless baskets of freshly baked rolls, I heard something about the bank's success and the nature of Kindersley Provisioners. Several years earlier, the Whitefish Bay Bank had financed a man named William Kindersley, who had been head cook at the Caribou Narrows Iron Mine. He was an ambitious man for a company cook, and he worked hard at making innovations in what he was calling the "Short Line Cooking Process" and had soon developed a method of cooking good-quality food for about a hundred men with only two assistants. About this time, a Frenchman named Thomas Véline came to him in search of a job, and Kindersley discovered that he had once been a chef at a well-known restaurant in Biarritz. He had fled to Canada after killing the husband of his lover and, not really liking Montreal very much, had headed west to "lose himself in the North American wilderness." Véline had studied to be an engineer at the Bordeaux Polytechnique before becoming a cook and was interested in things like food preservation, particularly the quickly expanding technology of flash freezing, and he and Kindersley formed a business partnership in the hope of taking what they learned at the Caribou Narrows Mine to other companies in the region.

There were a number of hurdles to be crossed, particularly with things like refrigeration, storage, and trained labor. And investors didn't seem to think mining and timber workers had much use for food made by a French cook. But a man who cuts trees for fourteen hours a day is surprisingly happy when his pot pie is made with first-rate chicken stock and frozen with some sense of how the product should look when it is finally unfrozen and cooked. The Whitefish Bay Bank was eventually convinced of the potential of all this and put up most of the capital, claiming a 20 percent stake in the firm above the interest on the loan. It was the best investment they ever made. Within two years, the company was providing food for nearly all the mines in the Iron Range and had begun to expand to other industries, quickly winning contracts with shipping traffic on the Great Lakes and the Mississippi, military bases in the region, and timber operations as far as Maine and the Pacific Northwest.

I asked if I could meet Kindersley and Véline, but the bankers said this would be impossible. Kindersley had just recently died after drinking an entire pint of benzene, which was explained by the fact that he had been blind drunk already and the benzene was stored in an old vodka bottle. Strangely, Véline had also come to an untimely death. The wife of the man he killed had not been particularly happy to lose her husband in this way. She had always been very much in love with him, despite her sexual transgressions, and because she had access to substantial resources—her family owned a textile mill in Pérouges—she was able to locate Véline without too much trouble. While he was in Crandall, Michigan, visiting a food-science laboratory, she met him outside a small luncheonette and shot him to death with a Beretta M1934. After a speedy trial in Lansing, Véline's murderer was executed, despite vigorous protests from the French government.

But the company (the Whitefish Bay men assured me) was being well managed by three of Kindersley's nephews, each of whom had a degree in business from the University of Michigan. And, in fact, it was true that the company was being well managed, although I never met any of the nephews. I had only one day to spend in Whitefish Bay because I had to return to Interlaken for a wedding, and the nephews were away on a hunting trip. Instead, I spent the next day shooting grouse and drinking more of the sawmill liquor before beginning my journey back to Switzerland.

The Horse Eaters

During a brief stay in the city of Duluth in 1954, I joined a club called the German Workingman's Club, although I was neither German nor did I work in anything like the manner these German men did. But I did have a fairly clear and compelling baritone, and spoke German fluently, and was invited to join during a time that they were staging a small version of Strauss's *Die Fledermaus*. They had once had their own baritone—something of a virtuoso, apparently—but he had been killed on an ore boat when a cable snapped and a yardarm fell on him.

These German men drank endless amounts of "brandy," which was

143

not brandy at all and really just the variously flavored grain alcohols so popular with people who live in freezing and lightless climates. I developed a taste for the brandy as well, and found that I could drink enormous amounts and still manage to carry out my fairly demanding vocal duties. We would drink all evening—during rehearsals and afterward—singing wildly and with great enthusiasm as we practiced our parts. I have to say that it was so pleasurable that I regretted not having performed more in my life, although when I was a boy I made protracted appearances in the choirs at the St. Sebastian chapel in Trieste and the Kyrka Gustavus Adolphus in Stockholm.

At any rate, I was so pleased with everything, and so looking forward to opening night, that I sent a courier to Chicago to buy cocaine for the after party of the first performance, such things not being easily available along the shores of Lake Superior in the 1950s. The performance was a huge success, and we received a standing ovation (although from an audience that had probably never heard another performance of *Die Fledermaus* to compare it to), and afterward we all went to a brothel on nearby Kipling Lake that was popular with the club members. The brothel was built in the style of a fishing and hunting lodge, and had something of a large meeting hall where an elaborate dinner had been prepared for us. Since many of the Germans came from the so-called Schauinsland foothills, we were served, among other items, large platters of roasted horse meat, a thing all people from that region love. The party carried on for several hours, men disappearing from the dinner table every so often to follow a woman into one of the back rooms, and at two in the morning the German Workingmen were still carrying on the celebration with no intention of stopping. By this point, we were also using the cocaine I had brought. Unfortunately, though, one of the members of the club used too much, and, after trying to swallow what appeared to be an undercooked horse tendon, choked to death beneath a high-standing Hamburg sideboard as we were singing a very raucous version of "Come Hither Woman, Young and Supple."

To my surprise (because, after all, I was new among them), I was asked to sing Mahler's "Lied des Verfolgten im Turm" at the funeral, which I did with an enormous amount of emotion and intensity, and afterward we all went to a large Italian restaurant to discuss the tragic event and take comfort in each other's company.

The American Sun

In 1949 the newspaper consortium American Sun bought nine paper mills in northern Wisconsin from a man named Harris Rollings. The exact sum paid for the mills was not reported since the companies involved were privately held, but by most estimates the deal was worth around fifteen million dollars, which, given the time and the place, was a very sizable amount of money.

Rollings immediately left northern Wisconsin, telling everyone that he had always hated it there, and moved to Key West, where he threw lavish parties, went out with popular actresses, and invested in various hotels along the Keys, including the Excelsior, the Union, and the Windsor. After about ten years of this, however, he decided that the warm climate had eroded his "masculine stamina," and in 1959 he returned to northern Wisconsin with dreams of establishing another business there. About this time, early models of the modern snowmobile were becoming popular, and since Rollings now had some experience in the hotel business, he quickly began work on a sort of luxury winter sportsmen's resort which might cater to wealthy businessmen from places like Chicago and Detroit. He invested his own money but solicited capital from other sources as well, insisting to everyone that he was building the "Chamonix of North America." The resort was completed in two years and quickly became exactly the sort of luxury retreat for the well-heeled sporting men of the northern Midwest that Rollings had hoped for.

I went to the resort one winter with W. H. Auden and John O'Hara. We were in Minneapolis attending a conference on Cervantes when we met the industrialist Christian Hoffman, who was staying in the room next door to me at the then famous Finnmark Hotel. Hoffman offered to take us to Rollings's resort (called "Nordholm" at that point) in his plane, and the next day I was snowmobiling through the Chequamegon National Forest equipped with two Colt .38 Specials and a large flask of bourbon. I rode all morning, learning how to fire my guns while weaving through trees, and around 1 P.M. redezvoused with Auden and O'Hara, both of them having flatly refused to ride snowmobiles themselves.

We met at what Rollings had named Der Spielzimmer, which was a large outpost built from lodge-pole pines on the north side of Lake Nicolet. There were several cooks and waiters in residence at this particular place, and the lunch we were served included turtle soup, fried walleye pike, and elk backstrap covered with a tart cranberry sauce. We also got extremely drunk during lunch, and O'Hara was nearly shot to death by Auden, who started playing with one of my Colts and (astonishingly) managed to accidentally shoot it inside Der Spielzimmer three separate times.

Several years later, I was passing through Chicago and decided I might like to spend another weekend at Nordholm, but after one of my secretaries made inquiries about the trip, I learned that it had closed down. Apparently, Rollings had fallen in love with the daughter of the plant manager at one of the pulp mills he had long ago sold to the American Sun, and although her father was against the marriage at first, he had acquiesced when it was discovered that she was pregnant. Just before the wedding, however, then early December, they took a snowmobile ride together, and she and her machine fell through the ice, just at the edge of Lake Nicolet. Both Rollings's future wife and his unborn child were dead within minutes, and after the funeral Rollings moved, brokenhearted, back to Key West, never re-opening Nordholm or selling it to another party. Years later, however, he did open a very popular hotel in Key Largo called the Madison, and embarked on an affair with the cabaret singer Fiona Maxwell that lasted for two decades, although he never married her.

The Little Elk Timber Cooperative

In 1966 I acquired a large timber company in northern Minnesota called the Little Elk Timber Cooperative, and in an effort to show that I was not interested in some sort of aggressive relationship with the people who worked there (I unexpectedly received the cooperative in repayment of a surprisingly sizable gambling debt) I invited the executives and the head of the lumber workers union to spend some time on my estate in Tromsø, Norway. I hosted a party there every year over the spring solstice and always had hundreds of guests pass through, and I decided that the Little Elk men might enjoy a visit to Scandinavia and a lavish party thrown in the custom that was fashionable in Europe at that time.

Among the notable events at the party, Steve McQueen arrived at midnight on the second night of the party entirely naked except for a scrap of reindeer fur that he had stretched across his loins. I had befriended Steve on the set of *Baby, the Rain Must Fall*, although we didn't spend much time together then, so I was happy he came to my party. Unfortunately, he and John O'Hara got into a terrible fistfight because both of them evidently wanted to sleep with the wife of Tromsø's mayor, which was inexplicable given the fact that she was the sort of dour Nordic woman who never would have slept with anyone, including (probably) her husband. But that's what they insisted the fight was over, and as they stumbled around in a state of drunken and violent fervor, with bloody noses and large gashes in their cheeks, they said all sorts of unusual things like, "Lena is my fucking property, so back the fuck off," and "I will take my dick and fuck her with it; I will fuck her with my dick." It was fairly shocking behavior, but I was distracted at the time and never really found out how things ended. Steve had brought the stage actress Anna Marshall to the party, and we walked by just as the fight was escalating. I was taking her to a fourteenth-century church that sat on a knoll on the south end of my property where I planned to seduce her. I did this, in fact, and commenced an annual ritual that took us to places like Cairo and Buenos Aires, although nothing more serious ever unfolded between us.

I never found out what the men from the Little Elk Timber Cooperative thought about the event. They left the day following the fight between McQueen and O'Hara without saying good-bye, although this wasn't unusual given how many guests were there, and it's very possible I was off somewhere and couldn't be found. I retained ownership of the company for exactly one year, at which point I sold it to a financier in Minneapolis, and I never spoke to any of these guests again. Surprisingly, though, I did get word that the union leader was indicted on corruption charges the following year after it was discovered that his six-year-old son was on the union payroll. The charges, however, were later dismissed, for reasons I never quite understood.

The Jorstad Shipyards

In 1901 a boat builder from Kristiansund, Norway, named Johann Ovdahl arrived in Moose Bay, Minnesota, on Lake Superior and went to work for the Jorstad Shipyards as a wheeltapper. He was almost entirely silent at first because he refused to speak anything but English and his English was abysmal. But after a year he was able to communicate with some facility, and he began spending his time explaining to those who would listen that the world was about to end and that nearly everyone on earth would soon suffer the eternal torments of hell.

Generally, people in Moose Bay disliked Johann, mostly because he spoke so violently against alcohol, which was the main interest of many of the local residents, in particular the Croats and the Finns. But Johann persisted, and was eventually able to persuade the pastor of the Lutheran church to let him speak on Sunday evenings in their basement fellowship room. No one came at first, but Johann was a surprisingly charismatic man, and he made up for his deficiencies in the English language with wild and terrifying descriptions of pain and suffering. Before long, the church was packed on Sunday evenings with people listening with great intensity to his denunciations of various vices and failures of the local community and the world at large. In particular, Johann began to speak out against his homeland, describing Norway as a "demonic and flesh-obsessed society," and said that if people really cared about their relatives they would write letters to urge them to come to Moose Bay, where together they could begin to prepare for the deluge that was soon to occur.

One of the men who became persuaded by Johann owned a shipping company that transported iron ore between points in Lake Superior and Lake Michigan, and he finally offered to build a church for Johann, if that was what he wanted. Johann said a church was exactly what his now growing congregation needed, although his concept of a church involved much more than a house of prayer. He told the owner of the shipping company (named Gordon Bakken) that what they really had to have was a compound with a dormitory and a communal dining room so people could spend as much time as possible under his tutelage. It was a radical proposal, but Bakken was a believer, and work was soon under way.

The buildings took about eight months to erect. They were simple, wood-framed structures built in the stark northern Minnesota custom, and Johann persuaded seventeen families to leave their homes and take up residence at what was now being called the Assembly of the Resurrection. It was tough going at first. People were not used to living in such tight quarters and on the very basic diet that Johann insisted on. But after about six weeks, and the defection of four families, the community began to function fairly well. It was at this point (and for reasons nobody entirely understood) that Johann left the dormitory late one night, placed approximately forty sticks of dynamite around the foundations of the structure, and blew up every single member of the Assembly.

Johann was not among them, which was understood because, shortly before dawn of the same day, the Jorstad Shipyards unexpectedly caught fire, and authorities later found substantial evidence of arson, including large black painted letters on a stone wall that said, "I am thiyne [*sic*] judge." Needless to say, both incidents were shocking to everyone in Moose Bay, although several people claimed that they had expected exactly this sort of thing all along.

Interestingly, the federal government took over the investigation and quickly discovered that Johann had done the exact same thing in Malaga, Spain, and Mannheim, Germany, blowing up 134 people in all in dormitories built with the help of sympathetic businessmen. Johann was never found, despite a substantial reward put up by the city of Moose Bay and the Jorstad Shipyards. It was reported, however, that he had been spotted, first in San Francisco and then in Tromsø, where, apparently, he had contacted several shipbuilders, offering his labor as a wheeltapper.

St. Benedict

In the medieval town of Verona the fairly bloodthirsty Bishop Aldo Urbino carried out his own version of the Inquisition by personally clubbing to death infidels with a bronze statuette of St. Benedict. The infidel would be strapped to a large stone altar and the bishop would crush the skull of the nonbeliever while reciting a variety of Latin declarations that he liked to write late at night while drinking wine in his reading room at the so-called Palazzo Urbino. Strangely, during the era of Mussolini, the unusually loyal Ras of Verona took up this practice again, claiming that it was the only way to properly deal with Communists and free-market liberals. And it certainly did have a very strong effect in terms of convincing people to cooperate with the fascists.

Following the war, the statuette changed hands several times and eventually ended up in the possession of the owner of a commodities firm in Chicago. The man's name was Charlie Fitzwater, and I had helped to finance a fairly complex venture of his that involved buying kola-nut plantations in Senegal. But the plan failed for reasons that were beyond his control, and when I came to Chicago to give a small talk as part of the University of Chicago's Blackthorne Lecture Series on French History, I arranged a meeting with him to discuss an equitable and manageable plan for repayment. He was an art collector and had impressed upon me that cash was short for him, and because I hardly wanted to put him out of business, I agreed to meet him in the bar at the Coventry Hotel, where he was going to show me the St. Benedict statuette, a thing he believed might be a first payment toward settling what he owed. I was not a collector of this sort of thing, but I did understand its value, and because I wanted to continue to do business with him I agreed to at least consider his offer.

We decided to meet at 9 o'clock, but I was early for the appointment and ran into another man I knew, who had, in fact, been waiting for me. The man's name was Cal Lundquist and he had been a tight end for the University of Minnesota, and then for the Detroit Lions and the Chicago Bears. I slept with his wife on several occasions and over several visits to Chicago, and he found out about it. He didn't waste time getting to this matter, and as he pulled out a fairly long knife, all he said was, "You know why I'm here." But just as he held up the knife (while bystanders quickly bolted away) Charlie Fitzwater arrived, stepped up behind him, and clubbed him with the bronze of St. Benedict. Ironically, he did not club Lundquist on the head, as was the custom with this particular statuette, but hit him on the left side, just under the rib cage, causing Lundquist to drop to the ground immediately, but without inflicting any permanent damage. After the police came and took my attacker away, I sat down at the bar to inspect the statuette, and, needless to say, gratefully accepted it in repayment of his debt.

Nominated by The Yale Review, Scott Geiger

A POETICS OF HIROSHIMA

by WILLIAM HEYEN

from THE GREAT RIVER REVIEW

Imperial Air Force pilot Sachio Ashida, unable
to fly over the burning city to report
to his superiors what had happened to it,
landed his plane, borrowed a bicycle,
& pedaled into it. He'd remember
a woman in front of her smoldering home,
a bucket on her arm. Inside the bucket
was a baby's head. The woman's daughter
had been killed when the bomb fell.

This is atrocity. You've just now descended
from a stanza wherein a baby's head—
were its eyes open or closed?—was carried
in a bucket by her mother.
An Imperial Air Force pilot stopped his bike
in front of what had been her home.
I've wanted us to breathe ashes & smoke,
but we cannot. This, too, is atrocity.

What's true for me is probably true for you:
I'm tired of trying to remember this.
Somewhere in Hiroshima the baby's head

is dreaming, wordlessly. No, it is not—this, too,
is atrocity. Ashida went on
to live a long life. He felt the swing & weight
of that bucket on his arm. No,
he did not. He did. He sometimes dreamed himself
pedaling backwards away
from that mother. I don't know whether
he did or not. Meanwhile,
we rave about the necessity of a jewel-center in every poem.
I've used a baby's head
in a bucket on her mother's arm. Whether
this is art, or in the hands of a master could be, or whether
art is atrocity, or not, I'm sick of being,
or trying to be, part of it, me
with my weak auxiliary verbs which vitiate
the jewel-center, me
with my passives, my compromised stanzaic integrity,
my use of the ambiguous "this"
which is atrocity. No, it is not. It is.

For years my old high school coach visited my home
with dahlias in a bucket,
big red-purple & blue-purple heads
my wife & I floated in bowls on our tables.
Have I no shame? This, too, this story
that evokes another, this narrative rhyme, this sweet
concatenation of metaphor,
is atrocity. Coach fought on Iwo Jima
for ten days before & ten days after
the flag-raising on Mount Suribachi.
He returned there fifty years later, brought me
a babyfood jar half-filled
with black sand from one volcanic blood-
soaked beach. He did. But at Marine reunions,
he couldn't locate any of his buddies
from his first outfit. No, he could not.
He once laid out on my desk aerial photos of runways
the Japanese used to "wreak havoc"—his words—
& said that hundreds of thousands of GIs would have died
if HST had not given the order.

As a participant in necessary atrocity, I agreed.
I still agree. But it doesn't matter if I agree—
what matters is whether poetry itself agrees. Incidentally,
Ashida was in training to become
a divine wind, a kamikaze.

1945. I was almost five. Col. Tibbets named
our *Enola Gay* for his mother.
The 6th of August. Our bomb, "Little Boy," mushroomed
with the force of 15 kilotons of TNT.
"A harnessing of the basic power of the universe," said HST,
as though the universe were our plowhorse.
In the woman's home, her daughter was beheaded.
I don't know if Ashida learned exactly how,
though we & the art of atrocity would like to know.
In any case, what could this mother do?
She lifted her daughter's head. She laid it
in the aforementioned jewel-center.
She was not thinking of the basic power of the universe.
Did she place oleander blossoms on her baby's face?
Did she enfold her daughter's head in silk, which rhymes with *bucket*,
& *sick*, & *volcanic*, & *wreak havoc*? . . .

(Buckets appear often, as a matter of fact,
in the literature of exile, for example
in Irina Ratushinskaya's prison memoir *Gray is the Color
of Hope*—coal buckets & slop buckets,
ersatz food placed in what were toilet buckets.
"Time to get up, woman. Empty your slop bucket."
Irina drags her bucket daily to the cess pit.
She doesn't know if she can ever become a mother.)

Ashida attained the highest black belt, went on
to coach the American Olympic judo team.
He did. I spoke with his daughter
at an event where I received a poetry prize,
a check for a thousand George Washingtons
& an etched glass compote
for a book on the Shoah. I said I once heard her father
lecture on Zen—the moon in the river,

153

River flowing by that is the world with its agonies
while Moon remains in one place,
steadfast despite atrocity.
I remember that she seemed at ease,
she who had known her father
as I could never.

While teaching at the University of Hawaii,
I visited Pearl Harbor three times, launched out to the memorial
above the *Arizona*. Below us, the tomb
rusted away—a thousand sailors,
average age nineteen—for nature, too, is atrocity,
atoms transformed within it, even memory.
We tourists, some Japanese, watched minnows
nibble at our leis.
No, we did not. This was my dream:
I knelt at a rail under a Japanese officer with a sword,
but now there are too many stories for poetic safety,
for stanzaic integrity—woman & daughter,
Ashida at his lecture, my high school coach carrying heads
of dahlias grown from bulbs
he'd kept in burlap to overwinter in his cellar,
even persona Heyen at Pearl Harbor
above the rusting & decalcifying battleship that still breathed
bubbles of oil that still
iridesced the Pacific swells as jewel-centers iridesce
our most anthologized villanelles. . . .

A bombing survivor said, "It's like when you burn
a fish on the grill."

I end my sixth line above with the word "home."
My first draft called it the woman's "house," but *home*
evokes satisfaction, *mmm*, a baby's
contentment at the breast, the atrocity
of irony, & *home* hears itself in *arm*, & *bomb*, & *blossom*,
& looks forward to *shame* & *tomb*.
I cannot not tell a lie.
Apparently, I am not so disgusted with atrocity
as I'd claimed to be—my atoms

154

do not cohere against detonation, but now time has come—listen
to the *mmm* in *time* & *come*—for closure,
as, out of the azure,

into the syntax of Hiroshima, "Little Boy" plunges—
I've centered this poem both to mushroom
& crumble its edges—
& "Fat Man," 21 kilotons of TNT,
will devastate Nagasaki. What is your history? Please don't leave
without telling me. Believe me,
I'm grateful for your enabling complicity.
I know by now you've heard my elegiac ē.
I hope your exiled mind has bucketed its breath.
I seek to compose intellectual melody.
I fuse my fear with the idea of the holy.
This is St. John's *cloud of unknowing* in me.
This is the Tao of affliction in me.
Don't try telling me my poetry is not both
beguiling & ugly.

"There was no escape except to the river," a survivor said.
but the river thronged with bodies.
Black rain started falling, covering everything the survivors said.

I have no faith except in the half-life of poetry.
I seek radiation's rhythmic sublime.
I have no faith except in atrocity.
I seek the nebulous ends of time.
This is the aria those cities have made of me.
I hope my centered lines retain their integrity.
I have no faith except in beauty.

Nominated by The Green River Review, Michael Waters.

THE CRYING INDIAN

by GINGER STRAND

from ORION

IF YOU WATCHED TELEVISION at any point in the seventies, you saw him: America's most famous Indian. Star of perhaps the best-known public service announcement ever, he was a black-braided, buck-skinned, cigar-store native come to life, complete with single feather and stoic frown. In the spot's original version, launched by Keep America Beautiful on Earth Day 1971, he paddles his canoe down a pristine river to booming drumbeats. He glides past flotsam and jet-sam. The music grows bombastic, wailing up a movie-soundtrack build. He rows into a city harbor: ship, crane, a scrim of smog. The Indian pulls his boat onto a bank strewn with litter and gazes upon a freeway.

"Some people have a deep, abiding respect for the natural beauty that was once this country," intones a basso profundo voice, "and some people don't." On those words, someone flings a bag of trash from a passing car. It scatters at the Indian's feet. He looks into the camera for the money shot. A single tear rolls down his cheek.

"People start pollution. People can stop it," declares the narrator.

Rewind. Replay. Thanks to YouTube, you can watch this ad over and over, framed by excited viewer comments: "A classic!!" "Very power-ful." "Best PSA ever made." Most YouTubers agree with the trade journal *Ad Age*, which included the campaign in the century's top hundred. Some netizens even claim the ad motivated them to pick up trash or chide litterers. The Advertising Educational Foundation de-clares the spot "synonymous with environmental concern." Wikipedia says it "has been widely credited with inspiring America's fledgling environmental movement." The crying Indian wept for our sins, and from his tears sprang forth a new Green Age.

This is remarkable, since the ad was a fraud. It's no big secret that the crying Indian was neither crying nor Indian. Even some You-Tubers point out that he was played by character actor Iron Eyes Cody, whose specialty was playing Indians in Hollywood westerns. The Italian-American Cody—his real name was Espera Oscar DeCorti—"passed" as a Cherokee-Cree Indian on and off camera. His long black braids were a wig, his dark complexion deepened with makeup. His fraud was not ill-willed: he also supported Indian rights, married an Indian, and adopted Indian children.

The fraudulence of Keep America Beautiful is less well known. In a recent survey, respondents were given a list of "environmental groups" and asked "Which organization do you believe is most believable?" Thirty-six percent chose Keep America Beautiful—it beat out the Nature Conservancy (29 percent), the Sierra Club (17 percent), Greenpeace (15 percent), and the Environmental Defense Fund (3 percent). Over two million Americans acted on that belief in 2006, volunteering for Keep America Beautiful activities: picking up litter, removing graffiti, painting buildings, and planting greenery. Many may not have realized they were handing their free time to a front group for the beer bottlers, can companies, and soda makers who crank out the containers that constitute half of America's litter. Or that this front group opposes the reuse and recycling legislation that might better address the problem. The information is not hard to find. Ted Williams wrote about it in 1990 for *Audubon*. Online, you can find many more narratives of KAB's real motives, including a summary by the Container Recycling Institute.

And yet, even with Cody outed as Italian and KAB unmasked as a trade group, the crying Indian remains a beloved environmental icon. Why did he touch such a chord? One day in June, while visiting family in Michigan, I decide to find out.

TO GET TO Illinois from western Michigan, you ease round the bottom of what Michiganians call "the Lake," then drop down into Indiana. Almost immediately, the landscape becomes classic heartland: seemingly endless, flat cornfields like the one where Cary Grant flees a crop-dusting plane in *North by Northwest*. Each small town pivots on a grain elevator, the horizon's only transect. I stick to blue highways, remarkably free of generic sprawl, and head west. I think, *Indiana.*

As a child, I had a puzzle of the United States, each state a separate wooden piece. I liked stacking them in two piles: Indian names, European names. I was always fascinated by place names, especially Indian ones. Even as a kid, I found it odd that pioneers should name their homes after the people they had displaced to build them.

But that's frequently the role Native Americans are given by American culture: marker of loss. Early American landscape paintings often included a token Indian: America was the new Eden, complete with mournful, expelled Adam. In the early nineteenth century, as "Indian removal" became federal policy, artists like George Catlin traveled the West, painting Plains Indians in war paint or ceremonial dress. Their still, solemn faces have a funerary tone. At the same time, hugely popular "Indian dramas" swept stages, almost always ending with an Indian character's noble death. Yet even as these stage natives reassured audiences with their disappearing act, they embodied the young nation's ideals: sacrifice, nobility, and honor. Depicting Indians as a "vanishing race," these works registered an odd anxiety about their vanishing. What if in building our new world, they asked, we actually destroy its founding values?

At nine a.m. I arrive at my destination, the Advertising Council Archives at the University of Illinois at Urbana-Champaign. The UIUC library is classic land-grant college architecture, monumental yet homespun: huge hallways with soaring ceilings, wide staircases with thick wooden railings. The Advertising Council Archives are in the basement, down a long, tunnel-like hallway. Before going in, I stop to examine a glass display case outside the door. It celebrates "the Advertising Council's commitment to the environment." Typical is an ad from a 1994 "Clean Water" campaign. "There are toxic chemicals in our water," it declares. "Such as oil. And pesticides. You might think industry is to blame. But they're only part of the problem. You and I, in our everyday lives, are also responsible for a tremendous amount of water pollution."

People start pollution. People can stop it.

KEEP AMERICA BEAUTIFUL first came to the Advertising Council for support in 1960. An advertising trade group, the Ad Council recruits and oversees ad agencies as they create pro-bono public service ads for nonprofits and government. The Council then coordinates donations of media for the ads. They are famously successful. Working with the Council, volunteer agencies have churned out loads of catchy

158

taglines for righteous causes: "Buckle up for safety;" "A mind is a terrible thing to waste;" "Friends don't let friends drive drunk." They created Smokey the Bear, McGruff the Crime Dog, and Vince and Larry the Crash Test Dummies.

Perhaps even more famous are the Council's World War II campaigns: "Loose lips sink ships" and Rosie the Riveter's "We can do it!" Formed in 1941, the Council was originally intended to mitigate the antibusiness, collectivist side of the New Deal. Its founding mission was defined as "reteaching a belief in a dynamic economy." But after Pearl Harbor, the ad men teamed up with the Office of War Information to crank out propaganda, encouraging Americans to buy war bonds, enlist, work in factories, and save tin cans, scrap rubber, and waste fats. At war's end, however, the Ad Council happily returned to its true role: prophet of endless growth.

Looking back from America's current position as global missionary of free-market gospel, it's easy to forget that enterprise American-style—dedicated to the proposition that consuming equals happiness—once needed the hard-sell here, too. But the ad men knew it. In 1945, the Council issued a pamphlet outlining its new purpose. The war was over, but a new battle was on: the "battle for markets." Europe, they declared, was in ruins. State socialism was creeping through the Old World. America, too, would move left, unless advertising could "resume its star role as a profitable seller of goods." This meant recasting the American Dream as the endless pursuit of plenty.

"Only if we have large demands can we expect large production," wrote economist Robert Nathan in 1944. "Therefore, it is important that in planning for the postwar period, we give adequate consideration to the need for ever-increasing consumption on the part of our people as one of the prime requisites for prosperity." This was more than economics: it was politics. An ongoing cycle of "mass employment, mass production, mass advertising, mass distribution and mass ownership of the products of industry," wrote the *Saturday Evening Post*, would make the U.S. "the last bulwark" of democracy. Consuming became national policy: the 1946 Employment Act named "purchasing power" as one of the things government was meant to promote.

Thus prompted, Americans of the late 1940s got down to the business of buying things. In the first five years of peace, consumer spending increased by 60 percent. People bought cars and boats and clothing. They bought furniture and appliances. They bought Tupper-

159

ware. Most of all, they bought houses. Housing starts went from 142,000 in 1944 to 2 million in 1950. The Ad Council cheered them on, casting consumption as what distinguished happy capitalists from those poor benighted souls living under the communist boot.

A 1948 Ad Council pamphlet, "The Miracle of America," is typical. In it, Uncle Sam—shown striding across the cover with a toolkit and rolled-up sleeves—explains American free enterprise to an average family. The key, Uncle says, is ever-more-efficient production: "The mainspring of the American standard of living is High and Increasing Productivity!" America's high rate of consumption—"We take abundance for granted"—is a sign of superiority. The U.S. has only one-fifteenth of the world's population, the booklet explains, but consumes "more than half of the world's coffee and rubber, almost half of the steel, a quarter of the coal and nearly two-thirds of the crude oil." This, the Ad Council assured the nation, was Success.

"I HAVE OBSERVED that they will not be troubled with superfluous commodities," wrote Thomas Morton about New England's Indians in 1637. Arriving in the Plymouth colony in 1623, Morton, a freethinking Anglican who'd hung out with a group of libertines (including William Shakespeare) in law school, quickly grew tired of Pilgrim prissiness. He set up a rival trading post called Mare Mount, where he commenced retail and revelry with the natives. His paganish Mayday beer bash particularly outraged the Pilgrims; they chopped down his maypole—twice. (The episode became a famous Nathaniel Hawthorne story.) Finally, Miles Standish—"Captain Shrimp," the reprobate Morton called him—was sent to arrest him. Standish cleverly arrived when Morton and his band were drunk, and the New World's first frat party summarily ended. Back in England, Morton wrote a book about his experiences, *New English Canaan*. In it, he gives an atypically glowing early account of native ways. "According to human reason, guided only by the light of nature," he declares, "these people lead the more happy and freer life, being void of care, which torments so many minds of so many Christians: they are not delighted in baubles, but in useful things."

Morton kicked off an American stereotype, one all the more powerful for having some basis in truth: the ideal of the "noble savage" who rejects European commodity culture. The reality is more complicated: the natives, of course, were savvy traders. But Morton highlights an essential contrast between Native American markets and

160

those of the colonists: Indians valued acquisition for use, not for its own sake. "They love not to be cumbered with many utensils," as Morton puts it. They knew the word "enough." Their markets weren't based on an ideology of infinite expansion.

Markets tend to get saturated. Even with planned obsolescence— another postwar innovation—people's needs eventually level off. After the initial postwar exuberance, American consumption slowed. That fact alarmed the captains of industry. In 1953, economist and Lehman Brothers banker Paul Mazur fretted that "it is absolutely necessary that the products that roll from the assembly lines of mass production be consumed at an equally rapid rate." Throughout the fifties, the Ad Council tried to jump-start consumption with ad campaigns like 1954's "The Future of America" and 1956's "People's Capitalism," all of which equated American freedom with mass consumption. Nevertheless, in 1958, people bought even less stuff. The Council launched "Confidence in a Growing America," designed to "encourage consumer spending." Supported by forty-one companies, it was nicknamed the "Buy Campaign."

But how do you get people to buy if their demands are sated? That's where the folks of Keep America Beautiful—rejecters of reusability— come in. Things that last forever you only buy once. But something you use once and throw away: that's the perfect product.

"THEIR NATURAL DRINK is of the crystal fountain," Morton wrote of the natives, "and this they take up in their hands, by joining them close together." He was fibbing a bit—he himself sold the Indians spirits—but he was making a point. Hydration, too, has its politics.

After the hand-cupping came the pewter mug, the canteen, and then eureka! the glass bottle. Before the 1950s, most beverage bottles were refillable. As late as 1960, refillables still delivered 95 percent of the nation's soft drinks. But the beer industry, shifting from local small brewers to large, centrally located corporate producers, was finding transporting all those empties increasingly expensive. They began turning to new "one-way" or disposable bottles. By the end of the 1950s, half the nation's beer would be in throwaway containers. Many of them were ending up as roadside trash.

In 1953, Vermont's state legislature had a brain wave: beer companies start pollution, legislation can stop it. They passed a statute banning the sale of beer and ale in one-way bottles. It wasn't a deposit law—it declared that beer could only be sold in returnable, reusable bottles. Anchor-Hocking, a glass manufacturer, immediately filed suit, calling the law unconstitutional. The Vermont Supreme Court disagreed in May 1954, and the law took effect. That October, Keep America Beautiful was born, declaring its intention to "break Americans of the habit of tossing litter into streets and out of car windows." The New York Times noted that the group's leaders included "executives of concerns manufacturing beer, beer cans, bottles, soft drinks, chewing gum, candy, cigarettes and other products." These disciples of disposability, led by William C. Stolk, president of the American Can Company, set about changing the terms in the conversation about litter.

The packaging industry justifies disposables as a response to consumer demand: buyers wanted convenience; packagers simply provided it. But that's not exactly true. Consumers had to be trained to be wasteful. Part of this reeducation involved forestalling any debate over the wisdom of creating disposables in the first place, replacing it with an emphasis on "proper" disposal. Keep America Beautiful led this refocusing on the symptoms rather than the system. The trouble was not their industry's promulgation of throwaway stuff; the trouble was those oafs who threw it away.

At the same time, the container industry lobbied hard behind the scenes. In 1957, with little fanfare, Vermont's senate caved to the pressure and declined to renew its reusable bottle law.

In 1960, the year Keep America Beautiful teamed up with the Ad Council, disposables delivered just 3 percent of the soft drink market. By 1966, it was 12 percent, and growing fast. As was the Ad Council. By then it was the world's biggest advertiser.

WHEN ASKED if their family tree contains any Indian branches, most Americans will say yes. In my own family, the putative native progenitor was said to be a great-grandfather some times removed. Cherokee is what we were told as kids. Given the family's deep Michigan roots this doesn't seem likely, unless someone took a serious wrong turn on the Trail of Tears. As an adult I learned that this family mythology was common—though its most common manifestation is a mythic Cherokee matriarch. Considering this syndrome—you might call it delusions of Pocahontas—only fuels my obsession with the crying Indian. Keep America Beautiful tapped into something very deep in the American psyche. But it took them a decade to figure out how to do it.

In 1962, Michigan considered a ban on no-return bottles. Keep

America Beautiful openly opposed it. Throughout the sixties, Keep America Beautiful and the Ad Council battled a growing demand for legislation with an increasing vilification of the individual. They spawned the slogan "Every litter bit hurts" and popularized the term "litterbug." In 1967, meeting at the Yale Club, they decided to go negative. "There seemed to be mutual agreement," wrote campaign coordinator David Hart, "that our 'soft sell' used in previous years could now be replaced by a more emphatic approach to the problem by saying that those who litter are 'slobs.' " The next year, planners upped the ante, calling litterers "pigs." The South Texas Pork Producers Council wrote in to complain.

At the same time, KAB's corporate sponsors made sure their own glass containers and cans never appeared as litter in the ads. This hypocrisy did not go entirely unnoticed. In the late 1960s, a noncorporate faction within the Ad Council, led by Dartmouth President John Sloan Dickey, began to call for Keep America Beautiful to move from litter to the larger problem of environmental pollution. They threatened to scuttle Ad Council support for further anti-litter campaigns. Backed into a corner, KAB directors agreed to expand their work to address "the serious menace of all pollutants to the nation's health and welfare."

Clearly a more subtle approach was necessary. The Ad Council's volunteer coordinator for the Keep America Beautiful campaign was an executive from the American Can Company. With him at the helm, a new ad agency was brought in—Marsteller, who happened to be American Can's own ad agency. The visual arm of Burson-Marsteller, the global public relations firm famous for its list of clients with environment-related publicity problems*, Marsteller crafted the new approach. The crying Indian campaign, premiering on Earth Day

---

*In more recent years, Burson-Marsteller performed crisis management for Union Carbide after the Bhopal disaster, for reactor builders Babcock & Wilcox after Three Mile Island, for British Petroleum after their Torrey Canyon oil spill, for Dow-Corning after silicone-breast-implant lawsuits, and for the government of Saudi Arabia after thirteen of its citizens helped carry out the attacks of September 11. One of Burson-Marsteller's key accomplishments was helping to invent the concept of *astroturf*. Corporate-sponsored groups designed to look grassroots, astroturf organizations are able to reach the media, and in many cases, the hearts of the public, in ways that corporate flaks never could. Their particular specialty was astroturf environmental groups: they helped spawn the *Coalition for Clean and Renewable Energy*, bankrolled by Hydro Quebec; the *Foundation for Clean Air Progress*, a consortium of energy, industry, and agricultural companies formed to fight clean air legislation; and the *American Energy Alliance*, which lobbied to defeat President Bill Clinton's proposed BTU tax. Until his April 2008 ouster, Burson-Marsteller CEO Mark Penn was also a chief strategist for the Hillary Clinton presidential campaign.

1971, had it all: a heart-wrenching central figure, an appeal to mythic America, and a catchy slogan. There was a pro forma gesture in the direction of ecology—the Indian paddles by some belching smokestacks, after all—and the language had shifted from "littering" to "pollution." But the message was the same: quit tossing coffee cups out of the window of your Chevy Chevelle, you pig, and America's environmental problems will end.

IN 1970, as Marsteller hatched the ad that would seal his fame. Iron Eyes Cody was busy making film westerns. He played a medicine man in *A Man Called Horse*, Apache chief Santana in *El Condor*, and a character named Crazy Foot in a comedy called *Cockeyed Cowboys of Calico County*. As in the earlier Indian plays, Indians in westerns are usually allied with nature, wilderness, old codes of vengeance and honor—the vanishing past that civilization must replace.

But in the questioning sixties, the inevitable march of manifest destiny began to be examined for its dark side. As social unrest accelerated, the counterculture began taking up Indianness to express a rejection of the status quo. In 1969, Native American Vine Deloria published *Custer Died for Your Sins*, a scathingly hilarious manifesto diagnosing the epidemic of bad faith in Indian-white relations, and advocating a new "tribalism" bent on "rejection of the consumer mania which plagues society as a whole." In 1970, Dee Brown published his influential *Bury My Heart at Wounded Knee*, a history of U.S. government treachery toward natives that questioned the inevitability of empire. The same year, the tragicomic epic *Little Big Man* played Custer's last stand as an analogue for the moral morass unfolding in Vietnam. Anti-war protesters adopted fringed jackets, beads, and braids. The Indian was still a symbol of America's lost principles. But, in a Mortonesque revival, he was also becoming a living alternative to the postwar culture of consumption.

In adopting the Indian as a symbol but turning his rejection of consumerism into a rebuke to individual laziness, Marsteller and Keep America Beautiful—underwritten by the Ad Council—struck greenwash gold. Their Indian evoked the deep discontents afoot in the culture. But they co-opted the icon of resistance and made him support the interests of the very consumer culture he appeared to protest. There he stood, stoic and sad, a rebuke to individuals rather than a rejection of the ideology of waste. But then, that was the very ideology the Ad Council had promoted all along.

It was an elegantly closed circle. The titans of packaging pushed throwaways into production. The Ad Council preached the creed of consumption, assuring Americans that the road to prosperity was paved with trash. The people bought; the people threw away. Then, the same industries and advertisers turned around and called them pigs. The people shamefacedly cleaned up the trash. And the packagers, pointing to the cleaned-up landscape, just went on making more of it.

ON MY WAY HOME from central Illinois, I stop to get a sandwich at the only place I can find: Subway. It's just off a highway exit, and I can hear the gears shifting on trucks as they accelerate up the on-ramp next door. I stand in front of the fridge staring at my options. Soda, water, energy drinks, juice. Plastic, aluminum, plastic. At Subway even apples—one of nature's most perfectly packaged fruits—come pre-sliced in plastic bags. I ask the clerk for a paper cup of tap water. She eyes me as if suspecting I'm the Unabomber's unknown accomplice. I *feel* like the Unabomber's unknown accomplice, because this small act, I know, is ridiculous. It's not enough.

Symbolic protest rarely is. In 1976, after KAB testified against a proposed California bottle deposit law, the EPA and seven environmental groups, including the Sierra Club and The Wilderness Society, resigned from its advisory board. Activists declared KAB a "front group." But by then, being outed didn't matter. The group's work was largely done. In 1976, two-thirds of America's soft drinks and nearly four-fifths of its beer came in disposables. Today, every American throws away about three hundred pounds of solid waste a year, about one-third of it packaging. Sixty percent of that comes from food and beverages.

Eleven states have succeeded in passing bottle bills. Beverage container recycling rates in those states are roughly double rates in non-deposit states. But in shifting the debate to bottle deposit legislation—which it opposed—KAB still won, because it shut down debate over whether disposable beverage containers were a good idea in the first place. Vermont's original 1953 law would have required manufacturers to accept and refill their empties. No one's talking about that now.

ENVIRONMENTALISM URGES us to consider the consequences of our actions. But what if by focusing on our individual actions—what we can do—we lose sight of the larger issue of what we can't do—what has been made impossible by the way the world now works? I leave Illinois with a nagging feeling that I'm missing a piece of the puzzle. I find it in an unexpected place: about sixty miles east of Portland, Oregon, on the banks of the Columbia River.

The Dalles, Oregon is the site of one of the Pacific Northwest's most longstanding and cherished Native American trading sites: Celilo Falls. Once a waterfall with a peak flow about ten times that of Niagara, today Celilo has vanished. It lies at the bottom of the reservoir behind The Dalles Dam, a mile-and-a-half-long concrete mouth, gates lined up like teeth, that has swallowed this stretch of the Columbia. At a Citgo station near the dam, a few Indians are parked in lawn chairs by a cooler with a hand-lettered sign: SALMON. The red plastic box sweats in the sun, entombing the sorry remnants of Celilo's once-famous salmon runs. At the dam visitors center, on the Oregon side, talk quickly turns to Google. The sachems of search have built a giant data center about five miles downstream, in The Dalles industrial park. "I hear they're running an extension cord over there from here," jokes the Army Corps of Engineers docent. Outside, the reservoir glints flinty blue in the sun.

I drive to the data center and park in order to circumnavigate it on foot. The facility sprawls across the riverfront, the size of a shopping mall. Its chillers, humming like a Dreamliner on take-off, cast waves of heat across the Columbia in an effort to keep the thousands of servers inside from melting. Across the street, a silent, cold blast furnace looms in stark contrast. It's an idled aluminum smelter. Both industries—aluminum and information—came to this spot for the same reason: cheap electricity from the government-built dam. The smelter used about 85 megawatts. Based on projected square footage, the Google data center can be expected to use about 100—enough to power a small city. I scramble onto a dirt hill and gaze at the data center's private substation—two 100 megawatt transformers—until a guard dog chases me away.

The federal government began damming the Columbia in the 1930s, but things really got going in the forties. With the advent of World War II, Uncle Sam needed aluminum—more than Alcoa, a near-monopoly up until then—could make. The War Production Board hired Alcoa to help Uncle Sam build twenty new aluminum plants between 1941 and 1943. Many were sited near government-built dams, especially on the Columbia River. In fact, beefing up

166

aluminum production was used as a reason to build new electricity-producing dams.

The result—especially after the war, when the government sold off its wartime plants to Alcoa competitors—was a glut of aluminum. Even as Cold War fears were used to justify building more dams, the aluminum industry scrambled to find new, peacetime uses for its product. The tail of production began to wag the dog of demand: Alcoa and their new competitors began inventing scads of new uses for aluminum: toys, boats, appliances, golf clubs, cookware. But the real break-through was the aluminum can. John D. Harper, Alcoa's young and innovative president, boldly led the company into the production of rigid container sheet for can companies, gambling that the disposable market could use up his excess aluminum. The first aluminum beverage can was introduced in 1958. The aluminum industry never looked back.

In 1960, the year Keep America Beautiful and the Ad Council joined forces, containers and packaging composed just over 7 percent of the U.S. aluminum market. But Harper's gamble paid off. Within twenty years, aluminum containers would produce more revenue for Alcoa than its second-, third-, and fourth-largest markets combined. John D. Harper spent much of that time as a member of the Ad Council's Industry Advisory Committee.

WE'VE COME a long way from our crying Indian. Or have we? The day the waters rose at Celilo Falls, the town's tribal elders looked on in tears. It wasn't the first such event. In June of 1940, Colville, Tulalip, Blackfoot, Nez Perce, Yakima, Flathead, and Coeur d'Alene Indians gathered at Kettle Falls, another beloved trading and fishing spot that was soon to be ninety feet beneath the reservoir of Grand Coulee Dam. For three days, elders spoke, fishermen recalled fantastic salmon runs, children played games, and the community mourned the end of an ancient way of life. It was called the "ceremony of tears." When the reservoir was filled, more than two thousand Indians were displaced from their homes.

The federal government built thirteen more Columbia River basin dams in the 1950s, another seven in the 1960s, and six in the 1970s. Many destroyed Native American towns and fishing sites. But this didn't just happen in the Pacific Northwest. It went on all across America. After World War II, the Bureau of Reclamation and the Army Corps of Engineers built scores of dams, a shocking number of

167

them on tribal land. The result was always misery for Native Americans. Kinzua Dam on Seneca land in Pennsylvania. The Moses-Saunders Power Dam on Mohawk land in New York. Tellico Dam, drowning Cherokee towns in Tennessee. Oahe, Fort Randall, and Big Bend Dams inundating Sioux land in South Dakota. The larger, hydroelectric dams quickly attracted power-intensive industries, often aluminum plants.

In 1948, a deal was reached for the Three Affiliated Tribes (Mandan, Hidatsa, and Arikara) in North Dakota to sell thousands of acres—at thirty-three dollars each—to the federal government for its new Garrison Dam. Three Tribes' Council Chairman George Gillette reluctantly went to Washington to sign the contract. In a widely published picture of the event, the secretary of the interior signs the document, his face impassive. Flanking him, several suited bureaucrats look anywhere but at George Gillette, rakishly handsome in his double-breasted, pinstriped suit. Gillette has taken off his glasses, put his face in one hand, and begun to weep.

Ironically, perhaps unwittingly, the Ad Council and Keep America Beautiful got it right. The crying Indian hints at the root cause of the problem he mourns: it's not just roadside trash. It's the culture of consumption that created that trash—with government subsidized power—and sold it to the public as the American Dream, when in fact it was that very dream's death. Iron Eyes Cody may have wept on cue, but George Gillette wept for the land.

IS THE CRYING INDIAN the root of environmentalism, as Wikipedia would have it? Or is he its sole mourner, weeping its silent dirge? In the thirty years following his debut, Americans landfilled or incinerated more than a trillion aluminum cans—enough to encircle the Earth 3,048 times.

I watch the crying Indian again on YouTube. Here's the genius of it: the ad appeals to a vague feeling of national guilt that—following in a long iconic tradition—is associated with Native Americans. What we've done to this land is not right, and the Indians know it, because we did it to them, too. As the Indian contemplates the trashed landscape and car-choked freeway, a dark possibility opens up: our way of life is destructive. The cars, the pollution, the factories: it's not, despite what we've been told, the best of all possible worlds. Something must change. And then that bag of trash arcs out the window and explodes like a revelation at his feet. Oh, we think, relaxing, so that's it.

That's what we've done wrong. We can stop doing *that*. It's the same move by which we're told to buy local food—that buying local will make things change—as if the government were not providing farm subsidies to agribusiness and highway subsidies to the trucking industry and zoning incentives to chain stores, thus shifting the costs of bad environmental choices invisibly to the taxpayer and making "buy local"—the best choice—often the most difficult and expensive one. How can we expect individual choice to right the wrongs of collective decisions?

Tracing the crying Indian to his real-life counterpart reminds us to focus not just on symptoms, but on the system. Keep America Beautiful and the Ad Council planted the seeds of a feel-good "shop for change" form of environmentalism that urges us to forgo regulation in favor of personal choice. We can do it! But in a world where federal funds continue to subsidize energy squandering, individual action is important, but it's not enough. In today's disposable market, aluminum is being edged out by resource-intensive plastics that are even harder to recycle. The aluminum industry has gone abroad in search of cheaper power, and their subsidized hydropower is being taken over by energy-guzzling data centers. Microsoft, Ask.com, and Yahoo have all joined Google on the harnessed Columbia's banks.

It's another elegant circle: Whenever you want to see "the best PSA ever made," you can go to YouTube and search for "crying Indian." Bytes will stream to your computer from a shiny digital factory, perhaps one sitting on the Columbia. The ancestral fishing grounds mourned by crying Indians will thus generate the electricity that activates Iron Eyes Cody's tear, falling once more for a trashed world.

Nominated by Orion

169

HARE AT ALDERGROVE

by PAUL MULDOON

from VALLUM: CONTEMPORARY POETRY

A hare standing up at last on his own two feet
in the blasted grass by the runway may trace his lineage to the great
assembly of hares that, in the face of what might well have looked
    like defeat,
would, in 1963 or so, migrate
here from the abandoned airfield at Nutt's Corner, not long after
    Marilyn Monroe
overflowed from her body-stocking
in *Something's Got To Give*. These hares have themselves so long
    been given to row
against the flood that when a King
of the Hares has tried to ban bare knuckle fighting, so wont
are they to grumble and gripe
about what will be acceptable and what won't
they've barely noticed that the time is ripe
for them to shake off the din
of a pack of hounds that has caught their scent
and take in that enormity just as I've taken in
how my own DNA is 87% European and East Asian 13%.
So accustomed had they now grown
to a low level human hum that, despite the almost weekly atrocity
in which they'd lost one of their own
to a wheeled blade, they followed the herd towards this eternal city
as if they'd had a collective change of heart.
My own heart swells now as I watch him nibble on a shoot

of blaeberry or heather while smoothing out a chart
by which he might somehow divine if our Newark-bound 757 will
    one day overshoot
the runway about which there so often swirled
rumors of Messerchmitts.
Clapper-lugged, cleft-lipped, he looks for all the world
as if he might never again put up his mitts
despite the fact that he, too, shares a Y chromosome
with Niall of the Nine Hostages,
never again allow his Om
to widen and deepen by such easy stages,
never relaunch his campaign as melanoma has relaunched its
    campaign
in a friend I once dated,
her pain rising above the collective pain
with which we've been inundated
as this one or that has launched an attack
to the slogan of "Brits Out" or "Not an Inch"
or a dull ack-ack
starting up in the vicinity of Ballynahinch,
looking for all the world as if he might never again get into a fluster
over his own entrails,
never again meet luster with luster
in the eye of my dying friend, never establish what truly ails
another woman with a flesh wound
found limping where a hare has only just been shot, never again
    bewitch
the milk in the churn, never swoon as we swooned
when Marilyn's white halter-top dress blew up in *The Seven Year Itch*,
in a flap now only as to whether
we should continue to tough it out till
something better comes along or settle for this salad of blaeberry and
    heather
and a hint of common tormentil.

Nominated by Vallum

WE HAD WONDERED WHAT ANIMAL MIGHT ARRIVE

fiction by LYDIA DAVIS

from NOON

We had wondered what animal might arrive and then learned from another neighbor that the man across the street was acquiring Black Angus calves to fatten for his table. The calves were delivered early on Palm Sunday—from an upstairs window, we watched them run down the ramp of the livestock van—and soon after, the man's friends and family began to gather to take a look. They came by car, truck, and motorcycle, and stood by the fence or by the wooden gate, one foot up on a crossbar. The calves, bewildered, lowed and cantered here and there, side by side. Some of the men and boys walked inside the fence trying to approach them. A woman went around to the far side to take photographs.

We were having our own excitement by then. A skilled cabinet-maker who lives up the road from us had at last finished making a large bookcase for one of our rooms, after weeks of painstaking planning and building. It is made of local oak and runs the length of one entire wall. It is seven feet tall and trimmed with crown molding and flutes. The cabinetmaker wanted to bring his wife to see it. We said he should bring anyone he liked, and we would celebrate with a glass of wine, but he said it would be just his wife and she didn't drink wine, only soda.

But when he arrived that morning, as we saw out the window, there were more people with him. We went out and discovered not only his

172

wife but his four grown daughters, all of them tall and slim with dark ponytails. One was accompanied by her boyfriend, and another had a baby in her arms. They were standing in the driveway and looking at the garden, and he explained that they were waiting for his mother-in-law, who, though she was blind in one eye, was coming in her own car. Just then she drove up and got out, saying "Here I am, One-eyed Jack!" We went inside and moved slowly, as a group, through the big old building, looking into every room. They were curious to see it, since it had once been a grammar school. It was built in 1930, among the first of the central schools that replaced the many one-room schoolhouses that we still see around here, some of them as small as a small bedroom.

When we were approaching the room, upstairs, where the bookcase was, we heard a voice calling from downstairs. A friend of one of the daughters had arrived late. Her father was with her, and she was carrying a very small puppy they had just adopted. With the puppy looking frightened and the baby content, the group at last arrived at the bookcase and were properly impressed. I took their picture standing in front of it.

About one month later, a third calf arrived. During the first week, it was nervous and broke out of the enclosure twice, once running up the road all the way past the Rural Cemetery. Then it settled down, and now the three cattle graze together. They are very quiet and do not low unless one happens to be shut in the barn and separated from the others. Two of them have strange white faces, like masks, but they rarely look up. They switch their tails constantly and vigorously from side to side as they graze, because of the flies. The other day, I realized they were growing up, because I saw two of them charging each other for the first time and butting their heads together. In another few months, perhaps, they will be large enough to slaughter for their meat. Then, I will miss their deep black against the green field, and their peaceful occupation.

Nominated by Noon

CINDERELLA

by DAVID MOOLTEN

from EPOCH

Among Oswiciem's vast heaps of shoes luck
Has left one of yours on top so that you,
Whoever you were, become the absence
Which blossoms from it, the girl for whom one seeks
Fitting thoughts or words. Forget the rot
Which has alchemized a vague gray from blue or beige,
Easy to imagine its mate, perfect opposite
Like a lover, still clinging to your foot
As the story would insist, that you jolted
From here holding up a gown's dainty flounces
While clopping through the sullen woods, spurned
The barracks and faux showers, the industrial hearths.
So any notion of identity or restitution
Might reduce to juvenile romance, a prince
In search of a shy, mistreated debutante,
When everyone knows the other lies elsewhere
In those piles with its Jewish sole, that after you
Emerged ragged and shorn, they ordered women
To kneel and sift, picking out the best.
Perhaps they missed yours, or hadn't yet
Got to them. But others just like them
Might have ridden a train back to the world
So that a Fraulein in Stuttgart in 1944
Could probe with her curious toes a snug pump
With a modest heel her mother has received

In a bundle of government surplus.
And this stepsister of sorts, maybe she doesn't appear
Cruel or ugly, doesn't even know when she waltzes
About her kitchen to Strauss from the radio
And waits for her beau, for the war to end,
How readily a person becomes a metonym,
A hat, a ring, a shoe, transferable, interchangeable,
How only the truth retains its magic fidelity
Like a glass slipper worn by a girl of cinders
And smoke, impossibly fragile and lost for good.

Nominated by Epoch, Daniel Hoffman

THE ARMS AND
LEGS OF THE LAKE

fiction by MARY GAITSKILL

from ZOETROPE: ALL-STORY

Jim Smith was riding the train to Syracuse, New York, to see his foster mother for Mother's Day. He felt good and he did not feel good. Near Penn Station he'd gone to a bar with a green shamrock on it for good luck. Inside it was dark and smelled like beer and rotten meat in a freezer—nasty but also good because of the closed-door feeling; Jim liked the closed-door feeling. A big, white bartender slapped the bar with a rag and talked to a blobby-looking white customer with a wide, red mouth. A television showed girl after girl. When Jim said he'd just gotten back from Iraq, the bartender poured him a free whiskey. "For your service," he said.

Jim looked out the train window at the water going by and thought about his white foster father, the good one. "You never hurt a little animal," said his good foster. "That is the lowest, most chicken thing anybody can do, to hurt a little animal who can't fight back. If you do that, if you hurt a little animal, no one will ever respect you or even like you." There had been green grass all around, and a big tree with a striped cat in it. Down the street, ducks walked through the wet grass. Jim had thrown some rocks at them, and his foster had gotten mad.

"For your service," said the bartender, and poured another one, dark and golden in its glass. Then he went down to the other end and talked to the blob with the red mouth, leaving Jim alone with the TV girls and their TV light flashing on the bar in staccato bursts. Sudden flashing on darkness: *Time to tune that out*, thought Jim. *Time to tune in to humanity.* He looked at Red Mouth Blob.

"He's a gentle guy," said Blob. "Measured. Not the kind who flies off the handle. But when it comes down, he will get down. He will get down there and he will bump with you. He will bump with you and, if need be, he will bump *on* you." The bartender laughed and hit the bar with his rag.

Bump on *you. Bumpety-bump.* The truck bumped along the road. Jim was sitting next to Paulie, a young blondie from Minnesota who wasn't wearing his old Vietnam vest. Between low, sand-colored buildings, white-hot sky swam in the sweat dripping from Jim's eyelashes. There was the smell of garbage and shit. A river of sewage flowed in the street, and kids were jumping around in it. A woman looked up at him from the street, and he could feel the authority of her eyes as far down as he could feel—in an eyeless, faceless place inside him where her look was the touch of an omnipotent hand. "Did you see that woman?" he said to Paulie. "She look like she should be wearing jewels and riding down the Tigris in a gold boat." "That one?" said Paulie. "*Her?* She's just hajji with pussy." And then the explosion threw them out of the truck. There was Paulie sitting up with blood geysering out his neck until he fell over backward with no head on him. Then darkness came, pouring over everything.

The bartender hit the bar with his rag and came back to pour him another drink.

He looked around the car of the train. Right across from him was a man with thin lips and white, finicky hands drinking soda from a can. Just beyond that was a thick-bodied woman, gray like somebody drew her with a pencil, reading a book. Behind him was blond hair and a feminine forehead with fine eyebrows and half-ovals of eyeglass visible over the frayed seat. Beyond that, more foreheads moved in postures of eating or typing or staring out the window. Out the window was the shining water, with trees and mountains gently stirring in it. She had looked at them and they had blown up. Where was she now?

"Excuse me." The man with thin lips was talking to him. "Excuse me," he said again.

"Excuse me," said Bill Groffman. "You just got back from Iraq?"

"How did you know?" the guy answered.

"I got back myself six months ago. I saw your jacket and shoes."

"All right," said the guy, as if to express excitement, but with his voice flat and the punctuation wrong. He got up to shake Bill's hand, then got confused and went for a high five that he messed up. He was a little guy, tiny really, with the voice of a woman. Old, maybe forty, and obviously a total fuck-up—who could mess up a high five?

"Where were you?" asked Bill.

"Baghdad," said the guy, blatting the word out. "Where they pulled down Saddam Hussein. They pulled—"

"What'd you do there?"

"Supply. Stocking the shelves, doing the orders, you know. Went out on some convoys, be sure everything get where it supposed to go. You there?"

"Name it. Ramadi, Nasiriyah, Baghdad."

"They pulled down the statue . . . pulled it down. Everybody saw it on TV. Tell me, brother, can you . . . what is this body of water out the window here?"

"This is the Hudson River."

"It is? I thought it was the Great Lakes."

"No, my man. The Great Lakes is Michigan and Illinois. Unless you're in Canada."

"But see, I thought we *were* in Illinois." He weaved his head back and forth, back and forth. "But I was not good in geography. I was good in *math*." He blatted out *math* like it was the same as *Baghdad*.

But he was not thinking about Baghdad now. He was tuned in to the blond forehead behind him, and it was tuned in to him; it was focused on him. Jim could feel it very clearly, though its focus was confused. He looked at its reflection in the window. The forehead was attached to a small, pointy face with a tiny mouth and eyeglass eyes, a narrow chest with tits on it and long hands that were turning a piece of paper like a page. She was looking down and turning the pages of something, but still her blond forehead was coming at him. It did not have authority; it was looking to him for authority. It was harmless, vaguely interesting, nervous, and cute.

While Bill was gone he'd realized that nobody at home would understand what was happening. He realized it, and he accepted it. You talk to a little boy in broken English and Arabic, make a joke about the chicken or the egg, you light up a car screaming through a checkpoint and blow out a little girl's brains. You saw it as a threat at the time—

and maybe the next time it would be. People could understand this fact—but this was not a fact. What was it? The guy who put a gun in his mouth and shot himself in the portable shitter, buddies who lost hands and legs, little kids dancing around cars with rotting corpses inside, shouting, "Bush! God is great! Bush!"—anybody could understand these events as information. But these events were not information. What were they? He tried to think what they were and felt like a small thing with a big thing inside it, about to break the thing that held it. He looked out the window for relief. There was a marsh going by—soft, green plants growing out of black water—and a pink house showing between some trees. House stood for home, but home was no relief. Or not enough. When he came home, his wife told him that the dog he'd had since he was sixteen was missing—had been for weeks and she hadn't told him. On at least six occasions during that time, when they'd been on the phone and he'd asked, "How's Jack?" she'd said, "He's good."

"Hey," said the little guy. "You sure this a river?"

"Positive."

Positive. She said she didn't tell him about Jack because Bill had only a few weeks left and she wanted him to stay positive. Which was right. They both agreed it was important to stay positive. And so she'd said, "He's good," and she'd said it convincingly, naturally. He hadn't known she was such a good liar.

"The reason I'm asking is it looks too big to be a river. A lake is always going to be bigger than a river. I remember that from school. The river leads to the lake; the river is the arms and legs of the lake. Only thing bigger than the lake is the ocean. Like it says in the Bible, you know what I'm saying?"

Bill didn't answer because the smell of shit and garbage was up in his nose. The feel of sand was on his skin, and he had to try not to scratch it or rub it in public like this crazy ass would surely do. Funny: The crazy ass, he should have some idea of what it was like, even if he was just supply. But if he did, Bill didn't want to discuss it with him—all the joy you felt to be going home, how once you got home you couldn't feel it anymore. Like his buddy whose forearm had been blown off, who still felt his missing arm twitch—except it was the reverse of that. The joy was there, almost like he could see it. But he couldn't feel it all the way. He could make love to his wife, but only if he turned her over. He could tell it bothered her, and he didn't know how to explain why it had to be that way. Even when they lay down to sleep, he could relax only if she turned with her back to him and stayed like that all night.

"But that don't look like the arm or the leg. That look like the lake. Know what I'm saying?"

Bill looked out the window and put on his headset. It was Ghostface Killah and he turned up the volume, not to hear better, but to get his mind away from the smell and the feel of sand.

Like it says in the Bible, you know what I'm saying? The white guy across the aisle laughed when he heard that, a thick, joyless chuckle. *Puerile*, thought Jennifer Marsh. Like a high school kid. Probably racist, too. Jennifer had marched against the war. She didn't know any soldiers, had never talked to any. But she was moved to hear this guy, just back from war, talking so poetically about rivers and lakes. *I should reach out to him*, she thought. *I should show support. I'll get up and go to the snack car for potato chips, and on the way back I'll catch his eye.*

The idea stirred Jennifer, and made her a little afraid. Afraid that he would look at her, a middle-aged white woman, and instantly judge her to be weak, artificially delicate, a liar. *But I'm not weak*, thought Jennifer. *I've fought to get where I am. I haven't lied much.* Her gaze touched the narrow, oval shape of the soldier's close-cropped head, noticing the quick, reactive way it turned from aisle to window and back. *Sensitive*, thought Jennifer, *delicate, and naturally so.* She felt moved again; when the soldier had stood to shake hands with the guy across the aisle, his body was slim and wiry under the ill-fitting clothes. He looked strong, but his strength was tensile—the strength of a fragile person made to be strong by circumstance. His voice was strange, and he blurted out certain words with the harshness of a sensitive person trying to survive the abrading force of the world.

See me comin'—Blam!—start runnin' and—Blam! Blam! Phantom limb, phantom joy. Music from the past came up behind Ghost's words: longing, hopeful music. *Many guys have come to you*—His son, Scott, had been three when Bill left; now the boy was nearly five, healthy, good-looking, smart, everything you would want. He looked up to his father as if he were somebody on TV, a hero who could make everything right. Which would've been great if it were true. *With a line that wasn't true*—"Are you going to find Jack tonight, Daddy?"

asked Scott. "Can we go out and find him tonight?" *And you passed them by—*

"The lake is bigger—but wait. You talking 'bout the ocean?"

Jennifer's indignation grew. The soldier's fellow across the aisle was deliberately ignoring him, and so, stoically adjusting to being ignored, the soldier was talking to himself, mimicking the voice of a child talking to an adult, then the adult talking back. "The ocean is bigger than the lake," said the adult. "The ocean is bigger than *anything*."

He hadn't meant to look for Jack; the dog was getting old and after two weeks must have been dead or far away. But Wanda had done the right thing and put up flyers all over their town, plus a town over in every direction. He saw Jack's big, bony-headed face each time he went to the post office or the grocery store, the gas station, pharmacy, smoke shop, office supply, department store. Driving home along back roads where people went for walks he glimpsed Jack, torn and flapping, stapled to trees and telephone poles.

Jennifer tried to imagine what this man's life was like, what had led him to where he was now. Gray, grim pictures came half-formed to her mind: A little boy growing up in a concrete housing project with a blind face of malicious brick; the boy looking out the window, up at the night sky, kneeling before the television, mesmerized by visions of heroism, goodness, and triumph. The boy grown older sitting in a metal chair in a shadowless room of pitiless light waiting to sign something, talk to somebody, to become someone of value.

The first time he went out to find Jack he let Scott go with him. But Scott didn't know how to be quiet, or listen to orders; he would suddenly yell or dart off, and once Bill got so mad he thought he'd knock the kid's head off. So he started going out alone. Late. After Scott and Wanda were in bed. They lived on a road with only a few houses on it, across from a stubbly field and a broken, deserted farm. There was no crime and everybody acted like there never could be any. But just to be sure he took the Beretta Wanda had bought for protection. At first he carried it in his pocket with the safety on. Then he carried it in his hand.

Jennifer grieved; she thought, *I can't help. I can't understand. But I can show support. This man has been damaged by the war, but still he*

181

is profound. He will not scorn my support because I'm white. As if he had heard, the soldier turned around in his seat and smiled. Jennifer was startled by his face—hairy, with bleary eyes, his mouth sly and cynical with pain.

"My name's Jim," the soldier said. "Glad to meet you."

Jennifer shook his proffered hand.

"Where you headed today?" he asked.

"Syracuse. For work."

"Yeah?" He smiled. His smile was complicated: light on top, oily and dark below. "What kind of work?"

"I'm giving a talk at a journalism school—I edit a women's magazine."

"Yeah? An editor?"

His smile was mocking after all, but it was the sad mocking men do when the woman has something and they don't. There was no real force behind it.

"I heard you talk about being in Iraq," she said.

"Yeah, uh-huh." He nodded emphatically, then looked out the window as if distracted.

"What was it like?"

He looked out the window, paused, and began to recite: "They smile and they say you OK/Then they turn around and they bite/With the arrow that fly in the day / And the knife in the neck at night."

"Did you make that up? Just now?"

"Yes, I did." He smiled again, still mocking but now complicit, too.

"That's good. It's better than a lot of what I read."

Did you make that up? Just now? Stupid, stupid woman, stupider than the drunk nigger she was talking to. Carter Brown, the conductor, came down the aisle wishing he had a stick to knock off some heads—not that they were worth knocking off, really. That kind of white woman—would she never cease to exist? You could predict it: put her in a car full of people, including black people who were sober and sane—hell, black people with PhDs—and she would glue herself, big-eyed and serious, to the one pitiful, lame nigger in the bunch. He reached the squawk box and snatched up the mouthpiece.

"To whoever's been smoking in the lavatory, this message is for you," he said into it. "If you continue to smoke in the lavatory, we will, believe me, find out who you are, and when we do, we will put you off the train. We will put you off where you will stand on the platform and

182

smoke until the next train comes sometime tomorrow. Have a nice day."

Not that the sane and sober would talk to her, it being obvious what she was: another white jackass looking for the truth in other people's misery. He went back down the aisle, hoping against hope that she would be the smoker.

"Did you talk to the Iraqis?" she asked.

"Sure. I talked to them. I talked mostly to kids. I'd tell 'em to get educated, become a teacher. Or a lawyer."

"You speak their language?"

"No, no, I don't. But I still could talk to 'em. They could understand."

"What were they like?"

"They were like people anywhere. Some of them good, some not."

"Did any of them seem angry?"

"Angry?" His eyes changed on that word, but she wasn't sure how.

"Angry at us. For tearing up the country and killing them."

She thinks she's the moral one, and she talks this way to a soldier back from hell?

Mr. Perkins, sitting behind, could hear the conversation, and it filled him with anger. Yes, the man was obviously not playing with a full deck. No, the war had not been conducted wisely; and no, there were no WMDs. But anyone, *anyone* who knew what war was should be respected by those who didn't. Perkins knew. It was long ago, but still he knew: The faces of the dead were before him. They were far away, but he had known them. He had put his hands on their corpses, taken their personal effects—*Schmidt, Heinrich; Grenadier; Grenadier-Regiment 916 . . . Zivilberuf: Oberlebrer.* He remembered that one, because those papers he'd kept. God knows where they were now, probably in a shoe box in the basement mixed up with letters, random photos of forgotten people, bills and tax statements that never got thrown out: *Schmidt, Heinrich.* His first up-close kill. He'd thought the guy looked like a schoolteacher, and, by Christ, he had been. That's why he'd kept the papers—for luck.

Yes, he knew, and obviously this black man knew—and how could she know, this "editor" with her dainty, reedy voice? More anger rose in him; he wanted to get up and chastise this fool woman for all to hear. But he was heavy with age and its complexity; and anyway, she just didn't know better. As an educated professional, she ought to, but obviously she didn't. She talked and talked, like his daughter used to about Vietnam, when she was a seventeen-year-old child.

"Angry?" said the soldier. "No. Not like you."

She said, "What do you mean? I'm not angry."

The soldier wagged his finger slowly, as if admonishing a child. "The thing you need to know is, those people know war. They've known war for a long time. So not angry, no. Not like you think angry."

"But they didn't—"

The finger wagged again. "Correct. They don't want this war. But they know . . . See, they make a life. The shepherd drives his animals with the convoy. The woman carries water while they shoot. Yes, some, they hate—that's the knife in the neck. But some smile. Some send down their good food. Some like the work we do with the kids, the schools . . ."

He could walk for hours, every now and then calling the dog and stopping to listen. He walked across the field and into the woods and finally into the deserted farm. When he walked he didn't always think of Iraq. He thought of Jack when he was a pup, of wrestling with him, of giving him baths, of biking with the dog running alongside, long, glistening tongue hanging out. He thought of how patient Jack was when Scott was a baby, how he would let the child pull on his ears and grab his loose skin with tiny baby fists.

But the feeling of Iraq was always underneath, dark and liquid and pressing up against the skin of every other thing, sometimes bursting through: a woman's screaming mouth so wide it blotted her face; his own foot poking out the doorless Humvee and traveling over endless gray ground; great piles of sheep heads, skinned, boiled, covered in flies; the Humvee so thick with flies they got in your mouth; somebody he couldn't remember eating a piece of cake with fresh brains on his boot; his foot, traveling, traveling. In the shadows of the field and the woods and the deserted farm, these things took up as much space as his wife and his child; they mingled with the memories of his dog. Sometimes they took up more space. When that happened, he switched off the gun's safety.

Like an angry, cripple, man, don't push me!—Ghost's voice and the music, close but never touching, even though Ghost tried to blend his voice with the old words. Sad to put them together, but somehow it made sense. Bill took off his headset and turned back toward the guy across from him, feeling bad for ignoring him. But he was busy talking to the blond behind him. And she seemed very interested to hear him.

"And the time I went out on the convoy? See, they got respect, at least those I rode with. 'Cause they didn't fire on people unless they knew for a fact they shot at us. Not everybody over there was like that. Some of 'em ride along shooting out the window like at the buffalo."

"But how could you tell who was shooting?" asked Jennifer. "I hear you can't tell."

"We could observe. We could observe from a distance for however long it took—five, sometimes maybe even ten minutes. If it was a child, or somebody like that, we would see. If it was an enemy—"

If it was an enemy, thought Bill, he would be splattered to pieces by ten people firing at once. If it was an enemy he would be dropped with a single shot. If it was an enemy she would be cut in half, her face gazing at the sky in shock, her arms spread in amazement as to where her legs might've gone. If it was an enemy his or her body would be run over by trucks until they were dried skins with dried guts squashed out, scummed-over eyes staring up at the convoy driving by. Oooh, that's gotta hurt!

"Still," said Jennifer, "I don't see how they could not be mad about us being there."

Oooh, that's gotta hurt! Six months before he would not have been able to hold back. He would've gotten into it with this woman, shut her up, scared the shit out of her. The war was stupid, OK. It was probably for oil. But it was also something else. Something you couldn't say easily with words. There was enemy shooting at you, and then there was the thing you could say with words. There was dead, squashed enemy, and there was the thing you could say with words. There was joking at squashed bodies, and nothing else to be said.

"Here," said Jim. "Let me ask you something now."

"OK," said Jennifer.

"Do you ever feel guilty?"

"What?"

"Do. You. Ever. Feel. Guilty." He smiled.

185

"Doesn't everybody?"

"I didn't ask about everybody. I asked 'bout you."

"Sometimes," she said. "Sometimes I feel guilty."

"Good. Because guilt is not a bad thing. Guilt can instruct you, you can learn from guilt. Know what I mean?"

"I think so." Something opened in her, some feeling she couldn't identify as manipulated or real.

He smiled. "So here's what I want to say: Guilt you can live with. But you can't live with regret. Can't learn from it, can't live with it. So don't ever feel regret."

The thing was, Perkins couldn't really understand this man either. He didn't know if it was because he had forgotten or because war was different now or because the man was black or because—well, the man was not right, that was obvious. But a lot of them didn't seem right. You supported them, absolutely, you wanted to be proud; what happened after Vietnam should never be allowed to happen again—but then you read someplace that they didn't care about killing civilians, that it was like video games to them. Stuff about raping young girls, killing their families, doing sex-type things with prisoners, taking pictures of it—and then you'd read somebody sneering that the Greatest Generation couldn't even fire their guns while these new guys, they *liked* to kill.

"Now I have another question. Is that OK?"

"Yes."

"When you look out that window, what do you see?"

Jennifer looked and thought; though he was crazy, she wanted to give a good answer. "Trees," she said. "Sky. Water. Plants. Earth."

He smiled. "All of that *is* there. I see it, too. But that's not all I see."

"What do you see?"

In his head Bill saw a horror movie, one he'd seen a long time before. It was a fight between good—or maybe just normalcy—and evil. Evil had gotten the upper hand. "We can't stop them now!" cried the scientist. But then by mistake the evil people woke something deeper than evil. They woke things underground called Mogred or some shit, things that knew only destruction and didn't care who was destroyed; they made the earth come open, and humanoid monsters without

186

faces emerged from the crack. They weren't on anybody's side; but because evil had disturbed them, they attacked evil.

Jim saw trees and shining water. He saw lake water, river water, sewage water. He saw the eyes of God in the water, and they were shining with love. In the eyes of God even the sewage water in the street was shining. In the eyes of God a woman came out on the street, moving very quickly. She drew up her robe and walked into the shining sewage and pulled out a child by the hand. She led the child and looked at Jim, and the mouth of God roared.

Outside the train window the mouth of God was silent. It was silent and it was chewing—it was always chewing. That was OK; it needed to eat to keep the body going. And the eyes of God were always shining with love. And the nose of God—that was something you grabbed at on your way to the chewing mouth. Like those people in the old television movie climbing on the giant presidents.

The war was like the crack in the ground that let the Mogred out. The crack in the ground had nothing to do with arguments about smart or stupid, right or wrong. The crack in the ground was even sort of funny, like in a movie with shitty special effects, monsters pouring out the crack like a football team.

How could anybody say they couldn't shoot their weapons? That's what Perkins wondered. If the United States Army couldn't shoot, who killed all those Germans and Japanese? True: straight off the ramp, chest-deep in the ocean, fighting its sucking, wet muscle toward the shore with machine-gun fire hammering down around you and shells slamming your eardrums, pushing on floating corpses as you got close—you couldn't see what to shoot at then. They hadn't been chasing a ragged third-world army with inferior weapons, and they hadn't been wearing body armor. They came out of the ocean into roaring death, men exploding like bloody meat, and all of it sucked into the past before memory could remember or the nerves had time to react. At least that must be why he could not recall most of it as anything but a blur.

The war was a crack in the ground, and the Iraqis were the Mogred, pouring out. Then somehow he and his buddies had become Mogred.

187

Then it was nothing but Mogred, clawing and killing. Bill glanced at the guy sitting across from him; that was no Mogred. No way.

"I can't tell you what I see," said Jim. "And what I see you will never see. Because I have been touched by God." There was a wheel of colors spinning in his mind, gunfire and music playing. A ragged little boy ran down the street, a colored pinwheel in his hand. A ragged little boy tried to crawl away, was stopped by a bullet. Laughter came out an open window. "You never hurt a little animal," his foster father said.

Unseeing and unhearing, she stared impassively at his face. "By Jesus, you mean?"

He felt himself smile. "Not by Jesus, no. Lots of people have been touched by Jesus. But I have been touched by God."

Unfeeling spread through her face like ice, stilling the warmth and movement of her skin. With unfeeling came her authority. "How'd you get to skip Jesus?" she asked.

"If I told you that, we'd have to be talking all day and all night. And then you'd be like me." He smiled. Ugliness bled through his smile, the weak, heartbreaking ugliness of the mentally ill.

Dear God, could they really have sent this man into combat?

When his daughter was a little girl, sometimes she would ask him to tell her a war story, her eyes soft and shining with trust, wanting to hear about men killing each other. But he never told her about killing. He told her about the time he was standing guard one night, when he thought he heard an enemy crawling through the brush to throw a grenade; just before he squeezed the trigger, a puppy came wiggling into his foxhole. He told her about the time in Italy, when he and his buddies saw a tiny woman carrying a great jug of water on her head, and he'd said, "Hell, I'm going to help that woman!" He'd stopped her and taken the jug off her head and almost collapsed it was so heavy; his buddies had fallen about laughing.

"Were you in the National Guard?" she asked. "Were you a reservist?"

"Naw," he said. "I was active duty."

"Well," she said. "I really appreciate talking to you. But I have to get back to my work now."

"All right." He extended his hand across the seat.

"And thank you for your service," she said. "Even if I don't agree with the cause."

This pitiful SOB had been in *Iraq*? That was one fucked-up piece of information, but it made all the sense in the world, thought Carter Brown as he took the ticket stub from the overhead. They deliberately went out and got the dumbest, most desperate people for this war—them and kids like his nephew Isaiah, who *were* in the National Guard so they could go to school. Isaiah, who got A's all through community college and who would be in a four-year school now if he wasn't busy being shot at. He tapped the spooky-looking white guy on the shoulder, maybe a little too hard, to let him know his stop was coming up, and—hell, everybody on this train was nuts—the man just about jumped out his seat.

Perkins was relieved to hear her finally become respectful, even if the guy was half-wrapped. At least liberals had changed since Vietnam. Everyone had changed. His daughter supported this war less equivocally than he did. She told him about attending a dinner for a returning soldier who'd said, "I'm not a hero. I'm a killer. But you need killers like me so that you can go on having all the nice things you have." Some of the people at the dinner had been disturbed, but not her. She'd thought it was great. She'd thought it was better than platitudes or ideals; she'd thought it was real.

He looked at his watch. When they got to the station, he thought, he'd go to the bathroom for another smoke.

One night when there was a full moon, out in the field across from the house where his wife and child slept, he remembered his first night in Iraq. There had been a full moon then, too, and its light had made a luminous path on the desert, like something you could follow out of the world. He remembered thinking, *We are going to do something great here. We are going to turn these people's lives around.*

"Your stop, comin' up."

Now there was the man across the aisle, talking to himself and nodding. Now there was Bill in the dark field, holding a loaded gun pointed at nothing. There were all the people criticizing him for not getting a job, for being cold to his wife, for yelling at his son, for spending too much time looking for a dead dog. He put away his iPod,

189

shouldered his pack. They didn't get it, and he didn't blame them. But alone in the field or in the woods, looking for his dog, was when he could feel what had happened in Iraq and stand it.

The train pulled into the station; people got up with their things; conductors worked the doors. The silent soldier stood with his pack and briefly clasped hands with the crazy soldier. Perkins fingered his packet of cigarettes.

He had been a returning hero, then people forgot the war ever happened. Then war was evil and people who fought it were stupid grunts, crazy upon return. Then people suddenly called them the Greatest Generation. Then just as suddenly they were the assholes who couldn't shoot their weapons. No, not assholes, just nice boys who didn't know what was real. These guys now, some people said they were killers, some said heroes, some said both. What would they be in fifty years?

As people disembarked, Jim rose and wandered away; and for a moment Jennifer thought he'd gotten off, too. But then she saw him walking toward the back of the car, talking to himself and to others. She turned her attention to the short essay she'd been editing before their conversation. It was by a novelist who was in love with a vegetarian and who had tried to impress her by pretending he was vegan. It was light and funny, and she felt too bitter now to appreciate those things.

Coming out of the bathroom, Perkins noticed the couple, the woman first. She was black and normally he didn't like black, but she was beautiful and something else besides. Her soft eyes and full presence evoked sex and tenderness equally, and he could not help but hold her casual gaze. Or he would have, if she hadn't been sitting next to a giant of a man with quick, instinctive eyes.

Old white fool, look away quick—good. Shouldn't have looked at all, and wouldn't if they were anyplace else. Chris put one hand on Lalia's arm and worked the game on his laptop with the other. He wasn't mad; old man couldn't help but look. Lalia was all beauty beside him, shining and real in a world of polluted, pale shit. He killed the dude crawling at him in the street, then got the one coming out the window. He moved down her arm and put his hand over hers; her fingers re-

190

sponded to his. His feelings grew huge. Dudes came rushing at him in the hallway; he capped 'em. He was looking forward to that night, to the hotel room he'd reserved that was supposed to have a mirror over the bed and a little balcony where they'd drink champagne with strawberries in chocolate. He killed dudes coming out the door; he entered the secret chamber. He wanted it to be something they'd always remember. He wanted it to be the way it had been the first time with her.

It was humiliating to be old, to shrink before the glowering eyes of a stronger man. But just mildly. He understood the young gorilla—you'd have to protect that woman. He thought of Dody, when she was young, how it was to go out with her; he always had to be watching for trouble, for some idiot wanting to start something. You always had to watch for that if you were with a good-looking female; it became automatic. Sometimes it made him scared and sometimes angry, and the heat of his anger got mixed up with the heat in Dody's eyes, in the curves of her small body, the heat she gave off without knowing it. That was all gone now, almost. They still kissed, but not with their tongues.

It took a long time to get with her, years, but when it finally happened it was like the song his aunt used to listen to when she sat by the window, her glass of Bacardi and juice tilted and the sunlight coming in, her knees opening her skirt—the song that made him run and hide in the closet the first time he heard it, because it was too much of something, something with no words, but somehow living in the singer's voice and words, high-voiced, sweet-strong words that made him remember his mama, even though everybody said he was too young to remember. *If I ever saw a girl / That I needed in this world / You are the one for me*—The words like the poems on cheap cards, like the poems nerds wrote to get A's in class—but the way this singer said them, they were deep and powerful, and they said things no words could say, things his mama said with her hand, touching his face at night, or his aunt, just brushing against him with her hip . . . A trapdoor opened; the secret chamber was flooded with dudes wearing masks. Shit, one of them capped his ass.

Oh, my little love, yeah—He had her every way with no holding back, with his shirt over the light to make it soft. She was a quiet lover, but the warm odor that came off her skin was like a moan you could smell, and though she moved like every other woman, she said things with her moves that no other woman said. When they finished, she'd turned around and pushed the hair off her dazed eyes and—*oh, my little love*—took his face in her hands. Nobody ever touched his face, and the move surprised him so that he almost slapped her away. Then he put his hands over hers and let her hold his face.

He remembered when the war ended the Italians invited the victorious Americans to see a local company put on an opera. They went, but it was mostly boring, too hot, everybody smelling bad up in the little balcony, the orchestra looking half-asleep, flies swarming—but then there was this one woman singing. He made his buddies quit horsing around and they did, they turned away from their jokes and listened to the small figure on the stage below, a dream of love given form by her voice and pouring from her to fill the room. When he and his buddy Bill Steed went backstage to meet her, it turned out she was older than they'd thought, and not pretty, with makeup covering a faded black eye. But he still remembered her voice.

In the essay Jennifer was editing, the writer claimed that sometimes who you pretend to be is who you really are. He said that sometimes faking was the realest thing you could do. She thought, *This is how I make my money. This is how I use my mind.*

"Bitch! What you think you doin', bitch!"

Her heart jumped; she looked up to see a huge black man looming over somebody in the seat behind him, yelling curses—oh no, it was Jim. He was yelling at Jim. A woman stood and grabbed the huge man's shoulder, saying, "Nuh, nuh, nuh," a beseeching half-word, over and over. She meant *no, don't*, but the big man grabbed Jim up and shook him like a doll. The woman shrank back, yet said it more sharply, "Nuh, nuh!" Ignoring her, the man stormed down the aisle to where Jennifer sat, holding Jim off the ground like he was nothing. Jim was talking to the man, but words were nothing now. She felt the whole train alert with fear but distant, some not even looking. She stood up. The man threw Jim, threw his whole body down the aisle of the train. She tried to speak. Jim leapt off the floor with animal speed and put his arms up as if to fight. She could not speak. Next to her, an old man stood. "I'ma kill you!" shouted the big man, but he didn't. He just looked at the old man and said, "He touch my wife's breast! I look over and saw his hand right on it!" Then he looked at Jennifer. He looked as if he'd waked suddenly from a dream and was surprised to see her there.

"It's all right," said the old man mildly. "You stopped him."

"It's not all right," said the young man, but quietly. "Nothin' all right." He turned and walked the other way. "You ruinin' my vacation," he said as he went. "Pervert!" He didn't look at his wife on his way out of the car.

The old man sat down. Jennifer looked at Jim. He was pacing back and forth in the aisle, talking to himself, his face a fierce inward blank.

There's no God, no face, you weak, lying—*you lying sack of shit!* There is just the woman and the roaring and the world and the pit. Jim fell into the pit; and as he fell, all the people in it screamed things at him. Teachers, fosters, social workers, kids, parents, all the people he'd ever known standing on ledges in gray crowds screaming at him as he fell past. He landed hard enough to break his bones. He was under an overpass, standing with his backpack and crying while his father drove away with his mother yelling in the front seat and his sister crying in the back, looking out with her hands on the window. Paulie sat next to him with no head and blood pouring up. His uncle said, *No, I cannot take those children.* Paulie fell backward and blood ran from him. Dancing children lay in pieces, guns shot. The woman and the child ran, fell, ran, far away. His foster mother opened the door and let in the warm light of the living room; the bed creaked as she sat and sang to him. The trees shivered, the giant fist slammed the ground, they shivered. The long grass rippled in the machine-gun fire. The pit opened, but Jim stayed on the shivering ground. He did not fall again. His sister came to him and held him in her arms. *La la la la la la la la la means I love you.* He closed his eyes and let his sister take him safely into darkness. She could do that because she was already dead. He didn't know it then. But she was.

The door between cars exploded open and they came rolling down the aisle, two conductors and a human bomb, the bomb saying, "And we're on our honeymoon! In Niagara Falls! The only reason we even took the train is she's afraid to fly—and this happens?"

"I know just the one you mean," sighed the black conductor. "I know just the one."

"And she's pregnant!"

"Don't worry, we'll get him off," said the white conductor. "We'll have the cops come get him. He won't bother you no more."

Carter had no pleasure in putting the man off the train, couldn't look at his sad, weak-smiling face. He even felt sorry for the blond woman, with her dry, pale eyes way back in her head, looking like she'd been slapped. He got the clanking door open, kicked down the metal steps, heaved the man's bag, and thought: *Cheney should have to fight this war. Bush should have to fight it. Saddam Hussein and Osama bin Laden should fight it. They should be stripped naked on their hands and knees, placed within striking distance of each other, each with one foot chained to the floor. Then give them knives and let them go at it. Stick their little respective flags up their asses so they can wave their damn flags while they fight.* "Utica," he yelled, "this stop, Utica."

He didn't seem to mind being put off the train; he was even pretty cheerful about it. Jennifer looked out the window and saw him talking to two policemen who stood with folded arms, nodding politely at whatever it was he was saying. She heard the big guy up ahead of her, still going over it. "I heard him talking to you," he said to someone. "What was he saying?"

"Crazy stuff," answered a woman. "I was real quiet, hoping he'd go away, but he just kept going."

"Why did he *do* that?" asked the big man. "I don't usually do nobody like that, but he—"

"No, you were right," said the woman. "If you hadn't done something, the next person he grabbed might've been a little girl!"

"Yeah!" The big man's voice sounded relieved. Then he spoke to his wife, loudly enough for Jennifer to hear him several rows away. "Why didn't you *say* anything?" he asked.

Because he like my brother. I could feel it when he touch me. My brother grab a teacher butt in the sixth grade, he do it for attention, it not even about the butt. I can't talk about it here, Chris, all these people listening, I can feel them, and this too private. But my brother coulda turn out like this man here. Kids beat on him when he was like six, he had to be in the hospital, and for a long time after, he talk in this whisper voice that you can't hardly hear, like he talkin' to himself and to the world in general, talkin' like a radio with the dial just flippin' around, givin' out stories that don't make no sense, but all about kickin' and punchin' and killin' people. He get older and anything anybody say to him, he bust out, "I'ma punch him! An' then do a double backflip an' kick him in the nuts! An' then in the butt! An' then—" It so annoying, and he still doing it when he get older, only then he talk about how somebody does this or that, he gonna pull out a gun and shoot him. He talk like he a killa, but he a baby, and everybody know it. My brother now, he work as a security guard in a art museum where he sit all day and read his books and play his games. But he could've got hurt real bad—and looked at one way, he talk so stupid he almost deserve it. But look the other way, Chris. You do that, you see he live in imagination, not the world; shit don't mean for him what it do for us. You see that and you wanna protect him even if he is a damn fool, and also I don't want you into any trouble over me, our baby is in me, and it is our day. I love you, that why I don't say nothin', Chris—

She put her hand on his arm and felt him withdraw from her without moving. She looked out the window; they were moving past people's yards. Two white kids, just babies, were standing in wet yards with their mouths open looking at the train, one with his fat little legs bare, wearing only shoes and a hoodie. Her heart hurt. *Please come back*, she said with her hand. *I love you. Don't let this take away our beautiful night.*

Disgraceful all around, thought Perkins. That they would treat a vet like that, that a vet would act like that. He looked out the window at small homes set beyond overgrown backyards, broken pieces of machinery sitting in patches of weeds, a swing set, a tied-up dog barking at the train, barbed wire snarled around chainlink so nobody could climb over. A long time ago he would've gone home and told his wife about the guy being put off the train; they would've talked about it. Now he probably wouldn't even mention it to her. They used to talk about everything. Now silence and routine were where he felt her most. He looked out on marshy land, all rumpled mud and pools of brown water with long grasses and rushes standing up. His reflection in the glass floated over it, a silent, impassive face with heavy jowls and a thin, downward mouth. And there, with his face, also floated the face of Heinrich Schmidt.

He didn't touch that lady's breast, he touched her shoulder. Maybe the train rocked or something, made his hand move down, but he was just trying to talk to her. The conductor knew that, he told him so, but they'd had to take him off the train anyway. It wasn't good but it wasn't bad. The police said there would be another train. But there was no lake to look at here. Where you sat down here, there were just train tracks and an old train that didn't work anymore. He would sit for a while and look at them, and then he would call his foster mother. He would tell her there'd been a problem he'd had to solve, a fight to be broken up, and he couldn't get back on the train. His foster mother had strong hands, she could break up fights, using the belt when she had to. She served food, she rubbed oil into his skin, she washed his back with a warm cloth. She led a horse out of the stable, not her horse, the horse of some woman down the road, that sometimes his sister Cora would ride. She was so scared to get up on it at first, but then she sat on it with her hands up in the air, not even holding on, and they took her picture.

They said Cora died of kidney failure and something that began with a *p*. They had the letter when he got back to the base. By then, they'd already had the funeral. He read the letter and then he sat still a long time. Before he left for Iraq, she'd had her toes cut off, and she said she was going to get better. When she took him to the airport, she walked with a fancy cane that had some kind of silver bird head on it. He couldn't picture her dead. He could picture Paulie, but not Cora. When he came home, he still thought he might see her at the airport, standing there looking at him like he was an idiot, but still there, with her new cane. He thought he might see her up in Syracuse, riding her horse. Even though he knew he wouldn't. He thought he might see her on her horse.

Riding her horse across a meadow with flowers in it, riding in a race and winning a prize, everybody cheering, not believing she'd really won, cheering. Then they'd have a barbecue like they used to, when the second foster father was there, basting the meat with sauce and Jim helping out. The cats walking around with their tails up, music turned up loud so they could hear it out the window, his foster father singing him a dirty song to the tune of "Turkey in the Straw." It was mostly a funny song so it wasn't dirty, and his foster father always told him not to hurt anything, so it wasn't bad. Or his other foster father did; he wasn't sure. He'd tell his foster about lying on the ground and feeling it shiver in terror, watching the grass and the trees shiver. He might tell his foster about seeing a little boy trying to crawl away and getting shot. Because his foster father had known Jesus. But he did not know the face of God.

Or did he? Softly, Jim sang: *Way down South where the trains run fast / A baboon stuck his finger up a monkey's ass / The monkey said, Well fuck my soul / Get your fucking finger out of my asshole.* A family came down the stairs, little girls running ahead of their mother. They wouldn't think his sister would win the prize but she would, she would race on her horse ahead of everybody, her family cheering for her. Not just her foster family, but her real family, Jim's real family. Like the Iraqis had cheered when they first came into the town. Before they had shot.

Nominated by Zoetrope: All Story, Daniel Henry

ZINC LID

by TED KOOSER

from THE VIRGINIA QUARTERLY REVIEW

It's the gray of canning season rain,
neither cool nor warm, and mottled
with feeble light. There's a moony
milk-glass insert ringed by rubber
and a dent where somebody rapped it
to break the seal. But its cucumber
summers, dill and brine, are over.
No more green Mason jars cooling,
no generations of dust beneath
the cellar stairs, the ancient quarts
of tomatoes like balls of wax,
the pickles slowly going gray
as kidneys, pale applesauce settling
out of its syrup. Today, on a bench
in a dark garage it's upside down,
a miniature galvanized tub adrift
on time, and in it two survivors,
a bolt that once held everything
together, season in and season out,
and a wing nut resting its wings.

Nominated by Virginia Quarterly Review

HER OWN SOCIETY

by BRENDA WINEAPPLE

from THE AMERICAN SCHOLAR

In 1862 EMILY DICKINSON ASKED the well-known abolitionist Thomas Wentworth Higginson, "Are you too deeply occupied to say if my Verse is alive?" Her question spawned one of the most extraordinary correspondences in American letters, between a man who ran guns to Kansas, backed John Brown, and would soon command the first Union regiment of black soldiers in the Civil War and the eremitic, elusive, strikingly original poet who cannily told him she did not cross her "Father's ground to any House or town."

For the next quarter century, until Dickinson's death in 1886, the poet sent Higginson almost 100 poems, many of her best, their metrical forms jagged, their punctuation unpredictable, their images honed to a fine point, their meaning elliptical, heart gripping, electric. Poetry torn up by the roots, he later said, that took his breath away. And yet today it seems strange that she would entrust them to someone conventionally regarded as a hidebound reformer with a tin ear. But Dickinson had not picked Higginson at random. Suspecting he would be receptive, she also recognized a sensibility she could trust: that of a brave iconoclast conversant with botany, butterflies, and books and willing to risk everything for what he believed.

At first she knew him only by reputation. His name, opinions, and sheer moxie were for years the stuff of headlines: as a voluble man of causes, he was on record as loathing capital punishment, child labor, and the laws depriving women of civil rights. As an ordained minister, he had officiated at the suffragist Lucy Stone's wedding; he read from a statement prepared by the bride and groom, which he later distributed to fellow clergymen as a manual of marital parity.

But above all, he detested slavery. One of the most steadfast and famous abolitionists in New England, he was far more radical than William Lloyd Garrison—if, that is, radicalism is measured by a willingness to entertain violence for the social good. Inequality offended him personally; so did passive resistance. Braced by the righteousness of his cause—unequivocal emancipation—this Massachusetts gentleman of the white and learned class had earned a reputation among his own as a lunatic. In 1854 he had battered down a courthouse door in Boston in an attempt to free the fugitive slave Anthony Burns. In 1856 he had helped arm antislavery settlers in Kansas and, a loaded pistol in his belt, admitted almost sheepishly, "I enjoy danger." Afterward he preached sedition while furnishing money and morale to John Brown. All this had occurred by the time Dickinson asked him if he were too busy to read her poems, as if it were the most reasonable request in the world.

"The Mind is so near itself—it cannot see, distinctly—and I have none to ask," she politely lied. Her brother, Austin, and his wife, Susan, lived right next door, and with Sue she regularly shared much of her verse. "Could I make you and Austin—proud—sometime—a great way off—'twould give me taller feet," she confided. Yet Dickinson in 1862 was seeking an adviser unconnected to family. "Should you think it breathed—and had you the leisure to tell me," she told Higginson, "I should feel quick gratitude."

Should you think my poetry *breathed; quick gratitude:* if only he could write like this.

Dickinson had opened her request bluntly. "Mr. Higginson," she scribbled at the top of the page. There was no other salutation. Nor did she provide a closing. Decades later Higginson still recalled that "the most curious thing about the letter was the total absence of a signature." And he well remembered that smaller sealed envelope in which she had penciled her name on a card. "I enclose my name—asking you, if you please—Sir—to tell me what is true?" That envelope, discrete and alluring, was a strategy, a plea, a gambit.

Higginson glanced over one of the four poems. "I'll tell you how the Sun rose— / A Ribbon at a time." Who writes like this? And another: "The nearest Dream recedes—unrealized." The thrill of discovery still warm three decades later, he recollected that "the impression of a wholly new and original poetic genius was as distinct on my mind at the first reading of these four poems as it is now, after 30 years of further knowledge; and with it came the problem never yet solved, what place ought to be assigned in literature to what is so remarkable, yet so elusive of criticism." This was not the benign public verse of, say, John Greenleaf Whittier. It did not share the metrical perfection of a Longfellow or the tiresome "priapism" (Emerson's word, which Higginson liked to repeat) of Walt Whitman. It was unique, uncategorizable, itself.

The Springfield Republican, a staple in the Dickinson family, regularly praised Higginson for his essays in *The Atlantic Monthly*, the prestigious magazine of the moment. "I read your Chapters in the Atlantic—" Dickinson would tell him, mailing her letters to Worcester, Massachusetts, where he lived and whose environs he had lovingly described: lily ponds edged in emerald and the shadows of trees falling blue on a winter afternoon. She paid attention.

He read another of the indelible poems she had enclosed.

> Safe in their Alabaster Chambers—
> Untouched by morning—
> And untouched by noon—
> Sleep the meek members of the Resurrection,
> Rafter of Satin and Roof of Stone—
>
> Grand go the Years,
> In the Crescent above them—
> Worlds scoop their Arcs—
> And Firmaments—row—
> Diadems—drop—
> And Doges—surrender—
> Soundless as Dots,
> On a Disc of Snow.*

White alabaster chambers melt into snow, vanishing without sound: it's an unnerving image in a poem skeptical about the resurrection it proposes. The rhymes drift and tilt; the meter echoes that of Protestant hymns, but derails. Dashes everywhere; caesura where you least expect them, undeniable melodic control, polysyllabics eerily shifting to monosyllabics. Higginson knew he was holding something amazing, dropped from the sky, and he answered her in a way that pleased her.

And would continue to do so. For Higginson, by the time of his death in 1911—the year Ronald Reagan was born—was fully alive to and part of the 19th-century experience: transcendentalism, abolition, war, Reconstruction, suffrage, *Looking Backward*, Teddy Roosevelt. "He reflected almost everything that was in the New England air, of vibrating with it all around," Henry James would say of him. Higginson coedited *The Woman's Journal* for the National American Woman Suffrage Association, which he had helped found; he adored Thoreau and admired Stephen Crane and Turgenev, whom he recommended to Dickinson; and by studying stressed syllables, he compiled songs, then called Gullah spirituals, that he had heard sung in South Carolina during the Civil War.

He replied to Dickinson's first letter right away, asking everything he could think of: the name of her favorite authors, whether she had attended school, if she read Whitman, whether she published, and would she? (Dickinson had not told him that "Safe in their Alabaster Chambers" was printed in *The Springfield Republican* just six weeks earlier.) Unable to stop himself, he made a few editorial suggestions. "I tried a little,—a very little—to lead her in the direction of rules and traditions," he later reminisced. She called this practice "surgery."

"It was not so painful as I supposed," she wrote back on April 25th, seeming to welcome his comments. "While my thought is undressed—I can make the distinction, but when I put them in the Gown—they look alike, and numb." As to his questions, she answered that she had begun writing poetry only very recently. That was untrue. In fact, she dodged several of his queries, Higginson recalled, "with a naive skill such as the most experienced and worldly coquette might envy." She told him she admired Keats, Ruskin, Sir Thomas Browne, and the Brownings, all names Higginson had mentioned in his various essays. Also, the Book of Revelation. Yes, she had gone to school, "but in your manner of the phrase—had no education." Like him, she responded intensely to nature. Her companions were the nearby Pelham hills, the sunset, her big dog Carlo: "they are better than Beings—because they know—but do not tell."

What strangeness: a woman of secrets who wanted her secrets kept but wanted you to know she had them. "In a Life that stopped guessing," she once told her sister-in-law, "you and I should not feel at home."

Emily Dickinson and Thomas Higginson, seven years apart, so seemingly different from one another and yet raised in a climate where old pieties no longer sufficed, the piers of faith were brittle, God was hard to find. If she sought solace in poetry, a momentary stay against mortality, he found it for a time in activism; for both, friendship was a secular salvation that, like poetry, reached toward the ineffable. Opting for the seclusion he could not sustain, Dickinson had walked away from public life. "The Soul selects her own Society— / Then—shuts the Door." The fantasy of isolation, the fantasy of intervention: it creates recluses and activists, sometimes both, in us all. "The Soul selects its own Society" is a beloved poem; so too was the "Battle Hymn of the Republic."

In the summer of 1870, the death of Higginson's elder brother, who had been staying near Amherst, gave him an opportunity to meet at last the strange poet who'd dropped into his world so abruptly, who alternately appeared fragile and sturdy, who bewildered him with an intelligence and a wryness and a will unlike that of anyone he had ever encountered. As far as he could tell, she confounded everyone. In Worcester he had spoken to one of her uncles, who shed no light on her at all, and though he would soon chat with the current president of Amherst College, he learned little more than he had already divined in their eight-year correspondence—that "there is always one thing to be grateful for—," as she would tell Higginson, "that one is one's self & not somebody else." She was definitely her own self.

She cowed him. He admitted to her in one of the few letters of his that survive: "Sometimes I take out your letters & verses, dear friend, and when I feel their strange power, it is not strange that I find it hard to write & that long months pass. I have the greatest desire to see you, always feeling that if I could once take you by the hand I might be something to you; but till then you only enshroud yourself in this fiery mist & I cannot reach you, but only rejoice in the rare sparkles of light."

What did he want to be to her? He hardly knew. "I am always the same toward you, & never relax my interest in what you send to me," he told her. "I should like to hear from you very often, but feel always timid lest what I *write* should be badly aimed & miss that fine edge of thought which you bear. It would be so easy, I fear, to miss you." He knew his limits.

If only he could see her, touch her hand, assure himself that she was real. Otherwise, she would remain a fantasy, even an obsession. How was it that she had such an unaccountable way of saying things? Perhaps because she lived with and for herself and her poetry? But to live so alone, so cut off from the rest of the world? "Of 'shunning Men and Women'—," she answered in an early letter, "they talk of Hallowed things, aloud—and embarrass my Dog—He and I dont object to them, if they'll exist their side." Higginson came to see that she was not really isolated; it was as if he was thinking out loud: "It isolates one anywhere to think beyond a certain point or have such luminous flashes as come to you—so perhaps the place does not make much difference."

It did not. Remarkable.

He now stood at the door of the frowning Homestead, brown brick, with its gracious side garden and its tall, unwelcoming trees—a country lawyer's place, he noticed with uncharacteristic condescension. Dickinson said she would be waiting. "I will be at Home," she had written him, "and glad."

He pulled the bell. A servant opened the heavy door. After offering his card, Higginson was shown to a dark, stiff parlor cluttered with books and decorated with the predictably dim engravings. The piano lid was raised, but what caught his attention was the table where someone had conspicuously placed his *Out-Door Papers* and his recently published novel, *Malbone*. He had been welcomed.

In a few minutes he heard what sounded to him, as he later said, like a child's step rushing in the hall. Then an airy, slim form appeared: Emily Dickinson, her dress white, her shawl blue, her hair Titian red, parted in the middle and pulled back. She carried two daylilies in her hand which she placed in his. "These are my introduction," she whispered. "How long will you stay?"

After the war, when he wrote *Malbone*, his one and only novel, Higginson had not yet met Dickinson in person, so he freely imagined her as lovely but intangible, with "a certain wild, entangled look . . . , as of some untamed out-door thing, and [with] a kind of pathetic lost sweetness in her voice, which made her at once and forever a heroine of romance." Here the protagonist, Malbone, is Higginson recast as the artist who falls in love with his fiancée's untamed half-sister, Emilia, often referred to as Emily. And this Emily/Emilia is Higginson's ideal, his Laura, his symbol of the unadulterated, untrammeled pursuit of art. For, as Malbone says, "Every one must have something

204

to which his dreams can cling, amid the degradations of actual life, and this tie is more real than the degradation; and if he holds to the tie, it will one day save him.

But, also like Higginson, Malbone cannot attain his dream lover: he cannot utterly lose himself to his pursuit of the ideal, and thus the affair between Malbone and Emilia ends tragically when, late one night, Emilia drowns in a stormy, featureless sea.

Emilia gone, Higginson thus restores the order of things, as convention prescribes. But convention had nothing to say about the nooks and crannies of an unusual friendship.

Dickinson and Higginson stood together in the same room in the Homestead parlor after eight years of correspondence and tantalizing bafflement. "Forgive me if I am frightened," she apologized. "I never see strangers & hardly know what I say." Nervous, she talked without stopping. Occasionally she paused to ask him to speak and then started all over again. "Manner between Angie Tilton & Mr. Alcott," he noted, referring to the two gabbiest people he knew, "but thoroughly ingenuous & simple which they are not & saying many things which you would have thought foolish & I wise."

He listed a few of her pungent observations:

"I find ecstasy in living—the mere sense of living is joy enough."

"How do most people live without any thoughts."

"Is it oblivion or absorption when things pass from our minds?"

"Truth is such a *rare* thing it is delightful to tell it."

She told him more about her family. Her father read only on Sunday, "*lonely & rigorous* books," she added for emphasis. She made bread for her father because he liked only hers, Higginson noted, "& says, 'people must have puddings' this *very* dreamily, as if they were comets—so she makes them." Doubtless she was ironic. And hyperbolic. She claimed she had not known how to read a clock until she was 15. "My father thought he had taught me but I did not understand & I was afraid to say I did not & afraid to ask any one else lest he should know." Her mother was weak. "I never had a mother," she said. "I suppose a mother is one to whom you hurry when you are troubled." Dickinson endured alone.

They discussed literature. She said that she and her brother had hidden Longfellow's novel *Kavanagh* under the piano cover to outfox their strict father, who forbade it. A friend concealed other books for them in a bush by the door. To read was to defy with pleasure.

They discussed poetry. Suggestively. Here was another form of transgression and transformation, erotic and inflammatory. "If I read a book," she declared, "[and] it makes my whole body so cold no fire ever can warm me I know *that* is poetry. If I feel physically as if the top of my head were taken off, I know *that* is poetry. These are the only way I know it. Is there any other way."

Poetry, again, as an explosive force: he must have felt the pull, the energy, her sexuality. He left in the evening exhausted but walked back to the house. Afterward, hinting at the sexual tension—and release—of the whole experience, he admitted he had never met anyone "who drained my nerve power so much. Without touching her, she drew from me."

"I am glad not to live near her," he concluded.

The remarkable encounter, far exceeding his expectations, was too much for him.

He had flirted with the writer Helen Hunt, he had flirted with others, but in his private life, unlike his public one, he had chosen the straight and narrow. Emily Dickinson demanded nothing short of a full commitment. Irreducibly herself, without compromise, she took everything, drained the cup, was irresistible. And was to Higginson, in this instance, far too dangerous.

When he took his hat for the last time that day, he promised the poet he would come again some time. "Say in a long time," she mischievously answered, "that will be nearer. Some time is nothing."

As usual, she was right.

Nominated by The American Scholar

EPITHALAMIUM

by BOB HICOK

from THE GETTYSBURG REVIEW

A bee in the field. The house on the mountain
reveals itself to have been there through summer.
It's not a bee but a horse eating frosted grass
in the yawn light. Secrets, the anguish of smoke
above the chimney as it shreds what it's learned
of fire. The horse has moved, it's not a horse
but a woman doing the stations of the cross
with a dead baby in her arms. The anguish of the house
as it reveals smoke to the mountain. A woman
eating cold grass in Your name, shredding herself
like fire. The woman has stopped, it's not a woman
but smoke on its knees keeping secrets in what it reveals.
The everything has moved, it's not everything
but a shredding of the anguish of names. The marriage
of light: particle to wave. Do you take? I do.

Nominated by The Gettysburg Review, Rachel Loden, Ed Falco, David Jauss

TWO STUDIES
IN ENTROPY

fiction by SARA PRITCHARD

from NEW LETTERS

T O RAE-JEAN'S FACE, people said things like, "Ohmygod, thank god you're alive," or "Ohmygod, it's a miracle," or "Ohmygod, just think: *What if* you'd forgotten something? *What if* you'd gone back inside?"

What if . . . . Always, *What if . . . .*

People would say something gruesomely speculative like that, prefaced with *What if*, and then they'd shudder and grimace in that horrible way that is almost a smile—that bizarre expression that grips people when they're relating details of life-threatening events. An expression that made Rae-Jean think of Munch's "The Scream"—the same soul-sucking posture and the same face-gripping gasp of abomination—but with a big, happy smile like Curious George.

Behind Rae-Jean's back, the same people said to each other: "Jesus, what a nincompoop!" "How stupid can a person be?" "Didn't she read the damn directions? For chrissake, there's a big friggin' warning on the label!" and "It's a wonder she didn't blow us all off the face of the earth!"

It was a miracle. It was a true miracle that no one had been killed or maimed or even slightly injured. There was a bus stop just across the street, at the corner of Callen and Mississippi, and only moments before the blast, three junior high school boys stood there smoking cigarettes, punching each other in the chest, and jumping up to slap and

208

bend the street sign. A few minutes before that, Renata Creech stood in the same spot, waiting for the Mountain Line bus.

Kids called Rae-Jean "Bombs Away Baker" and "The Flea Bomber." "Here comes (or there goes) The Flea Bomber," they'd call out every time she passed by.

Rae-Jean heard them, too. She heard them all right. They meant her to hear them. She'd never be able to live it down.

Rae-Jean was the woman who set off eighteen flea bombs in her house at 8:30 a.m. on the morning of August 27, 2002, before going to work. She was about eight blocks away, heading up Dorsey Avenue with Alice James and Ralph Waldo Emerson in the back seat, heading up to the kennel where Alice and R.W. had reservations to spend the day while the house fumigated itself. The explosion—detonated by the tiny pilot light in the furnace, no bigger than the flame of a Bic lighter—literally blew Rae-Jean's bungalow to smithereens. The windows exploded, and the front and back doors were ripped off their hinges and hurled into the alley and street. Rae-Jean's dining room wall with its built-in corner cupboard displaying her collection of carnival glass, slammed through the next-door neighbor's garage. A shrapnel cocktail of glass shards, nails, and little pieces of plaster shot up high into the air like fireworks.

Five minutes after the explosion, chunks of fiberglass insulation still floated in the sky like pink clouds. 3M, some of them said. 3M or R-18, R-36, broadcasting their insulation factors. Shreds of fabric—chintz, tweeds and tattersalls, corduroy, damask, black watch plaid—pieces of upholstery, clothes, linens, old soft-bodied suitcases, and dog beds wafted about like chrysanthemum petals, coming to rest in trees and shrubbery over a mile away.

Hunks of cement from the foundation and bricks from the fireplace, buoyed up by the force and gust of the explosion, wafted about, giddy as wishing pennies atop Old Faithful.

An eyewitness on West Virginia Avenue had just stepped out of the shower, she said, when she heard the big bang. She thought it was the end of the world. She looked out her bathroom window and saw the roof of a house two streets below lifted up like the lid of a cookie jar and set back down again, as if by an invisible hand. Lifted how high? "Oh, about ten feet," she said. She thought it was a psychedelic flashback, a little wiggle in reality. She thought she was seeing things again. She thought maybe she'd had a little stroke. She thought maybe she was in a movie. She just didn't know what to think, she said. She got down on her knees right then and there on the bathmat—in her birthday suit—and said four Hail Marys and two Our Fathers before drying her hair.

Rae-Jean kept driving. Sure she heard the rumble. She felt it all right. It felt like a run-away underground freight train barreling down Dorsey Hill, she said. It felt like the earth had terrible gas. In Rae-Jean's rear-view mirror, the sky blossomed orange like a Japanese lantern.

What would you do? Make a U-Turn? Keep going? There was a lot of commotion in the streets, in cars. It was morning rush-hour traffic. People frantically dialing their cell phones. Cars speeding up and cars slamming on breaks. Cars pulling off onto the shoulder and cars pulling up onto sidewalks. Sirens began to scream, blue and red lights to whirl and flash. One woman got out of a minivan and ran around with her arms thrown up in the air, two men chasing after her in a kind of Keystone Kops routine that reminded Rae-Jean of something people used to call a Chinese fire drill.

Rae-Jean's first thought when she heard the bang and felt the shudder and saw the orange pop-sky behind her was: terrorist attack. But terrorist attack on what? Wal-Mart? Giant Eagle? Maybe the same thing was happening at the same time all over America. It never occurred to Rae-Jean that her house could be involved in any way whatsoever. Her instinct was to get away from it, whatever it was. So Rae-Jean kept driving.

At the sound of the explosion, R.W., who was startled by loud noises (even a bar of soap falling in the shower) started barking while holding his hedgehog in his mouth, a trick he'd taught himself years ago in order to muffle his bark so he could keep barking and Rae-Jean wouldn't be annoyed and get on his case. Employing the hedgehog mute, R.W. could carry on for sometimes as long as fifteen minutes before Rae-Jean got after him. The hedgehog was R.W.'s constant companion. Actually, in the name of hygiene, there were two hedgehogs, but R.W. didn't know that. He thought they were one in the same. R.W. slept with his hedgehog and kept it close by at all times, retrieving it at any barking opportunity, then barking the hedgehog-bark while keeping an eye out for Rae-Jean, calculating the extent of her patience, and then running away from the bark-inducing scene a split second before Rae-Jean was about to smack him.

R.W. took the hedgehog with him everywhere he went. Holding the hedgehog in his mouth, R.W. ran back and forth, back and forth, back and forth, back and forth across the back seat of the CRV, barking his *Mmwwoff Mmwwoof* at the mayhem, trying to make it stop. Alice James began to whimper and quiver and jumped up into the front seat, into Rae-Jean's lap, furiously licking Rae-Jean's ears and seriously interfering with her driving.

R.W. was a chocolate Lab mix. A big goofy guy the color of a Duncan Hines double chocolate cake mix, with a brown nose and pinkish brown lips that looked like—there was no denying this: night crawlers. Alice James, another rescue like R.W., was part Chihuahua and part pug. A "pughuahua," the advertisement on petfinder.com had described her, "with maybe a little bit of rat terrier thrown in for the sake of confusion." Alice James was small and black, except for her pale, polka-dotted belly, and with disproportionately large ears like Yoda.

The day after the explosion, a very unflattering color photograph of Rae-Jean, Alice James, and R.W. appeared on the front page of *The Dominion Post* (and all over the Internet), under a hideously large headline that shouted: *Woman blows up house trying to rid residence of fleas.* The photo was taken in the harsh fluorescence of the police station, and Rae-Jean's face was blotchy and puffy; she looked like a criminal. Like both the assailant and the victim. R.W. sat slobbering on the bench beside her, hedgehog squashed in his soft, wormy mouth, and Alice James was sitting on Rae-Jean's lap, looking like a fruit bat. Alice James had a startled look on her sweet face, and her big ears stuck out like satellite dishes. Her bulgy eyes, rendered even more prominent by the camera's flash, made Rae-Jean think of poor Christina Rossetti after she'd developed Graves' disease. A very unflattering photograph indeed.

Another photo on the page-two continuation of the lead story showed the remains of Rae-Jean's house, looking like the first of the Three Little Pigs' houses—the one made out of straw—after the Big Bad Wolf had had a go at it. Still another photo showed a white clapboard house with a steep green roof, a thick circle drawn around the top of the chimney. An inset to that photo—an enlargement of the circled chimney area—zoomed in on Rae-Jean's Oster toaster perched atop the chimney like a chrome Christmas tree topper.

Up until August 27, 2002, Rae-Jean had led a nice, quiet, uneventful, if boring and conventional life. She went to work every day. She went home. On weekends, instead of going to work, she went to Giant Eagle and Wal-Mart and Blockbuster, and then she went home.

Rae-Jean had worked for twenty years as a copyeditor at a university press that published mostly esoteric and incoherent textbooks that it then sold for exorbitant amounts of money to destitute students who had no choice but to use their student-loan money to buy these books. Rae-Jean had edited such arcane manuscripts as *The Postmodern Beowulf*, *Homosexuality and Deuternaopity in Squirrels*, *The Synthesis and Antithesis of Polypeptotes*, *Freemasonry for Dummies*, and *Whither the Witch Hazel: Piles-Driven Imagery in the Poetry of Elizabeth Barrett Browning and Alfred Lord Tennyson*.

For twenty years, Rae-Jean had worked in the same dank, old building on the University of West Virginia's campus. Stansbury Hall was undeniably a dump, the worst building on campus, an embarrassment, an eyesore—a gothic, dilapidated, dirty brick monstrosity with a defunct gymnasium and locker room in the basement. The university press' offices—along with English, creative writing, philosophy, and ROTC—were, likewise, housed in this crypt that was permeated by a peculiar and foul odor, an odor with a base note of B.O., mold, and stinky Chuck Taylors; middle notes of Lysol and something sharp and indescribable but primarily uric; and high notes of burnt Maxwell House coffee and Krispy Kreme donuts.

The press' director was a jolly little man, a foremost Samuel Pepys scholar who earned his weight times one thousand and seemed to spend a lot of time traveling to international conferences and giving basically the same paper over and over again on Samuel Pepys or spending all day in his office downloading Broadway show tunes from iTunes, which he then sang along with in a robust, off-key baritone.

"Oh, I got plenty o' nuttin'," you might hear him in there singing or, *"Where are the simple joys of maidenhood?"*

Rae-Jean's "office" was a dirty beige upholstered cubicle right outside the director's door. Sharing a cubicle wall with Rae-Jean—a sort of sororal work-twin—was Wanda, the loud-mouthed production assistant with the chronic yeast infection. At least once a week, Wanda called her OB-GYN nurse practitioner to discuss her odious condition.

"Yes, cottage cheese," Wanda could be heard saying behind the nubby façade of privacy, and Rae-Jean would cover her ears and make "The Scream" face.

"Yes, yellowish . . ." Wanda would say. "Yes, fishy."

So there was all that: the ordinary twill of life; the hohum *sturm und drang* of the workplace: the ubiquitous absurdities, the anathematic coworkers, the bloody deadlines and even bloodier bottom lines; the bland, eternal, Sisyphean, absolute, unrelenting, surreal certainty of the day-in-and-day-out of it all. Life as a slice of white bread, moistened with spit, and rolled into a messy glob, a doughy ball that couldn't make the slightest dent in the iron gates of life.

Then, on August 27, 2002, all that changed. Rae-Jean's uneventful life began to leaven and swell with hypotheticals. Gravity grabbed a hold of it and pumped it a few times in its death grip. *What ifs* . . . entered the picture and beefed things up a bit. *What if* Rae-Jean really *had* gone back inside?

In minutes, with the help of only eighteen Orkin flea bombs (each with a $2 mail-in rebate), Rae-Jean's little monochrome life was rendered a glorious, full-color graphic novel, each frame decorated with the words °KA-BOOM!° °BAM!° °MOMENTS LATER . . .° and °WATCH OUT!° in red and yellow starbursts all around it.

And this is only the half of it. Unbeknownst to Rae-Jean, Jamie Archer, a 47-year-old homeless man, had found a home in Rae-Jean's basement and had been living there for nigh on three months. Every weekday around 10:00 a.m., hours after Rae-Jean left for work, Jamie let himself into Rae-Jean's basement by jimmying the lock on the basement door, an entrance obscured by two ugly, overgrown yews and which Rae-Jean never used. Every afternoon by 4:00 p.m.—plenty of leeway before Rae-Jean came home—Jamie let himself back out and headed downtown for dinner at the Salvation Army soup kitchen, followed by a walk along the bike trail and an evening at the library, the park, or the Friendship Room, before heading down to the Cottonwoods—or "Cottonwoods Estates" as the sojourners called it, or "Cotton-on-the-Mon"—the old hobo camp between the train tracks and the river, a twenty-some-acre area that city law enforcement officers pretended didn't exist.

At the Cottonwoods, you could count on being left alone, at least by "the man." As long as you stayed down there all night and didn't wander up across the tracks into the edges of downtown, you were OK. You could do anything down there: get drunk, get high, get down; nobody cared. But just you stay there. There was trouble sometimes, and every year or so someone turned up dead. What happened was, now and then, somebody just got fucked up and wandered too close to the slippery riverbank and drowned, and though *The Dominion Post* always said the death was being investigated, the case was always closed the same day it opened.

One time, though, a baby turned up dead, found floating in the river, and that was the only time the law ever stepped in, arresting the mother and eventually convicting her of second-degree murder. The trial was a continuing front-page story in *The Dominion Post*. Another time a sojourner known as Prophet Jimi was run over by a train. Prophet Jimi often wore a choir robe and a string of miniature Christmas lights wound into something resembling a crown of thorns around his head. Prophet Jimi could be found during rush hour on the street corner by Pita Pit downtown, preaching to the traffic, waving Bob Dylan's "Highway 61 Revisited" album cover at the pedestrians and cars. Rae-Jean recognized pieces of the prologue to *The Canterbury Tales*, allusions to *The Waste Land*, and lyrics from "Maggie's Farm" in his sermon as she walked by.

"They hand you a nickel / They hand you a dime," Prophet Jimi would shout. *"Every fuckin' month is the cruellest month whan that Aprill, with his shoures soote / The droghte of March hath perced to the fuckin' roote. Are you having a good time?"*

After dark, the street people all disappeared back into the Cottonwoods and the abandoned warehouses and the old General Woodworking lumberyard and the condemned glass factories, and the slum houses along the railroad tracks and around Stansberry Hall. From across the river, you could see their campfires burning in the Cottonwoods, and sometimes, faintly, voices and music carried across the river, but most people didn't know the old hobo camp was even there.

During an eight-month period that had ended in early 2002, Jamie had actually been paid to live in someone's basement in Rae-Jean's neighborhood. A woman named Shirley Durnn was pursuing an MSW at the university and conducting a study on the movement of street people around the city. The study, entitled "Analysis and Mapping of Diurnal Migration of Transient Populations in a Mid-Atlantic, University City with a Population of Approximately 100,000, July 2001—February 2002," was designed to evaluate the usefulness and popularity of urban social services for the homeless and to serve as a tool for planning and siting such services in comparable areas. Shirley Durnn's husband, David Durnn, a geographer and the other principal investigator on the project, was using a geographic positioning system to map the movement among services. The Durnn & Durnn Report eventually came to be published by the university press where Rae-Jean was employed and became a classic in the study of homelessness and social services, used in college classrooms across the country.

Jamie was one of ten sojourners participating in the study. "Sojourners" was a term Shirley Durnn preferred over "homeless," because, she said, "homeless" defined a person by what they didn't have, what they were not. Sort of like the term "nonfiction." "Street person," likewise, Shirley Durnn said, was demeaning, and they should object to that title, too. Was a person who lived in a condo called a "condo person"?

Shirley Durnn came to the Friendship Room one evening to explain her study and its benefits for sojourners. To participate in the study, all sojourners had to do was wear a homing device—an ankle bracelet like prisoners under house arrest wear—and go about their business. No questions asked. If they completed their obligations to the study, which also included agreeing to be interviewed twice by Shirley Durnn in what she called the entrance and exit interviews, sojourners would be paid $500. Plus, sojourners would be contributing to the welfare of other sojourners by helping to evaluate services, and every sojourner would be given free housing for the duration of the study period, in the basement of "host households" around town participating in the study. Who got what basement—some were in commercial buildings, some in residences—would be determined by a lottery.

Jamie volunteered. In the lottery, he drew the Durnns and was given full access to their cellar for the eight-month study period. He could come and go as he pleased; no questions asked. He had to agree to sign a contract with the Durnns saying he would not bring visitors or illegal substances to his basement and that he would not conduct any illicit activities there and that he would not deface any property or smoke in bed and that he would "maintain the peace." Other than that, he could do what he wanted. Sometimes, Jamie stayed away for days at a time, spending his nights and days at the Cottonwoods. Sometimes he stayed at the Durnns' for days on end, venturing out only for meals at the soup kitchens or a visit to the library.

Jamie's sojourn at the Durnns' was one of the best times of his life. David Durnn was a true dump hound. Before Jamie took possession of the Durnns' basement, David Durnn fixed it up with items neighbors had put out for the trash, which included an old office cubicle. It was beige with nubby fabric walls and had a Formica-topped desk and bookshelf with sliding doors. There was even a newspaper clipping still push-pinned to one of the fabric walls. "*Worker dead at desk for five days*" the headline on the yellowed newsprint said.

Jamie would like to have stayed there forever in the Durnns' basement, coming and going as he pleased, but when Shirley Durnn's study was complete, the Durnns moved and sold their house. Shirley tried to negotiate a provision with the realtor that the new owner would allow Jamie to continue to occupy the basement rent free for as long as he wanted, but no realtor would touch that with a ten-foot pole. When Shirley told Jamie the bad news, he cried.

Adhering to the basement-dwelling etiquette established by the Durnns, Jamie never went upstairs in Rae-Jean's house, and he never disturbed anything in the basement without returning it to its original place. When scouting the neighborhood for new digs after receiving Shirley Durnn's bad news, Jamie chose Rae-Jean's house because it reminded him of the Durnns', because it had a concealed basement entrance, and because he liked Rae-Jean's dogs. He had often walked down the alley, passing by R.W. and Alice James in their fenced-in yard. R.W. always ran up to the fence, barking with a hedgehog in his mouth. Jamie would lean over the fence, R.W. would pass him the hedgehog, and Jamie would throw it a few times, which made R.W. immensely happy, and if R.W. was happy, so was Alice James, his devoted companion.

Every morning when he arrived at Rae-Jean's, Jamie opened the cellar door leading to the kitchen, and R.W. and Alice James came bounding downstairs. After a few games of hedgehog, rewarded by a few "street treats," Jamie unrolled his bed roll and took a long, peaceful nap behind the furnace, R.W. and Alice James curled up beside him.

Rae Jean's house, like many houses in her working-class neighborhood, had been built by or for coal miners or glass factory workers in the first half of the twentieth century. Most of the houses, including Rae Jean's, had an outside entrance to the basement, which had a crude but fully functional bathroom in one corner, complete with claw-foot bathtub.

These basements offered ideal accommodations for a sojourner. Jamie liked them. He liked the perspective—eye-level with the crust of the earth. He liked the dirty windows, the way dust and dirt filtered the low-angled sunlight into cellars and the way smooth cement absorbed heat and light. And he liked the quietness, the guttural sounds of plumbing, the barely audible ticking of upstairs clocks, and the furnace thermostat that clicked on and off like castanets.

He liked living close to the basics—an "urban Thoreau," he thought of himself—close to the machinery that kept things going, the old well-built contraptions that kept chugging away year after year like a stout-hearted old Scandinavian farmer. He liked concrete and poured cement floors and cinderblock walls, big weight-bearing posts and beams, rusty tools and ice skates hanging from pegs and three-penny nails, furnaces and hot water heaters, pipes and plumbing (especially copper and lead), dehumidifiers, washers, dryers, freezers, lawn mowers and rakes, old snow tires and snow shovels, bags of rock salt, arthritic bicycles, sleds, fishing poles, paint cans and shoe polish, odd nuts and bolts glinting from Skippy peanut butter jars, dented folding chairs, plastic bins and boxes that said things on the outside like "1985 TAXES" and "CHRISTMAS," Ball canning jars and lids, wilted amaryllises under the stairs, and dried-out geraniums hanging by their rootballs from the joists.

Jamie's favorite plant was the homely snake plant, sometimes called mother-in-law's tongue because it grew in long, sharp, tongue-like spears. Along with the Boston fern, the snake plant had been a favorite in Victorian parlors, but now snake plants, like a lot of things that have seen their day, lived mostly in basements, where they thrived on neglect. People bought snake plants on impulse and then after a few months of moving them around, grew disillusioned with them because they did nothing. But snake plants had come into their own, so to speak, in basements. They'd found a home.

Always there was running water and electrical outlets, warmth in winter, coolness in summer, in cellars. Quite often there were multiple rooms: a laundry room permeated with the smell of Bounce fabric softener; a coal bin; a furnace room; a root cellar full of cobwebs and plank shelves, often with a lonely corroded jar of bread & butter pickles or tomato juice dated 1962, left behind as testimony to some former industry and abundance. One house had a secret passageway leading from the cellar to an underground bomb shelter stocked with tasty gourmet canned foods, including potted Argentine beef, caviar, tinned cashews, and fancy apricots in heavy syrup, plus a keg of beer, cartons of cigarettes, and three cases of Spanish wine.

There was even a washer and dryer in Rae-Jean's basement, which Jamie used on a regular basis. Plus, there were discarded things, like boxes full of books. Jamie was on page 510 of *The Postmodern Beowulf*, lost deep in the bowels of literary theory, reading an essay by some dude named Michel Foucault, who was surely tripping. Jamie was so taken by Foucault that he'd gone to the university library and "borrowed" another book by the author, entitled *Madness and Civi-*

lization. Jamie would have legitimately checked the book out of the library, but the library made that difficult. He knew they would want things like a permanent address, a phone number, an e-mail address, a student I.D., a passport, a driver's license—any number of positive forms of identification impossible for a sojourner to produce.

That was the problem, too, with the shelters. They wanted to book you. It was the same thing with jobs. To get a job you had to have a number where you could be reached. To have a number where you could be reached, you needed a job to pay for a cell phone and phone service and an address to where the phone company could mail your bill.

At heart, though, Jamie was an optimist. He rolled with the flow and dodged the flow's punches. He took his chances. Without a second thought, he stuffed *Madness and Civilization* under his coat, into the back of his pants. So what if some sensible-shoed librarian caught him with Michel Foucault in his trousers? So what if some buzzer went off? Big fuckin' deal: a slap on the wrist and back out on the street sans Foucault. But if he did walk boldly, defiantly, right past that electronic eye, with *Madness and Civilization* in his pants, well then, hey, good day!

Likewise, so what if the lady who lived in "his" house came home one day and heard the dryer rumbling downstairs and called the police. A few days in jail, and Jamie would be run out of town . . . with a paid bus ticket . . . to another town, another basement. No big deal. No city fathers or mothers wanted to keep a sojourner in jail; they wanted to get rid of him, pass him on. They were just waiting for the perfect opportunity, looking for excuses to hand a sojourner his walking papers.

"When you got nothin', you got nothin' to lose," Jamie told Shirley Durnn during his entrance interview, when she was constructing what she called his 'life narrative'.

"When you got nothin' to lose, you got everything to gain," Jamie added, smiling. "Everything you come by's a brass ring, a free ride. You find a quarter in a pay phone, and it's a prize. Trouble is, ain't so many pay phones anymore."

And when Shirley asked Jamie what it was like to have everything you own in one backpack or, in Jamie's case, everything you owned in one plaid suitcase on wheels, Jamie said it felt good. It felt like he was in control.

"When you got a lotta stuff," Jamie explained, "the stuff's got you.

218

You gotta work to keep your stuff, and you gotta worry about your stuff all the time. You gotta worry if it's all gonna be there when you get home. You gotta worry about it because it all costs a lot of money, and it ain't paid for. You gotta work, work, work to make it work.

"The secret is," Jamie told Shirley, "you gotta not want their stuff. That's the whole secret. Not wantin' stuff. Not bein' seduced by stuff you see."

When Rae-Jean read the transcript of the interview with Jamie Ray Archer, white Caucasian male, age 47, who gave his address as "Bulk Mail" and his occupation as "actor/philosopher," she was amazed to learn that Durnn & Durnn's background research on Archer indicated that the score on a 1972 Stanford-Binet would have placed him in the gifted category and that he had attended the state university on an academic scholarship and had shown promise in music, language arts, and math, but then had dropped out suddenly mid-semester the second semester of his freshman year. Something had happened. Something had gone awry.

When Shirley Durnn asked Jamie if he'd ever owned more than he did at present, more than what he had in that suitcase, Jamie said, yes, yes he had. He'd had it all, Jamie said. He'd had a house once—a house with a mortgage—a nice house with a wall oven, a washer and dryer, and a yard—and he'd had a Plymouth once, and once a 1987 Datsun. "Good car," Jamie said. He'd even had an entertainment center once, Jamie added, laughing, and he'd had all kinds of jobs. He'd worked as a house painter and as a house carpenter and he had had his own business on the side as a handyman. He'd been in five or six bands. He'd worked as a "lumper," too. A lumper is a guy who unloads trucks for cash, he said. You just show up someplace like Giant Eagle when you know a truck's comin' in, and the driver will give you $50 cash to unload it. If you're fast, if you do a good job, then the drivers get to know you, and they'll look for you among all the other lumpers standing around. If you let them down, if you don't show up a few times, you're out. Some other lumper will win their favor.

He'd worked for a bit, too, as an auto mechanic and as a taxi driver, and he'd worked for a few months at a Record Bar and for almost a year at Family Dollar, but always there'd been some kind of trouble. He'd spent some time in county jails, too. Here and there. Public intoxication. Vagrancy. Some other things that he didn't really do. "Mistaken identity," Jamie said. "Wrong place at the wrong time," Jamie said, laughing. He'd had a wife once, too, Jamie said, and two kids.

"Two boys. Two little boys," Jamie said, "ain't so little now, though, I suppose."

There was a long pause then when Shirley and Jamie said nothing.

"It was all too much," Jamie said.

Sometimes after work, on her way from Stansberry Hall to her car parked in the public garage downtown, Rae-Jean would pass a street person, a stocky, curly haired, middle-aged man, leaning against a utility pole or just standing in the middle of the sidewalk reading a book, a tattered plaid suitcase on wheels beside him. The street person was always dressed in green, and Rae-Jean thought of him as "The Green Man." In spite of the fact that he was obviously a street person, Rae-Jean looked forward to seeing him every day in his misshapen green knit hat with earflaps, his grungy green corduroy pants, his lime-green sneakers, his green puffy jacket with the pointed hood, and his unraveling, green, fingerless gloves. It was part of the routine. It was like when she was a kid and went to visit her grandparents who lived in the town in Pennsylvania where Planters Peanuts originated. All Rae-Jean and her sister wanted to do as soon as they got there was go downtown and shake hands with Mr. Peanut. Mr. Peanut was a giant peanut dressed in black tights and a black top hat and spats, and he wore the most wonderful, round, incredibly shiny, black shoes. He wore white gloves and carried a walking stick, and he walked around downtown Wilkes-Barre all day, handing out little red-and-white striped bags of freshly-roasted peanuts. And if Mr. Peanut wasn't out, why then the whole trip was a bust, as far as Rae-Jean and Dee-Dee were concerned.

Rae-Jean never made eye contact with The Green Man. She'd learned years ago that if you made eye contact with street people, nine chances out of ten, they'd ask you for money. At first she gave it to them: a dollar here, a dollar there, another dollar, but before she knew it, it was every day. Dollars and dollars. Word got around she was an easy touch, and sometimes three or four sojourners would be standing together on the sidewalk between Stansberry Hall and the parking garage, blocking her path, asking for money. But Rae-Jean got pissed. Wouldn't she like to spend the day in the park with R.W. and Alice James instead of going to work at the university press? Wouldn't she like somebody to pay her way?

Rae-Jean started crossing the street to avoid the homeless people. Soon, they left her alone, and she never made eye contact again. Still, every time she passed The Green Man in front of the Salvation Army, she had an urge to look up, to look right into his face. Once she did, but he was reading and did not avert his eyes from his book, although she had the feeling always that his eyes were on her back once she'd passed.

No matter what the weather, The Green Man was always on the corner by the Salvation Army when Rae-Jean left work. Rae-Jean thought many times about giving him something, especially during the holidays. Maybe an envelope with a $20 bill, or maybe just a Christmas card or a little penny valentine or a prayer card, but she never did, and then suddenly he wasn't there anymore.

Since not long after "that day"—the euphemism Rae-Jean's co-workers used to refer to August 27, 2002—Rae-Jean, R.W., and Alice James had been living in a one-bedroom apartment on Elysian Avenue. An old woman there had died after having fallen and broken her hip, and there'd been some apartment shuffling by other tenants, leaving Rae-Jean a nice, airy flat on the bottom floor. People—good people—were always trying to give Rae-Jean things for her apartment, but secretly, Rae-Jean had developed a liking for the austerity of her new home, its sort of Japanese minimalist space. She had next to no furniture. Only three dog beds; an apartment-size refrigerator; a hot plate, and some clothes, dishes, and housewares from the Salvation Army. Pretty soon, Rae-Jean's instincts to protect her uncluttered environment took root, and she got as good at rejecting charity as she'd become at averting sojourners. She just said, "No. No thank you. It's too soon." Or she said she had things "on order."

There was another thing about the apartment on Elysian Avenue that Rae-Jean loved: at night you could hear the train whistles and the furious rumble from the B&O tracks as the trains passed. You could *feel* the trains. The vibration from the trains made the windows in Rae-Jean's apartment chatter like wind-up false teeth, even though her apartment was blocks away from the tracks. There was a train always just around midnight, one that came flying up from Charleston, heading up toward Pittsburgh, and another one around 4:00 a.m., same direction. They were loud, all right, those trains, but not piercing and heart stopping like the fire whistles in the middle of the night, calling all volunteer firemen, or the mine whistles calling all the women, all the mothers and wives, signaling disaster. The train whistles were different. A different pitch maybe, but something about their passing gave them a different tone, a different presence, not alarming but almost benedictive. They started far away like a birdcall and then rushed by as if they were spreading some goodwill across the community, some peace, delivering some benevolent message about passing, about transience and life here on earth. They were regular and constant and reliable, the trains. They came and they went with the same plaintive call, the same schedule, come what may.

The trains' whistles reminded Rae-Jean of her father, who had ridden the rails as a young man. He'd lived a hard life, Raymond Walker Baker. The son of a Nebraska homesteader and one of thirteen children, he'd survived the Spanish influenza while five family members died. As a young man, R.W. Baker made his way east during the Great Depression, riding boxcars, laboring here and there for food and shelter, moving on. At a square dance outside of Huntington, West Virginia, he'd met Rae-Jean's mother, Regina, and that was that. He settled down, took a wife. But Ray Walker always loved the trains. He watched the trains. He knew the songs: the train songs and the hobo songs. *"Hallelujah, I'm a bum,"* he taught Rae-Jean and her little brother, Walkie, to sing, *"Hallelujah, bum again / Hallelujah, give us a handout / To revive us again."*

He knew the hieroglyphs of hobos past and had taught them to Rae-Jean and Walkie when they were kids. A circle with an "x" in the middle meant "good for a handout." A line drawing of a smiling cat meant "kindhearted lady." A rectangle with a line extending out of the top right-hand corner meant "here you can get a drink," a box intersecting a box meant, "don't stop here." Often, as she walked R.W. and Alice James, Rae-Jean studied the colorful spray-painted graffiti on the walls and bridges and the cliffs along the river, thinking of her father at the kitchen table, drawing on a brown paper bag. What did they mean today, the elegant swirls and alarming faces? What warnings and messages were they sending?

At night, lying on her dog bed, R.W. with his hedgehog, and Alice James close beside her, street light and pale moonlight leaking through her blinds, Rae-Jean often lay awake, smoking a cigarette and sipping a glass of bourbon, waiting for the midnight train whistle and thinking about her father as a young man with curly dark hair, her father in dungarees and a blue cloth jacket, lying on his back in a pitch-dark boxcar years before she was born, her father, head cradled in his laced fingers, dreaming, rolling east across America, head first, rolling from the Great Plains toward West Virginia and her mother, and when she heard the rumble and whistle of the B&O trains, Rae-Jean smiled and Rae-Jean rolled over and sighed.

After the flea bomb explosion, Rae-Jean had received a large settlement from State Farm Insurance. Even though, technically, the explosion was her fault, it was deemed an accident. There was a class-action law suit, too, against Orkin, which a young, aggressive, New York lawyer had convinced Rae-Jean to join. With the insurance money, Rae-Jean at first planned to rebuild—something small, modern, Usonian, and energy efficient—on the same lot. She'd hired an architect and worked with her for months on plans. Straw-bale construction, adobe, tile roof, passive solar, lots of light. A Roycroft-red, poured-cement floor in the main room, which would absorb sunlight and radiate heat. There was a landscape architect involved, too, and an interior decorator. A courtyard emerged; a boxwood-concealed dog run and a sophisticated, automatic, electronic dog door; a small atrium; a pantry; walk-in closet; and a terraced area with a water feature—a trickling waterfall: everything—and more—that Rae-Jean had ever dreamed of in a home. But then at some point the whole idea of building the house began to lose its appeal.

It was just too much.

After the explosion, there was a memorial service at the Cottonwoods for Jamie's suitcase. Jamie arranged it himself. He had narrowly escaped annihilation on August 27, 2002. Having arrived at Rae-Jean's house only moments before the blast, a palpable tension in the atmosphere and a terrible chemical odor made him turn and run, leaving his suitcase by the back door, and then: *KA-BOOM!* *BAM!* *MOMENTS LATER . . .*

What a story Jamie had to tell. He constructed it as a ballad. He could feel language squirming inside him like a tape worm. He could feel words burbling up inside like he'd swallowed hydrogen peroxide. He felt giddy. "It's the blarney," his grandmother used to say. "It's the blarney comin' out."

At the campfires that night in the Cottonwoods, Jamie roamed around and told again and again his great escapade, telling it each time a little more fantastically. At first he said the explosion knocked him flat. In the final version Jamie told, he said he flew over the rooftops, "like an angel," for miles and miles. Over Oak Grove Cemetery he flew, over the Gibson Brown angel and the statue of the Confederate soldier. And clear across town he flew, over the courthouse and the arboretum and over the coliseum, and then out across the Monongahela River in a big sweep, and that finally he landed on his feet in an abandoned lot full of Queen Anne's lace, out in the old Dupont Industrial Park, set down light as a feather next to a deer, set down so lightly that that doe didn't even look up or twitch an ear or flick her tail. And then he walked all the way down the River Road and across the Westover Bridge, and back into town.

That night, August 27, 2002, Jamie drank too much and smoked too much, and he wandered off to take a leak and stumbled and slid down the steep, muddy bank toward the Monongahela River. A big old buttonball tree took a step sideways and leaned over, reached down a white limb and scooped him up and set him down again, safe and sound, against her trunk, and when Jamie woke up the sun was high and a tugboat named Miss Ruby was chugging by.

The Durnn & Durnn report confirmed what Shirley Durnn had suspected all along and what any sojourner would have told her, without the services of her husband and GPS map-ping. Sojourners preferred the Cottonwoods and the sheltered places underneath bridges and overpasses; the abandoned, derelict houses like "The Castle" along the railroad tracks, near Stansberry Hall, with its boarded-up doors and windows and its shredded wallpaper and missing stairs and sagging ceilings, corroded bathroom, and precarious floors; and the old A&P parking garage that hung over Decker's Creek. They did not care for the regimentation and the rehabilitation that most of the social services downtown with their bright, fluorescent lights and antibacterial handsoap and rules had to offer. They went to the soup kitchens for meatloaf and mashed potatoes and gravy and canned French-style string beans, and they went to HealthRight, and they used the bathrooms at the library . . . if it was convenient. Otherwise, they lived outside, in the Cottonwoods—like twenty-first-century Indians, they said—drinking firewater, and peeing and pooping behind bushes.

A few years later, city officials, waving the Durnn & Durnn report, succeeded in appropriating $2.5 million to bring sanitary facilities, basic utilities, and cheap weather-proof housing to the Cottonwoods. The proposed housing was 150 large, portable, molded plastic igloos that came in two pieces and snapped together like big dog houses. The planned renovation also included a provision for the installation of a 12-ft-high chain-link fence for a two-mile stretch along the B&O tracks and an iron gate that would be used to "secure" the area at nightfall.

Stating their best intentions, designers and advocates of the Cottonwoods Upgrade—as it came to be known—described the use and condition of the century-old hobo village: It was "a narrow strip of riparian land between the B&O Railroad tracks and the Monongahela River, which had been used as a campground by vagrants since the heyday of railroads, gaining in popularity and use during the Great Depression and continuing on into the twenty-first century as more and more of the nation's indigent population took to the roads and the streets."

It was "an unsanitary and unsafe area," they said, "frequented by derelicts and public offenders." It was a "magnet for crime." It was "fouled with human waste and excrement," they said, "a breeding ground for disease and the spread of tuberculosis and other contagions." It was a "threat to nearby businesses and adjacent public property such as the rails-to-trails bike path where families recreated."

Supporters of the Cottonwoods Upgrade spoke of it as "a revitalization" as a "giant social step forward," and as a "renaissance in urban planning." Critics of the Cottonwoods Upgrade saw it as the blatant and unconscionable creation of a ghetto.

The sojourners, however, paid neither the city planners, the social workers, the construction workers, the politicians, the proponents of the Cottonwoods Upgrade, nor the opponents of it any mind. They simply moved up river a bit to build their fires and make their camps and construct their hives of cardboard and plastic sheeting. And from across the river at night you could still catch a whiff of smoke when the wind blew, and you could see the campfires gleaming like tiger eyes along the riverbank, and in the skim-milky moonlight, among the buttonballs and cottonwoods, the water snakes and Joe Pye weed, the poison ivy and touch-me-nots, hearts-a-burstin' and briery bushes, the sojourners continued to live, for the most part, outside, making do, come what may, guided only by serendipity, chance, and weather, world within world, fringe of fringe frayed, drinking the cheap, rotgut alcohol that—like its more expensive and sophisticated correlatives— takes the world away.

Nominated by New Letters

NOT THERE

by MAXINE SCATES

from THE AMERICAN POETRY REVIEW

Sometimes late at night
around 11:05 when I'm watching the local news
reporting traffic accidents and meth lab busts
and the reasons for the smoke that has sealed
the city in a breath-ending autumnal haze
in mid-summer, I cannot lift myself—
I'm not there. Then it could be any year,
but probably the early sixties, '63 or '64, a Friday
night, I'm watching Johnny Carson or Steve Allen
or maybe Jack Paar and Judy Garland who is swinging
her legs from a stool, half-singing, half-crying. The jets
are screaming overhead and in the intervals
after they pass the neighbors are arguing again
and it doesn't matter which house because they all do:
Big John and his nameless wife, Julia and Ted,
The Smiths, Rosie and Bob, or Lynne and Jack,
the ex-Hell's Angels who have settled down
with their four kids. They all pretend they can't hear
what the next is yelling but I'm the one who hears
nothing. My mother is sleeping and my father
has left for good and all the years I was not there
when my father was are gathered in the haze
of aftermath, of disconnect and I'm still not there,
the way kids aren't when they can't do anything
about what is happening so instead watch the bird

dissolve into the corner of the ceiling as nothing
continues to happen, certain everything has happened
before them as I know everything has happened
before me. And all of it, the war, the harm my parents
visited upon each other evenings after work,
and the long days of the weekend, has left me untouched,
a miracle, living in a sheath of numbed, stunned light
I will wear years into the future I cannot yet imagine
where I will overhear a woman in a drugstore
telling the pharmacist how a drunken driver has killed
her child and though I am sorry and understand she hates
all drunks I know I am not the drunk who killed
her child. I am not there or even trying to be. But
soon I will awaken knowing I have been absent so long
I am in danger of never returning, and then I do begin
to wonder where I have been and all I can tell you
now is that time has not begun. And though I can't
explain how it did maybe some clock slowly began
to wheel when I did remember how one night
I let the steering wheel slide out of my hands, the car
beginning its slow drift toward the slough, just
for the sake of seeing how it felt, maybe for the sake
of ending the not-thereness. But mostly I don't feel
that way anymore—just those few minutes late at night
when I am tired and for a moment outside and then
life resumes in a kind of flooding that I recognize
as my lifetime, broken as anyone's, the pieces floating up,
the one that knows I could have been that drunk,
the weedy smell of the river in late afternoon, the crickets
humming the day's small aches and pleasures in this
my present—which if I've learned anything, I've learned
is never possible without the past.

Nominated by Brigit Pegeen Kelly, Dorianne Laux, Joseph Millar

TIED TO HISTORY

by GREIL MARCUS

from THE THREEPENNY REVIEW

I'M GOING TO TALK ABOUT a doubled memory. It's a memory of an actual incident, but inside that memory is another memory—a false memory, an attempt to remember something that can't be found.

I was ten in 1955; my family had just moved into a new house in Menlo Park, California. There was a big radio set up, and I'd play with it at night, trying to pull in the drifting signals from stations from across the country: from Salt Lake City, Cincinnati, even (once or twice) New Jersey. One night a few lines came out. "When American GIs left Korea," the radio said, "they also left behind countless father-less babies. Once everyone talked about this. Now, nobody cares."

The words bothered me at the time, but I put them out of my mind. Or so I thought. For the next twenty years, that incident would reap-pear—crashing into whatever I was thinking like an invisible mete-orite. As I got older, I realized it was an echo of something other than what the words from the radio actually described—I knew it was an echo of an absent memory of my own father, whose name was Greil Gerstley, who was lost in a typhoon in the Pacific when his destroyer went down. Those were all of the facts of the event present in my head at that time: no date, no details, no story. I was born Greil Gerst-ley, but when those words came out of the radio, I wasn't Greil Gerst-ley anymore. And though those words made me an echo chamber for the memory they called up, I had nothing to remember: the memory that was called up was blank.

Still, we all have memories of things we did not experience: cultural memories that have taken up residence in our minds, built houses,

228

filled them with furniture and appliances, and commanded that we live in them. These sorts of memories come from all sources, but especially from movies—and so, before I come back to the blank memory I started with, I'm going to talk about David Lynch's *Blue Velvet*.

The famous opening of this 1986 picture seems to parody the American fantasy of home, peace, pleasure, and quiet—that is, the all-but-trademarked American dream—but what's most interesting about what's happening on the screen is that it may have no satiric meaning at all.

The title sequence has shown a blue velvet curtain, slightly swaying from some silent breeze, casting back to the black-and-white velvet or satin backgrounds that provided a gloss for the title sequences of Forties B pictures. The opening theme music for *Blue Velvet* is ominous, alluring, at first suggesting Hitchcock's *Vertigo*, then a quiet setting where predictability has replaced suspense, then horns cutting off all hints of a happy ending. Bobby Vinton sings "Blue Velvet," his soupy number-one hit from 1963—but with the sound hovering over slats of a white picket fence with red roses at their feet, the song no longer sounds soupy, or for that matter twenty-three years in the past. It sounds clean and timeless, just as the white of the fence and the red of the roses are so vivid you can barely see the objects for the colors. For an instant, the viewer is both visually and morally blinded by the intensity of the familiar; defenses are stripped away.

In slow motion, a fireman on a fire engine moving down a well-kept middle-class street waves at you, a warm smile on his moon face. Another picket fence, now with blazing yellow tulips. Children cross a street in an orderly manner as a middle-aged crossing guard holds up her stop sign. There is a house with a white picket fence and a middle-aged man watering the lawn. Inside the house two middle-aged women sit on a sofa; there's a Pierrot doll on the lamp behind them. They're drinking coffee and watching an old-fashioned TV set, a small screen set in a blond wooden box with legs, a set from the Fifties, when a television was sold as a piece of furniture, in this case an object reflecting values of taste and modesty: the box looks Swedish Modern, and also simple enough that the man in the yard might have made it himself.

Outside, the man watering the lawn seems to sway with Bobby Vinton; the camera shows the faucet where the garden hose is attached leaking spray. The hose catches on a branch. The sound of water coming from the hose and the faucet rises to a rumble that seems to be coming out of the ground; every predictable act is about to explode from the pressure it is meant to hide. The man clutches his neck and falls to the ground. He drops the hose. A dog rushes up and, planting its forefeet on the prone man, drinks from the spray. The rumble grows stronger, and the camera goes down to the ground, beneath the grass, to reveal a charnel house, the secret world, where armies of hideous beetles, symbols of human depravity, of men and women as creatures of absolute appetite, banishing all conscience, appear to rise up and march out of the ground to take over the world like the ants in *Them!* Then the hero finds an ear in a field and the detective story that will take up the rest of the movie begins.

But it's the pastoral that stays in the mind, not the nightmare bugs and things-are-not-as-they-seem. Lynch's picture of things-as-they-ought-to-be is elegant. It feels whole, not like a cheat—for its moment it feels like a step out of the theater and into an idea of real life. Watching it again, you can see that the slightly stiff nature of Lynch's framing and timing of the fireman, the children, the crossing guard, the too-bright images of the fences and flowers, are not a matter of making the familiar strange, but of getting at how familiar the familiar actually is.

These shots don't play like a dream, and they don't play like the beginning of an exciting new story. They play like memory, and they stay in the mind like a common memory laying itself over whatever personal memories a person watching might bring to the images—because what the sequence seems to be showing a viewer is a proof that the notion of personal memory is false. The details of the sequence could, perhaps, be excavated to match specific details of Lynch's own boyhood, but what is striking about these quiet, burningly intense images is that nothing in them is specific to anyone. They are specific—overwhelmingly specific—only as images of the United States.

Anyone's memory is composed of both personal and common memories, and they are not separable. Memories of incidents that seem to have actually happened, once, in a particular time, to you, are colored, shaped, even determined, which is to say fixed in your memory, by the affinities your personal memories have to common memories: common memories as they are presented in textbooks and television programs, comic strips and movies, slang and clothes, all the rituals of everyday life as they are performed in one country as opposed to the way they are performed somewhere else.

The images that open *Blue Velvet* are images of things anyone watching a movie made in the U.S.A. can be presumed to have seen before, and to have remembered as if he or she waved back at the fireman or picked up the hose—as if whatever it is that makes the image significant was determined by the person remembering it, and no one else. But this is not true—and you can take it farther. If personal memory is false, what happens when you try to construct a memory of something that, in fact, you do not remember, but should—that you desperately want to remember?

I think I always knew that the words about the Korean orphans, left behind and forgotten in the United States, lay behind what I ended up doing with my life: rewriting the past, pursuing an obsession with secret histories, with stories untold—with what, to me, were deep, fraternal connections between people who never met: such people as the Dadaist Richard Huelsenbeck in Zurich in 1916, the revolutionary theorist Guy Debord in Paris in 1954, and the punk singer Johnny Rotten in London in 1976. But I did not pursue the secret history, the unremembered history, that lay behind the words from the radio.

One can of course remember what one has not experienced. Older people tell children, *This is what it was like, this is what he was like, how he laughed, how he walked, the team he rooted for.* You absorb that: you meet someone who in fact you will never meet, and so that person, never present, becomes part of your memory. But in my case, none of that was true.

I was born six months and a day after my father was killed in the Second World War—I know that now, but growing up, I never had a date to work with. My mother is from San Francisco; Greil Gerstley, in 1944, at twenty-four, second in command on a destroyer named the *Hull*, was from Philadelphia. They hadn't known each other long when they married in San Francisco in September. My mother went with my father to Seattle, where the *Hull* shipped out.

I was left with the name, which became, for me, a talisman and a mystery. In 1948 my mother remarried, to Gerald Marcus, and he adopted me, and my name was changed. I don't remember myself as Greil Gerstley, but Greil was an unescapable name—I always had to explain it, but I really had nothing to tell. The story of the *Hull* was not told in my family. There were no pictures of my father Greil Gerstley in my house. When I visited my Philadelphia family, there were pictures, but I felt furtive, unfaithful, criminal, when I looked at them, and no one ever offered me a picture of my own to keep. There were memories—I was visiting my father's older brother and his older sister. There was even a professionally shot home movie, showing my father in his dress Navy uniform—in the way he looked, in the casual, commanding way he leaned back in a chair, so much a match, now, for John F. Kennedy, that the footage is hard to look at—but none of that was shared with me. It must have been that to tell the story of who my father was, what he had done, what happened to him and to so many others would be too much for a small boy to take in—or that to tell me such things would be, somehow, a breach of faith with my new father, or with my mother, in her new life.

The situation never changed. When I grew older, the habit of not speaking about the past became a kind of prison. I didn't know how to break out of it. I didn't ask, and nobody told. Like many children, I sometimes fantasized that I was not the child of my parents—but in my case, it was at least half true. Or more than half true: though I always knew I had had a different father than my brothers and sister, my mother might never have lived the life I came from. When, at first, I asked about my father, she would say she didn't remember—their time together was so short, she said. The letters he wrote to her from the *Hull*—he was in charge of censoring mail, which is to say he could write what he pleased—were thrown out. He might have told her that, one night, preparing a navigation chart, he renamed a star for her; if he did, she never told me. My mother gave her wedding book to her mother—and when, sometime in the late Fifties, my grandmother took it out and paged through it with me, she told me never to tell my mother she had showed it to me.

So in times of childhood or teenage unhappiness, the fantasy that I might have lived a different life, been a different person with a different name, was more a fact than a fantasy: if my father had lived, both my mother and I would have lived very different lives. But it was the kind of fact that, when you try to hold on to it, slips through your fingers like water.

Thus I developed my obsession with the past; I used the cultivated mystery of my own past as a spur to reconstructing events both as they happened and as they didn't—as they might have. I became a writer, and this is always the route I've traveled, whether writing about Elvis or Bill Clinton, Bob Dylan or Huey Long, John Wayne in *Rio Bravo* or Frank Sinatra in *The Manchurian Candidate*. I never expected my untold story to actually appear, as real life—to challenge, as real life, the fantasy that has always been the foundation of my work.

But the story did appear. A few years ago, my father—my second father—called to say there was a documentary on the *Hull* on the Weather Channel. I watched it, alone; when my wife came home, I said, "I just saw my father die." He wasn't in the film: rather, survivors from the *Hull* spoke over stock footage and still photos of the typhoon that destroyed over eight hundred men from their ship and from the two more that went down in the same storm. You saw their Navy photos, as they were in 1944; you saw them now, smiling, laughing, sober, crying, speaking of the countless men who made it into the open sea with life jackets, and who, when they were found, had nothing of themselves left below the waist—countless men eaten alive by sharks.

Then, two years ago, a writer named Bruce Henderson got in touch with me. He was looking for information about Greil Gerstley for a book on the *Hull*. Was I perhaps named for him by a friend? Was I a distant relative? Was there anything I could tell him?

The story he told, based on interviews he had conducted with survivors and people in the orbit of the ship, was terrible. The *Hull* had been at Pearl Harbor on December 7, 1941, but was not damaged; its captain then—the man who trained my father, who became the *Hull's* executive officer—was respected and trusted. In Seattle, he was replaced by a martinet from Annapolis, a man so vain and incompetent, so impatient with advice from experienced sailors and sure of his own right way, that, when the *Hull* set sail for the South Pacific, twenty men went AWOL, certain that to ship with this man was a death sentence.

With the typhoon looming, Admiral Halsey ordered the fleet to sail into it—"to see what they were made of." With the ship trapped in a trough, with waves on each side a hundred feet high, the captain determined to power the engines to full throttle and smash his way out, while his officers vainly tried to tell him that, in a trough, you cut the engines and wait. The captain panicked; he issued contradictory orders, rescinded them, issued them again. Other officers, who survived to tell the story to Bruce Henderson, begged my father—who was trusted as the captain was not, admired as the captain was reviled—to seize the ship: to place the captain under arrest, take command, and save the ship, in other words to lead a mutiny. There was no mutiny, but *The Caine Mutiny* was inspired by what happened in this typhoon, and by what might have happened.

My father refused. In the history of the Navy there had never been such a mutiny, he said. He knew, he said, that if he took command he would be court-martialed, and if he didn't, he and everyone else would probably die.

The ship was pitching at angles of seventy degrees. My father was thrown against machinery, breaking ribs, bones in his back, and the bones of one hand. Another sailor got a splint on his hand. The ship pitched over ninety degrees—and after that the only direction it could go was down. With the ship flooding, my father was pulled from a hatch into the open sea. One survivor says he said to a sailor who approached him, "Don't try to help me, I won't make it"; another remembers him asking for help, and the men near him knowing he had no chance.

As it happens, long after the war, when enough time had passed for those who had been part of it to talk about it, the survivors of the *Hull* began to hold reunions. In December 2006, in Las Vegas, they held what they determined would be their last, and one of my daughters went. She looks like my father, as I don't; my mother, in a rare unguarded moment, was the first to see it. The people in Las Vegas saw it. They told her stories, some of them as terrible as the one Bruce Henderson told: that when the original captain of the *Hull* was told, by one of the survivors, that if he had still been the captain the ship would never have gone down, he shot himself.

So now I know these facts, or I have heard, second or third hand, these stories. I have a story I can tell. If it had been told to me when I was a child, I might have, in a deep and true sense, remembered it as if I had been there when it happened, with at least the same instantly recallable immediacy with which I can summon up the exploits of Ty Cobb and Babe Ruth, who of course I never saw. But these facts, severed from the family history that might have given them flesh, are, really, no more mine than the images that open *Blue Velvet*.

I can make sense of them, or hold them in my mind, only as scenes from movies—the likes of *The Cruel Sea, Victory at Sea*, the documentaries *The World at War* or *Why We Fight*—or from the movie that, someday, someone might make (since the facts appeared my wife and I and our daughters and our friends have been casting it). But if any such movie were ever made, the story that I have, as a personal story, would be even less mine than it is now—and the truth is that, now, it isn't mine at all. It is a contrivance—it is a story that I might now remember, but don't. What might have been a personal story dissolves into the public domain of a much greater story, of the War, of heroism and stupidity, arrogance and decency, and hundreds of thousands of the dead—and in that sense, whatever personal memory might be found here, the common memory rightly takes away.

Nominated by Threepenny Review, Jane Hirshfield

METALLURGY FOR DUMMIES

by JAMES RICHARDSON

from TIN HOUSE

Faint bronze of the air,
a bell I can't quite hear,

The sky they call gunmetal
over gunmetal reservoir,

the launch, aluminum,
cutting to the center,

waters bittered with the whisk
of aluminum propellers

(your gold drink stirred
with a gold forefinger).

*

Faint tinnitus,
where is it?

Air silver with a trillion
wireless calls,

stop-quick stop-quick
of sweep hands,

crickets and downed lines,
their sing of tension,

that out-of-earshot
too-bright CD sun,

the heads of presidents
sleet sleet in your jacket.

*

They were right,
those alchemists.
Anything—

tin-cold
eye of salamander,

a fly's
green shield and styli

235

on your wrist,
distinctly six—
anything might—

mutterings in the wet,
two-packs-a-day
brass of sax, bright

tears pestled,

or your hair's backlit
(same as the rain's)
slender metals—

anything might flash out

*

Surely one sip,
mused Midas,
gin and silver,

surely her fine engine tuned
to a dial tone,

surely her famous sway
gone Gold, gone Double
    Platinum,
Rare Earth, gone Transuranic . . .

*

Anything slow,
slash-black and copper
monarch settling,

the shy key's glint and turn,

sunny-cloudy
brass-and-tarnish fruit
paused at your lips, reflecting.

Any velocity,

water under the bridge
my leap
like dropped change rings on,

or seen from a train
chicory's blue
extrusion to a wire of blur,

the train itself
(of thought)
on its track and track and track,

your soft, incredible metals.

*

. . . surely these vast reserves
(that treasurer surmised).
I must address

with a safecracker's
listening touch.

I'll be the anti-thief
slipping certificates of silver,
the slim faux-platinum

yen of credit,
palms flat,

over and over into her
skin-tight pockets.

*

Eyes, blank or deep,
a lake
gone bright dark bright.

(on thin ice giving way—
one: roll up the window
two: when the car fills . . .)

the fatal-in-seconds
keen cold of a mirror,
the blank bright blank

that any word might.
any word might not.

*

No one my touch
(that treasurer surmised)
can bear and tell

(apparently did not touch
  himself).

*

Wine so cold it's nails,
rings in the glass, poured,
your ring and its click
two-three, and click,
the bar awash

in digital and silver
whispers of the disc,

yes no yes
yes,
and This

Just In:
incredible metals

the shifting of your silks
imagines, unimagines,

the thought-blue
alloy of your lids,

the pistol
chill of your lips
my lips might freeze to.

Nominated by Tin House, Judith Kitchen

EDGE BOYS

fiction by CHARLES McLEOD

from CONJUNCTIONS

$\mathbf{B}$OUGHT IN MOTEL ROOMS, in public park bathrooms, the edge boys have highlighted their hair. The boxes of Clairol are plucked stolen from shelves and tucked into boxer-brief waistbands. The store clerks are busy asking for price checks. The edge boys have very white teeth. They stride the linoleum, smiles shining out. The clerks think: no one that pretty would take things. The doors whoosh to open; here is the sun, here is the blacktop, shimmering. The edge boys wear shorts that go past their knees. The edge boys wear oversized T-shirts. They buy gum at gas stations and pace the grass strips between pump bays and street intersections. When cars slow in passing, the edge boys blow bubbles. Tucked in their anklets are prepackaged condoms. They have earrings in both of their ears. Last week was the last week of their high-school semesters. The edge boys are ready to earn. In parentless houses, the kitchen tap running, they work water down to their scalps. Blond with red streaks or brown with blond streaks or black transformed to white blond. They wrap the dyed locks in lengths of tinfoil and wait, watching game-show reruns. Their yearbooks, in backpacks, sit signed and forgotten: *have a great summer. i'll see you in autumn. thanks for being such a good friend.* The edge boys are gay. The edge boys have girlfriends, meek girls with glasses or cheeks stained with acne, who hide their girth under loose batik skirts, girls who ask less per their subpar aesthetic and thus function as near-perfect foils, the edge boys needing only to take them to movies, to malls, to infrequently dine them at some neoned franchise and then later take their clothes off, this last part disliked but understood as essential, as requisite for the upkeep of hetero visage, manda-tory for avoiding all manner of bullshit in locker-walled, fluorescent-lit halls, so these girls' hands held in high-ceilinged lunchrooms, these girls taken to prom, their taffeta dresses like bright shiny sacks, their matching sling backs rubbing their fat ankles raw, and the edge boys make clear on spring nights in late April that it has been fun but just not enough, that it's in both parties' best interests to move on from each other, to let summer heal wounds and meet up in fall, and by the week after finals the edge boys are working, are putting in hours, are taking their knocks, have had their foreheads put hard against corners of nightstands, have been bruised by closed fists, have been robbed, have been taken to dark lonely lots off the parkways, the mood chang-ing, the date going wrong, and sometimes the edge boys flee into nighttime, hoping their sneakers don't scuff, as the body in youth will start itself over, can reset with nearly no flaws, but the shoes are ex-pensive, were purchased, must last, possess sharp lines and clean looks, traits that the edge boys must also possess so the skin tanned in backyards on slow afternoons, the teeth brushed and whitened and flossed, the hair kept to flawless, shampooed and then sculpted, the back tightly tapered, sharp as the bristles on a brush—their image rechecked in the bathrooms of Chevrons as the day turns itself into dusk, and when the dye fades the edge boys repeat the process of dye-ing, and when cars stop the edge boys lean through the frames of car windows, asking for rides to some other place, asking how much and for what.

And here the edge cities, the car-fervent boomburbs, Levittown's sprawling kempt spawn, more jobs than bedrooms, the streets dead by evening, the office parks sleeping it off; here the coiffed glow of postindustrial society, the middle class outsourced, the farmlands paved over, gone, practical know-how no longer important so goodbye to Pittsburgh's Steelworkers Union, goodbye to Baltimore's docks, the stevedores half starved from nothing exported, the labor halls places of rot, production supplanted by codified knowledge, the making of goods replaced by the selling thereof, the old urban centers un-wanted, not needed, high crime and high rent, the drug-addled dozing at bus stops, so development set down in between freeways, acreage near airports bought cheap and built up, and from this Bethesda and Scottsdale and Reston; Irving, Texas, and White Plains, New York; here Costa Mesa in LA's choked basin; here Downers Grove and Og-den, Utah, here the midlevel skyscraper of mixed office/retail, the arterial road ten miles long, where sidewalks are largely parachronistic as sidewalks are *places of sloth*, made for the beggar and stroller, the uncertain, the person too full of free thought, for the edge cities are kingdoms of *the action efficient*, progress optimized, apologism constantly scoffed—realms of the stem cell, the spreadsheet, the lepton, where the hum of the lathe has never been heard, where absent is the din of the die caster's punch, these sounds replaced by the light constant clacking of flesh on computer keyboards, the new assembly lines well-lit partitioned desk cubicles one floor up from the whir of juice bars, and rolled out from these factories datum not item, patent not part, as the things we make now are not things at all, are service or research, advice or idea, theory mapped out or thought up—here Science unbridled, here plugs cords and wires, here bits bytes and pixels replacing the orchards, all produce imported by plane and then truck, here nanotech labs with federal contracts, here the cybernetics startup, *here green even sod between rows of parked cars outside of the Mall of America;* here wetlands demolished, here cell towers erected, here all the bees dying off, here bigger and faster and smaller and brighter, here the twenty-screen Cineplex showing ten action titles, teens texting on handhelds through all the slow parts, here drive-thru windows on pharmacy walls, here Zoloft and Lustral passed out like fast food, here tax breaks enormous for new corporate tenants, here regional outlets inside megacenters, here firms expert in hedge-fund investment and intellectual property law; here unclassified research in the hills east of Berkeley, Houston's Sugarland, Denver's Aurora, here Cool Springs between Memphis and Nashville, here Clearwater due west of Tampa, each place a nexus of postwar success, these cities we fought for, these cities we won.

The edge boys do oral. The edge boys do anal. The edge boys will do half and half. On laptops, in bedrooms, listings are posted, published to Web sites with classified sections accepting of this sort of fare. The edge boys were born 1990 or after. The edge boys can type very fast. Cross-legged on throw rugs, on low thread-count bed sheets, the edge boys' shoulders hunch over flat screens, searching for what to say next. When their eyes blink, the edge boys don't know that they're blinking. On walls are taped posters of rock bands or rap stars or harmonizing Caucasian quintets. Square fans fill windows, their blades quickly turning. The rooms of the edge boys are never a mess. The rooms of the edge boys are kept swept and dusted, clothes hampered, corners absent of lint—quick work that functions as high-gloss veneer should parents, at some point, peek in. The edge boys do poorly on standardized testing; for them it will be junior college at best. There is flash on the brainpan and their bodies hunch tighter and their fingers, crookedly, tap: *versatile bottom seeks high-class encounter. tan toned and ready right now. if you have the quarters come see my arcade. i have the best games in town.* The edge boys review; the edge boys make edits. The edge boys are junk food, sweet cheap and addictive, so the edge boys call themselves twinks. With driveways vacated, with the highways now humming, with the sun burning dew from the grass, the edge boys are mid-morning entrepreneurs, undertaking new enterprise, assuming all risk. The edge boys are merchant fleet, caravan, troupe. The edge boys are both song and dance. The edge boys offer companionship, not fucking: *any money exchanged is a gift for time spent.* Pictures are uploaded alongside the squibs, photographic self-portraits in which the edge boys are shirtless, their faces made blurry or blacked out, as the edge boys must show what they have to offer without revealing too much of themselves. A lawnmower whirs; a car honks a street over. Hummingbirds hover inches from blossoms; the edge boys can see them through cracks in the blinds. Light falls in threads onto desktops and dressers. The rooms of the edge boys are often so still that the edge boys sometimes believe themselves dead. From hallways chime wall clocks; it's seconds past ten. Windows are closed out and e-mail then opened and soon after the ads of the edge boys go live. The edge boys stand up and step out of lounge pants. The edge boys own phony IDs—crude fakes they self-publish on laser-jet printers while their parents, exhausted, succumb to canned laughter on prime-time TV—as the edge boys must be young looking but legal, twenty-one, twenty, nineteen, some age that confirms them as virile and nubile but rules out anything *statutory*, and with music put on and their wardrobe selected, the edge boys walk briskly to white-tiled bathrooms where towels hang folded in halves, the shower knob pulled out or turned right or left, the steam rising over the basin's glass door, the wall mirror growing fogged in.

And here the respondees, the white-collar lustful, alumni of Schools of Letters & Science, men in their twenties, their thirties, their fifties, men of all races and sizes, men who were born on American soil and men who at one point were naturalized, men who have been with the company for decades and men only recently hired, men who lean left and men who lean right and swing-voting men who will cross party

241

lines should they really believe in the candidate, men with no voting record, men who watch sports ten hours each weekend and men who do not own a television, men who ride Harleys and men who drive hybrids; dumb men, who will not last through the next round of layoffs, and men who are workers upstanding, men who wear suits with ties Windsor knotted, men who wear lab coats and bow ties, men who are lead-end application designers and men who once worked on Wall Street, men with full knowledge of the Doha Round's implications and men unsure of where Doha is located, men with low tolerance for processing lactose, men allergic to peanuts, to buckwheat; bearded men, bland men, men with thin fingers, men who are wearers of rings, men with tan lines where these rings once were but most aptly *men of duplicity*, men of the mask worn under the skin, men of coarse acts and good hygiene, men at once members of neighborhood watch groups and blackguards for their local sex industry, and these men of the condo, the townhouse, the Tudor, these men of argyle and khaki, who stay late or rise early and work hard or don't, all of these men double-dealing—men of two forms, two positions in space, makers of both song and painting, men who are crooners of stanzas threnodic, peddlers of anapest, of trochee, men who know which sounds to stress and not stress to sell fables in a manner convincing: men of the midday trip to the dentist, men of cars whose oil needs changing, men who are fathers of very sick children, small boys or girls who abruptly fall ill at desks inside school buildings, and these children needing *care*, needing parent and transport, needing warm soup and cold remedies, so grave faces worn while approaching coworkers, or bosses in the middle of e-mailing: *I just got a call from, You won't believe this, He said and She said and Well they just told me*—lines near canonical for each of these men, these scholars entrenched in the oral tradition of lying, as the edge boys are canvas that can't be left blank, are these men's passion, their calling, what they would choose if there was nothing else, no yard work, no anniversaries, no pushing of paper or processing words to sustain and increase yearly salary, so all manner of untruth composed and conscripted, the devotion to craft close to boundless, and here is the cell phone purchased in secret, and here the bank account no one else knows of, and here the PO box for these bills and statements, rented the next city over, as the lunch breaks of these men do not involve food but do very much include *hunger*, so daily or weekly, in the stalls of work bathrooms, or in cars parked in the dark of garages, the ads of the edge boys perused via BlackBerry,

242

flipped through using touch screens on iPhones, and when the right hue is found, the precise chiaroscuro, these men then envision their paintings: art made amongst cheaply starched sheets of queen beds in rooms advertised as having free cable, or the bought trysts transpiring well into evening, subject and object in states of undress at rest stops on the city's periphery, and sometimes the process goes very smoothly and on occasion the practice is rougher, but more important than outcome *sustained feasibility*, that these actions are able to be tried and retried, to be done again over and over.

The edge boys want their donation up front. The edge boys take cash and cash only. The edge boys will wear any items you like, providing they then get to keep them. The edge boys can tell you which parts of lots can't be seen from the street, from the freeway. The edge boys don't ever kiss on the mouth though the men that they meet *will lean in*, will keep trying, and by now, my midforties, still married, still scared, still fake small meek and unsure, a member of gyms, a father of daughters, as someone who dishonored oath long ago but has largely upheld every contract, as owner of a house now fully paid off, as possessor of matching brass shoehorns, as someone who never stood up for himself and finds richness in acts done in shadow, in darkness, the edge boys, for me, serve as *opera omnia*, comprise a life's work collected, and here *early works*: my third year at Lehigh, a major in civil engineering, freshly admitted to Tau Beta Pi and possessed by the deeds of Telford, of Jessop, both preeminent builders of canals, of artificial channels of water, this '83, Rock Hudson infected, the disease often still called gay cancer, AIDS known to Reagan, who was two years away from using the term while in public, and *winter in Bethlehem*, bright but cold days, the steel plant still up and running, the historic downtown lined with bare elms, the clothiers and bookshops brick walled and stately, and for ten months by this time letters to parents, verse that spoke often of Daphne: Daphne of Cleveland, Daphne a senior, Daphne who too soon was graduating, and included therein our fake union's minutiae, trips to Ohio or north to the Catskills or hikes to the top of South Mountain, the posts detailed but also disjointed, meant to seem rushed, to seem done in one breath, to convey I was in constant hurry, whereas in truth there was only course work and near-daily walks, done close to sunset, down to the bank of the river, brisk peregrinations from my Fountain Hill in-law past one side of St. Luke's Memorial, where often a nurse, in pink scrubs and peacoat, stood smoking by a low bank of generators, and with eye contact made and a quick nod hello his shoe tramps on the dirt path behind me, and these men my seniors by a decade or more—there were eight in two years, in total—and while I remember their faces and where they said they grew up and the deep grove of white pines we went to, I cannot recall a single one of their names or if they once ever told their names to me, but nonetheless *closeness*, something near respite, relief from a bleak way of seeing, as while I adored all the things human beings had made I mainly despised human beings: saw their design as shortsighted, their construction haphazard, their maintenance needing too much maintaining, but hidden by trees, dusk sinking to night, *the singing of near-perfect industry*, here pressure and density, here equations of state, here balance, breath measured, entropic, and when we were finished, had switched ourselves off and parted from each other's company, within me was calm, flat neutral and static, the job done, the stars still indifferent, and so over time, and through acts of this manner, I came to see love as *duty to work*, a viewpoint not that uncommon, as I held great affection for accomplishing task, for procedure done forthwith and fitly, and by May of my last year in North Appalachia, that region of limestone and sinkholes, I knew I would always live two lives at once, a life seen and a life more invisible, and knew also that these lives would transpire in parallel, would move forward in space at a similar rate while remaining at all points equidistant, but ignored in this thinking *Euclidean principle*, as according to Euclid *on a spherical plane all straight lines are turned into circles*, bend warp and wrap, are bound by their globe, and thereby become geodesic, and with earth a sphere this meant points intersecting, meant contact made between two different things that I'd thought I could always keep separate.

And here *midcareer*, the Near North Side loft, my wife holding a torn condom wrapper, the two of us poised on opposite sides of our kitchen's marble-topped island, light pouring in through the balcony's sliding-glass doors, reflecting from off Lake Michigan, this '97, the boom in full swing, the country choking on money, and with one arm akimbo the person I married releasing the ripped piece of plastic, the object suspended and then falling slowly to the smooth beige Biancone counter, and on this woman's wrist a chain of white gold, and on her finger a ring of white diamonds, and the condom itself, once contained in the wrapper, in a trash can at Anna Page Park west of Rockford, used in conjunction with a junior in high school, a boy named Brandon O'Cleary, taller than average and lithe and light haired and

244

dressed in grunge-era trappings: ripped jeans and cloth high-tops and plaid flannel shirts, worn despite the damp heat of deep summer, button-down items undone by myself on at least ten separate occasions, the two of us coming to know one another per work for the firm that employed me, endeavors involving repeated site visits to dozens of area cities, as these places were ready to take on more people, were building hundreds and hundreds of houses, and along with these houses new schools and boutiques and plazas and fire departments, structures intended to be *flanked by small ponds*, by fountains and banks of bright flowers, and lawns would be needed and toilets and bathtubs and all this depended on *water*, as without water no dwellers could dwell, and no shoppers could do all their shopping, and no roads would be tarred and no sprinklers would hiss and the juice bars would have no crushed ice for their smoothies, so watershed checked for all types of pollutants, farmland surveyed for new aquifers, and *here's where to pipe in to existing storm drains* and *here's how to maintain water tables*—all of this data determined and gauged, collected for further analysis, and at night in hotel rooms in Schaumburg or Elgin calls home to the woman I married: *I'm just checking in* and *yes things are fine* and *I can't wait to get home and see you*, sayings that in some ways were not utter lies as I loved my wife then and I still do, but with the receiver set down on its cream-colored base a walk to my car to start *trolling*, cruising each village—the malls and gas stations—for boys who were in need of money, who were willing to part with one type of resource in order to then gain another, as I wanted something soullessly epicurean and the edge boys had this to offer, could promise me dividend with low overhead if I was willing to become a partner, and at tables in food courts not far from arcades or in restrooms out west toward the toll roads, the edge boys and I would come to terms quickly, as we were living within a bull market, and yes there were blips—a kidney infection, a stop at a DUI checkpoint—but the tech bubble was big and said bubble was growing and past the continued growth rate of this bubble few other events seemed to matter, so *repeated foray* while my wife sat at home with first one and then both of our children, and the paychecks were big and I had money in hedge funds and things just kept growing and growing, and the first of our daughters grew out of her onesies and went to her first day of preschool, and the suburbs expanded, spawned acres of homes, replete with skylights and bird feeders, where young men and women, the moon overhead, supplemented their own genealogy, while beneath them new pipes pushed out all their sewage, carried their waste to *wherever*, but what I mean to say is there was no need to think, only an urge to keep doing, so when the condom's torn wrapper touched down on the counter I looked at my wife very calmly, crossed my arms on my chest, and leveled my eyes and explained *that confer-ence in Denver*, where by true chance I ran into someone that I knew from my days back at Lehigh, and her name was Daphne and she was from Cleveland and one drink had led to three others—and the story was seamless (there were parts told while weeping), and I beseeched my wife not to leave me, to accept my mistake and think of our daugh-ters and think of the concept of family, something that I, for one night of my life, had so foolishly placed by the wayside, and while this tale was spun into something metallic, into something expensive and shiny, my thoughts went again, as they still sometimes do, to the image of Brandon O'Cleary, his long body leaning on a tall granite wall littered with weaving graffiti, his hair to midear, deep blond and unwashed and parted straight down the middle, the locks grimy enough to keep a clean angle, to roof his face in an A-frame, and Brandon liked music and Brandon liked pot and Brandon liked shooting home movies, and set up his parents' bulky camcorder on a tripod each Sunday evening, where before dusk and until shortly after he filmed from his small bedroom's window, the lens looking down the length of his street, looking, he told me, *at nothing*, at cars leaving driveways and children on bikes, at snowfall and rainfall and hail, and stacked in his closet were columns of tapes, some years old and some very recent, these acts of surveying disclosed to me while I set up my firm's *total station*, a device that like Brandon's sat too on a tripod, and was also used in surveying, and when Brandon approached and said *what the hell is that* I told him of angles and distance, of sight via prisms and data recording and how to look under and over and straight through the earth, how to see measure test and tell everything.

But now it is summer and I've rushed through my life, only to find other summers, more seasons of heat, doubleheaders and picnics, more evenings of lush thrumming stillness, more weeks of monoto-nous unchallenging work, more checks written for property taxes, more vacations taken to mundane locales: lighthouses or churches or statues or bridges, trips now made most often without me, my wife and two daughters wanting time to themselves, a concept I don't find surprising, as while I've been a good father in a number of ways I am also quite guilty of *distance*, of supporting my offspring with money, not love, of remaining *emotionally absent*, a shortcoming my spouse has said she equates to our children being not male but female, that I have had a hard time accepting my role in our family and that from this our family suffers, but when they pack up the Jeep for points west or east there is, within me, real sadness, deep melancholy that I've failed at my task, that I couldn't perform any better, that on car rides to St. Louis to lay eyes on the Arch or to Wyoming to hike in the Tetons, I am spoken of poorly—not called spiteful names in tones bright with rage but wondered at, frowned upon, questioned, the way the favored team's fans, having watched their club lose, leave the stadium bewildered and empty: *they should have done better* and *what were they thinking* and *man, I just can't believe that*, and to provide counterbalance to these feelings of shame I walk to my den and computer, boot up the hard drive, and sit down at my chair and see who is working this evening, who will meet me at street corners close to the mall, where the big summer sale is happening, where nightly the blacktops, like still inland seas, wait for the next day's sojourners, temporary residents of these declining Edens, as America is reaching its summer, that point where all bloom has happened, where what has sprung from the earth shows off what it's got and waits patiently for *decomposition:* the peaking of oil, the drying of rivers, the crops lying wrecked in their rows in the heartland or some other crippling paucity, and for this reason the edge boys are genuine artifact, Americana that's highly collectible, each one like the last one but also unique, made individual via small details: a birthmark or scar or small discoloration, a type of deodorant whose scent is brand-new to me, a way of dyeing their hair that I'd never thought of or a piercing in some place that I had not seen, and on these evening drives to the malls or motels, I allow myself time to wander my city, take in each billboard and juice bar and gas pump, every neon, glowing marquee, and here is the semi just in from the freeway, its trailer filled with plasma TVs, and here the grease franchise, burgers and shakes, cars ringing three sides of the building, the doors locked but the drive-thru window still open, its panes retracting hydraulically, and out farther from town landfill and power plants and all manner of *infrastructure unsightly*— squat concrete structures where sewage is treated, as the clean must be kept from the dirty.

And Brandon, my favorite, do they know what their acts bring, these people of cities on the edges of cities? Do they know that all this is ending? That how things are now is not how they will be? That this grand experiment's over? That the Feds have cut rates per blowback from subprime and still these places are failing? That homes being built now will never be lived in? That at the auto plazas, units aren't moving? That people work longer than ever before and earn less than they did at midcentury? That the petals have dried out and the stalks are all rotting? Because, Brandon, I know it, and this is why last night I put in my two weeks after being telephoned by a headhunter, an anonymous man two time zones away representing a firm working in *catastrophe modeling*, in the scientific prediction of disaster, in detailing what type of wrath to expect when the next Level Five descends on the Gulf Coast, or the big one arrives to shake down San Francisco, or the Southwest has its next batch of fires, or the Singapore Causeway succumbs to tsunami or a flood eats some county in Kansas, for these events, now, are just short of certain, and insurers want to cover their asses—need to know what kind of odds are in play, if gross loss will be millions or billions, and for this *computer-assisted scenarios*, software eschatological in nature, programs designed to map out the End Times second by second by second, and here's what to expect when the Bay Bridge collapses, and here's what this zip code will look like as rubble, and here's what turns to ash if winds blow from the west as opposed to blowing northwesterly and Brandon, the money's terrific, the sum offered much more than I would have expected for my input on our slow apocalypse, and for this reason I will again move my daughters and wife, and will sell my house and then buy a new house, and find yet another tree-lined tranquil street in a newly made master community, where each house looks just like the last one, some split-level in which I may hide a bit longer and wait while things turn truly sour, for coastlines to shrink and shelves to go bare and gas to hit twenty a gallon, and perhaps I won't ever see it, will expire before we fully lose balance, and fall from our perch on the roof of the world, spiraling downward and downward, and it was to be different, *there were to be bluebirds*, there were to be grills near the shore of a lake, a postwar aria of infinite refrain; we were to applaud, and be applauded. There was the promise of promise. We had solved something. The dead were brought back from French beaches and honored. The dollar held. Wheat grew. We made things of substance. But it all went perverted, we purchased each other, and we left you, Brandon, with *nothing*, with hair dye and game shows and modified food, with the ghost of Social Security, with lead in the paint on the walls of your schools, with electromagnetic pollution, with esplanades of red brick where the hollow walk shopping, the headsets of their cell phones like blinders, with some small bit of wealth that can never make up for the damage inflicted upon you and Brandon, I'm sorry, I should have known better, I should have made more prudent choices, but what I loathe most about the person I am is also the thing that completes me so Brandon, please, one kiss, I'm done asking, we have financialized your humanity, we have taken and taken, and there's no stopping this and there's no cure for this and so coated in fear lust and haste are our happenings that we forget wholly *implication*, that these cities, like rash on the skin of the land, are emblematic *of more dire virus*, and once in a host will not go away but replicate over and over, and, Brandon, my pet, we're low on vaccine, and the antibiotics are useless, and small bits of plastic float in our seas, debris no bigger than plankton, sharp brittle shards that won't biodegrade, not now and not ever—proof we were here, in our miserable way, have washed up on every island, and wrecked every acre and nautical mile, and spun the hand on our moral compass, and without any pride or belief in ourselves exist without any power, and supplanting this *war*, and replacing this *purchase*, and we give ourselves over to skirmish and item, and our guilt gels around us, forms into things that we can't escape so more things are built to contain them, and if we don't like how they look they can always be brightened so Brandon, keep bleaching, burn through every root, because if you're not pretty then you'll get no money, and if you don't feed us, we promise, we'll eat you.

Nominated by Conjunctions, Don Waters

THE FAVORITE

by ALISON TOWNSEND

from RIVER STYX

You know you're not supposed to have favorites,
but can't help liking most this girl
with auburn hair, and the name of your best
friend in high school, the one who recites
swathes of Emily Dickinson aloud, standing out
like a shining blade among the bored, pasty faces
in Freshman English, announcing that she
wants to write *her* research essay on love,
eighteen after all, despite her way with language.

You don't know yet you'll be her favorite too,
happy whenever you see her name on your roster,
as you watch her hammer a house of words together,
board by shining board, turning your slightest
suggestions into windows and doors—apertures
that could open on almost anything. And do,
the day she comes to your office, an essay
cradled in her arms for you to read before
class—the one thing (she tells you)

she is afraid to write. Though she has
written it, fighting her way back inside
her fourteen-year-old self so convincingly
you can feel lilies blooming inside her skin
and the way her eyelids flutter, taste Juicy

250

Fruit, smell the talcumed longing that pulls
her to the carnival that night with her best friend,
flat-bellied and sparkling, looking for the kind
of boys she doesn't even know to watch out for.

But this is where things jumble and blur, her story
suddenly yours, the twinkling Ferris wheel
a circle of boys with joints you and your friend—
the one with your student's name—
found yourself trapped inside one New Year's
decades ago, the memory pushed down the way
those boys pushed the two of you from one
to another, The Beatles' "Come Together" loud
in the back of your head. As your student flirts

down the midway, through the hot scent of cotton
candy and popcorn, everything about her unbearably
young, from the small, hard apples of her knees
to the way her braces cage the candy-cotton-stained
red of her mouth. To the moment you know is ahead
when the boy she shunned a few steps back grabs
her arm, then yanks her under a tent flap,
the way a boy pulled you under the stairs
at that basement party. Pushing her down the way

that boy pushed you, his friend there too, and another,
then more, then you fighting free, and somehow
your girlfriend underneath them all while you
tried to think how to make it end, *Come together,
right now* playing over and over. Or is it
that carnival honky-tonk, sweat and beer and
sawdust and dope, the short skirt pushed up,
the boys' movements jerky and sharp?
Because you got away didn't you? hitch-

hiking home in the dark with your friend,
who couldn't talk about what happened.
And they didn't—your friend, and your student
who was held down, the secret of it clamped
deep inside like a hideous pearl. Until this week

when she sat in her dorm and typed
what you now read aloud. So she can see how clear-
sightedly she reaches back and puts her arm
around that girl, washing her off, throwing

the torn skirt out. So she can know
it was not her fault, the most beautiful
room in her whole house built from the ugliest
mud, terror a blue vowel that kisses
the hurt. As you read back to her
what she has written, thinking of your lost
and silent friend, the iodine sting
of your student's words burning,
healing, alive in your mouth.

Nominated by River Styx

TWO EXPERIMENTS AND A CODA

by LIA PURPURA

from AGNI

Street Experiment

All things go. Snow comes, stays, hardens, then melts. We expect its behavior. Along one block, dropped and unfound, or unsearched for, things surface in the thaw. First a penny, and I see the cent mark in my head—*who writes that anymore?* I know I wrote a lot of them as a kid, in my play stores making play price tags to stick to the fast-sale things. I think, "Nah, leave the penny," but a few steps later there's a nickel, bright as an open eye on the gray stones, and it earns, in that way, my attention. As coin number two, it suggests a series, little coin-crumbs leading up to a Susan B. Anthony prize. (Wordless all this, the intrigues of finding and finding a way to proceed, stirred together, forming an inclination, steps toward.) I go back for them both.

Next comes a tiny feather. I have to go back for that, too, since I passed it, thinking, "Too small to be worth it," and "Not of the series." But it's so fresh, so dry in the slush, just-come-down, unmatted and perfect, from somewhere. The proper name *pin feather* attaches and helps; such precision lends weight. At first I thought, "It's enough just to note this," that noting alone would seal the feather in mind (remember, the rules are not yet worked out), and it's at just this moment that the experiment starts, the challenges firm, the rules finesse: *everything* found in the space of a block will be picked up and kept, and by way of that decision a synchronic study, *some* kind of picture, will emerge. The likelihood of finding stuff asserts, now that I'm saying "experiment," and the awareness of things-to-be-found is a form itself.

The things themselves are not talismans, not the result of magical spells (step-on-a-crack stuff, or if-I-reach-the-fence-before-the-light-turns). It's better than that. Things are evidence of a way of behaving, and the experiment's a form of alertness to take part in. A turning-toward, where slowly, one possibility shades into the next. Moves bear forth things. Thing begets thing.

Come two stalks of silver milkweed, dried and uprooted, blocks from the riverbank where they grow. And with them, the word *berm*, from way back, from nowhere—the place where so strangely, precisely, they've landed. Then a red ribbon. A cork. A weird lanyard crimped into a stiff, uncomfortable curl. Each rough, hempy end is wound like a noose with black plastic. It's the shape of the thing that complicates— too short for a bracelet, too lumpy to mark a place in a book. The materials tooth into each other, grip tightly, and pinch into hard spines at each side. That I can't tell what the lanyard is for makes me off-kilter. I want to drop it and change the rules, but the experiment's already in motion. Now I have a thing that just *is*. As a place for making knots, it reflects an afterthought, like the making smooth of a branch with a knife for the hell of it, practice, alleviation of boredom. A tension twists it, suggesting tendon/scar/pod. Broken finger or tail. Dendrite, those sprouting, frayed ends. The urge to go longer or to flatten asserts. I may be wrong about *afterthought*. There are intentions I cannot know. The story's still going, the end still furled. Discovery is current. Now. Right this minute. I pocket the thing and keep walking.

I find a rubbery fishbone skeleton. It's a cartoonish form with a triangle head, center bone, and three requisite ribs intersecting. It's ready to choke a mean cartoon cat. It fits in my hand. How it came loose from a whole is not clear. If it broke from a key chain, its eye isn't ripped and there's no telling grommet; if it fell from a necklace, there's no silver link. Decoration, fishing gear, useless cereal-box prize—I can't tell, but into my pocket it goes.

Stubby pencil with hospital logo, bottle cap, and wet envelope come. Then I see—I'm pretty sure—what will be the last thing. There's a lot of traffic today for some reason. My experiment's running along Linn St. between Market and Jefferson, and here I am, at the corner of Jefferson, my planned destination. A woman sees me eyeing the thing and together we laugh at its clear incongruence, right there in the street and so out of season, at how I'm timing my move because the traffic won't stop, and probably, too, because the sun's finally out and the town's finally warming after a very long winter. All this makes the present moment shine, the white golf tee shine on the wet, slushy cobbles, and the tether between us, the woman and me, firm up. I let all the cars pass. I dart out for the tee and she applauds as she crosses.

My path is complete now, here at the corner. But crossing with my pocket of loot, I wonder right off what to do if I find more stuff. If something comes, will I stop and reach down? Will extending the rules invite disappointment, the little deflations of staying too long, of trying to rekindle? Will overriding the experiment's frame wreck the objects' odd preciousness, stain the control, dilute the results—as second-guessing and too many choices dilute the good firm finality of a decision? These questions are part of the experiment, too. If the experiment's over and the boundaries marked off—does that mean it *ends*? Does the looking stop, do the objects stop coming and collecting cease? If I am not there, won't things still appear? I consider the notion of unclaimed surprises. Will anyone else's eye wander as mine does, and after the pleasures of finding and taking, wonder *now what* and *what's next?* I cross the street. In my pockets, all the stuff jangles.

I think there's more to it. I'm certain there is.

And though I didn't know it then, the experiment really wasn't over.

Months later, at my last dinner party, I gave away everything I found to ten friends. Before they arrived, I laid the things out on my bed and considered what would be best for each friend. The objects found their recipients easily, each attaching naturally to a certain person. To Brooke, the split hooves of milkweed spilling their down; lanyard to Jeremy; weird fish to Ryan, who also was puzzled by its origins. And one by one, as the things left my hands, I saw it: the experiment was still in motion! When the coins came, first they suggested *series.* Then *series* broadened. Parameters firmed: *allow everything, take it all in.* Then, when the time came to leave, things came to mean "remember me"—though there on the street, they spoke of this not at all, or so softly I heard nothing at the time.

I have to believe the experiment's end is disguised, even now, as "giving away." I have to believe orange fish/feather/lanyard, the experiment itself is underway still, and that my starting point on the cobbly street was no starting point at all. And that my room, that night, emptied of stuff, was not at all empty.

This seems like a lot to come to. This seems like enough to me.

It takes only a moment to decide.

I let the phone ring and ring and don't answer. And now I'm in it.

My breathing is loud. Drinking coffee is loud. Keeping silent is a thing I'm doing with the whole of my body and I hear things anew. I take deeper breaths the better to expel more air, because voice isn't here to help me sigh, to shape a thought with sound.

Ice breaks loose and slides roughly down the big skylight, and I startle, but let no brisk exhalation escape. Will someone I absolutely *must* talk to come? Will I scribble comments on my yellow pad in response, or just stay away? Outside, everything is icing over. A guy scrapes his windshield, no gloves at all. With no words at all, I'm thinking that I'd last not three minutes like that before freezing up. It's windy and the trees are swaying stiffly. My breath catches when they bend lower than it seems they can bear, when it looks like they'll snap. If they snapped, how loud would it be? And ice pelting the skylight, is it lovely, is it lonely to eat uninterrupted by even the possibility of talk? I have terms to abide, rules to attend as I consider these things.

I'm reading an article about Roger Staubach and realize I don't know how to pronounce his name. I try an "au" then an "ow" in my head. I clear my throat after a jalapeño and hear my voice, way back there, against bone. Without my voice, something else rests too. Even listening feels loud, especially to the radio report about tin masks made for WWI soldiers whose faces were burned off or ruined in combat. Soldiers had not yet evolved instincts for trench warfare, and when they stuck their heads up and looked out they got blasted. Mirrors were banned in hospitals. Suicide was rampant. I conjure the sound of knuckles-on-tin-cheek. The disbelieving rap in air. The writer being interviewed, Caroline Alexander, has done an article about the masks for *Smithsonian Magazine*. Her voice is hard, righteous, assured. When asked about new prosthetic technologies, she refuses the shift in conversation, suggests that perhaps it would be better not to make war in the first place. She lets the words sit. She won't fill the quiet. An extra beat slips past the interviewer, into which the author's corrective tone seeps and stills. I very much admire her ferocity. I very much admire the effect of the silence.

The trees move without talking. Not that they were chatty before, but such a conjecture leads to all kinds of what-ifs. Their bent-to-near-snapping leads and leads. What do you say to a tree in peril? In my way I am answering: tension in the back confirming, ache in the neck abiding. According to the plan, I'm not going to speak all weekend.

And, yes, I am bored at times. Boredom is a state in which hope is secretly being negotiated. I keep that phrase on my bulletin board. A friend of mine advocates boredom for kids, so they might learn to rely on their inner resources. I think it's good to support certain states-of-being—fragile ones like boredom, in danger of being solved or eliminated. Similarly, I fear for aimlessness, restraint, reverie. On my watch list are the sidelong glance, the middle distance, chatting with strangers, frisson, navigating a body by scent, wandering. Anyway, I don't want to stop the experiment now. Phone calls come that can wait, though there's the call from a friend checking to see if I've lost power since the storm picked up and inviting me to his warm house for dinner—and for the night if I want. I do want. But I don't take the call.

By midnight I feel I can't breathe all that well. So I force myself to sleep. And who knows what I say then.

It's the next day—though the experiment makes a kind of continual present. As does the ice, silvering, encasing. I'm wondering what my first word will be. Should I choose, then, to say "LOVE" and set that in motion, to send my love a little telegram by way of my voice, by way of a clear stage from which he might feel it, many states and thousands of miles away? What's the one word I will choose to mark and measure the end of my silence? Should I let it surprise me, that first chancy word by which I buy back my voice? I'm of two minds: draw around the event something like a veil, and stage and perform the word—or let it slip out, like a secret under pressure, tired of holding back a force. It might be something like "Excuse me" after bumping someone in the tight aisles of the Coop, or "Ah" or "Um" as I gather my wits to answer a simple question. Or it may be a barely audible sigh, floating a vowel out, "O," for which, now, still, this morning, my breath alone serves richly. In my head, I try on various collisions with Big Expectations.

The snow blowers are a deep bass distraction, and when they still for a moment, regaining their strength, the thick voices of men at work fill in the silence. The sound rises and falls as the machines are crashed into banks of hard snow and the snow draws up into chutes then explodes in an arc like water from an uncrimped garden hose, hose I liked to stand on and fuss with, quietly hidden around the side of the house as my grandmother watered her extravagant roses. In that way, by silencing the running water, I could make her speak: "What?" and "Huh?" and eventually, "Hey, someone's up to something." In the garage, made for hiding, post-trickiness, is the oil-soaked concrete, the scent of lime/fertilizer/grass seed, rakes and hoes with worn wooden handles, beach pails and shovels, fringed canvas umbrella, inflatable seahorse, garden chairs whose scratchy weave marks your thighs with red lines.

It's a little past noon when I say it: "Hi." And then "No" in response to my housemate's offer of coffee. Two small, clear words. No rallying gems. No symbols or portents. Up in my room, I repeat the words to myself to feel the effect more privately: "Hi. No." My nose and throat engage, and some empty spaces fill up with reverb. The words sound good. Younger and rested. More necessary. Relieved of something and freshened.

Coda

I found pearls. I found a diary. I found a black thong and blue condoms in a pile. I found five T-bones still wrapped and frozen. A set of house keys with an address tag nearly led to my first big crime. I found a packet of private-stash pictures. I found a thesis red-slashed on each page. I found a cold jay with its heart still beating. I found a phone, an iPod, a joystick. I found tinned caviar perfectly chilled. I found a wallet stuffed with Euros, a man's shoe, a Swiss army knife, plane tickets to Prague. I found an old mercury thermometer unbroken, and it confirmed a balmy 35 degrees. My name appeared in the cobbles' damp pock marks. I plucked a single blade of grass, very fresh, very green, from a crack in the sidewalk: the first blade of the year, and *I* found it—amazing!

What loot! Such a cache and a trove!

Tell me then—are these better finds? Are they somehow more than coin/feather/lanyard? Wilder things confer on me . . . *what*? Lend the experiment undercurrent, scent of an unnamed district/arrondissement/sector, and make the very stones underfoot remarkable? There's a rhythm, I know, *a drive* to this list. Doesn't it, though, blast my quieter point about discovery—its ongoingness, the surprise of that? Doesn't all this excitement override thoughts about beginnings and endings—that they're wobbly and unfixed and slip past their boundaries? Is it *not enough* to know that a street with its stuff, its overlooked prizes, curves and bends, makes its way to my eye, my hands, makes its way to my room for one very rich season, then passes into the hands of others?

As for experiment #2, the words, the "Hi" and the "No"—how my housemate, a visiting philosopher from Italy, hoped for better ones. We discussed it a lot. She wanted the experiment refined, improved— for me to have undertaken it on a sunny day, to have kept the silence rolling for a week. To have dealt with others, shopping and teaching, and encountered problems that required rerouting all the usual vocal solutions. She wanted to see me negotiate harder. And yes, of course, the experiment could have been revved. But what happened that weekend moved by degrees. It was about small adjustments and deepening time. Silence in its most animate form. It included sensations, their span from icy, darkened moments to those blowing and flying, cracking and pelting—time and sensation slipping from worn, gray sky to frayed hose, the gray weave below the green casing, precise pressure I had to apply, all my weight on one foot, making sure the hose crossed the concrete path so I might properly clamp off the water, stop the brown, threaded O-mouth from gushing—or spraying, if my grandmother was using the nozzle to mist her roses somewhere in the long, hot core of summer.

Surely there is a calibration for all this. Surely such moments are worth noting, small as they are, moving forth and retracing, mildly roving. Surely nothing more amped—stop the noise, kill the hype— need happen to make one certain of existing. Existing precisely, existing acutely—as, say, after a fast, when eating commences, the tongue rides slowly the slick curve of a green olive, singular morsel, whose skin resists just a little, then gives, and there comes a burst of briny, sharp pleasure. Then the paring away, down to rough pit. Rolling the pit. Holding it, shifting—all those tender and ordered attentions.

Then comes a cool sip.

Ice against teeth. Sweat on the glass.

A breath. Conversation.

Abundance dosed out so as not to confound with its rush of riches.

Nominated by Agni, B.J. Ward, Paul Zimmer, Andrea Hollander Budy

DEVOTION: FLY

by BRUCE SMITH

from AGNI

A FLY LIKE AN ENVOY for the Lost Boys or a delegate sent to dicker with the dead. Does it want in or out? Does it belong to the generations of generations or descend from one who grazed the face of Dickinson and whispered in her ear the middle octave key of F? Does it want nectar or the dead, and which am I? Vectors for fugue and spontaneous bruising. Vectors for pestilence and gods who call for sacrifice. Shit seraph, heaven worm, world eye, scholar bent over the heated pages of the Coptic translating the words *matter* and *heaven* in its three-week Paradiso. Fly worries everything. Fly walks on the ceiling. Fly works its rosary, a discalced nun of doubt, our intercessionary, while we are free to be evermore certain about our God and the war. Fly buzzes in the blown-open pages of the tiny novellas everyone carries scattered like dreams in which we were all the characters. Fly already at it, its story, a secondhand story, before smoke and a steel-blue wash over everything. Looking up the way the Myrmidons looked up at the sun, skeptical, sweaty while they killed the ram and ewe, strung the bow, lifted timbers. It was their job to fight for someone's love and rage, someone's beauty worth dying for.

Nominated by Agni, Diann Blakely

WHAT THE WORLD WILL LOOK LIKE WHEN ALL THE WATER LEAVES US

fiction by LAURA VAN DEN BERG

from ONE STORY

MADAGASCAR WAS NOT THE FIRST EXPEDITION on which I had accompanied my mother. We'd started traveling together the year I turned seventeen, after my father called from Alaska to say he wouldn't be returning from his ice-fishing trip and my mother, a biologist who specialized in rainforest primates, told me it was time I saw the world.

As we landed in Fort Dauphin, south of Madagascar's capital, the morning sun blazing copper through the small windows, my mother told me to stop calling her *mother* and to start calling her *June*, adjusting her oversized black sunglasses—she'd started wearing them all the time, even at night and indoors—as she explained *mother* made her feel old and undesirable. In the year without my father, the same year she turned forty-five, her age had appeared on her face like a terrible secret. The delicate half-moons underneath her eyes had hardened and crinkled, lines appeared in her forehead. Her hair grayed, though she'd dyed it blonde to cover the evidence. It was even startling to me, the person who saw her day after day. Sometimes I wondered if she wasn't in Madagascar to research deforestation and primate populations for her latest book, but to charge through the vines and bushes in hope of finding some fountain of youth, to splash river water on her face and paste mud against her skin; to look for a cure.

My mother was a leading expert on primate habitats and a tenured professor at Cornell, though she'd been on leave since my father left us. Antananarivo University's biology department, concerned about the drop in primate populations, was funding her Madagascar expedition. She had a theory that the lemurs, who consumed much of the fruit in the rainforests and buried the seeds after eating, were trying to re-plant their damaged habitats. But since lemur populations were lower in deforested areas, she believed the rainforests would never regenerate, because the lemurs weren't there to plant the seeds. This theory, she had told me, would be the centerpiece of her next book.

After landing, we entered a black taxi and my mother directed the driver to Hotel Le Dauphin, where we would be staying for the next twelve weeks, on the island's eastern tip. Nearly everyone in Madagascar spoke French, although my mother had taught me some basic Malagasy on the plane. Outside the airport, the taxi lurched down a pot-holed road, jostling us in the backseat. Such was the nature of travel in these remote corners, but my mother loved it all, the frantic car rides, getting off the plane, walking down the little stepladder, and going right onto the tarmac, the sky opening before her, dangerous and romantic.

By the time we embarked on the Madagascar trip, I'd been on sabbatical from high school for nearly a year and had given a lot of thought to what I wanted to do with my life. Somewhere between our first trip together—in the past year, we'd been all over South America and to New Guinea—and arriving in Madagascar, I'd decided to become a long-distance swimmer.

I first saw the ocean in my tenth year, when I visited Montauk with my parents, who dressed me in flippers and goggles before sending me into the Atlantic. I remembered turning around, the water closing over my shoulders, and waving to my parents, their distant silhouettes blending together on the shore. It was the only time I recalled them standing so close. After Montauk, I joined the school swimming team and by the time I started traveling with my mother, I had accumulated a bedroom full of trophies.

I didn't see that much open water again until I spent a month in Uruguay, near the Southern Atlantic. That was the first trip I took alone with my mother, who was there to study marmosets with a South American scientist named Alfonso. After my father announced his plans to stay in Alaska, my mother had collected me from the high school I attended in upstate New York on a December afternoon, my hair still wet from swimming practice, and instructed me to pack a suitcase for Uruguay. Travel light, she'd said, and bring some bug spray. We'd stayed in a village inn outside the port city of Montevideo. I had my own room and only a few nights passed before I heard Alfonso's voice next door and my mother's laugh rising and falling like an echo. I spent my days staring at the marmosets she and Alfonso trapped in the rainforest for observation, small creatures that thrived on leaves and insects and had plumes of fur for tails. I ate eggs and sweetbreads and let the boy who sold me empanadas slip his hands underneath my shirt. Some nights, I sat outside for hours and watched the river rush behind the inn.

During those days, there was so much I didn't know. I hadn't yet traveled to Argentina in a small airplane that shuddered as it passed over emerald-colored fields. Or returned to South America after only a few days of being back in New York, of sleeping in my own bed and pocketing eyeliner from the neighborhood drugstore, because my mother's contact had called to tell her that after a logging company deforested a primate habitat, the marmosets started pushing each other from trees, and she wanted to see it for herself. I didn't yet know what it felt like to be too jet lagged to sleep or eat, to get bitten by a jumping viper and have a medicine woman suck the poison from my arm, to have boys throw empty beer cans at my bare legs because I was young and foreign and wouldn't let them lead me into a windowless room with a door that locked. Or to watch my mother disappear into the dark canopy of a rainforest—her camouflage baseball cap pulled low, binoculars swaying from her neck, a knife tucked into her belt—and wonder if she would ever come back. Whenever I confessed my worries, she told me that if I kept brushing against death, little by little, fear would become a memory and I'd be able to face anything.

In the taxi my mother elbowed me and pointed at a tall, crusty tree. "That's a triangulated palm. They're endangered, Celia, like everything else on this island." Then she described the lemurs I would see in the rainforests outside Fort Dupain: Black-and-Whites, Makis, Sifakas, Indris. "And in a few days, we'll meet Daud, a zoologist from Antananarivo University," she continued. "He's coming all the way from the capital to work with me."

The space inside the taxi felt too small, the air heavy and sour, so I rolled down the window. I was hanging my head outside, gulping down the breeze, when I heard the most terrible noise, shrill and gloomy, like an off-key trumpet. The sound came again and again, until I finally sank back into the car and closed the window.

"That's the mating call of the Indri lemurs," my mother said. "Ancient tribes in Madagascar believed that if you listened to the Indris long enough, your body would turn to stone from the inside out."

I leaned back in my seat and sighed, thinking of upstate New York, our pale yellow house with air conditioning and running water. I wondered what my father would say if he could see me here. Things between my parents had been tense for years before he decided to stay in Alaska. From my room, even with the door closed, I would hear them arguing about my mother's incessant traveling, "incessant" being a word my father used to describe many of the things she did.

The taxi dropped us at Hotel Le Dauphin, a fancy name for a two-story white stucco building with rooms like closets. Before I could unpack, my mother was at my door, ready to go exploring. We wandered through a market, the drumbeats and hissing fires drowning out the Indris, which had been even more audible from my hotel room. I wondered about swimming, how far we were from water. My mother ordered us red rice with grasshoppers from a food stand. No knives or forks were used in Madagascar, only large spoons. I started flicking the grasshoppers onto the ground with the lip of my spoon and my mother said, after all the traveling I'd done in the last year, that I should be more accepting of local customs, though I could tell she was dismayed by the food stand's use of paper plates. At home, she would, for conservation, wring the water from paper towels and hang them to dry. Once, when I invited over friends from school, they made the mistake of commenting on the paper towels, and my mother lectured them about the earth's dwindling reserves, and after dinner, instead of driving us to the video store, she made us watch a documentary on the Gibbon population in the Congo.

I poked the charred grasshoppers until they disappeared into the mound of red rice, then stared at my mother, trying to see her eyes through her sunglasses, a constant shield between herself and the world. We were physical opposites: my mother bronzy and tall, all sinew and bone, while I was dark-haired and small, soft around the shoulders and belly. It wasn't until I began eating that I realized the earth, the dust, was red too—deep and dark like an open wound. It had already stuck to the legs of my mother's jeans and stained the toes of my sneakers. I told her I couldn't eat any more rice, soothing her protests by remembering to call her *June*.

Daud arrived from the Capital on a Sunday. He was in his mid-thirties, handsome and broad-shouldered and wearing a pair of hiking boots so old the soles were worn thin. When I first saw him, I was starting down the hotel stairs. There was no running water that morning and I was going to see what could be done. Daud stood in the small space between the stairs and the hotel entrance. The sun beating through the skylight gave his skin a deep sheen. His nose was slightly crooked, as though it might have been broken once, and there was an unexpected delicacy to his ears. Their shape reminded me of seashells. A large patch from Antananarivo University was stitched onto his backpack. I stopped moving down the stairs. He turned towards me, his eyes narrowed in the light. I could hear the Indris; the heat was pressing. I had already gotten terrible sunburns, my shoulders flushed and peeling. My mother had joked that it looked like I was molting.

Before I could say anything, I saw my mother in the hotel entrance. If she noticed me standing at the top of the staircase, she didn't let me know it. She swept into the room, dressed in khaki pants and a loose white blouse, wearing her sunglasses.

"I just watched two Sifaka lemurs nearly kill each other over a mate," she told Daud. "Don't they have an amazing way of fighting, the way they spin across the dirt like dancers?"

"Their kind of love makes ours look easy," he said.

"Did you know I was one of the first to photograph Golden-Crowned Sifakas?" my mother asked. "They were so rare, it took us weeks of trekking in the rainforest to find them. You've probably seen some of my footage." I watched her take Daud's arm and lead him outside, struck by how the light that made his skin glow only turned hers dull and gray. I knew she'd been rising before dawn to observe the lemurs—I'd often wake as she was washing her face and dressing in the other room, as though our bodies were synchronized—and the malaria medicine had probably been giving her bad dreams. Her hair had looked brittle in that hotel lobby, her cheeks shadowed and sunken, although she'd also somehow never looked so beautiful, wearing her exhaustion with a regalness that seemed new to me. If I'd passed her quickly or been watching from another angle, if she'd turned her head towards the light a little more, I might have mistaken her for a stranger.

At the end of each day in the field, Daud returned to the hotel with red dirt streaked across his white T-shirt, his skin gleaming from the heat, humming a familiar-sounding song, which I eventually recognized as *The Impossible Dream*. He spoke English fluently, and I loved the way he could make my own language sound alluring. He told me about life in Antananarivo, teal and red motorbikes weaving around pedestrians, street vendors selling cotton shirts and Zebu meat; about tribes in Madagascar that believed spirits dwelled in trees and planted one at each village entrance to keep away evil; about how the sprits abandoned the trees at nightfall and no one left their house after dark.

Daud spent his days with my mother, observing lemurs in the rainforest and trapping and tagging a select few, so they could analyze how deforestation had changed their patterns of eating and mating and nesting. Afterwards, the three of us would have dinner together on the concrete terrace that extended out the back of the hotel. At these dinners, I became a kind of pet for my mother and Daud. During the day, they had lemurs in common and at night, they had me.

"Celia has the most astonishing memory," my mother said one evening, after we'd finished our bowls of lichee and mango, and then asked me to recite one of the lists she'd taught me since my father left, like European cities with the highest crime rates or the most polluted places on earth.

"Come on," my mother urged. "Don't be modest. Why don't you do pollution this time?"

I would have preferred to list the names of everyone who'd swam the English Channel, like Lynne Cox, who'd done it when she was only fifteen, or talk about Lewis Gordon Pugh, who broke the record for the coldest long-distance swim in Antarctica.

"Ranipe, India," I began. "Then La Oroya, Peru, and Linfen, China." From there, I moved to Dzerzhinsk in Russia and Haina in the Dominican Republic and Kabwe in Zambia.

"And of course," I finished. "There's Chernobyl." My mother had always been fascinated by the ruined landscape of Chernobyl. Anyone who keeps a nuclear power plant in business, she liked to say, should have to eat their own plutonium.

266

"Peru?" Daud said in response to my list. "I wouldn't have guessed that."

"It's because of the metal processing plant in La Oroya," I replied. "And the toxic emissions of lead."

"What else have you got?" he asked, ladling lichee juice into his spoon.

"A list of all the famous scientists who've committed suicide," I said. "And how they did it."

"I didn't know that many had," he replied, then sat back in his chair and waved his hand, as if to say *but prove me wrong*.

I cited Adolphe d'Archiac, who threw himself into the Seine River, and Garrett James Hardin, who committed suicide with his wife, and Percy Williams Bridgman, who shot himself, and James Leonard Brierley Smith, who took cyanide, and Viktor Meyer, who also took cyanide. When my mother taught me this list, she said I needed to understand the toll answering important scientific questions could take on a person. After Viktor Meyer, I could have continued, but Daud was staring at me, holding his spoon in midair, and I grew shy from his attention.

"Seems cyanide was the way to go," he said after I'd stopped.

"It does kill you pretty quickly," I said.

"June." He turned to my mother. "You certainly have given your daughter quite the education."

"Most parents shield their children from reality," she said. "But I wanted Celia to learn about hardship early on."

My mother started going on about pain being the root of knowledge, a Simone Weil quote she never attributed, but I had stopped listening. Instead, I looked at Daud, who was gazing at my mother, entranced, no doubt, by the way she spoke. The lilt in her voice still got my attention, even though I'd been hearing it all my life.

I kept in touch with my father after he settled in Alaska. He wrote me long letters about the endless dark of winter and the way the ice glowed silver during twilight and Lana, the woman who had been his ice-fishing guide. He was living in her cabin outside Fairbanks. I never told my mother how much I looked forward to his letters. Sometimes, if we'd been traveling for a few months, I'd find two or three waiting for me in New York. I was careful to not let her know when I started writing back.

My father was concerned that I wasn't going to school anymore. I

267

assured him that while I wasn't in the classroom, I was still getting an education of sorts. I had, for example, become fluent in Spanish and French and, in a letter sent from Hotel Le Dauphin, I wrote him some words in Malagasy—*Tsy azoko* for *I don't understand, veloma for goodbye.* I knew rainforests once covered fourteen percent of the earth, but now it was down to six. I could identify the medicinal sedges used to treat dysentery and fevers and explain how carnivorous plants digested insects. *As soon as she finishes her lemur research, I'll be studying right angles and Beowulf in New York again*, I kept promising my father in my letters, adding on more than one occasion that my mother had worked something out with the school's headmaster, which was a lie. I didn't know where my mother and I were headed after Madagascar, although I had a feeling it wasn't upstate New York. She'd always been a light traveler, but when she finished packing for this trip, her closet was nearly empty. Something had changed. I just didn't know what.

There were several times when I considered asking my father if I could live with him, but I never did—somehow sensing, without him ever saying as much, that Alaska wasn't an option for me. I did visit him once at Lana's cabin, three months before my mother and I left for Madagascar (I had convinced my mother to let me go by saying I was interested in studying polar bears). Lana turned out to be a lanky, dark-haired woman, elegant in a quiet, vaguely sad sort of way. She had lived in Alaska all her life and had no desire to travel elsewhere. My father and I never talked about his leaving: we seemed to have a mutual understanding that what was in the past should stay there. He took me bird-watching every morning, and we observed great gray owls and American dippers through binoculars. In the afternoons, we went to a lake near Lana's cabin—a pond really, small and sunken and rimmed with brown grass—and listened to the arctic loons howl in the distance.

At night, Lana would fry fish and after dinner, we sat on the porch and drank beer until the stars pulsed. Our time together was pleasant, but cautious, like a trio of acquaintances leery of attempting more than small talk. One night, Lana told us the Inuits believed death dwelled in the sky and pointed out the aurora borealis, where you were supposed to see images of loved ones dancing in the next life. I searched for my mother, but didn't see anything that reminded me of her and was relieved. At the time, she was finishing a river expedition in the Amazon and if something had happened, I probably wouldn't have known about it yet. I stayed in Alaska for eight nights and during every one, I dreamt of Amazonian snakes: silvery blindsnakes and banded pipesnakes, giant vipers and anacondas. I would wake in the early morning, kicking away the sheets in a panic, to make sure nothing was coiled at the bottom of the bed.

One evening, after my father and Lana left for a walk, I searched a chest drawer for matches to light the kindling I'd arranged in the fireplace and came across a bundle of letters. They were the letters I had sent my father during my travels, and as I unfolded them one by one, I was struck, despite less than a year having passed, by how young the handwriting looked: loopy letters that couldn't hold a straight line on the page. A child's handwriting, I'd thought when I finished reading them, the house dark and the fireplace still cold. A child's promises.

Every morning my mother and Daud went into the field and didn't return until dusk. One afternoon, my mother, wanting me to do some exploring of my own, arranged for a villager to take me down the river in a *pirogue*, a canoe made from a hollowed log. At first, I thought the stretch of water that divided the rainforest might be a good place for practicing my butterfly, but every time I saw a crocodile basking on the banks, something in my chest clutched.

I tried staying in my room and passing the time by reading. It was cooler in the hotel and I'd snuck some fashion magazines into my suitcase (my mother disapproved of magazines unless they had to do with science). After reading each one twice, I grew bored and moved onto the books my mother had packed for me, books about women having adventures: *Out of Africa, Jane Eyre, Delta of Venus.* But I couldn't concentrate with the Indris and the stories didn't really appeal to me, the mess of love and longing, women adrift—not when I wanted to be reading about swimming techniques, breathing control and resistance training. Some afternoons, I would spend the whole day counting and recounting the money I'd been hoarding since I began traveling with my mother: the pesos left over from what she'd handed me to buy chajá cakes for her and Alfonso in Uruguay, the fifty-peso note she'd given me for a camera in Argentina (I'd picked the cheapest one, then told her it was expensive and there was no change), the stack of ariarys she'd allotted me when we arrived in Madagascar, for food and souvenirs. Eventually I began leaving the hotel, but without the excitement I had earlier in the year, when life with my mother was still enticing. Instead there was a heaviness, a feeling of premature exhaustion and age.

I started taking long walks, stopping to pry open pitcher plants and examine termite hills and scorpions and huge Malagasy tombs—stone compounds decorated with bright geometric paintings and animal skulls. I said prayers outside the tombs, my folded hands smudged with red, and asked whoever was supposed to be listening to not let my organs morph into stone, for I kept dreaming everything inside me was oblong and gray. I took pictures until my film ran out. The last photo was of a passing bus. The hubcaps were dented and rusted, the windows rolled down. Everyone on the bus was singing. Sometimes, for no reason at all, I would break out running and keep going until my knees gave and I was gasping for air.

I found a little bar on the village outskirts, a tin-roofed shack with dust and spiders and an old radio that played electronic dance music. On my first visit, the bartender filled my glass with a clear liquor that burned my throat. I returned every day for two weeks. I never saw another customer, but I didn't mind. I thought the solitude would help me sort out my life. I liked to think of what I would do once I returned to New York. Re-enroll in high school and get back on the swim team. Practice with more dedication than anyone else, swimming before and after school, forgoing lunch to be in the water. Sometimes I wondered what Daud would think if he saw me sitting in the bar, my sweat-soaked tank top clinging to my skin; I had seen the way my mother touched his forearm when she laughed, detected the smoothness in his voice when he called her *June*. One afternoon, after leaving the bar, I got dizzy and vomited on a plant with pointed leaves. I didn't go back again. In all the time I spent there, the only words the bartender and I exchanged were when I thanked him—*misaotra*—for the drinks.

It wasn't much longer before I heard Daud's voice in my mother's room for the first time. I listened carefully, but the sound of the Indris increased at night, and I just heard whispers and laughter and then Daud's humming. At dinner the next evening, my mother kept throwing significant glances in his direction, and he reached across the table to brush strands of hair from her face. It soon became their habit to only discuss fieldwork, rarely speaking to me directly. I sometimes caught my mother looking at Daud with a kind of possessiveness as she closed me out of conversations by talking science. I was left to drift in my imagination, to picture what my life would look like if I was away from here.

"Did you hear about the spider monkeys that attacked a tourist in Manja?" I asked them one night, just to see if I could get their attention. They had been talking about the nesting patterns of Pygmy Mouse lemurs for an hour. "I heard they scratched out an Italian woman's eye."

"Spider monkeys aren't naturally aggressive," Daud said. "They must have been provoked."

"And there aren't spider monkeys in Manja." For the first time that evening, my mother turned to me. "It seems your source was wrong, Celia."

She and Daud resumed their conversation about Pygmy Mouse lemurs. I went upstairs and pulled the shoebox that held my money from underneath my bed, fanned the brightly colored foreign bills across the floor and made uneven stacks with the coins. I spent the rest of the evening using my stash to create little towers and bridges and moats, a city of paper and metal, an escape.

My walks started getting longer, bringing me all the way to the coast. It took over an hour, but being near the water made me feel less restless. By the shoreline, the foliage was paler and drier, the hills lower, and then the landscape broadened into a wide curve of sand, speckled with gray rock and sea foam. I would wade up to my knees, nervous of going too far, of riptides and sharks. Each time I went, I promised myself I'd go far enough to feel the sandy floor disappear beneath me, the chill of deeper waters, but I never did. I was always looking for a point I could swim towards—another shoreline, a little clump of land, a large rock—but there was nothing: no land, just the sea, beaming like the sun had cracked open and seeped into the waves.

Once, as I walked down the path that led to the sea, I heard a rumbling noise and turned to see a Jeep slowing beside me, Daud in the driver's seat, alone and waving. He rolled down the window and offered me a ride. When I got in, I asked why he wasn't in the field with my mother, and he said they'd been working nonstop for weeks and he was taking a break.

"Thought I'd go for a drive," he said. "Maybe see the ocean."

"I go there all the time." I took my hair, stiff from sun and seawater, down and shook my head. I used to keep my hair short, but since I started traveling, I'd let it keep growing.

"Long walk," he said.

"It's worth it."

When we arrived, he parked on the edge of the beach and we got out. The ocean was blue and quiet. Daud removed his hiking boots, then peeled off his T-shirt and tossed it onto the hood of the jeep. I touched the point of his shoulder and, trying to channel the confidence of my mother's voice, asked if he wanted to swim with me.

"You should be careful," he said. "There are strong currents if you go out too far."

"It's not so bad," I said.

"Then you lead the way."

I smiled and dropped my backpack in the sand. I jogged into the ocean, hesitating when the water crossed my knees, but heard Daud's footsteps behind me and kept going. Once the water covered my shoulders, I swung my arms until I could no longer see the bottom, trying to look practiced and at ease, imagining Lewis Gordon Pugh paddling through the arctic and Lynne Cox crossing the English Chanel. When I finally stilled, the muscles in my legs quivering, I turned in the water. The coast was about half a mile away, shimmering like cut glass, and Daud was moving towards me in a leisurely freestyle.

"You've got good speed," Daud said when he reached me. His face was wet and gleaming.

"I won two division swimming championships in high school," I said, thinking of the trophies in my bedroom, made from fake marble with little plastic swimmers affixed to the top. "And I was a runner-up in the state championship. I would have gone to regionals if I hadn't left school to travel."

"Your mother must have been proud," he said.

I looked across the water, not telling him my father was the only one who ever attended my meets or photographed me with my trophies. I asked Daud about what surrounded Madagascar, and he said the Mozambique Channel was six hundred miles to the west, the Mascarene Islands five hundred miles to the east.

"The record for long-distance swimming is just over two thousand miles, set by Martin Strel when he swam the Mississippi," I said. "So it would be possible to swim the Mozambique Channel or reach the Mascarene Islands."

"Open water swimming is different," Daud said. "There are no lanes, no one to blow the whistle."

"I know." I pictured us going out even farther, the low roar of the ocean filling my ears. "That's why I want it."

We didn't say anything more for a while. We bobbed in the water, the sun bright against our faces. The longer we stayed, the farther the shore seemed. I found the openness both terrifying and intoxicating— a part of myself fighting the impulse to swim back to solid land, another part wanting to plunge myself into this kind of vastness again and again. I was afraid of so many things, I had come to realize during my traveling year. My mother seemed to have a perplexing immunity to fear, the way she hurled herself into foreign lands and the arms of men, while I was always entangled in ideas about penalties and peril.

I started to ask Daud what being in the field with my mother was like when he disappeared underwater, leaving only a blanket of ripples where his head had once been. I spun around, looking for him, waiting to feel his hands graze my knees. I stared across the water and shouted his name. When he didn't surface, my body got heavy and slow with panic, with thoughts of sea creatures and underwater black holes. But then he appeared in the distance, grinning and flapping his arms. Before I could call to him, he vanished again, this time staying under even longer, until I felt vibrations around my legs and he reappeared right in front of me, bursting through the water with the force of a sea god.

"How did you learn to do that?" I asked. "To hold your breath for so long?"

He told me that when he was young, he'd go swimming in the ocean with his brothers after school. "Some afternoons we'd race," he said. "You need to be strong. And to be able to hold your breath for a long time. We'd take turns pushing each other underwater."

"Can you show me?" I drifted closer to Daud, wondering if it was possible to cure fear. "Teach me the way you learned?"

He rested his hands on my shoulders, our noses nearly touching. Water had beaded in his eyelashes, making them darker and longer. He stared at me for what felt like a long time. Then he thrust me underwater and held me there for maybe twenty seconds. He released me long enough for me to take a single breath, then pushed me down again. I opened my eyes the second time, saw the shadows in the water and Daud's legs. By the time he pulled me up, my lungs were aching. His hands slipped down my chest, his fingers momentarily clinging to my breasts before he regained a grip on my shoulders. Each time he took me underwater, he kept me there longer, until I started scrambling against the weight of his hands. His palms were like stones against my shoulders; I twisted and squirmed, getting wild with panic, my fingers thumping his chest and stomach. The last time he took me under, I felt the back of my brain go fuzzy and my vision waver, started to imagine death swooping down from the sky like a great black bird, and in the instant after a weightlessness washed over me, he let me rise for air.

We swam back to shore slowly, Daud's hand on the center of my back. "It's good for you to struggle against the water," he said, "in case you ever get sucked down by a strong tide. You have to know how to fight."

When we reached land, I lay in the sand, exhausted. It was late in the afternoon and the sky had started to darken. Daud sat next to me, asked if I was okay, and I nodded. My shorts and tank top were soaked, my white bra straps exposed. I looked down and saw the small ridges of my nipples. I didn't try to cover myself, feeling too tired and too brave. Daud's body was lean, his forearms and calves roped with muscle. He had a pale scar in the shape of a horseshoe on his chest. I wanted to touch it, but sensed I should not. I told him about the lists I'd started keeping on my own, different from the ones my mother encouraged me to memorize. The one I thought about the most was famous disappearances: Amelia Earhart, Jimmy Hoffa, Ambrose Bierce. I wondered if the mysteries of their lives would ever be solved, how long someone would look for me before my name was added to such a list. He didn't ask me questions, just let me talk. We stayed there— close but never touching—until it was nearly dark.

We returned to the hotel forty-five minutes late for dinner. My mother was waiting for us on the terrace, her plate empty. As Daud and I took our seats, I noticed our plates were heaped with food. My hair, still wet, stuck to the back of my neck, my clothes dusted in sand. Before I started eating, I tucked my bra straps back underneath my tank top. I was relieved Daud had put his shirt on before we arrived at the hotel.

"Turnips with garlic and ginger tonight," my mother said. "I'm sure it tasted better when it was hot."

"How did it go this afternoon?" Daud asked.

"I got amazing footage of the Red-Ruffed lemurs," my mother said. "When you see the clips, you'll wish you'd been there."

"It sounds like you managed well enough without me," he said.

"I always manage well on my own." My mother sat a little straighter in her chair before telling us meaningful scientific research was best done in solitude, that collective thought only diluted the strongest ideas. "Did Walter Buller have research teams?" she asked us. "Did William Swainson?

"June," Daud said. "They were working at the turn of the century."

"That's not the point," she said.

In the dusk, I couldn't see my mother's eyes through her sunglasses, though I suspected she was looking at me. I focused on scooping turnips with my spoon.

"Celia took me swimming today." Daud pushed away his plate. "I didn't realize she had such talent."

"You do have a few trophies at home, don't you?" My mother tapped her upper lip with her index finger for a moment, pretending to not remember.

She stood and dropped her napkin. "I already checked with the cook, and there's no dessert tonight." The sky was dark, the terrace lit only by the dim glow of lightbulbs hanging from a wire. She walked away from the hotel, towards the tall grass and trees. Daud looked at me, started to say something, then followed her.

I called my father from the hotel owner's office. Lana answered and when she heard my voice, she passed him the phone without saying anything. He asked after my mother and I told him that I didn't think she'd be returning to New York after all. I had been longing to tell someone about the way she was changing, how much she seemed to have aged in the last year and how hard she was pushing against it.

"She's not changing," my father said. "She's just laying her cards on the table."

"But why now?"

"Because she doesn't have to pretend she wants to live the same life that I do anymore."

"She's making me call her by her first name."

"When your mother turned thirty, she cut off her hair and went to Mexico for two weeks. She's never taken aging well." He sighed and shifted across the line. "And I never understood why she was so inter-

275

ested in those lemurs. I always thought they looked like deformed cats."

"It's because they're starting to die. Too many trees are being cut down."

"It's just like your mother to pick something like that," he said. "It's not the lemurs she really cares about. It's being able to alter something bigger than she is."

"But couldn't she find another purpose? Something closer to home?"

"That's the problem," my father said. "She only has one. And it's not you or me, either."

I rubbed the receiver against my cheek. Even in the hotel owner's office, the windows and door closed, I could still hear the Indris faintly. "I've decided to become a professional swimmer," I said.

"You mean like the competitions you did in high school?"

"Not exactly," I said. "I mean long-distance, open water."

"Why would you want to do that?"

"To go as far as I can."

"Celia," my father said. "Couldn't you pick something a little less dangerous?"

I told my father that I had been swimming every day and had never once been afraid. I wondered if he thought long-distance swimming was the kind of thing my mother would do, grueling and lawless. I didn't tell him that when I was in the water I always imagined a world famous coach, like Paul Blair or Doug Frost, trailing me in a motorboat and shouting commands through a megaphone—*straighten your legs, keep breathing, reach like you're grabbing onto the person you love most*. Or that when I was frightened by powerful tides or strange shadows in the waves, I thought of Daud holding me under, of the way he made me struggle, and kept swimming. Or that when I paused to catch my breath, I would sometimes turn in the water and see my parents on the shoreline, as I had as a child, two ghosts in my memory.

Not long after my swim with Daud, I heard shouting in my mother's room. It was late in the night. I had wrapped myself in a white sheet and was trying to read enough *Delta of Venus* to fall asleep. I sat up in bed and pressed my ear against the wall, but I only caught footstomping and door-slamming, which made my room shudder.

It occurred to me then that I should go to my mother. When I opened the door, she was sitting on the edge of the bed, facing away, head in her hands. She was naked, her clothes heaped in the corner. Her sunglasses and the postcards she usually traveled with—pictures of the Andes Mountains and the Amazon River and the desert where the Aral Sea had once been—were scattered across the floor. Some of the cards had unfinished messages written on the back, notes to friends and colleagues that had never been sent. Her hair sat stiffly on her shoulders, her back dotted with freckles. She'd lost weight since coming to Madagascar, and I could see her spine, curved and stretching her pale skin into translucence. She looked small and frightened, a huddled child. The sheets were tangled; the unshaded lightbulb hung from the ceiling at an odd angle. She was not crying, just sitting there, unmoving, and I did not know what to say. And so I closed the door, gently as possible, and went back to my room.

The morning after her fight with Daud, my mother woke me early and said she was taking me to the rainforest. When I asked about Daud, she told me the lens on their spotting scope had cracked and he'd gone to a nearby village to have it repaired. We drove down a grooved dirt road for about a mile before she parked in front of the dense treeline, fat with spade-shaped leaves and vines. She sat in the driver's seat for a moment longer, pale and sweating, and I thought of the way her naked back had looked the night before.

"Celia," she said. "Why have you been avoiding the forest?"

"I didn't know I had been."

"We've been here for six weeks and you've never once asked to come into the field with me. Don't you care about what's happening to the lemurs? Don't you want to see them?"

"I hear enough of them." Closer to the rainforest, the Indris were louder than ever, cawing in a way that made me want to scratch my ears. "I really don't think I'd mind if they went extinct."

"Which would leave me with nothing," my mother said, getting out of the car.

We carried backpacks; binoculars hung from my mother's neck. As we moved into the forest, the light darkened, shadowing leaves and vines. She was already a few feet ahead and I had to hurry to catch up. We walked down an overgrown path, thick with tree roots, and while the Indris must have been unbearably loud by then, the noise was not what I remembered. I remembered walking behind my mother, the sweat seeping through the back of her T-shirt, the sway of her blonde ponytail. Her telling me about lemurs having symbiotic relationships with tiny birds and the five layers of the rainforest: the overstory, the canopy, the understory, the shrub layer, and the forest floor. She said each part had its own little ecosystem, its own little universe. And weren't people like that too, she continued, worlds unto their own. I began to wonder if I had been avoiding the rainforest after all, wanting so badly to carve out a purpose that I'd had to find my own landscape. Or maybe I had been frightened of what existed here, scared that whatever had intoxicated my mother would reach me too, that my own desires would disappear into the mist and heat and ceiling of green.

My mother stopped to peer at two ringtails through her binoculars. She told me it was unusual to see a pair, since they typically traveled in groups. I was glad we didn't spot any of the lemurs she and Daud had trapped and tagged. It pained me to imagine these ringtails, who reminded me of small raccoons, being captured and sedated, my mother clipping little plastic bracelets around their spindly ankles and staring at them through the bars of a cage.

When my mother's right leg began cramping, we rested underneath a tree. I asked if she'd been getting cramps in her legs frequently and she nodded, adding that Daud got annoyed if she slowed them down. "Which is why you can't slow down," she said. "If you do, no one will wait for you."

"You've been working in jungles too long," I said. "People don't think like that everywhere."

"That's what you say now."

"Maybe we should go back to New York for a few months," I said. "I think I'd like to give school another try."

"You don't need high school," my mother said. "Algebra, sentence diagramming, spelling quizzes. None of that matters."

"But you have a doctorate," I said. "You couldn't be here if it weren't for your education."

"Nothing I learned in the classroom is helping me."

"I miss our house." I picked up a handful of dirt, then let the red earth fall through my fingers.

"There's nothing for us in New York," my mother said.

"But what will you do?" I looked away when I realized I'd said you and not we.

She stretched her arms. Her sunglasses were crooked on her face. "We should head back to South America. More primate habitats are scheduled to be deforested. A group of scientists are planning to protest outside the logging companies, to stand in front of machines. We could be part of a resistance."

But what was there for me in South America? I wanted to ask. My mother must have seen something in my expression because she pointed out a Crested Ibis swooping between the trees. She always drew my attention to birds when she wanted to change the subject.

In thirty minutes, she was paler and sweatier and the cramp in her leg still hadn't passed. "I think we should go back," I told her.

"I promised to get images of the Black-and-White lemurs today," she said. "They're at least a mile deeper into the forest."

So we got up and we walked. My mother didn't tell me the names of plants or tree frogs or anything else we passed. I knew she was unwell. She photographed the Black-and-Whites, who had a peculiar way of balancing atop bushes, and then we returned to the Jeep and went to the hotel. Daud was still not back. In her room, she lay down on the bed without undressing. I took off my shoes and lay next to her. Swimming had changed my body; the muscles in my legs were harder, the skin on my stomach darker and tighter. I looked at my mother's arms. Her wrists seemed fragile, the points of her elbows too angular.

"Maybe I should call the hotel owner," I said, my voice nearly a whisper. "If you're not feeling well."

She shook her head. Her sunglasses slipped down a little. "So you really want to be a swimmer?"

"I think so."

"When did this start?"

"While we've been traveling," I said, though I knew it had really begun long before.

"You have too much fear right now," she told me. "The man who took you canoeing said you wanted to turn back after passing the first crocodile." She rested her hands on her stomach. "When you commit yourself to swimming a river or across an ocean channel, you're committing yourself to the possibility of death. Your team, the people you train with, won't care if you drown or die of exhaustion. They'll only care if you break the record. And so that's all you can care about too."

"I've been practicing," I said.

"Do you swim until your legs are so tired that you can't kick anymore? Until you begin to sink?"

"No."

"See?" she said. "Still too much fear."

"That doesn't sound reasonable."

"Reason is overrated," she said. "Caution and beauty too."

We were quiet for a while, lying close enough for me to feel the heat of her skin, to smell the dirt and sweat. For a brief time, it was as calm as floating in a waveless body of water, someplace still and boundless.

"Celia," she finally said, her voice low and hoarse. "Do you think of me as *June*?"

"I've been calling you that, haven't I?"

"But in your mind. Am I *June* to you there?"

"Thinking of you as my mother is a pretty hard habit to break."

She sighed. And then she fell asleep. I stayed with her a little longer, staring at the cracks in the ceiling, spidery lines that reminded me of split earth. The room was hot. I was hearing the lemurs again, a blanket of noise like falling rain.

Daud returned late in the night and by the time I heard him climbing the stairs, my mother had been vomiting for hours. It had started soon after I returned to my room, when I heard retching through the walls and found her hunched over her small, rusted bathroom sink. Her sunglasses had fallen off and when she looked at me, I saw dark pockets underneath her eyes.

"Cholera," Daud said from the doorway. "She's been showing signs for a few days. Leg cramping, drowsiness. She's been filling her canteen with river water. I told her that wasn't a good idea, but she wouldn't listen."

"Why would you do that?" I shouted into the bathroom.

"I've been traveling for years and never been sick once." My mother was still leaning over the sink. "I'm supposed to be immune."

Daud said he needed to get an ORS packet, a powder of sugar, salt, and electrolytes that would be mixed with boiling water. The cholera would pass in a few days, but in the meantime, dehydration was a danger.

"I have some packets in my room," Daud said. I noticed he was still standing in the doorway, that he hadn't gone to my mother.

While he was away, my mother became delirious. She said the lemurs were dead and the forests were burning, that a flood was going to sweep away the hotel and crocodiles would rule the island. I was relieved when Daud returned, carrying a canteen filled with a mixture of hot water and the ORS powder. He handed me the canteen and I kneeled on the bathroom floor and cupped the back of my mother's head in my hand. She drank without protest.

We moved her to the bed and I took off her shoes. I was surprised by the narrowness of her feet, the little clusters of blue and purple veins bunched on her skin like constellations. The tops of her hands were beaded with sweat and for a moment I was afraid to touch her. I smoothed her hair and noticed gray roots coming in, as though someone had painted the peak of her head with ash.

Just as I was drawing my hand away, my mother wrapped her long fingers around my wrist. "This is why I need you here," she said before turning from me and drifting off.

Daud and I went into the hallway and sat on the floor, next to each other, our backs against the wall. He gave me another ORS packet for the morning.

"I'm going back to Antananarivo," he said.

I asked Daud what my mother had done. Things hadn't ended well in South America when Alfonso saw her passport and discovered she'd shaved a decade off her age. Maybe she'd done the same to Daud. Or wanted to take all the credit for their lemur research.

"Her theory is wrong," he said. "That's what we've been fighting about. Or that's part of it, anyway. Lemurs don't impact rainforest regrowth the way she thought. Rainforests are shrinking, but the deforested parts don't do better or worse without the lemurs and their seed-burying. The trees still start regenerating."

"Does she know she's wrong?"

"Knowing and believing are two different things," he said.

"Maybe when she gets better, she'll come around."

"We both know that's not going to happen," Daud said. He drummed his fingers against the scuffed floorboards. "Have you given any thought to getting out of here?"

"A little." I knew all those moments of closeness, when we talked in the rainforest and in her room, when I poured the hydration mix into her sick body, would be forgotten once she'd recovered, once she was back to acting like all those human concerns, even love, didn't touch her.

"You could come back to Antananarivo with me. Stay in the city a little while, see if we can't find you someone to train with." Daud touched my elbow. His fingertips felt warm and smooth.

"I can't leave my mother like this," I told him.

Daud shrugged. "Would she stay for you?"

"I don't know," I said. "But I'm not her."

He rested his head against the wall, his throat curved and muscular, and started humming. I wondered what it would feel like to be in the company of a man who didn't know my mother, who saw me without the shadow of my origins. I would be free to offer a self I had selected and shaped, to pretend I knew nothing of science, that I'd never traveled beyond the New York state lines, that I only understood water and openness and quiet.

"You can't hear the Indris as much from here," I said. "If only I'd known that sooner. I might have slept in the hallway."

"The lemurs have gotten used to people over the years, gotten lazy," he said. "But some people think they drove the first British colonists who attempted to settle the island mad." He told me the Latin root of *lemur* meant *ghost* because of the way they could blend noiselessly into the rainforest and dart from tree to tree so swiftly, they were nearly invisible. He'd read travel journals from British sailors that described being awakened at night by screams, but never finding the culprits, and entering forests with the sensation of being followed, but never understanding what was tracking them, if something was there at all.

"Hard to believe they were actually feared," I said. "They just look like sad little monkeys now." I recalled the way some of them clung to the trunks, as though their homes might topple at any moment.

"I wanted to give you these before I left." Daud took an envelope from his back pocket and handed it to me. "I shot them a few weeks ago."

I opened the envelope and found two pictures inside: one of an Indri, the creature that had been tormenting me so, crouched in the crook of a tree, timid and pitiful under the glare of Daud's camera. The other was of my mother kneeling on the rainforest floor, elbow-deep in black mud, as though she had hooked her fingers around a treasure and was dragging it to the surface.

Once my mother had fully recovered and Daud had been gone for a few days, I announced my plans to leave. I told her in the evening, while we had dinner on the patio. I had been swimming that afternoon—for the last time in those waters—and let myself bob in the sea like a buoy. My hair was still damp and smelled of brine.

"I'm tired," I said. "I need to go someplace familiar."

"You mean New York."

"I mean home."

"What will you do there?"

"Daud said your theory about the lemurs is wrong." We'd had a special dinner of curried fish, and I stared at the fine white bones on my plate. "What if he's right? Do you have other theories you could write about?"

"Important ideas are often discouraged by lesser people." She picked at her fingernails, which were rimmed with red dirt. She had started going back into the field, but still looked pale and tired. "You didn't answer my question."

"I'm going to swim," I said, thinking of all the other things I was looking forward to: white bread and mayonnaise, my own apartment with clean sheets and hot water, movie theaters and grocery stores.

"You won't make it far, Celia." My mother straightened her sunglasses. "You don't have it in you."

"You have no idea what I have."

"Strangeness is everywhere and everything makes you tired in the end," she said. "When you figure this out, you'll be back."

I asked the hotel owner to arrange a taxi for the morning and then packed my bags. In my room, I counted my money, making sure I had enough for a car and a plane ticket. I planned to show up and wait until I could get a flight to the States, eventually ending up back in New York, where I would look for a job and an apartment near the Atlantic. I couldn't imagine ever making my way through the lanes of a swimming pool again; I had grown used to the expanse of the ocean, the sensation that I could, at any moment, vanish within it.

When I came out of my room the next day, I found one of my mother's postcards by the door. A desert was on the front and on the back she had written: *what the world will look like when all the water leaves us,* along with some statistics on the evaporation of the Aral Sea, formerly the world's fourth largest lake and once a popular training ground for distance swimmers. I tucked the card into the side pocket of my backpack, next to Daud's pictures. I did not know what my mother would do after Madagascar—travel to another foreign place and join a different research team or extend her stay in Fort Dauphin, though I was sure she wouldn't return to New York. She reminded me of a skydiver who'd cut the strings of her own parachute, volatile and doomed.

The taxi was waiting for me outside. The driver was a small man with a white beard. The top of his head barely reached the headrest. I was climbing into the backseat when I saw, in the far distance, a tall figure moving towards the rainforest. The sprawl of trees looked bright and endless, an ocean of green. I asked the driver to wait and followed my mother down the road, wanting a chance to say goodbye, to say the things we might, after this moment passed, not ever be able to again. I stayed just close enough to keep her in sight. She had to know I was there, had to hear my feet tapping the red dirt, but she never turned around, never spoke a word.

When the driver honked, I stopped walking, as though I had been yanked by an invisible string. I watched until she became dark and slanted, imagining the cries of the Indris swelling, the vines bending underneath her boots; a moment that, over time, became like a scar on my brain—my mother moving down that crimson path, the ancient, knotted trees parting for her like a secret, the tall grass bowing like waves breaking on a beach, before her shadow disappeared into the sea.

Nominated by One Story, Shannon Cain

"THIS DREAM THE WORLD IS HAVING ABOUT ITSELF"

by CAROLYNE WRIGHT

from THE IOWA REVIEW

"This dream the world is having about itself . . ."

—William Stafford

won't let us go. The western sky gathers
its thunderclouds. It has no urgent need

of us. That summer in our late teens we
walked all evening through town—let's say Cheyenne—

we were sisters at the prairie's edge: I
who dreamed between sage-green pages, and you

a girl who feared you'd die in your twenties.
Both of us barefoot, wearing light summer

dresses from the Thirties, our mother's good
old days, when she still believed she could live

anywhere, before her generation
won the War and moved on through the Forties.

As we walked, a riderless tricycle
rolled out slowly from a carport, fathers

watered lawns along the subdivisions'
treeless streets. We walked past the last houses

and out of the Fifties, the Oregon
Trail opened beneath our feet like the dream

of a furrow turned over by plough blades
and watered by Sacajawea's tears.

What did the fathers think by then, dropping
their hoses without protest as we girls

disappeared into the Sixties? We walked
all night, skirting the hurricane-force winds

in our frontier skirts so that the weather
forecasts for the Seventies could come true,

the Arapahoe's final treaties for
the inland ranges could fulfill themselves

ahead of the building sprees. We walked on
but where was our mother by then? Your lungs

were filling with summer storms, and my eyes
blurred before unrefracted glacial lakes.

Limousines started out from country inns
at the center of town, they meant to drive

our grandparents deep into their eighties.
Our mother in her remodeled kitchen

whispered our names into her cordless phone
but before the Nineties were over, both

of you were gone. Mother's breath was shadow
but her heart beat strong all the way in to

the cloud wall. You carried your final thoughts
almost to the millennium's edge, where

the westward-leaning sky might have told us
our vocation: in open fields, we would

watch the trail deepen in brilliant shadow
and dream all the decades ahead of us.

In memory of my sister

Nominated by The Iowa Review, Joan Swift

THE BONEYARD

by BEN QUICK

from ORION

THE FIRST THINGS I SEE are the tails of the planes. Theyre just like hundreds of dorsal fins rising from prehistoric fish that have been lined up by a butcher on a massive table of thin brown grass. It is a surreal sight, and I allow my eyes to settle into the rhythm of motion—not quite focused, not quite gone—watching the rows of sharp metal ridges whir past at fifty miles per hour.

As I crest a small rise, the bodies of the craft come into full view: rows and rows of warplanes, all shapes and sizes, stretching on forever, it seems. I force myself back to the task at hand, navigating the approach to the Aerospace Maintenance and Regeneration Center (AMARC) on the southeast side of Tucson, Arizona. I turn right at the traffic light on Kolb Road into a small parking lot and find a space.

Ten minutes later, I'm riding shotgun in a black van with government plates. My driver, head of public relations at AMARC, is Terry. Middle-aged, handsome, and soft in her talk and manners, Terry asks me what I want to see. I hesitate—not because I don't know, but because I'm not sure how to tell her that I've come to bear witness to American folly, to rest my eyes on the flying machines that flattened the forests of Southeast Asia, poisoned its people, and changed my life.

"The C-123s," I say.

She looks at me quizzically, pushes her index finger to her lower lip. I'm nervous to begin with, having never been on an air base, having very little in the way of credentials, and having tried, however awkwardly, to obscure the true reason for my visit. I'd told her I was doing a piece on Vietnam-era warplanes for graduate school when we talked on the phone.

I mutter these words—*My father is a veteran*—and I'm suddenly taken by the irrational fear that I may have given the impression of an apologist looking to take some photos for a nostalgic slide show. My fear is compounded by the fact that today is September 11, the anniversary of the day some folks, especially those in the military, have come to view as off-limits for dissent. That I find myself moderately attracted to Terry only complicates matters. I'd expected a formal woman in military garb, spit-shined boots, and the works, but AMARC employees are civilian contractors. And the loose-fitting sundress, designer shades, and casual tone of the woman beside me have caught me off guard. I'm entirely unsure of myself and my purpose.

"The C-123s? I'm not sure if we have any of them. They might have one in the museum."

"Well I saw one in this book." I reach down between my legs, flip open my bag, and produce the picture book I'd found at the public library. Glossy and oversized, *The Desert Boneyard* by Philip Chinnery is filled with aerial photos of AMARC, snatches of aviation history, and nostalgic recollections of past commanders and famous aircraft. An honest appraisal of the Air Force arsenal and its capacity for destruction it is not, but like many seemingly frivolous research tools, it has served a vital purpose. It has shown me that AMARC—known affectionately as The Boneyard—had, at one point in time, housed the airplanes I came here to find.

"Oh, you got you a book. Let's see . . ." Resting the book on the cup holders in the space between the seats, I turn to page seventy-five. I can feel beads of sweat on my forehead.

"Oh. Those. Oh sure, we have two of them on the west side, but the rest are fenced off. You can't get to 'em. Nobody goes in there."

"Why?"

"Well, the toxin."

January 20, 1961: Eight inches of snow fall on Washington DC, initiating one of the worst traffic jams ever in the nation's capital as John F. Kennedy takes his inaugural vows. Up to this point, American involvement in the turmoil of Southeast Asia has been secondary, mainly involving the grudging flow of money and arms to the fragile Diem regime in South Vietnam. But conservatives in the capital are calling for more than a half-hearted attempt to fill the vacuum left by

France's withdrawal from the region. And the new American president is young and Irish-Catholic, a suspect combination in midcentury American politics. He is worried that Republicans will paint him pink if he doesn't hold the South from Communist guerillas. So he sets out to do so, and to do it with gusto, expanding U.S. military operations in a manner later described by Noam Chomsky as a move "from terror to aggression."

The word *counterinsurgency* begins to appear more and more frequently in the speeches of American politicians. A long and awkward utterance, it is a word that depends on the existence of the root word *insurgency*, defined by Webster's as "a condition of revolt against a government that is less than an organized revolution and that is not recognized as belligerency." In the case of Vietnam, the people charged with perpetuating the state of revolt—the insurgents—are a loose but growing number of Communist soldiers recently given the tacit approval of the Hanoi government in North Vietnam. They have begun conducting night raids on military posts and villages in the South under the name National Liberation Front and have become known condescendingly to Diem supporters as the Viet Cong.

In Vietnam, countering these insurgents means denying the Viet Cong and their allies in the countryside and hills the apparatus of survival: food and forest. Before long, the primary method of denial becomes the aerial application of a variety of defoliants. In 1961, accepting a joint recommendation from the State and Defense departments, President Kennedy signs a resolution accelerating the program. Spraying will intensify in three distinct plant communities: the dense broadleaf vegetation that blankets the Vietnam outback and turns roads and supply routes into ambush zones, the mangroves that line swamps and provide habitat for the catfish and shrimp that are staples of the Vietnamese diet, and the fields of foodstuffs—rice, manioc, and sweet potatoes.

Before 1961 is up, Kennedy sends scientist James Brown to the newly established United States/Vietnamese Combat Development and Test Center (CDTC) in Saigon to explore the effectiveness of a variety of herbicides for use as counterinsurgency tools. The results of Brown's work are a cluster of compounds that come to be known as the "rainbow agents" for the colors of the identification bands that encircle barrels of the herbicides. Agents White, Purple, and Blue will all see use in the jungles of Southeast Asia, but the most intensively employed by far will be Agent Orange, a fifty-fifty mix of the n-butyl esters 2,4-dichlorophenoxyacetic acid (2,4-D) and 2,4,5-trichlorophenoxyacetic acid (2,4,5-T).

The origins of Agent Orange lie in an obscure laboratory at the University of Chicago where, during World War II, the chairman of the school's biology department, E. J. Kraus, discovered that direct doses of 2,4-D can kill certain broadleaf vegetation by causing the plants to experience sudden, uncontrolled growth not unlike that of cancer cells in the human body. Kraus, thinking his findings might be of use to the Army, informed the War Department, which initiated testing of its own but found no use for the stew of hormones prior to the end of the war. But experiments with 2,4-D and 2,4,5-T continued through the 1950s.

Late in 1961, Brown and the technicians at the CDTC decide the time is right, the testing complete, the dispersal methods sound. On January 13, 1962, three Air Force C-123s—twin-propellered short-range assault transport planes—lift off from Tan Son Nhut airfield in South Vietnam, each loaded down with more than a thousand gallons of Agent Orange. The planes fly low over the canals and deltas of the Ca Mau Peninsula—the claw-shaped tip of the nation—occasionally taking fire from the swaths of jungle below. When they finally reach the prescribed site, the chemical cargo is sprayed continuously from three groups of high-pressure nozzles jutting from internal dispensers, the entire load dropped in minutes. A mist can be seen settling over mangroves as the planes turn back toward Saigon. Operation Ranch Hand is underway.

Fifteen thousand gallons of herbicide will be sprayed over the forests and fields of Vietnam that first year. By 1966, the annual application will have increased to 2.28 million gallons. In retrospect, the ecological and human consequences of the spraying program will seem catastrophic. But in 1962, in the thick of an increasingly desperate conflict with a silent enemy hiding in the bush, the extermination of mangroves and rice crops, the destruction of hundreds of thousands of acres of forest canopy, and the desertification of land adjacent to supply routes are embraced as steps toward creating the conditions for winning the war, conditions that nevertheless seem to be slipping farther and farther away from American military strategists in Washington and Saigon.

The kerosene stench of chemical rain that falls on American troops as they slink through the hinterlands in search of Viet Cong is seen as a bearable nuisance. The lethality of the fog that settles on the farms of South Vietnamese peasants and the convoys of American soldiers, like so many war costs, will remain hidden.

My father returned to the Midwest after his tour in the jungles of Vietnam accompanied by a dehumanizing terror. But along with the images and the guilt was something more tangible, a rash that covered his back, raised hivelike splotches that didn't go away for five years—until I was nearly three. The name for this rash is chloracne; its cause, prolonged exposure to herbicides.

I entered this world on a muggy July evening in 1974, the sun beginning to sink down into the hardwoods that separate the town of Morrison, Illinois, from miles upon miles of cornfields—fields that would have been at least six feet tall by then, ripening with line upon line of fat yellow ears sheathed in green. The delivery went without complication. There was my mother's low moaning, the usual frenzy of female nurses, and the old doctor reaching his latexed hands to cradle my small wet head as it emerged from the birth canal. There was much crying and celebration, the ceremonial cutting of the cord by the father, the grandparents waiting anxiously in the hallway, aunts and uncles, friends. But there was something else as well, something curious: although in every other way I fit the normal profile of a baby boy, my left hand was almost round, and at first glance, fingerless. Looking closer, one could see that there were indeed fingers in the flat bell of flesh and bone, but no space between them, and the bones were either misshapen or missing altogether. Instead of clutching at nipples and beards, it flew from side to side like the club on the tail of a pre-historic beast. My grandmother was horrified.

Despite my evident uniqueness, I ran through the first half of my childhood like any other midwestern boy, playing soccer and baseball, fishing, running around the neighborhood with other children in packs. I played war games in the local woods, snuck off to the candy store with my younger brother, dug up earthworms in the big garden between rows of tomatoes and hot peppers, watching with delight as aphids and sow bugs crawled over my hands. Although I endured a number of surgeries in a prolonged attempt to separate fingers, and although I was forced to wear a series of uncomfortable bracelike contraptions to bed—sterile plaster meant to force the bones to bend into a more functional formation—these were happy times for me. Too young to feel self-conscious, stubborn and creative enough to circumnavigate any limitations, I didn't really stop to think that I was differ-

292

ent from other children. I climbed trees, played catcher in little league, kept goal for my soccer team, won sprints in swim meets.

Still, I have to believe an awareness was growing. There must have been innocuous comments from neighborhood boys, partially hidden conversations, questions. And parents, even kind and well-meaning parents, can fumble with answers.

I must have been close to ten years old the day my mother and I ambled through the automatic door of Eagle's Supermarket and across the chipped green and white checkers of tile. We came for just a few items, the only memorable one being the ice cream. We were gliding across that tile, headed straight for the open freezers of the dairy section, me in my shorts and t-shirt, my mother in her gardening clothes. We were moving fast, were so close to the freezers that I could almost feel the chill, could almost see the dense coating of hoar-frost on the inner chambers, when she ran her eyes from my face to my shorts and asked with impatience: "Why do you keep your hand in your pocket? Don't you think people know?" Hiding my flaw was beginning to become second nature, an act of instinct rather than will.

Terry's been at the boneyard for eighteen years. She shoots down the gravel road like a person who's done it a thousand times before, pointing out an array of aircraft, telling me stories as we bounce through the past. Here sit the Grumman Tomcats. There, in the tall grass, the Rockwell B-1Bs. And over there, on the near side of the wash, the Lockheed Hercules, the Huey transporters, the Cobra gunships. This F-14 bombed one of Saddam's bunkers in the second Gulf War. That 119 was Westmoreland's ride. Airplanes, helicopters, and missile casings, all in different shapes, sizes, ages, and states of dismemberment, are lined up like trinkets in a jewelry booth at a country fair—the earrings in this quadrant, the bracelets in that, the bolos over here, the brass buckles over there. Three thousand acres' worth.

Some are stripped for parts. As evidence I see the glint of naked metal on exposed engines and radiators and, in big black drums beside hoodless frames, the jumbled masses of fuel pumps and belts. Some will be called back to service with the Air Force or Navy, maintenanced and flown away to bases in Utah and Nevada. Others, especially the historic planes, are destined for museums. And still others will end up in the hands of foreign armies, sold to the highest—and often most unsavory—bidder or shipped off, at discount rates, to allies in Tel Aviv or Seoul.

Through this broad yard of history we roll, the faded marks of the military all around us. Terry gradually slows down and comes to a stop. On one side is a row of unarmed nuclear warheads; on the other, the noses of two green and tan cargo planes.

"Here we are."

Stepping down from the van, I tear my disposable camera from its foil package, unpack my tape recorder, and walk toward the aircraft.

"So these were not part of Ranch Hand?"

"No. I think these guys were just transporters."

"Just transporters."

They look like smiling whales, these two transporters. Smiling whales with propellered wings. Like all the planes in The Boneyard, the windows, air ducts, and doors of the 123s are covered in thick white latex. Spraylat, it is called, and it keeps the interiors of the planes cool. Without the Spraylat, temperatures in the cargo holds and cockpits can rise to two hundred degrees Fahrenheit, baking everything inside. The white coating makes the planes look like ghost ships, mummies in an aviation graveyard. But I came to see the other planes, the ones that devastated a vast and peopled landscape, the ones that maimed me before I was born.

Operation Ranch Hand dissolved in 1970 under intense pressure fueled by increasing awareness of the dangers of Agent Orange. By then, one-seventh of Vietnam's total land area had been sprayed with herbicides, one-fifth of its forest flattened. Studies would eventually show that the spray missions flown by the men of Ranch Hand had little or no effect on the path of the war, that the millions of gallons of herbicide dropped on nipa palm and mangrove, on tropical rainforest, on trails and swamps and roads, on military barracks and rice paddies, saved few American lives. Studies would also show that the substance held in the striped barrels was more dangerous than its handlers had realized, and that American military leaders had known this for a long time.

Peter Schuck, author of *Agent Orange on Trial*, notes that, "as early as 1952, Army officials had been informed by Monsanto Chemical Company, later a major manufacturer of Agent Orange, that 2,4,5-T was contaminated by a toxic substance." The substance he refers to is dioxin, a chemical that the Environmental Protection Agency has described as "one of the most perplexing and potentially dangerous chemicals ever to pollute the environment." Lab tests in the 1940s had shown that even the tiniest amounts of dioxin, concentrations as small as 4 parts per trillion—an amount equivalent to one drop in 4 million gallons of water—induced cancer in rats. In slightly larger doses, the substance brought on virulent symptoms leading to quick death. When barrels of Agent Orange were shown to congress questions about the effects of human exposure began to swell.

By the 1970s, for Vietnamese living and working in spray zones, the answers to these questions had already started to become clear and painful: babies born with massive birth defects, some with skeletons that bended and twisted as they grew, some with organs on the wrong side of skulls and ribs, some with conditions so bad they survived only days. Even though American servicemen came into contact with the toxin over the course of months rather than years, soldiers—particularly those serving at the apex of Ranch Hand, men dropping on knees to fill canteens with odd-looking water pooled in bomb craters, men walking with handheld weed sprayers around the flanks of base camps, men sleeping on naked ground—still ran the risk of lethal exposure. The risk was so real, in fact, that as Yale biologist Arthur Galston put it, all soldiers "who worked with Agent Orange or saw duty in the heavily defoliated zones of Vietnam have a legitimate basis for asking the government to look into the state of their health."

Concern about long-term effects on the people and ecology of Vietnam and the health of American G.I.s prompted groups of critical American scientists to publicly denounce the use of Agent Orange and other herbicides as early as the mid-1960s. In 1966 and 1967, a coalition led by the well-respected American Association for the Advancement of Science sent petitions to the Johnson White House calling for an end to all chemical and biological warfare. At the same time, international anxiety was growing. In 1969, after three years of failed attempts, the United Nations succeeded in passing—despite sustained and often menacing opposition from the U.S.—a resolution declaring Operation Ranch Hand a violation of the 1925 Geneva Convention Protocol limiting the use of chemical weapons. Still, the spraying continued.

Finally, evidence showed up that was too damning to be stonewalled or intimidated away. In late 1969, Matthew Meselson, a broadshouldered Harvard scientist fond of bow ties and no friend of war boosters, obtained a copy of a National Cancer Institute report confirming the teratogenicity—the ability of a compound to cause embryonic or fetal malformation—of 2,4,5-T in rats and mice. Meselson convinced Lee DuBridge, his former colleague at the California Institute of Technology and science advisor to the then newly elected Richard Nixon, to convene meetings to discuss the implications of the findings. In spite of the continued reluctance of many in the Pentagon to acknowledge the seriousness of the data, administration officials could read the changing tea leaves of public tolerance, and on April 15, 1970, application of Agent Orange and most other defoliants was suspended indefinitely.

Years later, a sad and fitting epitaph for the Agent Orange saga would come from James Clary, an Air Force scientist and author of the official history of Operation Ranch Hand, in a statement to Senator Tom Daschle: "When we initiated the herbicide program in the 1960s we were well aware of the potential for damage due to dioxin contamination in the herbicide. We were even aware that the military formulation had a higher dioxin concentration than the civilian version, due to the lower cost and the speed of manufacture. However, because the material was to be used on the enemy, none of us were overly concerned."

By the time I reached adolescence, there was no longer any doubt as to whether I was like other young men. I was different, less than, not quite whole. Instead of attempting to come to terms with what I have now come to realize is a minor glitch in DNA, instead of facing up to my own uniqueness, the shape of my particular handprint, I tried hard to deny it, to prove to myself that I was in no way distinct from the two hundred boys and girls I entered Dixon High School with in 1988. On the surface, I succeeded. I joined sports teams and—I'm sure this was a conscious act of rebellion—put myself in positions that required the use of both hands in order to succeed. I wrestled and won matches as a freshman, earned four varsity letters as a soccer goalkeeper, brought home trophies and plaques. What's more, I had awkward sex with teenage girls, drank beer and smoked pot, grew my hair long, hung out with the right crowd, took a cheerleader to the prom.

Inside, I was a wreck. I recall the summer between my junior and senior year and a girl named Krista, younger than I, brown hair, green eyes, slender, carrying always the smell of Elizabeth Taylor Passion. Krista was the first girl I spent more than one or two nights with, and I fell for her hard. Along with my friend Josh and his girlfriend Billy, we spent the better part of the summer together. It was a hot summer, hot in the manner that all mid-western summers are, so thick with vapor that even the loosest clothing sticks to skin, and sunglasses slide down noses. That whole summer, when I was in the company of Krista—which was most of the time—I wore long sleeves. I would rush into my bedroom to change clothes each time she came to my house. There was a particular red cotton shirt a friend had loaned to me that I must have worn three times a week. I wore it in the water when we swam in the moonlight at the abandoned rock quarry; I wore it during sex on the gravelly shore; I wore it when to do so must have been agonizing. I thought the sleeves would hide my hand.

And the long-sleeved t-shirt was not the only mechanism employed for hiding the truth of who I was. I took to wearing thick goalkeeper's gloves that kept the shape of their fingers against gravity when I shook hands with players from opposing teams after soccer games (in retrospect, I wonder if the gloves weren't part of the appeal of the position). I would bury both hands deep in the pockets of my letterman's jacket as I flirted with girls from other schools at track meets or wrestling matches. I became skilled at striking a variety of postures to keep my dreaded deformity out of sight, turning this way or that, sitting down just so. I learned to live in a state of contortion.

It would be comforting to look back and to sense some kind of turning point, some theatrical beginning of a healing process, a link between the discord of those years and the relative stillness of the present. The truth is this: like most authentic change, most real letting go, mine has happened gradually, and beneath the surface of things. A decade and a half of life—of marriage and divorce, of fatherhood and graduate school, of love affairs and rafting swift rivers, of university teaching and Buddhist meditation—have swept away much of the hidden shyness and dread. But still, at the age of thirty-three, I'm finding that old habits die hard. If I've lost myself momentarily while driving, reading a book, or engaging in some other task that requires a chunk of my brain, I sometimes find that, without intending to, I have tucked my left hand gently behind my right elbow. Lying in bed at night before sleep takes hold, I'll notice my left hand resting underneath the ruffles of the blanket while my right hand sits bare and comfortable on top. Or I'll think about a class I've taught on a particular morning, coming to a sudden realization that all the gesturing and hand-waving was done with one arm. I will pause for a moment and make a mental note. Sometimes, I will curse.

Terry pumps the brakes to keep from skidding, drags the gearshift into park, and points out the driver's-side window. From behind a chain-link fence, I stare at a fleet of seventeen C-123s beached on the desert playa. A two-foot square of aluminum, white with red block letters, clasped to the fence at shoulder height, reads AUTHORIZED PERSONNEL ONLY, meaning Air Force specialists wearing hazmat suits. I must make do with the view from the fence line, which is fine with me, since the nearest contaminated aircraft are less than fifty feet away.

I climb out of the van and gawk. Forty years before, these olive planes, arranged before me now like neglected toys on the top shelf in a child's bedroom, unloaded over 10 million gallons of dioxin-laden herbicide on a countryside halfway across the world, the same countryside my father tromped through with a gun at his side for one full year at the peak of the spraying. And now, on the edge of the desert metropolis, beneath wisps of cloud shifting and breaking in the morning sky, in the checkered shadow of the chain-link fence, as much as I would like to deny it, I find myself looking for catharsis—a burst of emotion that will finally and emphatically wash it all away.

I know how lucky I am—that things could be much worse. I've seen the pictures of the Vietnamese tending the earth after the fire. The parents who cut and burned the trunks of leafless trees to keep their children warm in winter. The beautiful young girls with jet black hair and loose blouses trimming grass for baskets. The peasants planting saplings in barren ground.

And I've seen the photos of jars filled with the stillborn at the Tu Du hospital in Ho Chi Min City. Babies born with two faces and three ears. Dead babies with limbs like ropes, long, slender, twisted like pale pretzels in formaldehyde. Siamese twins with melting heads, gathered in a lovers' tangle, the lips of one pressed to the neck of the other in the softest kiss. Shelves full of pickle jars holding the rawest fruit.

And the living, the children of the damned. Children with eyes like marbles, huge and rolling and blank. Children with skin like birch bark, skin that peels and flakes in small squares, covering their bodies in checkerboards of dying flesh, pushing up from scalps like duff on a forest floor. Children with alien heads, their skulls ten times the size of their jaws. I've seen the feet turned in on themselves, the blackened arms, the hands like clamps.

I look down at my hand in its present state, nearly three decades after the last surgery, after I finally said no more—no more casts, no more stitches, no more IV needles, no more Darth Vader masks spewing anesthesia into my lungs. I look down at the rumpled flesh, the grafts sewn between the spaces opened up to give me fingers, grafts of crotch skin, grafts that grow hair, and the lines of scars from the stitching, and the two tiny inner digits, and the middle knuckle that bears no crop, and the pinky that juts straight out, and the short, thick thumb, and I am glad that at six years of age I finally said no. They wanted to do more surgeries, wanted to cut a little more here, tweak the bone structure a little more there. And I said no.

A gust of wind rakes an old Pepsi can along the base of the fence. It rattles to a stop on the crown of an anthill, teeters for a moment, and rolls to my feet like an empty shell. Out here on the scabland of memory where scorpions scurry under B-52s, jackrabbits bound over chopper blades in tufts of never-green grass, and the sun burns through everything, there are no epiphanies. There are only dirt and space, dreams and loneliness, and—I realize with a start—confrontations with the past that will never quite fill the gaps. Taken with an incredible urge to urinate, I snap one last photo and hop in the van, trying hard not to look back.

Nominated by Orion

I TURN MY SILENCE OVER

by **KARY WAYSON**

from THE JOURNAL

I am in the tenth month of the ninth life
of my silence.
My baby's grown fat enough to feed me.
I turn my silence over. I turn it
towards my mother. It wears
the expressionless face of an oscillating fan.

Each day, at intervals, a bell brings
enormous horses to the middle of my alphabet.
I turn my silence over.
I'm not speaking to my mother.
My mute has balloons for his hands.

O Underbite!
With your mailbox of a jaw.
O Nothing! When I ask what's wrong.
I turn my silence over: an astronomical number.
O, How I could go on!

Market to market I go and come home.
My silence runs parallel to the direction of my travel.

My silence makes a district with just one
constituent: I am the legislator of my mother.

My silence doesn't ask, doesn't eat, doesn't act.
I am sick on it, celibate
and exhausted. Each night
I am up with it: Sublunary Thing! My silence
is an insomnia.

Let's ask the throat what the mouth wants tonight.
I've grown fat on my refusal to say a word.
I turn my silence over and there's a doubling
of my mother. I've been doing
little sit-ups with my sense of reserve.

So I'll wait. I'll waste my turn. I have my way—my one!
I turn my silence over. I'm not speaking
to my mother. Like God I guess
I've already come.

Nominated by The Journal, Angie Estes

IN AFRICA

fiction by EDWARD HOAGLAND

from NEW LETTERS

IN AFRICA, everything is an emergency. Your radiator blows out and as you solder a repair job, Lango kids emerge from the bush, belonging to a village that you'll never see, and reachable by a path you hadn't noticed. Though one of them has a Kalashnikov, they aren't threatening, only hungry. Eight or ten of them, aged eight or ten, they don't expect to be fed by you or any other strange adult. Although you know some Swahili, you can't converse, not knowing Lango, but because there is plenty of water in the streams roundabout, they are fascinated that you choose to drink instead from bottles you have brought. Gradually growing bold enough to peer into the open windows of your Land Cruiser, they don't attempt to fiddle with the door or reach inside, seeing no food or curious mechanical delectables. The boxes packed there white-man-style are cryptically uninformative. Meningitis and polio vaccines, malaria meds, deworming pills, Ringer's solution, folic acid, Vitamin A and similar famine-fighters. However, they will remain as long as you do, and you don't dare leave to take a leak because this fabric of politesse would tear if you did, as it would have already if they were five years older.

You wish you could ask them if mines have been laid in the road recently by either the rebels or the government forces. Their fathers, the men of the village, haven't emerged because they're probably off with the guerrillas, and the women would not in time of war anyway— even the nun whom you are going to visit (a lay sister, although to all the Africans, a nun) has been raped, judging from what her radio message to the Order's little villa in suburban Nairobi appeared to convey. That's why the footpath to their tukls is maintained indecipherably. The problem is your diarrhea. To pee in front of the children would be no big deal; the boys themselves pee in front of you. But diarrhea might amuse them enough to demystify you. They could open the car and loot it if you did that, or disappeared for a few minutes to relieve yourself. It's a balance you must maintain as you work on the engine: friendliness and mystery.

Disasters can swallow you in Africa, and yet the disasters too get swallowed up: which may be why we rolling stones roll there. Visas are fairly informal and the hotels wildly variant, so you can live a while on almost nothing if you need to, as your troubles seem to piffle in the face of whatever else is going on. To shuffle tourists around on a safari route or manage a bunch of Kikuyu truck drivers who shuttle loads from Mombasa up to Nairobi or on to Kisumu and Kampala takes no special skill. I'm nominally a teacher (if I haven't had some kind of contretemps with an individual on the school board), and originally came over from America on the Salvation Army's nickel to work in one of their schools for the blind. It went well. Needless to say, I cared for the kids, and supervisors who live beyond their selfish interests I don't quibble with. But I did feel, over time, as if I might be going blind too, which becomes a bit absurd when you are under these skies, in the midst of landscapes such as Africa's. I went to Alexandria on a business venture, but returned.

Tourists want to be good guys in roughing it, and I can cook over an open fire, chauffeur a Bedford lorry, and recognize the planets or make a rainy evening more interesting by telling yarns, while keeping the Samburu from taking advantage of the Ohioans, and vice versa. Good will is not the problem; mainly just incomprehension. The former are living on a dollar a day. But expats in a stew like Nairobi's may also barter for their daily bread—clerk in a store that caters to Europeans, selling fabrics, carvings, baskets, masks, with a crash pad in the back for that extra pair of hands boasting New England English and a whitely reassuring smile, who's been hired for a stretch. Helps discourage robbers, in fact, to have a lug like me bunking in the place. Then there's always the blond Norwegian girl who arrived on an international internship of some sort but is staying on for an indeterminate number of months because an Ismaili merchant of advancing years but local wealth (gas stations, an auto agency, an office building and adjoining mart) is loaning her his garden house for the pleasure of her

303

company occasionally at the dinner table, presided over by a portrait of the Aga Khan. The gent just likes to see her beauty in the room. He has a plump, swarthy wife as old as himself, so doesn't intrude upon her privacy after supper, or object if she accepts within the villa's high brick walls a presentable Western freeloader of her own for fleeting visits. The Masai watchman has been clued in—it's Kukuyu thieves he is hired to deter—but of course will turn away a *mzungu* like me, as well, if her nod turns to a frown.

But when you get a gig with a safari company, they will have a barracks to put you up in for the couple of days between the Amboseli and Serengeti trips. A schoolteacher like me probably "plays well with others," so you may meet richer clients who, after the Tsavo and Masai-Mara jaunt, will want to hire a knowledgeable companion for a solo expedition west into Uganda's wilder parks, or south down the Indian Ocean coast, and not just to Malindi and Lamu, where everybody goes. This free-lancing may then piss off an employer, but we're speaking of a city splitting at the seams with squatter camps, swollen by an enormous flux of displaced refugees from within hungry Kenya itself, not to mention all the illegals from the civil wars afire in the countries that surround it: Somalia, Sudan, Ethiopia, Congo, Rwanda. Look on a map—dire suffering—need I say more? And if you can drive an SUV or a Leyland lorry or ride herd on the Africans who do, and have the say-so of that Salvation Army major behind you, another do-good agency will have an opening in relief work for you pretty soon.

I do that too. From gorillas right to guerrillas. I've chaperoned a perky Japanese fellow with binoculars hanging around his neck to eyeball the silverbacks in the Rwenzori Mountains; and next I'm venturing—or pussy-footing—slowly through Lord's Resistance Army rebel territory in northern Uganda with tons of corn and sorghum for one of the refugee camps up in the war zone of southern Sudan. But, between those ventures, there'll be the new San Francisco divorcée I ran into on the terrace of the Casino Club or the Thorn Tree Café who has deplaned in Kenya to do the Karen Blixen, Isak Dinesen, *Out of Africa* thing in the very suburb—Karen, verging on the Ngong Hills—named for her. Nearing forty, like me, she's just bought a villa from a South Asian or an Anglo-colonial former grandee at a fire-sale discount, which appeared to have everything—the tamarind and flame trees, passion-flowers and bougainvillea, the leopard foraging in the garbage cans at night, killing the cat and dog if they go out, and the faithful Kamba manservant, Mutua, who accompanied the house but now is becoming nearly as fearful of staying in it as she, with no white man in residence who knows how to handle a pistol. Her first car, a romantic, vintage Land Rover, has already been hijacked from her at a stoplight at terrifying gunpoint; and bandits armed with machetes boost themselves over the neighbors' walls, but when she tries to call the police—if the phone line does connect—they will ask her if she has "any petrol," because they don't. "Can you come and get us?" Wonderful colored tiles, crafted doorways of mahogany, teak beams, an inherited library of all the appropriate books—Adamson, Kenyatta, Lessing, Moorehead, Soyinka, Paton, Cary, *Things Fall Apart*, etc.— and a fairytale, gingerbread roof, but some nights she goes to the Norfolk Hotel to sleep, when she can't raise a friend closer than America on the telephone, if it works. She hasn't had time to find many of these in Nairobi yet, or an escort to take her places where she might begin to. So a "Middle School History Teacher," from America, no less, but who knows some Swahili, and about motors, firearms, and the general East African maze, might be welcome to move in rent-free, after a look-over, if her long-distance harangues with her lawyer in California didn't bore me to tears, once the novelty of the stage-set wore off. She had pals in the Bay Area who, like the lawyer, told her she ought to have sunk her settlement money into Napa Valley real estate instead of this. Now nothing could be renegotiated.

I escorted her to the Carnivore night club, where harlotry and brutality acquired new imageries for her, and to croupiers' tables at other places where the bouncers have you lift your hat to show them that no pistol is concealed underneath, but a white man who doesn't score can solace himself with little girls and boys waiting outside at three a.m. to offer him a blow job for the equivalent of twenty cents. Also, however, to the Leakeys' marvelous National Museum, and the slightly swank Dog Show at the old Race Track, where the *West With the Night* lady, Beryl Markham, used to hang out: plus the fabled patio of the Muthaiga Club, which Beryl had already managed to join—Beryl played tennis and golf—where divorce, according to legend, was the primary sport. Yes, Beryl was my landlady's name as well, although she wasn't a pilot, a horse trainer or an author, like B. Markham. But she could brush her ash-brown tresses without the services of her Russian Hill hairdresser, glad to forego being a bottle-blonde for this cleansing period, while in Africa, she said. Quite a nice woman, who missed her therapist and paid for regular sessions on the telephone rather than trying our local quacks. Her son was a sophomore at Andover, so her trips home were going to be timed with those of his vacations that weren't slated to be spent with his father.

Once she had rendered it crystal-clear that my position as a temporary live-in did not entail conjugal rights, she granted me some, if only because it was so much easier to vent her feelings in dishabille. She enjoyed tantalizing me at cocktail hour, and I didn't need to flatter her; she *was* wenchy as she mixed the drinks. I did tease her, though, because she'd finally bought a handgun for protection, when there were plenty of macho unemployed white hunters or former mercenaries around—now that shooting elephants was out of style and the apartheid wars were over and African dictators preferred black thugs—who could have run interference for her in an emergency much better than me. I wasn't beefy, red-faced and recognizable around town as the type that if bandits broke into their girlfriend's house in the dead of the night, could leap from a sound sleep, grab her ornamental, six-foot, Karamojong spear off the wall, and hurl it through the first of them. (A Frenchman, a Foreign Legionnaire, had actually done that—what a boyfriend!) But those guys, being even more downscale than me, were less presentable in the circles she aimed for or felt comfortable in. What in fact they were mostly doing for a living, now that no more Mr. and Mrs. Francis Macombers were seeking tutelage on the veldt, and in order to expiate their numerous sins, was lying behind sandbag emplacements in the desert heat defending U.N. and NGO enclaves in Mogadishu and other bad spots in Somalia that Hemingway would not have enjoyed either.

I couldn't go to visit my Norwegian damsel at her Ismaili pasha's villa in Thika and keep in Beryl's good graces, but since she, that damsel, didn't care, neither did I. Yet we were tiring of each other, nevertheless, Beryl and I. Beryl was used to computer innovators, wine splicers, or else still whizzier, glitzier men with inherited capital to live on—even a polo player, whose photo, in whites, graced her coffee table. Politely, after a couple of weeks, I began to pack to leave without needing to be told; then was delayed because my glasses were stolen off my nose by a thief who reached in through the car window one noonday while we were stopped for a light, Beryl driving, which made it seem more stupid, since I didn't have the excuse that my hands were gripping the wheel. We talked about our poor parents: how what had looked apathetic or shortsighted or lackadaisical to a kid now appeared more throttled, and of course you feel sorry for them anyhow once they're safely in the ground. Her father made his money as a go-getter, until he'd been shelved, and sat home for a year or two, running a comb through her hair every morning before sending her off to school. Earlier, I had noticed she liked me to do something resembling that, while perching on my knee. But if she was mainly playing Meryl Streep, I wasn't an adequate leading man.

More important, the neighborhood had changed. Our faithful Kamba houseboy, Mutua, cooked and served our meals on Irish linen and Spode plateware with cut-glass fingerbowls from checkerboarded, fine-wood cabinetry. Yet one block down, an elderly white woman—a lifelong Kenyan resident and the widow of a coffee rancher from the highlands toward the Aberdare Range—who had chosen not to decamp in the general white stampede after Independence, but live out her seventies and eighties alone in the outskirts of Nairobi with five or six African women as companions—defenseless, penniless Kikuyu crones, with no villages or relatives of their own, they said, to go to, and whom she offered protection in return for some few services, in their penury—was smothered in her bedsheets. It had supposedly been a charitable arrangement. Not having quite outlived her money, she took them in, one by one, in exchange for the house being kept reasonably well dusted, behind its shrubbery, and being served breakfast in bed and perhaps other minor amenities. She could have hired more energetic retainers, but two or three of these wrinkled ladies had known her husband, and how she and he preferred their tea and scones, plus Scotch in the evening. A gentle presence—a thread of continuity on the wooded street—she simply disappeared from view: not puttering in her garden or looking in her mailbox. No housekeepers were visible around, although taxis were seen entering and an unfamiliar young man opened the gate. She was stiff and decomposing in her bed when her accountant and a security bruiser from his office forced the back door. No autopsy would have been performed on such an individual, snugly tucked in, with no untoward marks on her skin, if the house hadn't been stripped of whatever moveables could possibly fit into a cab on a series of trips, and the help had all vanished. Nobody really knew who they'd been. But they must have possessed plenty of relatives and a web of villages out near Mount Kenya to flee to for a comfortable old age.

Nairobi's beleaguered, superannuated white community remembered other suspicious, inconspicuous deaths and looked at their own impassive retainers: not that they would have wanted to risk hiring

307

any young strangers as an alternative, however. Few pensions exist for old people. Without an extended family, they starve. So you continue to take somebody in, with no wages necessary, if you happen to have run through your own resources and just have a roof and rice and beans to offer. The bewildering sheer size of this new megapolis, with fetid, unmapped shantytown add-ons, its eclipsed police force carrying rifles on foot patrol through the downtown avenues to try to shoot the car-thief gangs, since there was no other way of stopping them, scared the old hands as well as Beryl. Pickpockets are simply kicked to death by a mob of civilians, when anybody manages to grab one. I myself have seen it happen to a whimpering little boy not over ten or eleven—all those polished, sharp-toed, office workers' shoes—you couldn't have squeezed through the tightening circle of fifty or more middle-class men in suits to save him. I tried—it was iron—and left. The joke, if you can call it that, among us expatriates is if you feel a hand grope for your wallet, the second thing to do is try to save the life of the pickpocket. This is a city veering into calamity, where transient whites like me still dribble in because it's a hub for aid groups, and yet a traditional wash-up spot for Anglo ne'er-do-wells who try to define themselves by where they have been, or, in another case, those parents, savvy parents, who want their children to see wild animals before it's too late and are sometimes my bread and butter. With the AIDS pandemic, it will soon be too late for a number of things.

I'm guide, ne'er-do-well, aid worker, what-have-you, but a nice guy, and I'd been supplanted at Beryl's trophy house by a natty English newspaperman (I can't blame her) who'd been brought in by the Aga Khan's business organization to spruce up the daily tabloid it owns in Kenya. Apart from a few design changes and feature additions, his job was really to hearten the idealistic employees who wanted the illusion of a free press in this country that's so stuffed with corruption, as well as a Fleet Street veteran to witness and even help them stand up to the intimidation they are often subjected to. He was energetic, conscientious, supple, and when working-class Fleet Street met San Francisco divorcée burning through her alimony, I didn't stand a chance. Being packed, as I say, and having given Beryl in her chic Land Rover a tour of Tsavo Park she would always remember, with the hippos at Mzima Springs particularly effusive, and where we'd glimpsed rarities like African wild dogs, hartebeest, oryx, while camping by an elephant herd's watering hole, with no schedule to follow—for both of us it was an idyll, and she'd ceased being ironic about making love for that half a week—I was content to go back to my hotel downtown. It's a hole-in-the-wall, owned by an Arab but across the street from the New Stanley, a famous old hostelry with bulletin boards on a thorn tree in the café patio, where Euro-American travelers traditionally leave notes for each other, and a swimming pool up on the roof. I'd registered there earlier because they give you a free safe deposit box when you do, then never check on whether you've actually left. Living cheaply just across the street in my Arab's seedy brownstone (these are the tatty details of a roamer's life), I was a frequent figure on the Thorn Tree's patio, or at the glass tables beside the swimming pool, up twelve stories, where the black kites and vultures sail and scud, and where I'd met both the Norwegian and Beryl, for example—my valuables secure behind the New Stanley's desk in the meantime.

But even at the Arab's, with less than ten guest rooms—and as in many Third World countries—the barman, like the doorman at the New Stanley, would let in local university students who had bribed him or maybe were related to him and trolling for adventure or else for a sugar daddy or simply a helpful foreign friend. Though I had pals with various flats roundabout the city, if I was otherwise unoccupied after a day of trolling for a new job myself, or temporarily filling in at an NGO's office, I could wiggle a finger (by which I only mean to suggest how easy it was) and be joined by one of these anxious, rather pretty but thin young women, who sat down obediently at my table but scrutinized me carefully to size me up. I'd make it plain that I was not an ogre, only lonely, and offer to feed them if they were hungry, which they usually were. Even on a scholarship, some students need to skip a meal or two per day. Yes, she could have the chicken, instead of the measly bean dish (might not have tasted chicken for a month), and a soft drink—was not required to get drunk. This was not a prelude, in other words. There would be no after-cost, so we could relax and ease our mutual solitude; then possibly a night or two later, as well. I'm not suggesting we were now on terms of equality—a man with hundreds in his wallet, and thousands in the money belt he is wearing underneath his clothes around his waist, with more in the hotel safety-box across the street, facing a college girl fifteen or twenty years younger in threadbare clothing, who lives on a dollar a day—but that I generally had the decency not to ask for a quid pro quo.

What she wanted wasn't really the meal so much as either a visa out or an employment opportunity right here in Kenya when she graduated; and the power of the white stranger from abroad was not just the beefsteak and green salad he could provide for the moment, but the implication implicit in his presence that he must know executives in the several office buildings that cut the paltry skyline of Nairobi who could find a slot for a stenographer in a city where ten recent university graduates wanted such a modest boon immediately. Although her chances of achieving that result with me were almost nil, nevertheless our conversations were not going to be valueless to her, but could add to her fluency in colloquial English, and insight into how to cultivate a European, her grip on reality, and how she fathomed white men, the mentality of older men from northern continents, and become a sort of low-rent therapy on a succeeding night, too, if she poured out her heart. The classes she was enrolled in at college were huge, the professors aloof, the families that the students came from often wracked and shackled by grief and hardship, even over and above the threat of AIDS. Five extra dollars could pay for a doctor visit and medicines that were needed for a sister who was sick. But on the other hand, there would be girls who strode right past my table, eschewing my relative sobriety and the proffered French fries and drumsticks, to a drunken construction engineer from Rotterdam who wants to haul her upstairs across one of his shoulders and fuck her in three ways in exchange for enough cash for her whole family to live on for three weeks, even after the bartender and elevator man have grabbed their cut as she leaves, past midnight, in her brother-in-law's heap.

The city turns so risky after dark that, much as with the pickpocket, you need to take responsibility for their lives if you keep one of these girls chatting with you over beer and pretzels till closing time. Hire a taxi, sure, but even the taxis become dangerous, or the drivers frightened to leave the downtown area toward the wildlands where the girl lives. She may not get safely home, so you tip a bellhop to allow her to sleep in his broom closet until dawn, or take her into your room under whatever terms you dictate, which in my case would be her call. These fastidious girls, with their four-year degree in hand, but still underfed, delicate, fit for an office career, though no employment is in sight because of the stove-in economy—no husband either, because of the AIDS tragedy—they panic after a year of walking the streets, trying every agency, bureau and store, cadging tea and a cookie perhaps at the interviews, as their good clothes wear out. Their aunt is a cleaning woman at some place such as my Arab's establishment, so, while pretending to visit her, they will eye me over her shoulder.

I'm alone, hunched over rice and a goat kebab, the generous helping at supper that paying guests get. I crook my finger and scrape half of my dinner onto my butter plate, give the girl my spoon to eat it with, tear my roll in half, pour half of my Tusker beer into my glass and hand her that, drinking the rest out of the bottle. Having noticed that day that music is advertised in a club window down the block, I say we're so close we could sprint back here at one a.m. without getting mugged. O.K.? Tears glisten in her questioning eyes, as she nods. So we go. There, I buy her a pizza to fill her small stomach some more, as she tells me that her mother died of appendicitis not long ago, as the cleaning woman, her aunt, already had. Her father is becoming disabled with arthritis. She has siblings with H.I.V. I change the subject to what she studied in school, to avoid hearing more unsettling details. Economics, history, art. She is of the Kalenjin, a tribe allied with the Kikuyu, who control the government at the moment and flaunt their power in public places by speaking Kikuyu instead of Swahili or English, which other people could understand. But we dance and gradually feel a rapport. I ask her if this purple blouse, flattering in color but with a hole in it, is her best. She says no, her second-best; she didn't know she was going to score on this particular evening out. Her bra strap is also frayed, but I observe without comment and assure her that she smells good, when, sweating, she confesses that her family has no running water. I say I do and we laugh. The music is Afro, on handmade instruments, but I wouldn't have come here without her presence at my table to save me from the assertive importunities of the muscular Kikuyu prostitutes.

We ask the bouncer please to watch us from the door as we run back through a sudden rainstorm to the Arab's building from the club—where I have my key ready to quickly get in. The girl must have had some bad experiences, however, because her face dissolves into a beseeching fear: Will I just mumble goodnight and leave her outside to the mercies of the muggers? She opens her purse on an impulse, not like a prostitute asking for payment, but a girl showing that she has no money to go anywhere. Hugging her with one arm, I lead her upstairs, start the tub in the bathroom, and wave her in. I then sit on the bed, look for CNN on the tube, after hiding my wallet and money belts (yes, I have two, because my regular belt, holding up my pants has a secret zippered section that you can also fold twenty hundred-dollar bills into), and watch a snatch of an Indian movie dubbed from Hindi into English instead. "Take your time," I reassure her through the door. "Enjoy yourself. Please. No hurry."

I hear her fill the tub again to rinse, or perhaps to double-do her hair. Then I hear her at the sink, washing her jeans, blouse and underclothes, I suppose. Finally she emerges, saronged in a towel.

"I did my wash so you couldn't kick me out," she explains. I smile. Her face is pretty, winsome, and small; I wonder whether her breasts are, as well.

"Can I see you some time?"

"You mean some time tonight?" she asks.

"Yes, some time tonight."

"Are you an art student? I was an art student," she says.

"Yes, I'm an art student. I promise."

"Sit where you are," she instructs me; then drops the towel, her arms upraised in a classic life-model pose, which she holds for my edification as if this were a class, while only watching to see whether I think she is exquisite.

"Exquisite!" I exclaim. When I move one hand very slightly, she turns round very slowly to display the small of her back and her buttocks. Her color is different from mine, but that distinction has vanished.

"Do you want to violate the code?" she asks.

"Yes, whatever that means."

She lowers her arms and comes to me, kneels and puts her hands on top of my thighs, as I sit on the edge of the bed. I cuddle her, fondle her, bury my hands in her hair, while figuring what we could possibly do with no risk of AIDS. I carry condoms, of course, but with an African woman, just thinking of the odds can distract and unman you, even if you theoretically have protection.

She remains in that supplicant position, not play-acting like a college student anymore. Her mind is not on sex.

"I want you to take me to America. Sponsor me, please. I know I need somebody," she elaborates bluntly, pleadingly, ignoring how my hands are cherishing her breasts. "I could be your maid. I'd work to repay you and go more to school."

Raising her up, shutting off the TV, I move to the little table where we can look at each other. "In other words, go bail for you? I'm your friend, not your father," I answer, masking my confusion with unjustified irritation. "Do you know what it costs to guarantee somebody for a visa? What they would make me sign as an indemnity?"

Naked across from me, crossing her arms now, Leli, as she wants to be known—Nyawera is her African name—who just wants to escape

312

from her country, nods. She has done her homework, been to the Western embassies, tried for student visas.

"You hurt my feelings," I complain again, a bit selfishly, as though the poor girl had picked me up more from calculation than straight, impromptu necessity. Waitresses in restaurants, who don't know you, will ask to be your "maid" also, occasionally. But, glancing at Leli's sadness, I have to soften and repeat that I am her new friend, and in fact am looking for work myself, and wave her close to me, to begin to cherish her again.

In the morning, as she dresses, the contrast is so poignant between how pretty she is and the threadbare underwear and outerwear she has to wear that I take her shopping for inexpensive clothes that aren't incongruously ragged. Afterward, she surprises me, however, by declining to go to a storefront I am temping at, where we feed street kids and treat them with skin ointments, antibiotics, inoculations, minerals, vitamins, whatever we happen to have. Powdered milk, powdered eggs, surplus soups or porridges that another Non-Governmental Organization may have given us.

I say bye-bye. She gets on a bus.

We have a basketball hoop up, and soccer balls, board games, playing cards, a tent fly hooked to the back wall in the courtyard with cots arranged underneath it, as a shelter where the children can feel some safety in numbers at least. What makes you burn out are the ones dying visibly of AIDS. Yet you don't want to banish them again to the furnace of the streets, or, on the other hand, specialize merely as a hospice, where salvageable kids aren't going to want to come. Many of them wish to go to school but have no home to go to school from or money for the fees. So I'd scrounged a blackboard and taught addition, subtraction, geography, the English alphabet, when I had a break from refereeing a gritty soccer game or supervising the dishwashing or triaging kids with fevers or contusions who ought to go to the hospital (not that that Dickensian trip was often in their best interest). We had artful dodgers eating our fruits and sandwiches, between excursions into robbery, drugs, peddling, or the pederasty racket—knives, guns, money, fancy sneakers, or the other wicked chimeras that adults around the corner might be offering them—but also earnest tykes, plenty of them, who your heart absolutely went out to. Yet triage isn't teaching, is frustrating, and I switch back and forth between such street work and the safaris and far-flung aid deliveries to conflict regions I've sometimes specialized in.

313

The girls were housed in a church anteroom nearby, spending the daylight hours with us; but I'd been surprised that Leli had promptly shook her head, from an antiseptic distance, with her new panties and bras in a shopping bag, much as Beryl might have done, and said she'd maybe see me at the Arab's another time. We *were* rather a rattled crew: a couple of dumbstruck interns from Swarthmore College in Pennsylvania, plus me, presently a little distracted by the red tape of renewing my Kenyan working papers, not to mention by Beryl's recent summons to return, since her Oxbridge yet working-class Fleet Street newshound had begun to be unfaithful to her with a Mongol-cheeked fellow Brit, whose brown hair hung down to her coccyx, instead of promising to go home to the Sonoma land of milk and honey with Beryl. Our boss at the shelter was a kind of born-again hangdog with a tolerant wife who was admirably cool during berserk emergencies, and those hundred young souls wouldn't have been fed without the two of them—would have been out purse-snatching, jizzim-swallowing, courier-running, and other deathly gambits as dangerous as walking a parapet. I used to suffer dreams of doing that whenever one I'd had a chance to come to care about would inexplicably vanish. Our funding originated with an umbrella relief organization called Protestants Against Famine, Baptist-financed from the States and run by a friend of mine named Al, who was married to a Dinka woman from the southern Sudan, whom he had met during a stint of working in the war zone there.

✿

So, intermittently, I'd free-lance on one-shot contracts with Al's or another agency which found itself short of personnel to shepherd a fleet of trucks from Mombasa's port to Kakuma Camp for thirty thousand Sudanese and Somali refugees in northern Kenya, or to deliver half a year's food and supplies to some man-and-wife evangelical outpost spotted almost off of the map in the outback. If you are genuinely feeding and medicating the locals, authorization for such missions will not be withheld. And that's how I'd met Ruthie the year before. Her station, at an abandoned church on the hairy periphery, had been temporarily vacated after somebody had a nervous breakdown or underwent a flame-out and nobody else could fill the bill. But before the structure was pillaged inside out, a new communicant, Ruth, rather shaky but fervent, volunteered to reestablish it, whose intentions were

314

of the best (who else would imaginably come?), though she was or-
dained as neither a doctor nor a preacher. The closest authorities, who
were rebels of the Sudanese People's Liberation Army, accepted her,
and that was all that mattered, apart from Al's say-so.

You don't have to be a doctor to help people who have no aspirin or
disinfectant or malaria, tuberculosis, dysentery or epilepsy pills, no
splints or bandaging, and no other near facility to walk to in the bush.
Kaopectate, cough suppressants, malnutrition supplements, antibi-
otics for bilharzia or sleeping sickness or yaws. If you were a nurse,
patients would be brought to you with these or hepatitis or broken
limbs. The old stone and concrete ruins of a Catholic chapel that had
been forgotten since the colonial powers left could be reoccupied, if
you chased the leopards and the cobras out, because joy is what is
partly needed, especially at first, and joy, I think, is, like photosynthe-
sis for plants, an evidence of God. Whether it, like photosynthesis,
provides evolutionary advantages is arguable. People may have sexual
intercourse out of boredom or simple hormonal pressures or vaguely
sadistic motives as often as in love and joy, and so human nature is re-
produced in all of its continuing imperfections. But joy, like beauty, is
a continuum, too, and in temperate climates it waxes with the sun
somewhat as plants do.

What I'm explaining is that, even if I'm not of their exact denomi-
nation, directors of small missionary programs in a pinch for person-
nel may see fit to hire me for jack-of-all-trades assignments. I can do
the basic mechanics if we break down on the road, and know when to
speed up or—equally important—slow down, when figures with guns
appear to block our passage. (If it's soldiers, you never speed up, but
the decision is not that easy because every male can look like a soldier
in a war zone, and the soldiers like civilians.) The big groups such as
Doctors Without Borders, CARE, Oxfam, Save the Children, have
salaried international staff they can fly in from Honduras, Bangkok or
New Delhi to plug a momentary defection or a flip-out—dedicated ca-
reer people, like the U.N.'s ladies and gentlemen, with New York,
Geneva, London, Paris, Rome, behind them, who've been vetted: not
much fooling around. But there are various smaller outfits, whose fly-
ers you don't receive in the mail back home, that will hire "the spiri-
tual drifter," as Al put it to me, to haul pallets of plywood, bags of
cement, first-aid kits in bulk, and bags of potatoes, bayou rice, cases of
your basic tins, like corned beef, tunafish, salmon, peas, what-have-
you, and trunks of medicine to provision the solo picayune apostle out

doing Christ's appalling work in the hinterlands. ("Wouldn't you get a little picky, picayune, washing dysentery doo-doo off of cholera asses, with toddlers with blowfish bellies and kwashiorkor red hair staggering around? The marabou stork stalkin' about, too" he added, "Waitin' for his meal?")

You draw up lists of refugees, so no one gets double their ration by coming through the corn queue twice. Use ink stamped on the wrists if you have to—if their names are always Mohammed or Josephine. And you census the children, as well, and weigh a sampling of them in a sling scale, plus measure their upper-arm fat, if they have any, with calipers to compile the ratio of malnutrition in the populace, severe versus moderate, and so on. I've helped inject against measles, tetanus, typhoid, when not enough licensed people were there, having been a vet's assistant at one point in my teens. I've pow-wowed with the traditional clan chiefs and tribal healers, the leopard-skin priests and village shamans and elders, or hard-butt young militia commanders, and delivered babies when nobody competent was around. I've squeezed the rehydration salts into babies' mouths when they're at death's door, or mixed the fortified formula, which you spoon into them, and chalked the rows of little white squares in the dirt where you have them all sit individually at their feeding hours so that every individual gets the same amount of protein, the same units of Vitamins A, C, E, B, calcium, iron, phosphorous, out of the fifty-five-gallon steel drum you're stewing the emergency preparation in. *Hundreds* of passive, dying children sitting cross-legged in the little squares, waiting for you to reach each of them. You don't think that breaks your heart? Chalk is never gonna look the same, even when you're teaching sixth grade again.

So, I'd met Ruthie one time the previous year, when her group, Protestants Against Famine, received a shipload of corn at Mombasa and needed to distribute it fast because of limited warehouse space. In fact the sheds were full of other organizations' beans and sorghum and corn, storehoused for Somalia, and it was expensive to guard outdoors, against the nightly pilferage, or protect from the rains. Better to have the pilferage going on close to the refugee camps than in Mombasa, anyway. I was hired to supervise part of this hasty dispersal. PAF had eight or ten small splinter missions in East and Central Africa, all serviced from Nairobi, and I took the overnight train down to the coast, getting a compartment easily at the last minute because of tourist cancellations after a washout and a wreck two weeks before, in which a lot of people had been killed. A hundred-seven bodies were trucked back to the capital and displayed for identification on open tables, naked or practically so, in the Nairobi morgue. I'm ashamed to say I went to stare, like every other rubbernecking lout in the city, because, along with the zaftig Africans laid out here and there, among the less intriguing corpses, was a Nordic-looking white girl, as if at some dirty peep show. Her passport, in her purse or baggage, had washed downriver like everybody else's after the crash, so the authorities, instead of turning her remains over to the Swedish or British embassy sensibly, decided, perhaps with relish, to treat her just as bad as everybody else. That was before my phone call. So, on the same railway route, after enough jerry-built repairs had been performed to get us across that particular river where it joins the Athi, I felt doubly regretful, as if I were going to be lying on that self-same slab myself pretty soon: and serve me right. Not to mention, coincidentally, the news from the PAF office manager, Al, that I ought to be forewarned that one of their mission women, Ruth Parker, had recently been captured at an isolated clinic in Sudan by a rump ("no pun intended") guerrilla group of the Sudan People's Liberation Army, which had overrun it in order to seize the supplies and medicines. Eventually they'd turned her loose to walk naked ("as is their wont") twenty miles south to the nearest outpost that had white people at it. Whether she'd been raped, like the Maryknoll I'd mentioned earlier, he didn't know ("couldn't ask over the radio, could I?"). But since she was refusing evacuation, he asked me to try to evaluate ("yes, I know you're not a therapist") her state.

What with the sudden cancellations, I got a roomette for the rattling rail trip across the lion-colored gamelands of the Athi Plains—wildebeests, zebra herds, Tommy-gazelles, and a cherry sun when it set—down to the sisal farms, sugarcane fields, and coconut palms on the coast. I thought I might have the adjoining accommodations to spread out in, too, on account of the scare; but no, just as the conductor was about to hoist the steps, two German business types came huffing-puffing along the platform toward my sleeper, hauling suitcases-on-wheels, with two brawny, blowsy African women keeping up with them, panting and hollering bye-bye, who were obviously going to stay behind. The Germans, in German, appeared to be amused by, but at the same time now wished to be well rid of, them. And now one did turn back, as if giving up the hope of wangling a parting tip for her services performed, muttering as much in Kikuyu to the other. But the bolder woman, after hesitating, pressed ahead. The Germans were wrestling their bags up the stairs into the vestibule, but she called out, "Please take me! I've never been to Mombasa. I'm a Kenyan and yet I've never been to Mombasa!"

It's a refrain I hear often in Nairobi. Americans will be standing around in safari togs—twill pants, brim hat, open-collared tan shirt—and the desk clerk, bellhop, taxi driver, restaurant greeter, recognizing me as a regular, say with more of a twist of irony: "You know, I've never seen an eland or a leopard." So, speaking again in English, which was apparently their lingua franca, she pleaded: "Save money! You can fuck me there instead of new people."

The laggard of the Germans, who looked more sensual in the shape of his mouth, was tempted. He let her mount the steps, though motioning to the conductor please to wait until they'd made their minds up. He glanced into the compartment their tickets had paid for; then at me for a reaction, because their side door opened into my own space.

"Save money. You can fuck me there instead of new people!"

"Are you broadminded?" he asked me. I nodded, so he nodded and turned. "Must go back on the bus. We fly to Europe," he explained to her—the bus of course being joltier and cheaper. Probably about thirty, she'd never ridden on a train before, and was so eager that she promised him she'd sleep on the floor. She opened a window so she and her friend could squeeze hands and exchange purses because the other woman's was bigger and had more inside.

Otto, the German who was her champion, told me he was a vintner, his pal a hydraulic engineer. As the train began to rollick and roll, he pumped his arm like his joystick. "Ava, maybe," he said to her, the rocking "will make me come too fast."

Ava—as she called herself, she later told me, because a customer who liked Ava Gardner had dubbed her that—assured each of us that he was "very strong, very strong." A tall highlands woman from the Nairobi slums, she was excited to be speeding along in this famous Mombasa sleeper train—not just a jam-packed, plebeian, pothole-bumping bus—and on the same railroad roadbed where we could see thousands of her fellow citizens traipsing home at this evening hour from their jobs downtown. I asked her where she lived; whether she had walked beside the tracks innumerable times into or out of the city herself from Mathare, a railway-siding slum, to save the bus fare, like all these countless men in office shoes and shabby, respectable suits

318

using the cinders as a thoroughfare. She smiled and waved her hand, only vaguely agreeing. I didn't ask whether she'd told the Germans about the crash, or mention it myself. The lower and upper berths where they were going to sleep fascinated her, and the windows, with a cooling, exhilarating wind, despite the muddy fetid slums going by and people in torn jerseys shitting in the open—until the limitless horizons of the veldt began.

"I want to see a lion," she said, when I pointed out how each railway section master's bungalow was high-fenced for protection.

The dining car had spacious windows, too, that complemented the table linens, crystal glasses, and silverware, although we kept them closed so our soup and rounds of beer and plates of fish and beef would stay clean. Sunset bled into dusk, as Ava ate a herculean meal, reaching over exuberantly to finish the leftovers on each of our plates, even to the last string bean or sliver of fat and strand of carrot or dab of mashed potato. This was a banner trip and she wouldn't deny herself any of its perks. The attitude of the waiters or other diners didn't faze her. Yes, she was going to be able to handle all three of us who were at the table with her tonight, if I was given to her as well—though of course I didn't intend that.

Sitting next to her, facing the grinning Germans, with their vacation fares (this jaunt was part of the advance package for them, Otto said, and Ava's company was only costing them an extra coach ticket because she was going to sleep on the floor), I was only nonplussed when I tried to ask her a serious question, such as what she thought of Daniel arap Moi, the nation's new president, or if the accent of the Mombasans, when they spoke Swahili, would be recognizably different, and she apparently thought I was patronizing her—bristled at being talked to like an African. She stared at me as though to say *do you think I'm an African?* But, realizing I meant no offense, then she would put her hand on my knee and slide it to my crotch to reassure me that she was competent to handle everything.

Munching cake, after Ava had finished the trimmings off the steak on their plates, Otto and Hans kept talking about getting inside her after supper, pistoning their fists. Should we rename her Betty, after Grable? We could decide when she was naked, during the gymnastics, when they could see her legs. Meanwhile, outside, a maintenance shed occasionally provided a bulb or two in the darkness, where a generator had been placed. Our twenty yellow-lighted railway cars coiling raffishly around the curves behind a black-plumed engine was a more

319

glamorous spectacle, and we might hear kids faintly shouting from a hovel beside a campfire. At first I'd be alarmed on their behalf—they sounded as if they were dashing toward the train—was their mother dying in childbirth?—till I realized they were only wildly seeking to register their existence on our consciousness.

We had three hundred miles to go in about ten hours from the relatively recently British-built city of Nairobi (previously a Masai watering hole), to the Arabs' eleventh-century port settlement on the Indian Ocean, which had been conquered by the Portuguese six hundred years later. Ava's English was better than that of Otto and Hans, and she knew a smattering of German, too, so could translate a bit when we talked European politics, besides quizzing the waiters for us in Swahili or Kikuyu, while reaching out to finish off a rind of cheese or scrap of cake frosting on anybody's plate. She took my mind off the train crash and rested her hand on my knee rather pleasantly whenever she fathomed that I might be on the point of mentioning it. Although she ate like a survivalist, she drank watchfully, clutching her purse. No one could have snatched it.

Later, however, as I fell asleep, I could hear them fucking her in the adjoining compartment like an athletic event. Having told them Ava could sleep in my extra berth whenever they were through with her, I hoped they wouldn't actually wake me up, it began to take so long. And they didn't. But I felt guilty in the morning, she looked so bedraggled from slumping on the floor through the wee hours. Didn't even go to breakfast. Napped on a bunk disgruntledly, complaining that she missed her children; her auntie was taking care of them. Her first train trip was ending badly. "Good jig-jig," Otto complimented her, handing her enough money for the bus ride home. Hans told me they'd decided that they wanted to find themselves new women in Mombasa who had "some India in them. The Goa eyes, the Bombay brown."

Barefoot toddlers waved at the train, and older kids were running to register their presence on us from the huts they lived in on the citrus plantations. It was tropical here at sea level, with vegetation rioting for any foothold along the roadbed, as I leaned out the half-door of the vestibule to feel the warming wind. On the causeway to the island, Mombasa-bound workers were hiking to their jobs, much as they would be in Nairobi just now. On my last trip down, I'd picked up the companionship of a Canadian professional woman with a heavy knapsack full of asthma medications, who was on the touching mission of trying to meet an English boyfriend who might resemble the one she had suddenly lost. He'd broken off with her, and from Toronto, she'd flown to Nairobi and gotten on our rattly train, and from Mombasa I soon put her on a bus for Malindi. Not that *they* had met in Malindi, but her beau had talked about this string of Indian Ocean beach resorts and she believed a man like him might be found vacationing there. It was a slender and forlornly different agenda than mine, but we went together to the massive stone watchtowers of Fort Jesus and climbed into a high, snug cranny to gaze out toward the crinkly bay. She was haggard from her asthma seizures and the loss of her love— inaccessible to me, of course, when I'd knocked on her hotel room door the night before—but another of the gallery of lovelorn whites you meet in Africa, who at least have the grace, I suppose, to try to do something about it. I still remember her grim, plaintive face, battling for breath, when she opened to my knock. "Don't you think it would kill me?" she said.

Hungry Somalis sail down the coast from Kismayu, and hungry Tanzanians drift up from Dar es Salaam, to make the warren of Mombasa's Old City a dangerous place. No more so than a dozen others on the continent, but its flavor combines Islamic complexities with the Hindu and the Byzantine: plus it's prostratingly hot. I found that our smart local fixer had already pre-loaded PAF's corn onto trucks to keep it dry, and loaned the rest of the grain to other organizations, like the Lutherans' and Catholics', who could use it quicker and later pay us back. So we got started.

✿

One delivery was headed up into Turkana and Toposa country, past Nairobi (where they picked up Al), into northernmost Kenya, past Lodwar, Kakuma, Lokichoggio, to Chukudum, in Sudan near the Ethiopian border area. Another, including my own bunch of trucks, turned west from Nairobi, through Gigil, Nakuru, Kisumu, and Jinja and Kampala, in Uganda, continuing from there on into the Congo, via Fort Portal. I was going to turn north, like the Nile, from Lake Victoria toward Masindi and Gulu, in Uganda, and then Equatoria in the southern Sudan. But first I accompanied the Congo trucks to Kisangani, which I always take the opportunity to do, even though my

321

French is bad and it's scarier than anywhere else. Thus a couple of weeks had passed before I did meet Ruthie at last: altogether a couple of months after her ordeal.

Wiry, though going a little sneakily toward pudge (no aid worker in a famine zone is going to be fat)—and quite sputteringly electric, as if plugged into a faulty cord—Ruth did not greet me as placidly as Dr. Livingstone had Henry Stanley. Her feeding station at Loa was in a moribund church school, built of fitted stones with an iron-sheet roof. We could imagine the stones being rolled laboriously into place a century ago by the Italian priests or monks and their convert crew; then the original rats' nest of a thatch roof proudly replaced later on. This section of the Nile had been delegated to the Italians to Christianize, whereas the Anglicans were granted more northerly and southerly pieces of the river, and the Belgians, needless to say, the Congo and its watershed.

Not that the rats disappeared with the thatch. Along with a new medicine chest and personal staples, Ruth and her Aussie assistant had asked for traps, which she now set strategically, as men unloaded the bags of millet and corn, and little boys collected whatever kernels spilled—as would the rats. Except for one truck to bring me back, I only let the drivers stay overnight because they were being paid per diem, but could report at once in a note to Al that it was Ruthie's Aussie assistant who was having panic attacks, more than her. Yet neither was quite ready for evacuation. I had no right to raise the "R" question in so many words because a war was underway, with no one to complain about a crime to. Her captors had been Nuer—enemies of the Dinka people we were feeding, and who they themselves might be surrounded by. The Dinkas were no doubt committing comparable daily crimes up the road toward Juba a ways. Her limp did give me an opening, without being personal, to ask if they had kept her shoes when they let her go.

"Sure," she said. "Anything and everything."

I'd been primed to extract either of them chivalrously from their precarious position, but they didn't leap at the offer, not even the jittery Aussie, who I should have perceived was cracking, and stuck into one of the trucks when they departed the next morning. I was still preoccupied with my trip into the Congo because my bad French had been a disaster. In the complexity of a "mission of mercy," and a tribal web that is extravagantly hallucinatory, with Lendu massacring Hema, or vice versa, I also buy diamonds, frankly, when I'm in the Congo—

which, unlike Sudan, has them—whether stolen rough from an open-pit mine or from a stream bed. In your hotel room, or to your restaurant table, a guy comes sub rosa to present you with a pouch you can sell afterward to a Ganda in the Chinese hotel in Kampala, who also knocks on your door, once you've registered, and gives you a three-hundred-percent profit for defying death, going through those roadblocks on the track back from Kisangani or Bunia to Fort Portal and Kampala.

I'd been primed, too, to flinch here at the hunger. But we'd arrived soon enough to prevent these skeletal scenes. I'd had a companion on this last leg north, a CIA guy, as it turned out, when three passports spilled out of his luggage when we roomed together in Ruthie's parsonage, as he unpacked. One "Herbert" had been born in Ipswich, Mass., and another in Tunis. He grabbed the third away from me before I could look at it. "Are you with Mossad, or our own Spook?" I asked. I'd made him travel in the cab with another driver, not to be squeezed for many hours against his professorial chest on the bumpy road. But he insisted he was a genuine Baptist preacher and preached at me like an Anabaptist to prove it until I said uncle: "You know your Bible."

"Do I look Jewish?" he joked. He was a funder, he claimed, out to "witness first-hand" how the money being generated in church collection plates in the U.S. was being spent by Ruthie. Just as the Spooks do, in fact, who fund the Sudan People's Liberation Army guerrillas that we were feeding, who were fighting Khartoum's army and militias. Mossad arms them, too, off and on, if we don't, in order to bleed the Arabs.

Herbert kept calling us Baptists Against Famine, instead of Protestants Against Famine, but prayed like one of those missionary pilots you have to fly with, if you can't go by truck. My friend Ed prayed loudly before he took off, and flew his Cessna with one finger on the map in his lap, peering downward to see if the lakes that the plane's shadow crossed were the same shape as the cartographer said they ought to be, being fresh out of a flying school in Iowa where people who feel called upon to become missionary pilots train.

"Shortest name you can pick," Ed liked to say of his. "Been to the Holy Land, but not Africa before this. But it's more Biblical here. That is, Christ would surely have his work cut out for him." Ed, with an Iowa Adam's apple, who sometimes flew Al to Ruthie's, was flabbergasted at how "biblical" this setting could be. The ancient illnesses, like polio—people crawling around on all fours right into adulthood as a result—and yellow fever, bladder prolapse, and the numbers of the blind, each one led about by a small child with a stick because there was no cataract surgery or treatment for glaucoma or trachoma. And leprosy: grandchildren caring for grandparents with hands or feet eaten away. Babies dying simply from diarrhea so frequently. He'd been dumbfounded at how any corn kernels that leaked from the floor of a truck or the seams of a Gift-of-the-American-People bag onto the dirt road were snapped up.

Herbert wasn't bogus enough to pretend to be surprised, but admired how Ruth had strings of Christmas tinsel hanging in the wind year-round to twist and throw off reflections of a spectrum of colors. We sat underneath a banyan tree, watching how huge the stars grew after dark, hearing a hyena giggle, a lion grunt. Herbert was gray-haired, which the local people understood as indicating in a white man—a *Kawaja*, not a *Mzungu*, in Arab-speaking Sudan—power as well as age, the power demonstrated in obtaining emergency deliveries of food. With his fine boots—when they were barefoot—one aged man asked him the following day if he were a king, and maybe had he walked from America? Or was he the leader of the United Nations, because of his imposing, professorial bearing, due to shuttling from the Third World to Washington, D.C., I suppose, which he hardly attempted to disguise. Could he therefore save their lives? Several told their children he could, and dozens soon ran to surround him, until tears filled his eyes. A mortar shell had gone through the roof of the defunct church in whose rectory we were sheltering, but this rendered it somehow more austere—did not detract from its dignity. In the right light, it was lovely, like old stone spiritually imbued. Herbert had not been told by either his office or ours about Ruth's ordeal, so that she could avoid gratuitous comforting, but when we were alone, I did ask her if she was okay.

"An old bag like me? A tough old bird? All right," she answered flatly, her challenging gaze not letting me escape the suspicion that my question was partly prurient. She wouldn't give an inch toward satisfying the office's curiosity as to what had happened to her when the Nuer seized her. The Nuer, who were former allies of our Dinkas, were now fighting them on behalf of Khartoum's Arabs, after, by their account, being betrayed by the Dinkas. And all three wore "biblical robes," as she pointed out, remembering our Ed, who amused her.

"Over-the-shoulder, like Jesus and the Prophets," she said. Nuer had different forehead scarifications than the Dinkas, and were being executed by firing squad by the Dinka commander at Loa if they were captured, which angered her.

My drivers slept late, before starting the mammoth drive back to the coast of Kenya. The Catholics had work for them next. But wherever they delivered it, they usually held out a little extra corn or sorghum for women who slept with them on these overnights; and so they were likely to come to the trucks stretching and yawning luxuriously. Wrong as it was, even a feminist like Ruthie worried mostly that they were bringing AIDS from the cities to camps such as this one that were so isolated the new diseases were slow to approach. What you had to remember before yelling righteously at them was the chance they ran of being blown up by a mine, machinegunned, grenaded, mortared, shot, or just pistolwhipped, or having their arms deliberately broken at a rogue roadblock when passing through the territories of guerilla groups that we weren't bringing any food to, like the Lord's Resistance Army, that Khartoum armed in exchange for the Lord's Resistance Army's attacking our relief convoys. The Nuer, in fighting our Dinkas, were being fed, oddly enough, by the U.N., though armed by Khartoum. And then there was the so-called West Nile Democratic Alliance, in northern Uganda, which was fighting Kampala and didn't mean to attack us, but sometimes mistook our trucks for the Ugandan army's, and who were supplied by dissidents in the Congo.

In the dispensary, at sunrise, laying out her replenished supplies, with a line of patients already waiting outside, Ruth glanced at her watch ironically. "Long night for your boys?" Hunched, obsessive, workaholic, she'd touched me from the start of our acquaintance, and, seeing my softening expression, she softened too. They had a dangerous drive ahead of them. After we'd been tending the ailing side by side for a while, and after our pale, brainy Herbert had woken up, breakfasted, and then mysteriously been escorted off to meet with the Sudanese People's Liberation Army's military folk, she took a break and led me out a side door and to a basketball-court-sized patch of elephant grass into which—I hadn't noticed—she'd tramped a continuously whorling, puzzling path. She needed to explain it was a Labyrinth because I'd never encountered one before: A Helix, or a Double Helix, or an earlike, snail-shell scroll to walk assiduously

325

around during a crisis or merely a meditative time. "The Archangel" had helped her plot its nine levels, she confided to me. "It saved my life."

I nodded as well as shook my head to indicate a promise not to blab about her in Nairobi. She must have sensed I had no intention of doing that, because she also showed me that she kept a regular Roman Catholic rosary to help her out, and Greek worry beads, as well as a North American Indian "spirit stick," chest-high, that she'd scratched angel or Celtic figures on, with a crescent-shaped quartz crystal suspended in the wooden circle at the top, plus a "gazing globe" of a blue mirror material, set on a pedestal, that witches supposedly couldn't look into. It all seemed quite as logical as the cruel anarchy hereabouts, with the Dinka and the Nuer tribes split apart from an effective alliance which had previously been winning both of their homelands back from Khartoum's army; and some of the nearby hill-country Acholi tribesmen fighting alongside the Dinkas but others joining the lunatic Lord's Resistance Army—who specialized in kidnapping children, and who cut people's lips off if they'd ever bad-mouthed them. The similarly disaffected local Baris were now enlisting in what they called the Equatoria Defense Force, to protect themselves against our Dinkas, and the Arabs, and everybody else. (The Kakwas, who were interspersed among the rest, sometimes got the West Nile Democratic Alliance to fight for them.) And, piercing this dismaying mess, Ruth's duty was to do her best for the hungry children, the civilian injured, the helpless bystanders, of which I saw more complexities later on. Meanwhile a large Arab garrison was being besieged by the Dinkas in the city of Juba, the regional capital, about an hour's drive in peacetime up the road from where we were. The siege was a loopy one, however, because the Arabs were equipped with tanks and armored personnel carriers and the Dinkas were not, and the Arabs held the airport, too, for resupply, so they could probably break through at will; were probably biding their time. Not for the first time, they could blitz through to the Uganda border, then withdraw to the bastion of Juba once again, because of the constant sniping along their supply line. No doubt Herbert and his masters in Washington would keep the Dinkas undersupplied for real warfare.

We bade Ruth goodbye and got back to Nairobi safe and sound, except that I had to tell our Kenyan driver, halfway, that I'd heard over the radio

326

from headquarters that a brother of his had been shot in a political quarrel, Luo vs. Kikuyu, in Kitale, his hometown, and killed. Cryptic Herbert (kiddingly, I'd asked him if Protestants Against Famine was just a front for the CIA) soon flew on to Joburg, and I returned to my storefront, with some side jobs occasionally up at Lokichoggio, Kakuma, or down at the port facilities in Mombasa, for World Vision, or Catholic Relief Services, whose country directors were acquaintanced with me. I could have applied for a regular post, but preferred the knockabout role—bringing authentic Congolese masks across the border and through Uganda to the classier specialty shops that high-end tourists stop at after their flying safaris. I did some fly-ins also, because sometimes the outfitter has to hire a personal guide for each family for them to feel catered to. "That is a giraffe," I will say. "Oh, how graceful!" they remark, "I didn't know they were so graceful." Then the gap-toothed Masai spearman who is hired to come along, in his warthog-hide sandals and red toga, with a sword in his scabbard, ocher makeup, beads, amulets, and neck bands, tells them that giraffe flesh is "the sweetest" of all meats, to add a frisson of life's ambiguities to the trip.

As before, I stayed at the Arab's otherwise, paying him a reduced weekly rate, and tipping a few key service people at the New Stanley, across the street, so I could frequent its rooftop swimming pool, street-level café and bar, etc., as if they really belonged to me. I never let a pretty girl go hungry late at night, or asked for a quid pro quo, if she'd found no customer, and when my Arab landlord happened to hear I'd been in the southern Sudan, I told him I'd worked for the Lutheran World Federation, who were known to be flying food to the populace of Juba, on the Arabs' side, and over the Dinkas' siege. That pleased him.

You meet many travelers in such a venue—businessmen with attaché cases full of banknotes to persuade the bureaucrats in Government House to sign onto a certain project scheme; ecologists on a mission to save the chimpanzees; trust-fund hippies doing this route overland, now that you couldn't go from Istanbul into Afghanistan; specialists from one of the U.N.'s many agencies studying a developmental proposal, or transiting to the more difficult terrain of Rwanda, Zimbabwe, Somalia, then resting for a spell on the way back. The New Stanley's taxi stand was busy from sunrise to pitch dark, and the pool on the roof was patronized by African middle-class parents, some of whom were teaching their kids how to swim, as well as the KLM airline pilots and Swissair stewardesses, the Danish or USAID water-project administrators waiting for permanent housing, or bustling missionaries passing through. It was so spacious high up, overlooking the central city, with Tiny Rowland's few Lonrho skyscrapers standing about on the same level, while the savage street dangers were segregated twelve stories below—so terraced and gracious, with iced drinks, potted trees, a luncheon grill, umbrellas over the tables to buffer the midday sun—that I could retreat there for a respite whenever I had ten or a dozen dollars to burn.

Nominated by New Letters, Gary Gildner

THE GOOD NEWS

by DAVID YEZZI

from POETRY

A friend calls, so I ask him to stop by.
We sip old Scotch, the good stuff, order in,
some Indian—no frills too fine for him
or me, particularly since it's been
      ages since we made the time.

Two drinks in, we've caught up on our plans.
I've sleepwalked through the last few years by rote;
he's had a nasty rough patch, quote-unquote,
on the home front. So, we commiserate,
      cupping our lowballs in our hands.

It's great to see him, good to have a friend
who feels the same as you about his lot—
that, while some grass is greener, your small plot
is crudely arable, and though you're not
      so young, it's still not quite the end.

As if remembering then, he spills his news.
Though I was pretty lit, I swear it's true,
it was as if a gold glow filled the room
and shone on him, a sun-shaft piercing through
      dense clouds, behind which swept long views.

In that rich light, he looked, not like my friend,
but some acquaintance brushed by on the train.
Had his good fortune kept me from the same,
I had to wonder, a zero-sum game
        that gave the night its early end?

Nothing strange. Our drinks were done, that's all.
We haven't spoken since. By morning, I
couldn't remember half of what the guy
had said, just his good news, my slurred good-bye,
        the click of the latch, the quiet hall.

Nominated by Dick Allen, Diann Blakely

THE POINTS OF SAIL

by SVEN BIRKERTS

from ECOTONE

THE NERVE OF FATHERING is woven through the moment—and here and now is the place to start. Late July of 2008, Cape Cod. We have come down almost every summer for the last twenty years. This time we are staying in Truro, my wife Lynn, our son Liam and his friend Caleb, and I. Our daughter Mara will take a few days off from her job next week to join us, arriving when Caleb leaves. There will be three days when we are all four together, the basic unit, taken for granted for so many years, but now become as rare as one of those planetary alignments that I no longer put stock in. *This*, though, I do put stock in. The thought of us all reassembled reaches me, wakes me with the strike of every blue ocean day.

It's mid-afternoon and I'm in Provincetown, sitting on a deck on the bayside, at one of those rental spots. Liam and Caleb have persuaded me to rent two Sunfish sailboats so they can sail the harbor together. Caleb has been taking sailing lessons all summer at home, and Liam had some a few years back, though as was clear as soon as they launched out ten minutes ago, he has forgotten whatever he learned. As Caleb's boat arrowed toward the horizon, Liam's sat turned around with sails luffing, and I watched his silhouette jerking the boom and tiller this way and that until at last he got himself re-pointed and under way. I was smiling, not much worrying about the wisdom of letting him out in his own boat—he's fourteen and as big as I am—though I did take note of a smudge of dark clouds moving in behind me.

Once Liam joined up with Caleb, the two little Sunfish zigged and zagged for the longest time in the open area between the long pier and the dozens of boats anchored in the harbor and I fell into a kind of afternoon fugue watching them. The book I'd brought lay face-down on the little table where I sat. I tracked the movement of the boats and half-listened to two men behind me talking about the perils of gin and various hangover remedies, and every so often I stood up to stretch and to glance up at the sky. Shielding my eyes with my hand, I panned left along the shoreline, past the clutter of waterfront build-ings and pilings toward Truro and Wellfleet.

I don't remember what year we first started coming to the Cape regularly. We had been down once or twice for shorter visits before we had kids. Massachusetts was still new to us—Lynn and I are both Midwesterners—and going to the ocean felt like adventure, a splurge. Fresh seafood, bare feet in the brine. What a sweet jolt to the senses it all was. And isn't this one of the unexpected things about getting older: suddenly remembering not just the specifics of an event, but the original intensity, the *fact* of the original intensity?

Those first times have mostly slipped away, replaced—overruled—by the years and years, the layers and layers, of family visits. The place, which is to say the *places*—the many rental spots in Wellfleet and Truro, including some fairly grim habitats early on—has become an archive of family life. Driving along Route 6 in either direction, I have only to glance at a particular turnoff to think—or say out loud, if Lynn is beside me—"that was the place with the marshy smell," or whatever tag best fits.

All of which is to say that this whole area, everything north of the Wellfleet line—which for me is marked by the Wellfleet Drive-In—is dense with anecdote. I have this storage box with its twenty-plus years of excerpts, all of them from summer, all from vacations away from our daily living and therefore of a kind, a timeline separate from every-thing else. "That first summer we . . ." Except that memory does not obey timelines, but associations. Shake the photos in the box until they are completely pell-mell, then reach in. That dark path by the Bayside rental fits right next to the place with the horses and that fits next to the field where we threw Frisbees, Like that. So when I shade my eyes and follow the shoreline, I am not so much seeing the things in front of me as pointing myself *back*. I am fanning the pages of a book I know, not really reading, just catching a phrase here, another there.

But now I turn again. I look across the tables on the deck and over the railing and out along the line described by the pier to my right. I see the two Sunfish, Caleb's with the darker sail heeling nicely into the wind, cutting toward the open water past pier's end, Liam's lagging, not quite right with the wind, but at least making headway. And I check over my shoulder to see how the clouds have gained, feeling a first tiny prick of anxiety. The boat rental people said the bay just past the pier was fine, but they also said they were a bit shorthanded today, that they wouldn't be taking their boat out quite as much to patrol. This flashes back to me as I see Caleb's boat slip out of sight behind the end of the pier, though I find that when I sit up straight I can follow the top part of his blue sail—accompanied, some distance behind, by Liam's, which is red.

We came those first summers when Mara was little, just the three of us, so often renting on a shoestring and ending up in some places that in retrospect seem rankly depressing, but then, when we were in them, were mainly fine. We ignored or joked about smells and bugs and cupboards lined with floral sticky-paper and those molten-toned seascapes bolted to the walls. We took pride in "making do," and I think now that we had endless patience for the clattery busywork of being young parents, the stroller-pushing, pretend-playing, all the up and back repetitions. I remember one summer we set ourselves up in a box-shaped little house—it was one of a dozen or so—on a hillside near Wellfleet. And in our largesse, before ever even setting eyes on the place, we invited my mother to visit for a few days, with Lynn's sister to arrive as soon as she left. It turned out that there was barely room for all of us in the living room, with its huge picture window fronting the road. It rained most of the week. I was beside myself with boredom. But I also wanted to be a good father. I played and played with Mara, trying to make her vacation a happy one. Alas, we had nowhere to go. My only diversion was a box of dominoes found in the closet. I sat Mara down on the floor beside me and we built towers. Over and over, piece by ticking piece, always the same basic design. How high could we make it? And how irritated I got if Mara knocked one of my good towers down! I was building for myself, desperate to stay amused. Somewhere we have a Polaroid of the two of us sitting beside our prize construction. Looking at the photo, I think what a stunning, unbelievably sweet little girl she was—and how ridiculous it was for me to get so serious about stacking those bones.

What kind of a father was I? I know that I tried to be different from my father, who all through my childhood maintained that he loved us—and clearly did—but who also told us, often, that we would appreciate him only when we were older and more intelligent. *Then* we would talk. But I could not imagine having that kind of detached deferral with my own child. I wanted entry to Mara's world, a role in shaping her mind, her sense of things. I wanted to get as close as I could.

My problem was that I had no idea how to proceed. I was never one for playing. The sight of a spinner on a gussied-up board game, or some molded plastic doll, filled me with fatigue. I hated almost all toys, nor could I endure the infantilized pretend chatter that was the required accompaniment to all forms of parent-child play, at least from what I'd observed. "Snuffy is a *niiiiiice* kitty . . ." Yikes! I could finally do only what I knew to do, what I *liked* to do. I could talk. I invented characters, told stories, created plot situations that grew into one another and became more and more elaborate over time. Steffie and Kevin, their friend Lenny, the villains Moe and Joe, Steffie's rival Cherry Lalou—and the world they lived in, the street, neighborhood, town . . . I worked hard at these; the adventures were good ones—so I thought, anyway—full of surprises, resisting pat endings but still upholding a basic picture of a moral universe, a triumph of idealism over low impulse. And Mara loved them. Every night, or whenever we had time together, she would beam at me: "Tell me a Kevin and Steffie, Dad." This went on for years.

Mara is almost twenty now. She is taking a break from college, living with roommates in an apartment in Belmont, ten minutes from where we live. She has a forty-hour-a-week job in a stationery store in Harvard Square, though she barely makes ends meet. She is, by her own admission, unsettled, experiencing vivid and frightening dreams and moods that can suddenly plummet and leave her feeling sad and exposed. The sensations she describes are familiar to me—they reach all the way back into my own young years.

I wasn't thinking about Mara just then, as I stood again on the deck to stretch, but I was very much aware of her. Her funks, the tone of her recent phone calls, knowing that she would be coming soon. I peered out at what I could see of the bay but all these things were there in my peripheral awareness.

I was having my first real doubt now. I could still see the tips of both sails, moving toward the other part of the bay, just above the edge of the pier, clean little shark-fin shapes. But the sky was definitely darkening and the wind was picking up slightly and the farther out Liam took his boat, the less confidence I had in his bluster about knowing how to sail. I turned around to see if there was a clock in the rental shed. The girl who worked there had left her counter and was standing on a crate, shading her eyes and peering at the harbor. She must have picked up on my agitation, because just then she said: "They'll be fine—but they shouldn't go too far out." I nodded. *They would know that*, I told myself. Then—*they're fourteen-year-old boys, they* won't *know*. I looked back quickly to make sure I could see the sails.

Liam has always been different from Mara. Six years younger, he is made from other material. While she is delicate, slightly wan, he is fleshy and boisterously solid. He always has been. Since preschool, he has never *not* been the biggest boy in his class. Barely into his teens, he has already caught up to me, and I am not small. The other night I told him to stand up straight against a wooden beam in the Truro house. I put the top of a DVD case flat on his head and drew a faint line. Then I told him to do the same for me. We had to laugh—we were the thickness of a pencil lead apart.

Given his size and his point-blank confidence, I tend to forget his age and essential vulnerability. When I have to face it I can get overwhelmed. He could hurt himself, cry a child's tears. Or be in danger. The worst was years ago. He was seven or eight years old, in summer camp. Lynn and I got a call at noon one day that we should come get him, that he was in the infirmary, having what appeared to be an asthma attack. We hurried over to bring him home, worried, but also thinking he had just overtaxed himself. We told him to rest in his room. Suddenly he was standing at the top of the stairs, red in the face, making a noise that was almost a bleat, terror on his face. He couldn't breathe; he was choking for air. Without hesitation we sat him down there on the top step and called the doctor, who told us to get an ambulance right away. Which we did. And moments later— time was a jumble—I was behind the wheel of our car, following an ambulance across town, hurtling through red lights, my calm life gone into a hyperventilating free fall that would not stop until more than an hour later, when a doctor came out to assure us that Liam's breathing had been stabilized and that he would be fine.

How long it took—maybe years—for that shock to fully ebb, for some trace of that anxiety not to be there every time he went outside to play, daily breathing treatments notwithstanding. I think of the way we look at our children when we are afraid, the way we read their eyes to see if they are telling us everything, and the terrible sense we have of their fragility, which for me goes all the way back to the very first night we brought Mara home from the hospital and set her up in a little crib. I remember how I just lay there listening to the breathing sounds, sure that if I tuned them out for an instant they would stop. A superstition, much the same as how I used to believe that if I relaxed my will for an instant while flying the airplane I was in, it would instantly plummet. Life has taught me much about my fears and about my grandiose presumptions, but only gradually.

Liam and Mara, what a strange distribution of personalities—no, what a pairing of souls. I have to think in terms of souls where my closest people are concerned. To think of them as personalities diminishes them, a personality being something one can put a boundary around somehow. They could not be more different in who they are, or in what each drew forth from us as parents. We never had a program or a plan. I have never had a clear instinct for what kind of father to be, not in terms of what I should be doing, modeling, instructing. I have somehow trusted to being myself. Maybe a better version—kinder, more attentive, and more consistent in my responses than I might be if I did not feel the responsibility of children.

My idea—and feeling—of being a father has changed from year to year, if not week to week. The father of a newborn is very different from the father of a toddler or a school-age child or a pre-teen or . . . Is there anything constant in it, besides the love and care, the great givens, the fact that I would do anything at any time to ensure their safety and well-being? But in terms of who I *am*—well, it stands to reason, doesn't it? The father of newborn Mara was thirty-six, the father of teenage Mara was fifty, and the man looking out for some trace of his teenage son is slowly pushing sixty.

I keep an image that I refer to from time to time to orient myself, from an afternoon moment on a Wellfleet side road some years ago. We had a week-long rental, an upstairs apartment in a frowsy old house that had been divided up to accommodate people just like us. It was grassy, though, and shady, with a nice stretch of road to walk, and nearby we had discovered a small horse farm, which became a popular destination for keeping the kids amused. We would stand by the roadside, pressed against the wooden fence, and watch the horses being exercised in the corral. Mara might have been ten or eleven that summer, Liam four or five, and I somewhere in my late forties. I do all this approximate figuring because my epiphany—I think it counts as one—had everything to do with ages and proportions.

It was the very end of a beautiful summer afternoon, the light beginning to slant. But though I was vacationing, I was also trying very hard to get some writing done, to bring a book project around to completion. It was because I wanted to think, to stew in my own notions, that I begged off when Lynn and the kids started off down the road on another walk. I waved them off, I remember, and then sat myself down on a steep, grassy verge in front of the house and watched. They were moving slowly, one or both kids dawdling. I sat and stared at them, and as I did I felt come over me, gradually, the clearest and sweetest melancholy. It was as if I had suddenly moved out of myself, pulling away and rising like some insect that has left its transparent shell stuck to the branch of a tree. It was as if the needle on the balance had drawn up completely straight; the string I plucked was exactly in tune, I watched my wife and two kids walking away from me down the road and I got it. I was *exactly* in the middle—of the afternoon, of the summer, of an actuarial life, of the great generational cycle. Outlined against the horizon in front of me were those three shapes, and behind me, imagined on the opposite horizon, were my own two parents, both still alive and in health, just coming into their seventies. I was in the middle, at once a son, a father, and something else: a man with plans and projects in his head, no one's person. It was the frailest and most temporary alignment, and the sensation just then of everything holding steady, hovering in place, exalted me, just as the knowledge that it had to change filled me with sorrow. I took a breath and swallowed my metaphysics. I headed in to use the bit of time I had to do my work. For if parenting held any practical lesson for me, it was that I had to learn to stake out time, to filch every little scrap I could.

Something's happened just now, here between one glance and the next. There were two sails in view beyond the line of the pier, but when I look I see only one. The blue sail. Caleb's. Fatherhood compresses into a single pulse, long enough for me to jump off the edge of the deck to the sand and start jogging around the ropes and old buoys to where the pier meets the shore, and when I reach that point I duck and go under to get to the other side, where I can see. As I straighten up I see just the one boat, and I can't get a clear picture of the rest.

337

There are other boats, sailboats, bobbing at anchor, just masts. I scour the water surface between—nothing. I am not afraid, exactly, but definitely anxious. Liam can swim, he has a life vest, he is right there somewhere. And yes, yes, there—I center in—I spot something moving right next to one of the anchored boats. A small commotion. Caleb's sunfish appears to be heeling around in that direction. Liam has obviously tipped over; he is there fussing in the water next to his capsized boat.

I know, sure as anything, that he will not be able to right the thing by himself. And Caleb won't be able to do much. Still not worried, I also realize I should tell the girl at the rental shack so that she can send someone out to give him a hand.

When I get back, the girl is standing on her crate with binoculars. She is ahead of me. "I've got Jimmy on his way to check it out." When I turn, a small launch is chugging toward pier's end. "He'll just bring them in," she says. "It's getting kind of blowy out there." And so it is. A glance up reveals that our blue day has gone completely cloudy, and that the water is getting choppy. I return to my chair to wait.

There is no guide to any of this. Kids get older in sudden jumps and with each jump the scramble begins. Strategies that worked so reliably one day are useless in the face of the new. Moods, secrecies, distances, brash eruptions. You know things are shifting when you suddenly find yourself choosing your words, reading cues like you never had to before. I had thought the family, our blustering foursome, immutable until Mara arrived at adolescence. Then she changed. She grew moody, and these moods were not something she could leave at home when vacation time came. This altered everything. It marked out before and after. *Before* was all of our innocent routines: walking to the beach or to the pond, or getting ice cream, or lounging in front of a rented movie cracking jokes. *After* was a new unknown that threw so much about family life into question. Who were we that this young person would find a thousand reasons not to be with us? Who was she to take us in with evaluating eyes, to wander off on solitary errands that left the rest of us wanting? "Family" now felt like something picked apart. What had happened to our invincibility?

To be a parent, a father, was suddenly to contend with the world washing in. Or adulthood. Adulthood is a force that no wall of childhood can ultimately withstand. Fatherhood has its first incarnation as a presiding and protecting. Later it becomes a kind of brokering. We start to run interference between the world as we know it and the world as our children are learning about it. If early parenting is about the fostering of innocence and the upholding of certain illusions—to give the child's self time to solidify—the later stage of parenting asks for a growing recognition of sorrow, cruelty, greed, of the whole un-adorned truth of things, the truth that the child, now adolescent, will encounter, but marked and annotated and put into perspective.

The last few of our Cape summers have made me feel this acutely, more than our daily-world interactions. The idea of vacation is so im-bued with heedlessness and innocence—the stock imagery of families relaxing together—that any small sadness or disaffection is amplified. The kitschy menu board at the clam shack seems to mock us, the shop-window posters, the happy blond groups bicycling along the beach road. For there is our teenager moping in the backseat, or on her beach towel, or lying curled up in bed as if nothing in the world is worth the exertion of sitting up. At times the daily business left be-hind can seem like the real vacation, the place to get back to.

I'm on my feet again. Foreground and background—my thought and my immediate awareness—seem to merge as soon as the procession comes into view from behind the pier. The launch with two silhou-ettes—one of them Liam's. And then, behind, the Sunfish with sail down, on a tow. Caleb's blue-sailed boat trails behind. All's well, I think, shaking my head. The girl from the rental desk makes her way down to the beach. I wave to Liam, wait for some nod. But though he seems to take me in, I get no response. He is sitting up very straight in the back of the launch, looking the way prisoners always do in movies.

I jump down from the deck and join the girl on the beach. Jimmy has unhooked the Sunfish and pushed it toward shore; he turns the boat to dock it at the pier. Liam remains upright in his seat. He doesn't respond when Caleb passes the launch on his way in.

A few minutes later, he moves toward me along the pier, his life vest still buckled tight. He looks pale, and when he draws closer and I reach to touch his shoulder, I catch something new in his expression. He's afraid.

The story comes out in jags, and not right away. First we all have to gather together again. Lynn arrives from her errands around town and we mill around for a few minutes collecting our things. And then the four of us are back on the main street, scouting for a restaurant. Only when we get a table and sit does Liam open up. It jars me. He switches into an edgy sort of agitation, not like him, talking fast and using his hands. I'm expecting some dramatic bluster, but I'm wrong. "I thought I was going to drown," he says. The voice itself, the tone, is flat. I know he's serious. "I was in irons—facing right into the wind— and then I got pushed into this other boat." We're at our table on the enclosed patio of a big bayside restaurant, paying full attention. In the five minutes since we arrived the sky has gone black—the wind is shaking the plastic around us, the first drops trailing down.

It's not until we've placed our order that the whole story finally comes out. And now I start to put it together, the way he was sitting in the launch, the look on his face when he walked toward me. I get the surface of it, then I get more. And even now, as I write, I'm feeling still other layers. I feel the shadow of the wing—the dread—as I did when he was talking. Liam could have drowned; it could have happened. He will need to tell it again and again to us before that look on his face goes away.

He was doing fine, he claims, until he passed the pier and found himself headed toward the moored boats. "I started to get scared," he says. The boats were coming up fast, and he tried to turn. "I messed up." I stare at his hands, big and red. "I got turned around and all of a sudden I was in irons." I can see he likes the phrase. "My boat got pushed back into this other boat and then my tiller got caught in its rope." He pauses to get the sequence straight, takes a breath. I think how I'd seen none of this, only the triangular peak of his red sail stalled in the distance. He explains how he was trying to work the tiller free with one hand while using his other to jostle the boom back and forth in hopes of catching some wind. And then—

"I don't really know what happened, something screwed up. I got the tiller free but the boom whipped around and all of a sudden it pulled the rope around my neck." That was when it happened. His boat had heeled over with a rush, jerking him into the water—with the rope suddenly around his neck. The force of capsizing instantly tightened the noose and as the mast pulled down to the water he could barely get his hand in between the rope and his throat. He was being pulled down by the boat. He panicked, thinking he was drowning. And then somehow, he doesn't know how, he slipped his head free.

He told his tale a number of times that night, getting his version the way he wanted it, gradually putting the picture outside himself, giving it over to us. As we listened, we all did that primitive thing. We kept reaching over to touch him. I put my hand on his, Lynn leaned her head against him, Caleb tapped his shoulder. The three of us were making him real again, planting him in our midst, taking him back from that "almost."

"You could have drowned, my God—" We said it again and again as the rain hammered down. And we talked about it for the rest of the night. We hovered around, bringing the "almost" in close and then fending it off again. I thought of myself there on the deck, oblivious, and could not resist extrapolating: a big obvious message about how it is between parents and their children—between any people who are close, really—how it snarls up together, all the vigilance and ignorance, luck and readiness, love and fear. We know nothing.

Four days before we have to leave the Truro house, Mara arrives. We are the basic unit at last. Caleb took the ferry back to Boston the day after the sailing episode. Reunion is sweet. But the ground feeling, the joy, of having everyone together in the same place, with nothing on the schedule except trips to the ocean and the making of meals, is overlaid with darker tones. Mara is still in her mood, it's obvious. She tells us that she has been having bad dreams and feeling anxious every night. I see her on the couch, reading a magazine, looking for all the world like a young woman relaxing with her family, except that something in the shoulders, the tilt of the head, gives her away.

Mara gets through the first night easily enough. In fact, she sleeps like she hasn't slept in a long time, deadweight sleep. Sleep like I have not had for decades. She told me to wake her early, that she would join me for my walk, and once I've had my coffee I try. But after a few separate prods I give it up. I go alone all the way down the long hill to the deli market to buy the papers. Heading back, I think about our long season of morning walks. It lasted for years, that season, and I remember it often. How we moved in companionable solitudes, rarely breaking into talk. We walked almost every day, miles at a time. She told me once, later, that she did it to keep me from being sad. I may have been doing it for the same reason—we were tunneling the mountain from opposite sides. But then our morning schedules changed and we tapered off.

I open the sliding door off the deck quietly—everyone is still sleeping—and I drop the *Times* and *Globe* on the kitchen counter. I see Mara sprawled on her bed much as I left her. I pause in the doorway and study her. I forget in which Greek myth one of the gods drapes a

341

cloth woven from gold over a sleeper's body, but I think of that as I stand there. I see how her face goes all the way back to first innocence.

Mara does seem happier now. Being away, or being with us, has given her a lift. She starts to crack wise, which is always a sign. And she is eager to go shopping with Lynn in Provincetown. That next day they disappear for a few hours. And then in the late afternoon we all go to the beach. The tide is low, the light spectacular. Lynn and Liam take their boogie boards down to where the waves are breaking. Mara wraps herself in a towel and reads Nabokov's *Ada*. I just stare, first to the left where the beach gradually merges into dune line, then, with a visceral pleasure—*There is nothing like this*, I think—over to the right, where the flat sand reaches into the faintest mist and the shoreline at every second takes that quicksilver print of water, and where silhouettes stand and wade and swim in the distance.

Mara doesn't go in this afternoon, or the next. There was a time when she would just *fling* herself into the tallest waves she could find. She would yowl and shake herself and do it again. I feel, though, like something about all this water is beginning to reach up to her now, like she might be almost ready to push up off her towel and march down. But not yet. We sit side by side and watch Liam, our appointed stone gatherer.

Lynn asked him to find some large ocean stones for her garden. Liam likes this kind of thing, a task. He has his big goggles on and every few seconds we see him go arsey-turvey into the waves, and then up he comes, arm lifted high, clutching the next prize, which he stops to inspect for a moment and then either hurls to the shore or releases back into the water. The Sunfish episode has receded. This is in keeping with his style. If for Mara life backs up and grows scary, for Liam it catches, pauses, and then rushes on again. They are so very different, and I look from one to the other as if recognizing that essential fact. It's the kind of thing I might say out loud to Lynn, but she's not here. She's out swimming—I see her paralleling the shore, a small moving shape down to my left. I would tell Mara, but Mara is all at once up. While we were both sitting there watching Liam the moment came. She has dropped her towel and is on her feet. With a quick over-the-shoulder glance she tromps down the sand and right to the water's edge. No running back and forth to work up to action. She pushes her hair back behind her ears and steps thigh-deep into the water. A flinch—I feel a sympathetic shock—and then she's in, under, three seconds vanished, and up with a thrust. And in again. I want to shout something, but I don't. I wish for the cold salt to scour her clean.

Liam, I see, has noticed his sister in the water. This makes him happy. I can tell. He turns away from the rock project and goes dol-phin-bounding toward her. He loves company, and the company of his sister, especially. When she can be gotten to. He wants to cruise the waves with her now, standing by her side. Nothing in common be-tween their body types—he dwarfs her. But they are brother and sis-ter, something in the way they stand side by side tells on them. They share humor—it's invisible, but I recognize it—and care. They share a certain brashness, too. When the big wave they've been waiting for ar-rives they push into it with the same slugging lunge. Two heads, and then, right when the wave thins to breaking, two tumbling oblongs flashing against the green.

Nominated by Ecotone, Tom Sleigh

FOR WHAT THE HELL
THEY NEEDED IT FOR

by JOEL BROUWER

from NEW ENGLAND REVIEW

For Crazy Horse came to Fort Robinson
to set a rumor straight and died. For he
brought white lilies to the clinic and asked
a nurse for water. For he woke from dream-
less sleep to a child pounding on the door
of the bookmobile and the sense no time
had passed. For whoever cried for water
from the stockade. For South Dakota, land
where he drove the country bookmobile and
she adopted practical methods to
set straight abstract problems. For the rumors
about how Crazy Horse died passed around
the stockade like blankets rank with pox. For
no time passing. For no time passing. For
time passing and already September
and the practical problems of the kids
crowding around the bookmobile. For pox
rising in a dreamless dark. For her still
dreamy beneath the sedative seeing
the lilies between the water pitcher
and tissues and saying aren't lilies for
a funeral. For whoever pounded

the stockade door in fear having woken
with the sense no time had passed. For the book
about Crazy Horse and the water he
drank reading it. For manual vacuum
aspiration and related methods.
For a rumor set straight. For the mother
who told him what my kids need ain't in no
damn book so what the hell they need it for.
For my lands are where my dead lie buried.
For what they did with it after. For time
passing in the century's dreamless sleep
as forts rose on the prairie like lilies.
For the last time and for the final time.
For the book about the methods he read
under water. For Crazy Horse dead by
his own hand. For a lily will crumble
beneath its strangling gilt. For Crazy Horse
murdered. For gilt obscene and abstract, but
steadfast. For Crazy Horse wore no paint or
war bonnet into battle, but covered
himself with dust and ash mixed with water.
For it came to him to do this in a dream.

Nominated by New England Review, Michael Martone

STOLPESTAD

fiction by WILLIAM LYCHACK

from PLOUGHSHARES

WAS TOWARD THE END OF YOUR SHIFT, a Saturday, another one of those long slow lazy afternoons of summer—sun never burning through the clouds, clouds never breaking into rain—the odometer like a clock ticking all these bored little pent-up streets and mills and tenements away. The coffee shops, the liquor stores, laundromats, police, fire, gas stations to pass—this is your life, Stolpestad—all the turns you could make in your sleep, the brick-work and shop fronts and river with its stink of carp and chokeweed, the hills swinging up free from town, all momentum and mood, roads smooth and empty, this big blue hum of cruiser past houses and lawns and long screens of trees, trees cutting open to farms and fields all contoured and high with corn, air thick and silvery, as if something was on fire somewhere—still with us?

The sandy turnaround—always a question, isn't it?

Gonna pull over and ride back down or not?

End of your shift—or nearly so—and in comes the call over the radio. It's Phyllis, dispatcher for the weekend, and she's sorry for doing this to you, but a boy's just phoned for help with a dog. And what's she think you look like now, you ask, town dog-catcher? Oh, you should be so lucky, she says and gives the address and away we go.

No siren, no speeding, just a calm quiet spin around to this kid and his dog, back to all the turns you were born, your whole life spent along the same sad streets. It has nothing to do with this story, but there are days you idle slow and lawful past these houses as if to glimpse someone or something—yourself as a boy, perhaps—the apartments stacked with porches, the phone poles and wires and side-walks all close and cluttered, this woman at the curb as you pull up and step out of the cruiser.

Everything gets a little worse from here, the boy running out of the brush in back before you so much as say hello. He's what—eight or nine years old—skinny kid cutting straight to his mother. Presses him-self to her side, catches his breath, his eyes going from you to your uniform, your duty belt, the mother trying to explain what happened and where she is now, the dog, the tall grass, behind the garage, she's pointing. And the boy—he's already edging away from his mother—little stutter steps and the kid's halfway around the house to take you to the animal, his mother staying by the side porch as you follow to-ward the garage and garbage barrels out back, you and the boy wading out into the grass and scrub weeds, the sumac, the old tires, empty bottles, paint cans, rusted car axle, refrigerator door. Few more steps and there—small fox-colored dog—lying in the grass, a beagle mix, as good as sleeping at the boy's feet, that vertigo buzz of insects rising and falling in the heat, air thick as a towel over your mouth.

And you stand there and wait—just wait—and keep waiting, the boy not saying a word, not looking away from the dog, not doing anything except kneeling next to the animal, her legs twisted awkward behind her, the grass tamped into a kind of nest where he must have squatted next to her, where this boy must have talked to her, tried to soothe her, tell her everything was all right. There's a steel cooking pot to one side—water he must have carried from the kitchen—and in the quiet the boy pulls a long stem of grass and begins to tap at the dog. The length of her muzzle, the outline of her chin, her nose, her ear—it's like he's drawing her with the brush of grass—and as you stand there, he pushes the feather top of grass into the corner of her eye. It's a streak of cruel he must have learned from someone, the boy pushing the stem, pressing it on her until, finally, the dog's eye opens as black and shining as glass. She bares her teeth at him, the boy painting her tongue with the tip of grass, his fingers catching the tags at her throat, sound like ice in a drink.

And it's work to stay quiet, isn't it? A real job to let nothing happen, to just look away at the sky, to see the trees, the garage beyond, the dog again, the nest of grass, this kid brushing the grain of her face, the dog's mouth pulled back, quick breaths in her belly. Hours you stand there—days—standing there still now, aren't you?

And when he glances up to you, his chin is about to crumble, the boy about to disappear at the slightest touch, his face pale and raw and ashy, scoured-looking. Down to one knee next to him—and you're going to have to shoot this dog—you both must realize this by now, the way she can't seem to move, her legs like rags, that sausage link of intestine under her. The boy leans forward and sweeps an ant off the dog's shoulder.

God knows you don't mean to try to chatter this kid into feeling better, but when he turns, you press your lips into a line and smile and ask him what her name is. He turns to the dog again—and again you wait—wait and watch this kid squatting hunch-curved next to the dog, your legs going needles and nails under you, the kid's head a strange whorl of hair as you hover above him, far above this boy, this dog, this nest, this field. And when he glances to you, it's a spell he's breaking, all of this about to become real with her name—Goliath—but we call her Gully for short, he says.

And you ask if she's his dog.

And the boy nods—mine and my father's, he says.

And you go to one knee, touch your hand to the grass, ask the boy how old he is.

And he says nine.

And what grade is nine again?

Third.

The dog's eyes are closed again when you look—bits of straw on her nose, her teeth yellow, strands of snot on her tongue—nothing moving until you stand up and kick the blood back into your legs, afternoon turning to evening, everything going grainy in the light. The boy dips his hand in the cooking pot and tries to give water to the dog with his fingers, sprinkling her face, her mouth.

A moment passes—and then another—and soon you're brushing the dust from your knee and saying, C'mon—let's get back to your mother, before she starts to worry.

She appears out of the house as you approach—out of the side door on the steps as you and the boy cross the lawn—boy straight to her side once again, his mother drawing him close, asking was everything okay out there. And neither of you say anything—everyone must see what's coming—if you're standing anywhere near this yard you have to know that sooner or later she's going to ask if you can put this dog down for them. She'll ask if you'd like some water or lemonade, if you'd like to sit a minute, and you'll thank her and say no and shift your weight from one leg to the other, the woman asking what you think they should do.

Maybe you'll take that glass of water after all, you say—the boy sent into the house—the woman asking if you won't just help them.

Doesn't she want to call a vet?

No, she tells you—the boy pushing out of the house with a glass of water for you—you thanking him and taking a good long drink, the taste cool and metallic, the woman with the boy at her side, her hand on the boy's shoulder, both of them stiff as you hand the glass back and say thank you again.

A deep breath and you ask the woman if she has a shovel. To help bury the dog, you say.

She unstiffens slightly, says she'd rather the boy and his father do that when he gets home from work.

In a duffel in the trunk of the cruiser is an automatic—an M9—and you swap your service revolver for this Beretta of yours. No discharge, no paperwork, nothing official to report, the boy staying with his mother as you cross the yard to the brush and tall weeds in back, grasshoppers spurting up and away from you, dog smaller when you find her, as if she's melting, lying there, grass tamped in that same nest around her, animal as smooth as suede. A nudge with the toe of your shoe and she doesn't move—you standing over her with this hope that she's already dead—that shrill of insects in the heat and grass as you nudge her again. You push until she comes to life, her eye opening slow and black to you—you with this hope that the boy will be running any moment to you now, hollering for you to stop—and again the work of holding still and listening.

Hey, girl, you say and release the safety of the gun. You bend at the waist and gently touch the sight to just above the dog's ear, hold it there, picture how the boy will have to find her—how they're going to hear the shots, how they're waiting, their breaths held—and you slide the barrel to the dog's neck, to just under the collar, the wounds hidden as you squeeze one sharp crack, and then another, into the animal.

You know the loop from here—the mills, the tenements, the streetlights flickering on in the dusk—and still it's the long way around home, isn't it? Wife and pair of boys waiting dinner for you, hundred reasons to go straight to them, but soon you're an hour away, buying a sandwich from a vending machine, calling Sheila from a payphone to say you're running a little late. Another hour back to town, slow and

349

lawful, windows open, night plush and cool, roads a smooth hum back through town for a quick stop at The Elks, couple of drinks turning into a few—you know the kind of night—same old crew at the bar playing cribbage, talking Yankees, Red Sox, this little dog they heard about, ha, ha, ha. Explain how word gets around, ha, ha, ha—how you gave the pooch a blindfold and cigarette, ha, ha, ha—another round for everyone, ha, ha, ha—three cheers for Gully—the next thing you know being eleven o'clock and the phone behind the bar for you.

It's Sheila—and she's saying someone's at the house, a man and a boy on the porch for you—be right there, you tell her. Joey asks if you want one for the road as you hand the receiver over the bar, and you drink this last one standing up, say goodnight, and push yourself out the door to the parking lot, the darkness cool and clear as water, the sky scattershot with stars. And as you stand by the car and open your pants and piss half-drunk against that hollow drum of the fender, it's like you've never seen stars before, the sky some holy-shit vastness all of a sudden, you gazing your bladder empty, staring out as if the stars were suns in the black distance.

It's not a dream—though it often feels like one—the streets rivering you home through the night and the dark, the déjà vu of a pickup truck in the driveway as you pull around to the house, as if you've seen or imagined or been through all of this before, or will be through it all again, over and over, this man under the light of the porch, cigarette smoke like steam in the air, transistor sound of crickets in the woods. He's on the steps as you're out of the car—the lawn, the trees, everything underwater in the dark—and across the wet grass you're asking what you can do for him.

He's tall and ropy and down the front walk toward you, cigarette in his hand, you about to ask what's the problem when there's a click from the truck. It's only a door opening—but look how jumpy you are, how relieved to see only a boy in the driveway—the kid from this afternoon cutting straight to go to his father, the man tossing his cigarette into the grass, brushing his foot over it, apologizing for how late it must be.

How can I help you?

You're a police officer, says the man, aren't you?

And Sheila's out on the porch now—the light behind her—a silhouette at the rail, she's hugging a sweater around herself, her voice small like a girl's in the dark, asking if everything's all right, you taking a step toward the house and telling her that everything's fine, another step and you're saying you'll be right in, she should go back inside, it's late.

And once again, the man apologizes for the hour and says he'll only be a minute—your wife going into the house—this man on your lawn pulling the boy to his side, their faces shadowed and smudged in the dark, the man bending to say something to his son, the kid saying yessir, his father standing straight, saying that you helped put a dog down this afternoon.

And before you even open your mouth, he's stepping forward and thanking you for your help—the man shaking your hand, saying how pleased, how grateful, how proud, how difficult it must have been—but his tone's all wrong, all snaky, a salesman nudging his boy ahead to give you—and what's this?

Oh, he says, it's nothing, really.

But the boy's already handed it to you—the dog's collar in your hand, the leather almost warm, tags like coins—the guy's voice all silk and breeze as he explains how they wanted you to have it, a token of appreciation, in honor of all you did for them.

And it's a ship at sea to stand on that lawn like this—everything swaying and off-balanced for you—and before you say a word he's laughing as if to the trees, the man saying to put it on your mantle, maybe, or under your fucken pillow. Put it on your wife, he says and laughs and swings around all serious and quiet to you, the man saying he's sorry for saying that.

Nice lady, he says—the boy milk-blue in the night, cold and skinny as he stands next to his father—the man telling you how he made it home a little late after work that night. Was after nine by the time he and the kid got around to the dog, he says, dark when the two of them get out to the field—flashlight and shovel—almost decide to wait until morning.

Can't find her for the life of us, he says, but then we do—not like she's going anywhere—takes us a while to dig that hole, never seen so many stones, so many broken bottles.

He nudges the boy—startles the kid awake, it seems—and then turns to the house behind them, the yellow light of windows, the curtains, the blade of roofline, the black of trees, the shrubs. He lets out a long sigh and says it's a fine place you seem to have here.

You say thanks—and then you wait—watch for him to move at you.

Any kids?

Two boys, you say.

Younger or older than this guy here?

351

Few years younger, you say.

He nods—has his hand on the boy's shoulder—you can see that much in the dark, can hear the sigh, the man deflating, his head tipping to one side slightly. So, he says, like I was saying, took us a while to get the hole dug. And when we go to take the collar, she tries to move away from us—still alive—all this time, she's been out there—imagine seeing how ants had gotten all into her.

He hums a breath and runs his palm over the boy's hair, says the vet arrives a little later, asks if we did this to the dog, makes us feel where you're supposed to shoot an animal, this slot just under the ear. He reaches his finger out to you and touches, briefly, the side of your head—almost tender—the smell of cigarettes on his hand, your feet wet and cold in the grass, jaw wired tight, the boy and his father letting you hang there in front of them, two of them just waiting for whatever it is you will say next to this, the man clucking his tongue, finally, saying, Anyway—helluva a thing to teach a kid, don't you think?

A pause—but not another word—and he starts them back toward the truck, the man and the boy, their trails across the silver wet of the lawn, the pickup doors clicking open and banging closed—one, and then another—the engine turning over, the headlights a long sweep as they ride away, the sound tapering to nothing. And in the silence, in the darkness, you stand like a thief on the lawn—stand watching this house for signs of life—wavering as you back gently away from the porch, away from the light of the windows, away until you're gone at the edge of the woods, a piece of dark within the dark, Sheila arriving to that front door, eventually, this woman calling for something to come in out of the night.

Nominated by Ploughshares

THE KAYAK AND
THE EIFFEL TOWER

by FLEDA BROWN

from THE SOUTHERN REVIEW

The white sheet I remember, flashing across
the bed, and I was watching my mother and the crying
and the bed disappeared and all was white
but it was not snow, it was my mind, and then, oddly,
she took us in a taxi to the movies, I think
it was *Ben Hur*. It was his postcard, now I know,
from that woman in the Philippines, back when
he was a soldier. All this, a movement
of shapes, nothing to hold on to. The kayak
is like that. It slides through the water and the paddle
goes on one side then the other, and there is the sway
of the boat and then the correction. It was
like that, and it was like the Eiffel Tower, all filigree
and lace, because I couldn't see anything solid,
but of course it was night and the movie was over,
I guess, but I remember the feel of her body,
her coat against my coat and the sidewalk rough
the way a child remembers the sidewalk: closer
than it will ever be again, grain after grain, and down
inside the grains, the press of earth that made
the grains, and the grinding that broke them apart,
and there were cracks in the sidewalk, and I swayed

a little as if I were in a kayak, not breathing but
sliding through with my mind so far away it was
on a lake, far out, and the shore wasn't the wool coat
my mother wore, not the coat, not anywhere.
And where was my father? Home, maybe, while
all this was rising from the bottom like a log, or a huge
gar, all the way to the top of the Eiffel Tower, while
my kayak dreamed its way off into some other story.

Nominated by Stephen Corey, Lia Purpura

ACCIDENT, MASS. AVE.

by JILL MCDONOUGH

from THE THREEPENNY REVIEW

I stopped at a red light on Mass. Ave.
in Boston, a couple blocks away
from the bridge, and a woman in a beat-up
old Buick backed into me. Like, cranked her wheel,
rammed right into my side. I drove a Chevy
pickup truck. It being Boston, I got out
of the car yelling, swearing at this woman,
a little woman, whose first language was not English.
But she lived and drove in Boston, too, so she knew,
we both knew, that the thing to do
is get out of the car, slam the door
as hard as you fucking can and yell things like *What the fuck
were you thinking? You fucking blind? What the fuck
is going on? Jesus Christ!* So we swore
at each other with perfect posture, unnaturally angled
chins. I threw my arms around, sudden
jerking motions with my whole arms, the backs
of my hands toward where she had hit my truck.

But she hadn't hit my truck. She hit
the tire; no damage done. Her car
was fine, too. We saw this while

we were yelling, and then we were stuck.
The next line in our little drama should have been
Look at this fucking dent! I'm not paying for this
shit. I'm calling the cops, lady. Maybe we'd throw in a
You're in big trouble, sister, or *I just hope for your sake*
there's nothing wrong with my fucking suspension, that
sort of thing. But there was no fucking dent. There
was nothing else for us to do. So I
stopped yelling, and she looked at the tire she'd
backed into, her little eyebrows pursed
and worried. She was clearly in the wrong, I was enormous,
and I'd been acting as if I'd like to hit her. So I said
Well, there's nothing wrong with my car, nothing wrong
with your car . . . are you OK? She nodded, and started
to cry, so I put my arms around her and I held her, middle
of the street, Mass. Ave., Boston, a couple blocks from the bridge.
I hugged her, and I said *We were scared, weren't we?*
and she nodded and we laughed.

Nominated by The Threepenny Review

LONDON &
A FRIEND

by PAUL ZIMMER

from THE GEORGIA REVIEW

THESE DAYS I saunter along the snow-plowed gravel road that extends over the top of our Wisconsin ridge and look down through bare woods to where I once plugged heartily through heavy drifts. Now it looks so cold and hard in those trees.

I well remember the obscurity of my numb toes and fingers, the exhaustion and breathlessness of struggling up and down the slopes as I once vigorously attended the winter.

There were favorite places I visited—a stand of tall, contorted hickories; red oaks that held their foliage through the winter; maples divided and leaning away from each other; clusters of birches; even the bones of blighted elms. I touched certain trees in special places to remember them as I passed. Some large oaks surely had been saplings about the time my parents were born early in the last century. These trees have stood through at least four human generations—and through our Depression, two world wars, and four or more of our lesser conflicts.

I remember, too, the tentative creature tracks I found in the snow. It pleased me to have nothing else on my mind except checking those small maps to see who had been hanging out on our land through the winter.

Now it is late February. Spring still seems remote in Wisconsin as I walk the ridge and look down—but I imagine I feel a slight easing off of the cold.

Before my retirement, I worked at several universities as a scholarly book publisher, and each spring I traveled to London to seek and sell American rights for copublications with British publishers. The trip was a marvelous perk for me—escaping the end of winter after a full year of toiling with author correspondence, contracts, invoices, administrative problems, staff meetings, financial statements, stacks of manuscripts.

For twenty-five years I was privileged to visit venerable British publishing houses each year and meet cultivated people who sometimes, when we finished working, would ask me to join them for an evening. In turn I would invite them out for drinks or meals, so that they could be my guests. I came to know central London rather well—the theaters, restaurants, jazz clubs, opera houses, bookstores, pubs, markets, record shops, concert halls, museums.

How does one recount the events and pleasures of a quarter century of visits to London every year in the spring? It was a delightful, dependable miracle. I first made the trip as an uncertain traveler, to spell an editor who had become too ill to make the trip. Quickly I recognized the pleasures and opportunities, and after this I continued my annual visits until my retirement in the late 1990s.

I miss those trips excruciatingly, especially when spring comes—the work and discovery, the excitement of evaluating interesting manuscripts, the decision making and careful selectivity on the run, the chance taking and bargaining, the satisfaction of making a good deal. Then there was the great city itself and its people.

In the early years of my London trips most of the publishing offices were cozy, worn digs in Bloomsbury, smelling of tea and Latakia, paper and proof ink. The editors and rights managers were urbane, articulate people who had *read* the manuscripts they presented and were enthusiastic sponsors of their author's works. They were intellectually nimble, friendly, and dedicated to making certain I was comfortable in London—going to the right plays, seeing the good exhibitions, locating the better bookstores and restaurants. If my appointment occurred toward the end of the workday, the editors often invited me to their favorite pub for a pint afterward. After a decade of retirement, I think of these people and wonder where they are now, in

358

the distance, like the winter trees I used to visit and touch in my rambles through the woods.

Now I'll risk sounding like a grumbling Luddite—but in my last years of visiting London I noted with some uneasiness that things had started to change. Of course I had no right to feel proprietary. I was an American who came for a short time to do a little business each year. The industry *was* updating and becoming more efficient with new technology, following the international trend to largeness. But I was wary of some of the changes that I saw.

I used to fear sentimentality and believe it was dangerous to my artistic and professional viewpoint, but as time goes on, I find myself clinging to old memories. Now I have lived enough years to be absolutely selfish about these recollections; I still harbor nostalgia about the London I knew.

The changes began in small ways. Old upright typewriters began to be replaced by keyboards and computer screens. Telephones gave way to programmed answering machines. Copiers, fax machines, and printers began to crowd the narrow hallways between the offices.

Far worse than this, great editors I had known for years began to disappear, were hustled into redundancy or simply replaced by accountants. Venerable publishing imprints were absorbed into the cold, massive portfolios of international conglomerates. Those that survived as entities were generally relocated to new high-rise corporate buildings near the Thames. The receptionists wore Gucci. The "editors" I visited referred to computer printouts instead of manuscripts when they pushed their "products" to me. They wanted to know how many "pieces" I might order if I were to do an American edition. They spoke of percentages and sales thresholds rather than relevance, research, quality of writing, and style. These people did not wear worn cardigans and have gas grates in their offices. They did not offer me tea from the cart, and they had not read the manuscripts they were hawking.

I missed the long walks after lunch through London streets and parks, the good talk about novels, poetry, history, paintings, symphonies, scholarship, and fine writing. The Thatcher-bashing. Of course I did, and do still.

Along with this, I was growing older myself. My energy levels were dropping, and in time I had to cut down on my daily schedule of hustling for taxis and Tube connections. Instead of four daily appointments, I made two or three. I often returned to my hotel room in midafternoon for a nap. I could no longer range out *every* night to the delights of theater and pub crawling. I stopped taking a drink with lunch. Some evenings I even stayed in my room and read proof, or watched rugby and British football on the old black-and-white television in the downstairs lounge of my small hotel.

For twenty-five years I stayed at the St. Margaret's Hotel on Bedford Place near the British Museum, an endearing establishment run by an Italian family named Marazzi. Although it "modernized" slowly over the years, in the early seventies the St. Margaret's was still an old Bloomsbury establishment—no credit cards, tea trays available in the sitting rooms on order from the desk, a small television lounge, full English breakfast, a sink in the room, loos and showers down the hall. Legend had it that T. S. Eliot once had rooms there. Some eccentric permanent residents talked to themselves in the hallways and carried umbrellas out to the street even on sunny days.

As the St. Margaret's gradually updated its facilities, in time it began to offer rooms with television sets and private baths. Did I really miss groping down the darkened hallway in the middle of the night to take a pee? You will accuse me of being a twisted fuddy-duddy if I say yes. In our day and age, to claim such things risks bathos. But yes, it is this very past that I miss: Zimmer feeling his way down the hall to the water closet, paying the price for all his pub pints; Zimmer sitting in the hotel lounge with other denizens, cheering madly for Chelsea or Manchester. All of this built my character.

Over the years the price of hotel rooms, food, taxis, pints, Tube tickets, museums, and theater tickets doubled, tripled, quadrupled, quintupled. The cost of opera tickets became impossible. The marvelously grubby rare bookshops on and near Charing Cross Road began to disappear or were renovated into "shoppes." The small specialty bookstores that sold new books caved in to the monster chains. Many of the quiet, historic pubs were remodeled and wired for rock music and video games.

Toward the end of my years of trips to London, as my retirement approached, it sometimes came to me with a pang that soon I would not be happily scurrying to springtime appointments in quirky, sacrosanct offices. I would not be enjoying chats in the pubs or attending plays in the West End. I was becoming a sort of circumspect American phantom lumbering in the London streets, mumbling to myself, resentful of the changes in myself and in the city.

Facing this was difficult. Already memories were swarming in my mind: A veteran editor who always poured our leftover tea into her potted plants, another who loudly blew his nose into a red handkerchief after his elegant recitation of the menu in a French restaurant. The ancient offices of John Murray Publishers, where I once covertly—when their editor left the room to fetch a manuscript—lay my head on a cushion that Lord Byron had used for a nap. Mincing my way through teetering, five-foot stacks of manuscripts and proof to a chair in Tim Farmiloe's office at MacMillan. ("Yes-yes-yes-yes-yes" Tim would rat-a-tat at me as I talked to him. It must have been his way of wearing me down.) Salty Colin Haycraft of Duckworth advising me not to visit Ireland ("Where would you go? All those sheep and priests.") Peter Owen smoking scented tobacco and playing Egyptian music while we passed manuscripts back and forth over the naked-women paperweights on his desk. Profane, ambitious David Croom, who would tell me to "piss off" when I pushed too hard on prices. Tony Seward, like a humanities angel in his walk-up attic office, five floors up just off Baker Street. Unsmiling Livia Gollancz pronouncing that the Tube had become uncivilized, "full of Americans smoking in the smoke-free cars." Sean Magee, who traded shots of calvados with me and loved race-horses almost as much as books. Diminutive Murray Mindlin, who would hold my arm and walk me all the way down the street to the Tube station after our meetings (he seemed never certain I could find it on my own) with his unceasing good talk and recitations. One year Murray was gone from his office, devastated by a cerebral hemorrhage that emptied his lively mind and left him permanently vacant eyed in a hospital bed. When I visited his old office and expressed my sadness to his replacement, the young man impatiently moved some papers on his desk and pronounced, "We don't make them like that anymore."

I also met a few writers and poets over the years. Battered, eighty-year-old Hugh MacDiarmid telling me the story of how he had rejoiced over his doctor's speculation that he might live to be a hundred, and hurried out to give the good news to his wife in the waiting room. "Ya know," he told me earnestly in his distinctive brogue, "I think herr face fell." Dannie Abse, his white hair plastered down by a London shower, forgetting where he had parked his car on the London streets after offering me a ride. Handsome young Kevin Crossley-Holland amongst ladies at a literary party, with his tweed coat grandly spread over his shoulders. Ted Hughes scowling forbiddingly by himself in a corner at the same party. The poet/publishers Peter Jay of Carcanet Press and Michael Schmidt of Anvil Press. A delightful conversation I had with a congenial man named Alan, whose last name I had missed when we were introduced; as we were beckoned to dinner I ashamedly asked him to repeat it. "Sillitoe," he said. Ancient Stephen Spender sipping tea in a publisher's office, barely flicking his eyes up at me as we were introduced.

Since retiring I have not returned to London. Undeniably that world has mostly disappeared by now—the dear, articulate dowdiness I loved, the wonderful "inefficiency" that produced such wondrous literature.

If I went to London now, where would I go? I think about this sometimes as I walk the ridge above my snowy woods and anticipate spring. Yes, of course, the great attractions and theaters would still be there, but what of my old friends and associates? They seem down the hill in the cold trees, a place where I can't easily go anymore.

And what of Tim Floyd, who was my friend even before I knew he was my friend? Tim with a face that enfolded you from a distance as you watched him talk to others. For several years early in my visits to London, when I stopped in for my usual nightcap in the Hedge—a pub just off Great Russell Street near the British Museum—I observed him holding forth to his coterie of mates. I was usually alone and tried to find a chair near them to eavesdrop. Although I am unavoidably American, I attempted to look earnest and intelligent so that they might tolerate me.

The talk was mostly social and political, occasionally literary. The neighborhood was discussed, the postal service, interest rates, construction at the museum, Benny Hill, the Arsenal football club—but eventually Tim would steer the talk to a book he had recently read. He'd tell the others stories from it, and he was good enough to hold their attention through a long narrative.

As I listened and watched, I thought surely this man was a teacher, a writer, or an artist. But when I finally worked my way into the group, Tim told me he was a "hauler," a driver and deliverer of construction materials around London. His mates were mostly workers themselves—in offices, warehouses, and stores—but they gathered around

Tim most evenings for conversation. Eventually I was permitted to sit as a "regular" on the edge of their group. Occasionally one of them would chat with me. If anything "American" came up, sometimes I was consulted.

After a year or so, I mentioned to one of them that I was a publisher doing business in London. He asked what I published. "Mostly scholarly books," I told him, "and books about our region in America, and some fiction and poetry."

"Tim's a poet," the man told me. "He's always writing in his little book."

"I write poetry, too," I told the man.

Of course, word got to Tim. The next time I went into the Hedge he came over to talk with me. A few nights later, after several requests, he showed me some of his poems. He kept them in a small gray leather book in his coat pocket. The pages were ruled in little squares, and his printing was small and neat within the blocks. The poems were a few lines each, many of them notes on things he fancied. He made oblique, interesting connections. A few had morals, but mostly he kept them open and didn't try to be didactic. They were intelligent and sensitive. He was shy about them, but proud, and seemed pleased that I praised or commented on some of them. He said he had never tried to publish. But he was acquainted with John Betjeman—had made deliveries to his house and been invited in for tea—and he had once been introduced to C. Day-Lewis in a pub.

One early summer in Iowa City, I was home after a long day of work at the university press, sorting through the mail and sipping a beer. In the stack was a small, pale blue airmail envelope with a London postmark—a note from Tim Floyd's wife. The message was brief:

> Dear Paul,
>   Tim has died. It was very difficult for him in the end. I am quite lost.
>   You know that he loved you. If you look out your window you might see his spirit soaring past.
>
>   Kindest regards,
>   Helga

I had not known Tim was sick. Oh. I had seen him only a few months before in London.

Earlier that day in Iowa rain had fallen, and the temperature had not yet risen. A sweet green breeze came through the living room screens. I had not known Tim was sick.

Over time we had become good friends. "You're very necessary," he once told me, when I appeared for my spring visit. For almost two decades, each year Tim invited me to his apartment for a Sunday lunch with Helga.

He would do the cooking. The kitchen was just off the living room behind some bookshelves. Over the stove, facing out, was a square opening through the shelves so that Tim could look out into the living room as I chatted with Helga. I commented to her once about how perfect it was to be able to converse with her and then look up and see Tim's benign face framed like a picture as he cooked for us—usually a curry, the smell of it wafting pleasantly into the room.

Those were very special Sunday afternoons in London. I often tried to invite Tim and Helga out for a lunch or dinner. Helga seemed interested, but Tim said that they did not like restaurant food. He would rather eat at home. I always brought along a very good bottle of wine and a book for them.

How privileged I was. After lunch we would watch together a Sunday afternoon television show they favored, about English working dogs being trained in the field. They had two cats who rubbed up against my ankles as we watched—Macavity (Tim loved Eliot's cat book) and another ginger-colored one whose name I can't remember.

We watched the dogs on the telly circle, run out, fetch, do some other maneuvers, and then return at the beckoning of their handlers. Only once did we see a dog break the rules and go off on a toot by itself, followed by the camera as it sniffed other dogs and peed on a distant post before returning to its master's frantic whistle. Everyone on the program was embarrassed.

Helga said, "Bad dog."

"Not so," said Tim. "Not so."

On our library shelves in Wisconsin is a little known book called *The Diary of a Nobody*, which I have read several times—a delightful Victorian novel by George and Weedon Grossmith about a priggish, lower-middle-class London clerk named Charles Pooter, who keeps up appearances and survives many misadventures with home improvements and cheeky tradespeople, which he carefully-records in his diary.

As the jacket copy says, Pooter "has an over-developed sense of dignity." But Pooter is always tripping over some rug. His entry for April 15 reads only, "Burnt my tongue most awfully with the Worcester sauce, through that stupid girl Sarah shaking the bottle violently before putting it on the table." *The Diary of a Nobody* is one of the most pleasurable books I've ever read. "I fail to see," Pooter writes, "because I do not happen to be a 'Somebody'—why my diary should not be interesting." I note that the book was a favorite of John Betjeman and T. S. Eliot, and Evelyn Waugh called it "the funniest book in the world."

Tim Floyd had walked to the Saint Margaret's and left this copy of *The Diary of a Nobody* at the desk for me one evening when I'd attended the theater instead of going to the pub. This was toward the end of my stay in London, and I never saw Tim again. Occasionally I take the book down and read passages to myself, and always I rediscover the note and small poem tucked in its pages, written on little square-ruled papers ripped from a pocket notebook. On one side of the note is written:

> <u>By Hand</u>
> *Paul Zimmer, Esq.*
> *P.T.O.*

On the other side is a note in a neatly printed hand:

> *38 Museum St*
> *Sorry to have missed you last night. This is the*
> *book I told you of last year. Always in the*
> *Hedge after nine-ish, except Thursdays when*
> *I go to the <u>Bloomsbury Tavern</u> at the bottom of*
> *Museum St. off Shaftesbury Ave.*
>   *Hope to see you*
>   *Tim—*

I looked for Tim in the Bloomsbury the next Thursday evening, but he was not there.

On the other slip of paper, in the same hand, is a small poem about a forlorn miniature tree that had been kept on a shelf over the bar in the Hedge pub for many years until one day, worse for its wear, the tree was no longer there:

<u>*R.I.P. for the Tree Poem*</u>
The tree that was only there
It leant across the mirror over the bar
Too far perhaps?
                    is gone.
Yet in my memory
Trees walk in innocence with elephants
And are triumphant.

Not a perfect poem, but Tim was pleased with it. I like it very much myself.

Nominated by Stephen Corey, Gary Gildner, Michael Heffernan

THE HOMING DEVICE COMPREHENDED AT LAST

by LIZ WALDNER

from NEW AMERICAN WRITING

When my god leaves me—
She doesn't leave you
When I don't know she's there, then
And now?
She's here
And now?
How to know which apartment to rent or whether to live with the
    other homeless women in the downtown SRO
No longer pressing
I breathe away the particles of impressing perfection
Permission to not know granted
And inhaled gratefully
What about Holly Springs?
It's all casino boats now
What about Crystal Springs?
The horrible chicken factory
Where to live is less important
At long last
As long as you can sing her
As long as I can sing her
You will be breathing

I will be the breathèd name of god
Some, more, longing.
Some. more. longing.
But this one gets you even closer
To living somewhere I belong

Nominated by New American Writing, Donald Revell

ETHAN: A LOVE STORY

fiction by J. C. HALLMAN

from TIN HOUSE

MY PARENTS' HOME sat inside a gated community called Sky Meadow, a set of forty builder-designed mansions sprinkled over a topographical elevation as neat as a cupcake. Sky Meadow was protected at its base by a gatehouse and a team of geriatric guards in gray uniforms who controlled the white tube arm that blocked passage into the community. The arm wouldn't really stop anybody, but there was a hydraulic bollard beneath the pavement as well, an explosive mechanism that would fire metal rods into the engine compartment of undesirable vehicles.

Sky Meadow was veined with the green wending swaths of a golf course, and my parents' home sat on the last of these, the eighteenth fairway, the home hole. They had furnished their house with a stratum of knickknacks that described their five-decade-long ascent from poverty. The three-dollar bowl that my mother had once broken and glued back together, bit by bit, was as precious to her as her baby doll, a collectible figurine she had won at auction. My father kept on his desk his beaten old slide rule—his BS in physics, nearly half a century old, had been more than enough to make him a successful corporate inventor—but alongside it was a bust of himself that he had once commissioned on a whim. My parents thought of themselves as retired, and their main activity now consisted of occupying that weird collection: the odd bits of fantastic art of the truly wealthy, the framed family portraits that charted their passage through middle class, and the kitsch—a variety of plastic Mickey Mouse figurines, a cheap oil lamp once used for actual light—set about like displays of the primitive culture from which their kind had evolved.

When I went home for Christmas that year, I hadn't ever seen my six-year-old nephew, Ethan. But even this was a point of disagreement for me and my family—my parents and brother and sister and their spouses—a group who had decided to respond to the world's basic intricacy so differently from me that just recognizing myself in them, in their mannerisms and bad habits, made me kind of lonely. Nobody could figure out why I had turned out so differently; it might have been a mutation I was born with. I tended to avoid family gatherings, as useless argument always ruled the day. I was still unmarried—that was surely part of it—and I was the youngest, too, though none of us was still young.

My sister-in-law insisted that I had met Ethan when he was nine months old, and my mother swore to an even more recent meeting. But the truth was I had never been within three states of the boy. Every family has its odd uncle—for the last generation it had been my Uncle Billy, who had become a monk—and it had been several years since I realized that I had become the odd uncle of the new generation. I didn't forget the birthdays of my nieces and nephews, I ignored them. I failed entirely in slithering those insipid greetings into their sleeves and weighing them down with crisp bills for toys or candy. I was an utter failure as a relative. Or so the family would have concluded, and perhaps they weren't wrong about that. I've given up trying to articulate the etymology of the dreads to which I seem to be prone, but it was precisely a sense of failure that had sent me home that year in the first place. A malevolent mood had struck, so disturbing that even the thought of family seemed a comfort. I agreed to go home. For, despite all the scuffles and ricocheting ridicule, despite my established unwholesomeness, my family still wished to see *me*. This was an intricate puzzle, like the little hokey bits of mangled wire, which, in their dismantling, are meant to make a diverting amusement and are often exchanged as presents at family Christmases. I didn't know why they wanted me—perhaps for the opportunity to turn the other cheek.

The sense of enclosure to my parents' home, at least for my mother, had resulted in an insidious agoraphobia—often she would not step outside the house for four or five days at a stretch—and, like each of

370

the last several houses the family had lived in (there were thirteen in all), this one had come outfitted with a sophisticated security alarm device. The windows and doors at home were all wired; infrared beams latticed the rooms at night. The exact technology had grown more ominous from home to home, but the alarm paraphernalia, whatever it was, came to be known in the family cant as "the system." We children had first been given special keys for the system, then were forced to memorize codes. One false alarm, long ago, had brought to the house a helicopter and half a dozen police cruisers running red light and siren.

I came home that year equipped with an early present from a beautiful lady friend. That was how I thought of her—my beautiful lady friend, married to another. The gift was a green sweater, and I swooned when my friend told me it would ignite the color in my eyes. I wore it home with a kind of dumb hope that it would armor me against the volleys I expected from my family—my own private security system. The general anxiety of being home took added jolt when, just two days into the sentence, I made the fool mistake—indeed, it confirmed that somehow I had wandered onto intellectual flatland—of washing the sweater and throwing it into the tumble dryer, which was set to "High/Cotton." The lint shield felted over like a pool table. The sweater came out in perfect miniature. I presented it to Ethan, whom it now fit perfectly. I tugged the collar over his head, and told him the sweater had come from a lovely girl. The boy's eyes tested this, and he decided to take a chance. "I like pretty girls," he said. "They make my eyes turn to hearts."

Ethan and I fell in love.

Ethan was a bright boy, dark-haired and dark-complexioned, and as he was now the youngest member of our unit—the only one who still believed in Santa Claus—he behaved with the requisite hyperactivity, frantic pleas for attention from us adults and those teenaged children passing themselves off as adults by joining the family table and waiting for the moment when their experience would let them chime in. Ethan was too young for that transition and knew it. So instead he would stalk us all from across the room, so that my mother would flutter her eyes to detach herself from whatever thought she'd been having and announce, "What's that noise? I heard a noise! Roger, did you turn on the system?" Ethan would giggle and pop out from behind the grandfather clock. Or he would turn sets of track lights off and on, or up and down if there was a dimmer switch, so that my brother or sister might ask loudly whether the house was haunted, and the phantom giggling would sound again. We returned to our loveless talk after these interruptions, and Ethan returned to the activity that kept him occupied the vast bulk of the time. This was his video game device, transported from his home in Florida and played on a television in the downstairs guest quarters. He spent hours with the gadget. Its complicated instrument of interactivity, a handheld controller pad with toggles and triggers and buttons, was for him as familiar a device for communicating his orientation to the world as were his legs or fingers. He preferred games targeted at adults, stories of mayhem and blood-lust, American valor transported to a future where the slaughter of aliens offended no one.

His favorite of the moment—surely about to be displaced by Santa's team of programmers—was called Halo, the name of an imaginary space-borne ship. The bad guys were called the Covenant, animal-like men and robots. The boy, oblivious to the game's religious subtext—the sound-track was Gregorian chant—focused on damage. He destroyed heavy ma-chinery, murdered at will, and generally found expression for a child's amorality. He rarely played the actual game, though he did sit fixed through the storyline that held the whole thing together. The boy simply inhabited Halo, the character he became for its duration. Even when he wasn't in the game—when he was neither haunting my parents' comfort-able home nor finding his eyes turned to hearts by pretty girls—he spoke in quotations from its script. "I'm too pretty to die," he might say at a quiet dinner of tender scallops, citing some madman soldier. "You want some of this? Come on, Sarge. That's what *I'm* talking about. I'm too pretty to die."

If all houses are museums of personal archaeology, then my parents' house was even more—a cultural cross-section of the Dream, the fan-tasy my parents had executed so well. It took me until I was an adult to understand that, all those years, my mother's alarm system had ac-tually kept us trapped inside. Open a door somewhere in that house and no matter where you were you heard the beeps registering the possible intrusion, data transmitting to the security firm's log of tres-passes. The system had been born of my mother's fear; but it had long since amounted to a transfer of angst—I felt claustrophobic in that house. It gave me the creeps. So on this particular junket east I took up the habit of leaving frequently to walk through the pine woods adjacent to Sky Meadow's golf course. The links were empty; the chill had scared off the last of the golfers a month before. The fairways themselves had frozen over. The expensive grass crunched loudly underfoot, and I left trails like the footprints of a ghost.

I am prone to loneliness, so I was pleased when Ethan, a day after he inherited my sweater, asked if he could join me. The family tensed at this request. How to protect the boy from his sordid uncle's influence? How to reject the request without trompling over the battery of politeness and common sense the family had crafted into its version of etiquette? They wanted me present, but they certainly didn't want my influence spread about. They must have thought of my journey home as a kind of inoculation for the teenagers, political homeopathy. I told Ethan that I would be glad for his company, but that he needed to ask permission. The boy complied by simply turning his head to the others. This produced the room's discomfort, and the family responded with a vocabulary of twitchings and shiftings. There were too many of them to just say no. Ethan was baffled by the delay, but waited silently for the adults to catch up and grant a grudging approval. The following interval spent clothing the boy against the weather might as well have been an effort to insulate him against nefarious dogma.

The stillness at the onset of winter stops time, or at least slows it, as though the cold has shriveled the works. It was morning still, but the dew of the night had frozen in midair and dropped down across Sky Meadow like a sheet of cellophane. Even the wasted space of the golf course felt like wilderness compared to the prison of the house. Ethan and I rejoiced in a sense of escape, and from here we could see how Sky Meadow was poised between the steeple of the downtown church and the flat roofs of the strip malls, studded with exhaust fans and air conditioning units. The boy bounced along as a fat mound of goose down and bunched wool, but thought of it as body armor from his video game, chunky Kevlar. He immediately scrounged from the underbrush a gun-like stick, branches protruding like stocks or magazines, and shoved it up into his armpit. "Come on, Sarge," Ethan said. "Move it up there, Jenkins. I've got contact on the motion sensors—keep it tight."

I dug around among some limbs until Ethan indicated a branch as thick as a baseball bat. I took it up, dooming a family of phosphorescent grubs. I lodged the branch under my arm.

"That's a rocket launcher," Ethan said.

"You bet it is," I said, patting the barrel.

The boy grimaced. "You don't hold it like that." He clean-jerked his own rifle up onto his shoulder and balanced it. "Like this."

"I see. Like a bazooka."

"A what?"

"It's an old kind of gun."

Ethan shook his head and swaggered forward, in character, his breath showing from his nose. "That's an AR-15 rocket-assist grenade launcher. It can fire armor-piercing shells against tanks. You're packing a ton o' fun there, soldier."

"I understand, sir." I settled the branch more firmly on my shoulder to show it new respect. "Am I Sarge, or am I Jenkins?" I said.

"Jenkins gets killed."

"Gotcha. And who are you?"

"I'm still Ethan," Ethan said. He took a step out into the woods, creeping across the crisp needles that made the forest's carpet. *"I'm too pretty to die,"* he whispered.

I don't think a child can truly have a conversation at six years of age. They have the tools, the words and the grammar, and they fake it well, but a six-year-old is still stuck at monomania and all they can believe in with certainty is themselves. Fantasies—video games or Santa Claus—are every bit as real as that which can be felt or touched. Childhood is the lack of a value distinction between fact and fantasy. The only real use of conversation is to pry the two apart.

Ethan and I found the Covenant in the woods. We rooted them out and massacred them for their violent manners and heathen ideologies. Ethan used "Choochoochoochoochoo," for the sound effect of his assault rifle, and corrected me when I tried, "bangBang!" for the rocket launcher. We coordinated our attack on the unsuspecting golf course. We ran the Covenant over and suffered only the loss of Private Jenkins. When we were done, when we had crisscrossed the stand of trees and our victory was a fact on the ground, I sat down against a stump and tipped back my imaginary helmet.

"Lieutenant Ethan?" I said.

"Yeah?"

"It's wrong to kill, isn't it? I mean for real?"

Ethan's eyes wandered off into the woods where he could still see the blood-lathered forms of our victims. He searched his memory for a prerecorded reply to my question, some macho aphorism. He shrugged, but I pretended not to see.

"Hm?"

He tilted his head. "This is just for fun. It's not real, Uncle C—." He tossed his rifle, his stick, onto the frozen ground. "See? It's not even the real *game*."

Ethan and I became inseparable at that point. He demanded that I sit next to him at dinners, he pulled out chairs for me, he pounced into my lap or onto my back, he knocked lightly on the door when I took naps or was in the bathroom. He touched me whenever he could, as though the cushion of flesh was a sufficient emotional umbilicus. The others became jealous. They who had carefully monitored his difficult birth, they who had followed his growth with 4x6s magneted to their refrigerators, they who had sent boxed treats and gifts for holidays when gatherings proved impractical, they who had fulfilled all the obligations of relatives—where was their reward for commitment and hard work? Why did this odd uncle deserve the boy's affections? They did not discuss this, as it was a failing they would rather not admit, but it was a thought as common as a faith. Even Ethan seemed aware of it and began conducting our romance in secret. When the family was gathered on the opposing sofas of the living room, verifying the futility of debating the sanctity of embryonic life, for example, or calculating the proper reaction to hostile nation-states, Ethan would walk up stealthily and whisper in my ear, "*Uncle C—, would you come downstairs with me?*" He meant that I should come play Halo with him, the real Halo. The rest of the family took a dim view of the game's violent nature. But it was hypocrisy. As it happened, that Christmas our entire nation was poised on the brink of military imperialism—the republic was casually in favor of the slaughter of thousands of innocents to justify the removal of an unruly dictator a couple of continents over. The family flicked a hand and argued for war. It was just, the threat was real, and there was nothing else to do. The violence of the video game was distasteful to them, but the real thing was palatable, even delectable. But I didn't make the point. It meant I had Ethan to myself.

Ethan taught me the use of the controller pads—they were tricky—and we each took a character. Somehow, he split the television screen in half so that we had separate subjective views. The first time we entered the game's broad arena, we just slaughtered the aliens for a while. I slowly grew accustomed to Halo's map, its obstacles and trenches and structures. But Ethan bored quickly. Before long, he sauntered his character up beside mine, raised his weapon, and fired. My screen fizzled into hibernation mode. In Ethan's view, my character showed a fist-sized exit wound and a haze of atomizing blood pixels. I clutched my chest and fell. Ethan hurried forward to harvest my ammunition. The boy giggled.

"I *got* you, Uncle C—."

Resurrection was a toggle away. My screen fluttered back to its intimate first person. I scanned for Ethan. He hovered over my old dead form. I scrolled quickly through my armory of weapons and chose the self-loading assault shotgun meant for close quarters. I loaded, leveled the thing at my nephew's back, and sprayed his shoulder blades. He buckled and bled and began to limp away. I discharged the shotgun twice more, until he groaned and fell and his blood colored the ground. Beside me, Ethan laughed uncontrollably. Our legs touched, and in the moment before his own reincarnation he laid his head softly against my shoulder. Then he revived himself, and I used my toggles to weave through the blocky landscape, Ethan's projectiles swishing past me in the little lasers of tracer rounds.

Over the next several days, the Covenant stood by as Ethan and I devastated each other. The boy might find the game's elusive minigun and administer its lead enema. Or I would stumble across the flamethrower and crisp my nephew head to toe. "I'm too pretty to die," I told Ethan once, as I sneaked up behind him to attach an anti-personnel mine to his belt buckle. "You want some of this?" he cried later, as he climbed into a tank and leveled its huge trunk at my chest. We tittered and played that violent tag until my head ached from the overload. Ethan would never be ready to quit, but he could recognize when he had worn me out, and we would head upstairs again.

By then the family had begun their own virtual war, the talk finally fixed on an ongoing discussion of that unruly dictator, and each of them would offer up bits of propaganda they had memorized verbatim, or, like a team of assistant coaches, they would hash out the likely strategies of the coming conflict, brandishing smart euphemisms. They spoke as though their words tasted good, and from inside the hyperbaric chamber of Sky Meadow their war must have seemed as easy to orchestrate as a feast. They moved troops, directed infrastructure, anticipated collateral loss, negotiated treaties, purchased allies, formed coalitions, passed bills and resolutions. Without me there to calcify their beliefs, they could explore the gradations that separated each from the other. Were smart bombs economically efficient? Was it wise to invade in February? What level of civilian casualty was acceptable? The teenagers would listen and chuckle at the expectation of sanctioned death. When I arrived, they would all pause to recalibrate. As a rule, the family tended to react to me as though I had just suffered some great loss, or perhaps not too long ago I had attempted suicide, and a certain delicacy was called for. I was one of extreme sensitivity—I couldn't confront the harsh evils of the world without dissolving into a slithering mess, and to accommodate me was to provide a kind of nurturance, to assure themselves they were capable of pity. But if I sat quietly for a time among them, if I squeezed in on a sofa and kept to myself, the intersecting lines of debate would begin again, three or four beams of misinformation. It was the basic Christian two-step of justifying atrocity in the name of civilization. It was a celebration of fused, contradictory platforms. If I stopped listening completely, it would come to sound like a honeycomb of bees dancing out an accidental message sure to infect the hive, and I could block it out as that kind of drone, pleasant in a way, once it lost that which was recognizable in it.

Two days before Christmas found us all in just such a pose, my post-Halo headache wavering through the song of the worker bees. The family was ironing out the details of what to do with the nation-state once they had achieved victory. "I don't think we're operating with a complete definition of treachery here," my brother said. The talk turned to the nature of evil and a precise definition of war. "State-level belligerents engaged in military action" was met with "organized inter-group violence." "Conflict to control geographical territory" fell to "political terrorism intended to expand sovereign rule." On this note, Ethan launched himself over the arm of the sofa and into my lap. He had been stalking us again. I grunted, and he threw his arm around my neck like a monkey. The family ignored us. "Of course those people want democracy," my mother said. Ethan fingered the back of my neck and looked at my eyes for a moment, measuring me.

And then, quite suddenly, he reached between my legs and grabbed my penis through my pants.

It was so casual a motion that it seemed perfectly normal, really. It lasted only a fraction of a second, and to react to it would have been to appear to have reacted to nothing at all. "Quite frankly, the international community is hardly a community without us," my father said. Ethan smiled, and leaned in next to my face. *"I touched your wee-wee!"* he whispered.

377

I looked about to make sure no one had seen. The buzzing was turning heated. There wasn't anything unusual about Ethan sitting in my lap, and I palmed the boy's spine. *"I know. You shouldn't do that,"* I whispered.

"Why should the Kurds have their own country? Can someone explain that?" my sister said.

"Why not?" Ethan said.

"Sure it's about oil," my brother said. "Should it be about something else?"

"Because it's a private spot."

"Realistically, imperialism is the only true solution to world chaos. That's historical fact."

Ethan's lip touched my earlobe. *"Why is it private?"*

My penis had shrunk back against my body, but I could still feel his fingers there. Why was it private? There were reasons. We had descended from a culture that had used a religion based on shame and perverse asceticism as its organizing principle. Our nation, lusty and promiscuous in the media, was in reality repressed on all matters sexual and even physiological. There were reasons, but they weren't really very good reasons, and Ethan wouldn't have understood them anyway. Childhood was made up of suffering in the sense that eventually you figured out the adults were all lying to you. What was there after the scam of Santa? When you were ready to give up fantasy, all there was to replace it was faith, and nobody had answers for the questions that really mattered.

"It's private because that's the rule," I said. *"Do you understand?"*

"I just don't want to go into this thing unless I can see a favorable end-game on the horizon."

Ethan didn't like it, but he nodded. It was the first moment when I had slipped into the role of adult for him. He became sullen.

"Promise," I said. *"Promise you won't touch me there again."*

"Why should we trust the Turks? They got a Muslim government. Elected!"

Ethan sighed. *"Promise,"* he whispered, and he slid off my knee to go play Halo, alone.

Ethan stayed away for a day or so. Christmas came looming up like a kind of countdown to niceness, that moment when the conductor would tap his baton and signal for regulated harmony. The family

378

gathered in the living room. Someone had hit the remote that ignited the fireplace, and the six-disc stereo sifted through Johnny Mathis and Bing Crosby. My brother offered the argument that Christmas trees— the one that loomed above us was eleven feet tall and filled with antique ornaments—actually predated Christianity. There was gathering evidence, he said, that bringing trees into homes and decorating them began with animist religions. This received mixed reviews from the family. They exchanged uncertain looks and touches. It may have all been a trap; without Ethan there to buoy me, I decided to take it as an opening and launched into a theory I had been preparing in my mind. I made some loose segue from Christmas trees to America (it wasn't hard—the decoration of the tree as a form of play, capitalism as an expression of game theory—I sort of fudged the details) and then argued that our nation itself had become a kind of video game. To be American had long since come to mean spectating, being a fan of one's country instead of a team player, investing in domestic interpretation and spin, inserting faith in a slot that triggered a show that gave an illusion of control, a vote that may or may not mean what you thought it did. Didn't we now have colleges for video games, commercials for them, competitions in them, didn't we think like a video game, export their philosophy, and wage war with the hope that it would resemble them? The republic seemed to think of civilization itself as a kind of video game—take control and blaze the terrain until you run out of lives. To be a superpower meant obtaining an infantilized super-skill, an ultra- or mega-weapon, the silly language was all the same, and the only goal was to retain the sanctity of power for as long as possible, because having it meant more lives and a prolonged version of one's society. This brought us back to the unruly dictator— the whole world just then preoccupied with weapons that meant validation. The dictator wanted mega-power. He wanted in the game. Didn't we want to destroy him, I said, just to keep him on the sidelines?

The family took all this in silently. It was too much for them. They knew I was crazy, but it was as though I had blasphemed, and you just couldn't chalk that up to insanity.

"Are you even an American? my father said.

There followed a melee of raw insult. We called a truce almost at once, and in deference to the descending holiday we attempted to establish some common ground, a no-man's-land of morality we could all obey. War is bad, I tried. No, remember the Great War, or the war after that, you couldn't really say they were bad. Evil is a uselessly relative and abstract concept. Hardly, look at the unruly dictator. Killing is wrong. No, they insisted, killing was sometimes the right thing to do.

"Well, that gives you all," I said, "a good deal in common with your average psychopath."

The family looked at the coffee table and held their breath against the noxious air. I couldn't hurt them, or even communicate with them. We all sat for a long moment wondering what family really meant if it was possible to wind up staring at one another across such broad vistas. Then Ethan reappeared. He walked among us quietly. He was wearing my sweater, and the green, I noticed, put a kind of light in his eyes. But the sweater wasn't the reason for his visit.

"Uncle C—, would you come downstairs with me?"

"Not right now, Ethan."

He stared a moment, and I came to understand that it wasn't a usual request; he wished to share some secret with me. He stacked his hands on my knee, and leaned forward.

"*Something happened,*" he whispered.

He took my hand as though to lead me to a dance floor. He was entirely intent on our mission. I didn't look back. What would have been the point? The family was relieved, and they spoke of me, I'm sure, in pithy tones of condescending mercy, as though I had just presented with some ghastly symptom of mental illness, some explosive habit that put a strain on all of them, but they could bear that cross if they just stuck together. I didn't hear them speak again.

Ethan's hand fit perfectly inside mine, but his skin was chilled. Something had spooked him. I stopped him on the landing halfway down the stairs.

"Santa already came," he said. "He came *early*."

I hid a smile, thought I understood. Ethan would be receiving dozens of presents that year, and the house was a minefield of stashed toys. The boy had rooted through some closet and turned up something meant for him.

"What did you find?"

"A game," Ethan said. "But I don't understand it."

I was confident. It was whatever program Ethan was to be given in replacement for Halo, and surely I could shepherd him through it. We continued to the television and nuzzled on the sofa. Ethan turned on the game and, while we waited for the program to load, put his head against my arm. But he was still disturbed. He opened his mouth to speak. He paused, and it was perhaps the first time in his life when he would step outside his tiny frame of reference to speak to the larger world.

"I saw Grandpa," he said.

I nodded. "Grandpa's upstairs."

He squared himself so that he could look me in the eye. "No. I saw Grandpa *in the game.*"

For what happened next I offer neither reason nor explanation. The screen twitched and sizzled and blanked, and then called up a fanciful sloping world of perfect streets and pine trees. It was not dread, not exhilaration, but a nameless hybrid of the two that sparked inside me when I recognized it. It was Sky Meadow. The game had begun its story at the base of that apocryphal hill, where the gray-haired guards played gin rummy in their tiny heated hut.

"You see?" Ethan said.

Our view was subjective, and Ethan toggled us toward the gate. The guards popped out, and the boy quickly produced a pistol and shot them both. He stepped around their bodies, then around the hydraulic bollard, which had fooled him the first couple times. It wasn't pretty, he said.

"How . . ." I said.

"I don't know. But wait."

We jogged through the clean landscape, past shrubs so well-groomed in reality that their virtual twins rendered them perfectly. Ethan stopped next to a fire hydrant.

"Now watch," he said.

He kicked forward another step, hitting some kind of trigger in the game's programming, and a few yards ahead a little man stepped out from behind a tree. He was unarmed, and took two steps forward before stopping and putting his hands on his hips. It was my father.

"I've come to realize that I just don't enjoy talking to you anymore," the little man said.

Ethan left the controller pad limp in his lap. "That's as far as I've gone."

I asked to see the game's packaging, but it was only a blank container he'd found in a shabby-chic end table. There was no box or manual. The game didn't have a soundtrack, but every few moments the little version of my father, Ethan's grandpa, shifted his weight and repeated his line.

"I've come to realize that I just don't enjoy talking to you anymore."

Ethan tried to step around Grandpa, but the game wouldn't let him. My father blocked the only path in a labyrinth with one solution. Ethan tried several directions, but we were stuck. Finally I said, "Lieutenant, what weapons do we have?"

There was the pistol he'd used on the guards, a machine gun, and a sniper rifle. "And there's some kind of light-modulating beam weapon," Ethan said.

"Like a laser gun?"

"I guess."

"Use the laser, Ethan," I said. "Use the laser, and blast Grandpa."

Ethan looked back at the screen and shuffled through our armory until the tip of the laser gun aimed out in front of us. He hesitated.

"You do it," the boy said.

He balanced the controller pad on my knee. He squeezed in tighter against my side, splicing our elbows together. I took up the pad and nestled it into my hands, arranging my fingers to the toggles. My father's expression was dense and somewhat annoyed, an expression I probably wear myself on occasion. Only the thought that the game might be some legitimate black magic gave me pause. But then the little man humped again from one leg to the other and began to speak, "I've come to realize—" and I yanked back hard on the trigger.

The weapon glowed an instant before it fired, and its energy shot forward in a sharp beam of pointed bright. It caught my father just above the navel, and two waves quickly spread over him—the first a shine as the power of the weapon began to destroy him, and then a hole, an expanding void as the beam took him apart, shuttling him off disassembled to some awful dimension. He was half gone before he had time to react, this by lifting his hand to watch it precede him into purgatory. Then he was gone and all was still.

We listened for a shriek from above, but the real Sky Meadow was as quiet as its tiny counterpart. It was just a game. Residual power from the laser flicked once in the air where Grandpa had stood, and then the path was clear.

"Keep going," Ethan said.

The game led to my parents' house, a maze within the maze, and once there we were confronted with versions of the entire family, each delivering some accusation before I vaporized them. "Admit it, you think everyone who has children is just wasting their time," my choppy mother said. I hit her as she dived behind the dining table. My sister popped out of a bathroom, compact in hand. "Sometimes, C—, even your vocabulary, it's like you're saying you're better than us." The light modulator turned her inside out. "Quite frankly," Ethan's father said, "liberals are the brainwashed masses of the Cult of the Academy." I got him with a head shot, and Ethan didn't even flinch. When Grandpa reappeared—"I'm Christian like the next man, but . . ."—I realized it wasn't murder, even in the game. The family kept reappearing. They were a multiplying immortal army of horrifying rhetoric. "Of course I vote my checkbook—isn't that what you're *supposed* to do?" "They buy our movies. We *gave* them television. They should love us." "Capitalism is all about competition, and war is the purest expression of economics—or whatever." I ticked them off as they appeared, but soon they were coming too quickly; the game had an automatic difficulty adjustment, and it was learning from my pattern of fire. The family was all onscreen at once, multiclones burbling rubbish, and when I could no longer hold them back I turned and ran us down the stairs, to the guest quarters, to where Ethan and I then sat, and when the game pulled up the room, there we were, two heads on the sofa watching a screen inside the screen, and another screen, and an infinity there too tiny to see.

Ethan climbed up on his knees to look behind us, but of course there was nothing there. Back on the television, my double climbed from the sofa and announced, "We inhabit a post-classic failing democracy!"

I stopped to consider a version of mortality. Would the act of annihilating myself amount to murder or suicide, would it be wrong or noble? Ethan swiveled back to await my decision. He was poker-faced about it, and I realized that our affection would never be greater than this, that it was based in binary code and cathode ray tubes, and that our version of compassion was best understood in those terms, in that space. My time with Ethan was an affair, and it would end as affairs ended. I would look back on a pleasure initially so complete that it would seem virtual in remembrance, an impossible fiction. We had arrived for this instant at an identical plane of concern and desire, but we had descended to that spot from opposite poles, and soon enough we would be yanked back to separate realities like puppets on puppet strings.

I fired, and because we were still pressed together, the laser treated us as one.

From there, the game became more familiar. Our invasion had

tripped my mother's alarm system, and as once had happened so long ago, law enforcement personnel descended on the house. FBI burst through the doors, SWAT repelled down the walls, all of them armed and anxious to deliver justice. They were the bad guys, but Ethan didn't seem to notice. "My turn, Uncle C—," he said, and he snatched the controller pad away to enter the fray.

Christmas arrived on time and the predictable civility came about quite naturally. We acted out the script of the morning, exchanges that gave the family a warm sensation of ritual and custom, as though we were a company reunited to act out an old play. Familiar lines came spiced with tradition. We traded books we thought the others should read, clothes we thought the others should wear. We warmed in the heat of the artificial fire and sang a birthday ditty to Baby Jesus. Ethan tore through his pirate's treasure of gifts. There was pot roast for dinner. "I'll take the cooked part," I told my father, as he sliced the rare beast and passed the slabs around.

The peace held until I left, and I distributed hugs and farewells across my packed bag as a taxi sat in the drive burping clumps of fume. It had snowed Christmas Eve, an idyllic storm laying a comforter across the Northeast. Ethan managed only the briefest of goodbyes at my departure—an embrace of consolation, the hug one gives a stranger when a moment nevertheless calls for affection. Our real goodbye had come some time before. The family had shuttled Ethan off to bed early on Christmas Eve, far too early for him, really. It gave the rest of us time to finish our wrapping, and position the presents for that year's photograph, and sip our eggnog and brandy, and hold that kind of holiday court that is possible when the world is at peace. My father engaged the alarm system when the lights of the Christmas tree lulled us with their foggy sheen. He turned off the fire. We all retired to our quarters. Mine for the week had been my father's study, furnished with a large contoured globe at perfect scale, and a tattered old leather armchair that was the third piece of furniture my parents had ever owned. My father's sculpted bust sat on the desk and watched me climb into a bed like a cot in a makeshift ward. Out the window, Sky Meadow knew nothing of the holiday except for a street lamp near the house that had burned out, a malfunction that would have been repaired at once if anyone had been on duty. The community took on an inky brand of black.

I wasn't quite asleep, but was already dreaming of my beautiful lady friend, when Ethan's knock on the door entered my fantasy as her touch on my cheek. The boy crept into the room and sat on the bed. He had detached his video device from the television downstairs and brought it with him. He had the new game as well.

"Can't sleep. Want to play?" he said.

We tiptoed out of the room. We moved forward a few steps through the dark before Ethan stopped and held me back. He pointed down to one of the infrared beam boxes shooting its invisible motion sensor across the floor. He indicated the angle it took. That's what he had been doing all the while he had hunted us in the living room. He knew where all the tripwires were. He straddled the light, and I followed his high-stepping lead through the musty museum. He stopped at the Christmas tree, the presents he would raze come morning, and bulged his eyes—the night's ghost had already come and gone. It wasn't that Ethan still believed in Santa Claus. It was that he resisted disbelieving, and that might have been the only good definition of innocence left. We were a nation with an alarm system. The family believed it was too pretty to die. In the face of all that, what could you say to anyone to address good and bad, right and wrong?

Ethan connected the game to the television in the kitchen. He sat in my lap and left the volume low. It all started as it had before, the gatehouse and the guards and the hydraulic bollard, but it began to change as soon as we jogged into its perfect light. Sky Meadow morphed to an alien forest, my family to the troops of some hostile regime. It was similar to what we had seen the day before, but different enough so that it seemed possible that Ethan and I had simply made a mistake in observing it. The boy weighed against me, warm and twitching as he played. I touched his heavy head. It's natural enough to question the validity of daylight from the stupor of a dreamy night, and love for my nephew seemed inevitable just then.

Nominated by Tin House

GOD'S TRUTH IS LIFE

by CHRISTIAN WIMAN

from IMAGE

W<small>HEN</small> I <small>WAS TWENTY YEARS OLD</small> I spent an afternoon with Howard Nemerov. He was the first "famous" poet I had ever met, though I would later learn that he was deeply embittered by what he perceived to be a lack of respect from critics and other poets. (I once heard Thom Gunn call him a "zombie.") My chief memories are of his great eagerness to nail down the time and place for his mid-day martini, him reciting "Animula" when I told him I loved Eliot, and asking me at one point—with what I now realize was great patience and kindness—what I was going to do when I graduated later that year. I had no plans, no ambitions clear enough to recognize as such, no interest in any of the things that my classmates were hurtling toward. Poetry was what I spent more and more of my time working on, though I found that vaguely embarrassing, even when revealing it to a real poet, as I did. Equivocations spilled out of me then, how poetry was all right as long as one didn't take it too seriously, as long as one didn't throw one's whole life into it. He set down his martini and looked at me for a long moment—I feel the gaze now—then looked away.

§

The irony is that for the next fifteen years I would be so consumed with poetry that I would damn near forget the world. One must have devotion to be an artist, and there's no way of minimizing its cost. But still, just as in religious contexts, there is a kind of devotion that is, at its heart, escape. These days I am impatient with poetry that is not

386

steeped in, marred and transfigured by, the world. By that I don't mean poetry that has "social concern" or is meticulous with its descriptions, but a poetry in which you can feel that the imagination of the poet has been both charged and chastened by a full encounter with the world and other lives. A poet like Robert Lowell, who had such a tremendous imagination for language but none at all for other people, means less and less to me as the years pass.

§

I once believed in some notion of a pure ambition, which I defined as an ambition for the work rather than for oneself, but I'm not sure I believe in that anymore. If a poet's ambition were truly for the work and nothing else, he would write under a pseudonym, which would not only preserve that pure space of making but free him from the distractions of trying to forge a name for himself in the world. No, all ambition has the reek of disease about it, the relentless smell of the self—except for that terrible, blissful feeling at the heart of creation itself, when all thought of your name is obliterated and all you want is the poem, to be the means wherein something of reality, perhaps even something of eternity, realizes itself. That is noble ambition. But all that comes after—the need for approval, publication, self-promotion: isn't this what usually goes under the name of "ambition"? The effort is to make ourselves more real to ourselves, to feel that we *have* selves, though the deepest moments of creation tell us that, in some fundamental way, we don't. (What could be more desperate, more anxiously vain, than the ever-increasing tendency to Google oneself?) So long as your ambition is to stamp your existence upon existence, your nature on nature, then your ambition is corrupt and you are pursuing a ghost.

§

Still, there is *something* that any artist is in pursuit of, and is answerable to, some nexus of one's being, one's material, and Being itself. The work that emerges from this crisis of consciousness may be judged a failure or a success by the world, and that judgment will still sting or flatter your vanity. But it cannot speak to this crisis in which, for which, and of which the work was made. For any artist alert to his own soul, this crisis is the only call that matters. I know no name for it besides God, but people have other names, or no names.

387

This is why, ultimately, only the person who has made the work can judge it, which is liberating in one sense, because it frees an artist from the obsessive need for the world's approval. In another sense, though, this truth places the artist under the most severe pressure, because if that original call, that crisis of consciousness, either has not been truly heard, or has not been answered with everything that is in you, then even the loudest clamors of acclaim will be tainted, and the wounds of rejection salted with your implacable self-knowledge. An artist who loses this internal arbiter is an artist who can no longer hear the call that first came to him. Better to be silent then. Better to go into the world and do good work, rather than to lick and cosset a canker of resentment or bask your vanity in hollow acclaim.

§

Dietrich Bonhoeffer, after being in prison for a year, still another hard year away from his execution, forging long letters to his friend Eberhard Brege out of his strong faith, his anxiety, his longing for his fiancé, and terror over the nightly bombings: "There are things more important than self-knowledge." Yes. An artist who believes this is an artist of faith, even if the faith contains no god.

§

Reading Bonhoeffer makes me realize again how small our points of contact with life can be, perhaps even necessarily *are*, when our truest self finds its emotional and intellectual expression. With all that is going on around Bonhoeffer, and with all of the people in his life (he wrote letters to many other people and had close relationships with other prisoners), it is only in the letters to Brege that his thought really sparks and finds focus. Life is *always* a question of intensity, and intensity is always a matter of focus. Contemporary despair is to feel the multiplicity of existence with no possibility for expression or release of one's particular being. I fear sometimes that we are evolving in such a way that the possibilities for these small but intense points of intimacy and expression are not simply vanishing but are becoming no longer felt as necessary pressures. Poetry—its existence within and effect on the culture—is one casualty of this "evolution."

§

The two living novelists whose work means most to me are Cormac McCarthy, particularly in *Blood Meridian*, and Marilynne Robinson. Both of these writers seem to me to have not only the linguistic and metaphorical capacities of great poets, but also genuine visionary feeling. My own predispositions have everything to do with my preference, of course: I *believe* in visionary feeling and experience, and in the capacity of art to realize those things. I also believe that this is a higher achievement than art that merely concerns itself with the world that is right in front of us. Thus I don't respond as deeply to a poet like William Carlos Williams as I do to T.S. Eliot, and I much prefer Wallace Stevens (the earlier work) to, say, Elizabeth Bishop. (To read his "Sunday Morning" as it apparently asks to be read, to take its statements about reality and transcendence at face value, is to misread—to *under*-read—that poem. Its massive organ music and formal grandeur are not simply aiming at transcendence, they are claiming it.) Successful visionary art is a rare thing, and a steady diet of it will leave one not simply blunted to its effects but also craving art that's deeply attached to this world and nothing else. This latter category includes most of the art in existence (even much art that seems to be religious), and it is from this latter category that most of our aesthetic experience will inevitably come.

§

The question of exactly which art is seeking God, and seeking to be in the service of God, is more complicated than it seems. There is clearly something in all original art that will not be made subject to God, if we mean by being made "subject to God" a kind of voluntary censorship or willed refusal of the mind's spontaneous and sometimes dangerous intrusions into, and extensions of, reality. But that is not how that phrase ought to be understood. In fact we come closer to the truth of the artist's relation to divinity if we think not of being made subject to God but of being *subjected* to God—our individual subjectivity being lost and rediscovered within the reality of God. Human imagination is not simply our means of reaching out to God but God's means of manifesting himself to us. It follows that any notion of God that is static is not simply sterile but, since it asserts singular knowledge of God and seeks to limit his being to that knowledge, blasphemous. "God's truth is life," as Patrick Kavanagh says, "even the grotesque shapes of its foulest fire."

What is the difference between a cry of pain that is also a cry of praise and a cry of pain that is merely an articulation of despair? Faith? The cry of a believer, even if it is a cry against God, moves toward God, has its meaning in God, as in the cries of Job. The cry of an unbeliever is the cry of the damned, like Dante's souls locked in trees that must bleed to speak, their release from pain only further pain. How much of twentieth-century poetry, how much of my own poetry, is the cry of the damned? (By "damned" I mean simply utterly separated from God, and not condemned to a literal hell.) But this is oversimplified. It doesn't account for a poet like A.R. Ammons, who had no religious faith at all but whose work has some sort of undeniable lyric transcendence. Perhaps this: a cry that seems to at once contain and release some energy that is not merely the self, that does not end at despair but ramifies, however darkly, beyond it, is a metaphysical cry. And to make such a cry is, even in the absence of definitions, a definition, for it establishes us in relation to something that is infinite. Ammons:

> . . . if you can
> send no word silently healing, I
>
> mean if it is not proper or realistic
> to send word, actual lips saying
>
> these broken sounds, why, may we be
> allowed to suppose that we can work
>
> this stuff out the best we can and
> having felt out our sins to their
>
> deepest definitions, may we walk with
> you as along a line of trees, every
>
> now and then your clarity and warmth
> shattering across our shadowed way:

§

Reading the Scottish poet Norman MacCaig and thinking again of how some poets—surprisingly few—have a very particular gift for

390

making a thing at once shine forth in its "thingness" and ramify beyond its own dimensions: "Straws like tame lightnings lie about the grass / And hang zigzag on hedges"; or: "The black cow is two native carriers / Bringing its belly home, slung from a pole." What happens here is not "the extraordinary discovered within the ordinary," a cliché of poetic perception. What happens is some mysterious resonance between thing and language, mind and matter, that reveals—and it does feel like revelation—a reality beyond the one we ordinarily see. Contemporary physicists talk about something called "quantum weirdness," which refers to the fact that an observed particle behaves very differently from one that is unobserved. An observed particle passed through a screen will always go through one hole. A particle that is unobserved but mechanically monitored will pass through multiple holes at the same time. What this suggests, of course, is that what we call reality is utterly conditioned by the limitations of our senses, and that there is some other reality much larger and more complex than we are able to perceive. The effect I get from MacCaig's metaphorical explosiveness, or from that of poets such as Heaney, Plath, Hughes, is not of some mystical world, but of multiple dimensions within a single perception. They are not discovering the extraordinary within the ordinary. They are, for the briefest of instants, perceiving something of reality as it truly is.

§

Encroaching environmental disaster and the relentless wars around the world have had a paralyzing, sterilizing effect on much American poetry. It is less the magnitude of the crises than our apparent immunity to them, this death on which we all thrive, that is spinning our best energies into esoteric language games, or complacent retreats into nostalgias of form or subject matter, or shrill denunciations of a culture whose privileges we are not ready to renounce—or, more accurately, do not even know how to renounce. There is some fury of clarity, some galvanizing combination of hope and lament, that is much needed now, but aside from some notable exceptions of older poets (Adrienne Rich, Eleanor Wilner) it sometimes seems that we—and I use the plural seriously, I don't exempt myself—are anxiously waiting for the devastation to reach our very streets, as it one day will, it most certainly will.

§

"The intellect of man is forced to choose / Perfection of the life, or of the work, / And if it take the second must refuse / A heavenly mansion, raging in the dark." Lord, how much time—how much *life*—have I wasted on the rack of Yeat's utterly false distinction. It is not that imperfections in the life somehow taint or invalidate perfections of the work. It is, rather, that these things—art and life, or thought and life—are utterly, fatally, and sometimes savingly entwined, and we can know no man's work until we know how, whom, and to what end he did or did not love.

Nominated by Image

BEAUTIFUL COUNTRY

by ROBERT WRIGLEY

from MARGIE

They had five cigarettes going. Also a joint
      and a foot-and-a-half high hookah brimmed
with cannabis above and 3.2 beer below.
      A pale blue amaze against the high ceiling.
The six who lived there were lotused around
      four unfolded pages of the San Antonio Express-
News, stemming and seeding several resinous pounds of pot,
      three of them still in uniform, fatigues at least,
just back from a day at "Special Training Detachment,"
      or as it was emblazoned on their helmet liners
"STD" (a sequence of letters not having, in 1971,
      the resonance or implication they have today).
It was a holding company for the hopeless
      and the hopeful. American soldiers, that is, such as they
  were.
Also in uniform, person number seven, call him Sergeant Blinks.
      He'd lost an eye in Vietnam, and he was
their dealer, their source, and he liked them more
      than seemed reasonable or right and promised them
each a free nickel bag for their custodial work.
      And even as they worked he was strapped off and shooting
  up
with one of the good sterile syringes
      they'd copped from Central Medical Supply.
That was why he liked them, they figured.

Come home a junkie, he seemed happy
to be here, since they were to have been medics
        and had stolen those syringes long before
Porter developed the bed-wetting problem and Denton
        and Speigel decided they were queers (gay, in those days,
meaning only excessively happy), and before the rest of them
        pleaded not merely ordinary cowardice
but conscientious objection. They said they meant it, in other words,
        even as they wondered how killing Nixon could be anything
    but right.
When they could talk at all they had those kinds of conversations.
        They thought about what was wrong and more wrong.
Blinks sat in the room's only chair, spike withdrawn now,
        head lolled off to the side, a kind of fractured baleen
of spittle lip to lip across his open mouth.
        The pot was so sticky they each paused now and then
to work the goo of it up and off each digit, and rolled it
        into black boluses they dropped in a communal coffee
    cup—
finger hash, it was called, and they couldn't take their eyes off it,
        redolent, drop deadly, and very much desired.
It would be, at the end of their stem-and-seed-parsing,
        what Sergeant Blinks offered in exchange for his lark:
if he could skin-pop them all with a drop or two of his horse
        in the backs of their six left and mostly white hands, it was
    theirs.
A long pause then. How bad could it be? they wondered.
        Meaning how good. Meaning they wanted what they wanted
and didn't want what they might come to want more
        or too much of, though what was too much
and what did they really want, after all?
        Well, they wanted that cup of finger hash
enough that no one said no, so happily
        Blinks rigged up five new times: syringes
from the dozens in the stolen box,
        a couple cc's from the cent-back cooking spoon,
and then, in between each of the four metacarpal ridges
        across the backs of their newly brave and unheroic hands
he eased—so gently, so skillfully—the needle's slender bevel
        just under this skin and made a series of blisters there,

wens, tear-shaped sebaceous cysts of the same stuff
        he had not long before plunged a pistonful of into his vein.
As per his instructions, they flexed their fists
        and slapped the dabbled backs of their hands
with their undabbled others, and felt come rushing up their arms
        a kind of other-coming, overcoming smolder.
Wilson, the one black man among them, studied his biceps
        and said again and again *hot fudge, hot fudge*.
It was like entering a large perfect mouth,
        a kind of woman-wetness they were up to their shoulders
  in,
their necks and ears, until there wasn't anything to say
        and even if there had been no mechanism by which to say
  it.
But it didn't last long, and as far as they would ever know none of
  them
        did it again. And Blinks left them their nickel bags and the
  sticky stuff,
and Spiegel boiled up the stems and made iced tea from the water.
        They were so wrecked they forgot to eat and eat
on the sun-busted front porch for hours, watching swallows cruise for
  moths.
        They even stood to salute at sundown and faced up the
  block
to the base's back gate at Taps,
        and for some reaction this was not at all ironic.
Tra-la they would not kill alas, they would not die.
        They couldn't see the base flag going down,
but the gloaming coming on from the east
        promised another day when everything would be better.
There were bats coming out, hunting
        America, someone said. Beautiful country.
And it was.

Nominated by Margie, Jeff P. Jones, Claire Davis, Brandon Schrand,
Grace Schulman, Andrea Hollander Budy

PUT ON THE PETTY

by AMOS MAGLIOCCO

from THE MISSOURI REVIEW

Aᴀᴛᴇʀ Eʀɪᴄ ᴀɴᴅ I sᴜʀᴠɪᴠᴇᴅ an F2 tornado in Tulia, Texas, I thought we'd live forever. We rode out the tornado in a high-profile SUV—precisely the wrong kind of shelter—and after we'd crashed into a brick wall and ducked under a one-hundred twenty-knot jet that screamed through the blown-out windows, it seemed as if the Angel of Death had roared, in a breath choked with debris, and then fled, leaving us alone and lucky. We were unscathed, but for a scratch on Eric's ankle and a cut on the back of my neck—or at least that was how it seemed for days and even weeks after the event. We were okay. We'd made it. Our chief complaint was embarrassment: two experienced storm chasers with almost two hundred tornado documentations between them weren't supposed to wind up inside one. But the vortex had formed in an unexpected portion of the storm and reached full strength almost instantly. After we climbed from Eric's totaled Nissan Xterra and studied the devastated town around us, he turned to me. "Well," he said, thinking of the next chase, "I guess we'll take your car on Monday."

I laid my camera on the ground and cleared a pile of Abilene brick away from the passenger door, the sensation of good fortune already forming in my chest. Not a broken bone or even a gash that would require a stitch. A miracle.

Four months later, I reminded Eric of this good fortune in the hallway of an Arlington, Texas, psychiatric hospital. My friend and chase partner, who always wore white T-shirts and khaki shorts, was leaning against the wall in blue hospital scrubs and a bright red wristband that marked him as "actively suicidal." Even his regular shoes were a potential threat, and so he wore laceless plastic ones, more like slippers. He was losing weight, looking younger every day, as if he were retreating into the safety of boyhood.

I said, "We can get through this"—one of the many rehearsed lines I always used when I visited Eric, though my top priority was to listen and make "normal" conversation. From then until my next visit or phone call I would compose more such lines, desperate to talk him out of a chronic mental illness I'd learned about just days before his hospitalization, before what he would describe in his journal as an "adamant" desire to kill himself "in a sudden and violent way."

On my visits we talked about the weather—of course—and a coffee-table book he was publishing with another storm photographer. Eric's storm images are among the most widely reproduced in the world. Days before his admission, I'd helped him copyedit the captions of his pictures for the book. When I reminded him of our unlikely survival back in Tulia, a light appeared in his eyes. His odds were better this time around, in a hospital, receiving treatment. I thought this logic would appeal to a meteorologist with a minor in mathematics. But after visiting hours ended and the hallway marked "Extreme Elopement Risk" emptied of friends and family, Eric's rational mind battled compulsions that I would never dispel with one-liners, however smoothly delivered. It started late at night, when the urge to cut himself, for "relief," rose like a blue-gray thunderhead on the empty prairie. One night he asked a nurse if they could draw blood. She tried to humor him, undoubtedly noting the bizarre request in his chart. The doctors would take vitals in the morning, she promised, and a few vials of blood in the process. He pondered injuring himself with the pencil he used for his journal but didn't want to lose his writing privileges.

Bob Fritchie and Rachael Sigler, meteorologists and friends of Eric's from college, were outside Tulia when the tornado hit. They knew Eric and I were close to the storm, and they saw the tornado descend and rip northward along the industrial park on the town's western edge. "I wonder where they are," Bob said and gripped his steering wheel. They called on the two-way radio, but by then Eric and I were roaming the littered streets, snapping pictures and high-stepping over power lines. Emergency sirens punctuated a chorus of bleating car alarms. A sheriff's cruiser raced toward us and struck a power line that snapped with a booming twang like a giant banjo string. The sheriff slowed beside us and started to roll down his window. I waved him on. We were fine, I yelled. The last thing we wanted was to distract emergency services. Eric remembered Bob and Rachael and called them on his cell to say that yes, we'd been struck, but we were okay.

"You guys keep chasing," I heard Eric say. "We'll go to somebody's house and find a ride tomorrow."

It was a magnanimous gesture, a convention of chaser courtesy. Keep going. Don't miss the next tornado. But this was not a typical situation: we'd taken a direct hit. Eric's car was mangled; the upper corner of a building, bricks still mortared together, had landed on the hood and now protruded through the windshield. A whole semi truck leaned on the front passenger bumper, threatening to topple. The town smelled of shredded vegetation and motor oil. I sure as hell didn't want Bob and Rachael to keep going, didn't mind a bit if they missed the next tornado, especially with darkness and more storms headed our way.

A thin line of blood grew on Eric's ankle. He said he might have glass in his eye, and I was having a harder and harder time disguising my own disorientation, as if I'd been clubbed in the head. I couldn't tell if it was physical or emotional, some lower order of shock. But I wasn't fooling Eric.

"Are you sure you're okay?" he asked.

"I am," I lied. "Just a little slow."

We gathered our bags and arranged them on a wooden pallet above the wet ground while Bob and Rachael crept into town from the south, entering the damage path. Bob pounded the steering wheel. A paramedic who recognized the scale of destruction, he also knew something about Eric I did not; he'd helped him through a suicidal episode two years before, when they were in college, and he understood Eric's ability to mask illness. Later I would come to regard Bob as the one who had saved Eric in 2005, where I would fail when it was my turn.

When I met Eric for the first time he was twenty years old, thin and square-jawed with a teenager's boisterous smile, already married and the father of a one-year-old boy. His last name, Nguyen, didn't fit—he was Caucasian and had taken his wife's name. In those days Eric didn't know much more about the weather than I did, but that would change quickly. After he graduated from Oklahoma University's prestigious School of Meteorology, he gave me an anthology of severe storm research, a leather-bound volume awarded to all freshly minted atmospheric scientists. He already owned a copy, but the gift was a sign of respect for what an amateur nonscientist like me had managed to learn on his own.

We chased together often, usually in separate cars since we lived far apart—Eric in Norman and I in Bloomington, where I attended grad school. In the summer of 2005 we both relocated to North Texas, each happy to have a familiar chase partner in close proximity. I was especially lucky. Not only was Eric a friend, but he'd been chasing since he was seventeen and by now was regarded as one of the best in the world. His photo of the Mulvane, Kansas, storm is one of the most recognizable tornado images of all time: a narrow white funnel curves down behind an antebellum-style plantation house (a sort of residence rarely seen in Kansas). Silvery debris like the spray of a waterfall rises from the point of impact, and, crossing the tornado, a bright rainbow arcs smartly to the ground. Chestnut horses buck and spit before a stable, and a white picket fence frames the scene. Though violent, the image renders the beauty of severe weather and is an eloquent reply to the question of why chasers do what they do.

We chased together for three years, compiling an impressive string of tornado intercepts; other chasers joked about attaching a tracking device to our vehicle. In the dry season of 2006 we found tornadoes shrouded by rain or hiding in twilight, monsters one could never really "see" until reviewing video later, frame by frame, for the sudden glimpse of a lightning-backlit twister. Yet in good years or bad, chasing hardly resembles what you've seen on television. We drive thousands of miles each year for that handful of minutes in which we witness tornadoes, and on most days nothing happens at all: even the best chasers fail in eight of every ten attempts. Afternoons fizzle into "blue-sky busts."

Bob and Rachael drove us out of Tulia on the dark highway toward Amarillo. Eric was excited and antsy. He leaned into the front seat and talked about the storm ahead and the one we'd escaped. He reminded me of a nervous little boy. I looked him over again and saw only that same cut on his ankle.

The supercell in front of us had already produced a tornado, and another storm was approaching from the west. We were sandwiched between them, and Bob tried to conceal our predicament, making awkward small talk with Eric.

"Look!" Rachael shouted and tapped her nail on the passenger window. In the next flash, a tall cone tornado appeared far to our north-east, moving away. Nobody suggested we stop and film it; no one reached for a camera. The tornado was an object of detached curios-ity, a silhouetted funnel, cousin of the beast that had smashed our truck.

Chasers do not ignore luck. Though most are meteorologists, trained to approach forecast problems from a scientific perspective, there remain much art and instinct to the process, what pros call "pattern recognition." And chasers are superstitious, too. One of my superstitions evolved from noticing how almost every time I played Tom Petty's album *Wildflowers*, the storm I was chasing produced a tornado. Eric thought it was silly, of course, as any self-respecting "met" would, until he saw it happen repeat-edly. He was a scientist, but he wanted to photograph tornadoes, too.

When I bought a car adapter for my iPod, he questioned whether the Petty would still "work" when played from a digital file instead of the CD I'd always used. We brought the disc just in case. In October 2005 the Petty induced a tornado from a storm that had looked hope-lessly serene, and Eric was convinced. After that, rather than his rolling his eyes or feigning disdain for my hocus-pocus, we debated which storms "deserved" the Petty. We waited for a storm to show a hard crown, gleaming knuckles under the back-sheared anvil and a cylindrical updraft base, cloud matter crisp and rounded like fresh clay. Tornadoes are never guaranteed, no matter how impressive a storm's appearance, but we sought to "help" those storms that seemed to be trying to produce one. They had to demonstrate intent. Occa-sionally it was obvious, and Eric would turn and say, "Better put on the Petty."

We had not been playing *Wildflowers* when we entered Tulia, though. As we reached town, I leaned over Eric's computer to find our next turn on the mapping software. Another program displayed radar data. We'd used the Petty an hour earlier when we'd intercepted a beautiful tornado in a flawless pursuit near Olton, Texas. Now we were simply repositioning for the storm's next cycle. A disorganized lowering beneath the updraft signaled no imminent danger. While I was studying the roads, Eric glimpsed a dust whirl over his left shoul-der. "Oh, shit," he yelled. "Tornado!"

When we reached the Amarillo hospital, I didn't check in as a patient. I assumed I was okay, as is my habit. But when a nurse called Eric back, he glanced to me and I was glad to join him. The truth was I didn't want us to be apart anytime soon. It was as if we both sensed there was more danger ahead, some kind of unforeseeable debris bearing down on us still.

I followed him to the examination room. The doctor was a young guy from Boston, a Johns Hopkins grad who seemed glad that someone recognized his dialect. He wore a navy-blue suit under his lab coat, and gold cufflinks gleamed from beneath the long white sleeves. "I've just returned from a banquet," he explained. I wondered what he thought of the Texas Panhandle, where local culture revolves around high school football and historical oil wealth.

"Who's the patient?" he asked.

Eric raised his hand. "I think I have glass in my eye."

The doctor patted the table, and Eric hopped on. The doctor searched each eye with a narrow penlight and applied drops that caused Eric's pupils to dilate completely; it was the first time I'd seen his usually bright, clear eyes so full and strange. I would see this again when the antipsychotics caused full dilations.

And then a third and final time.

After the drops, Eric described the room as "overexposed." In storm imagery, sunlight below a cloud base can "burn out" that portion of the picture. Settings for clouds and sun are entirely different. It is impossible to adjust for both.

The doctor asked what had happened.

"Car wreck," Eric said.

"Did the car roll?"

"No. It didn't."

I assumed the doctor was asking out of more than curiosity. "We got hit by a tornado," I volunteered. Eric blinked a few times and then smiled and nodded slowly. I choose now to see that as a moment of relief for him, a release from yet another secret.

"While you both were in the car?"

"Yes," I said.

He looked me over. "And you're okay?"

"Right as rain."

Eric shook his head no. "He seems a little loopy to me."

The doctor began searching my scalp. "Did you take a blow to the head?"

"I don't think so."

"Well, we haven't had anybody else from Tulia. I guess you boys are the only victims." And it was true. Nobody else was treated for injuries. All businesses in Tulia had closed for the night; staff and customers were secure in their home basements or shelters when the sirens blew. The mangled Sonic drive-through, normally a hive of cruising teens and preening middle schoolers on Saturday nights, was empty because a new location had opened the night before, on the other side of town.

Eric and I kept chasing in the days and weeks after Tulia. We ventured out two days later, in fact, though we were tense. He said we were chasing differently, and I agreed. It was logical. Intelligent creatures learn from mistakes. They adjust. He became fascinated with the statistical improbability of meeting such a small tornado at the moment of its maximum power. Later, he assisted another meteorologist on a paper dissecting the data collected by Eric's onboard weather instruments. In Tulia we recorded the most dramatic pressure drop in history: nearly two hundred millibars—the equivalent of being thrust three thousand feet into the air from sea level. The data were so extraordinary that to survive peer review the author had to establish a theoretical basis by which such measurements were conceivable.

The paper concluded that we were struck the instant before the "supercritical vortex" began the process of "vortex breakdown" and that we experienced the "corner flow region," where the greatest pressure falls are theorized to be. In layman's terms, a tornado is never more violent than the moment before it unravels.

I returned to teaching, though within a week the flashbacks started, and my concentration broke. During a workshop, I found myself staring at a young student writer and imagining how the fibrous insulation had drifted down long after the winds calmed. Three weeks after the accident, I canceled classes and called Eric. We had spoken frequently and chased together since Tulia but never discussed the psychological effects.

"Are you having flashbacks?"

"Yeah," he said. "All the time."

We talked about their random appearance, how there seemed to be no identifiable prompt. He was relieved to hear it from me first, and I was glad to share it with him. I did not mention that it made me reconsider chasing and how absurd it would be to die in a tornado before I'd published a book. I was a writer first, not a weather geek. I never threatened to quit, but the shift in my tone was surely apparent to Eric.

Our last chase was June 6, 2007. In Valentine, Nebraska, near the Sand Hills just south of the Dakota border, we waited in a restaurant parking lot with dozens of other chasers. Eric met his longtime photography agent in person for the first time and gave the man a hug, as though they'd been close for years. The day's storm erupted in the foothills of the Badlands, and we rushed across the border and turned west on Interstate 80 as a tornado snaked out from under the storm. It was so far away that we could only see the funnel in our peripheral vision, the faintest outline on the rolling terrain. We drove and drove but never seemed to close the distance. It was Eric's last tornado, and it already looked like a memory.

When he entered the hospital two months later, medicines wrecked his short-term memory. He forgot that he'd invited me to visit the same day as his new girlfriend. She waited ahead of me in line, a small, shapely girl with a rose tattoo on her ankle, and I guessed who she was. When the doors swung open, Eric spotted her, and they hugged and started down the hallway together. I thought of leaving, giving them time alone, but it had taken an hour through heavy traffic to reach the hospital, and I wanted to see him. I decided to stay a few minutes and then head back. When he saw me, a smile spread across his face. "There he is," he said. "Showing up unannounced."

"We talked about it yesterday," I said.

He shook his head. "Damn meds." The three of us leaned against the wall and chatted for a half hour. Eric's beard was coming out patchy and blond. They wouldn't let him anywhere near a razor, he said.

His girlfriend tucked herself under his arm, and he looked relaxed, even confident. He gave no indication that he wanted me to leave. He directed the conversation, in fact. When his girlfriend asked if I'd been in the tornado, I nodded. "He's a survivor," Eric said. A week later, he revealed that he'd been hallucinating during this entire conversation, seeing a fence opening and closing around the three of us.

"I know so much about suicide I could make it happen right now if I wanted," he wrote in his journal. "Sometimes I wonder if being an expert has condemned me."

I was not an expert, nor did I know, while Eric was hospitalized, the meaning of the word "survivor" in the context of suicide. Instead, I absorbed everything I could find about Eric's disease, schizoaffective disorder, and the meds he took. I could diagram the molecular structure of Effexor and explain, as I did the last time I spoke to him, how the drug could produce a temporary serotonin deficiency before the desired increase. "Good," he said. "That gives me some hope." Now I know how, in the lexicon of suicide, the word "survivor" stands for the six people closest to the victim.

Eric's wife later found his journal in the evidence bin at the Arlington Police Department. I'd seen it on my very last visit. He had clutched it to his chest for an hour while we talked. It was a typical student composition book with a mottled black-and-white cover, bound with glue along the spine. At one point he had lowered it and fanned dozens of pages filled with his small, neat script. He said he was writing about "whatever I'm feeling . . . things that piss me off." He lifted an eraserless pencil from a pocket in his scrubs, and I studied the lead tip. I imagined he was making progress if they allowed him such potentially harmful objects.

He may have noticed me studying that pencil. He was quick, hyperintelligent, and he knew me better than I knew him, but he didn't know everything. He didn't know the most important things. I never told Eric how I understood why we hide sickness, why it sometimes feels most urgent to keep it from those we love best.

"Eric was an action guy," a friend offered later. "You were visiting him. You were calling. You asked him to eat more—that's an elemental expression of care." But what I see now are the clouds that skewed his perception of himself and others, how truth spun and lifted into dark condensation. Didn't he need to hear what reality was every day and every hour? The answer, it seems to me, is yes, he did. He needed to hear each day all over again what was real and what was vapor. A week after my last visit, as Eric lay in a coma, a neurologist leaned inches from his ear in the twice-daily and always unsuccessful effort to wake him. "Eric!" the doctor shouted. "Eric, can you open your eyes? Can you squeeze my hand? Eric!"

When I was a boy I tried to imagine the shape and depth of "forever," a child's idea of God's lifespan soon giving way to a young boy's conception of the universe, then an adolescent's nightmare of death's endless spooling dark. Now I measure forever by Eric's absence, the immutability of his death. Nonnegotiable. No second chance. I can write no scenes to change the outcome, though I imagine dozens of conversations that never happened, gratifying for us both, redeeming and potentially life-saving. Could one revelation have made a difference?

In composing a forecast, meteorologists understand that any unaccounted-for element in the "initial conditions" can alter the outcome entirely—simplified chaos theory. The thinnest layer of dry air at two thousand feet sparks a tornado outbreak where there might have been clear, muggy skies. And Eric was unstable at the time, his mind in chaos, so who can say what would have changed the equation? No forecast has a chance.

When my mother suffered a toxic reaction to the drug Heparin after bypass surgery, I imagined no point of intercession to keep the poisonous medicine from her system. I wrote no scenes to change the world. But suicide is a volitional death, the victim's choice, and for survivors, each memory returns as a lost opportunity. With Eric, there are an infinite number of moments when I could have said more, acted more kindly, begged him not to hurt himself or explained how much he meant to me. And there was one thing I certainly should have told him.

When my father died in 1998, we buried him back home in Binghamton, New York, in a graveyard overlooking the Chenango River Valley. After the service, my mother and I climbed the steep hillside to the car, hurrying to escape the January wind.

"Amos," she called from behind me, "are you having some weakness in your upper legs?" The answer was yes, for years now, and the unusual gait I was developing could not escape the eye of a lifelong nurse, especially one whose only brother had developed the same trait forty years earlier. But all I knew on that day was that my mother was thinking of her dead brother, the Uncle Billy I'd never met, and having just buried her husband, she needed no more disquieting news. Besides, I thought, I was only a little out of shape, a few pounds overweight. Nothing a jogging regimen couldn't fix.

"No," I answered. "There's nothing wrong with my legs. What makes you say that?"

"You walk like Billy did at your age. I hadn't noticed it before."

In 1951, my uncle had been diagnosed with progressive muscular atrophy, a catchall term common before the discovery of the dystrophin gene, and as his mobility deteriorated over the years, all the doctors could say was take plenty of vitamin E. Enjoy brisk evening strolls. Billy died in gall-bladder surgery the same way most Becker's

405

muscular dystrophy patients go: sudden cardiac failure. A year after my father died, two muscle biopsies confirmed my own diagnosis: the same as my uncle's. In the womb, I'd had a fifty-fifty chance.

Eventually I told my mother and wrapped the news in promising discoveries—gene therapy and myostatin inhibitors—that I hoped would compete with her memory of Billy's deterioration. She wept on the phone but tried to hide the guilt she felt for having passed along a bad gene. "It could be worse, Mom," I said. "Those kids with Duchenne's." Those are the ones you see on television. Unlike them, I had enjoyed a normal childhood, running and playing sports with my friends, just like Billy, who pitched a no-hitter for the Deposit Lumberjacks when he was seventeen.

And this is how I would have told Eric, if I had ever revealed my secret to him. It's the scene I imagine most: a brief preamble and then the hard news, with the offer that now he knew someone else, someone he loved and trusted, who understood about hidden illness and the aversion to being seen as sick or broken or doomed. You're not alone. It could be worse.

On the first Monday in August, he told me his own diagnosis. I thought, *Tell him now*, but then, *No, don't make this about you*. I had just resigned my position as a lecturer at the University of North Texas, and when he answered the phone I had said, "Guess what I just did."

"You quit your job."

I was amazed. "Wow," I said.

"I know you."

We talked about why it was a good idea to invest time in finishing my novel. Then he gave me his news, and we talked about what his doctor had said about the medicines and their side effects. I was stunned but humbled by his confidence—things he might have felt if I had had the courage to reveal my own illness. I didn't know yet about his suicidal impulses or the hospitalization two years before. And I did not tell him later, after he was hospitalized, because I thought the information was too heavy. I would wait until he was stronger. I borrowed against the time I thought Tulia had granted us.

Now I understand my ungenerous silence as a resistance to my own disease, an instinct to preserve in Eric's eyes the reflection of who I was when we'd met ten years before. In this way we were the same. His sister would later tell me how much he feared that I'd stop chasing with him if I learned of his suicidal impulses.

406

One day when I was visiting Eric, a poor woman lost in deep schizophrenia approached us in the hallway. She wore a hospital gown tied loosely in back and nodded toward Eric's comparatively fashionable scrubs. "Can I have your clothes?" she asked.

"I think they have some at the nurse's station," he said. He pointed in the direction he wanted her to walk.

"I don't like the clothes up there," she said. She studied his face. "Can I have your education?" Her hair was short, and she was thin as a prisoner, with needy, searching eyes.

"I left my diploma at home."

The woman cocked her head in confusion and leaned into him. "What are you doing here?"

Eric pointed to me. "I'm visiting him. He's the craziest guy in the place."

"Tomorrow is a new month," Eric wrote at 3:00 P.M., three and half hours before we spoke for the last time, four hours and fifteen minutes before he mortally wounded himself. "Let's hope it's a good one." I often wonder how far the ambulance traveled to arrive at the psychiatric facility, only to carry him just across the intersection to Arlington Memorial Hospital. From that night until September 9, the nine days he lived in a coma, I would pass that intersection each day; it can't be more than three hundred yards from the front door of the psych ward to the emergency room entrance.

Six weeks after Eric died, I appended to our last phone call, then playing over and over in my head, the sequence of events that must have followed. During our talk, I had mentioned to him that my contact at a magazine, for whom I'd written an interview with a novelist, no longer worked there, and the new editor wanted a formal query letter. But I was still confident the magazine would take the interview. I was upbeat about the prospects and even my small chance to make the cover. He was glad to hear it. I thought it was important to share something from my own day and offer evidence that I was still working, that his crisis wasn't a burden to me. I wanted to say that I loved him like a brother—but I was afraid to imply that things were somehow worse than they seemed to me. It would have been abnormal, and I wanted him to feel as though his normal life was waiting for him. Perhaps I wanted so much for things to be normal that Eric played along.

He had forty-five minutes of consciousness left.

407

He ended the call abruptly: "They're going for a smoke break," he said. (He'd started a cigarette-a-day habit in the hospital, Marlboro Lights 100s.) We agreed I would visit over the weekend, on whichever day his mother didn't come. He reminded me of the visiting hours on weekends. The last words I ever said to him were, "I'll see you tomorrow or Sunday."

"Okay," he answered. Then he hung up the phone.

If he went for a smoke, he would have reentered the ward about 6:45 P.M. The next thirty minutes are unaccounted for. What we know for sure is this: at 7:15 P.M., visiting hours started with the normal commotion as family and friends entered together in a group. Eric's wife, from whom he was separated, was stuck in traffic and would arrive twenty-five minutes later. In the bustle, Eric slipped from his "line of sight" supervision into an empty, unlocked and apparently unmonitored room. He stripped the bed of a single sheet and walked into the bathroom.

Before we reached Tulia on April 21, Eric and I saw a tornado near the town of Olton, a beautiful laminar cone. It approached the road ahead of us, and the funnel lit up like a bulb when the sun peeked from under the shadow of the anvil, a magical translucence. Filaments at the base swirled like dancers. I planted my tripod in the dirt beside the shoulder of the road. Eric ran to the fence line and began shooting stills. "This is awesome," he said and hopped a little, overcome with joy. I locked my camera in place and stepped away to take in the view. Tiny hailstones fell in spurts and stung my arm. From the back of the storm, rain curtains rippled across our vehicle. I cleaned my lens with the bottom of my shirt.

"It is awesome, man," I answered. And it was.

When the tornado crossed the road to our east, we chased it. It swung north, away from us. Having watched it form to our south, mature to our southeast and continue to our east, we knew without saying so that our strategy was perfect. We'd waited inside the bear's cage—the center of a thunderstorm's rotation—but we'd kept the wall cloud in sight and noted all the signals of tornadogenesis. We readied our cameras, cool and quiet, Tom Petty in the background. We'd been here before.

As we drove up behind the tornado, I joked, "Let's not drive right into it. Exciting as that might be."

"I know," Eric said and chuckled.

The tornado scraped a row of houses and peeled shingles from the rafters. We held our breath, hoping those inside were huddled under-ground or in interior rooms or closets. Our invincibility made us gen-erous, freed our spirits for unconditional empathy. There are necessary illusions all storm chasers hold: the sense of control, of risk calculated to such a degree that they can boast of how it is safer to hunt tornadoes than to drive to work in the suburbs. The walls of those houses remained intact. The people inside, the victims, would survive. The tornado moved on. In ten years it would be a story for family reunions.

When it was well off the road, we pulled up alongside. Eric shot photos from the driver's side, and I leaned over with my camcorder.

"Can you see around me?" he asked.

I said that I could.

Eric pointed. "Look at that debris in the air. There's debris way up in the air, lofted debris. It disappeared in the funnel." I lowered the camcorder to look. There were roofs and trees and cars, none bigger than your fingernail, floating into the upper reaches of the storm, higher and higher until they slipped from view as if they were weight-less and would never crash back to earth in a field covered with fresh rain and hailstones, into softened dirt vulnerable to their terrible im-pact.

Nominated by The Missouri Review

WHY THE NOVEL IS NECESSARY BUT SOMETIMES HARD TO READ

by **MARIE HOWE**

from TIN HOUSE

It happens in time. *Years passed until the old woman,*
one snowy morning, realized she had never loved her daughter . . .

Or *Five years later she answered the door, and her suitor had*
*   returned*
almost unrecognizable from his journeys . . .

But before you get to that part
you have to learn the names—you have to suffer not knowing
   anything about anyone

and slowly come to understand who each of them is, or who each of
   them
imagines themselves to be—

and then, because you are the reader, you must try to understand
   who you think

each of them is because of who you believe yourself to be in relation
    to their situation
or to your memory of one very much like it.

Oh, it happens in time, and time is hard to live through.
I can't read anything anymore, my dying brother said one afternoon
Not even letters.
Come on; Come on—he said, waving his hand in the air
What am I interested in—plot?

You come upon the person the author put there
as if you'd been pushed into a room and told to watch the dancing—
pushed into pantries, into basements, across moors, into
the great drawing room of great cities, into the small cold cabin or

to here—beside the small running river where a boy is weeping,
and no one comes . . .

and you have to watch without saying anything he can hear.

One by one the readers come and watch him weeping by the running
    river,
and he never knows

unless he too has heard the story where a boy feels himself all alone.

This is the life you have written, the novel tells us. *What happens
    next?*

Nominated by Tin House, Ellen Bass, Dorianne Laux, Katrina Roberts

MY FIRST REAL HOME

fiction by DIANE WILLIAMS

from POST ROAD

IN THERE, THERE WAS THIS MAN who developed a habit of sharpening knives. You know he had a house and a yard, so he had a lawn mower and several axes and he had a hedge shears and, of course, he had kitchen knives and scissors, and he and his wife lived in comfort.

Within a relatively short time he had spent half of his fortune on sharpening equipment and they were gracing his basement on every available table and bench and he added special stands for the equipment.

He would end up with knives or shears that were so sharp they just had to come near something and it would cut itself. It's the kind of sharpening that goes beyond comprehension. You just lean the knife against a piece of paper.

Tommy used to use him. Ernie'd do his chain saws.

So, I take my knives under my arm and I drive off to Ernie's and he and I became friends and we'd talk about everything.

"I don't sharpen things right away. You leave it—and see that white box over there?" he'd said. That was his office. It was a little white box attached to the house with a lid you could open and inside there were a couple of ballpoint pens. There was a glass jar with change. There were tags with rubber bands and there was an order form that you filled out in case he wasn't there.

He wasn't there the first time I came back, at least I didn't see him.

I went up to the box and those knives were transformed.

As I was closing the lid, he came up through the basement door that was right there and we started to chat and he has to show me something in the garden, so he takes me to where he has his plantings. It's as if the dirt was all sorted and arranged, and then, when I said he had cut his lawn so nice, he was shining like a plug bayonet.

All the little straws and grass were pointing in one direction.

"I don't mow like my neighbor," he said.

Oh, and then he also had a nice touch—for every packet he had completed there was a Band-Aid included. Just a man after my own heart. He died.

I was sad because whenever I got there I was very happy.

Nominated by Post Road, Clancy Martin, Kim Chinquee

EVERYTHING, ALL AT ONCE

fiction by AUSTIN BUNN

from THE SUN

"I HAVE LICHEN," my mother says. "On my vagina."

What am I supposed to do? I am her daughter.

"Lichen is a woods thing," I say over the phone. "A hiking thing."

My mother lives on the tenth floor of a high-rise that overlooks New York Harbor from a New Jersey bluff. She leaves only to shop, to return half of what she has bought, and to eat lunch at the Quick Check. She has not been hiking or on lichen or lichen-adjacent since before I knew she had a vagina. Her adventures are happy hours in the penthouse bar, where she counts the freighters and container ships with Al, a retired sea captain.

"Well, the Internet says I have it inside me," she says, "and you can't tell a soul."

It is Saturday morning. I open my garage door, the phone wedged between my ear and shoulder. Inside, the mausoleum of my marriage—the shelves and stacks and piles—greets me with a grim exhale. The papers arrived from the lawyer yesterday. Soon I will be officially divorced from Scott. I'm selling what I can.

"You have to come with me to the doctor," my mother says.

But I have buyers coming. I'm expecting to get money for my past life. The pleasures of subtraction, of seeing things go.

"This is your mother speaking," she says. "This is your mother in need."

What ever can I do?

I say, "Give me an hour."

At noon a girl drives up in a pickup with her Mexican boyfriend. They saw my ad on Craigslist and are trying to outfit their entire life in one day. Already they look numb, zombified by exertion. A scrunchie cinches the girl's blond hair on top and makes her look like a pineapple. She sucks the final drops from a Gallon Guzzler, pegging the ice with the straw for more. Her boyfriend wears a sweat-soaked red-and-yellow T-shirt that reads, "YALE." He massages her shoulders when she stands still, but he is shorter and has to reach up a little. In the bed of the truck, an old mint green refrigerator is lashed down haphazardly with straps, like an escape trick.

"How come you want to get rid of so much awesomeness?" the girl asks, her fingers tracing the scalloped rim of a Waterford crystal bowl: a wedding gift that I used for loose change. Her boyfriend picks through a basket of shells and conches, carefully spaced and layered with towels, that I displayed in a glass cabinet at our old apartment. Scott and I had a place a hundred yards from the shore, yet I thought we needed reminding. My whole marriage was a reminder to have a marriage.

"I left my husband," I say. "All this reminds me of him, of us."

The girl glances over at her boyfriend. "Don't tell him that," she says, sotto voce. "He's wicked superstitious."

I see their relationship unscroll in front of me—his fears, her fears of his fears, the double braid of accommodation and resentment—and I want to tell her: *Run.* The divorced aren't jaded; we're clairvoyant.

"Hey, that basket of shells?" I say to the boyfriend, who presses two conches against his ears, grinning. "I'll give it to you. No money. *Mi casa, tu casa.*"

He looks surprised, then honored, then seems to see the basket for what it is: a wicker container of beach trash, another weight he'll have to carry. He deposits the conches and turns to a shelf of puzzles. I had a jigsaw period.

They leave with the crystal bowl, coffee maker, nightstand, single mattress, artificial Christmas tree, and miter saw. Without asking, I carry the basket of shells to their truck. I smell the creamy coconut of suntan lotion and a funky undertone, brackish and tidal. Shards of sanded glass, like fogged irises, rumble inside a cookie tin. Scott and I lived at the beach for five years, and if you could watch just our beach episodes, we looked happy. Scott would fish in the surf or play his guitar, and I would read or just listen, jealous of his aptitudes. I'm a librarian at Highlands Elementary; what I'm good at is cataloging. After every good time we had, I gave myself an assignment to bring one shell home, something singular and beautiful. Proof that I'd felt loved, that I was experiencing what there was to experience. That display case was my own library, a library of moments.

I set the basket down in the truck bed and wonder what the girl will make of it. Will she see the bounty of the Jersey coast, or just me, a forty-one-year-old woman, alone and childless, her diseased mother for a best friend? I am her future. I want to tell her that after their marriage ends—after he cheats, or spends his days stoned, or gambling, or gets up from the table when she asks him for a child—she should pass the shells right on down to the next girl: mementos of what's next.

But this girl sees nothing in the shells but souvenirs from someone else's bad trip. She peels the money from a roll as thick as her fist. "We don't want that basket," she says.

"Good," I say, "because I don't like your look."

Doctor Stecopolous is Greek, in his midthirties, and my mother adores him. Every time we've met, he seems as if he's just come from an exam that he knows he aced. He patiently allows my mother to pry into his parents' immigration, his years of school, his new marriage. After every detail, my mother throws a look in my direction: *Thessaloniki! Isn't Thessaloniki wonderful?* He is my mother's ideal man at a time when her interactions have become transactional: He has warm hands, walks her to the reception desk. He wears patent-leather Italian shoes ("He doesn't skimp," my mother said) and tolerates her jokes, the signal flares of her personality.

She has her legs up in the stirrups, holding her breath with her hands crossed over her belly. Dr. Stecopolous probes under the paper gown while I perch on a stool by his desk. A bluish plastic model of a uterus rests next to the computer monitor and looks drained and baleful, as if it doesn't belong in the light. A little door is open in the front, like a dollhouse entrance. What's inside? A pink secret. I could crawl in and rest.

"Well, you were right," the doctor says. "This is definitely lichen sclerosis." He pokes his head up from under the gown. "Do you want to take a look?"

"Ah, no thank you," I say.

"He wasn't talking to you," my mother says. He positions a mirror for her to see. I don't want to look, not even by accident. My phone says I have a message, from Scott. He got the papers too. The end is here, and I'm sure he wants to talk. I fiddle with the uterus model. The tiny door in front will not close properly, and I want it closed, in place.

"Are you sexually active?" Dr. Stecopolous asks.

"No," I say. "She is not."

My mother remains quiet, staring up at the ceiling.

"Edith?" the doctor asks.

"Mom?" I ask.

She closes her eyes and sighs. "Yes," she says.

"What? With who?" I ask. The tiny door snaps off in my hand.

"I don't need to know that information," Dr. Stecopolous says. "But you will need to adjust your sexual activity." He delivers this line as if it were conceivable that my mother had activity to adjust. My mother is seventy-one. She is in menopause. There is no menoplay. Then he tells her she'll need to apply a steroid cream to her labia—I see the zincky, frosted lips of skiers, or the flaps of an undersea coral fan—and he writes her a prescription.

"Will my labia become stronger?" my mother asks, dressing.

"Gross," I say, and hand Dr. Stecopolous the door to the uterus. It looks like the piece that covers a battery compartment on a remote— the part that inevitably breaks. "I think I messed up your model."

Dr. Stecopolous has no idea what I'm talking about.

"Your uterus," I say. "I broke it."

"Oh, that's all right," he says. "My uterus broke a long time ago."

My mother pats his hand. "You're not missing anything," she says.

In the car, my mother hunts in her purse for Coffee Nips, as though she were the person I remember her being. "I need your support right now," she says. "Not your judgingness."

"Fine," I say. "But I'm allowed to say, 'Ew.' "

She closes her eyes, leans back against the headrest, and sucks on her candy with immeasurable delight. She's wearing the clip-on sunglasses I bought for her and a white sport fleece, collar up. I notice now that she got dressed up for the doctor visit—her gold, drapey pants and sapphire blouse from Shine Daughters!, a fashion catalog she loves, even though it's for African American women—on the off

417

chance that Dr. Stecopolous would run away with her. The poignancy of my mother's life is that she still thinks people are looking at her. On her bureau she keeps a framed photo of herself in the Atlantic City parade: a red-haired mermaid on a papier-mâché splash, gazing upon the crowd with a royal look. When I was a girl, after she divorced my father and went feminist and vegetarian—oh, my God, the lentils, the antinuke walkabouts, the woven totes of my youth—I used to stare at the photo and wish for it to come alive, for her to see me and invite me up onto the parade float. I ached to be her so badly I made her bookmarks with declarations of love. From our porch I would watch her leave to go jogging, braless and single and alive, and wait patiently with her pack of cigarettes to reward her upon her return.

Now she uses a cane, tucked next to her in the passenger seat; she's used it irregularly since her foot surgery, and I know it humiliates her. Men seem almost regal with canes, but women are expected to keep their balance forever. Dimesized freckles blot her skin, the star chart of her body gaining constellations yearly. A youth spent at the shore is catching up with my mother: the skin of her face looks like wax paper that has been crumpled, then flattened. Studying her, I want to run my fingers over my own wrinkles to stretch and smooth them.

A smile collects on her face. This doctor visit has given her a sense of drama, an urgency that cuts a path through the hours. Otherwise she could spend a day moving bills around.

"What are you looking at?" she asks.

"I'm trying to see you how your lover sees you," I say.

"Oh, please." She scratches at the corner of her mouth. "I'm starving, and I need my prescription."

"I have to get home," I say. "I have more people coming."

"Good," she says. "There's a Quick Check near you."

As we drive, I'm bothered, I realize, by the thought that someone finds my mother attractive. I feel excluded. When my mother married my father, she was a good Catholic girl, a virgin. "Mistake number one," she told me once. "I hadn't even been down there yet." She divorced my father thirty years ago, and somewhere in her apartment is a photo cube with pictures of all her boyfriends since: Val, the therapist; Devon, my elementary-school teacher; and the ape with sideburns who worked in the anthropology department at the college.

"It's Al, isn't it?" I say. Al, the retired ship's captain, who wears blue khakis and a little anchor pin on his cardigan. Al, who plies her with highballs and Manhattans at dusk. He has furry Popeye forearms and a dimly lit Pacific back story. I picture him on top of my mother, gritting his teeth and thrusting upward, like a ship cresting a wave.

"Wasn't it funny how you broke the uterus?" my mother says.

"Just tell me if it's Al," I say.

She adjusts an air vent. "You should know that he is very gentle," she says. "And appreciative."

I shiver. My mother can't bend over and instead has to spread her legs and squat. Her skin itches constantly, a side effect of her Parkinson's medication. She keeps a back scratcher in her car and another, the telescoping kind, in her purse for emergencies. She can eat a half gallon of ice cream for dinner. People like her should not be having sex; sex is the reward for not eating a half gallon of ice cream.

"What's your problem?" she says.

"I'm just surprised," I say, "and worried about you."

She gazes out the window as if she hasn't heard me. "It's not too late for you," she says. "You've been separated for six months. It's time to meet new people."

"I'm not ready."

"What about that one man I showed you?" she says. "The guy from the Internet?" She has taken to trolling the Craigslist personals for me, trying to matchmake. She'll call and read me the postings: "He says he'll be at the Harborside having a drink for the next hour. I'll go by and check him out for you." *No!* Or: "This one says he likes Bruce Springsteen." *We live in New Jersey; that's redundant!* She is unable to understand that Craigslist is where people sell their junk, including their personalities. No genuine, non-pot-smoking, nongambling, non-fucking-a-teacher-at-your-school man will let the universe know he's having a drink at the Harborside. It's an SOS from the bottom of the dating pool.

"There is no 'guy from the Internet,' and there will never be," I say, my pronouncement punctuated by the speed bump at the entrance to my parking lot. Outside my garage, a man leans against the trunk of a Mercedes convertible. His legs are crossed, and while he talks on his cellphone, he digs at his molars with a pinkie. He's dressed in the Manhattan palette: charcoal pants, a black short-sleeve dress shirt, and ribbony sandals that make his feet look bloodless. His skin is woefully untan. No wedding ring. I park, and he finishes his call. "What about him?" my mother whispers. I bound out of the car.

"You're fifteen minutes late," the man says. "I thought you were going to be a no-show."

419

"I'm sorry. My mother had a doctor appointment."

"That's me!" My mother waves from the passenger seat.

He peers in at her as if she were a zoo animal. "I'm just here for the baby shit," he says.

I throw open the garage door and point. The "baby shit" is in the back, where I could throw a blanket over it and pretend it was a mountain in the distance. I have a bassinet, a baby chair, a stroller, and a play "environment." When Scott and I were trying for kids, I made the mistake of accepting all of this from friends who had had their children, who were done having them. But I never got pregnant. Scott refused to get a fertility test because it was "annoying," then "expensive," then finally "against his religion"—the religion of morning bong loads, apparently. My fallopian tubes weren't cooperating either; maybe they knew better. When I moved out, I wasn't quite ready to see it all go, not because I hadn't given up on kids—I have, I'm fine, don't pity me—but because I felt like playthings were for *me*. My first night in the apartment, my mattress pinched at the back of the moving van, I laid out the play environment and fell asleep in it. I slept historically.

He pulls back the blanket as if uncovering a body in a morgue. "How much for everything?" He is driving a fifty-thousand-dollar car and buying third-hand baby furniture. I don't press.

"I'll take seventy-five," I say.

"Done," he says. On his way out with the stroller, he picks up the biggest shell in the basket. It's a fan the size of a dinner plate and bleached white. "You giving these away?" he says.

I found that shell one night when Scott and I were fooling around under a pier. I had taken a black-and-white photography class—I wanted a hobby; it seemed important and complicating—and we'd gone there to fill out my portfolio. Scott was high and determined to go down on me, but first I made him pose nude. Afterward, in a post-coital glow, I plucked the shell from the sand, feeling like an amateur naturalist. The photographs, though, were bad, dark and indistinct.

This morning I was eager to give the shells away. But now I don't want this man to have them.

"Sorry," I say. "Keepsake."

He picks up a mottled brown-and-pink conch, flawless. The flare looks like the interior of a lip. "What about this one?" he asks, and I'm back in the tide, our first summer together, bonfire on the beach.

"Look what I found," I say, and Scott pulls me to him. "Look what I found," he whispers and squeezes my hips.

I don't want these memories.

"Look, you can find these shells on the beach," I say to the man with the convertible.

"I don't have time for the beach," he says.

I won't relent, and he gives up in a way that makes it seem like my issue. I help him with the stroller, happy to see it fit sideways, recklessly, in his passenger seat, ready to launch at the first bump.

"It seems like you're shedding," he says.

"Shedding?" I say, irritated. He wants to teach me a word.

"You should call me," he says. "I'm a therapist. I see things." A business card flags out in his hand. I take it and give him directions back to the turnpike. My mother remains in the passenger seat, a heap of Coffee Nip wrappers in her lap.

"He seemed like a hot prospect," she says.

"He just bought baby stuff off Craigslist," I say. "Not a prospect."

"Well, you sold it there," she says.

My phone has four messages: two cancellations and two from Scott.

My mother and I buy burritos at the Quick Check and pick up her prescription at Walgreens, but the fact of the two items—the vaginal steroid and our food—in the same bag erases my appetite. On her balcony, with its sweeping view of the parking lot, I watch her chew her carefully managed bites. My mother has one brave molar left. A heavy breeze brushes the plants and lifts our napkins.

"You need to call Al," I say, fetching the phone. "He could be a carrier."

"It's not contagious. Dr. Stecopolous said."

"Dr. Stecopolous is not God," I say. "And he has ear hair."

She sets down the half-eaten burrito and carefully folds it up in the tinfoil. "You love me when I'm vulnerable," she says. "It makes you feel whole."

"I'm being cautious," I say. "I'm being you." How true and how awful that is. There must be a place in between parent and child, a way to take care of each other without resentment and hating yourself.

"Well, stop," she says and stands unsteadily. "Don't be me. Nobody should be me." She walks inside without her cane, lurching from one piece of furniture to another, phone in hand. One of the sad aspects of age, I think, is that you lose control over the quality of your entrances and exits. She sits on the couch, in the dark, and I hear her dial and leave a message. A small happiness—the pride of her following my instructions—rises in me.

"What happened?" I call to her.

"Leave me alone."

"What? He's not there?"

"He does his power walking on Saturdays," she says. "Why don't you go upstairs to the bar." She wants to shower and apply her salve in private. I'm happy to leave and take the good magazines with me.

When the elevator door opens into the Penthouse Lounge, I feel as if I'm stepping onto the pleasure deck of a 1970s cruise ship, all aquamarine-and-pink extravagance, smelling vaguely of pizza dough and shrimp cocktail, the aroma of recent fun. I pull a chair over to the floor-to-ceiling window. At this hour, the building's shadow stretches way out into the Atlantic. Scott and I came up here just once, right after my mother moved in, and he pointed out the whole sweep, from the Palisades to the knobby tip of Long Island. Right below the window, Sandy Hook arcs out toward Manhattan. The people on it are just dots of color; maybe one is collecting shells, trying to hold the afternoon still. I could call Scott.

I should call Scott.

Living at the beach was his idea. I'd thought of other places for us—Philadelphia, Hoboken, the city—but he wanted to sit in the sun and think and "see what surfaced." Here I am, at the top floor, doing it without him. What we take from each other, without knowing. I remember Sundays he'd prop his fishing pole up in the sand, park himself in a lawn chair, and stare out at the water, watching night come. Once, near the end, I showed him a perfect nautilus I'd found. He palmed it. "This used to be something's house," he said with an emphasis that told me he was high, long after he'd promised to stop. "A house, until something died." And I saw the curl of emptiness inside the shell, and it was all I could see. All that armor protecting what? A darkness, really; an ending, more hollow than special.

The elevator dings, and old men in baseball caps and windbreakers spill out. They discover me alone at the window and give me a wide berth. I'm probably some fantasy they've all had: the teary girl in the penthouse bar. They begin stretching on the floor, their legs up on tables, flexing. Not one has broken a sweat. It's impossible to tell if they're about to leave or are finishing up. I recognize Al in a yellow tracksuit and white sneakers without a scuff. His headphone-radio, a novelty of twenty years ago, loops around his neck. His eyebrows need pruning. He smiles, and all I can see is complicated dentistry.

"You need to talk to my mother," I say to him.

He looks concerned, almost as if he cared. "What's the matter?"

"She'll tell you about it."

"Is she hurt?"

"She's . . . coping," I say, righteous and inviolable. I am her daughter. I have her interests at heart.

"I'll do that," he says with chronic gentlemanliness. I smell a peppery gust of after-shave, cologne, and soap. When he asks if I'm all right, I huff at him. He backs away, giving me my space, except now I don't want it.

"Look, I just want you to take responsibility for your actions," I call out. He's bent over now, fingers about three feet from touching his toes. Al cranes himself out of position, his hands on his lower back, and comes back.

"Do you love her?" I ask.

"Your mother and I are good friends."

"Friends with benefits?"

"I don't know what that means."

The words boil out. "What is it with you people?" I yell. "Do you all just go ahead and have orgies? Is this some sort of fuck castle?" The men step toward the elevator. I know I sound insane, but I feel like I'm right. If I'm not having sex, they're not allowed to either. "You've ruined her!"

Al pats my shoulder, as though he had the right to touch me. "Grow up," he says.

I take the stairs, shame firing my face. I can't believe I didn't slap him. I can't believe he touched me, soiled me. I might have lichen now too! Revenge flurries through my head: I'll report him. I'll tell the doorman of the building. I'll take it to the Internet. He'll see.

In her apartment, my mother lies on the couch in her bathrobe, napping. I kneel next to her, wanting to protect her from what she'll soon know. No one wants my judgingness, not even me. But where can I put it?

Two cucumber slices cover her eyes. She looks like a surprised cartoon character. And in her face—in the small cool fact of the cucumber—I see that my mother has not given up. She is not done, not over, and I must make allowances.

"Shhh," she says. "The cream is doing its magic. It's tingly."

"I need to leave," I say. "I need to be alone."

She takes my hand and holds it to her. "Go be you."

I call Scott from the beach, the empty shell basket at my feet.

"I'm falling apart here," he says.

"Remember those shells," I say, "the ones I put in that cabinet?"

"No, not really," he says. "Wait. Maybe. Yeah."

"They're all in the ocean now." A wave comes, splashes up to my knee. I feel the last shell brush against my leg as it goes. "The tide just came and took them," I tell him. "Everything, all at once."

Nominated by The Sun, Anna Solomon

1814: THE LAST FROST FAIR

by RITA DOVE

from NORTH AMERICAN REVIEW

was something to be happy about,
wasn't it? Four days in a short cold month

when even one's breath, upon exit,
instantly condensed into a shower of snow.

The sky was black. The river shone,
a marble corridor dulled by its awestruck traffic—

charred coal, crushed underfoot and smeared
the length of this vast, dim spine of ice

dubbed City Street by the amused vendors
—as if those walking there, terrified to drop

too bold a footfall, slid booth to booth
instead. Banked fires hurled sooty issue

against the frigid air so that smoke hung
nearly gelatinous, in wreaths of drab warmth

from Blackfriar's Bridge to Three Cranes Stairs;
it was difficult to breathe. Games abounded—

skittles for the squeamish, bowling for the bold,
donkey rides for the ladies and dancing for all.

A small sheep was roasted whole on the ice
and plates and knives laid out, with penny loaves;

and an elephant led across the river by rope
just below Blackfriars—wasn't that

a sign? The Fair began on a Tuesday,
followed by Candlemas, which meant

even if the coaches still weren't running
the northern roads, and yet another man

was found frozen near Dove's Inn, having
drunk freely there, then fallen into a snowbank—

all the same, winter's grip was loosening. Soon
there'd be no more sleighs-for-hire come evening,

no more Punch and no Judy duking it out
for the children crowding the makeshift stalls;

and as for the three men propped up
on hay bales when the gin tent broke loose

and skimmed downriver—
before ice water sluiced over their boots

and the sweat broke out, wasn't it
the best damn drunk ever?

From Temple to Westminster, a curve of soft fire
alive on the ice. Lanterns bobbing. No time

for din and rabble when the King was calling,
when one was near a Professor of Music, when . . .

Christ, the night's bitter.
Move on, before you start to like

freezing to death.

Nominated by North American Review, R.T. Smith

TIME AND
DISTANCE OVERCOME

by EULA BISS

from THE IOWA REVIEW

"**O**F WHAT USE IS SUCH AN INVENTION?" *The New York World* asked shortly after Alexander Graham Bell first demonstrated his telephone in 1876. The world was not waiting for the telephone.

Bell's financial backers asked him not to work on his new invention anymore because it seemed too dubious an investment. The idea on which the telephone depended—the idea that every home in the country could be connected with a vast network of wires suspended from poles set an average of one hundred feet apart—seemed far more unlikely than the idea that the human voice could be transmitted through a wire.

Even now it is an impossible idea, that we are all connected, all of us.

"At the present time we have a perfect network of gas pipes and water pipes throughout our large cities," Bell wrote to his business partners, in defense of his idea. "We have main pipes laid under the streets communicating by side pipes with the various dwellings. . . . In a similar manner it is conceivable that cables of telephone wires could be laid under ground, or suspended overhead, communicating by branch wires with private dwellings, counting houses, shops, manufactories, etc., uniting them through the main cable. . . ."

* * *

Imagine the mind that could imagine this. That could see us all connected through one branching cable. The mind of a man who wanted to invent, more than the telephone, a machine that would allow the deaf to hear.

For a short time, the telephone was little more than a novelty. For twenty-five cents you could see it demonstrated by Bell himself, in a church, along with some singing and recitations by local talent. From a mile away, Bell would receive a call from "the invisible Mr. Watson." Then the telephone became a plaything of the rich. A Boston banker paid for a private line between his office and his home so that he could let his family know exactly when he would be home for dinner.

Mark Twain was among the first to own a telephone, but he wasn't completely taken with it. "The human voice carries entirely too far as it is," he remarked.

By 1889, *The New York Times* was reporting a "War on Telephone Poles." Wherever telephone companies were erecting poles, homeowners and business owners were sawing them down, or defending their sidewalks with rifles.

In Red Bank, New Jersey property owners threatened to tar and feather the workers putting up telephone poles. One judge granted a group of homeowners an injunction to prevent the telephone company from erecting any new poles. Another judge found that a man who had cut down a pole because it was "obnoxious" was not guilty of malicious mischief.

Telephone poles, newspaper editorials complained, were an urban blight. The poles carried a wire for each telephone—sometimes hundreds of wires. And in some places there were also telegraph wires, power lines, and trolley cables. The sky was filled with wires.

The War on Telephone Poles was fueled, in part, by that terribly American concern for private property and a reluctance to surrender it to a shared utility. And then there was a fierce sense of aesthetics, an obsession with purity, a dislike for the way the poles and wires marred a landscape that those other new inventions, skyscrapers and barbed wire, were just beginning to complicate. And then perhaps there was also a fear that distance, as it had always been known and measured, was collapsing.

The city council in Sioux Falls, South Dakota ordered policemen to cut down all the telephone poles in town. And the Mayor of Oshkosh, Wisconsin ordered the police chief and the fire department to chop down the telephone poles there. Only one pole was chopped down before the telephone men climbed all the poles along the line, preventing any more chopping. Soon, Bell Telephone Company began stationing a man at the top of each pole as soon as it had been set, until enough poles had been set to string a wire between them, at which point it became a misdemeanor to interfere with the poles. Even so, a constable cut down two poles holding forty or fifty wires. And a homeowner sawed down a recently wired pole then fled from police. The owner of a cannery ordered his workers to throw dirt back into the hole the telephone company was digging in front of his building. His men threw the dirt back in as fast as the telephone workers could dig it out. Then he sent out a team with a load of stones to dump into the hole. Eventually, the pole was erected on the other side of the street.

Despite the War on Telephone Poles, it would take only four years after Bell's first public demonstration of the telephone for every town of over 10,000 people to be wired, although many towns were wired only to themselves. And by the turn of the century, there were more telephones than bathtubs in America.

"Time and dist. overcome," read an early advertisement for the telephone. Rutherford B. Hayes pronounced the installation of a telephone in the White House "one of the greatest events since creation." The telephone, Thomas Edison declared, "annihilated time and space, and brought the human family in closer touch."

❈ ❈ ❈

In 1898, in Lake Comorant, Mississippi, a black man was hanged from a telephone pole. And in Weir City, Kansas. And in Brook Haven, Mississippi. And in Tulsa, where the hanged man was riddled with bullets. In Pittsburg, Kansas, a black man's throat was slit and his dead body was strung up on a telephone pole. Two black men were hanged from a telephone pole in Lewisburg, West Virginia. And two in Hempstead,

430

Texas, where one man was dragged out of the courtroom by a mob and another was dragged out of jail.

A black man was hanged from a telephone pole in Belleville, Illinois, where a fire was set at the base of the pole and the man was cut down half-alive, covered in coal oil, and burned. While his body was burning, the mob beat it with clubs and nearly cut it to pieces.

Lynching, the first scholar of the subject determined, is an American invention. Lynching from bridges, from arches, from trees standing alone in fields, from trees in front of the county courthouse, from trees used as public billboards, from trees barely able to support the weight of a man, from telephone poles, from street lamps, and from poles erected for that purpose. From the middle of the nineteenth century to the middle of the twentieth century black men were lynched for crimes real and imagined, for "disputing with a white man," for "unpopularity," for "asking a white woman in marriage," for "peeping in a window."

The children's game of "telephone" depends on the fact that a message passed quietly from one ear to another to another will get distorted at some point along the line.

In Pine Bluff, Arkansas a black man charged with kicking a white girl was hanged from a telephone pole. In Long View, Texas a black man accused of attacking a white woman was hanged from a telephone pole. In Greenville, Mississippi a black man accused of attacking a white telephone operator was hanged from a telephone pole. "The negro only asked time to pray." In Purcell, Oklahoma a black man accused of attacking a white woman was tied to a telephone pole and burned. "Men and women in automobiles stood up to watch him die."

The poles, of course, were not to blame. It was only coincidence that they became convenient as gallows, because they were tall and straight, with a crossbar, and because they stood in public places. And it was only coincidence that the telephone pole so closely resembled a crucifix.

Early telephone calls were full of noise. "Such a jangle of meaningless noises had never been heard by human ears," Herbert Casson wrote

431

in his 1910 *History of the Telephone*. "There were the rustling of leaves, the croaking of frogs, the hissing of steam, the flapping of birds' wings. . . . There were spluttering and bubbling, jerking and rasping, whistling and screaming."

In Shreveport, a black man charged with attacking a white girl was hanged from a telephone pole. "A knife was left sticking in the body." In Cumming, Georgia a black man accused of assaulting a white girl was shot repeatedly then hanged from a telephone pole. In Waco, Texas a black man convicted of killing a white woman was taken from the courtroom by a mob and burned, then his charred body was hung from a telephone pole.

A postcard was made from the photo of a burned man hanging from a telephone pole in Texas, his legs broken off below the knee and his arms curled up and blackened. Postcards of lynchings were sent out as greetings and warnings until 1908, when the Postmaster General declared them unmailable. "This is the barbecue we had last night," reads one.

"If we are to die," W.E.B. Du Bois wrote in 1911, "in God's name let us not perish like bales of hay." And "if we must die," Claude McKay wrote ten years later, "let it not be like hogs. . . ."

In Danville, Illinois a black man was hanged from a telephone pole, cut down, burned, shot, and stoned with bricks. "At first the negro was defiant," *The New York Times* reported, "but just before he was hanged he begged hard for his life."

In the photographs, the bodies of the men lynched from telephone poles are silhouetted against the sky. Sometimes two men to a pole, hanging above the buildings of a town. Sometimes three. They hung like flags in still air.

In Cumberland, Maryland a mob used a telephone pole as a battering ram to break into the jail where a black man charged with the murder of a policeman was being held. They kicked him to death then fired twenty shots into his head. They wanted to burn his body, but a minister asked them not to.

The lynchings happened everywhere, all over the United States. From shortly before the invention of the telephone to long after the first trans-Atlantic call. More in the South, and more in rural areas. In the cities and in the North there were race riots.

Riots in Cincinnati, New Orleans, Memphis, New York, Atlanta, Philadelphia, Houston. . . .

During the race riots that destroyed the black section of Springfield, Ohio a black man was shot and hanged from a telephone pole.

During the race riots that set fire to East St. Louis and forced five hundred black people to flee their homes, a black man was hanged from a telephone pole. The rope broke and his body fell into the gutter. "Negros are lying in the gutters every few feet in some places," read the newspaper account.

In 1921, the year before Bell died, four companies of the National Guard were called out to end a race war in Tulsa that began when a white woman accused a black man of rape. Bell had lived to complete the first call from New York to San Francisco, which required 14,000 miles of copper wire and 130,000 telephone poles.

❋ ❋ ❋

My grandfather was a lineman. He broke his back when a telephone pole fell. "Smashed him onto the road," my father says.

When I was young, I believed that the arc and swoop of telephone wires along the roadways were beautiful. I believed that the telephone poles, with their glass transformers catching the evening sun, were glorious. I believed my father when he said, "My dad could raise a pole by himself." And I believed that the telephone itself was a miracle.

Now, I tell my sister, these poles, these wires do not look the same to me. Nothing is innocent, my sister reminds me. But nothing, I would like to think, remains unrepentant.

One summer, heavy rains fell in Nebraska and some green telephone poles grew small leafy branches.

Nominated by The Iowa Review

GRADUATES OF WESTERN MILITARY ACADEMY

by GEORGE BILGERE

from FIELD

One day, as this friend of my father, Paul,
    was flying over Asia,
he vaporized a major Japanese city.

True story. They'd been chums
    at a military academy in Illinois,
    back in the thirties.

My father was the star: best in Latin,
    best in riflery and history,
best in something called "recitation,"

    and best at looking serious.
In the old yearbooks he has exactly the look
    you were supposed to have back then:
about fifty-two percent duty, forty-eight percent integrity.
    Zero percent irony.

But somehow, all my father got to do later on
    was run his own car dealership. A big one,
but still. While Paul
    got to blow up Japan. My father

ushered in the latest models.
      Paul ushered in the nuclear age.
It seems unfair, but there you are.

Paul had been an indifferent Latin scholar. Weak
      in history and recitation. For these and other reasons
my father took a refreshing swim
      across a large, inviting lake of gin,
complete with strange boats and exotic shore birds,
which resulted in his interment
      under some shady acres I occasionally visit.

While Paul went on for decades,
      always giving the same old speech. Yes,
he'd done the right thing. No doubt about it.

      He improved his skills at recitation
and developed a taste for banquet food.
      To this day he struggles with his weight.

Nominated by Field, Robert Wrigley, Mark Halliday

BIJOU

by MARK DOTY

from CONJUNCTIONS

THE MOVIE I'M WATCHING—I'm hesitant to call it porn, since its intentions are less obvious than that—was made in 1972, and couldn't have been produced in any other era. A construction worker is walking home from work in Manhattan when he sees a woman in a short fake fur coat knocked over by a car when she's crossing an intersection. The driver leaps out to help her up, but the construction worker—played by an actor named Bill—picks up her purse and tucks it in his jacket. He takes the subway to a banged-up-looking block, maybe in Hell's Kitchen, climbs up to his tiny, soiled apartment, nothing on the walls but a few pinups, women torn from magazines. On his bed, he opens the purse, looks at its spare contents, keys and a few dollars. He opens a lipstick and touches it to his tongue, tastes it, does it again, something about his extended tongue touching the extended lipstick . . . Then he's lying back, stroking himself through his jeans, getting out of his clothes; he's an archetypal seventies porn guy, lean, with thick red hair and a thick red mustache, a little trail of hair on his wiry belly. Then he's in the shower, continuing his solo scene, and he begins to flash on images of women, quick jump cuts, but just as he's about to come he sees the woman in fur falling when the bumper of the car strikes her. That's the end of that; the erotic moment is over, for him and for the viewer, once that image returns.

Chastened, toweling off, he's back in the bedroom, looking again at what spilled from her purse. There's an invitation, something telling her about—a party? an event? someplace called Bijou at 7 p.m.

Then he's walking in Soho—the old Soho, long before the art glamour and even longer before the Euro-tourist-meets-North-Jersey shopping district: garbage in the streets, cardboard boxes in front of shuttered cast-iron facades without windows. He finds the address, goes in and up, and the movie shifts from the gritty Warholian vocabulary it's trafficked in thus far to another cinematic tongue. An indifferent woman in a lot of eye makeup sits in a glass booth; Bill proffers the invite; she gestures toward a door and and utters the movie's only line of dialogue: *Right through there.*

"There" turns out to be a hallucinatory space, its dominant hue a solarized, acidy green. Within that color, Bill moves forward. He confronts the image of his own body in one mirror and then in many, reaches out to touch his own form with pleasure. Time dilates, each gesture extended, no rush to get anywhere, only a little sense of forwardness. In a while there's another body—man or woman?—prone, facedown, and Bill's on top of him or her, they're fucking in a sea of all that green. In a while we can see the person beneath Bill is definitely a man. Then, much later, Bill's alone, lying prone on the floor as if now he's let go, all his boundaries relinquished, and one man comes to him and begins to blow him. Bill lies there and accepts it. In a while another man enters the scene, and begins to touch and cradle Bill's head, and then—no hurry here, no hurry in all the world—there's another. Now the pattern is clear, one man after another enters the liquid field of green that sometimes frames and sometimes obscures—and they are all reverently, calmly touching Bill. They have no end save to give him pleasure, to make Bill's body entirely, attentively, completely loved.

This is the spiritualized eroticism of 1972 made flesh, more sensuous and diffuse than pointedly hot, a brotherhood of eros, a Whitmanian democracy. It makes the viewer feel suspended in a sort of erotic haze, but whatever arousal I feel in imagining Bill's complete submission to pleasure suddenly comes to a halt, as surely as if I'd seen that woman struck down in the crosswalk again, because I realize that all the men in the scene I'm watching are dead. Every one of them, and the vision they embodied, the idea they incarnated gone up in the smoke and ashes of the crematoriums, scattered now in the dunes of Provincetown and Fire Island.

Or that's one version of what I felt, watching *Bijou*, Wakefield Poole's weird period piece of art porn. Of course it is not news that the players are all gone now. How beautiful they look, the guys in the movie, or the men in the documentary *Gay Sex in the 70s*, posing on

437

the decks in the Pines or on the porches of houses in San Francisco, eager for brotherhood and for knowledge of one another. That is a phrase I would like to revive: to *have knowledge* of someone. It suggests that sex is, or can be, a process of inquiry, an idea that Poole would certainly have embraced.

Watching the movie is just one of countless experiences in which the fact of the AIDS epidemic is accommodated somehow. *Accommodated* doesn't mean understood, assimilated, digested, interpreted, or integrated. Accommodated: We just make room for it because it won't go away.

I don't know what else I expect. What could lend meaning to the AIDS crisis in America? Hundreds of thousands perished because there was no medical model for understanding what was wrong with them, and no money or concerted effort offered soon enough to change the course of things in time to save their lives. They died of a virus, and they died of homophobia. But this understanding is an entirely social one, and it doesn't do much to help the soul make meaning of it all. I have no answer to this problem save to suggest that a kind of doubling of perspective—an embracing of the layered nature of the world—is one thing one could carry, or be forced to carry, from such a shattering encounter. AIDS makes the experience of the body, a locus of pleasure and satisfaction, almost simultaneously the site of destruction and limit. What if, from here on out, for those burned in that fire, the knowledge of another body is always a way of acknowledging mortal beauty, and any moment of mutual vivacity understood as existing against an absence to come? Presence made more poignant, and more desirable, even sexier by that void, intensified by it.

Maybe the viewer's involuntary gasp, when Bill thinks of the woman hit by the car as he's jerking off, is two-fold—first, the shock of the inappropriateness of it, and then the secondary, deeper shock—that the particular fact of her body is differently understood, differently longed for, when it is seen where it really is, in the world of danger—and that such a perception shakes the desirer out of simple lust and into some larger, more profound realm of eros.

I used to like to go to a sex club in the East Village, a place now closed through some combination of pressures from the Health Department, the police, the IRS, and the real estate developers who are remaking

438

Manhattan as a squeaky-clean retail zone. A combination Whole Foods/condo development has opened right down the block.

Beyond a nearly invisible doorway (shades of the one Bill entered in Soho, long ago), there was a bouncer inside the door, a flirty man who loved jazz music, and then an attendant in the ticket booth ("Right through there . . .") and then a sort of living room where you could check your clothes with the two attendant angels, one black and startlingly shapely, one blond and ethereally thin. They were loving, kind, and funny boys; they looked at the goings-on before them with a sly combination of blessing and good humor, which is just what you'd want in an angel.

Then, beyond a black vinyl curtain shredded so that you could part it dramatically with a swipe of the hand, were two floors, with a kind of stripped industrial look to them—bare brick and cement, a certain rawness, and structures of wood and metal in which to wander or hide, all very plain the first year I went there, and later redone with branches and dried leaves everywhere, as if an autumn forest had sprouted in the ruins of a factory.

Sometimes it was a palace of pleasure, sometimes it was a hall of doom. Sometimes when you thought you wanted to be there, you'd discover you just couldn't get into the swing of it. Sometimes you weren't sure you'd wanted to go and it was marvelous. Often it felt as if whatever transpired had little to do with any individual state of mind, but rather with the tone of the collective life, whatever kind of spirit was or wasn't generated by the men in attendance that night, or by the city outside busily thinking through the poem of this particular evening. There were regulars who became acquaintances and comrades. There were visitors who became dear friends. There was a world of people I never saw again, once the doors closed.

Whoever made the decisions about what music to play preferred a kind of sludgy, druggy trance, often with classical or operatic flourishes about it. The tune I'll never forget was a remixed version of Dido's great aria from Purcell's *Dido and Aeneas*. It's the scene where the Queen of Carthage, having been abandoned by the man she's allowed to wreck her kingdom, watches his sails disappear out to sea and resolves to end her life. As she prepares to bury a knife in her breast, she sings, unforgettably: *Remember me, but—ah!—forget my fate.*

It seems, in my memory, that they would play this song every night

I attended, always late, as the evening's brighter promises dimmed. There was a bit of a backbeat thrown in that would come and go, in between the soprano's great controlled heaves of farewell and resignation, but the music always had the same effect. I'd take myself off to the sidelines, to one of the benches poised on the edges of the room for this purpose, lean back into the swelling melancholy of the score, and watch the men moving to it as though they'd been choreographed, in some dance of longing held up, for a moment, to the light of examination, the perennial hungry quest for whatever deliverance or release it is that sex brings us. It was both sad and astonishingly beautiful and now it seems to me something like the fusing of those layers I mentioned above: the experience of desire and the awareness of death become contiguous—*remember me*—one not-quite-differentiated experience.

My partner Paul's mother has Alzheimer's, or senile dementia. The first sign of it he saw was one morning when, for about a forty-five-minute period, she didn't know who he was. Now she doesn't know who anyone is, or if she does it's for seconds at a time. I was sitting beside the condo pool with her—the Intercoastal Waterway behind us, so that we sat on delicate chairs on a small strand of concrete between two moving bodies of water—along with one of her other sons. *Who are you*, she said to him. *I'm Michael, your son*, he said. She laughed, the kind of humorless snort that means, *As if* . . . Then he said back to her, *Who are you?* And she answered, *I watch.*

That's what's left for her, the subjectivity that looks out at the world without clear attachments or defined relations. She is completely obsessed with who everyone is; she is always asking. I wonder if this has to do with her character, or if it's simple human need; do we need to know, before we can do or say anything else, who people are to us?

Not in *Bijou*; abstracted subjectivities meet one another in the sheer iridescent green space of sex. They morph together in patterns, they lose boundary; they go at it so long, in such fluid ways, that the viewer does too.

Paul's mother's state is not, plainly, ecstatic; she wants to know where she ends and others begin. The desire to merge is only erotic to the bound.

The other day my friend Luis asked me if I thought there was anything spiritual about sex. We happened to be walking in Soho at the time, on our way back from some stores in the Bowery, so we might have passed the very door through which Bill long ago entered into his acidulated paradise. That prompted me to tell my friend about the movie, and my description prompted Luis's question. Luis has a way of asking questions that seems to say, *You really think* that?

I am not ready to give up on Whitman's vision of erotic communion, or its more recent incarnation in Wakefield Poole's pornographic urban utopia. But the oddest thing about Poole's film, finally, is that woman knocked down by the car; why on earth was she necessary to the tale? I suspect it's because even in the imagined paradise of limitless eros, there must be room for death; otherwise the endlessness of it, the lack of limit or of boundary, finally drains things of their tension, removes all edges. Poole can almost do this—create a floating, diffuse, subject-and-object-less field of eros. But not quite; the same body that strains toward freedom and escape also has outer edges, also exists in time, and it's that doubling that makes the body the sexy and troubling thing it is. *O taste and see.* Isn't the flesh a way to drink of the fountain of otherhood, a way to taste the not-I, a way to blur the edges and thus feel the fact of them? Cue the aria here: *Remember me*, sings Dido, *but—ah—forget my fate!* That is, she counsels, you need to both remember where love leads and love anyway; you can both see the end of desire and be consumed by it all at once. The ecstatic body's a place to feel timelessness and to hear, ear held close to the chest of another, the wind that blows in there, hurrying us ahead and away, and to understand that this awareness does not put an end to longing but lends to it a shadow that is, in the late hour, beautiful.

Shadows, of course, lend objects gravity, attaching them to earth.

Luis is right, sex isn't spiritual. The spirit wants to go up and out; it rises above, transcends, flies on dove wings up to the rafters and spies below it the form-bound world. Who was that peculiar French saint who died briefly, returned to life, and then could not bear the smell of human flesh? She used to soar up to the rafters in church, just to get away from the stench of it. Sex is soulful; sex wants the soul-rich communion of other bodies. The sex of *Bijou* isn't really erotic because what it wants is to slip the body's harness and merge in the lightshow of play, the slippery forms of radiance. That's the aspect of the film that's more dated than its hairstyles, as if it were desirable for sex to take us up out of our bodies, rather than further in. That distance is a removal from knowledge, the guys who are pleasuring Bill aren't anyone in particular, and do not need to be individuated. But that's not soul's interest. Back in the sex club in the East Village, soul wants to know this body and this, to seek the embodied essence of one man after another, to touch and mouth the world's astonishing variety of forms. Spirit says, I watch. Soul says, Time enough to be out of the body later on, the veil of flesh won't be set aside, not tonight; better to feel the heat shining through the veil.

Nominated by Conjunctions, Joyce Carol Oates

SOAP AND AMBERGRIS

fiction by YOUSEF AL-MOHAIMEED

(translated by Anthony Calderbank)

from PEN AMERICA

I LIVE IN A SMALL, single-story house in Al-Atayef Quarter. My husband didn't leave me anything, apart from a mud house that shakes when the thunder crashes and the rain pours. I live off the kindness of other Muslims, either from charity or zakat. I wash the dead for Allah's sake, and take whatever kindness or generosity the family of the deceased offers in return.

One day, an hour before the afternoon prayer call, I heard a knock at the door. It was a bearded man, his beard full of gray hair. He spent quite a while asking Allah to preserve me and grant me a long life before asking me to go with him to wash the corpse of a deceased woman. He said, by way of reassurance, that there was another woman with him in the car so it would be lawful for me to go with him. Anyway I was comfortable with the man. There was a look of goodness and faith in the features of his face.

I quickly put on my abaya and picked up my equipment and followed him into the street. I got into the back seat of a pickup truck, a Datsun or a Hilux, I can't remember. I sat next to a young woman who didn't return my greeting. She was wrapped in black and made a gesture with her index finger as if she were saying "la ilaha illa allah" inaudibly. The car set off and I uttered a blessing for the dead woman and asked Allah to have mercy on her soul. I asked Allah to grant them patience and consolation but I never heard the voice of the woman next to me at all. She never even said "Amen." Not a single cry or sob, and her body didn't shake with weeping.

The driver, the old sheikh, was calm and composed. He drove carefully, never went too fast. When we had been going for a while I asked him, "Is the place far?" He didn't answer. When I asked him the third time he said, "Put your trust in Allah, woman! We're almost there."

I stole a glance at the woman's feet. She was wearing cheap black plastic shoes and her heel and the side of her leg that showed under the abaya almost glowed they were so white. I noticed a gold ring with a zircon on her middle finger and felt convinced that she really was a woman. I had begun to fear that she was in fact a man in an abaya, and that the two of them had hatched some plot against me and were spiriting me out of the city. The man who was driving didn't look like someone who would do such a thing, but then we're always hearing how criminals can mislead their victims by acquiring innocent, honest, and noble features.

Suddenly, after sitting with these doubts and misgivings a while, I realized we were heading down a steep hill to the west of the city, and there was nothing around us save the hills and the highway heading to Taif. I noticed a black barrel of water in the back of the pickup, lunging left and right, and I knew that things were indeed grave, and that my end might well have been near. But I decided to hide my fear and remain calm. I asked the woman next to me if the dead woman was her mother. She didn't answer. I said quickly, stammering with dread, "May Allah reward you handsomely," as if it were my own funeral, and I was asking Him to have mercy on me and my life as its end rapidly approached.

After a short while during which we heard nothing but the hum of the car as it devoured the tarmac I ventured to speak to her again. "My daughter, say you take refuge in Allah from Satan!" But she didn't. She didn't say a word. I reached out my hand to touch hers, and the coldness of her palm made me jump. The driver snarled, "Shut up, woman! Take refuge from Satan yourself, and don't take my mind off the road."

I was silent, but my heart was not. It trembled like a bird chased by marksmen from tree to tree. I thought maybe the woman was dead and had just been propped up in the back seat, and this man was the killer. But then why did he want her washed and buried? A murderer doesn't care if he stuffs his victim in a rubbish bag and throws it into a cesspit or a well or any other place.

The car turned onto a paved desert road. The sun was now to the left. The driver never hesitated or slowed down to check the road in front of him. He clearly knew it well, or was someone well versed in the secrets of the desert, the hills, wadis, and dunes. Yes for sure he knew the trees and found his way by the lay of the land and the acacia and the shafallah and the rimth and ghada trees. A man like that would never lose his way, not even at night. The daughters of Na'sh, the stars of Ursa would lead him, and the Pleiades, and Canopus and Bellatrix, and the morning star which all desert dwellers know.

He drove the car between two huge mountains and approached a sand dune. I remember how surprised I was that there could be a sand dune there on such rocky ground. Anyway he stopped the car and opened the back door for the woman who I'd imagined might be a corpse and would fall to the ground. But she got out slowly, calmly, obediently, and walked in front of him without closing the door. He walked behind her with deliberate steps as she headed with amazing posture and serenity towards the sand dune. Once they were on top of the dune he moved in front of her and she followed him down the other side. I saw their bodies gradually disappear until all I could see was the woman's head. Then that disappeared too without turning back once to look at me. It was as if she had made some resolute decision, or as if she were drugged and in a trance. She didn't say a word or interact with anything around her at all. My questions hadn't had any effect on her whatsoever.

After a few moments, as I sat alone in the car with the door open, I heard a gunshot shatter the silence of the mountains. Even now years later I hear the echo of gunshots in my little mud house and wake up terrified in the middle of the night. I don't know if there were three shots, one after the other, or if the echo bouncing round the mountains made it seem like the shots were repeated. My heart thumped wildly, as if it would fly out of my rib cage, and a shiver passed up my neck and made my hair stand on end. It was as if not a single drop of blood remained in my body.

After a few minutes, which seemed like an eternity, I spotted somebody coming into view from behind the hill. It was him, plodding heavily along as if he was dragging his outrageous crime behind him, as if he was dragging a million murdered people. He untied the barrel of water from the back of the pickup. "Get out!" he ordered. I couldn't refuse, or even speak. I got out and walked behind him as he rolled the barrel along in front of him. He reminded me to bring my bag with my washing tackle: soap and oils and musk and ambergris and other things. I was like the young woman had been a short while before, following behind him, stupefied and silent. I did not look back, just followed his huge feet as they sank into the sand and he lifted them out again with considerable strength and power.

As I walked down the other side of the dune I saw her, spread out on the sand, still wearing her abaya. I began my work, taking particular care to mop up the blood that had flowed from her chest. When he reached the bottom of the dune he must have turned round and seen her silent and submissive eyes, waiting to go to eternal death. Then he shot her, the most important thing in his life. And now he was digging in the dust with the spade he had carried over his shoulder. He wept incessantly and wailed like a woman and his beard soaked up the copious tears. When the grave was finished we wrapped the young woman in her abaya. As he was placing her in the hole, he slipped and fell in on top of her. He began to howl inconsolably. I was afraid he might do something to himself so I began to ask Allah to have mercy on her soul and I said some prayers and consoled him. After it got dark he took me home.

Nominated by Kenneth Gangemi

THE LOST GLOVE

by MARK HALLIDAY

from THE CINCINNATI REVIEW

There is this thing that we don't have yet.
What do we have? We know there's a woman
and we know there's a man. That's about it.

But are they together now? It depends on what you mean
by together. And what you mean by now.
There is a spicy peanut sauce.

Well okay that would imply an intensity, and like a zest
for life. But zest is not love. Right but anyway
where my confusion lies is, what exactly is going on

between these people in terms of this dune buggy.
That's what I'd love to see magnified. I mean
are they riding in it together? And are they kind of

out of control? I feel there's an unstated martini here.
The experience is like way out in front of the comprehension.
It's the kind of situation where he can only know what he thinks

after he's lost her. That's what the lost glove means.
What? Because he only focuses on the sadness of the glove
when he realizes the other glove is gone. Oh come on

it's just a glove! Okay but look at the last four letters of that.
The whole thing is one of those traumatic soufflé deals—
where this imaginary beautiful thing exists for somebody

but when it falls it's just all this embarrassing cheese.
That's why she keeps not saying what she starts to say
about the sailboat, or the song about a sailboat.

Think about it: two gloves—a *couple* of gloves—
it's like how we are doomed to exist in these two genders.
Sure, you know, the peanut sauce is spicy, but at what price?

Exactly. When you have a woman as such and a man as such
it just lends itself to this hugeness. Like a radiant cloud.
Fine; but I think the windup to the cocoon exploding

needs a little more windup. Because there's deep hugeness
and then there's soufflé hugeness. Unless you show us the Saturday
we don't know why he cries on Sunday when she says

"Oh, my monkey." What is up with that monkey thing?
Well, he was like swinging through the trees of her fantasy.
Right, and you know how sometimes you love someone

but you want them to dangle. She's into that dangle aspect.
All right. So, when you get to the lips, the whole lips focus,
there's that old how-bad-do-you-want-it type of vibe.

But isn't that *before* the sailboat part? And before the glove is
    missing?
I feel we just lose him till we get back to the lost glove.
But what about the birds? Which birds; the ones in her mouth?

But obviously those are in his mind, he *dreams* the birds in her
    mouth!
No wonder they don't work! Anyway I just feel this radiant cloud.
It's sexy, in a sad way, but it's still a cloud. You can't really

sleep with a cloud. Okay what it comes down to is, we feel
something missing. There is a missingness. There is definitely

this "she" and there is this "he" and his version of her and hers of
   him;

and there is this dune buggy. Yes. They don't know where they are,
so why should we? All they know is the lemons are ripe.
It's one of those. It's like, how much can we care about those lemons?

We don't not care; but something is beneath.

Nominated by The Cincinnati Review, Daniel Hoffman, Sydney Lea, David Rivard, Lloyd
Schwartz, Charles Harper Webb, Stephen Corey

THE SUTRA OF MAGGOTS AND BLOWFLIES

by SALLIE TISDALE

from CONJUNCTIONS

THE GREAT ENTOMOLOGIST Jean-Henri Fabre covered his desk with the carcasses of birds and snakes, opened the window, and waited.

He didn't have to wait long.

From the time I was quite young, I loved cold-blooded creatures. I had to be taught not to pick things up in the woods: To me it was all good, all worth examination, from beetles to mushrooms to toads. I was stealthy, and in the thistle-ridden fields near my house, I caught many blue-belly lizards to keep as pets. My father built a cage for them, a wonderful wood-and-screen contraption that smelled of pine and grass and reptile. I kept garter snakes and frogs and chameleons too. Once, someone gave me a baby alligator. I had several praying mantises, and built them elaborate branch houses in the cage, and fed them crickets. I don't know where this came from, my appetite for the alien; it feels like an old question, long and mysterious.

My study of living things, part inquiry and part the urge to possess, became inevitably a study of predation and decay. I had to feed my pets, and most preferred live food. The mantises always died, their seasons short. The chameleons died, too delicate for my care. The alligator died. I tried to embalm it, with limited success—just good enough for an excellent presentation at show-and-tell. When one of my turtles died, my brother and I buried it in my mother's rose bed to see if we could get an empty turtle shell, which would be quite a good thing to have. When we dug it up a few weeks later, there was almost nothing left—an outcome I had not anticipated, and one that left me with a strange, disturbed feeling. The earth was more fierce than I had guessed.

In time I became specifically interested in human bodies, how they worked and how they got sick and what they looked like when they died. This did not pacify my mother, who worried aloud about my ghoulish preoccupations. I did enjoy the distress I could cause by something as simple as bringing an embalmed baby alligator to school in a jar. But I was also—and for a long time I could not have explained why it was of a piece with my impassioned studies—exquisitely sensitive to the world's harsh rules. I regretted each cricket. An animal dead by the side of the road could bring me to tears, and I cried for each dead lizard, each mantis. A triad, each leg bearing weight: sensitivity, love, and logic. The weight on each leg shifts over time: now, a penetrating awareness of the cruelty seemingly built into the world's bones. Now, a colder logic, an awareness of the forces that balance systems at the cost of individuals. At times in brief pure blinks of my mind's eye, a love painful in its intensity, an unalloyed love. I love the tender, pale blossoms opening now on the cherry tree in my yard, the sudden pound of lush raindrops from the empty sky: Each thing I see is a luminous form in a sparkling world. Such love is a kind of grace; enshrined in it, all is right with the world. It is a little touch of madness, this kind of love—raw and driving.

Some years ago, I began to study the small things in the forest that I didn't understand, moving from the lovely and lethal amanita mushrooms to the stony, invincible lichens to the water skippers coasting lightly across the little creeks. I began to study insects especially and then flies in particular.

Flies are so present and innumerable that it is hard to see their presence clearly, hard to believe in their measure. There are around 120,000 species of flies, depending on who's counting, and they have many names: bee flies, cactus flies, papaya flies, warble flies, brine flies, nimble flies, biting midges, green midges, gall midges, mountain midges, dixid midges, solitary midges, net-winged midges, phantom midges—so called because the larvae are transparent and seem to disappear in water. Studying flies, my head begins to spin with suborders and divisions, tribes and clades, and the wild implications of the Latin names: Psychodidae and Sarcophagidae and *Calliphora vomitoria*.

451

The Order Diptera is old, as are most insects; it was well established by the Jurassic Era, 210 million years ago.[1] (Unlike all other insects, flies do not have four wings. Diptera comes from the word *di* for two and *ptera* for wings.) Fly biology is a vast and changing field. New species and subspecies of flies are always being discovered. Familiar species are found in new locations; variants between species are analyzed in new or more subtle ways, and so the taxonomic distinctions between flies are always being revised. But in the general term, flies are defined by their single set of wings, legless larvae, and mouthparts designed for biting, sucking, or lapping.

Inside these templates, there is stupefying variation. They are divided into families, genera, and species by the varied location of veins in the wings, their color, body size, type of mouthpart, the number of stages of larval development, the type and separation of eyes, antennal structure, the arrangement and number of bristles on the body, the length of the legs, and habitat—differences controversial and infinitesimally detailed.

We often know them as the most common and familiar things, as single things: individual flies rescued or swatted, struggling in webs, crawling dizzily across cold windowpanes on a milky October day. One finds flies in odd places, but so often they are not a surprise even in surprising locations—in the laundry basket or buzzing inside the medicine cabinet, or caught unaware in the wash water. Almost every fly you catch in your house will be a housefly, one of the family Muscidae, chubby and vigilant flies that can birth a dozen generations every summer. (Houseflies are found in virtually every place on earth save for Antarctica and a few isolated islets.)

Sometimes we know them as plagues: I've been battered by biting flies in forests, near mangrove and in sand, flies the size of pinheads in clouds so thick I couldn't walk twenty feet without getting a crop of angry red bites on every inch of exposed skin. These are the ones we call punkies or gnats or no-see-ums, the fly family known as Ceratopogonidae. There are more than four thousand species of them—tiny,

[1]We are one kingdom with flies: Animali, and then we diverge. (You can remember the taxonomic series of kingdom, phylum, class, order, family, genera, species with an appropriate mnemonic: *Keep Pots Clean; Our Food Gets Spoiled.*) Flies are found in the Phylum Arthropoda: exoskeletons, jointed legs, and segmented bodies, a group that includes crabs, centipedes, and spiders as well. The flies are in the Subphylum Mandibulata, which means mandibles on the second segment past the mouth opening, and just imagine that. We are not in Kansas anymore. Class Insecta means a body is divided into head, abdomen, and thorax. The insects from here on out—beetles, fleas, ants, scorpions, walking sticks, and many other types—are entirely separate orders.

almost invisible flies with stinging bites, inexplicable dots of pain.

The *Encyclopaedia Britannica* says simply, "It is not possible to discuss all dipteran habitats." Flies live in the air and the soil and under water and inside the stems and leaves of plants. They live high in the mountains, in sand and snow, tide pools and lakes, sulfur springs and salt lagoons. The brine fly lives in the thermal springs of Yellowstone at temperatures up to 43 degrees Celsius. There are flies in the volcanic hot springs of Iceland and New Zealand living at even higher temperatures. Certain flies handle extreme cold easily too, blessed with a kind of antifreeze and other strange gifts. The wingless snow fly lives underground in burrows, and wanders across the white fields during the day—wee black spots walking briskly along in the afternoon. The Himalayan glacier midge prefers temperatures around the freezing point, but has been seen active at minus 16 degrees Celsius. (When placed in a hand, it becomes agitated and then faints from heat.) One carnivorous fly lays its eggs in pools of seeping petroleum, where the larvae live until maturity. One wingless fly lives inside spiders. Certain flies can live in vinegar. There are flies munching contently on spoiled vegetables. When we eat them by accident, they just ride the peristaltic wave on through, exiting in our feces and moving along.

The single pair of wings that is crucial to the identity of flies may be very small or startlingly large or vestigial, may lie open or closed, look scaly, milky, beribboned with black veins, smoky or transparent. Instead of a second set of wings, flies have small bony structures called halteres. They are mobile gyroscopes for flight, beating in time but out of sync with the wings, twisting with every change of direction, to keep the fly from tumbling. Most are astonishing flyers, able to move in three dimensions at speeds hard to measure. Some can hover motionless and fly backward or forward or sideways like helicopters. (Flower flies, which look alarmingly like wasps but are harmless, will hover in front of your face, appearing to gaze directly into your eyes.) Midges beat their wings more than a thousand times per second; this is too fast for nerve impulses and instead involves a mysterious muscular trigger effect. A fruit fly can stay aloft for an entire afternoon, burning ten percent of its body weight every hour. There are clumsy flies: The march fly travels laboriously only a few feet off the ground, and so is continuous fodder for car radiators; march flies are often seen banging into people and bushes, and even the walls of buildings. Soldier flies can fly, but don't very often; they sit for long periods of time on leaves or flowers. Other species prefer to walk or run, sometimes on the surface of water; the louse fly, often wingless, walks sideways, like a crab.

John Clare wrote of flies that "they look like things of mind or fairies." There are flies so small they can barely be seen by human eyes; others are as wide and long as a man's hand. Their bodies may be lime green or shiny blue, glowing black, metallic or dull yellow, pearly white, leathery, variegated in browns, matted with dust. A few are flecked with iridescent gold and silver. They are squat or slender or wasp waisted. Their legs may be very long and fine or stubby, delicate as a web or stout and strong. Fly genitalia, one text notes, are "extremely polymorphous." Some flies have beards or even furry coats made of bristles; others seem hairless. The hover flies mimic bees and wasps, growing yellow-brown bristly hair like the fur of a bumblebee or striped like yellow jackets. The tangle-veined fly, which is parasitic on grasshoppers, has a loud, bee-like buzz. A fly's antennae may be akin to knobs or threads or whips or feathers or pencilline brushes. Insects do not breathe exactly; they perform gas exchange in a different way from mammals, through tubes called spiracles. Their larvae breathe in many ways, through gills and snorkels, or by taking up the oxygen stored in plant roots and stems. Spiracles show up just about anywhere: beside the head, in the belly, in a maggot's anus.

What great variety they have! When Augustine argued that the fly is also made by God, he spoke of "such towering magnitude in this tininess." The family Nycteribiidae, the bat ticks, are true flies but look like spiders without heads. They live only in the fur of bats, sucking bat blood, hanging on with claws. Exposed, the stunted bugs run rapidly across the bat's fur before disappearing underneath. But the family Tipulidae, the crane flies, fill your palm. They look like giant tapered mosquitoes, with very long, slender, spiderlike legs, three eyes, and big veiny wings that may span three inches. They do not bite. These are the ballerinas of the flies, delicate and graceful. Male crane flies form mating swarms that dance above treetops at sundown, or flow over pastures in a cloud, pushed by the breeze.

So one fly seeks light and heat; another avoids both. One is a vegetarian—another a terror. They flit like tiny shadows in the night skies, crawl across the windowpane and out of the drain and into the garbage and into our eyes. Sometimes flies migrate out to sea far from anything human, flitting across the white-capped waves of the ever-moving sea for miles, for days. The fly is grotesque and frail and lovely and vigorous, quivering, shivering, lapping, flitting, jerking, sucking, panting: Theirs is an exotic genius, a design of brilliant simplicity and bewildering complexity at once.

I study flies, I am stunned by them. I love them, with a fleeting love—with the triad: love, logic, sensitivity. Did you notice how calmly I noted that there is a fly that lives inside spiders? Another that is parasitic on grasshoppers? This is a humming, buzzing world; we live in the midst of the ceaseless murmur of lives, a world of strange things whispering the poems of old Buddhas. The world's constant rustling is like the rubbing of velvet between distracted fingers; it can drive one mad. Beside the cherry tree, under that bright sky, lives the sheep bot fly. It enters a sheep's nostrils, where it gives birth to live young. The maggots crawl up the nasal passages into the sinuses, where they feed until they are grown—a process that lasts nearly a year. The sheep's nose runs with pus; it shakes its head at this odd itch, shakes and rubs its nose into the ground, grits its teeth, jumps about, growing ever weaker. The condition is sometimes called the blind staggers. One day the sheep gives a great sneeze, and out shoot mature sheep bot flies. They are ready to mate and make more babies.

It is right here with flies that I face a direct and potent challenge: What do I really believe? What do I believe about beauty and the ultimate goodness of this world?

Jean-Henri Fabre lays out his corpses by the open window. A few days later, he writes, "Let us overcome our repugnance and give a glance inside." Then he lifts the bodies, counting the flies that have come, the eggs they lay, the larvae that form ". . . a surging mass of swarming sterns and pointed heads, which emerge, wriggle, and dive in again. It suggests a seething billow." He adds, as an aside, "It turns one's stomach." He examines and measures and counts, and then gently places a few hundred eggs in a test tube with a piece of meat squeezed dry. A few days later, he pours off the liquescent remnants of the once-hard flesh, which "flows in every direction like an icicle placed before the fire." He measures it, and keeps careful notes.

"It is horrible," he adds, "most horrible."

I have been a Buddhist for more than twenty-five years, since I was a young woman. My avid urge to understand bodies didn't stop at the bodies themselves; I sought for a way to think about the fact of life, the deepest query. Buddhism in its heart is an answer to our questions about suffering and loss, a response to the inexplicable; it is a way to live with life. Its explanations, its particular vocabulary and shorthand, its gentle pressures—they have been with me throughout my adult life; they are part of my language, my thought, my view. Buddhism saved my life and controlled it; it has been liberation and censure at once.

Buddhism is blunt about suffering, its causes and its cures. The Buddha taught that nothing is permanent. He taught this in a great many ways, but most of what he said came down to this: Things change. Change hurts, change cannot be avoided. "All compounded things are subject to dissolution"—this formula is basic Buddhist doctrine, it is pounded into us by the canon, by the masters, by our daily lives. It means all things are compounded and will dissolve, which means I am compounded and I will dissolve. This is not something I readily accept, and yet I am continually bombarded with the evidence. I longed to know this, this fact of life, this answer—that we are put together from other things and will be taken apart and those other things and those things we become will in turn be taken apart and built anew—that there is nothing known that escapes this fate. When one of his disciples struggled with lust or felt pride in his youth or strength, the Buddha recommended that the follower go to the charnel ground, and meditate on a corpse—on its blossoming into something new.

We feel pain because things change. We feel joy for the same reason. But suffering is not simply pain: It is our peculiar punishment that we know things change and we want this to be otherwise. We want to hang on to what is going away, keep our conditions as they are, people as they are, ourselves as we are. In Buddhist terms this is variously called thirst or desire or attachment or clinging. It means that we hold on to the hope that something will remain, even as it all slides away like sand in running water, like water from our hands. Knowing the answer does not stop the question from being asked.

Desire is not always about holding something close; it has a shadow, the urge to push things away. Buddhists usually call this aversion—the desire for the extinction of something, for separation from it. The original Pali word for aversion, *dosa*, is various and shaded, translated sometimes as anger or hatred, sometimes as denial, as projection, aggression, repulsion, and now and then as disgust or revulsion or distortion. Aversion has as much force and fascination as the positive desires we know. It may be simply a reflexive flinch, a ducking for cover, it may be much stronger. Like desire, aversion is a many-colored thing, flavored by circumstances. It is a kind of clinging—clinging to the hope of *something other than this.*

When I began to study flies, I couldn't seem to stop. Fabre wrote, "To know their habits long haunted my mind." I think of the violence with which we describe such prurient obsessions—we say we cannot tear our eyes away. My eyes are glued to flies and it is as though they are stitched open against my will. I feel revulsion; I flinch, I turn away, I duck for cover. I get squeamish, which is a rare feeling for me. But I also feel curiosity and admiration and a kind of awe. The buzz of a fly's blurred wings is one of the myriad ways the world speaks to us; it is one of the ways speech is freed from our ideas. I feel that if I could listen, if I could just listen without reacting, without judgment or preference or opinion—without reaching for a dream of how things might be otherwise—there is something I would understand that I have yet to know.

Compassion in all its flavors is woven through the enormous canon of Buddhist thought. Its root meaning is "to suffer with." We are able to feel compassion toward those beings who look like us and those who are most familiar. (These are not the same thing; dissimilar creatures can be deeply familiar, as we know from our time spent with dogs, with horses—even lizards.) At what point do we extend this circle past what is known, past what looks like us? At what point do we suffer with what is completely strange? And how far must that circle extend before it includes the sheep bot fly?

This mix of push and pull I feel when I look at insects is akin to the way the tongue longs for an acquired taste. The first time one tastes certain complex flavors they are unpleasant, even offensive. But in time it is that very flavor, its complexity—the bitterness or acidity mingling with other layers—that brings you back. Whether it is wine or chili powder or *natto*—a Japanese delicacy of soybeans bound into a sticky, cobwebbed mold—one returns in part because of the difficulty. We are sharply, pleasantly excited by the nearness of rejection, by skirting along the edge of things, the dank and sour things that instinct reads as dangerous. These shadings of flavor ever so briefly evoke poison and rot—the urine scent of beer, the lingering oily bitterness of coffee, the rank tang of certain cheeses (and I will return to cheese; it factors here). There is a brief shrinking away, perhaps very brief, minuscule, but there nonetheless.

This is a little bit of what I feel toward flies. Let us give a glance inside—a glance, a gasp, a shiver, the briefest reactivity: and then another look, a bit sideways though it may be, and then another. Then there follows the need to look: interest turning into inquiry into passion: the desire to know, to see, and something more, something crucial—the need to bear it, to be able to bear it, to be able to look as closely and thoroughly as I can.

Flies have long been considered the shells and familiars of gods, witches, and demons. They are associated with reincarnation, immortality, and sorcery. They are so unutterably strange, all swarming and speed and single-mindedness, and they cannot be avoided. I really mean that; we eat flies every day.[2] The FDA permits thirty-five fruit fly eggs in every eight ounces of golden raisins, up to twenty maggots "of any size" in a hundred grams of canned mushrooms, and a fair number of both eggs and maggots in tomato products. Last night's mushroom pizza? A womb of flies.

Flies sense the world in every way, its faintest textures: minuscule currents of shifting air, the vibration of a bird's approaching wings, the scent of decaying flowers or a mouse's corpse a half mile away. Some flies have a complex and unique ear, a flexible tympanal membrane in a complex structure behind the neck. A few parasitic flies listen for the distinct sound of their selected prey; one imagines a head carefully cocked.

They taste and smell in ways far more subtle than ours. There is no profound difference between the two senses anyway; both are a way of identifying chemicals, defining them, discriminating. They sense the sex pheromones released so hopefully by their prey, and follow; they smell the prey's feces, its breath, or the small damage done by other hunting insects. Biting flies are sensitive to stress chemicals, including the higher levels of carbon dioxide emitted when mammals

---

[2]Consider the cheese skipper, a kind of black fly found all over the world. They are so called in part because they skip, or leap, when disturbed; they curl up, grabbing the tail with the hooked mouth, tense, and then let go—springing like a coil, fast and hard. Cheese skippers are attracted to meat, cheese, and corpses, which develop a cheesy smell at a certain stage when butyric acid is present. Their family name, Piophilia, means milk loving. The larvae can be eaten accidentally, and may survive ingestion and burrow into the gut. One imagines the little thing shrugging its nonexistent shoulders and changing course. When the larvae infest a hard cheese like pecorino, they decompose the fats until the cheese turns creamy and pink, at which point the Italians call it *casu marzu*, "rotten cheese." Gourmets like it, and will blend *casu marzu* into a paste to spread on bread. Most people try to remove the maggots first. Selling this cheese is illegal in Italy, because even shredded maggot parts are dangerous—all those hooks. But not everyone does this. Some consider the maggots part of the delicacy—an aphrodisiac, or a peculiarly nutritious food.

exert themselves. The black flies respond directly to the scent of human sweat. Many flies have taste and smell receptors on their complex mouthparts, their antennae, the delicate legs, and fine-clawed feet. Walking, they sample the coming meal; instantly, the proboscis unwinds. Flies are sensitive to minute differences in the world's chemistry, and its surprising similarities: One of the parasitic *Lucilia* flies is attracted, according to one text, to "wild parsnips and fresh meat." One molecule attracts the male to the female; another causes the male's ritual courtship flight; a third causes the female to relax and hold still. Their world is a superdimensional pheromonal architecture, a mingled and vaporous mist multiplied by sight and sound and space.

Consider the compound eye, common to all insects, variously evolved in flies. A fly's eyes may be huge: the eyes of horse flies are bulging black caps filling the face. Other flies may have tiny eyes, and some flies have no eyes at all. (The pyrgotid flies have strangely shaped heads that protrude in *front* of their eyes, an evolutionary development hard to comprehend.) The eye may be flat or bulging, round or triangular in shape, shining like jewels. A deer fly's eyes are brightly colored, green or gold with patterns and zigzags. Tachinid flies have reddish eyes; dance flies have orange ones. Each facet of a compound eye is held at a unique angle, independent of all the others. They are capable of differentiating between the wavelengths of light and can distinguish the angle at which sunlight falls, allowing them to navigate off the surface of water. A fly has a thousand eyes, four thousand eyes, side by side without gap. The fly cannot focus on a single form, but sees each form from many angles at once. Each single thing is multiplied, the object broken like a mirror into shards, into shocks of light, and remade like water into a single lake, a prism, a drop of dew.

Flies eat blood and meat and feces and other insects and each other, but also pollen, nectar, algae, decaying seaweed, and fungi. Bulb fly maggots are tiny dilettantes, seeking only the inner tissue of hyacinth, tulip, narcissus, and lily bulbs. Fruit fly maggots are picky: One species eats walnut husks, another eats cherries. Pomace flies live on rotting fruit, but they don't eat the fruit; they eat the yeast that grows on rotting fruit. (This is a brief world indeed; a new generation is born every ten days or so.)

Flies bite, suck, slice, lap. Bee lice live in the mouths of bees, eating nectar. Stiletto fly larvae sometimes live in wool blankets and decaying wood. Among the black flies, which plague cattle, each species specializes in a cow part—one sucks blood from cows' bellies, one from cows' ears, and so on. The flat-footed flies, which run in a zigzag pattern across plants, include a variety called smoke flies; they are attracted to fires and eat the burned wood afterward. Eye gnats are drawn to tears, sweat flies to sweat, face flies to eyes and noses.

Flies hurt us, but only in passing; sleeping sickness, malaria, yellow fever, river blindness: mere accidents. The sheep bot fly can live in many places, including human eyes if eyes are more convenient than the sheep—but it prefers the sheep. We are simply more food, more warm and meaty beings among endless beings. But what food!—palaces of muscle and blood, rich and fertile fields.

I read otherwise sober and mechanical descriptions of flies, and trip over the anthropomorphic complaint. Both Pliny and Plutarch complained that flies were impossible to train and domesticate. Among modern thinkers, one fly is "good" and the other is "bad," one is a "pest" and another a "bane" and another a "benefit." The tachinid flies are parasitic on destructive caterpillars, and snipe flies eat aphids, so they are described with kind words. Their predation does us good, but all predation does something good and not just the predator. Predation makes way. It makes room.

Even entomologists hate flies, on principle. Edwin Way Teale, who wrote of the natural world his entire life with reverence and cheer, hated the housefly. He obsessed over the number and variety of bacteria, fungi, viruses, and parasites they carried from place to place, and finally seems to have simply flung his hands into the air and given up, declaring the housefly "an insect villain with hardly a drop of redeeming virtue." Leland Howard, a USDA entomologist, wrote an encyclopedic account of insects in 1904 that is still quoted today. He called the harmless saltwater flies "sordid little flies," and the wingless bird tick "apparently too lazy to fly." Of the bluebottle, which sometimes has parasitic mites, he wrote, "It is comforting to think that the house-fly has these parasites which torment him so. Such retribution is just."

Humans are a nightmare; we tear the earth apart. We trepan mountains and pour them into rivers, take the soil apart down to its atoms, sully the sea, shred our world like giant pigs rutting after truffles. We poison our nest and each other and ourselves. We eat everything, simply everything, but we turn away from flies.

The circles of compassion can suddenly expand. Federico García Lorca wrote that he rescued flies caught at a window; they reminded him of "people / in chains." And of course I've done the same. I often do—catch flies and crickets and spiders and let them go, careful of their frailty. This brief moment of the widening circle; it is easily challenged by the maggot, by the swarm. The larvae of the fungus gnat sometimes travel in great masses, for reasons no one can guess—huge groups called worm snakes piled several deep, squirming along about an inch a minute. I know why Beelzebub is Lord of the Flies; is there any other god who would slouch so towards Bethlehem?

I long sometimes for a compound eye. It is a tenet of my religious practice, an ever-present thorn, to remember that my point of view, that any point of view, is merely a point. My eyes cannot see a landscape, let alone a world. But how we judge things has everything to do with where we stand. Can I learn to see a form from many angles at once? Can I see other beings, this moment, my mistakes, my words, like this? Can I know multiplicity as a single thing?

So many flies: Mydas flies, sewage flies, robust bot flies, gout flies, scavenger flies, snipe flies. Big-headed flies, thick-headed flies, picture-winged flies, stilt-legged flies, spear-winged flies, banana-stalk flies, flower-loving flies, stalk-eyed flies, flat-footed flies, pointed-winged flies, hump-backed flies.

The literature of Zen Buddhism is thick with nature—nature images, metaphors, puzzles, and questions, but mostly the calm and serene inhuman world of clouds, seeds, spring shoots, meadow grasses, and ponds, the moon and the mountain and the wave and the plum blossom. (Kobayashi Issa, an eighteenth-century Buddhist haiku master, wrote: "Where there are humans / there are flies / and Buddhas." But he is talking, I think, rather more about humans than flies.) Such images are used as metaphors for all kinds of Buddhist concepts, but they are partly an effort to convey how Zen Buddhism describes reality itself, the world. Hongzhi, a great Zen master of China, described it as "sky and water merging in autumn"—a vast, shifting, unbounded world.

Central to Zen Buddhism is a belief in *busshō*, usually translated from the Japanese as Buddha Nature. (In English we like to capitalize words like *buddha* and *nature*, to distinguish subtly different ideas with the same sound. Today, glancing inside the seething billow of life, it seems to me an impotent fist shaking at the greatness of what we try to say with the words. But I will follow the rule.)

Busshō is shorthand for something that requires quite a few words to explain—or it is already one too many words for what can't be explained in words. Buddhism is founded on the idea that all things are impermanent, that nothing has a fixed self-nature that passes through time unchanged. Change is not an aspect of the matrix but the matrix itself. It is because no one thing is permanent that we are not separated from anything—not bounded, not contained. All beings are constantly appearing, constantly springing into existence, hurtling out of themselves, of what they were, what preceded. Buddha Nature is—what? Original nature. Perfect nature—the substrate or source of all things. But it is not God, it is not ether, it is not simply a womb that gives birth. It is all things; it is that which manifests as things—as the world—as people, rocks, stars, dewdrops, flies—all beings, all forms, all existent things. All existence.

What do I know about Buddha Nature, anyway? I can't even tell you what it is—and Buddha Nature isn't an "it" and it isn't really an "is" either; not a quality attached to anything or a state of being or a space in which things exist; Buddha Nature as I understand it—there's that "it" again—is this, this, this, here, this minuscule and gargantuan and muscular relational and organic now, the luminosity of the sparkling world, the vast inevitability of loss, and not that exactly either. I use that phrase, Buddha Nature, even as it fills my mouth with ash, to mean all those things and more—relation, aspects, moments, qualities, acts, aeons, and bodies—and I use it in a positive way, with pleasure, with outright joy, to mean that all of us—those of us who think we are something unique and those who never think about it, and all those creatures who don't do what I might call thinking but are yet alive, and all those things we bang up against and assume aren't alive at all—are in some way kin, in some way both source and effect, eternally and continually and without hesitation, spontaneously and instantaneously and infinitely giving birth to ourselves, spilling out of nothing into nothing, with great vigor—leaping, sliding, appearing, disappearing into and out of a lack of solidness, into and out of the nonexistence of permanent nature, and that because this is the law—the muscle, the hinge—of reality—it's good. It's all right. Everything is all right.

Everything is all right. The female horsefly favors large warm-blooded animals. They see quite well and will fly around their prey just out of reach, finally biting one's back or leg. (As is true with many other biting flies, including mosquitoes, only the females bite. The males live on plant pollen and juices. It so happens as well that the

462

males live brief lives while the females live the whole long, hot summer. The story is told that the Declaration of Independence was signed on July 4 because the horseflies in Philadelphia were intolerable that year, and the delegates called for an early vote so they could get out of town.) The "phlebotomus" insects, as they are called, have anticoagulant in their saliva; after a bite, the blood continues to run, sometimes dangerously so. (To be precise, the horsefly slices rather than bites; its mouthparts are like tiny knives.) In their turn, horseflies are eaten by robber flies, who capture them on the wing and then find a convenient twig to rest on while sucking them dry. Robber flies are sometimes called bee killers; they prize honeybees and will watch them from the shadows while the bees gather pollen, then suddenly dart out and seize one from behind, so it can't sting. They drain the bee dry and drop its empty shell; below a familiar perch, the bodies slowly pile up.

The cluster fly lays its children inside earthworms. If you crush a cluster fly, it smells like honey.

The female thick-headed fly hangs around flowers, drinking nectar, like a bully at a bar. She waits for a bee or wasp and when one comes close, she grabs it. The bee seems not to care, does not resist, while she deposits an egg before letting go. The bee flies away, the larva hatches, and burrows within. The larva eats the bee slowly until it dies, then falls to the ground within the bee's body and burrows underground to pupate. Flies are holometabolous, meaning the young undergoes a complete metamorphism into the adult form, into a completely different form. The pupa is the quiescent phase between, and may last days or weeks or even longer. The pupae of flies are not protected by cocoons like those of butterflies; they simply harden, or build a shell from soil or spit. Some flies make a puparium from their own skin. Eat the bee, crawl underground, sleep the winter through, and emerge as a fly, seeking bees. That is the cycle, the great web of its life, round and round.

Pyrgotid flies do the same thing to May beetles, except that instead of burrowing into the ground, they live in the empty beetle shell over the winter. Flesh flies live under the skin of a turtle and in the stomach of frogs. The sheep bot fly—I have described this creature already. But there is also a bot fly that infests rabbits, and a bot fly that lives in horses' throats, a bot fly that favors horses' noses, and another bot fly that prefers horses' tongues. There are bot flies specific to kangaroos, camels, warthogs, zebras, and elephants. The human bot fly, transmitted by mosquitoes, is cosmopolitan in its tastes; besides people, it infects dogs, cats, rabbits, horses, cattle, and sheep.

One of the drawbacks of a long Buddhist practice is that one sometimes has the urge to present one's self as more composed than one actually is. (Let's be clear here; I mean me.) Emotional equanimity is a Buddhist virtue, a reflection of one's ability to accept reality and a sign that one is not contributing to the heat of suffering in the world by resisting that reality. That this equanimity is a real thing to me, a true tranquility found through steady practice, is beside the point. My tranquility may be real but it is not immune to conditions; it is no more permanent or unchanging than my skin. At times there is a loud voice inside me, complaining indignantly: *Explain this!*

Someone please explain this.

In my dreams, I could not make *Apocephalus pergandei*. It is named after Theodore Pergande, a renowned entomologist of the latter nineteenth century who was particularly interested in aphids and ants. He was observing carpenter ants one day when he saw the heads of the ants begin to fall off one at a time. When he investigated, he found what has become known colloquially as the ant-decapitating fly. The mature fly lays eggs on an ant's neck. The larvae hatch and then bore into the ant's head, eating it from the inside. Eating, the larva grows, slowly killing the ant, which apparently expires just as its head pops off. But as many of us wish we could do, it does not leave its childhood home behind. Instead, the little vermin remains inside for a while, and if you look closely that is what you will see: ants' heads, walking around, filled with the children of flies.

A Buddhist practice requires rigorous self-disclosure—mostly to one's own self—and a kind of undefended willingness to be present in one's own crappy life as it is. This means noticing how often we tell lies about ourselves. I lie about many things, to myself and others. I lie about the way that triad on which I balance tilts: sensitivity, logic, love. It limps at times, or I find myself one-legged, just plain falling down. I am not always at home in this world, not always relaxed, not always in love with this great big Buddha-Nature-ridden place.

The Tachinidae is one of the largest, most selective, and successful fly families. "Ingenious," says one entomologist, for how they have solved the problems of their peculiar niche—"respiration in particular," since it is tricky to breathe inside things. Tachinid larvae are pure parasites, infesting virtually every kind of insect. One type lays its eggs on the leaves preferred by a certain caterpillar; the caterpillar eats the eggs, and the larvae hatch inside—born, as it were, at the buffet table. Another chooses crickets and katydids. The female fly can hear the precise frequency of the cricket chirp. (She can also hear, though the calls are many times higher, the ultrasound calls of the insectivorous bats she wants to avoid.) She follows the chirp carefully through a mechanism unlike human hearing. When she locates the host, she lays her live babies beside or on them. They burrow in and eat selectively to keep the host alive as long as possible.

Caught in a certain light, tachinid flies glow, their wings like violet veils, ovaline eyes the burnt orange of sunset. I sit in the dark summer night, pleasantly melancholy, listening to crickets and contemplating *busshō* in a pulsing world.

I can pretend to have this settled. I can pretend to not mind. Certain gall midges are parasitic on themselves: The larvae hatch inside the mother and eat her from the inside out. I am appalled, even as I recognize the marvelous efficiency. Then I turn away from my own appalled thoughts. I am practicing acceptance. I bow. I tell myself it is a kind of compassion. It is sacrifice. (As though I understand *that* in some way.)

The horsefly bites a horse, and the blood runs, and before the wound even closes the face fly creeps in and settles down to stay. The human bot fly captures a bloodsucker, such as a mosquito, and lays eggs on its body—just enough that the mosquito can still move freely. Then the mosquito finds a host and lands. The heat of the host causes the bot fly larvae to hatch; they slide off to the host's skin, down a follicle of hair, and in, another accidental gift. The larvae live just under the skin. They form a breathing hole with their hooks, keeping it open by digging constantly. This is called myiasis, flies developing in living flesh. (Many fly families indulge; the human bot fly is just one.) The maggots live under the skin until they are about an inch long. One observer of the condition wrote that myiasis causes "intense discomfort or pain," which is not a surprise. But the maggots are never still; he adds that people also complain of "the disquieting feeling of never being alone."

A person with myiasis must be patient; it is damaging to try to remove tiny larvae. One treatment is suffocation: coating the openings with paraffin or nail polish or turpentine, or lathering on chloroform dissolved in vegetable oil. One of the most effective methods for removing them is to lay strips of raw bacon across the wound; the larvae come running. Squirming, rather, in their roiling, systaltic wave.

Oh, well—parasitism is routine in the insect world. Can we call it cruel, this life governed by instinct? Consider this: Two flies glued down by their wings to a table, for convenience. A drop of paraffin is carefully poured on their backs and then scooped out into a crater. Each fly's thorax is opened into the crater with a tiny scalpel, exposing the muscle. Saline is dropped into the craters for moisture. The flies are then rotated and joined, back to back, the paraffin gently sealed with a hot needle to form a double fly. This new kind of fly can walk, sort of, each taking a turn riding the other piggyback—or it can be neatly glued to a stick. For convenience. Now the scientist has a wonderful thing, a little monster with which to study many things: metabolism, hunger, dehydration, decay.

Explain that.

The larva grows, then settles into pupation. After time, after a mountain of time, the maggot disappears, the cask opens, and a fly emerges. It is fully mature; it will grow no more. The larvae of black flies are aquatic; the matured fly secretes a bubble of air and rises in it like an astronaut to its new life in the air, bursting out of the bubble at the surface. One observer said that a sudden hatching of black flies leaves the water "in great numbers with such force and velocity" that it seemed as though they were being "shot out of a gun." In contrast, the net-winged midge makes a submarine, a stiff case that floats to the surface, where it bursts open; the adults rise from their boats as delicate as mist. At first it is a wrinkled and empty fly bag, without color or strength. The new being takes a great gulp of air and expands, incalculably vast and whole, the actualization of fly.

So many flies: tabanid flies, green bottle flies, bronze dump flies, stilt-legged flies, bush flies, stable flies, louse flies, frit flies, dung flies, rust flies, elk flies, seaweed flies, horn flies, scavenger flies, gadflies, skipper flies, soldier flies, Hessian flies, Richard flies, light flies, stone flies, sand flies, grass flies, eye gnats, wood gnats. A myriad mosquitoes.

There is something so simple and clear about the speech of flies; if I knew fly words, what would be clarified in my own? I study how flies use the world—how they make something of it that wasn't there before. They liquefy the dead, they slurp up the world, inhaling the bodies of others. They shoot out of lakes and the ground and out of bodies, joyous, filled with air. If I believe—and today, I think I do—

that every being is Buddha Nature, that there is no place Buddhas cannot or will not go, then I must give a glance inside.

I don't know what a Buddha is.

One fly, its passing hum, this we know—but they mob up, don't they, into masses of flies, into rivers and mountains of life, crawling and skipping and vibrating without rest, working at disintegration and change. Phantom midges form such enormous swarms they have been mistaken for smoke plumes, humming with such force that, in the words of one observer, they sound "like a distant waterfall."

Many fly swarms are birth explosions; others are orgies. Male dance flies join in huge mating swarms, graceful ellipses that flow up and down across meadows and gardens. They make frothy structures called nuptial balloons to carry on their abdomens for attracting females. Some species put seeds or algae in their balloons; others go straight for dead bugs—the bigger, the better, as far as the female is concerned. (Female dance flies routinely eat during sex—maybe from the nuptial balloon they have accepted as part of the bargain, but often, they eat another fly.) One type of dance fly uses only saliva and air, creating a lather of emptiness; as they dance, the empty bubbles glitter like lights.

Long-legged flies do their mating dance in slow motion, their rhythms complex and mysterious; they wave black and white leg scales back and forth in front of the female like a vaudeville stripper waves her fans. Pomace flies have tufts of dark hair on their legs called sex combs, with which they hold the female still during mating. The male penetrates from behind, the female spasmodically jerking in response. Already mated females are unreceptive; they curl their abdomens under, fly away, or kick at males.

The impregnated female seeks a nest. A few flies give live birth, and a few incubate their young. The tsetse fly, keds, and bat flies all hatch within their mother and are fed with something akin to a milk gland until they are ready to pupate, at which point they are finally expelled. But most flies lay eggs—a single egg, or hundreds, or thousands. She has a telescoping ovipositor, fine and small, which emerges from her abdomen and gropes its way inside—into the soft spaces, in the dark. Flies lay their eggs in the roots and stems of plants, in fruit, in the algae of a still pond, in shit, in hair and hide, in the bodies of other insects, the stomachs of cows, the dirty hunks of wool around the anus of sheep, in the pus of an infected wound. (The preference of many

467

carnivorous species is the corpse.) Blowflies deposit eggs in the eyes, ears, nostrils, mouth, vagina, and anus. Female flies are choosy; many have taste buds on the ovipositor to help them pick the best location— each fly to its own place. Insistent and shy, the ovipositor worms its way down: into garbage and wounds, into the rotten flecks of meat on the floor of a slaughterhouse, into stagnant water, between the membranous layers of a corpse, between fibers of living muscle, on the umbilical cord of newborn fawns—into "any convenient cavity," says the *Britannica*—and deposits tiny eggs shimmery and damp, masses of them. She is careful not to crowd them, filling first one newly made womb, and then another and another. A day later, she dies.

Horrible. Most horrible.

Larvae are the unfinished fly; they are like letters not yet making a word. Maggots are the simplest of larvae; they are the ur-fly, the refined essence of the fly, the marvelously simplified fly—its template, a profoundly primitive thing. Many maggots have no head, consisting only of a body and a mouth filled with hooks. They move by wavelets of muscular contraction and relaxation, grasping with the mouth hooks and other hooks along their sides. They can roll and spring and slide.

After they hatch, they eat and grow. This process may be slow or fast. The chironomid midge larva in West Africa grows in spurts, drying out and reviving through extreme temperature variations and waves of drought and rain. When it is almost completely desiccated, it enters into a condition called cryptobiosis—still alive but with no signs of metabolism. Sprinkled with water, it wakes up, takes a meal, and starts growing again until the next dry spell. Blue bottle flies require an almost totally humid atmosphere—something a corpse can easily provide in most cases—and in good conditions, hatch almost as soon as they are laid. They begin to eat, and never stop. I am being literal: They never stop. (Trashmen call maggots "disco rice" for the way they wiggle through the waste.) If undisturbed, a maggot will eat without ceasing until it is grown. There is a distinct advantage to maggots having anal spiracles; there is no need to stop eating in order to breathe.

Aristotle, like many others for most of history, believed that some flies "are not derived from living parentage, but are generated spontaneously . . . in decaying mud or dung; others in timber." They simply appear all at once from manure and corpses, with no sign of having been born. How else to explain this locomotion, this primordial fecundity?

Maggots can reduce the weight of a human body by fifty percent in a few weeks. In the decomposing of a body, there are several waves of insects, each colonizing in its turn in a strict sequence. The first wave is blowflies and houseflies of certain species; they begin to arrive within minutes of death. Their bodies are beautiful, glasslike in shimmering greens and blues, their eyes a deep, warm red. They glisten, tremble, and the larvae hatch and eat. They are ingenious little maggots. A dead body is in fact alive, a busy place full of activity—so much that the body seems to move of its own accord from their motion. The sound of all this movement, all this life, writes one entomologist, is "reminiscent of gently frying fat."

In time, other species of blowflies and houseflies arrive. The corpse begins to blacken, soften. (Corpses at this stage are called "wet carrion" by biologists.) The meat on which the maggots feed begins to liquefy and runs like melting butter. This is the fluid Fabre contemplated in quiet shock. "We here witness the transfusion of one animal into another," he wrote. If the maggots fail to move in time, they drown in the broth of the corpse they are eating.

By the time these larvae have fallen off into the soil to pupate, a third wave of flies arrives—fruit flies and drone flies and others, flies that prefer the liquids. Toward the end, the cheese skipper appears, drawn to the smell, and carefully cleans the bones of the remnants of tendons and connective tissue.

I contemplate my ordinary, imperfect, beloved body. I contemplate the bodies of my beloveds: individual, singular, unique, irreplaceable people, their skin and eyes and mouths and hands. I consider their skin riddled and bristling with that seething billow, I consider the digestion of their eyes and the liquefaction of those hands, my hands, my eyes—the evolution of the person into the thing, into wet carrion and eventually into a puddle, into soil, into earth, and flies. And it will come, whether I turn away or not.

We are nothing more than a collection of parts, and each part a collection of smaller parts, and smaller, the things we love and all we cherish conglomerates of tiny blocks. The blocks are built up; they will be taken apart the same way; we are nothing more. (And yet we are something more; this is one of the mysteries, I know. I cannot point to it, hold it, name it, except in the limited and awkward ways I have already tried. But there is something more, and it is the totality of this *nothing more.*)

Flies are wholehearted things, leading wholehearted lives. They understand dissolution, and by understanding I mean they live it. The parts are separated, they become something new. Pouring one's life into compoundedness without resistance, living by means of compoundedness and its subsequent falling apart—this is the wisdom of the creatures of the earth, the ones besides us, the ones who don't fight it. Because the human heart is devoted to compounded things and tries to hold them still, our hearts break. (One more thing to dissolve.) How can we know their lives? How can we understand the spongy proboscis, softly padded, with its small rasping teeth?

What better vision of the fullness of birth and the fullness of death than the maggot and the fly? A legless, headless, gill-breathing vermiform, giving way to the complete stillness of the pupa, and emerging as a land-based flyer—each stage utterly unlike the others, with nothing remaining of what was before. In their turn, maggots and flies help us along in our own fullness of birth and death, until what we were is completely changed. Decomposed, recomposed, compounded, dissolved, disappearing, reappearing—a piece from here and a fleck from there, a taste of this karma, a speck of that memory, this carbon atom, that bit of water, a little protein, a pinch of pain: until a new body and a new life are made from pieces of the past. The wee bit they claim, can you begrudge it? Dissolved, our flesh is their water, and they lap us up.

"Placed in her crucibles, animals and men, beggars and kings are one and all alike," wrote Fabre. "There you have true equality, the only equality in this world of ours: equality in the presence of the maggot." What lucky flies smelled the flowery scent of the Buddha's death, and came—flowing through the air like a river in the sky, a river of flies! What lucky maggots were born in his body, in the moist heat of the afternoon while the disciples still mourned! The maggots and blowflies are the words of the old Buddhas, singing of the vast texture of things, a lullaby of birth and death. They came and turned him into juice and soil, the Buddha flowing gloriously like cream into the ground.

After a night of more routinely menacing scenes—an insecurely locked door, a strange man in a wig—I woke in the early morning from a brief, vivid dream. There had been a series of burning rooms, and finally a room completely engulfed in flames. I saw several people walking calmly through the room, untouched, smiling. I woke as one

470

turned and looked at me, and said, "I can't tell you how safe I feel in this house."

One of the most famous parables of Buddhism is that of the burning house. The story is told by the Buddha in the Lotus Sutra. A man's children are trapped in a burning house, and won't leave when he calls them. In order to get them out, safe and free, he promises carts full of treasure, great treasure. Finally, tempted, they come out, and are saved. Fire is change, loss, the impossibility of holding on; fire is also the burning, ceaseless desire we feel to hold on to that which can't be held. The house is burning, and we stupidly stand there, refusing to leave—until we are tempted by the promise of treasure—the precious jewels of the Dharma, the practice, the Buddha himself.

Right here, what do I believe? I do believe in perfection, right here—and not just perfection existing in the midst of decay, but decay as a kind of perfection. I believe in beauty, especially in the moments when one least seeks it—not just the dewdrop, the grass, but beauty in the shuffling of papers on the desk in the little cubicle thick with the snuffles of the sweaty man a few inches away. Beauty in the rattle of the bus sliding halfway into the crosswalk right beside you. Beauty in the liquid aswim with maggots. In everything, in anything. I can believe this, without in any way really understanding. Even after I have my answer, the question is always being asked.

When I begin to truly accept myself as a flit, a bubble, a pile of blocks tilting over, my precious me as a passing sigh in the oceanic cosmos of change—when I accept this moment passing completely away into the next without recourse—when I begin to accept that its very fragility and perishing nature is the beauty in life, then I begin to find safety inside a burning house. I don't need to escape if I know how to live inside it. Not needing to escape, I no longer feel tempted, no longer need promises or rewards. I just walk through it, aware of fire.

The north woods in summer smell like blackberry jam, and in the pockets of sun the tiny midges dance in the heat-sweetened air. They are drunk with it, galloping round and round as their lives leak quickly away. They are points of light in the light.

Nominated by Conjunctions

FACE

by IDRIS ANDERSON

from MRS RAMSAY'S KNEE (Utah State University Press)

The bleeding head looked up from the black road,
A white shirt on the shoulder and the arm pushing up,
The asphalt gritty and black, the white staccato
Streaks of speed. An accident. I was driving east
In a black night toward the coast on a map, toward love.
Warm, I hoped, at the end of the road. Late
And so few cars on the wide, divided highway.
Fear of drift. Taste of salt. Sound of speed.
And then the headbeams of my car caught the face,
White like the shirt. Hair on the brow a lick of blood.
My car swerved to miss the bleeding face
In the road. Then I woke up. I knew who he was.

My father's brother, killed at the age of twelve
In a hunting accident, years before I was born,
Years before my father knew my mother.
They were taking guns out of the back floor
Of the car, doves still bleeding, fluttering in the sack,
And a gun his cousin lifted, loaded, his finger
On the trigger, carelessly. He didn't know what
He was doing. And my grandmother ran toward the shot,
Ran and ran at the sound of the shot—she couldn't know
What had happened. But she knew. Younger then
Than I am now, she got over it, and was kind.
There was no enduring sadness in her.

I admired how she killed a rat in her kitchen
With a flyswatter once, how she watered flowers
On her porch and they bloomed and bloomed.
She lived forty more years in the big house
With a gun under her pillow, his photograph
A large oval over the mantel in the living room.
Old women, great aunts, smelling sour
Like old flesh, sweet powder and mildew,
Would grab me, feel my bones, said I looked
Just like him—that I was a girl didn't matter—
The small mouth, the cheekbones. I used to
Stare at his handsome beauty—the dark eyes.

What the mind does for the mind should be a kind
Of healing, and maybe this is. I had forgotten
How their hands moved over me until the dream
Of the young man dying in the road, whom cars ignored
As I did, speeding toward love week after week
And never arriving—the oddly familiar boy,
The bleeding face looking up from the road,
The head without a body, none that I could see,
The mangled car in the dark burning up.
I didn't get a good look. It doesn't matter
How it happened, who abandoned the scene,
Just that he's bleeding. I did nothing but swerve.

I wake to birds in trees on another coast.
Nobody lives here that I know. Week after week,
I sleep dreamless. And I have made a pact
With desire. Affections sustain me. A quiet hour
With an open book and a dear face near me in the dark.
I wake to redwoods, firs, and a view over islands
North into Canada, a distant ridge of mountains
Rimmed with snow, and this comfortable oddness
Of feeling him sometimes alive in my shoulders,
In the way I hold my hand on my knee, as if waiting
In the woods with a gun in my arms, quietly searching
The white sky, the bare autumn trees for birds.

Nominated by Utah State University Press, Eleanor Wilner, Robert Thomas

BIRD FEED

fiction by ASHLEE ADAMS

from MCSWEENEY'S

Nurse Ox called up at the house that night to say that my Grandma Martin's lungs had tuckered and then petered out. I had asked him to call, day or night. I'd said, "Don't be bull-headed. You call me if anything changes. If she starts to breathe funny. I want to hear about it." Nurse Ox claims he descends from remarkable characters, big men who expect their boys to become big men. His granddaddy, on his mama's side, was responsible for the nickname, Ox. That granddaddy was called Moose at birth by his granddaddy, so there was tradition to uphold.

One forty-three a.m. was the time when the phone rung. Nurse Ox said, "Cora, I hate to tell you this." When I didn't respond, he said, "I heard her take the last one." He went on to describe that breath, and told me tales of how she got off easy compared to some. Some sick folks who've been cooped up for months will shoot straight in the air, their eyeballs straining. They'll gasp, gargle, fart, leave nail marks in metal. He assured me she took the last one in stride. She had buzzed him right after her supper, he said. Beef tips, English peas, canned peaches. She'd hardly touched the peas, one mouthful at best, but she'd gotten down three of the four peach slices. Still to this day, I can't get that lonely peach slice out of my head. I imagine it soaked in corn syrup.

Ox says he questions sometimes if he has filled out enough to warrant Ox. He worries that becoming a certified nursing assistant just tacked on an uphill battle.

My granddaddy, dead now for forty years, dropped by to get her, he said. The second time she buzzed, she said, "Tell me. Do you see that man sitting at the end of my bed?" He said he ought to have called me right then. I told him not to worry over it, he did fine. I thanked him for the details.

The longer Dr. Yang refused to let me give her back her home place, her fig bush, her pecan trees, her little riding mower, the more she and I had to open up in places we'd rather have left sealed off to the general public. I started telling Nurse Ox things, and he started telling me things. Ox has children, one a baby girl, two years old, and the other a boy, nine. They live with their mother, who swears Ox isn't fit to care for himself much less their babies. I told him I just could not see that for the truth. He did a fine job taking care of my grandma. I know, I know, he said. But some people will do you that way.

After I told Ox goodbye, I slipped the phone back on its cradle and raised myself. I'd begun sleeping in her bed, feeling like I needed to keep it warm until her return, and now I started toward her chiffarobe. I knew to hold steady. I gripped the edge of her nightstand and placed one foot flat on the floor before I tackled the other one. That was how I'd start living. Her corduroy coat, her favorite thing, was for some reason behind a a bunch of never-worn dresses. I pushed my hand through its armhole and inhaled a mixture of Beechnut chew, chalk dust from the kaolin mines nearby, peppermint and cold weather, black coffee, seeds and grains. She'd left two buckeyes inside the left-hand pocket, the one with the stuffing poking out.

In the kitchen, I tugged on the string hanging from the yellow bulb. That bulb always hummed, and it was humming then. I pulled my chair out from underneath our table, making the chair legs squawk across the linoleum. She was supposed to bang pots, wake the house, not me. I started some coffee perking, flipped on her weather radio. I didn't like my new role. I rubbed my fingers over her peach gingham oilcloth. Winds blew northeast at ten miles per hour. She had a thing for chicken paraphernalia. Chickens on hand towels, chickens on birdhouses, chickens on fly swatters. I held the salt shaker in one hand and the pepper shaker in the other and glided them, two roosters, across the oilcloth. I hummed them a waltz. A black iron skillet hung above her stove. It belonged to somebody way back, but I couldn't remember who. I spent the rest of that night thinking up questions that had answers only she could give. When the sun broke over her cow pastures and demanded another day out of me, I was thinking of my mother and of all the places she might have gone.

Uncle Roy, the businessman, the eldest, showed up first. Grandma Martin used to say he was a good son, the way he remembered to beat mud off his boots at the backdoor stoop. When I heard his boots knocking on concrete I said, "Come on in. I'm back here in the kitchen."

"Well, Cora," he said, his large frame filling our doorway, "none of us wanted it. But she had gotten feeble." He sighed and added, "So the story goes." His words sounded rehearsed, and I started to tell him so, just in case he thought I was too young and dumb to notice. I had learned what intuition meant, and I was intuitive. I could intuit, for instance, that he had a knack for pure jackass. He didn't put his arms around me, didn't pat me on the shoulder. He just moved right along, said, "I'll be in charge of arrangements."

Later, when I listened through the vent upstairs, I heard him on the phone, saying to his good buddy, "By God, she can stay on here, but she'll go to work full-time." And that was that. I started the breakfast, dinner, and supper shift uptown at The Red-Bellied Diner. I wasn't but eighteen, but then, as everyone told me, I am damn lucky she saw me to eighteen.

Her stories remain. During the summer months, on the edge of nightfall, Grandma Martin filled my baby hands with cracked corn and millet, bird feed for the bobwhite. Together, in our pajamas and housecoats, we stood at the edge of her two hundred and fifty odd acres of newly planted loblolly.

One day those pines will be worth something, Uncle Roy was known to say. I'll cut those suckers down and make a killing. Those pines are green gold. Even then he was famous for zapping a good thing going. Luckily he only popped by during daylight hours. In the evenings we didn't have to hear him talk about how much an acre of raked pine straw was worth.

In the evenings, only she and I stood at the cusp. *Bob White*, we mimicked in the darkness. *Bob White*, the brown-and-white-patterned bird resounded. *Cora*, she said, *it could be your granddaddy's spirit.* In good faith, we released the seed, which sprayed over the straw and sounded like pellets of hail. Feeding the birds became our ritual, a way for a widowed lady who lived nine miles south of town to entertain the gaps between her granddaughter's suppertime and bedtime. Most nights, after the birds were fed, we went inside and curled up on the ratty couch underneath her orange and brown afghan, Beechnut scented even still, and drifted off to reruns of *Bonanza*.

476

Once I heard her good friend Sandy ask if she ever felt stuck raising me. These are your best years, Sandy said, the retirement years. These are the years to see Jerusalem.

No, I heard her say. We invent things to pass time. We get by.

There were ladybugs always. By my bed, growing up, there was an endless supply of company trapped in gold-topped mason jars. Grasshoppers, katydids, butterflies, lightning bugs.

You're naked as a jaybird. I'd run through her old house, after my bubble bath, in all of my glory. *Jaybird died with the whooping cough,* she'd sing, her voice a tad hoarse. In the winter she kept blue flannel sheets on my bed, and when I got tucked in, she was ready with Rumplestiltskin and the Ugly Duckling.

"Mama," Uncle Roy used to say, "that gravel in your voice will kill you dead. Don't you remember Daddy? He hacked his way to heaven."

Nonsense, she'd say. She swore by buckeyes, bottle trees, calamine lotion, by not going out with a wet head, by not eating fish and ice cream at the same meal.

Later, we, the Hebron, Georgia community, a speck on the map they say survives because of the mines, would discover that kaolin, the shiny chalk the locals call white gold, could make our lungs patched as leopards. We became known for going down in coughing fits. Five years ago, when we first met at her bedside, in Room 104 of the Good Shepherd nursing home, it was Nurse Ox who clarified kaolin pneumoconiosis for me. He showed me the spots on her x-ray.

Just the other day, I returned to The Good Shepherd. I walked right down her hallway on the way to the hospital cafeteria. The nursing home is attached to the hospital, a real convenience, a selling point. If your mama or daddy needs the emergency room, well, they can be hooked up in five seconds or less.

I didn't have to go through the old folks' section to find food. I could have gone through Labor and Delivery, the mostly happy section, but I took the hard way. It has been five years. I felt like I was up for the test. New risks are finding me on a daily basis, it seems, so I figured what the hell.

Last month I started my first real job, a secretarial position in Right of Way at the Highway Department. All the ladies there, almost all of them two decades older than me, think they can control their blood pressure by eating at the hospital, which is just not the truth, seeing as how we still have to decide between lemon pie and chocolate fudge cake and banana pudding. I am going to make a habit of grabbing cold apple pie and turning it into a wonder. There is a microwave. There is a soft-serve ice cream maker. I can make a difference in that pie's life.

Around ten every morning, we, the ladies, take a break and discuss cravings. What we hope they are serving, what we hope they are not. They make good collards. Their meatloaf last week and the week before kind of stunk. Not enough ketchup on top. Too much gristle, I said on Wednesday, speaking up. When they agreed, I knew they were going to let me be one of the bunch.

I'd driven three of the ladies over: Dorothy, Mira, and Shelby. My car is a Civic with 240,000 miles racked up and cantankerous as all get out. When we made it to the hospital, I dropped them off at the entrance of Labor and Delivery and told them to scoot on through and snag us a table. I'd be back in a jiff, I said, I just needed to park in front of the nursing home and run in and hug my great aunt Ruthie's neck. I don't have an aunt Ruthie. But once upon a time, I did have a Room 104, and as I stood just inside that room for the first time again, what I heard was the familiar piano intro for *The Young & the Restless*. The sound of that piano, what Nurse Ox called the nursing home dinner bell, echoed all the way down the hall, every television glued to the 12:30 story. Will Nikki and Victor ever die?

A woman was propped up in the bed my grandma died on. Her tongue was caked with white film. Without trying, I could just about see her tonsils. Her head was cocked funny; she had large, hairy ears. Her toenails poked up from underneath a thin blue blanket. The room, it smelled of Pine Sol and eggs and shit. I didn't have the right to stare, but being in this place could make people forget their rights.

She never wanted to be dropped off here. She said she'd just as soon go out into her woods and find a bed of straw, but Uncle Roy said hogwash. They've got what you need up there, he said. He reminded her of the emergency-room perk.

I remember one of the nurses, the one not to be trusted, the one with boingy, uncontrollable hair, the red-haired one who flipped my grandma over and yanked her diaper off in front of me and said, smiling a not-sweet smile, "Whew. This itty bitty baby has made a stinky." My grandmother's butt bones were blades as thin and pale as bird ribs. Not much flesh left, just small sacks of bruised skin dangling from sharp edges. She used to sing to me: *Head and shoulders, knees and toes, knees and toes.*

"Cora, is that you?" Nurse Ox asked, startling me. He was pushing a cart filled with ice, grape juice, apple juice, orange juice, ginger ale, and Sprite into the room, smiling. I had sampled them all. Grape was best in the morning. "You come to visit Ms. Ellen?"

"No," I said, and watched him slide her body up by putting his hands on each side of her rib cage, exactly as you would do if you were lifting your baby from the crib. I am shocked by his lost weight, by the purple bags that have blossomed underneath his eyes. He is not well.

"Sweet pea," he said coaxingly, "you need to take a few sips. We can count them together."

"Who is that woman in my room?" Ms. Ellen's wobbly hand was tangled up in a line that hooked to her vein, and I could see she was angry with me. "I can hold it," she said, and grabbed for the child's-size plastic cup. "You tell her to get on. She doesn't belong in here. You hear me, Ox?" Her eyebrows were bushy and wild.

"Ms. Ellen, this is Cora!" He shouted a little, and I couldn't tell if she was hard of hearing or if he was just trying to lend her his enthusiasm. "You knew her grandmother. Ms. Martin, remember? You said you two went to grade school together. I'm about to take her granddaughter out for lunch."

"Oh," she said. "Oh." She bowed her head, changed her tune. "Well. That's fine then," she said, and straightened a crease in her blanket. "You need somebody, Ox."

I didn't eat lunch with him that day, but I did the next. I skipped out on the ladies and let Nurse Ox pick me up from a side road and drive me to Wendy's for a loaded baked potato and a Frosty. He bit into his old-fashioned burger and said I was good-looking, that that little tidbit had never flown past him, but that he was still working on not being separated from his wife and kids.

He was good company, but I wasn't thinking about dating him. No matter, he said, and told me about his cousin, John, who lives in Athens and who used to drive a chicken truck for a living. Granddaddy tried to call him Mule, Ox said, but John never cared for granddaddy much. Music, he said. John loves good music. I wouldn't find nobody more my speed, he said. "And what speed is that?" I asked him. All he allowed was, "I know what it is. Don't you worry, I know."

I didn't tell him I was married with a kid. He didn't ask. Besides, in a small town, there's no need to tell. You just go on and assume everybody is updated. I held on to his napkin; he'd written John's email address on it and called it a gift. "You stick this gift in your family Bible," he said. "Don't lose it."

"Ox," I said. "I'm finished with people thinking I need a handout."

"Gift," he said. "It's a gift, and I insist."

It was all weird, and yet Nurse Ox, the caregiver, could not have caught me more slumped. I had committed to somebody for the long haul, but that haul was looking even longer than I could have conjured.

Now, six weeks later, I hear a whippoorwill while waiting for Rick, the husband I don't imagine I've ever loved, to get our son, Daniel, out of his car seat. He has parked on the other side of Kentucky, afraid somebody might dent his new car.

I consider pointing this bird's voice out to him, but he said, just the other night, "Goddammit, honey. She is all you talk about. Do you really think people give a rat's ass about what she used to say?" He meant Grandma Martin, who used to tell me about the whippoorwills. He was rooting for Clint Eastwood, one of his shoot-'em-up movie stars, when I'd tried to convince him to walk out to our tiny concrete backyard and admire a chipping sparrow's nest lined with horsehair. Sometimes I think his ass could use a little birdshot.

Daniel slips out of the car seat and curls his arms around his daddy's neck. They have the same hair, wavy brown, prone to cowlicks. We are blocks over from La Hacienda, Madge's favorite restaurant. Madge is my mother-in-law. She requires that we come here for supper every Thursday. I'd rather wait in the parking lot and see if I can't hear what that whippoorwill is saying, but Rick wouldn't allow that. That would seem nutty.

"Let's hurry," he says, so we hurry. I rub my buckeyes together and head toward the sombrero hat lit up red and green.

Last night I discovered that I feel her presence best when I am blessed with a red bird in the yard. At work today I wrote this to John, who has been showing up in my inbox. I am discovering that sometimes I don't know I know things until I write them. I believe that red bird is her sticking close by me, I wrote.

John never says I'm nutty. He doesn't even imply such. He says anything is possible. Come to find out, John still lives in Athens, Georgia, plays old country and blues for WUOG every Friday night between three a.m. and six. Pooped or not, he's there. Holidays, it doesn't matter. Unless he's out on the highway, which he's cut back on over the years, he's there. No dead air. He says a lot of prisoners call in and make requests. He mentioned this in an email after I requested he blare Loretta Lynn's "Fist City" for his devoted listeners.

Inside, Madge has her eyes locked on me. She is wearing Rudolph on her sweatshirt, and his nose blinks red. Christmas Eve is tomorrow. Her mouth is pinched into a tight little bow, and she uses a bent spoon to crush the ice in her Coke. She says she can't stand ice unless it's crushed.

"Sorry we're late," I say, and slide into our usual booth, the one with ripped red vinyl.

"Well, Cora," she says, and pauses. "It's not like I expect the world."

She motions for Daniel to come over and give her some sugar, and I give him a gentle shove in her direction. I know she wonders about the glue caked in her grandson's hair, wonders why Daniel, being three and all, is out at La Hacienda in his Winnie the Pooh pajamas, the ones with the ketchup stain on the collar. Daniel kisses her left cheek, and she turns her head, expecting one on the right too. But Daniel drops underneath the table. Both shoes come off.

"Son," I say, and duck my head. "Come out from under there. It's nasty." These moments are tough. I search for Rick, but he's got his elbow propped up on the back of Trey Barker's booth. Trey Barker was valedictorian of their high school class. They're talking about shooting deer. "Please," I say. "If you want that ice cream when we get home, how is it you have to act?"

"Maybe you ought to just get him," Madge says to me. She told Rick one night on the phone that I cause her blood pressure to spike, and when they hung up Rick asked me in all sincerity why it is I am hell-bent on killing his poor mother.

"Please," I say again.

"No!"

"Kids," I say and give Madge a weary-mother smile, one of hopeful camaraderie, but she has a red tortilla chip sticking out of the right side of her mouth. Her nostrils flare a bit, like she might've just smelled something ferocious.

"Kids," she says, and admires a nearby couple whose one-year-old is distinguishing farm animals on a child's placemat. "How cute and well behaved," she adds. "So," she says, "are you still thriving as the secretary in Right of Way?"

"Just a minute." I slink underneath the table and find my son. Madge's feet, pasty and swollen, puff over her maroon shoes and remind me of muffin tops. Down here it's shaded, and I too wish I could

481

stay hidden. "Come here, Daniel," I say, and take his upper arm in the palm of one hand. He resists. "It's not polite to sit on the floor," I say. "C'mon. Let's stand up."

"Not now!" He claws my pants with a handful of saliva. I can feel every one of his small muscles go tense.

"Yes now!" I yank his arm with all of my strength, but he has nailed himself to turquoise shag and won't turn loose. He has more stamina than Jesus.

"Daniel," Rick says, suddenly there, startling both of us. "Your little behind better be out from under that table by the time I get to two. One." Rick's man-sized hands are on his bent knees, and he peers down into the corner where his son's mouth is frozen into a shocked O. "Don't you let me get to two."

Daniel's mouth unhinges, goes slack. His eyes become hound-doggish. He eases up through the gap between the cushion and the table and sits on Madge's side just as pretty as you please. He even gives his father an extra helping of emotional advantage, letting his shoulders slump forward dramatically, as if to say *I'm yours*.

"Now," Rick says, barrel-chested. "You stay there and act right."

I see Madge's teeth for the first time tonight. She does not even try to suppress the grin that sprawls across her face. "Here baby," she says, and shovels a spoonful of yellow rice into Daniel's mouth, says, "You mind your daddy. He's a good man. I know. I raised him."

Daniel falls asleep on the car ride home, which affords me about ten minutes before I have to cajole him. Then it's Please take off those pajamas so they can be washed, please get in the tub, please use soap, please get out of the tub, please don't slip, please put on these clean pajamas, please put the tag in the back, please brush your teeth, please brush the back ones, please get in the bed, please stay in the bed, please don't get up again, please, please don't make me get your daddy.

I glance back at our son and wonder if I could just leave him in the car overnight. What could possibly happen? It's December. Too cold. But maybe if it were fall, spring. I would leave the windows cracked. Could I do it, if I were alone, if no one would ever know? He almost always sleeps the night through. Getting him to go to sleep is the tough part. His eyelashes are long. He looks like the cherub he often is not.

I take my feet out of my shoes and prop them on the dashboard, a habit that irritates Rick. I remember walking beside her, early summer, late afternoon. We walked by dirt daubers clinging to skeleton shacks. We saw where termites had infested wood and eaten through aqua-outlined windowsills. In front of Mr. Wiley's place stood what she called a bottle tree, a funny-looking thing on top of a hill that always caught a breeze. Grandma Martin spoke of spirits trapped inside, their whistle, their endless *boo*. The branches, robbed of leaves, swayed in a way that made it known that the tree still lived.

Past Wiley's place was our white wooden church. One Saturday a month, she and I opened the front doors of Piney Mount Methodist to Windex and to Pledge. I slid down iron railings while she rearranged hymnals, dusted the vestibule. Just as often, it was our turn to stuff the preacher. Sky-blue asters were painted on the yellow dishes, the delicate ones, the preacher-come-to-visit dishes. Sweeping the church steps beside her renewed my faith. The worst sin, she said, is to withdraw from the fire of the spirit. *Cora, are you listening for the spirit?*

I look back again at my son, who has managed to twist his whole body over in his seat. Despite the buckle, his bottom rocks in the air defiantly. How could I have thought of leaving him alone in a car all night? I reach over and turn up the volume on the radio. I concentrate on getting my act together. Rick prefers 105.7, easy listening turned down low, which serves to remind me that whole seasons have passed since I heard music. Grandma Martin sang hymns for sustenance. To be born again, I imagine, would be to walk down that dirt road, her hand in mine, to be able to sing along to one more hymn, to introduce Daniel to her, to see what she could make of all my mess. But there is no use in thinking like that. The bulldozer came and tore Mr. Wiley's place down, and I don't know whatever happened to that bottle tree, but it is gone, stump and all. The road got paved. Even the church has fallen in.

Rick drums his fingers on the steering wheel. He drives a Toyota Corolla, white, beige interior, A/C, excellent condition. The passenger window turns into a mirror at night. I find the outline of my nose, my chin, my lips. I cannot see my eyes, although I reach up and touch the tips of my cheekbones, right where the sockets curve like gentle U's. I used to watch her pray for holy light. Her eyelids wrinkled tight, her palms clasped, knuckles turned white. At the kitchen table, I watched her lips move. With the sort of praying she could do, there was never need to worry that God might be unwilling to provide. I remember the grittiness of Dixie Crystals spread across oil cloth, granules that slipped from her morning cup of Sanka. While she blessed breakfast, I peeked, patted each sugar square, licked my fingertips clean. After the blessing, she never failed to turn up the local radio station so we could hum and sway, listen to the obituaries made less alarming by the doses of Seeds From the Sower that followed them, the sixty-second daily devotional all the way from Metter, Georgia.

"Cora," Rick says. He clicks the music off. "Honestly, it is embarrassing."

He wants me to probe, but I won't.

"Are you listening?" he asks.

"Yes."

"It's embarrassing how you can't control Daniel in public."

I nod in agreement but without devotion to the matter, a nod that says fine, fine, you're right, of course you are, now let's drop it. He's not going to drop it, though. He uses his pointer finger to turn my chin toward him. Here we go.

"What?" I am forced to stare into his eyes. I look, a rare occasion. His eyes are solid brown, lifeless loafers. "What?"

"You listen," he says, revving up. "And I mean, you listen good." His tone is a mixture of dependable irritation and split-second panic. It is the dash of panic that intrigues me; I detect an unusual hint of shrillness in him. "I saw Ms. Evelyn in the bank this afternoon. She came up to me, and I *knew* it wasn't good. She said she hated to bother me, but she just thought I should know that you can hardly get Daniel in the car when you pick him up. She says you're always trailing in after everybody else has been picked up. That true?"

I turn away and roll the window down. I try to inhale all of Hebron, this town that is proud of its technical school, Hebron Technical Institute, where Rick teaches. He calls himself a Professor of Electricity.

"Tell me," Rick says.

I don't tell him that I think I should have just had dogs. He wouldn't go for that. He's not particularly fond of that sort of honesty. We've tried open communication. It doesn't work. Our Shepherd mix got its little head crushed by a FedEx truck last summer.

"Are you deaf?" he asks. The twinge of fear I thought I heard has faded. He's gone to the other side. Meanness. "You're useless," he says. "And close the damn window. You're letting all of the heat out." He turns the radio up, just a hair, enough to let me know I can't really hear it.

At the red light on Washington Street, I look over at Hebron brightening with high hopes. It is Christmas. The town, which did not get connected to the interstate, has turned on white bulbs that dance in a canopy of otherwise spindly trees. A large spruce pine leans to one side in front of the courthouse. Hundreds of bulbs weigh it down. One shines in memory of her. The light turns green and we circle the courthouse, which is surrounded by empty stores, one right after another. This time of year, locals, daring anyone to call their town dead, strand colored lights around deserted windows, doorframes. All of these stores are known for what they used to be. That used to be James Brantley's shoe shop, and that used to be Doc Johnson's dime store. Their emptiness is hard to imagine.

But everyone talks about the coffee shop, the one real bright light. Avis Horton who lived in Atlanta and moved back to Hebron said that a town without a coffee shop is a town without a college. She calls the Technical Institute "Hebron College." So there her storefront sits, alive and well, advertising peppermint hot chocolate, eggnog lattes. A young woman, not much younger than me, auburn hair, natural looking except for bright red lips, stands underneath the tin awning, pretending to read a thick book in the dark. She seems to be anxiously awaiting someone. Her skirt is short, dark green tweed. She's not from around here. She looks like her life is about to begin.

We round the corner, and I reach down to roll the window up. I think of telling Rick every truth, how lately I have been bringing sixty dollars with me every afternoon when I go and get Daniel, how they charge two dollars for each minute parents make teachers wait after six o'clock, how I can see bony Ms. Evelyn's face peering out from Daniel's classroom window, staring down the asphalt drive, ready to make the exchange. How thirty minutes of free time between getting off work as a secretary and starting work as a wife and mother is worth sixty dollars a day, three hundred dollars a week. I want him to know how broke I have become.

I want to tell him I am lost without my grandmother's home, her presence, her love, even though I know how silly that must sound, how flimsy and self-indulgent. I want to kick my feet against this dashboard, as our son does, to throw a pure hissy fit, the kind that makes your veins pop until someone notices your need and promises to fulfill it. I want to tell him how ridiculous it is that this John-stranger keeps writing, keeps asking for more, more stories of her, more stories of me. I want to tell my husband how all during supper tonight, all I wanted was to punch his mother in the face and push her over a cliff, then hurry home and begin again the game of crafting and waiting for Yahoo messages.

"They must be cleaning it," he says, matter-of-factly. We are passing by the technical school. The light is on in his classroom. His tone has flipped to nonchalant, and I know this line is supposed to propel us through the transition.

"Yes," I say. "They must be cleaning it."

He turns right on Deer Crossing. We never have to look for deer. They never cross. He makes a left on Mulberry and a right on Savannah, another left on Whispering Pines. We pull into our driveway at the end of the cul-de-sac. Our headlights shine on our green vinyled house, an institutional green. When Madge and Rick went to look for Rick's house, there were three colors to choose from: green, beige, and white. I didn't know Rick back then, but I know now that his mother chose.

Rick cradles Daniel's sleeping body, and I unlock our front door. Daniel's rabbit nightlight is on, a present given to him by Madge. The plastic bunny leaps into the air, his mouth agape with frozen joy, buck-toothed and unabashed. Rick pulls the Christopher Robin covers back with one hand and eases our son into bed. He strokes Daniel's head and uses his thumb to wipe shiny drool away from Daniel's chin. His son smells of tired little boy, salty and tart.

As soon as Rick hops into the shower, I rush to the dark nook near the kitchen where his laptop sits. Rick takes short showers. I enter my password. I wait. This computer is slow. Too slow.

Last month, Ms. Evelyn helped Daniel mail a wish list to Santa. It arrived in our mailbox a couple of weeks ago. I drove forty miles to the Milledgeville Mall, the nearest one, what people around here call the Small Mall, with the intention of buying all of the meaningful people gifts, all the cousins and coworkers, but I ended up with a chocolate chip cookie from The Cookie Factory and a Belk's plaid scarf for Rochelle, Rick's sister, whose name I drew at Madge's annual Thanksgiving get-together. She lives in Atlanta, and she looks and acts like it. Last year, when she drew my name, she presented me with a book called *The Purpose-Driven Life: What on Earth Am I Here For?*

I broke off some of my cookie and shared it with a tiny, respectful girl who rode a blue paint-chipped carousel horse. Santa was there. He sat between Walden-books and the U.S. Army Recruiter's. When I walked by Premier One Nails, he waved at me, and I realized he was young and thin, not at all Santa-like. I circled Eckerd Drugs and

486

Goody's and Hallmark to see if he would wave again, and when he threw his hand up, abundantly clear, I smiled and thought more about bringing Daniel.

Madge has been hounding me to take Daniel to sit on Santa's lap, telling me, "Cora, dear, if you don't have a picture of him on Santa's lap, you will live to regret it." Tonight I told her that of course, of course we went. I told her that I am having the photograph framed in silver and gold, a Christmas present to everyone, and that yes, yes of course he was wearing the green velvety vest with the nativity scene she gave to him.

Which of course is untrue. Inbox (3). I click. I wait.

It was wintertime, almost one year after she died, when I met Rick. He and his church buddies would come for Sunday-night supper at The Red-Bellied, and he always ordered the special: cubed steak, mashed potatoes, turnips, biscuit, never cornbread. When Rick asked around about me, one of his students who used to attend my high school and who now works for Uncle Roy told him that my uncle said that he could do the world a favor and save my life. This boy, Poochie, said, "Ask her out, man. It's obvious she needs somebody."

And so Rick thought he saw a life that needed saving. He tells me this from time to time. He says, "It doesn't matter if you want me. You need me." He claims he has gone on mission trips to the North Georgia Mountains. Four hours from Hebron is the farthest he has gotten, but he says he has seen enough to let him know that the whole world is wide open to his talents. He can pray with the needy, and he can fill their dark houses with electricity. What more could people ask for, Madge jokes proudly, than to have a son who is a man of the Lord, who can preach and bring light.

(1) Madge Branson: Don't forget! You have to bring potato salad tomorrow night.
(2) Your Saved Search @ 1-800-Save-A-Pet.com: We found a pet for you!
(3) John Hall: Do you want to sit in on my shift tomorrow night?

"Cora," Rick says.

I jump. He is walking down the stairs. Shit. Shift? Where? WUOG? I click the white X in the red box at the top right-hand corner. Suddenly there is nothing but a rolling hill, bright green grass, blue, blue sky and a smattering of icons.

"I don't have any clean socks," he says, hovering over me.

"Yes you do," I say, and point him to the laundry room.

Two months after my first date with Rick, I drove the nine miles from my Grandma Martin's house to the tech school. Rick was in Room 34, teaching Poochie and others the art of rewiring. I tapped on the glass, and Rick excused himself. We found the student lounge, a smoke-filled TV room with a drink-and-candy machine. He asked for a dollar. I dug into my pocket and found four quarters. Together, we waited for a Mello Yello to drop. A commercial advertised moisturizing lotion. An alligator crawled across the screen.

I told him about the test, how I had taken two of them. I told him about the clinic I'd heard about in Atlanta. I told him I didn't need a single thing from him.

"Marry me," he said, looking not at me but at the alligator. "Now you definitely need me. You'd be a fool to think otherwise."

I didn't argue. It was six a.m. when Dr. Davis placed Daniel, 9 lbs., 6 oz., on the outside of my stomach. I held his thumb. His eyes were grayish-blue, his head still anointed in my blood. Terrified, I told the nurse, when she asked how I was feeling. I am terrified by the holy responsibility of it all. She said, "Oh, it's not so scary. People do it all the time."

Madge, ever vigilant, stood by my bedside, right where Grandma Martin should have been. She grabbed my hand and held on tight, said, "Well, he is here now." Her face contained desperate disappointment. I reached for my skirt, which was draped over the metal chair, which hid the buckeyes in its pocket, but I didn't know how to ask for what I needed, and they would not let me get up from the bed.

"Yes, he is," the nurse said, happy, optimistic: "A big, healthy boy."

The way the nurse stroked my other hand reminded me of the way the Clinique lady at Belk's uses a makeup sponge to dab my cheeks lightly. Foundation will hide your flaws, she says.

"I'm taking the laptop with me," Rick says now, pulling the cord out of the socket. I know I will not be able to check my email again until work tomorrow. We never go to bed together. He stays outside in a shed he built for himself, doing God knows, praying for people and studying his Bible is what he says, and by the time he comes to bed I've been long asleep.

My boss leaves at noon. "Merry Christmas, everybody," he says, throwing his hand up over my cubicle. He has to scoot to Bi-Lo, where they have his wife's congealed salad—lime with pineapple chunks, not his favorite—and her deviled eggs waiting for pickup. He has to get ready to attend his mother-in-law's Christmas Eve shindig. "It would be great if you all stayed until three before shutting down," he says to me.

The ladies and I lock up at 12:10.

"Where are you heading?" Dorothy asks me.

"I don't know," I say, and watch Mira and Shelby pull out of the parking lot. A Christmas wreath is hooked to the grill of Mira's Beretta. Today Shelby wore dangling candy canes in her ears. Dorothy is unadorned, and I feel safe. "Yeah, I do," I say. "I'm heading to Athens later this evening."

This morning I wrote to him and said, "I can't imagine being anywhere else tonight." He forwarded a photograph of himself. He is bending over and offering a piece of beef to a skinny stray, a matted-hair mutt he found sniffing up Atlanta Highway. "That's Jack Sprat," the caption reads, "and I am going to make him fat." John's eyes, a bluish-green soda bottle. His grin, devilish but not smirky.

"Athens?" she asks. "What in the world for?"

"Hot date."

"You're joking," she says. She knows I'm married.

"I promise I'll tell you when I get back."

"All right," she says, and climbs into her truck, a red Nissan Frontier. "I'll be waiting."

She doesn't probe, a good sign. "Save a story for me too," I say.

"You know how it is," she says, and I nod and watch her drive away to what I imagine to be her own family drama. She has become my girl-crush, someone I hope I can let in one inch at a time. Years have passed since I've had what could be called a best friend. I feel rusty.

I've never been to Athens. I hear it's big, bigger than Hebron, smaller than Atlanta. The University of Georgia is there. Used to, Grandma Martin and I witnessed Dawg fans fly down Highway 15, their cars and trucks splattered with red and black. Madge says freaks go there. That's why she sent her darling Rochelle to Georgia Tech, even if it did mean her baby had to brave I-75. Suffering Atlanta is an act of courage. If you survive Atlanta, you gloat. Once a year, Uncle Roy has to drive up that way for a farm parts convention. I merged, he says. I about got swiped, he says. Juggled twelve lanes. You follow the speed limit, you're a dead duck.

Two lanes, country roads, take me to where I am heading tonight. I have fooled around town for as long as I can, and it is finally getting late enough to leave. I get on the Macon Highway and it starts to drizzle. What am I doing? What am I thinking? For the past five years, I have shown up for Madge's Christmas Eve, for every Thursday night #6 cheese enchilada, beef taco, rice plate. I called Madge on my coffee break this morning, told her she could pick Daniel up from day care. He'll curl up on her lap and they'll watch weatherman Bill Powell track Santa on radar over middle Georgia. I didn't say that I wouldn't be back tonight.

It was Christmastime, damp and cold, when they buried her. At the gravesite I bowed my head and focused on an inch of jaundice-colored Johnson grass between the tips of my shiny black shoes. The blades, soft as carpet during spring, had turned brittle as weak bones. Everything felt collapsed. You're weak, Rick has said. My mother raised me, Rob, and Rochelle with half the trouble. When are you going to grow up, stop looking for a mommy, and start acting like one?

Sometimes, in these emails, I go too far. I take flying lessons, tame mechanical bulls at honky-tonks, kiss rattlesnakes. Evel Knievel has nothing on me. I walk tightropes for fun. My mother is on tour, a Russian ballerina. I am younger than I am. My poor pop died crossing the Rio Grande. I have not mentioned Rick, or Daniel. The chapter in my life I have tried to give with complete precision is the years spent with her. The rest of the story has holes.

John started UGA, I know that much, a history-education major. He says he has two semesters left, but he doesn't know if he can finish them off. It's not looking too good. It's been four years since he quit. He got involved with WUOG, started working at Pilgrim's Pride's chicken-processing plant on Pryor Street, worked up to Transportation Logistics Specialist. The other night I got an email entitled *Anhydrous Ammonia Sucks*. A small amount is needed, he says, to produce methamphetamine. *Did you know a hundred pounds of ammonia escaped from a damaged valve and floated over Athens? Yeah. Some asshole at our chicken plant wanted to get hold of an ingredient. Ammonia will scrap your lungs and make you miss breathing.*

He misses the old Ox. My hard-headed cousin ought to leave that shit alone, he says.

Leaving Hebron is not nearly as damn difficult as people make it out to be. Athens is a pretty clear shot. The Texaco Station on Prince Avenue, where he said he'd be, isn't hard to find.

I'm in his truck now. John ekes two more drops of Regular. Jack

490

Sprat has named me friend. His big head is propped up on my thigh. I can see my Civic from John's passenger window, parked nearby his Ford. Once, I read a trash novel about a wife who is about to cheat. She pulls up into a parking lot, deserted, a seedy old motel's, and parks next to her lover's El Camino. A bluish yard light flickers, makes a zingy sound, shines down on her as she walks toward devilment. She climbs the stairs and finds the room number where the sin is going to take place. Just before she knocks, she leans over the balcony and notices how snuggly the roof of his vehicle looks next to hers. I bet she hoped the rest of her days were going to be cozy central.

"You need anything?" John asks.

"I'm doing fine," I say, and watch him go inside to pay. Fabric droops perfectly from his truck's ceiling. There are cracker crumbs, plastic wrappers. A few empty Coke cans and a smattering of CDs on the floorboard. He is tall, wiry, knobby-kneed. It's windy, and his thinning hair flies easily. Even-keeled, he is. Inside, he stands in front of the candy section. He holds a couple of sweets up to the store window, and I get to nod yes or no. I look down through the window and see my driver's seat. I stuck my wedding ring underneath there.

"Here," he says, when he returns. He hands me a bag of salt and vinegar potato chips and a package of peanut M&Ms. He lets Jack Sprat gnaw on beef jerky. "I found you something sweet and something not so sweet," he says. He doesn't ask what a young woman like myself is doing out with a stranger like himself on Christmas Eve. He doesn't allude to other lives, other plans. We ride on.

"Where are you carrying me?" I ask. He wrote that he has somewhere outside of Athens, out in the country, that he wants to show me before his radio shift. "What's the surprise?"

"It's a surprise," he says, reminding me.

I focus on taking enough breaths, slow and deep. Rhythmic. Last week, on aisle nine, I abandoned a whole cart of groceries. Going to the back of Bi-Lo for a jug of milk felt like too much of a goal for me. I nearly knocked over a display of guacamole Doritos trying to get me and Daniel out to fresh air. The other morning, I allowed that craziness to slip to Dorothy, but she just said, "Oh yeah, honey. A panic attack. When I was with Larry, I got them all the time."

"You mentioned your grandma liked music. You like this?" he asks.

"Sure," I say, but I haven't been paying attention. Rick hates it when I don't pay attention to everything he pays attention to. I listen, but inside I feel shaky. What am I doing? What am I thinking?

491

"You mind if I turn it up?" he asks.

I remember my mother's face. There was a photograph on top of Grandma Martin's pie safe. When I was a kid I'd drive a red tricycle through the kitchen and stare into my mother's eyes. The photograph was black and white, but Grandma Martin said the dress my mother wore was aqua with red buttons. All of my life I had stared at that one dress. She was thirteen, fourteen maybe, and she was smiling. What color, I wonder, was the dress she wore the day she left?

"God, no. That would be great," I say, sounding starved.

Both windows are rolled down. "You can move that if you need to," he says, and points to the floorboard.

I look down. Both of my feet are propped up on his jumper cables. Rand McNally's Road Atlas is on the dash. The cold night air fills our lungs, and as he shares his sour neon worms I start to realize that he has been in a place where he knows what it is like to need something badly. I take a swig of his Coke, and when I press my lips on the can where his have been, I think, if this was my real life, we might stand a chance. The lights of Athens are behind us, and we pass a sign that says we are heading toward Jefferson, another small town. I unlatch my seat belt and twist around. He turns on his signal and we climb up a dirt road called Mavis Lane. The brake lights turn the dust red, and I think about how many years it has been since somebody offered me a joyride into the country.

"My mother," I say for the first time, possibly ever, "left me when I was a baby. If we met on the road, we would not recognize each other." He touches my hand for a moment, just enough for the veins in my body to feel like they are sweating. Rick was my first and last. I'm not familiar with reactions.

But all he says is "Hold on a minute." He pulls the truck around to the side of a rust-splotched white trailer perched on nearly flat tires and pats my knee. "Thom," he shouts. "Are you here, buddy?" We sit for a moment, the engine idling, and stare at this man's spot. A pit bull is chained to a dead tree, making enough racket for ten dogs. I start to get spooked. "Don't let this place scare you," he says. "Thom's been down on his luck, but he's a decent fellow."

"All right," I say, and hold Jack Sprat, whose neck strains for all it's worth, barking sass right back.

"Let's hop out." He shuts off the ignition and comes around and gets my door. "Friendly won't bite you if you don't look him in the eye. Ain't that right, Friendly?" He tells the dog he's going to unhook him from the tree. He says he can't stand to see a chained animal. "Don't worry," he says to me. "I'll wait till we're set up inside." He grabs Jack Sprat by the collar and drags him along. We walk up to the porch and he pulls a key out from underneath a dying cactus drooped over in a clay pot. There is a window with three panes, a Kroger bag taped over the missing one. The wind causes the plastic to rattle. I can see a child's truck on the kitchen counter. Right now, I think, Daniel is under Madge's table. "Thom," he shouts. "We're coming in on you."

But he didn't need to hunt down a key. The door isn't locked. It swings open, and inside old handheld church fans are stuck to brown paneling. If there are lights, John doesn't flick them on. "Thom," he hollers again. Over the mantelpiece are photographs of MLK, JFK, Muddy Waters, Minnie Pearl. John names them all and turns my attention to a wall lined with albums. Two Christmas stockings are hung from a lopsided coat rack. One says Thom, the other says Friendly. "I reckon he's gone," he says, and slides a record out of its sleeve, holding it like a newborn. I watch him blow dust from vinyl. He throws a bunch of newspapers from the stained couch to the stained carpet and takes a seat. "Ox says you miss music. Why don't you put this record on?" He looks up at me, his eyes bright, the record a gift.

"All right," I say. I can't help the grin. "It's been a long time," I say. "I don't want to scratch it."

"You won't," he says.

"All right." I walk over to the record player and lift the plastic lid. I take a long, deep breath and slip the needle onto the first groove. A soft *shh* follows, a grainy static. I turn around and face John, but I'm thinking of her. The sound causes my chest to tighten. Jack Sprat is sitting in the middle of the couch, John on the right. I walk to the couch and sit on the left. He waits to see if I'll ask the dog to move, but I don't. I feel like I am on my first date, shy, new, and terribly excited.

John strokes the back of Jack Sprat's neck and tells me we are listening to Townes Van Zandt, a man who sings about the highway kind. "You ought to know I have a wife," he says between songs. "But we're separated. Who knows who the hell she's with tonight." He scratches Jack Sprat's head harder, his nails digging in. He looks out the window, away from me, long enough to let me know he hasn't separated from her at all. She's here in this room, tonight, right here with us. He needs somebody to talk to, but I'm not her. My heart aches. I feel like a fool.

"I didn't bring you here to talk about this," he says.

493

"I know you didn't," I say, and reach up and scratch Jack Sprat's neck, right below John's hand. I think of tidbits withheld: husband, child. The score is even-steven. I try to sit tall. I try to sit like I don't mind this.

"Go out there and take a look," he says, picking his hand up and pointing to the door. I ease up off the couch and stand in the doorway. I don't see much but what I believe is a pasture. I smell cow shit. It's not as green out there as I needed it to be.

"I don't see much," I say.

"Look harder," he says.

And then I see it. A yellow light near a cow trough shines down on what looks to be a bottle tree. Red and blue glass. The tree's archritic limbs, a deep purple in the night sky, curve to the breaking point, like a spine inflamed with scoliosis. The wind, an invisible sound, crosses the field's great expanse, whirs in and out, an eerie breath of familiarity blown through some homemade instrument.

"I'm going to see," I say.

"I'll be here," he says.

I don't need him to be. Outside, Friendly growls and jerks his chain, but he can't go anywhere. I walk an inch beyond his last inch, tempting him, pissing him off. I take a gulp of wind. I'm wearing her blue corduroy coat, the buckeyes secure in the pocket where I once found them. The scent of pines lines a cornfield, and I head toward the bottle tree. Never before have I gone into woods alone. My grandmother carried a .410 rifle on account of rattlers when she walked her acres alone in the morning hours before dawn. I hold on to a fence post and crawl over barbed wire. I keep walking forward, by myself, toward the darkness.

This is not what Rick meant when he said I should start acting like a mommy. I can't love him, but out here I feel like I can see the truth. My mother ran off, but I'm not her. I'm not eighteen. I have a boy to raise.

In the distance, strange hounds bark. Off to my right, a cow lows. John's record turns in the night air, and I keep moving. There is the sound of pine straw underneath my feet. There is a big truck out on the highway. A whippoorwill is close by. I walk until I can hear her. And then, dead still beneath that tree, I look up.

Nominated by McSweeney's

SPECIAL MENTION

(The editors also wish to mention the following important works published by small presses last year. Listings are in no particular order.)

POETRY

A Selective History of Los Angeles, In Seven Turns—Dorothy Barresi (Pleiades)
Barry Dickson 1945—Barry Dickson (North American Review)
On Deck—Alice Friman (Georgia Review)
This Time—Brendan Galvin (Shenandoah)
User's Guide to Physical Debilitation—Paul Guest (Paris Review)
November—C.G. Hanzlicek (Ploughshares)
Kurosawa's Dog—Dennis Hinrichsen (Field)
Powers—Tony Hoagland (Ploughshares)
Coleridge's Laundry—Maxine Kumin (Prairie Schooner)
Pentagon Orders Dead Officers To Report for Duty—Dorianne Laux (The November 3rd Club)
Zucchini Shofar—Sarah Lindsay (*Twigs and Knucklebones* (Copper Canyon)
So Norman Died, Of Course—Scott Owens (Main Street Rag)
Cancer—Kevin Prufer (New England Review)
Momento Mori—Jonathan Rice (Harpur Palate)
Jane Austen, Inventor of Baseball—Jay Rogoff (Salamagundi)
Quarantine—Gibbons Ruark (*Staying Blue*, Lost Hills Books)
Translation of My Life—Elizabeth Spires (American Poetry Review)
The Frail Boat—Michael Van Walleghen (Spoon River Review)
Open Field—Phillis Levin (Kenyon Review)
The North Side—D. Nurkse (Threepenny Review)
Night—Carl Phillips (New England Review)

NONFICTION

497

The Invisible Dead—Dustin Beall Smith (River Teeth)
Purity: It's Such a Filthy Word—Lee Upton (Triquarterly)

FICTION

Black Step—Daniel Woodrell (New Letters)
The Little Wife—Edith Pearlman (Ontario Review)
Skywriting—Andrew Malan Milward (The Southern Review)
How To Make A Shoe—Kelle Grom (Agni)
Muscle Memory—Katherine Karlin (One Story)
The Lives of Diamonds—Jennifer S. Davis (Epoch)
Divine Afflatus—Jane Gillette (Michigan Quarterly Review)
Safety—Anne Sanow (Kenyon Review)
Tell Him About Brother John—Manuel Muñoz (Epoch)
Temporary Love—Ha Jin (Shenandoah)
Debt—Sana Krasikov (A Public Space)
Won't You Stay, Please?—Paul Eggers (Prairie Schooner)
Love Song for The Mother of No Children—Melanie Rae Thon (Virginia Quarterly)
Pie—Richard Spilman (River Styx)
Saved—Hershella Smith (Appalachian Heritage)
Drei Alter Knockers—Barry Callaghan (Exile)
The Dead Kid—Gillian King (Carve)
Flashflood—Aaron Michael Morales (Momotombo Press)
After Everyone Else Has Left—Jack Driscoll (Idaho Review)
Robotics—B.J. Hollars (Bellingham Review)
Evacuation Instructions—Elliott Holt (Bellevue Literary Review)
Victory At Sea—Ron Carlson (Iowa Review)
Confessions—Tara Mantell (Gettysburg Review)
The Peripatetic Coffin—Ethan Rutherford (American Short Fiction)
Mr. Dabydeen—E.A. Durden (Glimmer Train)
The Weather—R.D. Skillings (Notre Dame Review)
Foreign Girls—Thomas Grattan (One Story)
Me And Big Foot—Jill McCorkle (American Scholar)
Rhododendrons—Jody Brown (New York Tyrant)
The Comfort of Taboos—Gary Fincke (Pleiades)
Loeka Discovered—Seth Fried (Missouri Review)
Being Dead In South Carolina—Jacob White (Third Coast)
The Devil I Know Is The Man Upstairs—Diana Joseph (Willow Springs)

Marginalia—Daniel Scott (*Pay This Amount*, Laughing Fire)
Pee on Water—Rachel B. Glaser (New York Tyrant)
Archangel—Andrea Barrett (One Story)
Fault—Urban Waite (Third Coast)
The Lover—Damon Galgut (Paris Review)
Harriet Elliot—Robin Black (One Story)
Departure—Alistair Morgan (Paris Review)
Echo—Jason Ockert (Witness)
The Final Cold—Charles Conley (Harvard Review)
Hurricanes Anonymous—Adam Johnson (Tin House)
Excommunicados—Charles Haverty (Agni)
Name—Tony Woodlief (Image)
Cattle Haul—Jesmyn Ward (A Public Space)
The Reader—Teolinda Gersáo (Threepenny Review)
The Dead At the Table—Antonio Tabucchi (A Public Space)
Safe Passage—Ramona Ausubel (One Story)
Uncertainty—Joshua Ferris (Tin House)
The Idiot, or Life In Wartime—Fred G. Leebron (Triquarterly)
Mandelbaum, the Criminal—Gerald Shapiro (Ploughshares)
Indignity—Kerry Neville Bakken (Gettysburg Review)
Entropy—Mathew Goldberg (American Short Fiction)
Intercourse—Robert Olen Butler (New Letters)
Ghost Dog—Molly Giles (Blackbird)
Amish In A Time of War—Lauren Groff (Five Points)
Superstar—Joseph Kim (Indiana Review)
Often I Mistook Other People For Abraham—Rivka Galchen
    (Zoetrope)
Tale of the Tea House—Kanishk Tharoor (Virginia Quarterly)
Cloudcroft—Darren Dillman (Shenandoah)
Pentimento—Uzodinma Iweala (McSweeney's)
Singing Worm—Marilyn Chin (Michigan Quarterly Review)
Burke's Maria—Skip Horack (Epoch)
Welcome Back—Theodore Wheeler (Boulevard)
Better Half—Sana Krasikov (Epoch)
The Structure of Bubbles—Emily Raboteau (Narrative)
Wanted Man—Nic Pizzolatto (Oxford American)
My Summer of Love—Alyce Miller (*Water*, Sarabande Books)
Return/Fire—Glenn Blake (Hopkins Review)
Sweet Nothing—Richard Lange (Southern California Review)
The Block Twice—Matt Sumell (Brooklyn Review)

Witness—Ashley Pankratz (Colorado Review)

Quality Snacks—Andy Mozina (River Styx)

Mama Godot—Jane Ciabattari (Chautauqua)

The Queen of Bass Fishing in America—Paul Lewellan (Timber Creek Review)

Shameless—Douglas Glover (Brooklyn Rail)

This Is The Story I Want to Tell—Philip Gerard (Water-Stone)

Railway Killers—Anthony Farrington (Indiana Review)

Pearl Diving—Adrianne Harun (Colorado Review)

Nowtrends—Karl Taro Greenfield (American Short Fiction)

Burning Bright—Ron Rash (Ecotone)

Deep, Michigan—Josie Sigler (Water-Stone)

First Girl—Elizabeth England (The Journal)

Old Gang—Thomas Cooper (Beloit Fiction Journal)

Killer Heart—E.B. Johnson (Glimmer Train)

A Difficult Man—Francois Camoin (Western Humanities Review)

The World, the Flesh, and the Devil—Pinckney Benedict (Image)

Sylvia Plath and Truman Capote—Brian Kiteley (The Pinch)

Looking For the Mule—Jerry D. Mathes II (Grist)

The Blue Hour Before Sunrise—Kimberly Verhines (Shenandoah)

Shilling Life—Thomas Lynch (Conjunctions)

Double Happiness—Mary-Beth Hughes (A Public Space)

The Farms—Eleanor Henderson (Agni)

Spin—Aurelie Sheehan (Ploughshares)

The World In Flames—Jess Row (Witness)

Little Man—Skip Horack (Southern Review)

Wilderness—Jean Thompson (One Story)

Caesar—Richard Burgin (Hopkins Review)

Insectuality—Jason Ockert (Ecotone)

Natural Citizens—Deb Olin Unferth (New York Tyrant)

An Incident At Pat's Bar—E.C. Osondu (Fiction)

Confession—Susan Hahn (Boulevard)

Kill Your Darlings—Lee Klein (Black Warrior)

The Santa Monica No. 2—Duncan Bock (Epiphany)

First Love—Cecilia Johnson (Beloit Fiction Journal)

More So—Michelle Brafman (Fifth Wednesday Journal)

As In Life—Sari Rose (Glimmer Train)

Another Sad, Bizarre Chapter In Human History—Benjamin Markovits (Paris Review)

Save The I-Hotel—Lysley Tenorio (Mānoa)
Covenant—R.A. Rycraft (Calyx)
The Peripatetic Coffin—Ethan Rutherford (American Short Fiction)
Assembling the Troops—Amber Dermont (Crazyhorse)
Den Mother—Kirstin Valdez Quade (Colorado Review)

PRESSES FEATURED IN THE PUSHCART PRIZE EDITIONS SINCE 1976

Acts
Agni
Ahsahta Press
Ailanthus Press
Alaska Quarterly Review
Alcheringa/Ethnopoetics
Alice James Books
Ambergris
Amelia
American Letters and Commentary
American Literature
American PEN
American Poetry Review
American Scholar
American Short Fiction
The American Voice
Amicus Journal
Amnesty International
Anaesthesia Review
Anhinga Press
Another Chicago Magazine
Antaeus
Antietam Review
Antioch Review
Apalachee Quarterly
Aphra
Aralia Press

The Ark
Art and Understanding
Arts and Letters
Artword Quarterly
Ascensius Press
Ascent
Aspen Leaves
Aspen Poetry Anthology
Assembling
Atlanta Review
Autonomedia
Avocet Press
The Baffler
Bakunin
Bamboo Ridge
Barlenmir House
Barnwood Press
Barrow Street
Bellevue Literary Review
The Bellingham Review
Bellowing Ark
Beloit Poetry Journal
Bennington Review
Bilingual Review
Black American Literature Forum
Blackbird
Black Rooster

Black Scholar
Black Sparrow
Black Warrior Review
Blackwells Press
Bloom
Bloomsbury Review
Blue Cloud Quarterly
Blueline
Blue Unicorn
Blue Wind Press
Bluefish
BOA Editions
Bomb
Bookslinger Editions
Boston Review
Boulevard
Boxspring
Bridge
Bridges
Brown Journal of Arts
Burning Deck Press
Caliban
California Quarterly
Callaloo
Calliope
Calliopea Press
Calyx
The Canary
Canto
Capra Press
Caribbean Writer
Carolina Quarterly
Cedar Rock
Center
Chariton Review
Charnel House
Chattahoochee Review
Chautauqua Literary Journal
Chelsea
Chicago Review
Chouteau Review
Chowder Review
Cimarron Review

Cincinnati Poetry Review
City Lights Books
Cleveland State Univ. Poetry Ctr.
Clown War
CoEvolution Quarterly
Cold Mountain Press
Colorado Review
Columbia: A Magazine of Poetry and Prose
Confluence Press
Confrontation
Conjunctions
Connecticut Review
Copper Canyon Press
Cosmic Information Agency
Countermeasures
Counterpoint
Crawl Out Your Window
Crazyhorse
Crescent Review
Cross Cultural Communications
Cross Currents
Crosstown Books
Crowd
Cue
Cumberland Poetry Review
Curbstone Press
Cutbank
Dacotah Territory
Daedalus
Dalkey Archive Press
Decatur House
December
Denver Quarterly
Desperation Press
Dogwood
Domestic Crude
Doubletake
Dragon Gate Inc.
Dreamworks
Dryad Press
Duck Down Press
Durak
East River Anthology

Eastern Washington University Press

Ecotone

Ellis Press

Empty Bowl

Epiphany

Epoch

Ergo!

Evansville Review

Exquisite Corpse

Faultline

Fence

Fiction

Fiction Collective

Fiction International

Field

Fine Madness

Firebrand Books

Firelands Art Review

First Intensity

Five Fingers Review

Five Points Press

Five Trees Press

The Formalist

Fourth Genre

Frontiers: A Journal of Women
   Studies

Fugue

Gallimaufry

Genre

The Georgia Review

Gettysburg Review

Ghost Dance

Gibbs-Smith

Glimmer Train

Goddard Journal

David Godine, Publisher

Graham House Press

Grand Street

Granta

Graywolf Press

Great River Review

Green Mountains Review

Greenfield Review

Greensboro Review

Guardian Press

Gulf Coast

Hanging Loose

Hard Pressed

Harvard Review

Hayden's Ferry Review

Hermitage Press

Heyday

Hills

Hollyridge Press

Holmgangers Press

Holy Cow!

Home Planet News

Hudson Review

Hungry Mind Review

Icarus

Icon

Idaho Review

Iguana Press

Image

In Character

Indiana Review

Indiana Writes

Intermedia

Intro

Invisible City

Inwood Press

Iowa Review

Ironwood

Jam To-day

The Journal

Jubilat

The Kanchenjuga Press

Kansas Quarterly

Kayak

Kelsey Street Press

Kenyon Review

Kestrel

Latitudes Press

Laughing Waters Press

Laurel Poetry Collective

Laurel Review

L'Epervier Press
Liberation
Linquis
Literal Latté
Literary Imagination
The Literary Review
The Little Magazine
Living Hand Press
Living Poets Press
Logbridge-Rhodes
Louisville Review
Lowlands Review
Lucille
Lynx House Press
Lyric
The MacGuffin
Magic Circle Press
Malahat Review
Mānoa
Manroot
Many Mountains Moving
Marlboro Review
Massachusetts Review
McSweeney's
Meridian
Mho & Mho Works
Micah Publications
Michigan Quarterly
Mid-American Review
Milkweed Editions
Milkweed Quarterly
The Minnesota Review
Mississippi Review
Mississippi Valley Review
Missouri Review
Montana Gothic
Montana Review
Montemora
Moon Pony Press
Mount Voices
Mr. Cogito Press
MSS
Mudfish

Mulch Press
Nada Press
National Poetry Review
Nebraska Review
New America
New American Review
New American Writing
The New Criterion
New Delta Review
New Directions
New England Review
New England Review and Bread Loaf
    Quarterly
New Issues
New Letters
New Orleans Review
New Virginia Review
New York Quarterly
New York University Press
Nimrod
9 × 9 Industries
Ninth Letter
Noon
North American Review
North Atlantic Books
North Dakota Quarterly
North Point Press
Northeastern University Press
Northern Lights
Northwest Review
Notre Dame Review
O. ARS
O. Blēk
Obsidian
Obsidian II
Ocho
Oconee Review
October
Ohio Review
Old Crow Review
Ontario Review
Open City
Open Places

Orca Press

Orchises Press

Oregon Humanities

Orion

Other Voices

Oxford American

Oxford Press

Oyez Press

Oyster Boy Review

Painted Bride Quarterly

Painted Hills Review

Palo Alto Review

Paris Press

Paris Review

Parkett

Parnassus: Poetry in Review

Partisan Review

Passages North

Pebble Lake Review

Penca Books

Pentagram

Penumbra Press

Pequod

Persea: An International Review

Perugia Press

Pipedream Press

Pitcairn Press

Pitt Magazine

Pleiades

Ploughshares

Poet and Critic

Poet Lore

Poetry

Poetry Atlanta Press

Poetry East

Poetry Ireland Review

Poetry Northwest

Poetry Now

Post Road

Prairie Schooner

Prescott Street Press

Press

Promise of Learnings

Provincetown Arts

A Public Space

Puerto Del Sol

Quaderni Di Yip

Quarry West

The Quarterly

Quarterly West

Raccoon

Rainbow Press

Raritan: A Quarterly Review

Rattle

Red Cedar Review

Red Clay Books

Red Dust Press

Red Earth Press

Red Hen Press

Release Press

Republic of Letters

Review of Contemporary Fiction

Revista Chicano-Riquena

Rhetoric Review

Rivendell

River Styx

River Teeth

Rowan Tree Press

Runes

Russian *Samizdat*

Salmagundi

San Marcos Press

Sarabande Books

Sea Pen Press and Paper Mill

Seal Press

Seamark Press

Seattle Review

Second Coming Press

Semiotext(e)

Seneca Review

Seven Days

The Seventies Press

Sewanee Review

Shankpainter

Shantih

Shearsman

Sheep Meadow Press
Shenandoah
A Shout In the Street
Sibyl-Child Press
Side Show
Small Moon
Smartish Pace
The Smith
Snake Nation Review
Solo
Solo 2
Some
The Sonora Review
Southern Poetry Review
Southern Review
Southwest Review
Speakeasy
Spectrum
Spillway
The Spirit That Moves Us
St. Andrews Press
Story
Story Quarterly
Streetfare Journal
Stuart Wright, Publisher
Sulfur
The Sun
Sun & Moon Press
Sun Press
Sunstone
Sycamore Review
Tamagwa
Tar River Poetry
Teal Press
Telephone Books
Telescope
Temblor
The Temple
Tendril
Texas Slough
Third Coast
13th Moon
THIS

Thorp Springs Press
Three Rivers Press
Threepenny Review
Thunder City Press
Thunder's Mouth Press
Tia Chucha Press
Tikkun
Tin House
Tombouctou Books
Toothpaste Press
Transatlantic Review
Triplopia
TriQuarterly
Truck Press
Tupelo Press
Turnrow
Undine
Unicorn Press
University of Chicago Press
University of Georgia Press
University of Illinois Press
University of Iowa Press
University of Massachusetts Press
University of North Texas Press
University of Pittsburgh Press
University of Wisconsin Press
University Press of New England
Unmuzzled Ox
Unspeakable Visions of the Individual
Vagabond
Vallum
Verse
Vignette
Virginia Quarterly Review
Volt
Wampeter Press
Washington Writers Workshop
Water-Stone
Water Table
Wave Books
West Branch
Western Humanities Review
Westigan Review

White Pine Press

Wickwire Press

Willow Springs

Wilmore City

Witness

Word Beat Press

Word-Smith

World Literature Today

Wormwood Review

Writers Forum

Xanadu

Yale Review

Yardbird Reader

Yarrow

Y'Bird

Zeitgeist Press

Zoetrope: All-Story

ZYZZYVA

CONTRIBUTING SMALL PRESSES FOR PUSHCART PRIZE XXXIV

A

A Cappella Zoo, 635 _ E. Benton, Pocatello, ID 83201
A.P.D., 280 South Main Ave., Albany, NY 12208
ABZ Press, PO Box 2746, Huntington, WV 25757-2746
The Acentos Review, CMR 459 Box 06112, APO, AE 09139
Aforementioned Productions, 47-32 41st St, 1C, Long Island City, NY 11104
Agni Magazine, Boston University, 236 Bay State Rd., Boston, MA 02215
Ahewlu Productions, 8633 Crossbay Drive, Orlando, FL 32829-8677
Alaska Quarterly Review, Univ. of Alaska, 3211 Providence Dr., Anchorage, AK 99508
Alice James Books, 238 Main St., Farmington, ME 04938
Alimentum, PO Box 210028, Nashville, TN 37221
Allbook Books, PO Box 562, Selden, NY 11784
Alligator Juniper, 220 Grove Ave., Prescott, AZ 86301
Alondra Press, 10122 Shadow Wood Drive, #19, Houston, TX 77043
American Literary Review, PO Box 311307, Univ. No. Texas, Denton, TX 76203-1307
The American Poetry Journal, PO Box 2080, Aptos, CA 95001-2080
The American Poetry Review, 117 South 17th St., Ste. 910, Philadelphia, PA 19103
The American Scholar, 1606 New Hampshire Ave. NW. Washington, DC 20009
American Short Fiction, PO Box 301209, Austin, TX 78703
Amoskeag, So. New Hampshire Univ., 2500 No. River Rd., Manchester, NH 03106-1045
Anderson Valley Advertiser, PO Box 459, Boonville, CA 95415
Anhinga Press, P. O. Box 10595, Tallahassee, FL 32302
Annalemma Magazine, 3300 University Blvd., 218, Winter Park, FL 32792
The Antioch Review, PO Box 148, Yellow Springs, OH 45387-0148
Appalachian Heritage, CPO 2166, Berea, KY 40404
Apple Valley Review, Queen's Postal Outlet, Box 12, Kingston, ON K7L 3R9, Canada
Aquarius Press, PO Box 23096, Detroit, MI 48223
Arestes, 2941 170th St., South Amana, IA 52334
Arizona Authors, 6145 West Echo Lane, Glendale, AZ 85302
Arsenic Lobster Poetry Journal, 1830 W. 18th St., Chicago, IL 60608
Arts & Letters, Campus Box 89, Milledgeville, GA 31061
Asheville Poetry Review, PO Box 7086, Asheville, NC 28802
Ashland Poetry Press, Ashland University, Ashland, OH 44805
Askew Poetry Journal #5, P.O. Box 559, Ventura, CA 93002
Asterius Press, PO Box 5122, Seabrook, NJ 08302-3511

Astounding Beauty Ruffian Press, 2155 Elk Creek Rd., Stuart, VA 24171
Atlanta Review, PO Box 8248, Atlanta, GA 31106
The Aurorean, PO Box 187, Farmington, ME 04938
Autumn House Press, 87 _ Westwood St., Pittsburgh, PA 15211
Avery Anthology, 630 W. 147 St; #2, New York, NY, 10031

B

Ballard Street Poetry Journal, PO Box 3560, Worcester, MA 01613
The Baltimore Review, P.O. Box 36418, Towson, MD 21286
Bamboo Ridge Press, PO Box 61781, Honolulu, HI 96839-1781
Barbaric Yawp, 3700 County Route 24, Russell, NY 13684
The Barefoot Muse, PO Box 115, Hainesport, NJ 08036
Barn Owl Review, 342 Olin Hall, Univ. of Akron, Akron, OH 44325-1906
Barrow Street, PO Box 1831, New York, NY 10156
Bartleby Snopes, *www.bartlebysnopes.com*, contact@bartlebysnopescom
Bat City Review, Univ. of Texas, 1 University Station B 5000, Austin, TX 78712
Bayeux Arts, Inc., 119 Stratton Crescent SW, Calgary, Alberta, Canada T3H117
Bayou Magazine, Univ. of New Orleans, 2000 Lake Shore Dr., New Orleans, LA 70148
bear parade, 228 Montrose Ave., #3, Brooklyn, NY 11206
Bear Star Press, 185 Hollow Oak Dr., Cohasset, CA 95973
Beloit Fiction Journal, 700 College St., Beloit, W 53511-5595
BelleBooks, 1092 Ridgeway Rd., Dahlonega, GA 30533
Bellevue Literary Review, NYU School of Medicine, 550 First Ave, New York, NY 10016
Bellingham Review, MS-9053, WWU, Bellingham, WA 98225
Beloit Poetry Journal, PO Box 151, Farmington, ME 04938
Beyond Art, 55 Sinclair Rd., Longdon, W14 ONR, England
Bidoun Magazine, 195 Chrystie St., #900 D, New York, NY 10002
Big Toe Review, 181 West St., Apt. D-3, Ware, MA 01082
The Big Ugly Review, 490 Second St., Ste. 200, San Francisco, CA 94107
Big Valley Press, 6737 N. Milburn Ave., Ste. 160, PMB 1, Fresno, CA 93722
Birmingham Poetry Review, University of Alabama, Birmingham, AL 35294
BkMk Press, UMKC, 5101 Rockhill Rd., Kansas City, MO 64110
Black Clock, Cal Arts/24700 McBean Parkway, Valencia, CA 91355
Black Rock Press, Art Dept./224, University of Nevada, Reno, NV 89557
Black Warrior Review, PO Box 862936, Tuscaloosa, AL 35486
Blackbird, Virginia Commonwealth University, PO Box 843082, Richmond, VA 23284
BlazeVox, 14 Tremaine Ave., Kenmore, NY 14217-2616
Blood Lotus, 1615 S. 20th St., Apt. D, Lincoln, NE 68502
Blood Orange Review, 1495 Evergreen Ave. NE, Salem, OR 97301
Bloodroot Literary Magazine, PO Box 322, Thetford Center, VT 05075
Blue Fifth Review, 267 Lark Meadow Circle, Bluff City, TN 37618
The Blue Jew Yorker, 415 Avenue C, #2B, Brooklyn, NY 11218
Blue Unicorn, 22 Avon Rd., Kensington, CA 94707
Blueline, 44 Pierrepont Ave., Potsdam, NY 13676-2294
BluePrint Review, 1103 NW 11th Ave., Gainesville, FL 32601
BOA Editions, 250 North Goodman St., Ste 306, Rochester, NY 14607
Bomb, 80 Hanson Place, Ste. 703, Brooklyn, NY 11217
Bone Print Press, PO Box 684, Hanover, MA 02339
Boston Review, Building E-53, Room 407, MIT, Cambridge, MA 02139
Bottom Dog Press/Bird Dog Publishing, PO Box 425, Huron, OH 44839
Boulevard, PMB 325, 6614 Clayton Rd., Richmond Heights, MO 63117
Bowery Books, 310 Bowery, New York, NY 10012
Boxcar Poetry Review, 401 S. La Fayette Park Pl. #309, LA, CA 90057
Brain, Child, PO Box 714, Lexington, VA 24450
Brass Tacks Press, 20001 Valley View Dr., Topanga, CA 90290
The Briar Cliff Review, 3303 Rebecca St., PO Box 2100, Sioux City, IA 51104-2100
Brick, Box 609, Stn P, Toronto, ON, M5S 2Y4, Canada
Brilliant Corners, Lycoming College, Williamsport, PA 17701

Broadkill Review, 104 Federal St., Milton, DE 19968
Bright Hill Press, PO Box 193, 94 Church St., Treadwell, NY 13846-0193
Broken Bridge Review, 398 Pomfret Street, Pomfret, CT 06258
The Brooklyn Rail, 99 Commercial St., #15, Brooklyn, NY 11222
Brooklyn Review, Brooklyn College, 2900 Bedford Ave., Brooklyn, NY 11210
Browser Books, 2195 Filmore St., San Francisco, CA 94115

C

C P Journal, 2413 Collingwood Blvd., B-323, Toledo, OH 43260
Café Irreal, PO Box 87031, Tucson, AZ 85754
Caketrain, 82588, Pittsburgh, PA 15218
Callaloo, 4212 TAMU, Texas A&M Univ., College Station, TX 77843-4212
Calyx Inc., Box B, 216 SW Madison #7, Corvallis, OR 97339-0539
Carolina Wren Press, 120 Morris St., Durham, NC 27701
Carve Magazine, PO Box 701510, Dallas, TX 75370
Cave Wall Press, PO Box 29546, Greensboro, NC 27429-9546
Celtic Cat Publishing, 2654 Wild Fern Lane, Knoxville, TN 37931
Center, 202 Tate Hall, University of Missouri, Columbia, MO 65211-1500
Cervena Barva Press, PO Box 440357, W. Somerville, MA 02144-3222
Cezanne's Carrot, PO Box 6037, Santa Fe, NM 87502-6037
Chandelle Press, 12106 Red Oak Crt. So., Burnsville, MN 55337
Chautauqua, UNC Wilmington, 601 South College Rd., Wilmington, NC 28403-5938
Chelsea Green Publishing, 85 North Main St., PO Box 428, White River Jt., VT 05001
Chicago Quarterly Review, 517 Sherman Ave., Evanston, IL 60202
Chimaera Literary Miscellany, 18760 Cypress Rd., Fort Bragg, CA 95437
Chroma, PO Box 44655, London N16 0WQ, England
The Chrysalis Reader, 1745 Gravel Hill Rd., Dillwyn, VA23936
Ciano Design, 678 Massachusetts Ave., Ste. 401, Central Square, Cambridge, MA 02139
Cider Press Review, 777 Braddock Lane, Halifax, PA 17032
Cimarron Review, Oklahoma State University, Stillwater, OK 74078
Cincinnati Review, Univ. of Cincinnati, PO Box 210069, Cincinnati, OH 45221-0069
The Classical Outlook, Montclair State University, Montclair, NJ 07043
Coal City Review, English Dept., University of Kansas, Lawrence, KS 66045
Coconut, 2331 Eastway Rd., Decatur, GA 30033
Colorado Review, 9105 Campus Delivery, Colorado State Univ., Fort Collins, CO 80523
Columbia, 415 Dodge Hall, 2960 Broadway, New York, NY 10027
Columbia Poetry Review, 33 East Congress Pkwy, Chicago, IL 60605-1996
Coming Together, PO Box 1273, Dellslow, WV 26531
The Comstock Review, 214 E. First St., E. Syracuse, NY 13057
Concrete Wolf, PO Box 1808, Kingston, WA 98346-1808
Conduit, 510 8th Ave. NE, Minneapolis, Minnesota 55413
Confrontation, Long Island Univ., 720 Northern Boulevard, Brookville, NY 11548-1300
Conjunctions, Bard College, Annandale-on-Hudson, NY 12504
Connecticut Review (CT Review), 39 Woodland St., Hartford, CT 06105
Convergence Review, 611 Courtland St., Apt. A, Greensboro, NC 27401-6231
Copper Canyon Press, PO Box 271, Port Townsend, WA 98368
Country Dog Review, 108 Gadwell Dr. Easley, SC 29642
Country Valley Press, 1407 Mission St. "A", Gardnerville, Nevada 89410
Court Green, Columbia College, 600 South Michigan Ave., Chicago, IL 60605-1996
Covert Press, 2413 Collingwood Blvd., #B-323, Toledo, OH 43620
Crab Creek Review, PO Box 1524, Kingston, WA 98346
Crab Orchard Review, Mail Code 4503, So. Illinois Univ., Carbondale, IL 62901
Crazyhorse, College of Charleston, 66 George St., Charleston, SC 29424
CRIT Journal, 215 163rd Pl SE, Bellevue, WA 98008
Cross-Cultural Communications, 239 Wynsum Ave., Merrick, NY 11566-4725
Cross-Cultural Poetics, College of St. Catherine, 601 25th Ave. So., Minneapolis, MN 55454
Curbstone Press, 321 Jackson St., Willimantic, CT 06226-1738

D

Dappled Things Magazine, 15 Newman St., Apt. B, Annapolis, MD 21401
Dark Scribe Press, Smith Point, New York (*www.DarkScribePress.com*)
Darkhail Publishing, PO Box 121, Fenton, MI 48430
Deaf-Blind Perspectives, 345 N. Monmouth Ave., Monmouth, OR 97361
decomP, 5440 5ᵗʰ Ave., Apt. 7, Pittsburgh, PA 15232
Denver Quarterly, University of Denver, 2000 E Asbury, Denver, CO 80208
The Distillery, MSCC, PO Box 5500, Dept. 210, Lynchburg, TN 37352-8500
The DMQ Review, 16393 Bonnie Lane, Los Gatos, CA 95032
Dogwood, Fairfiled Univ., 1073 North Benson Rd., Fairfield, CT 06824-5195
Dossier, 244 DeKalb Ave., Brooklyn, NY 11205
Drash, Temple Beth Am, 2632 NE 80ᵗʰ St., Seattle, WA 98115
The Driftwood Review, 1737 Windsor St., Salt Lake City, UT 84105

E

Ecotone, UNC Wilmington, 601 South College Rd., Wilmington, NC 28403-3297
Edge, PO Box 799, Ocean Park, WA 98640
Ekphrasis, PO Box 161236, Sacramento, CA 95816-1236
Electric Velocipede, PO Box 266, Bettendorf, IA 52722
Eleven Eleven Journal, California College of the Arts, 1111 Eighth St., S.F., CA 94107
Elkhound, PO Box 1453, New York, NY 10028
Empowerment4Women, 14845 SW Murray Scholls Dr., Ste. 110-227, Beaverton OR 97007
Emprise Review, 197 W. Lafayette #2, Fayetteville, AR 72701
The Enigmatist, PO Box 1455, Burnet, TX 78611
Entelechy International, New England College, 98 Bridge St., Henniker, NH 03242
Epiphany, 71 Bedford St., New York, NY 10014
Epoch, 251 Goldwin Smith Hall, Cornell University, Ithaca NY 14853-3201
Eskimo Press, 1050 Arapahoe Ave. #1105, Boulder, CO 80302
Esopus, 532 Laguardia Place, #486, New York, NY 10012
Etruscan Press, 84 W. South St., Wilkes-Barre, PA 18766
Eureka Literary Magazine, 300 E. College Ave., Eureka, IL 61530-1500
Europa Editions, 116 East 16ᵗʰ St., New York, NY 10003
The Evansville Review, Univ. of Evansville, 1800 Lincoln Ave, Evansville, IN 47722
Event, PO Box 2053, New Westminster, BC, V3L 5B2, Canada
Every Day Fiction, 108-1065 Howie Ave., Coquitlam, BC, V3J 1T5, Canada
Excaliber Press, 3090 Dauphin Square Connector, Mobile, AL 36607
Exit 13 Magazine—22 Oakwood Ct., Fanwood, NJ 07023

F

Failbetter, 2022 Grove Ave., Richmond, VA 23220
Fiction International, San Diego State University, San Diego, CA 92182-6020
Fiction Weekly, Box 92633, McNeese State University, Lake Charles, CA 70609
Field, Peters Hall, 50 North Professor, Oberlin, OH 44074
Fifth Wednesday Journal, PO Box 4033, Lisle, IL 60532-9033
Finishing Line Press, PO Box 1626, Georgetown, KY 40324
First City Review, 1014 N. Orianna St., 3ʳᵈ Floor, Philadelphia, PA 19123
The First Line, PO Box 250382, Plano, TX 75025-0382
Fithian Press, PO Box 2790, McKinleyville, CA 95519
5 AM, Box 205, Spring Church, PA 15686
Five Centuries Books, 1055 Kensington Pk Dr., Ste 216, Altamonte Springs, FL 32714
Five Points, Georgia State University, PO Box 3999, Atlanta, GA 30302-3999
Flame Books, 58 Springfield Rd., Kings Heath, Birmingham, United Kingdom
Flash Fiction Online, 10 Ridgeview Ave., West Orange, NJ 07052
Flatmancrooked Publishing, 3311 Franklin Ave., Sacramento, CA 95818

Fledgling Rag, 2848 Nolt Rd., Lancaster, PA 17601
Fleur-de-lis Press, Spalding University, 851 South Fourth St., Louisville, KY 40203
flipped eye publishing ltd, 17 St. Albans Ter, Waterloo Park, Manchester M8 8BZ, UK
The Florida Review, Univ. of Central Florida, PO Box 161346, Orlando, FL 32789
Flume Press, 400 W. First St., Chico, CA 95929-0830
Foliate Oak, University of Arkansas, Monticello, MCB 113, Monticello, AR 71656
Forge Journal, 1610 S. 22nd St., Lincoln, NE 68502
Four Way Books, P.O. Box 535, Village Station, New York, NY 10014
Fourteen Hills, SF State Univ., 1600 Halloway Ave., San Francisco, CA 94132
Fourth Genre, Michigan State University, Morrill Hall, East Lansing, MI 48824-1036
The Fourth River, Chatham University, Woodland Rd., Pittsburgh, PA 15232
Fox Chase Review, 7930 Barnes St., Apt. A-7, Philadelphia, PA 19111
The Fray Magazine, 505 Lexington Pkwy S Apt 9, Saint Paul, MN 55105
Free Books Inc., 1787 Rhoda, Lowell, MI 49331
Free Lunch, PO Box 717, Glenview, IL 60025-0717
Freight Stories, PO Box 44167, Indianapolis, IN 46244
From East to West, 12 Jonathan Dr., Brunswick, ME 04011
Fugue, PO Box 441102, University of Idaho, Moscow, ID 83844-1102

G

Gadfly, 12 Mantle Way, Stratford, London E15 4BT, England
Galleon, 36-A Sixth Street, Moncton, NB E1E 3G6, Canada
Gallinas Magazine, 1206 National Ave., Las Vegas, NM 87701
Gander Press Review, 10767 Richardsville Rd., Bowling Green, KY 42101
Gargoyle Magazine, 3819 13th St. N., Arlington, VA 22201-4922
The Georgia Review, Gilbert Hall, University of Georgia, Athens, GA 30602
The Gettysburg Review, Gettysburg College, Gettysburg, PA 17325-1491
Gilbert Magazine, 3460 N. Hackett Ave., Milwaukee, WI 53211-2945
Ginger Cat's Booksmyth Press, 102 Mechanic St., Shelburne Falls, MA 01370
Gival Press, PO Box 3812, Arlington, VA 22203
Glimmer Train Press, 1211 NW Glisan St., Ste. 207, Portland, OR 97209-3054
Gold Wake Press, 5 Barry St., Randolph, MA 02368
Gonzalez, 177 Amity St., #9, Brooklyn, NY 11201
Goose River Press, 3400 Friendship Rd., Waldoboro, ME 04572
Grasslands Review, English Dept., Indiana State University, Terre Haute, IN 47809
Grateful Steps, 1091 Hendersonville Rd., Asheville, NC 28803
Graywolf Press, 2402 University Ave., Ste. 203, Saint Paul, MN 55114
Great River Review, Anderson Center, PO Box 406, Red Wing, MN 55066
Green Fuse Poetic Arts, 400 Vortex St., Bellvue, CO 80512
Green Hills Literary Lantern, Truman Univ., 100 East Normal, Kirksville, MO 63501-4221
Green Mountains Review, Johnson State College, Johnson, VT 05656
The Greensboro Review, PO Box 26170, Greensboro, NC 27402-6170
Greystone Press, 2220 N.E. 131st St., Edmond, OK 73013
Guernica Magazine, 557 W. 149th St., Apt 19, New York, NY 10031
Gulf Coast, University of Houston, Houston, TX 77204-3013
Gulf Stream Magazine, 3000 N.E. 151st St., AC1-335, North Miami, FL 33181

H

H.O.W. Journal, 3000 47th Floor, Long Island City, NY 11101
Harbour Publishing Co., 4437 Rondeview Rd., Madeira Park, BC V0N 2H0 Canada
Harp & Altar, 240 Adelphi St., #4, Brooklyn, NY 11205
Harpur Palate, English Dept., Binghamton University, Binghamton, NY 13902
Harvard Review, Lamont Library, Harvard University, Cambridge, MA 02138
Hawai'i Pacific Review, 1060 Bishop St., LB7, Honolulu, HI 96813
Hayden's Ferry Review, Arizona State Univ., PO Box 875002, Tempe, AZ 85287-5002

Hazard, One Community College Drive, Hazard, KY 41701-2402
The Healing Muse, 725 Irving Ave., Ste. 406, Syracuse, NY 13210
Heart Lodge, 9707 W. Chatfield Ave., Unit D, Littlelon, CO 80128
The Hedgehog Review, UVA, PO Box 400816, Charlottesville, VA 22904-4816
High Country News, PO Box 1090, Paonia, CO 81428
Hobert, PO Box 1658, Ann Arbor, MI 48103
The Hopkins Review, 135 Gilman Hall, 3400 N. Charles St., Baltimore, MD 21218-6828
Home Planet News, PO Box 455, High Falls, NY 12440
Hotel Amerika, English Dept., 600 S. Michigan Ave., Chicago, IL 60605-1996
Hither & Yahn, PO Box 233, San Luis Rey, CA 92068
The Hudson Review, 684 Park Ave., New York, NY 10065
Hunger Mountain, Vermont College, 36 College St., Montpelier, VT 05602
Hyphen, 17 Walter U. Lum Place, San Francisco, CA 94108

I

The Iconoclast, 1675 Amazon Rd., Mohegan Lake, NY 10547
Ibbeson Street Press, 25 School Street, Somerville, MA 02143
The Ice Cube Press, 205 N. Front St., North Liberty, IA 52317
The Idaho Review, Boise State Univ., 1910 University Dr., Boise, ID 83725
If Poetry Journal, 1 Alsace Lane, Rockville, MD 20851
Illuminations, College of Charleston, 66 George St., Charleston, SC 29424
Illya's Honey, PO Box 700865, Dallas, TX 75370
Image, 3307 Third Avenue West, Seattle, WA 98119
Indiana Review, 1020 E. Kirkwood Ave., Bloomington, IN 47405-7103
Inglis, 2600 Belmont Ave., Philadelphia, PA 19131
Inkwell, Manhattanville College, 2900 Purchase St., Box 1379, Purchase, NY 10577
The Iowa Review, 308 EPB, University of Iowa, Iowa City, IA 52242
Iron Horse Literary Review, Box 43091, Texas Tech Univ., Lubbock, TX 79409-3091
Isotope, Utah State University, 3200 Old Main Hill, Logan, UT 84322-3200

J

J Journal, John Jay College of Criminal Justice, 619 West 54th St., 7th, Fl, NY, NY 10019
Jabberwock Review, Mississippi State University, Mississippi State, MS 39762
Jane Street Press, 1 Jane Street, New York, NY10014
Jefferson Press, PO Box 115, Lookout Mountain, TN 37350
Joggling Board Press, PO Box 13209, Charleston, SC 29422
Johnny America, PO Box 44-2001, Lawrence, KS 66044
The Journal, English Dept., Ohio State Univ., 164 West 17th Ave., Columbus, OH 43210
Journal of New Jersey Poets, 214 Center Grove Rd., Randolph, NJ 07869-2086
Journal of Truth and Consequences, 110 Scenic Dr., Hattiesburg, MS 39401
joyful!, PO Box 80054, Springfield, MA 01138
Juked, 110 Westridge Dr., Tallahassee, FL 32304

K

Karamu, Eastern Illinois University, 600 Lincoln Ave., Charleston, IL 61920
Kartika Review, 109 Schooner Ct., Richmond, CA 94804
Kaya Press, 2650 Durant Ave., SLG-09, Berkeley, CA 94720
KCLF-21 Press, PO Box 45035, 5845 Yonge St., Willowdale, ON, M2M 4K3 Canada
Kelsey Review, Mercer County Community College, PO Box B, Trenton, NJ 08690
Kenyon Review, Walton House, Kenyon College, Gambier, OH 43022-9623
The Kerf, College of the Redwoods, 883 W. Washington Blvd., Crescent City, CA 95531
Keyhole, 1307-B 15th Ave. So., Nashville, TN 37212

The King's English, 3114 NE 47th Ave., Portland, OR 97213
Kore Press, PO Box 42315, Tucson, AZ 85733-2315
Kudzu, Hazard, 1 Community College Dr., Hazard, KY 41701-2402
Kunati, 13575 58th St. No., Ste. 200, Clearwater, FL 33760-3721

L

The L Magazine, 20 Jay St., Ste. 207, Brooklyn, NY 11201
Lake Effect, 4951 College Drive, Erie, PA 16563-1501
Lake Oconee Living, 235 South Main St., Madison, GA 30650
Lamberson Corona Press, PO Box 1116, West Babylon, NY 11704
Lamination Colony, 2571 Beckwith Trl SE, Marietta, GA 30068-3114
Laughing Fire Press, 245 Coast Blvd., La Jolla, CA 92037
Left-Facing Bird, 228 Halpin Rd., Middlebury, VT 05753
Les Figues Press, PO Box 7736, Los Angeles, CA 90007
Lilies and Cannonballs Review, PO Bo 702, Bowling Green Sta., NY, NY 10274-0702
Limp Wrist, PO Box 47891, Atlanta, GA 30362
Linebreak, http://linebreak.org
Lips, 7002 Blvd. East #2-26G. Guttenberg, NJ 07093
Lit, The New School, Room 514, 66 West 12th St., New York, NY 10011
Lit Up Magazine, 200 E. 4th St., Yankton, SD 57078
Literary Imagination, Oxford University Press, 2001 Evans Rd., Cary   NC 27513
The Literary Review, Fairleigh Dickinson Univ., 285 Madison Ave., Madison, NJ 07940
Littoral Press, PO Box 3226, Berkeley, CA 94703
Long Island Sounds, 33 Woods Lane, Southampton, NY 11968-1719
Lost Coast, 155 Cypress St., Fort Bragg, CA 95437
Lost Horse Press, 105 Lost Horse Lane, Sandpoint, ID 83864
The Louisville Review, Spalding University, 851 S. Fourth St., Louisville, KY 40203
Low Rent Magazine, 305 Bergen St., Ste. 2C, Brooklyn, NY 11217-1964
Lumina, Sarah Lawrence College, Slonim House, 1 Mead Way, Bronxville, NY 10708-5999
Luna, University of Minnesota, 207 Church Street SE, Minneapolis, MN 55455
Lunch Hour Stories, 22933 Bothell Everett Hwy, Ste. 110, Bothell, WA 98021-9366

M

The MacGuffin, Schoolcraft College, 18600 Haggerty Rd., Livonia, MI 48152
Magrapoets, 13300 Tecumseh Road East, Tecumseh, Ontario N8N 4R8, Canada
Main Street Rag, PO Box 690100, Charlotte, NC 28227
MAKE Literary Productions, 2229 W. Iowa #3, Chicago, IL 60622
The Malahat Review, PO Box 1700 STN CSC, Victoria BC V8W 2Y2 Canada
Mandorla, Illinois State University, #4240, Normal, IL 61790-4240
The Manhattan Review, 440 Riverside Dr., #38, New York, NY 10027
Manoa, English Dept., University of Hawaii, Honolulu, HI 96822
Many Mountains Moving, 1705 Lombard St., Philadelphia, PA 19146
Marathon & Beyond, PO Box 161, 7050 Guisti Rd., Forestville, CA 95436
Margaret Media, Inc., 618 Mississippi St., Donaldsonville, LA 70346
MARGIE, PO Box 250, Chesterfield, MO 63006-0250
Marginalia, PO Box 258, Pitkin, CO 81241
Marriage Records Publishing House, 800 SE 10th Ave., Portland, OR 97214
Marsh River Editions, M233 Marsh Rd., Marshfield, WI 54449
The Massachusetts Review, South College 126047, Amherst, MA 01003-7140
Mayapple Press, 408 N. Lincoln St., Bay City, MI 48708-6653
McSweeney's Publishing, 849 Valencia, San Francisco, CA 94110
Memonons, 3424 Brookline Ave., #16, Cincinnati, OH 45220
Meridian, University of Virginia, PO Box 400145, Charlottesville, VA 22904-4145
Mezzo Cammin, Fairfield University, Fairfield, CT 06824-5195
Michigan Quarterly Review, Univ. of Michigan, 915 E. Washington St., Ann Arbor, MI 48109

Michigan Writers, Inc., PO Box 1505, Traverse City, MI 49685
Mid-American Review, Bowling Green State University, Bowling Green, OH 43403
The Minnesota Review, Carnegie Mellon University, Pittsburgh, PA 15213
Minnetonka Review, P.O. Box 386, Spring Park, MN 55384
MiPOesias, 604 Vale St., Bloomington, IL 61701-5620
Mississippi Review, 118 College Dr. #5144, Hattiesburg, MS 39406-0001
The Missouri Review, 357 McReynolds Hall, Univ. of Missouri, Columbia, MO 65211
Mobius, the Poetry Magazine, PO Box 671058, Flushing, NY 11367-1058
Modern Haiku, PO Box 7046, Evanston, IL 60204-7046
Momotombo Press, 230 McKenna Hall, Notre Dame, IN 46556
Mud Luscious, 2115 Sandstone Dr., Fort Collins, CO 80524
Muse-Pie Press, 73 Pennington Ave., Passaic, NJ 07055
Muumuu House, 228 Montrose Ave., #3, Brooklyn, NY 11206

N

N + 1 Magazine, 68 Jay St., #405, Brooklyn, NY 11201
Narrative Magazine, 1660 Westlake Dr., Kelseyville, CA 95451
Natural Bridge, UM-St. Louis, One University Blvd., St. Louis, MO 63121
New American Writing, Oink! Press, 369 Molino Ave., Mill Valley, CA 94941
New Century Publishing, 57 Waldron Rd., Lempster, NH 03605
The New Criterion, 900 Broadway, New York, NY 10003
New England Review, Middlebury College, Middlebury, VT 05753
New Issues Poetry & Prose, WMU, 1903 W. Michigan Ave., Kalamazoo, MI 49008-5463
New Letters, Univ. of Missouri, 5100 Rockhill Rd., Kansas City, MO 64110-2499
New Madrid, English Dept., Murray State University, Murray, KY 42071
New Ohio Review, Ohio University, 360 Ellis Hall, Athens, OH 45701
New Orleans Review, Box 195, Loyola University, New Orleans, CA 70118
The New Orphic Review, 706 Mill St., Nelson, B.C. V1L 4S5 Canada
the new renaissance, 26 Heath Rd., #11, Arlington, MA 02174-3645
New Verse News, *www.jamespenha.com/TheNVN.html*
New York Quarterly, P.O. Box 2015, Old Chelsea Station, New York, NY 10113
New York Tyrant, 676 A Ninth Ave., #153, New York, NY 10036
Nextbook.org, *www.nextbook.org*
Nimrod International Journal, 800 South Tucker Dr., Tulsa, OK 74104-3189
Ninth Letter, University of Illinois, 608 S. Wright St., Urbana, IL 61801
No Colony, 2571 Beckwith Trl SE, Marietta, GA 30068-3114
No Tell Motel, 11436 Fairway Dr., Reston, VA 20190
Nodin Press, 530 North Third St., Ste. 120, Minneapolis, MN 55401
Noon, 1324 Lexington Ave., PMB 298, New York, NY 10128
The Normal School, 5245 N. Backer Ave., M/S PB 98, Fresno, CA 93740-8001
North American Review, Univ. of No. Iowa, 1222 West 27th St., Cedar Falls, IA 50614-0516
The North Carolina Literary Review, East Carolina Univ., Greenville, NC 27858-4353
North Dakota Quarterly (NDQ), 276 Centennial Drive, Grand Forks, ND 58202-7209
Northwest Review, 5243 University of Oregon, Eugene, OR 97401-5243
Northwestern University Press, 629 Noyes St., Evanston, IL 60208-4210
Not One of Us, 12 Curtis Rd., Natick, MA 01760
The Notre Dame Review, 840 Flanner Hall, Notre Dame, IN 46556-5639
The November 3 Club, 66 Fairfax Rd., #3, Worcester, MA 01610

O

O Tempora! Magazine, 4511 Harrisburg Rd., Summerville, GA 30747
Oak Bend Review, 2901 Oak Bend Ct., Flower Mound, TX 75028
OCHO, 604 Vale St., Bloomington, IL 61701
Off the Coast, PO Box 14, Robbinston, ME 04671
Old Mountain Press, 2542 S. Edgewater Dr., Fayetteville, NC 28303

Old Red Kimino, 3175 Cedartown Hwy. SE, Rome, GA 30161

One Story, Old American Can Factory, 230 3rd St., #A111, Brooklyn, NY 11215

Ontario Review, 9 Honey Brook Dr., Princeton, NJ 08540

Open City, 270 Lafayette St., Ste. 1412, New York, NY 10012

Open Minds, 680 Kirkwood Dr., Bldg. 1, Sudbury, ON P3E 1X3, Canada

Opium, 114A Diamond St., Brooklyn, NY 11222

Oranges and Sardines, 120 N. 11th St., LaCrosse, WI 54601

Orchises Press, Geroge Mason University, Fairfax, VA 22030

The Orion Society, 187 Main St., Great Barrington, MA 01230

Osiris, PO Box 297, Deerfield, MA 01342

Oxford American, 201 Donaghey Ave., Main 107, Conway, AR 72035-5001

P

P.R.A. Publishing, PO Box 211701, Martinez, CA 30917

The Pacific Review, English Dept., 5500 State College Pkwy, San Bernardino, CA 92407

Paddlefish, 1105 West Eighth St., Yankton, SD 57078

Paradox, PO Box 22897, Brooklyn, NY 11202-2897

The Paris Review, 62 White St., New York, NY 10013

Parthenon West Review, 738 Minor Ave., Kalamazoo, MI 49008

Passager, 1420 N. Charles St., Baltimore, MD 21201

Passages North, English Dept., 1401 Presque Isle Ave., Marquette, MI 49855-5363

Pearl, 3030 E. Second St., Long Beach, CA 90803

Pedestal Magazine, 6815 Honors Court, Charlotte, NC 28210

PEN America, PEN American Center, 588 Broadway, Suite 303, New York, NY 10012

Perihelion, An Online Journal of Poetry and Mayhem, *www.perihelionreview.com*

Permafrost, University of Alaska, Fairbanks, Box 755720, Fairbanks, AK 99775

Perugia Press, PO Box 60364, Florence, MA 01062

Peterson Literary Review, Community College, 1 College Blvd., Paterson, NJ 07505-1179

Petigru Review, 8 Allegheny Run, Simpsonville, SC 29681

Phoebe, GMU, 4400 University Ave., Fairfax, VA 22030

Phrygian Press, 58-09 205th St., Bayside, NY 11364

The Pinch, English Dept., 467 Patterson Hall, Memphis, TN 38152-3510

Ping-Pong, Henry Miller Library, Highway One, Big Sur, CA 93920

Pistola Magazine, pistolamag.org

Pittsburgh Press, University of Pittsburgh, Pittsburgh, PA 15260

Pleiades, University of Central Missouri, Martin 336, Warrensburg, MO 64093-5046

Ploughshares, Emerson College, 120 Boylston St., Boston, MA 02116-4624

PMS poemmemoirstory, 1530 3rd Ave. South, Birmingham, AL 35294-1260

Poemeleon: A Journal of Poetry, 5755 Durango Rd., Riverside, CA 92506

Poems Against War, 2923 St. Paul St., Apt. 2, Baltimore, MD 21218

Poems and Plays, Middle Tennessee State University, Murfreesboro, TN 37132

Poet Lore, The Writer's Studio, 4508 Walsh St., Bethesda, MD 20815

Poetry, 444 N. Michigan Ave., Chicago, IL 60611-4034

Poetry Atlanta Press, 701 Highland Ave., NE, #1212, Atlanta, GA 30312

Poetry Bay, PO Box 114, Northport, NY 11768

Poetry Center, Cleveland State Univ., 2121 Euclid Ave., Cleveland, OH 44115-2214

Poetry International, English Dept., SDSU, 5500 Campanile Dr., San Diego, CA 92182-6020

Poetry Kanto, 3-22-1 Kamariya Minami, Kanazawa-Ward, Yokohama, 236-8502 Japan

Poetry Northwest, 4232 SE Hawthorne Boulevard, Portland, Oregon 97215

The Poetry Project, St. Mark's Church, 131 East 10th St., New York, NY 10003

Poetry Review, 22 Betterton St., London WC2H 9BX, England

Poets Wear Prada, 533 Bloomfield St, 2nd Floor, Hoboken, NJ 07030

Pool, PO Box 49738, Los Angeles, CA 98849

Possibilities, 23 Willabay Dr., Unit D, Williams Bay, WI 53191

Post Road, c/o Mary Crane, Boston College, Chestnut Hill, MA 02467

Potomac Review, Montgomery College, 51 Mannakee St., Rockville, MD 20850

Prairie Schooner, UNL, 201 Andrews Hall, PO Box 880334, Lincoln, NE 68588-0334

Presa Press, PO Box 792, Rockford, MI 49341

Press 53, PO Box 30314, Winston-Salem, NC 27130
Prick of the Spindle, PO Box 4087, Ft. Polk, LA 71459-1087
Provincetown Arts, 650 Commercial St., Provincetown, MA 02657
Provincetown Journal, PO Box 1525, South Dennis, MA 02660
A Public Space, 323 Dean St., Brooklyn, NY 11217

Q

Quarter After Eight, Ellis Hall, Ohio University, Athens, OH 45701
Quarterly West, 255 S. Central Campus Dr., Rm. 3500, Salt Lake City, UT 84112-0109
Quick Fiction 13, *www.quickfiction.org*, PO Box 4445, Salem, MA 01970
Quill and Parchment Press, 1825 Echo Park Ave., Los Angeles, CA 90026

R

Radiant Turnstile, PO Box 268, Kingsland, TX 78639
Ragged Sky Press, 270 Griggs Drive, Princeton, NJ 08540
The Raintown Review, 8400 Menaul Blvd., NE, Ste A #211, Albuquerque, NM 87112
The Rambler—PO Box 5070, Chapel Hill, NC 27514
Rapier, Marist School, 630 Cleburne Terrace NE, Atlanta, GA 30306
Raritan: A Quarterly Review, Rutgers, 31 Mine St., New Brunswick, NJ 08903
Rattle, 12411 Ventura Blvd., Studio City, CA 91604
The Raven Chronicles, 12346 Sand Point Way N.E., Seattle, WA 98125
Raving Dove, PO Box 28, West Linn, OR 97068
Real, Box 13007-SFA Station, Nacogdoches, TX 75962
Red Hen Press, PO Box 3537, Granada Hills, CA 91394
Redactions: Poetry & Poetics, 58 South Main St., 3rd Floor, Brockport, NY 14420
Redbone Chapbooks, Arts & Sciences, Macon State College, Macon, GA 31206-5144
Redivider, Emerson College, 120 Boylston St., Boston, MA 02116
The Redwood Coast Review, 35850 Old Stage Rd., Gualala, CA 95445-9563
relief, 60 West Terra Cotta, Ste. B, Unit 156, Crystal Lake, IL 60014
The Republic of Letters, Apartado 29, Cahuita, 7032, Costa Rica
Rhino, 630 Clinton Place, Evanston, IL 60201-1768
River Poets Journal, 1848 Finch Dr., Bensalem, PA 19020
River Styx, 3547 Olive St., Ste. 107, St. Louis, MO 63103-1014
Riverteeth, Ashland University, Ashland, OH 44805
Roanoke Review, Roanoke College, 221 College Lane, Salem, VA 24153-3794
Rock & Sling, PO Box 30865, Spokane, WA 99223
roger, Roger Williams University, One Old Ferry Rd., Bristol, RI 02809
The Rose & Thorn, 3 Diamond Court, Montebello, NY 10901
Rougarou, Univ. of Louisiana at Lafayette, Griffin Room 221, Lafayette, LA 70504
Rural Messengers Press, 356 E. State St., #2, Jacksonville, IL 62650

S

Sacred Fools Press, 45 Dean Ave., Johnston, RI 02919-1473
Saint Anne's Review, 129 Pierrepont St., Brooklyn Heights, NY 11201
Salamander, Suffolk University, English Dept., 41 Temple St., Boston, MA 02114-4280
San Francisco Bay Press, 900 Timber Creek Place, Virginia Beach, VA 23464
Santa Monica Review, 1900 Pico Boulevard, Santa Monica, CA 90405-1628
Sarabande Books, Inc., 2234 Dundee Rd., Ste. 200, Louisville, KY 40205
Scala House Press, PO Box 4518, Seattle, WA 98194
Schuylkill Valley Journal, 240 Gold Hills Rd., Havertown, PA 19083
SCR+II Poetry eZine, 18760 Cypress Rd., Fort Bragg, CA 95437
Scribendi, 1 University of New Mexico, Albuquerque, NM 87131-0001

Sea Stories, 21 Eldridge Rd., Jamaica Plain, MA 02130

The Second Hand, 1827 1st Ave., N #301, Birmingham, AL 35203

Semiotext (e) 2007 Wilshire Blvd., #427, Los Angeles CA 90057

Seneca Reviews, Hobart and William Smith Colleges, Geneva, NY 14456

Seventh Circle Books, PO Box 150107, Kew Gardens, NY 11415-0107

Seventh Quarry, Dan-y-bryn, 74 Cwm Level Rd., Brynhyfrd, Swansea SA 5 9DY, Wales, UK

Sewanee Review, University of the South, 735 University Ave., Sewanee, TN 37383

Shady Lane Press, 9138 Queen Elizabeth Ct., Orlando, FL 32818

SHALLA Magazine, 2440 S. Hacienda Blvd., Ste. 212, Hacienda Hgts, CA 91745-4768

Shape of a Box, 8324 Highlander Court, Charlotte, NC 28269

Shenandoah, Mattingly House, Washington and Lee Univ., Lexington, VA 24450-2116

THE SHOP, Skeagh, Schull, Co. Cork, Ireland

Short Story Library, 1014 Watts Dr, Charlotte, NC 28216

The Sienese Shredder, 344 West 23rd St. # 4D, New York NY 10011

Silenced Press, 449 Vermont Place, Columbus, OH 43201

Silent Voices, PO Box 11180, Glendale, CA 91226

Silver Boomer Books, 4925 South 5th St., Abilene, TX 79605

Skidrow Penthouse, 68 East Third St., Ste. 16, New York, NY 10003

Skyline Publications, PO Box 295, Stormville, NY 12582

Slipstream, Box 2071, Niagara Falls, NY 14301

Smartish Pace, PO Box 22161, Baltimore, MD 21203

SmokeLong Quarterly, 524 S. Sydbury Lane, Wynnewood, PA 19096

So to Speak, 4400 University Dr. MS2C5, Fairfax, VA 22030-4444

Solo Café, Santa Barbara City College, 721 Cliff Dr., Santa Barbara, CA 93109-2394

Song of the San Joaquin Quarterly, PO Box 1161, Modesto, CA 95353-1161

Sonora Review, English Dept., University of Arizona, Tucson AZ 85721

Sound Streettracks, 2115 Granberry Rd., DeRidder, LA 70634

Soundzine, 720 Mahlon St., Lansing, MI 48906

Sous Rature, 1149 Best Rd., E. Greenbush, NY 12061

The Southampton Review, 239 Montauk Highway, Southampton, NY 11968

The Southeast Review, English Dept., Florida State Univ., Tallahassee, FL 32306

Southern California Review, USC, Los Angeles, CA 90089-0355

Southern Humanities Review, 9088 Haley Center, Auburn University, Auburn, AL 36849

Southern Indiana Review, 8600 University Blvd., Evansville, IN 47712

Southern Illinois University Press, 1915 University Press Dr., Carbondale, IL 62902

Southern Poetry Review, 11935 Abercorn St., Savannah, Georgia 31419-1997

The Southern Review, Louisiana State University, Baton Rouge, LA 70803

Southwest Review, So. Methodist University, PO Box 750374, Dallas, TX 75275-0374

Sou'wester, Southern Illinois University, Peck Hall 3206, Edwardsville, IL 62026

Specs, Rollins College, English Dept., 1000 Holt Ave., Winter Park, FL 32789-4499

Spoon River Poetry Review, Illinois State Univ., Campus Box 4241, Normal, IL 61790

St. Petersburg Review, Box 2888, Concord, NH 03302

Stirring, 218 Stevens Dr., Hattiesburg, MS 39401

Stone Canoe, 700 University Ave., Ste. 326, Syracuse, NY 13244-2530

Storyglossia, 1004 Commercial Ave., #1110, Anacortes, WA 98221

The Storyteller, 2441 Washington Rd., Maynard, AR 72444

Studies in American Indian Literatures—UNL Press, PO Box 84555, Lincoln, NE 68501

Subtropics, PO Box 112075, University of Florida, Gainesville, FL 32611-2075

Summerset Review, 25 Summerset Dr., Smithtown, NY 11787

The Sun, 107 North Roberson St., Chapel Hill, NC 27516

sunnyoutside, PO Box 911, Buffalo, NY 14207

Superficial Flesh, 6320 Campbell Rd., #1442, Dallas, TX 75248

Superstition Review, 3931 E. Equestrian Trail, Phoenix, AZ 85044-3010

Skyline Publications, PO Box 295, Stormville, NY 12582

T

Take Five, PO Box 118, Elkton, MD 21922

Tampa Review, 401 W. Kennedy Blvd., Tampa, FL 33606

Tears of the Phoenix, 5 Devonshire Rd., Norwalk, CT 06850
10 X 3 Plus, 1077 Windsor Ave., Morgantown, WV 26505
Tertulia Magazine, 623 W. Broad St., Nevada City, CA 95959
Texas Tech University Press, Box 41037, Lubbock, TX 79409-1037
The Same, Box 494, Mount Union, PA 17066
The Write Perspective, Univ. of Texas, 702 East Dean Keeton St, Austin, TX 78705
Thermos Magazine, 64 Railroad St., Amherst, MA 01002
Third Coast, Western Michigan University, Kalamazoo, MI 49001
Third Wednesday, 174 Greenside Up, Ypsilanti, MI 48197
Third World Press, 7822 S. Dobson Ave., Chicago, IL 60619
13 Miles from Cleveland, 6846 Chaffee Court, Brecksville, OH 44141
Threepenny Review, PO Box 9131, Berkeley, CA 94709
Tiferet, 211 Dryden Rd., Bernardsville, NJ 07924
Tiger's Eye Press, PO Box 2935, Eugene, OR 97402
Tight, PO Box 272, North Bennington, VT 05257
Tikkun Magazine, 2342 Shattuck Ave., Ste. 1200, Berkeley, CA 94704
Timber Creek Review, PO Box 16542, Greensboro, NC 27416
Timberline, 6281 Red Bud, Fulton, MO 65251
Time Being Books, 10411 Clayton Rd., Stes. 201-203, St. Louis, MO 63131
Tin House, PMB 280, 320 7th Ave., Brooklyn, NY 11215
Tipton Poetry Journal, PO Box 804, Zionsville, IN 46077
TLOLP, PO Box 1266, San Clemente, CA 92674
Toasted Cheese Literary Journal, 44 East 13th Ave., #402, Vancouver V5T 4K7, BC
Toadlily Press, PO Box 2, Chappaqua, NY 10514
Traprock Books, 1330 E. 25th Ave., Eugene, OR 97403
TriQuarterly, Northwestern Univ. Press, 629 Noyes St., Evanston, IL 60208-4210
Tuesday: An Art Project, PO Box 1074, Arlington MA 02476
Tupelo Press, PO Box 539, Dorset, Vermont 05251
Twelve Stories, 5059 Anderson Place, Cincinnati, OH 45227
Two Rivers Review, 2209 Gridley Paige Rd., Keansboro, NY 13328

U

U.S. 1 Poets' Cooperative, U.S. 1 Worksheets, PO Box 127, Kingston, NJ 08528-0127
Umbrella, 102 West 75th St., Ste. 54, New York, NY 10023-1907
Underground Voices, PO Box 931671, LA, CA 90093
The University of Georgia Press, 330 Research Dr., Athens, GA 30602-4901
University of Pittsburgh Press, 3400 Forbes Ave., Pittsburgh, PA 15260
University of Wisconsin Press, 1930 Monroe St., 3rd Floor, Madison, Wi 53711-2059
University Press of New England, 1 Court St., Lebanon, NH 03766
Unsaid, Box 141, Robbins, NC 27325
Unsplendid, 306 Clemens Hall, University of Buffalo, Buffalo, NY 14260-4610
Up-Set Press, Inc., PO Box 200340, Brooklyn, NY 11220
upstreet, PO Box 105, Richmond, MA 01254
Utah State University Press, 7800 Old Main Hall, Logan, UT 84322

V

Valley Voices, State University, Itta Bena, MS 38941
Vallum, PO Box 326, Westmount Station, Montreal, Quebec H3Z 2T5 Canada
Valparaiso Poetry Review, English Dept., Valparaiso Univ., Valparaiso, IN 46383
Vestal Review, 2609 Dartmouth Dr., Vestal, NY 13850
Vibrant Gray, 280 Ocean Parkway #5V, Brooklyn, NY 11218
Vice Magazine, 97 North 10th St., Ste. 202, Brooklyn, NY 11211
Viking Dog Press, 501 S. Market St., Muncy, PA 17756
The Virginia Quarterly Review, 1 West Range, PO Box 400223, Charlottesville, VA 22904

Virtual Artists Collective, 5710 S. Kimbark #3, Chicago, IL 60637
Voices Anthology, PO Box 9076, Fayetteville, AR 72703

W

Waccamaw, PO Box 261954, Conway, SC 29528-6054
Wasatch Journal, PO Box 511281, Salt Lake City, UT 84151
Washington Writers' Publishing House, PO Box 15271, Washington, DC 20003
Water Forest Press, PO Box 295, Stormville, NY 12582
Water~Stone Review, MS A1730, 1536 Hewitt Ave., St. Paul, MN 55104-1284
Wave Books, 1938 Fairview Avenue East, Seattle, WA 98102
Wayne State University Press, 4809 Woodward Ave., Detroit, MI 48201-1309
West Branch, Stadler Center for Poetry, Bucknell University, Lewisburg, PA 17837
Whiskey Island Magazine, 2121 Euclid Ave., Cleveland, OH 44115-2214
Whispering Prairie Press, PO Box 8342, Prairie Village, KS 66208-0342
Whistling Shade, PO Box 7084, St. Paul, MN 55107
White Pelican Review, PO Box 7833, Lakeland, FL 33813
White Pine Press, PO Box 236, Buffalo, NY 14201
Wild Apples, PO Box 171, Harvard, MA 01451
Wild Writing Women, PO Box 2298, Los Gatos, CA 95030
Wilderness House Literary Review, 145 Foster St., Littleton, MA 01460
Willow Springs, 501 N. Riverpoint Blvd., Ste 425, Spokane, WA 99202
Willows Wept Review, 1928 Fairfax Ave., Cincinnati, OH 45207
Winged Halo Productions, PO Box 803, O'Fallon, IL 62269
Winterhawk Press, 9533 Caraway Dr., Boise, ID 83704
Wising Up Press, PO Box 2122, Decatur, GA 30031-2122
Witness, 4505 S. Maryland Pkwy, Box 455085, Las Vegas, NV 89154-5085
Woodley Memorial Press, Washburn University, Topeka, KS 66621
The Worcester Review, 1 Ekman St., Worcester, MA 01607
Word Worth, PO Box 221, East Aurora, NY 14052
Words and Images, Univ. of Southern Maine, PO Box 9300, Portland, ME 04104-9300
Workers Write!, PO Box 250382, Plano, TX 75025-0382
World Audience Publishers, 303 Park Ave. So., #1440, New York, NY 10010-3657
World Literature Today, 630 Parrington Oval, Ste. 110, Norman, OK 73019-4033
Write Bloody Publishing, c/o Todd Valentine, 11561 Luzon, Cypress, CA 90630
Writecorner Press, PO Box 140310, Gainesville, FL 32614-0310

Y

The Yale Review, Yale University, PO Box 208243, New Haven, CT 06520

Z

Zahir Publishing, 315 S. Coast Highway 101, Ste.U8, Encinitas, CA 92024
Zoetrope: All Story, 916 Kearny St., San Francisco, CA 94133
Zossima Press, 366 S. Brookvale Rd., Cheshire, CT 06410
ZYZZYVA, PO Box 590069, San Francisco, CA 94159-0069

THE PUSHCART PRIZE
FELLOWSHIPS

The Pushcart Prize Fellowships Inc., a 501 (c) (3) nonprofit corporation, is the endowment for The Pushcart Prize. We also make grants to promising new writers. "Members" donated up to $249 each. "Sponsors" gave between $250 and $999. "Benefactors" donated from $1000 to $4,999. "Patrons" donated $5,000 and more. We are very grateful for these donations. Gifts of any amount are welcome. For information write to the Fellowships at PO Box 380, Wainscott, NY 11975.

Siv Cedering
Dan Chaon & Sheila Schwartz
James Charlton
Andrei Condrescu
Tracy Crow
Dana Literary Society
Carol de Gramont
Daniel Dolgin & Loraine Gardner
Karl Elder
Donald Finkel
Ben and Sharon Fountain
Alan and Karen Furst
John Gill
Robert Giron
Doris Grumbach & Sybil Pike
Gwen Head
The Healing Muse
Robin Hemley
Jane Hirshfield

Helen H. Houghton
Joseph Hurka
Janklow & Nesbit Asso.
Edmund Keeley
Thomas E. Kennedy
Sydney Lea
Gerald Locklin
Thomas Lux
Markowitz, Fenelon and Bank
Elizabeth McKenzie
McSweeney's
Joan Murray
Barbara and Warren Phillips
Hilda Raz
Mary Carlton Swope
Julia Wendell
Philip White
Eleanor Wilner
Richard Wyatt & Irene Eilers

MEMBERS

Anonymous (3)
Betty Adcock
Agni
Carolyn Alessio
Dick Allen
Henry H. Alley
Lisa Alvarez
Jan Lee Ande
Ralph Angel
Antietam Review
Ruth Appelhof
Philip and Marjorie Appleman
Linda Aschbrenner
Renee Ashley
Ausable Press
David Baker
Catherine Barnett
Dorothy Barresi
Barrow Street Press
Jill Bart
Ellen Bass
Judith Baumel
Ann Beattie
Madison Smartt Bell
Beloit Poetry Journal
Pinckney Benedict
Karen Bender
Andre Bernard
Christopher Bernard
Wendell Berry
Linda Bierds
Stacy Bierlein
Bitter Oleander Press
Mark Blaeuer
Blue Lights Press

Carol Bly
BOA Editions
Deborah Bogen
Susan Bono
Anthony Brandt
James Breeden
Rosellen Brown
Jane Brox
Andrea Hollander Budy
E. S. Bumas
Richard Burgin
Skylar H. Burris
David Caliguiuri
Kathy Callaway
Janine Canan
Henry Carlile
Fran Castan
Chelsea Associates
Marianne Cherry
Phillis M. Choyke
Suzanne Cleary
Martha Collins
Joan Connor
John Copenhaven
Dan Corrie
Tricia Currans-Sheehan
Jim Daniels
Thadious Davis
Maija Devine
Sharon Dilworth
Edward J. DiMaio
Kent Dixon
John Duncklee
Elaine Edelman
Renee Edison & Don Kaplan

Nancy Edwards
M.D. Elevitch
Failbetter.com
Irvin Faust
Tom Filer
Susan Firer
Nick Flynn
Stakey Flythe Jr.
Peter Fogo
Linda N. Foster
Fugue
Alice Fulton
Eugene K. Garber
Frank X. Gaspar
A Gathering of the Tribes
Reginald Gibbons
Emily Fox Gordon
Philip Graham
Eamon Grennan
Lee Meitzen Grue
Habit of Rainy Nights
Rachel Hadas
Susan Hahn
Meredith Hall
Harp Strings
Jeffrey Harrison
Lois Marie Harrod
Healing Muse
Alex Henderson
Lily Henderson
Daniel Henry
Neva Herington
Lou Hertz
William Heyen
Bob Hicok
R. C. Hildebrandt
Kathleen Hill
Jane Hirshfield
Edward Hoagland
Daniel Hoffman
Doug Holder
Richard Holinger
Rochelle L. Holt
Richard M. Huber
Brigid Hughes
Lynne Hugo
Illya's Honey
Susan Indigo
Mark Irwin
Beverly A. Jackson
Richard Jackson
David Jauss
Marilyn Johnston
Alice Jones
Journal of New Jersey Poets
Robert Kalich
Julia Kasdorf

Miriam Poli Katsikis
Meg Kearney
Celine Keating
Brigit Kelly
John Kistner
Judith Kitchen
Stephen Kopel
Peter Krass
David Kresh
Maxine Kumin
Valerie Laken
Babs Lakey
Maxine Landis
Lane Larson
Dorianne Laux & Joseph Millar
Sydney Lea
Donald Lev
Dana Levin
Gerald Locklin
Rachel Loden
Radomir Luza, Jr.
Annette Lynch
Elzabeth MacKierman
Elizabeth Macklin
Leah Maines
Mark Manalang
Norma Marder
Jack Marshall
Michael Martone
Tara L. Masih
Dan Masterson
Peter Matthiessen
Alice Mattison
Tracy Mayor
Robert McBrearty
Jane McCafferty
Rebecca McClanahan
Bob McCrane
Jo McDougall
Sandy McIntosh
James McKean
Roberta Mendel
Didi Menendez
Barbara Milton
Alexander Mindt
Mississippi Review
Martin Mitchell
Roger Mitchell
Jewell Mogan
Patricia Monaghan
Jim Moore
James Morse
William Mulvihill
Nami Mun
Carol Muske-Dukes
Edward Mycue
Deirdre Neilen

W. Dale Nelson
Jean Nordhaus
Ontario Review Foundation
Daniel Orozco
Other Voices
Pamela Painter
Paris Review
Alan Michael Parker
Ellen Parker
Veronica Patterson
David Pearce
Robert Phillips
Donald Platt
Valerie Polichar
Pool
Jeffrey & Priscilla Potter
Marcia Preston
Eric Puchner
Tony Quagliano
Barbara Quinn
Belle Randall
Martha Rhodes
Nancy Richard
Stacey Richter
Katrina Roberts
Judith R. Robinson
Jessica Roeder
Martin Rosner
Kay Ryan
Sy Safransky
Brian Salchert
James Salter
Sherod Santos
R.A. Sasaki
Valerie Sayers
Alice Schell
Dennis & Loretta Schmitz
Helen Schulman
Philip Schultz
Shenandoah
Peggy Shinner
Vivian Shipley
Joan Silver
Skyline
John E. Smelcer
Raymond J. Smith
Philip St. Clair
Lorraine Standish

Maureen Stanton
Michael Steinberg
Jody Stewart
Barbara Stone
Storyteller Magazine
Bill & Pat Strachan
Julie Suk
Sun Publishing
Sweet Annie Press
Katherine Taylor
Pamela Taylor
Susan Terris
Marcelle Thiébaux
Robert Thomas
Andrew Tonkovich
Juanita Torrence-Thompson
William Trowbridge
Martin Tucker
Victoria Valentine
Tino Villanueva
William & Jeanne Wagner
BJ Ward
Susan Oard Warner
Rosanna Warren
Margareta Waterman
Michael Waters
Sandi Weinberg
Andrew Weinstein
Jason Wesco
West Meadow Press
Susan Wheeler
Dara Wier
Ellen Wilbur
Galen Williams
Marie Sheppard Williams
Eleanor Wilner
Irene K. Wilson
Steven Wingate
Sandra Wisenberg
David Wittman
Wings Press
Robert W. Witt
Margo Wizansky
Matt Yurdana
Christina Zawadiwsky
Sander Zulauf
ZYZZYVA

SUSTAINING MEMBERS

Anonymous (5)
Carolyn Alessio
Dick Allen
Russell Allen
Jacob Appel

Philip & Marjorie Appleman
Renée Ashley
Jim Barnes
Catherine Barnett
Charles Baxter

CONTRIBUTORS' NOTES

ASHLEE ADAMS teaches at UNC, Chapel Hill. "Bird Feed" is her first published story.

IDRIS ANDERSON has published poems in *The Hudson Review, Ontario Review, South Carolina Review, ZYZZYVA* and elsewhere. She is head of the English Department at Crystal Springs Uplands School in Hillsborough, California.

KIM ADDONIZIO's latest books are *Lucifer at the Starlite* and *Ordinary Geniius: A Guide for the Poet Within,* both from W. W. Norton. She lives in Oakland, California.

YOUSEF AL-MOHAIMEED lives in Riyadh, Saudi Arabia and has published several novels and story collections in Arabic. His *Wolves of the Crescent Moon,* a debut novel, was his first published outside of the Middle East.

FRANK BIDART won the 2007 Bollingen Prize in American Poetry. His latest collection of poems is *Watching The Spring Festival* (Farrar, Straus & Giroux), which includes "Collector."

GEORGE BILGERE's latest book, *Haywire,* won the 2006 May Swensen Award. He lives and teaches in Cleveland.

SVEN BIRKETS edits *Agni* and directs the Bennington Writing Seminars. "The Points of Sail" is part of an anthology just out from Ecco. *The Book of Dads: Essays on the Joys, Perils and Humiliations of Fatherhood.*

EULA BISS won two Graywolf Press nonfiction prizes for *No Man's Land: American Essays.* She holds an MFA from The University of Iowa and is artist in residence at Northwestern University.

AUSTIN BUNN's stories have appeared in *One Story, American Short Fiction, West Branch* and elsewhere. He lives in Grand Rapids, Michigan.

GEOFFREY BROCK is the author of *Weighing Light* and the translator of several books from Italian. He teaches at The University of Arkansas.

JOEL BROUWER is the author most recently of *And So.* He lives in Tuscaloosa, Alabama.

FLEDA BROWN won the Felix Pollak Prize for her recent collection of poems, *Reunion* (2007). She lives in Traverse City, Michigan.

HENRI COLE's latest poetry collection is *Blackbird and Wolf* (Farrar, Straus & Giroux, 2007). In 2003 he received the Kingsley Tufts Poetry Award. He lives in Boston.

BROCK CLARKE's most recent book is the novel *An Arsonist's Guide to Writer's Homes in New England.* He teaches at the University of Cincinnati.

LYDIA DAVIS is the author of *Collected Stories* (Farrar, Straus & Giroux, 2009). She lives in update New York and is on the faculty of SUNY Albany.

RITA DOVE won the Pulitzer Prize in poetry and was U.S. Poet Laureate from 1993–1995. Her latest book of poetry, *Sonata Mulattica,* is just out from W. W. Norton.

PETER EVERWINE lives in Fresno, California. His *From the Meadow: Selected and New Poems* was recently published.

B.H. FAIRCHILD won the National Book Critics Circle award in poetry and was a finalist for the National Book Award. He lives in Claremont, California.

MARY GAITSKILL lives in Red Hook, New York. She is the author of two novels and three story collections, most recently, *Don't Cry.*

LOUISE GLÜCK is the author of *Averno* (Farrar, Straus & Giroux), a finalist for the 2006 National Book Award. She teaches at Yale.

J.C. HALLMAN's selection appears in a collection of stories—*The Hospital for Bad Poets* (Milkweed, 2009). He is also the author of *The Chess Artist* and *The Devil is a Gentleman*.

MARK HALLIDAY has won three Pushcart Prizes. He lives in Athens, Ohio.

WILLIAM HEYEN teaches at SUNY, Brockport, New York. He is the author of several books of poetry, including *Shoah Train*, a finalist for the 2004 National Book Award.

BOB HICOK's *This Clumsy Living* received the Bobbitt Prize from the Library of Congress. *Words for Empty and Words For Full* is due out soon from The University of Pittsburgh Press.

EDWARD HOAGLAND's 20th book was published in 2009—*Early In The Season*. This Pushcart selection is the opening of his fifth novel, just finished. He lives in Barton, Vermont and Edgartown, Massachusetts.

CHRISTIE HODGEN is the author of the novel, *Hello, I Must Be Going*, and the story collection, *A Jeweler's Eye for Flaw*. She lives in Kansas City.

LAURA KASISCHKE is a previous Pushcart Prize winner. She lives in Chelsea, Michigan.

TED KOOSER served two terms as U.S. Poet Laureate and has won both Pulitzer and Pushcart prizes. He lives in Nebraska.

WILLIAM LYCHACK is the author of a novel, *The Wasp Eater*, and a forthcoming collection of stories, *The Architect of Flowers*. He teaches at Phillips Academy.

AMOS MAGLIORCCO's fiction has appeared in *Iron Horse Review*, *Oxford Magazine* and *Southwestern American Literature*. He lives in Denton, Texas. The late Eric Nguyen's work can be seen at w.w.w.mescale.ws.

LUTHER MAGNUSSEN is the pen name for an author, living in New York, who wishes to remain anonymous.

GREIL MARCUS is the author of *Lipstick Traces*, *The Dustbin of History* and two other books. He lives in Berkeley, California.

JILL McDONOUGH is the author of *Habeas Corpus*. She lives near Boston.

CHARLES McLEOD lives in Piedmont, California. His story collection, *National Treasures*, and his debut novel, *American Weather*, will be published by Random House UK in 2011.

DAVID MOOLTON is a physician specializing in Transfusion Medicine. He is the author of three poetry collections and won the T.S. Eliot Prize from Truman State University.

PAUL MULDOON lives in Princeton, New Jersey and is a professor of humanities at Princeton University. His latest book is *Horse Latitudes* (2006).

JOYCE CAROL OATES is a Founding Editor of The Pushcart Prize. Her next story collection is *Dear Husband*. She lives and teaches in Princeton, New Jersey.

GREGORY ORR's tenth poetry collection, *How Beautiful The Beloved*, was published by Copper Canyon in 2009. He founded the Graduate Program in Writing at the University of Virginia, where he teaches.

RICHARD POWERS is the author of ten novels. His *The Echo Maker* won the National Book Award. He lives in Illinois.

LIA PURPURA's essay collection, *On Looking*, was a finalist for the National Book Critics Circle Award in 2007. Her poetry collection, *King Baby*, was published in 2008, by Alice James Books.

SARA PRITCHARD is the author of *Crackpots*, a novel, and *Lately*, linked stories. She lives in Morgantown, West Virginia.

BEN QUICK lives in Tucson Arizona, teaches at The University of Arizona and is at work on a memoir about the war in Vietnam.

SPENCER REECE is a postulant for Holy Orders in the Episcopal priesthood. His book of poems, *The Clerk's Tale*, was published in 2004. He studies at the Berkeley Divinity School at Yale.

PAISLEY REKDAL is the author of three poetry collections and a book of essays. She lives in Salt Lake City.

JAMES RICHARDSON is professor of English and Creative Writing at Princeton. His *By The Numbers* will be published by Copper Canyon. He was a finalist for the 2004 National Book Critics poetry award for his collection *Interglacial: New and Selected Poems and Aphorisms*.

MAXINE SCATES lives in Eugene, Oregon. She is the author of two books of poetry: *Toluca Street* and *Black Loam*.

BRUCE SMITH is the author of five books of poems, and was a finalist for the National Book Award. He teaches at Syracuse University.

GINGER STRAND is the author of *Inventing Niagara* and *Flight*. She has contributed to *The Believer*, *Gettysburg Review*, *Swink*, *Raritan* and *New England Review*. She lives in New York.

SALLIE TISDALE lives in Portland, Oregon. Her most recently published book is *Women of the Way* (Harper, 2006).

ALISON TOWNSEND lives with her husband on four acres of prairie and oak savanna in the farm country outside Madison, Wisconsin. She is the author of two poetry collections and two chapbooks.

LAURA VAN DEN BERG is currently at work on a novel. She graduated from the MFA program at Emerson College, and has published stories in *Epoch*, *Story Quarterly*, *Boston Review* and elsewhere.

LIZ WALDNER teachers in the Creative Writing Program at the University of Houston and lives in Houston.

KARY WAYSON's *American Husband* won the 2009 Ohio State University Press / *The Journal* award. She also won the 2003 Discovery / *The Nation* award.

CHRISTIAN WIMAN is the author of three books, including the recent *Ambition and Survival: Becoming a Poet* (Copper Canyon). He is the editor of *Poetry*.

BRENDA WINEAPPLE's *White Heat: The Friendship of Emily Dickinson and Thomas Wentworth Higginson* (Knopf, 2008) was a finalist for the National Book Critics Circle Award, and a *New York Times* Notable Book. She teaches at The New School and Columbia University.

DIANE WILLIAMS is the founder and editor of *Noon*. She teaches at New Yorks's Mercantile Library, and won two Pushcart Prizes previously.

CAROLYNE WRIGHT has published eight books of poetry, four volumes of translations, and a collection of essays. Her latest book, *A Change of Maps*, was published by Lost Horse Press in 2006.

ROBERT WRIGLEY's *Beautiful Country* will be published by Penguin soon. He lives in Idaho.

DAVID YEZZI is executive director of *The New Criterion* and the author of two books of poetry. *Azores* (2008) was a *Slate* magazine best book of the year.

ADAM ZAGAJEWSKI, the distinguished Polish poet, teaches part of the year at The University of Chicago.

PAUL ZIMMER has worked in the book business for over forty years. He is now retired on a farm in Wisconsin. His latest book of poems is *Crossing To Sunlight Revisited* (University of Georgia).

INDEX

The following is a listing in alphabetical order by author's last name of works reprinted in the *Pushcart Prize* editions since 1976.

536

539

540

541

542

543

545

547

551

554

561